*Praise
The
Human
Season*

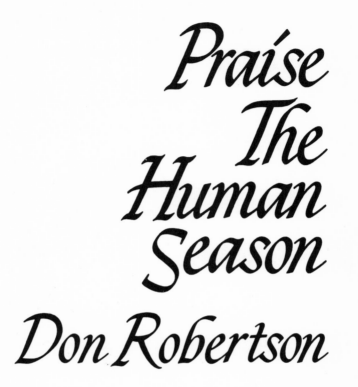

Praise The Human Season

Don Robertson

A

ARTHUR FIELDS BOOKS, INC. NEW YORK 1974

The title is taken from Archibald MacLeish's poem "Immortal Autumn" and quoted with the permission of Houghton Mifflin Company.

The author would like to thank Miss Carol Lucas, of WKYC-TV, Cleveland, for her valuable technical assistance.

Published simultaneously in Canada by Clarke, Irwin & Company Limited, Toronto and Vancouver
ISBN:0–525–63013–9
Library of Congress Catalog Card Number: 73–18891

For Anne, Stephanie, Rebecca and David H. Elliot

"I praise the fall it is the human season."
Archibald MacLeish

*Praise
The
Human
Season*

Weekend

In the spring of 1971, when it became apparent to Howard W. Amberson that neither he nor his wife had much time remaining, he walked to Woolworth's and purchased a large ledger, bound in red and gray. He also purchased a dozen of those throwaway Japanese felt pens. He returned home, seated himself at the kitchen table and began to write. (His wife was out visiting a sick friend, and so he was not disturbed.)

These words, *he began*, will be an attempt to sort out confusions. They will come in no logical sequence, but perhaps their total impression will make a sort of sense. I shall try to be careful and fastidious, and I shall try not to yield to exaggerations and melodrama. I always have respected the language, and I shall try to treat it with precision.

Therefore, in line with this wish for precision, let me say straight out: I am terribly afraid.

Amberson worked on the ledger in secret, usually late at night after his wife had fallen asleep. He worked at the kitchen table, and sometimes the cat watched him. He worked through the spring and he worked through the summer and he worked into the fall. He threw away nothing.

My wife had pain last night, and for once I did not have to urge her to take her medication. My own pain is also large, but there is no medication for it.

Amberson and his wife celebrated their golden wedding anniversary in June. Their daughter and her husband and children came from Dayton to be with them. The children all were girls, and Amberson read stories to them. He had a strong voice, and the girls were delighted.

He thought of the ledger as a journal of antique events. He kept it hidden in the cellar behind a pile of torn cardboard boxes. The ledger . . . or journal . . . became obsessive with Amberson. It gave him enormous pain, but he kept at it. By the autumn of 1971, he had written several hundred pages, and his obsessiveness led to another obsession that was even less reasonable. He decided it was imperative that he take his wife on a motor trip. He was seventyfour, and his wife (her name was Anne) was seventytwo, and she carried a large scar where her right breast should have been.

He said to himself: We do not understand this world. Do not we have an obligation to try? Is it fair to leave before we know what it is we are leaving?

He discussed the motor trip one day with his family doctor. The man's name was Groh. The subject came up after Dr. Groh said: "I really should be sending Anne back up to Columbus for more of the cobalt treatments, but they would be a waste of time."

"What do you mean by that?" Amberson asked the doctor.

"At a cost of perhaps five thousand dollars," said Dr. Groh, "we could perhaps extend her life by two months."

"You said 'perhaps' twice in the same sentence."

"Yes," said Dr. Groh. "I expect I did."

Amberson's hands were folded sedately in his lap. He glanced down at them, and he was pleased to see that his fingernails were clean. "I have always tried to be neat and precise," he said, "but there is no excuse for being such a fussbudget. I apologize for picking at your choice of words."

"All right," said Dr. Groh.

Amberson's hands came apart. Leaning forward a little, he pressed his palms against his legs. He rubbed his legs, and he rubbed his knees,

4

and then he said: "I'd like to discuss something with you."

"Discuss away," said Dr. Groh.

Amberson was seated in a straightbacked chair. It was not a comfortable chair. He stared at the floor. "I seek definitions," he said.

"Definitions of what?"

"Of what we are, of where we have been."

"Are they that important?"

Amberson looked up. "How's that? What?"

Dr. Groh sat erectly behind his desk. He was past sixty, but his hair still was dark. He was slight and a bit owlish, and his teeth were widely spaced. He leaned forward, resting his elbows on the desk. "I am not much good at this sort of talk," he said, "but there's one question I want to ask you, if you'll allow me."

"Go ahead."

"When you use a word such as 'definitions,' it sounds like some sort of intellectual exercise. Why is an intellectual exercise necessary? If you find any answers, what will you be able to do with them?"

"Anne and I have lived together a long time. Aren't we entitled to know what it's all meant?"

"But *why?* What the hell difference does it make to you? Why distract yourself? Why distract Anne?"

"I don't see why we have to die," said Amberson. His chest hurt.

"For Christ's sake," said Dr. Groh, "what kind of thing to say is that?"

Amberson folded his arms across his chest. "I am simply saying what I mean," he told the doctor.

Dr. Groh leaned back and shook his head. "This is the goddamnedest conver—"

Amberson abruptly stood up. The movement made him gasp a little. "As long as I draw breath," he said, "I shall remain interested in my life."

Dr. Groh stared at Amberson for a moment, then grinned up at him and said: "You goddamned pompous ninny."

"What?"

"Are you still seeking the secret of the universe, is that it? Who the hell do you think you are?"

"I am taking Anne on a motor trip," said Amberson.

Dr. Groh's grin went away. "I beg your pardon?"

"I am a human being, and I have occupied space on this planet for more than seventyfour years, and I have a right to know what it's all meant. What do you propose I do? Go crawl under someone's porch like a sick cat?"

Dr. Groh hesitated a moment before speaking. Then: "Now, hold on. Are you saying you're taking Anne off somewhere on a trip in your car?"

"Yes."

"Where?"

"I have no idea."

"My God," said Dr. Groh.

Amberson managed a sort of smile. "I have been working at the idea for some months now," he said. "There is an apparatus we do not understand, and Anne and I have a right to investigate it. We are not stupid, and perhaps we shall discover something."

"Howard, you are talking absolute crap."

"I am talking nothing of the sort. I have given it all a great deal of thought."

"You'll take her away from her *home* when she is *dying,* when *you* are dying?"

"Yes."

"Because of whatever the hell this *apparatus* is?"

"Yes."

"Then you're no goddamned better than the cat crawling under the porch."

"No," said Amberson. "That is not true." His arms still were folded across his chest. "It is not right for people to face their final days with no purpose. There always must be projects and goals."

"Jesus Christ Almighty," said Dr. Groh.

The purpose of these words is to seek a pattern. Once a pattern is determined, then the confusions should vanish. A summation becomes possible, and value can be judged. These considerations are important to me, and they are even more important than my fear.

Walking home from Dr. Groh's office, Amberson had to restrain himself from hugging his chest. He ran his tongue along the insides of his dentures, and he tried to ignore the sound of his heart. He was aware of an odor of dry leaves; it was all powdery, and it had a sort of sting to it, and it was not a bit unpleasant. He walked slowly, and he saw a little boy bouncing a basketball in a driveway, and he saw a pregnant woman beating a rug in a side yard. He thought back on the things Dr. Groh had said, and he knew the doctor had not understood. The doctor was a kind man and a good friend, but he had understood nothing.

6

Amberson rubbed his mouth. He blinked at the sidewalk, and he saw a wooly worm crawling across a fallen leaf. The wooly worm had a thick band; and perhaps the band meant the winter would be severe.

It's not as though I am doing anything indecent, said Amberson to himself. I do not have to question it.

Amberson bent over the leaf and picked it up. The wooly worm clung to an edge of the leaf. Carefully Amberson placed the leaf on a treelawn.

I have lived all my life in the small city of Paradise Falls, Ohio, which is southeast of Columbus about fifty miles or so. Its population is barely six thousand, a figure that has remained constant since shortly after the turn of the century. It is the seat of Paradise County, which in the mid-1960's was officially classified as an economic distressed area. The designation was rendered by someone in the Johnson Administration, and in 1968 Nixon carried the county with 61.8 percent of the vote.

"I believe I'll buy a movie camera," Amberson said to his wife at breakfast the morning after his conversation with Dr. Groh.

"What on earth *for?*" she wanted to know.

"Our trip."

"What trip?"

"The trip we're taking."

"Are you trying to tell me that we're going on a trip?"

"Very good, my dear. You have grasped the thrust of my words with great exactitude."

"Now. Don't be a snot."

"I'm very sorry," said Amberson.

Anne Amberson poured sugar and cream on her oatmeal. Then: "Where are we going? And when? And just give me a courteous answer, without any of your snot talk."

Amberson smiled. He looked up, and he saw that Anne also was smiling. "I don't know where we'll be going," he said, "but we'll be leaving Monday morning."

"Well, whoop de do."

"A movie camera will enable me to photograph changing leaves," said Amberson. "And relics in museums. And sunsets. And Indians weaving rugs. And then I'll splice all the film together and give illustrated lectures in church basements. I'll call them 'Footloose with the Ambersons.' "

"You have flapped," said Anne Amberson.

"I believe the word is flipped," said her husband.

Prior to my retirement in June of 1962, I was an English teacher at Paradise Falls High School for fortytwo years. I also coached the track team for thirtysix of those years. I always have been fond of track. I see it as the only gentle sport, noncombative and therefore good for the participant. In track, all injuries are self-inflicted. (In track, one never touches one's opponent. One tests one's *skills* against him, but never one's capacities for brutal behavior.)

My late father was the chief bookkeeper and later the secretary and treasurer of a tile and brick firm known as the Paradise Falls Clay Products Co., which has been the city's principal industry for more than a century.

My late mother was active in the White Shrine of Jerusalem. She disliked Catholics.

There were four of us children—three boys and a girl. My two brothers and my sister are long gone, and I don't visit their graves as often as perhaps I should. But, ah, that is really a moot point, considering how I feel and what I know is soon in store for me.

"Flapped or flipped," said Anne Amberson to her husband, "it's all the same. You have gone around the bend."

"No," said Amberson. "It's simply that I feel we should try to tuck in the loose ends and come to an understanding. Madmen do not concern themselves with loose ends."

"What are you talking about?"

"I want to understand."

"Understand what? Stop being such a sphinx."

"All right," said Amberson, spreading his hands, "to be as clear as I can, I'm only trying to say that you and I have lived a total of one hundred fortysix years, and we have seen a great deal, but what is the sum total of all our years?"

"And so we go gallivanting off, and you with a movie camera?"

"Yes," said Amberson. "To create a final resolution of the apparatus."

"I haven't the slightest idea what you're trying to say."

Amberson glanced out the window. "Yes you do," he said.

My two brothers and their wives, together with Papa and Mama, are buried near a cluster of rigid tulip trees in a declivity at the Oak Grove Cemetery, which some oldtimers (myself included) still call the "new" cemetery, even though it has been in use since 1911. The "old" burial ground was known as Oak Hill Cemetery, and it had pretty well filled up by that year.

My father was a member of the syndicate that purchased the land for the "new" cemetery, and the enterprise brought the old fellow a substantial profit. He died of a stroke in 1927, and his will divided the shares equally among myself and my two brothers. (My sister Caroline had died in 1922, and my mother in 1923.)

My brothers sold their shares, but I hung onto mine, and I always have been glad I did. The annual income averages about two thousand dollars, and it has enabled me to put our own three children through college. (Henry, the oldest and brightest, even was able to attend Kenyon.)

Our two sons are dead. Henry has been dead for more than a quarter of a century. My God, my memory is such a clamor of dead persons.

Anne Amberson shook her head. She was silent for a time, and then she said: "All right. The apparatus. Whatever you say."

"We'll enjoy the trip," said Amberson.

"Oh yes," said Anne.

"I think of dead persons a great deal."

"That's your age speaking."

"I think of them in the present tense."

"That's an affliction of us relics," said Anne.

"I love you very much."

"I know that."

Amberson reached across the table and touched one of his wife's hands. "How do you feel?"

"The pain is better this morning."

"Better how?"

"Duller," said Anne Amberson. "Now please stop asking about it. When you *ask* about it, I *think* about it. Which makes me *feel* it."

"I worry about you."

"Worry about yourself. Leave my pain alone. Worry about your own pain."

"I really do love you."

"Yes. Yes. *Yes,*" said Anne Amberson. "I know you do. I know all

9

about it." She hugged herself, and her arms were gray, and her skin was cracked at the elbows. She cleared her throat, sighed and asked him to go down cellar and change the sand in the cat box. He told her it would be his pleasure, and she smiled and said: Oh sure. I just bet.

I suppose I was reared in an atmosphere of serenity. My father was a quiet man, rimless and precise, with a snappish little voice that always put me a bit in mind of insects. Busy insects. Ants perhaps.

As for my mother, well . . . the memory of man has known not a woman dedicated so strenuously to warmth, and apple butter, and piano waltzes, and the works of Wilkie Collins, and the removal of dead leaves, and—most importantly—the White Shrine of Jerusalem, plus of course the Order of Eastern Star.

One evening (I was perhaps six or seven at the time) my father, speaking at the family supper table, allowed as how the Eastern Star initials, OES, really stood for Old Eviscerated Shrews.

The comment prompted my mother to say: "Alvin, that remark was about as amusing as scurvy."

But my mother laughed as she spoke, and so did my father, and so did all of us children. Potatoes were passed, and later there no doubt was music in the parlor. There was rancor in our family (there is rancor in all families, even the happy ones, and never mind what Tolstoy says), but most of the time it was successfully suppressed. We believed that existence was hard enough, which meant we believed that it was foolish to bring troublous things into the open.

I promise in this ledger not to be maudlin. I shall try to spare the reader (what reader? will there be a reader?) melodrama, selfpity.

Later, after he had changed the sand in the cat box, Amberson went for a walk with his wife. They strolled along Cumberland Street and High Street and West Main. It was late September, and the leaves had just begun to turn and fall. Here and there were smears of gold and crimson, but there still was a great deal of green, and the sun was warm. Amberson and his wife walked slowly, arm in arm. "I am perfectly serious," he said.

"Fine," said Anne Amberson. "You have a gift for seriousness. We've been married fifty years, and if there's one thing I've always admired about you, it's been your seriousness. That night in the Buick, for instance. *Well,* such *seriousness.*"

Amberson smiled. "Fifty years of marriage, and at least once a week the woman has brought up the matter of the Buick."

"The Buick memory is important to *me*. It is very funny. It is pleasant."

"If I concentrated deeply enough," said Amberson, "I probably could bring back the pain from my cramps."

"Well, I certainly *hope* so," said Anne Amberson, her voice sweetly innocent.

As a boy, I always sat quietly at stereopticon shows. I never was known to twitch, squirm or jiggle a foot. I did well in school, and I was the first in my class to grasp the difference between an Austrian and an Australian. When I was seven, I happened to read a campaign biography of Alton B. Parker. I read it, as the saying goes, from cover to cover, and then I gave a detailed report on it to my somewhat stunned teacher and classmates. The teacher, whose name was Mrs. Sonntag if my memory does not betray me, told me I was a wonder and a caution. And *I* told *her* I thought Alton B. Parker was an interesting and important man, and therefore what was so peculiar? Why was I such a wonder? Why was I such a caution?

The Ambersons walked for perhaps an hour and a half. By the time they returned home, they were a bit winded, and Anne Amberson fixed them some hot cocoa. She opened a package of Omar Bakery ginger snaps. For some years now Amberson had been fond of Omar Bakery ginger snaps. They stung his gums and teeth, but he liked them anyway.

The Ambersons sat at the kitchen table and drank their cocoa and munched on their ginger snaps, and Amberson said: "We'll drive at our leisure, and in no particular direction."

"But we're too old to go off gallivanting. And besides, you don't drive that well any more. If you want to know about the apparatus, read *Time* magazine."

"I already read *Time* magazine," said Amberson, sipping his cocoa. He shifted his weight, crossed his legs. His joints hurt. He had already eaten all of his first ginger snap, and its sweetness had brought pain to his gums and his eleven remaining real teeth. "We must see the apparatus firsthand."

"Isn't Paradise Falls part of the apparatus?"

"There is more to the world than Paradise Falls."

"Harrumph and ahem," said Anne.

"Yes, my pet," said Amberson, laughing.

I was the youngest of the four children of Alvin and Margaret Amberson. The oldest was Alvin Jr., born 1889. Then came Caroline, born 1890; then Ernest, born 1896; and finally me, Howard, born 1897 and (according to family legend) something of a, ah, Little Surprise.

We all were small (Alvin Jr. grew to be the tallest, at five-nine, if he stretched his neck; I myself am barely five-seven), but Alvin Jr. and Ernest were extremely combative, especially as far as Catholics were concerned.

Caroline, on the other hand, was quite timid, and she seldom said six words in the same hour, unless she was conversing with her dolls, who probably understood her better than anyone, including that strange fellow she eventually married.

To the best of my recollection, she was about seventeen before she stopped playing with her dolls. There were seven of them, and she had named them, and I remember all of the names. (My mind has always been an excellent repository of trivial information. I sometimes have trouble remembering the names of Ohio's two United States senators, but I am immediately able to recall the names of seven dolls from more than sixty years ago. This characteristic undoubtedly says something rather interesting about my personality— but just what?) At any rate, the dolls' names were Jennifer, Dorothy, Ermengarde, Juliet, Angelica, Imogen and Alicia. (The senators' names, incidentally, are Saxbe and Taft. I voted for neither.)

Caroline's favorite doll . . . the one she always took to bed with her . . . was Jennifer, a sad and shabby little thing that had had a pink bald head for as long as any of us could remember. I was a somewhat nosy boy, and occasionally I spied on my sister, and one night I overheard her talking to Jennifer. "Oh my goodness," said Caroline, "oh my dear Jennifer, if only I had a vial of Magic Gas. It would put the entire world into a delicious and restful sleep for maybe a day, and then I would be able to go to people as they lay sleeping. And I would be able to *touch* them. And they would not be afraid of me. And I would be able to *kiss* them. And hug the ones I wanted to hug. And there would be no anger and no bad words. And no bad faces. I hate bad faces. They get me all ascared and wet behind my eyes, you know what I mean? Oh, if only I could find some Magic Gas . . ."

Jennifer was not only bald. Her skull was cracked, and she had just one arm. Later, when I acquired an education and became at least partly aware of some of the more common interpretations of certain symbols, I became uncomfortable whenever I summoned Jennifer to mind.

In 1922, when Caroline died, I was at her bedside. I kissed her dead forehead, and it was moist, and her husband was drunk in the next room, and it occurred to me that I really should have tried to say something to her. And then I wept, which was most uncharacteristic of me in those days (but no longer) but at least gratifying to the rest of the family. In those days, *Noblesse Oblige* meant something.

"First thing tomorrow morning," said Howard W. Amberson, "I'll go to Heimrich's for the camera and the film. Pete will show me how to work it."

"I certainly hope so."

"We'll have a record. A definition."

Anne shook her head, folded her hands in her lap. "You give everything such a . . . such a *finality*. I keep hearing sighs between the words. If we're going on a little trip, fine—but for heaven's sake don't be so *moany* and *glum*."

"There is no such word as *moany*," said Amberson.

"Well, pardon me for living," said Anne.

Amberson's eyes began to itch, and so he rubbed them.

There are occasional times when I do not even think of myself as being old.

Ha! And double ha!

And yet the fact exists that on certain occasions I awaken in the morning with a lightfooted and tumblejumping optimism clamoring in my skull. My joints hurt, and my heart is fragile and murderous, and my saliva is forever rancid, and yet, and yet . . .

And yet my lungs fill themselves with sweet breath. And my mind clears away all the memories of all the dead persons I have known and—in many cases—loved. And I say to myself: I matter. What I do matters. My last days can be felt as well as endured. An old goat is still and all a goat, and goats have blood; goats have feelings. God has had a hand in their preparation.

Fortunately for me (my physical condition being what it is), this sort of lunacy invariably vanishes by the time I finish my first cup of breakfast coffee. Truth is age; truth is the pain I feel in my gums.

Why did I write the above paragraph? At my age, why must I qualify my excesses of feeling? Is someone keeping score?

Oh, God. The fact is: I do not particularly want to die.

The Ambersons watched a great deal of television. They were especially fond of daytime serials, and Amberson's favorite was one called *Somerset,* which was carried on Channel 4 out of Columbus. In the summer of 1971 he became interested in the female villain, whose character name was India Delaney. She had high cheekbones and she was, in Amberson's opinion, a beautiful woman—and forget her character deficiencies. One afternoon, after he had expressed this view to his wife, Anne said: "She reminds you of Regina Ingersoll, doesn't she?"

"Yes," said Amberson. "Of course she does."

"Honestly, sometimes I think *the walls* remind you of Regina Ingersoll."

"Now. Now. If she were alive today, she would be seventy."

"I bet she is. The ornery live long."

"I am seventyfour, and you are seventytwo—so what does that make us?"

"Never mind," said Anne.

"It is impossible for me to think of Regina Ingersoll as being seventy."

"It's a good thing she's off God knows where, dead or alive or whatever. If she were here, you'd probably run off with her. You always did favor younger women."

"I wonder what happened to her."

"She's probably senile, and she probably dribbles in her soup."

"Don't you wish," said Amberson, smiling.

"And I bet her nose runs. And I bet she has warts."

"Don't you wish," said Amberson, still smiling.

Anne Amberson laughed out loud. It sounded like sandpaper in a hole.

I was thirty when I met Regina Ingersoll, and she was twentysix. The year was 1927, and she had been hired to teach French at Paradise Falls High, replacing a Miss Katharine Frazee, who had retired after presiding over Romance Languages at the school since about the time of the Napoleonic Wars. (In point of fact, the poor woman had borne a profound resemblance to pictures I had seen of Blucher, the Prussian whose arrival at Waterloo had sealed the Little Corporal's defeat.) And so Regina Ingersoll was a decided improvement, but then so, too, would have been a ringtailed baboon. This is a cruel opinion, I know, and I must here stipulate that I did not originate it. The phrase came from my friend, old Fred Boyd, who taught chemistry. And it annoyed me. In those days I became easily exasperated by that sort of witless levity. I could not abide imprecision, and so I said to him: "If you think our glamorous Regina Ingersoll is in any way, shape, manner or form comparable to a ringtailed baboon, you have my deepest sympathy. You are hopelessly mad, and you should be put in a place that has soft walls, warm lights and strong keepers."

(Academic humor does not often amount to much, and that is a fact.)

But, at any rate, Regina Ingersoll. She was small, shorter than I, but she carried herself well and proudly, as though her forehead were about to scrape heaven's, ah, bottom.It was said she had been born and reared in Columbus, but no one seemed to know for certain. The rumor persisted that she had left Columbus (or wherever) because of some sort of scandal. She wore short skirts, and her stockings were rolled, and she had what appeared to be the dearest little breasts I ever had seen. (My wife's were considerably larger, but they also were heavier and less jaunty. In addition, I had become used to them. Regina Ingersoll's breasts, on the other hand, had what I defined as an elfin charm, perky and inquisitive and most enchanting. Now then, I realize I was somewhat aswoon in my own rhetoric, but I honestly saw myself as being the only man in Paradise Falls who truly appreciated those cunning little twin delights. In the sweaty lexicon of my increasingly feverish imaginings, I called them bubbies for the connoisseur. Well, after all, I *was* an English teacher, wasn't I?)

And yet, the supposed delights of Regina Ingersoll's body notwithstanding, it was her *face* that fascinated me even more. I believed then (and I believe now) that it was the most disconcertingly luminous and exquisite face I ever had encountered. Her eyes were green and often moist, and they had a way of becoming warmly opaque whenever she was emotional about something. The effect was enough to make me want to rub my palms against my thighs. It caused my armpits to become sticky, and it created in me an embarrassed awareness of my lips and my nose and my ears and all my other protuberances. I was thirty years of age, and I should have known better, but when Regina Ingersoll made her eyes all opaque and milky, I felt myself lapse into a sort of boyish diffidence, clammy and inarticulate and manifestly absurd.

Her eyes sat deep and immense in the lovely hollows formed by her cheekbones, and her mouth was warm and full, with a glistening sensuality that fair made me want to climb to a treetop and shout hallelujah. (There is no exaggeration here, and I should know.) And that glorious mouth framed tiny precise teeth that had no spaces between them and forever were alight with what I saw as being silvery spittle. That is correct—*silvery spittle.* Oh dear God, you have no idea how I mooned and groaned. (I am smiling as I write this, but I was not smiling *then.* No indeed.)

Regina Ingersoll's hair was reddish, and she kept it in a tight bob that curved ever so gently behind her ears, which were pinkly delicate and enough to shred the soul. Or at least my soul. Sometimes, when I saw Regina Ingersoll's ears in the proper light (and I was in the proper mood of what I must shamefacedly call incipient tumescence), I actually had to make a physical effort not to make some sort of gentle kissing sound. I had been married for six years, and I already was the father of two children (the third and last would be born in 1930), and I fancied myself as being responsible and decent, with a full knowledge of properties and obligations, and yet there it was—this lunatic desire to seize Regina Ingersoll and gnaw and nibble on her like some sort of dimwitted puppy. Or, more accurately, a great baying hound, foamy and relentless.

And Regina Ingersoll saw my stupid torment.

And understood.

Oh yes, she surely did understand.

Her eyes showed that she understood.

They became milky, and they laughed at me.

And I mooned. I groaned. I languished.

And my wife asked me was I feeling well. And I became angry, and I told her *of course* I felt well; what sort of question was that? And dear Anne, plumply pretty, heavybreasted and polkadotted, hugged me and told me there, *there,* I didn't mean to upset you. I suppose sometimes I'm just an old nagface.

That is absolutely correct, I said.

"You were touchy about her," said Anne. "I do remember that."

"Was I?"

"Whenever I brought up her name, you became very defensive. You were like a little boy trying to hide a stolen toy. I suppose you thought you were being deviously clever. Well, you were about as deviously clever as a . . . as a sack of lead weights."

"I've hid nothing from you about Regina Ingersoll."

"That's all right for you to say *now.* But *then* it was different."

"I told you what she said to me that night. It was the only time we ever even sat close together, let alone *did* anything."

"And I'm still shocked," said Anne.

"By what she said?"

"Yes. It may seem amusing to you, but to me it was and is outrageous."

"It wasn't until what, 1941 or 1942, that I told you. I thought it wouldn't have mattered after all that time."

"Well," said Anne, "it did matter. And it still does. She was a terrible woman, and it was a terrible thing she said."

"Oh yes," said Amberson. "Terrible."

"Oh, I do hope she still is alive. I can almost see the dribble."

"Now who's being terrible?"

"Well," said Anne, "I have a right."

Regina Ingersoll was not shy, and she apparently didn't care if the entire world saw the tops of her stockings. In the faculty lunchroom, her mouth moist, her fine teeth neatly munching on tiny sandwiches of jelly and cream cheese, she spoke of beaux and tea dances and the music of Vincent Youmans, and she allowed as how Charles A. Lindbergh has the most *adorable* hair a person could *imagine*. And, ah, the tips of her delicious little frontal apparatus moved in and out with each breath, pushing at her chemise and causing me (hound that I was) to drink numerous glasses of ice water and spend a great deal of my time taking large shuddery breaths at the nearest open window.

(Now I can laugh, but now I am seventyfour, not thirty.)

It just about goes without saying that all the female teachers thoroughly detested Regina Ingersoll. According to Hester Ridgely, who taught social science and had a cluster of wens on her neck, Regina Ingersoll had come to Paradise Falls in the aftermath of some sort of big stink allegedly having to do with an abortion. (The phrase "big stink" was Hester's, not mine. It is a sad fact that she never truly understood the meaning of delicacy, and I have several vivid recollections of her using the word "shit" in moments of distress and/or exasperation. Today that sort of word—coming from anyone, man or woman—would not be worth noting. But in 1927 it was enough to curl the gates of heaven, and that is the honest truth.)

Therefore, considering its source, I quickly discounted the abortion story. And anyway, such a word as "abortion" was an affront when used in connection with the resplendent Regina (or so I fervently believed). And it did not even matter to me that she *did* display her stocking tops too freely and often.

One day in the autumn of 1927 (it was one of the lunch periods, and I was in charge of the Hall Monitors, a task that necessitated my prowling the corridors and making certain no Unauthorized Persons were wandering about), I happened to be passing Room 214, where Regina Ingersoll taught. The room was vacant that period, and I knew it was vacant (I had long since put her schedule to memory), and so it was with a certain degree of interest that I hesitated after hearing what quite clearly were moans. And I remember that my immediate thought was: My Lord, she is entertaining a lover in there.

I hesitated. I could have walked past Room 214, but I am after all only human—and anyway, I had an obligation. As the teacher in charge of the Hall Monitors, I had no choice but to investigate. (As Anne would say, harrumph and ahem.)

And so I entered the room. I seem to recall that my heart was slamming, and that my mouth tasted like stones. I quickly looked around, and at first glance I thought the room was empty. A single word was written on the blackboard, JEUDI, so I suppose the day was Thursday.

At any rate, I was about to leave when I heard another of the moans, and it was loud, quite splintered and hoarse. It was then that I saw the boy. His name was Ferdinand Burmeister, and he was kneeling behind Regina Ingersoll's desk. One of his cheeks rested against the pale blue pillow that was on the seat of her chair. He was extremely fat, this Ferdinand Burmeister, and his face was an explosion of acne, and his hands were laced over his belly. I stood and stared at him, but he obviously had not heard me—or, if he had, he did not care. His eyes were closed, and his moans came wordlessly, in a sort of rhythm, and from time to time he moistly kissed the pillow.

What I now have to say should be obvious. I stood there and watched this poor, tortured Ferdinand Burmeister, and I knew precisely how he felt. That pillow was *her* pillow, and it couched *her* rump, and therefore it was a holy relic. In point of fact, it is a wonder that I did not say to him: All right, sonny, that's enough. It's my turn now.

But of course I did no such thing. Instead I backed out of the room and withdrew down the hall and out of earshot of the moans. Ferdinand Burmeister later married a girl named Sally Toombs (she had red hair), fathered seven children, inherited the family pharmacy, prospered, ran for Council, was elected, served seven terms, and in 1966 was chairman of the Paradise County United Appeal campaign, which realized 106.3 percent of its goal.

"Her name," said Anne Amberson, "is Marie Wallace."

"Whose name?" Amberson wanted to know.

"The actress who plays India Delaney. The one who reminds you of your erstwhile flame, old Dribble-Soup Ingersoll."

"How did you find out?"

"The credits ran today while you were out buying that ridiculous movie camera. I *believe* they are called credits. Her name was toward the end, and I wrote it down so it wouldn't slip my mind. I wrote it in the margin of my *Future Shock.*"

"You and your *Future Shock,*" said Amberson.

"*You* and your movie camera," said Anne.

"Do you understand the book?"

"Some of it."

"What do you get from it?"

"A feeling of being very old."

"Tremendous," said Amberson. He and Anne were sitting in the kitchen again, and he was eating a leftover dish of cold baked apple. It was in heavy cream. "Somehow I don't see her as a Marie. She is too imperious for such a name."

"You see her as a Regina," said Anne.

"All right. Perhaps I do. But what I mean to say is, the name 'Marie' calls to mind dimestore clerks."

"I'm sure Marie Antoinette would be delighted to hear that."

Amberson nodded, shrugged a little. Then: "And Marie Vetsera."

"Who?"

"She was one of the victims of the Mayerling tragedy."

Anne frowned. "Mayerling. That had something to do with a prince who killed himself and his girlfriend. Right?"

"His mistress. Marie Vetsera was the mistress of a man who was in line for the throne of Austria-Hungary."

"Yes. Now I think I remember."

"Your Ohio State education has come to the rescue," said Amberson.

"Listen to the pot calling the kettle black."

"Hello there, Mrs. Kettle."

"Good afternoon to you, Mr. Pot."

Amberson smiled.

Anne also smiled. There was no color in her face. She picked at the cracked skin on one of her elbows.

Amberson decided it was time he tried to make her feel better. He decided to bring up someone who probably was worse off than either of them. He said: "I saw Ferd Burmeister downstreet this afternoon. On Main Street, right outside of Heimrich's."

"What does Ferd Burmeister have to do with Marie Vetsera?"

"Nothing," said Amberson, eating another slice of the baked apple. "His name simply popped into my mind, that's all. Have we given Sinclair any of this cream?"

"Yes. He came in this morning and begged for a snack. I gave him some in his dish." Here Anne hesitated, picked at her elbow. Then she smiled and said: "But let's not change the subject. What's all this about Ferd Burmeister? You're not the sort to have things just *pop* into your *mind*."

Amberson was wearing spectacles. They had speckled brown rims. He pushed them to the end of his nose and blinked at his wife. "Honestly," he said, "there's no real reason."

Anne sighed. "All right," she said, "have it your own way. So what did you two discuss?"

"Movie cameras. He apparently knows a great deal about them."

"He knows a great deal about many things. He is a very important fellow. If you don't believe *me*, just ask *him*."

"Yes," said Amberson.

"But I can remember when he had pimples. Lots of pimples."

"So can I."

"That was an ugly thing for me to say."

"Well," said Amberson, "it's true."

"But he's never done anything to me. I shouldn't say ugly things about him."

Amberson shrugged.

Anne shook her head. "He must be about sixty by now."

"At least," said Amberson.

"So tell me. What else besides movie cameras did you and Ferd discuss?"

"The freeze."

"What freeze?"

"Nixon's freeze."

"Oh," said Anne. "He seem all right?"

"Fair to middling," said Amberson, shrugging.

"I think I recall somebody telling me he was having trouble with his pancreas. Or something down there."

"His gall bladder," said Amberson, spooning up the last of the apple.

"Isn't the gall bladder the same as the pancreas?"

"Hardly. The gall bladder receives the bile. The pancreas is a gland, and it makes discharges. The one receives, and the other . . . ah, emits."

"Howard W. Amberson, the fount of information. First Marie Vetsera, and now this."

"Thank you. Oh, and by the way, it is the cow's pancreas that provides sweetbreads."

"Really? How thrilling."

"Yes," said Amberson. "Very."

"Yum yum," said Anne. "I've always been so very fond of sweetbreads. Some nights I simply cannot go to sleep, just from the excitement of thinking about them."

"Yes. I know."

"What?"

"Sometimes I hear you groan in your sleep. 'Sweetbreads . . . oh how I pine for sweetbreads . . .' Your groans are very passionate."

"You are a nit," said Anne. She shook her head. "I've never eaten sweetbreads. Not in my entire life."

"You haven't missed much, take my word for it."

"I always thought they were brains."

"Well, they aren't. They are the pancreas."

"People who eat sweetbreads are eating a gland, right?"

"Right," said Amberson.

"Gland-eaters. Sounds terrible."

"Yes. Like a title for one of those science-fiction movies that always seem to be playing at the Paradise Valley Drive-In. *The Attack of the Gland-Eaters.*"

"Delightful," said Anne. "You were telling me Ferd seemed fair to middling. How did he look?"

"Prosperous. Freshly bathed and shaved. And he was wearing some sort of scent. Rather heavy."

"But how did he *really* look?"

"You mean the interior of his soul or whatever?"

"Yes."

"I'm not qualified to answer that."

"Yes you are."

"All right," said Amberson. "All right. He looked dreadful. He looked old."

"*Good* and old? All passions spent?"

"Yes."

"Thank you," said Anne, and she still was smiling.

Amberson also was smiling now. He loved his wife very much, and he had cheered her, and he supposed he owed Ferd Burmeister a small debt.

It was on Halloween night of 1927 that matters between Regina Ingersoll and me came to a sort of resolution.

Old Fred Boyd, the chemistry man, gave a costume party that night for all the teachers. Anne and the children had gone to Lancaster to visit her sister Christine, and so I attended the party alone. I came as a magician, and I wore an old top hat and suit of tails that I had inherited earlier that year from my father. My mouth was adorned with a large and villainously curling false black moustache, and I had dyed my eyebrows black as well, to heighten what I saw as being a devilishly sinister effect. My hair came down in a natural widow's peak (I still had hair in those days), which added to my rakish aspect, and old Fred told me I looked like pretty hot stuff, to use his phrase. I swirled my tails like a good fellow, and I stroked my moustache, and a number of the ladies giggled, and I was quite delighted.

There was some fairly decent bootleg Scotch on hand, and it gave me a splendid warmth, enabling me to dance with several of the ladies—including Fred Boyd's wife, and Muriel Johnson (who taught algebra) and even Hester Ridgely (wens and all). But I did not dance with Regina Ingersoll, and neither did any of the other men. She arrived quite late, with her smile at the ready and her eyes all milky and warm, and she was dressed as a sequined black cat. Her tail was long, made of yarn, and there were jimmies on her face, and she had exaggerated her eyes with immense smears of mascara. She had come to the party alone, and it would have been quite simple for her to have made some sort of Grand Entrance. But she did not do this. She simply went to the Boyds, shook hands with them, then drifted into a corner and chatted quietly with whomever happened to pass her way.

Oh yes, she was quiet and demure, but she had of course triumphed. Every man in that room was watching her, and her unspectacular entrance had been the act of a genius. She could not have been more conspicuous if she had arrived naked and playing a trombone. It was a remarkable performance, a true work of art.

For myself, I was terribly aware of her eyes, which were quite filmy indeed and certainly impossible to ignore, what with all the mascara. I made an effort to remain on the opposite side of the room from her, and for some reason I found myself bumping into chairs and lamps and tables, which was certainly uncharacteristic of me. (I hoped the others would think it was the Scotch.)

Old Fred Boyd came up to me and said: "You seem at loose ends. Are your wheels out of line?"

I remember laughing rather nervously and blaming my confusion on the fact that Anne and the children were away. And then I said: "I'm afraid I'm not able to function as a bachelor any more."

Old Fred Boyd was wearing a pumpkin over his head. There were holes for his eyes and mouth, and now I was able to see his dentures as his mouth spread in a grin. He leaned close to me and said: "Mr. Magician, you are a liar. Your distress is being caused by our friend Miss Pussycat, and you know it. She has been fastening you with those great big encrusted eyes of hers ever since she arrived, and so you are all asquirm. Pussy is away, and Mousie wants to play."

"That is a dreadful slander," I said, but I did not raise my voice. As a matter of fact, I was smiling a little.

Old Fred continued: "I can't say as I blame you. But my wife is here, and all the other men have their wives with them. Which means we don't even dare *dance* with the adorable Miss Pussycat. My God, how I envy you, what with your wife out of town and all. I wish you good fortune and great strength."

"How's that?" I said.

But old Fred moved away from me, his troublemaking pumpkin-head bobbing cheerfully. He embraced Muriel Johnson and began dancing with her to the music that came from the Victrola. It was a fast dance, a Charleston perhaps, and her breasts wobbled, and she laughed.

I watched them for a moment, and then I again was aware of Regina Ingersoll's eyes. There was nothing I could do to resist them. They were immense and undefeated, and they began to pull me across the room. (Does all this seem sophomoric? Well, it is sophomoric, but sometimes one has no choice but to behave like an idiot. Sometimes one is simply magnetized by one's loins. As my brother Alvin Jr. used to say, a stiff prick has no conscience.) And so, shambling and scuffing like a virgin farm boy, I walked across the room, past Hester Ridgely, past Mr. and Mrs. Bob Leonhard (he taught physics), past Irene Freeman (she taught English and was chairman of the department), past Mr. and Mrs. George F. Derwent (he was the football coach, and they both wore West Point cadet outfits), and past Karl Loeffler (he taught German, and he was perspiring freely in a polar bear suit), and advanced loose and flat-footed on a smiling Miss Pussycat, and now someone had put a foxtrot on the Victrola, and I asked Miss Pussycat would she care to dance, and my voice was raw and reedy.

Her smile enlarged itself, and I was very conscious of silvery saliva,

23

and she told me yes, she would be delighted to dance with me. She opened her arms.

We danced, and she permitted me to lead. I held her at arm's length, and I was aware that Hester Ridgely and Irene Freeman were frowning at us.

Miss Pussycat moved closer to me. Her jimmies glistened. "I appreciate this very much," she said.

I shrugged. I could not speak.

"I really do," said Miss Pussycat, moving even closer. Now she was humming with the music. Perhaps it was Vincent Youmans. I cannot remember.

I cleared my throat, and this time I was able to speak. "You . . . ah, there is nothing to appreciate," I said. "This is . . . ah, no big thing."

"Yes it is," said Miss Pussycat, and her cheek brushed my shoulder. "And you know it is."

I recall that my mouth held too much spittle. I swallowed damply, and I was able to smell her hair. I managed to tell her all right, if she wanted it to be a big thing, then it *was* a big thing. And so we danced, and within a minute or two we were dancing easily, and she kept moving closer, but we did not bump into anything, and I found myself wondering whether Hester and Irene's eyeballs had fallen out yet. That damned *provocateur* of a Pumpkinhead Boyd danced past with Mrs. Pumpkinhead Boyd, and chortling noises came from within the pumpkin, and Mrs. Pumpkinhead made a clucking sound and told her husband hush. I smiled at them, and Miss Pussycat squeezed my hand.

We danced three consecutive dances, all foxtrots, and her fragrance put me in mind of what? A field of clover after a summer rain? The breath of angels? The taste of some inexpressibly sweet honey? I have written of sophomoric behavior. All right then, choose whatever sophomoric metaphor pleases you—it will serve very nicely to describe the glory of her scent. She kept moving closer, and it is a wonder I did not whoop and clap and leap about the room. She held her tail of yarn in her free hand, and once she even tickled my chin with the tassel that was fastened all poofy and impudent at its end (I sniggered like a schoolboy), and I said to myself: Dear Lord, please spare me. I am too young to die.

Then someone put a fast number on the Victrola, and I managed to tell Miss Pussycat I was sorry, but fast numbers were beyond me. And she laughed and said yes, she just bet that was true. I seem to recall that my face then reddened, and so she again laughed. We walked across the room to the sofa and seated ourselves, and by that time I was absolutely convinced that something splendidly dreadful was about to happen to me. And I was correct. Oh yes. Very.

Idly holding her tasseled tail in her lap and from time to time fingering the nap of the tassel, Miss Pussycat spoke quietly of her life in Paradise Falls. She lived in a rooming house owned by an elderly spinster named Bagley. The place was on Mulberry Street, and it adjoined both the cemeteries. "I like Miss Bagley fine," she said, "even if the poor old girl *does* talk too often about some sweetheart of hers who vanished off the face of the earth at Gettysburg, but I must *say* that those awful *graveyards* really *do* give me the *willies*. My room looks right out on the mausoleum of a man named Wells, who I understand was a pretty big cheese around here thirty years ago."

"That he was," I said. "My parents used to tell me about him. And I remember his daughter. She was quite strange."

"Well," said Miss Pussycat, "*anyway,* that mausoleum has all sorts of *froufrou* and *fuss* on it, if you know what I mean—so vulgar and tasteless."

"I used to look at it when I was a boy," I said. "I remember a frieze of angels and lambs."

"Yes," said Miss Pussycat, "*angels* and *lambs.* Can you imagine?"

"I think the frieze was his daughter's idea of a joke. I understand he was a terrible old bandit. He died, you know, when a church bell fell on him. I am told she hated him."

"I can believe *that,*" said Miss Pussycat.

"I suppose the frieze was her way of making an ironic proclamation to the world."

"One of these days I must move out of Miss Bagley's place. I'm not very comfortable with ghosts and old hatreds."

"That certainly is understandable," I said.

Then, smiling, Miss Pussycat changed the subject, remarking that life was a great deal more pleasant than death, at least to those who had a choice, and she launched into a description of Paradise Falls and its inhabitants. "They haven't been terribly friendly," she said. "Most of the women seem to see me as some sort of threat, a painted *putain* out to wrest their dear husbands from them. And I'm sure you understand why only one man—namely, you—asked me to dance tonight. The others have their wives with them, and they don't *dare.* Oh, I tell you, it's almost funny. If those women only *knew* how dull, flat and colorless I find their husbands. Present company excepted, as I'm sure you know."

"Thank you," I said, beaming.

Miss Pussycat squeezed one of my wrists. "I absolutely *must* ask you a question," she said.

"Please do," I said, still beaming.

Briskly she patted my wrist, and then she said: "Tell me, do you have a large penis?"

Howard W. and Anne Amberson lived alone, there in 1971, in a spacious brick and tile house on West Cumberland Street just west of Market Street. It had been built in 1920, and the down payment had been a wedding present the following year from Amberson's father. The house's only other occupant, there in 1971, was the family cat, Sinclair, a neutered gray male of about eleven who liked to eat 9-Lives Super Supper and ride in the automobile.

"What'll we do about Sinclair?" Anne Amberson asked her husband.

"In connection with what?"

"Our trip. We'll have to hire a catsitter."

"No. We'll take him with us. He likes to ride in the car. He'll enjoy the scenery."

It was night, and the Ambersons were lying in bed. Anne had just taken a bath, and she smelled like Camay. She wore a pink nightgown, and it was fastened tightly at the throat. She did not like her husband to see her scar. "What about calls of nature?" she asked him.

"We'll take along his box," said Amberson. "We'll put it in the back seat, and he can do his duty whenever he likes."

"It will *smell.*"

"We'll take along extra sand and change it every day."

"*We'll* take along extra sand and *we'll* change it every day?"

"*I'll* change it every day," said Amberson, smiling.

"Good," said Anne. "I love Sinclair, but I do *not* love his *box.* Still, don't you think he'd be happier staying home, with a catsitter to take care of him? The little Williamson girl is very sweet, and she loves cats."

"No. Sinclair needs to learn that there's more to the world than the rhubarb plants out back. And the garage roof where he sleeps in the sun."

"You are a strange man, Howard Amberson."

"I am an *old* man, and I have a right to be strange."

"I suppose you do. You and your movie camera. Lord save us all."

"I'll take care of buying the extra sand," said Amberson. "I believe the Big Bear has extra large bags. Twenty pounds or so. Something like that."

26

"Make sure you have someone carry it to the car. I don't want you struggling across the Eastwood Plaza parking lot with twenty pounds of *cat sand* and having another of your heart attacks."

Amberson chuckled and punched his pillow.

"It would be some epitaph," said Anne. "RIP: Here Lies Howard William Amberson, Rudely Snatched Away by Twenty Pounds of Litter Green."

Amberson snorted, patted his wife on a knee.

"*Fresh,*" said Anne, embracing him.

To the best of my recollection, I had put away only two drinks of the bootleg Scotch before Miss Pussycat made her astonishing inquiry, I wasn't drunk; I hadn't *imagined* the question. Of course there was a great deal of noise in the room, and perhaps I hadn't *heard* it correctly. I therefore blinked at her and said: "I beg your pardon?"

Miss Pussycat stroked the tassel at the end of her tail. Speaking quietly and with a sort of vacant thoughtfulness, she said: "You are a small man, and I was rather hoping you had a small penis."

"Oh," I said. "Well."

"If a man has a large penis, I cannot accommodate him without suffering great pain."

"I see," I said.

"So tell me."

It all had to be a joke, correct? She was only trying to shock me, correct? She was testing the sophistication of my attitudes, correct? Therefore, it was necessary that I play the game, correct? It was necessary that I be suave and a bit coy, that I behave as though attractive young women inquired about the size of my penis every day of the week and twice on Sunday. And so, even managing to smile a little, I said: "I don't believe I want to tell you."

"Please do," said Miss Pussycat. "Pretty please."

"No," I said. My fingers were cold. I crossed my legs and jiggled a foot. I have already reported that I was not the sort to jiggle a foot, and yet there I was, jiggling away like some sort of poor dumbfounded spastic.

Miss Pussycat shook her head. "I thought you were different," she said, rubbing the tassel against one of my wrists. "I am very lonely. You would be too, if every night when you looked outside all you saw was a sea of *mausoleums* and *tombstones* and heard nothing but a terrible *silence.*" Here she looked me squarely in the eye, and then

27

she said: "I suppose you think I was being obscene when I asked the question—but, you see, I was married once, and I loved the man very deeply, but the *size* of him caused me such awful *pain*. He was so gentle, and he liked to read poetry aloud. I met him in Paris in June of 1920, and we were married six weeks later, but it was a fiasco, I tell you. A terrible *calamity*. You see, we just simply did not *fit*. We took many long walks, and he tried to talk away my pain with his romantic rhetoric, but it did no good. We saw a number of physicians, but they were of no help either. And so finally Carl began seeing other women, and that was when we were divorced. But I believe he still loves me. He has never remarried either, and he writes me every other day or so, and he keeps insisting he would marry me again tomorrow if I would have him. But of course that will not happen. My problem has in no way been alleviated. I . . . well, you see, I am simply unable to stand the pain . . ."

I nodded. Hester and Irene were staring at me, and I hoped my face was properly expressionless.

"Perhaps I am going crazy," said Miss Pussycat.

"No. You are not going crazy."

"Then please tell me what I want to know."

I cleared my throat. It was something to do. "I am unprepared," I said, "for any sort of quantitative analysis. I have never entered a contest."

Miss Pussycat smiled. She dropped the tassel to her lap, then held her forefingers six inches or so apart. "When distended, is it this large?" she asked me.

"Perhaps," I said, and for some reason I covered my mouth.

She moved the fingers until they were perhaps nine or ten inches apart. "Ah, Carl's was like this. He was a *stallion*, I tell you."

"Please," I said. My mouth still was covered.

"Please what?"

"Please don't use your fingers as a measuring device. We are being watched."

"By the Misses Ridgely and Freeman?"

"Yes."

"All right," said Miss Pussycat. She folded her hands in her lap. "They probably are only thinking I'm describing the size of a fish . . . *but,* if it makes you feel better, I'll sit here like a very prim and proper girl."

"I appreciate that," I said, uncovering my mouth.

"So?" said Miss Pussycat, staring straight ahead. "Is it six inches or smaller?"

"All I can say is: Perhaps."

"Anything larger just absolutely does me in."

"I see."

"If I have shocked you, forgive me."

"You are forgiven."

"You seem like a gentle person. And you are intelligent and sensitive. I would very much like you to take me to bed—provided of course you are not too large. And I wouldn't *dream* of demanding any sort of *commitment*. I know you are married, and I suspect you love your wife very much. All I want is some warmth and attention, and perhaps a little relief and enjoyment. I promise you there would be no large consequences. Well, what do you say to all that?"

I rubbed my knees, and my foot still was jiggling. "There . . . ah, there is nothing I *can* say," I told her.

"I am unattractive?"

"Hardly. But *I* am a coward."

"I was afraid of that," said Miss Pussycat. One of her jimmies slid down a cheek. For a moment I thought she was crying, but she flicked away the loose jimmy with a fingernail and said: "I am not weak, and I am able to live with disappointments. I thought you would understand. Well, perhaps you do, but it's a useless sort of understanding, isn't it?"

"Yes," I said. "I suppose it is."

"Will you regret your decision?"

"Absolutely."

She smiled. "That is something of a comfort."

"Good."

"I wonder what the Misses Ridgely and Freeman are thinking. For all they can tell, we are discussing the weather. Or the corn crop. Or whatever."

"Thank God," I said.

Miss Pussycat laughed. Her head went back, and her throat worked in spasms. "You rascal you," she said, sputtering, and she slapped me on a knee. But she kept her voice down. Finally, she said: "You are a dear man. I don't know why I say it, seeing as how you've rejected me, but there is something lovable about you."

"Thank you," I said.

"It would have been enjoyable. I sort of suspect you are small enough."

"So do I."

"*C'est la vie,*" said Miss Pussycat, and I seem to recall that she sighed a little.

"Vraiment," I said, and I seem to recall that I also sighed—and more than a little.

"Your accent is atrocious," said Miss Pussycat, smiling.

"Well, this is all something of a strain," I told her.

Again Miss Pussycat laughed, only this time much more loudly. Old Fred Boyd, still wearing the pumpkin, came across the room to her and told her he was pleased she was having such a good time. She wiped at her eyes and told old Fred that his friend Howard Amberson was a genuine wit. I quickly stood up and crossed the room and helped a woman named Iris Snell choose a new record for the Victrola. That was the first and last time I had a private conversation with Miss Pussycat . . . I mean, Regina Ingersoll. She taught at Paradise Falls High School for only one year. She left town in June of 1928 and was never seen or heard from again. I waited until about 1941 or 1942 before I told my wife of the incident, and she expressed strong disapproval. As well she should have. For, you see, Regina Ingersoll had torn at my dreams through all those years. And she continued to tear at them until I was well past sixty. And perhaps, in a sense, she tears at them yet (why else have I written so extensively about her?).

Amberson decided that they would take $2,000 in Travelers' Cheques with them on the motor trip. He and Anne had a savings account of more than $27,000 in the Paradise Falls State Bank, and he obtained the Travelers' Cheques the Saturday morning before they were due to set out. The teller who handled the transaction was a slender girl named May Soeder, and she had green eyes and red hair. "I hope you have a nice trip," she said. "It's a good time of the year to be going on a little vacation. The leaves and all."

"Yes," said Amberson. He was signing the checks, and they were in small denominations, and so there were many of them to be signed. He used one of his Japanese pens. His handwriting was fastidious and still quite schoolteacherish.

"Where are you going?" May Soeder wanted to know.

"I'm not quite sure."

"Oh?"

Amberson smiled. "I shall put one thousand dollars' worth of these checks in one pocket," he said, "and I shall put one thousand dollars' worth in another pocket. When the first pocket is empty, we'll turn around and head home."

"But where are you *going?*"

"Somewhere," said Amberson, shrugging. "Every day will be an adventure. We'll be footloose. We'll go in whichever direction suits our whim, and I'm taking along a movie camera, and I'll try to record as much of it as I can."

May Soeder handed Amberson the passbook. "Mr. Amberson," she said, "you are something."

"How so?"

"My boyfriend, Alan Barnhill . . . maybe you know him . . . he was in Viet Nam, and now he's working out at the refrigerator plant . . ."

"I know him. I know the family. He has an older brother, Ted, who ran track for me a number of years ago."

"Yes. That's right. Ted. Well, anyway, Alan says that all people should be allowed to do their own thing. He says there is nothing more precious than a single human being. He says we only live once, and so we owe it to ourselves to experience everything we can. Otherwise, he says, we sell out our . . . our *humanity.*"

Amberson finished signing the checks. He capped the pen, slipped it in a pocket of his suitcoat. He removed his spectacles and cleaned them with a handkerchief. No one was in line behind him, and so he was able to chat a bit with this girl. "Doing one's own thing is very important these days, isn't it? I hear the phrase a great deal. On television. In conversations. Everywhere."

"Well, it *is* important, isn't it?"

"Yes—as long as it's not a rationale for selfishness. We must still consider other people."

"Alan considers other people. He considers *me.* He is very considerate."

"Good," said Amberson. "In that case, he is a fine fellow. Has he discovered yet what his own thing is?"

"Not yet—but he's working on it."

"Does he propose to marry you?"

"Yes."

"Good," said Amberson.

May Soeder leaned forward and rested her elbows on the counter. Her throat was pink. Her hair was long, and it tumbled across her forehead. She brushed it back and said: "He is good to me in every way I can think of . . . That sounds like bragging, doesn't it?"

"A little . . ."

"I didn't mean it to sound that way. It's just that I'm not ashamed."

Amberson hastily cleared his throat. "Don't mind me," he said. "Different times have different mores, and I should be able to understand that."

May Soeder smiled. "Girls didn't talk this way in your day, did they?"

Amberson summoned the grinning jimmied image of Regina Ingersoll to his mind. "Some did," he said, "but not many."

May Soeder nodded.

There was nothing more Amberson wanted to say, and so he started out.

May Soeder called after him. "Mr. Amberson—?"

She still was leaning forward as Amberson turned. "Please don't be angry with me. I'm not ashamed of myself, and I'm not ashamed of Alan."

"That's fine."

"And you're not angry?"

"I'm not angry a bit."

May Soeder grinned and winked. "You are a doll," she said. "Go in good health. Do your thing."

"Right on, baby," said Amberson, and he gave May Soeder a jaunty wave as he went out.

I am writing most of this at night, after Anne has fallen asleep. Her pain is strongest at night, and she often requires pills. But the pills are quite potent, and she sleeps soundly, and she knows nothing of what I am doing. Some day I may show her all this material (or whatever it is), and then again I may not. I suppose that decision depends on what conclusion I reach, if indeed I reach a conclusion at all.

At the beginning, I stated that this would be "an attempt to sort out confusions." But the more I write, the more I wonder. Can a human life be defined in any terms other than confusions? And aren't confusions, by their very nature, impossible to "sort out"? Can man be described in the same terms used to explain an electrical wiring scheme?

The questions are rhetorical, and so why am I writing all this?

Perhaps because these words retain in me a sense of purpose—and are in effect a plea to the Almighty to spare me until I am finished. (Perhaps I am a curious sort of Scheherazade, a *very* curious sort of Scheherazade to be sure, but one whose motives are precisely the same.) My heart has been splintered, but I do not want to die.

Or perhaps I am writing all this because I am seeking to determine my worth. Isn't it all terribly stupid and pretentious? Stupid because there is no pattern. Pretentious because I can be judged only by God, and any conclusions *I* might draw would be prejudiced and probably selfserving.

So does this mean that it is only fear of death, and nothing more, that keeps me hunched over this ledger? Am I really only an elderly smalltown Scheherazade blabbering away in order to keep a sword from falling on my neck? Is *that* the only reason for all these words?

I deplore all these thoughts. I have loved, and I have mourned, and surely I am of some worth. I must write now of love . . . yes, honest love . . . of my wife and our courtship and the commitments we made. (By doing so, perhaps I shall be able to suppress some of my doubts.)

I met my wife (her name then was Anne Georgia Howell) at a Pi Phi dance at Ohio State University in the autumn of 1919, when I was a senior. Anne was a sophomore pledge, and she wore a blue dress that night, a blue dress with a velvet collar. Her escort was a large breathy fellow named Sam Chappell. I had come to the dance with a chattery little blonde named Joanna Lyman, and until that night I had been reasonably certain that within a year or so I would marry Joanna. She was from Cleveland, but she had read Edgar Lee Masters (in those days, who *hadn't* read Edgar Lee Masters?), and she had told me on numerous occasions that she was just *fascinated* by small towns, my dear, and goodness gracious, wouldn't it be fun to live in one?

Joanna's father was in the wholesale luggage business in Cleveland, and so there was a good deal of money in the family. In addition, she was an adroit kisser. She and I were forever grabbing at one another, and she squirmed when she kissed, and she was not reluctant to use her tongue. And now and then, on what she considered to be special occasions, she permitted me to reach inside the front of her dress and stroke her breasts, which were small but quite firm.

And, in addition to all this, she said she was quite sure she loved me. She told me on numerous occasions that she was perfectly willing to marry me whenever I saw fit to give the word. Her words made me puff like a frog; they gave me a feeling that I was God's ultimate earthly manifestation of virility; ah, they gave me all sorts of grandiose and pompous thoughts. She had a way of gasping and sighing, did that Joanna Lyman, and she was forever murmuring passionate speculations into my ear. I just *know* you will be absolutely *terrific,* she told me. I can tell from the way you kiss. Your *mouth* is so *sensual.* Ohhh, I could just absolutely *die.*

And so forth and so on, and she seldom paused for breath. With Joanna Lyman, the question always was: Just who was courting

33

whom? *My* words of endearment were *devoured* by *her* words of endearment; I barely could get in an ah, yes or no, and after a time another question began to scrape at my mind: How come, if my virility was such a great miracle of Creation, I did not have the initiative? How come my poor words were always being devoured?

These questions were of course flatulent and absurd, but I was a virgin, and they were not flatulent and absurd to *me,* no indeed. I was twentytwo years of age, and I had never even touched a girl's private parts, and it is an honest wonder I had not exploded. At twentytwo I was distressingly behind my contemporaries (most of my highschool classmates had married, and many of them already had children of their own), and this was giving me much anguish. As my dormitory bedsheets could attest. But, well, never mind about *that.* There is no reason to be explicit. I am certain that anyone who is still breathing air will know what I mean.

Joanna also was a virgin—or so she said, and there was no reason for me not to believe her. She liked to say she was . . . ah, *intacta,* my dear . . . absolutely and maddeningly *untouched* . . .

Well, I did find Joanna amusing, and I did not believe that marriage to her would be such a terrible state of affairs. And, beyond all the thrashings and gropings, we did have a certain intellectual affinity. We were neither of us aggressive or belligerent; we enjoyed books and the theater, and we both were majoring in secondary education. (Now, looking back on it with whatever passes for the wisdom of my years, I suspect that our real affinity lay in that particular area. The "learning process," as it is called today, gave us great delight. To us, Alexander Pope had flesh and warts, and fat Louis XVII aroused our pity, and the Organ Symphony of Saint-Saëns moved us beyond words. Oh yes, Joanna was the most dazzling and vivacious girl ever to have entered my life, but there was a good mind behind all that chatter, and it would be unfair of me to dismiss her here as a pleasant little nitwit with pretty breasts. There was more to her, and my memory of her is respectful and appreciative.)

We had met, Joanna and I, in the autumn of 1917. Several of the Pi Phi girls gave a tea for a group of sophomore ROTC cadets, and she came sashaying up to me and told me I was absolutely the *neatest* and most *resplendent* little fellow she had ever *seen.* And, even though she had called me *little,* I was immensely flattered. There were a great many neat and resplendent ROTC cadets on the Ohio State campus in the fall of 1917, but this sparkling little blonde had chosen *me,* and I suppose it was then that I began thinking about my cosmic and irresistible virility. And so, with a measured thoughtfulness most appropriate in a secondary education major, I began courting Joanna, and soon I was tasting her tongue, and she was speaking of Edgar Lee Masters and her interest in small towns, the *microcosm* and all.

I have written that Joanna was not aggressive or belligerent, and perhaps her behavior seems to contradict the denial. And yet, believe me, she was in most ways soft and even timid. I distinctly recall her telling me one night that she actually had to *swallow hard,* my dear, and take about *one zillion* breaths, before sashaying up to me that afternoon at the Pi Phi tea. As you get to know me, she said, you will discover that all my gush and chatter is not *natural.* It's an *act of will,* that's what it is. In my family, those who don't speak up are pushed into the trash bin, and so I've had to learn to speak up. I'm not all that I seem to be, and I hope you'll come to understand that.

I did come to understand it. In the two years that I courted Joanna, I must have visited the Lymans' Cleveland Heights home at least half a dozen times. It was an enormous Tudor structure on Fairmount Boulevard, and everything in it also was enormous—including the people who lived there. Joanna's father was perhaps six and a half feet tall, and her mother was staggeringly fat, and she had three immensely hairy and deepvoiced older brothers who looked as though they ate boulders and railroad locomotives for breakfast, and the atmosphere in the place was one of incessant clamor. The three brothers all were bachelors, and they and the father greatly enjoyed playing football in the parlor. Joanna and I were always drafted into their games, and they did not even bother to clear away the furniture. According to their way of thinking, this made the game more interesting—and provided stationary blocking for whoever had the ball. On one occasion they used the family goldfish bowl for a football. Naturally, the water slopped out of the bowl, and the fish (there were four of them) fell to the rug and died there. I tried to pick them up and carry them to the downstairs bathroom, but one of the brothers tackled me and told me it didn't matter about those damn fish; it was the game that mattered, and I would stay there and *play* the game, and never mind about those stupid fish; nobody could stand them anyway. And so the fish died, and I seem to recall that my side lost.

Whenever I visited the Lymans' home, I felt as though I had intruded on a gathering of Brobdingnags. The furniture was vast and institutional, made of dark and heavy woods, with colossal cushions and armrests. The drapes were like tarpaulins, and the floors resounded louder than doom. And everywhere were those braying elephantine Lymans—the father, the mother and the three sons. And there *I* was, a twig in the forest, clutching Joanna by the hand and hoping no one would step on me. And she said to me: See what I mean about my family? And I said: Yes. And she said: Now do you see why I have to speak up so much, even though it is against my nature? And I said: Yes. And she said: Survival. And I said: Yes.

It all was just about enough to make me want to weep for her, and that is no exaggeration. (I recall that the fish were kicked under the sofa so they would not get in the way and perhaps cause someone to slip and fall.)

It was an utter mystery—to both me and Joanna—how she came to be born into that tribe of lunatic giants. She told me she sometimes even wondered whether her father was really her father at all. Perhaps Mama was briefly enamored of a circus midget, she said. I mean, I am barely five feet tall, and just look at the rest of my family, will you?

I regret to say that this last point did not bother me at all. I am afraid I was too delighted by the fact that Joanna was shorter than I. In 1911, at the age of fourteen, I had reached my full height—five feet, seven inches, provided I kept my spine straight. (Today my spine is no longer straight, and I suppose I am barely five-six at the most.)

But, anyway, Joanna. Despite her frightening family, I was comfortable with her, and I was somewhat looking forward to what I saw as being a long and serene life with her. And surely, considering her background, she had to crave serenity as much as I did. Now then, one might ask why serenity meant so much to me. Well, consider this:

Like my father, I was (and am) precise. Or at least I fancy myself as having always had that characteristic.

Therefore, I sought (and still seek) definitions and dimensions. Why else would I, at this late date, take my wife and go off looking for something I call an apparatus?

So, once that is understood, it should be clear why I enjoyed Joanna for more reasons than those provided by the somewhat limited physical pleasure she gave me. With Joanna, there was a definite *pattern* to be seen, a reassuringly rigid *schedule.* You see, neatness lay within me like breath and blood. Unlike my brothers, I had never bullied Catholics or squandered my energies in any other sort of needless hatred. Unlike my sister, I had never held imaginary conversations, and I had never yearned for Magic Gas. To me, violence and daydreams had a curious similarity—they both were stupid, and they both were wastes of time.

As a result of all this, I was of course hugely annoyed when I fell in love with what I considered to be that silly ninny of an Anne Howell. The emotion she created in me was anything but precise, and she did great damage to the pattern I had established. I was forced to throw poor Joanna over the side and yield myself to what I saw as being a horrendous disruption. (I must say, though, that later events showed Anne to be not much of a disruption at all. But later was later, and the beginning was a much different proposition.)

The Pi Phi dance where I met Anne was what we called in those days a drinking affair. Hip flasks were just coming into use in 1919, and most of the young men brought them. But not I. To me, drinking was a waste of time; it robbed one of one's precision. And Joanna did not care much for whiskey, either. But most of the others did not share our distaste for the stuff. For instance, Anne's escort, Sam Chappell. He was a great hip flask man, and he was already a bit drunk by the time Joanna and I arrived at the dance. I had taken several classes with him, but I knew him only slightly and considered him to be something of a windbag. The sort of windbag who was forever boasting of sexual conquests that probably were imaginary. But he was larger than I, and so I had never called his attention to this character deficiency. It was also for this reason that I did not object when he cut in on me and wheeled away with a squealing and giggling Joanna, who told him: "Dear *me,* Sam, you are such an *animal!*" And Sam Chappell, grinning, whispered something in Joanna's ear that made her frown in a sort of mock bewilderment.

I was a bit annoyed, but what could I do about it? So I drifted off the dance floor, and it was then that I bumped into this plump little girl who was wearing a blue dress with a velvet collar.

I was first aware of her eyes, which were extremely blue, and—for some reason I could not understand—I promptly began to feel rather boyish and almost silly. Grinning clownishly at her, I said: "Hello there, Little Miss Blue Eyes, my name is Howard Amberson and a great big bully has just made off with my lady friend. It is a crime the way we little people are forever being picked on."

Little Miss Blue Eyes smiled. "The great big bully is *my* escort," she said.

"Really? Now why would such a nice girl come to a dance with the likes of a Sam Chappell?"

"It was either that or stay in my room and read John Stuart Mill."

"Oh," I said. I took Little Miss Blue Eyes by an elbow and steered her toward the punchbowl. "Please join me in a glass of nonalcoholic Pi Phi strawberry punch."

"It's cherry," said Little Miss Blue Eyes. "And my name is Howell. Anne Howell. The Anne has an E at the end."

"Pleased to meet you, Miss Howell."

"The E gives my name a more ethereal quality, I think. My name originally was Ann without the E, but two years ago I had the E legally tacked on. I went to the Fairfield County Court House and signed a document, and it was notarized and everything."

"I approve of the E," I said. "It not only makes your name more ethereal; it makes it more feminine."

"I have always tried to be feminine," said Anne Howell.

"Yes," I said. "I can see that. And you have succeeded brilliantly."

"Thank you," said Anne Howell.

"Incidentally, I think your collar is scrumptious."

"Feminine?"

"Very."

Now we were standing at the punchbowl. I did the honors, and we stood and sipped the stuff from tiny cutglass cups, and of course it was dreadful. Anne Howell made a face. "I honestly believe I have tasted more flavorful *dishwater,*" she said. "If this is the best Pi Phi can do, perhaps I should look somewhere else."

"Are you a pledge?"

"Yes. And I'm a thirsty pledge. I think maybe I'll take up Sam on his offer of something stronger. He has a flask, you see, and he's been after me to—"

"You sound very sophisticated," I said.

"I am not sophisticated *at all,*" said Anne Howell. "But I *am* a little bored."

"I have always been told that Pi Phi girls are too smart to be bored."

"I am only a pledge. My brains have not been fully certified."

"Is it important for girls to have brains?"

"Of course it is important for girls to have brains," said Anne Howell.

"Even girls who look so scrumptious in velvet collars?"

"Now you're being just plain silly."

"That is correct," I said, pressing my lips together and nodding thoughtfully. "It is an affliction common to short men whose lady friends have been abducted by great hulking brutes. We become silly; we laugh and joke; our mouths are saying tra-la, but our hearts are saying boo-hoo."

"Well, cheer up."

"Why?"

"For one thing, you are rather handsome—for a little fellow."

"Thank you," I said. "The Ambersons are a handsome race, I agree. Microscopic, but handsome."

"*Now.* I didn't say you were *microscopic.*"

"But it's what you were thinking."

"You have no way of knowing what I was thinking."

"That is an intriguing remark," I said.

"I meant it to be," said Anne Howell.

I sipped my punch. I made a pained noise, then said: "Sam Chappell is an idiot."

"Why do you say that?"

"To have abandoned you like this. He has no manners."

"I'm very sorry you're stuck with me."

"I do believe I'll survive. I really do."

"Thank you, kind sir," said Anne Howell. "Your compliments are exceeded only by your great height."

And so began my courtship of Anne Howell. Joanna was reasonably decent about it, and Sam Chappell did not seem to care much one way or the other. When I told Joanna, she smiled a little and said: "I never really showed as much as I should have, did I? I *should* have shown more, Howard, but I didn't know *how.* Bubbly little Joanna isn't really so bubbly after all, is she? What *is* it? My awful family? Are you afraid, is that it?" She hesitated for a moment, and I started to say something (to deny any fear, of course), but she squeezed one of my wrists and said: "No. Please. You don't have to say anything. Let *me* say what *I* have to say, and that'll be the end of it, all right? *Now.* I thank you for being so honest, for coming to me and being so straightforward about everything. A lot of fellows would have just let things *drift,* which makes girls think absolutely *horrid* things about themselves. But not *you.* Oh no. Never *you.* Honesty is the best policy, right Howard my love? *Isn't that right?*" And then, snorting and sniffling, Joanna wept, and I knew enough not to try to comfort her. She laced her hands over her face, muffling the sounds. I felt ridiculous, like an actor in a bad sentimental romance, but I did not touch her, nor did I say anything. We were sitting on a stone bench in a park not too far from the football stadium, and it was late November as I recall, and I looked away from Joanna and studied the clear autumn sunlight that came slanting, all golden and mottled, through the bare trees that lined the park. I was able to see Joanna's breath. It curled through her fingers. I also was able to see my own breath. It came placidly, in clouds. I leaned back and thought of nothing in particular. No. That is not true. I thought of Anne Howell.

"What should I take in the way of clothes?" Anne Amberson asked her husband.

"A good selection," said Amberson. "Since we don't know where we're going, you'd better be prepared for any sort of weather. Perhaps we'll go to Texas, or perhaps we'll go to Maine. I simply don't know."

"The more I think about all this," said Anne, "the crazier it seems. You've always been such a *meticulous* and *organized* man, and now you suddenly insist we go traipsing off like a couple of I-don't-know-whats."

"We are not a couple of don't-know-whats," said Amberson. "We are Mr. and Mrs. Howard W. Amberson, and we propose to inspect the apparatus."

"It still all sounds crazy to *me,*" said Anne.

"It is not crazy," said Amberson. "It is reasoned and logical."

Anne rubbed her right shoulder. "All right," she said. "All right. Fine."

It was Sunday morning, and they would be leaving the next day. Now they were drinking coffee in the kitchen. Its windows faced east, and there was a great deal of clear warm sunlight. It made Amberson's eyes smart a bit. He blinked at his wife, and she still was rubbing her shoulder. "How is the pain?" he asked her.

"Not good," said Anne. The words came tightly.

"Did you take your pain pills this morning?"

Anne nodded.

"Why are you rubbing your right shoulder?"

"It seems to have spread there lately."

"Is there anything I can do?"

"No," said Anne. "No thank you. The pills will do their work in just a little while."

Amberson blew on his coffee, then sipped at it. He glanced at the wall clock, and it showed 8:35. "If you want to go to church, we have time."

"No. I expect I've heard everything Mr. Saddler will ever have to say."

"Perhaps you should go lie down."

"Yes," said Anne, but she did not get up. Instead, she rubbed her right shoulder.

"Would you like me to help you?"

"No. I'd just like to sit here for now."

"All right."

"What I *need* to do and what I *want* to do are different," said Anne.

Amberson said nothing.

"Did you hear me when I got up the first time this morning?"

"No."

"It was a little after four o'clock. I had to go to the bathroom. I sat on the throne and opened my nightgown and looked at the scar. I rubbed the places where I hurt. When I was a girl, I prided myself very highly on my breasts. But then you know that, don't you?"

"Yes."

"I may have been dumpy, but I did have nice breasts."

"You were never dumpy," said Amberson.

"Thank you," said Anne. She began to weep.

Amberson reached across the table and touched her hand.

"I am . . . I am very foolish," said Anne, wiping her eyes with her napkin.

"No," said Amberson. "You are not foolish at all. You cannot let the pain distort what you know to be the truth about yourself. You are not now foolish, and you never have been foolish."

"Is your . . . is your coffee hot enough? Would you like me to . . . warm it up for you?"

"My coffee is fine," said Amberson.

"We sit in these rooms with so many old things."

"Yes."

"We . . . we never set out to harm a . . . a soul . . ."

"We never did. Not knowingly."

Anne blew her nose with a Kleenex she had tucked in a sleeve of her bathrobe. "All these rooms," she said. "All the old photographs, lamps, clocks, what-have-you. We weren't lazy, were we? We worked hard. We had energy. Why then does it come down now to all this silence? How can a person live most of his life one way, with the energy and all, and then end it another way, with all the pooping around, with all the groaning and all the complaining and all the scars and all the pain? Where's the mercy in it? How come it isn't neat? Sometimes I can *taste* the silence. It is like dust. I kiss the old pictures, and then I close my eyes, and then I see the boys, and I . . . well, I . . . just . . ."

Amberson looked down at his hands.

Anne was weeping again, and again she blew her nose.

Amberson glanced up at her.

Her eyes were just as blue as they ever had been, and now—what with their moistness and all the sunlight—they actually glistened. "There is . . . such a thing as surviving too . . . much," she said. "I . . . well, I just *hurt*, that's all . . ."

"I know," said Amberson.

"You really do?"

"Yes."

"About the dust and the photographs and all of it?"

"Yes," said Amberson.

"The other day, when you spoke of the past, what did you say about it?"

"I said I think about it in the present tense. And you said it was an affliction of us relics."

"That's true, isn't it?"

"Yes," said Amberson. "It means we think of ourselves as being less alive than we once were."

"It means we have . . . survived too long?"

"I don't want to believe that," said Amberson. "Which is precisely why we need to examine the apparatus. Either we are alive or we are not. If we are, then we must inspect the world."

"As a summation? Some sort of what—valedictory?"

Amberson said nothing.

Anne rubbed her shoulder. She shook her head, winced, then said: "I really sometimes can't . . ." She let her words trail away. She rubbed. She grimaced. Her tongue made sucking noises. She glanced out the window, at the sky and the garage and her rhubarb plants and whatever.

Anne Howell was from Lancaster, and she was an orphan. Her father and mother had been killed in an interurban trolley accident in 1912, when she had been just thirteen. The rest of her childhood had been spent in the home of an older married sister, Christine, a cheerful young woman with three children and a husband who was a reasonably prosperous attorney. Christine and Anne were separated by eleven years, and so it was almost as though Christine were Anne's mother—and strangers or casual acquaintances often told Christine gosh, she must have been a very young bride, considering the age of her *daughter*. (Christine had a large florid laugh, and it always erupted from her whenever the mistake was made. "Either *I* look very *old* or *Anne* looks very *young*," she once told me, "and I honestly never quite know whether I should laugh, or cry, or throw things or *what*. I tell you, maybe I ought to be carted off to a museum and stuffed like an auk or a wild Arabian goonybird." And then there came from this Christine another of her enormous laughs, and she beat her palms together . . . hollowly, like a child watching the circus clowns.)

Christine's husband was as large and hearty as she. His name was Ed Wohl, and he shared a law practice with his elderly father, who once had been an assistant Ohio attorney general. Ed was sixteen years older than Christine, and his skin was pale and puffy. He was bald, and there were liverspots on his hands. Admittedly then, he was not very impressive physically. But in this case the physical aspect belied the man. Droopy and enervated as he may have seemed, he was nonetheless quite a passionate fellow, and even something of a rascal. He abounded with genial nudges and winks and sniggers, and the very first time I met him he squeezed one of my elbows and said (his voice mock surreptitious): "I must say, my friend, you surely do know how to pick them. God strike me dead for criminal lechery, but my wife's baby sister is just about the juiciest little morsel I've seen in years. Those breastworks . . . great God. But, ah, well now, I expect you, ah, get what I mean."

"Yes," I said to Ed Wohl, "I get what you mean."

And then Ed sniggered, and what the devil, perhaps I shouldn't have liked him, but I did. (And I liked Christine as well. They both have been dead many years—Ed since 1931 and Christine since 1954 —but I remember them fondly. I remember their laughter and their love.)

To an outsider, I am sure my courtship of Anne Howell was conventional enough. But naturally *I* did not see it that way. I was a *participant* and not an outsider, and to *me* it was not conventional in the least. To *me* it was all steam and cramps, and since when were those things conventional? My soul clapped and smarted, and since when were *those* things conventional? Anne and I had discovered an uncharted and exalted plane of existence. We had grown great wings, and we flapped them, and the rest of the world became unutterably mundane and petty. I escorted Anne to dances at Ohio State, and I took her home to Paradise Falls to meet my parents and my brothers and my sister, and we went on picnics and sleighrides, and she allowed me to touch her breasts; she was victory; she was empire (I am convinced Tennyson would have adored her); she made my days whir and spin. And, praise God, my family approved of her. My father, speaking thinly and with precision, allowed as how she was a splendid young woman, so full of zeal. And my mother, upon learning Anne was a Methodist like ourselves, began cheerfully proselytizing for the White Shrine of Jerusalem and the Order of Eastern Star. And my brothers and my sister, all of whom were married by then (by 1920 I was an uncle three times over), agreed she surely did have a great deal of spunk and laughter, and on one occasion, after having lunch with Anne and me, my dear sister Caroline took me aside and said: "Your lady friend seems to be a kind person. It is rare to find kind persons. We hope you do not let her get away." And I said: "Don't worry. That's not about to happen." And it did not. There was no way in the world it could have. Anne and I had enormous wings, and there was nothing we could not attain together. It all had been written in heaven. (Or so we believed, knowing nothing of tired metaphors and the arrogant innocence of young lovers. We told one another we were *not* ordinary. We told one another we were *not* conventional. We told one another we were sublime.) We were married in June of 1921. She wore forgetmenots in her hair, and she smiled so broadly I was able to see her one gold filling. I told her good Lord, what a fine advertisement she was for some dentist. We were both virgins.

That Sunday afternoon, after fixing a light lunch of pea soup and ham sandwiches, Anne went upstairs and lay down in the bedroom. Amberson sat in the front room and watched the Denver-Cleveland football game on Channel 4. Sinclair hopped on Amberson's lap, curled up and went to sleep. Amberson stroked Sinclair, and Sinclair's claws went in and out. The Denver team chewed up the Cleveland team with great vigor, and the score was 24–0 at the half. Amberson dropped off to sleep for a bit and missed the halftime show. When he awakened, the game had resumed, and the score was 27–0, and his left leg had gone to sleep. Lifting Sinclair carefully so as not to disturb him, Amberson stood up and gently placed Sinclair in the chair. Sinclair awakened briefly, yawned, washed a foot, then went back to sleep. Amberson turned off the television set, then went into the kitchen and fixed himself a cup of cocoa. He seated himself at the kitchen table and rubbed the circulation back into the leg that had gone to sleep. He rubbed briskly, and the tingling went away. He blew on the cocoa and drank some of it. He said to himself: When in doubt, Anne and I always seem to come to this room and fix ourselves a snack. We live in here. The other rooms have become a museum.

Grimacing, Amberson placed his cup on the table. He pressed both his hands over both his ears and listened to the action of his heart. He had had two reasonably severe heart attacks in the past seven years, and Dr. Groh had told him: I'll not lie to you. The next one probably will put you away. So for God's sake take it easy.

Amberson's heart made sounds that were frail and uneven. He closed his eyes. His breath felt as though it were coming in spasms, and so he tried to control it. He said to himself: I am taking it easy. I am taking it easy. I *am* taking it easy.

He took his hands away from his ears. He opened his eyes. He glanced out the window. Leaves were coming down. Again he closed his eyes, and this time he tried to imagine springtime leaves, but he could not. He saw too much green. It was unreal, too pretty and candified. He shook his head and again opened his eyes. His back hurt. He decided it might be good if he went upstairs and lay down with Anne. He finished the cocoa, stood up, went to the sink and rinsed out the cup. Now there was a pain in his side to go with the pain in his back. He said to himself: I am trying to take it easy. I am trying to take it easy. I am *trying* to take it easy.

He went upstairs and lay down beside his wife. She was not asleep, but she did not say anything, and neither did he. He listened to his heart, and he listened to leaves, and sunlight nudged at the drawn blinds. A dresser was at the foot of the bed, and framed photographs of the children were displayed there in a sort of semicircle. They were old photographs, and they had been tinted by hand. They all had been taken at the same time—in the spring of 1932—by old George Vannice, who in those days had owned and operated a studio on Market Street. Henry had been nine that year, Lewis six and Florence just two. Old George Vannice had had to work quite hard to get Florence to smile, making faces at her and manipulating a hand puppet that had been in the shape of a duck. (These were the Bedroom photographs, as opposed to the Parlor photographs, or the Guest Room photographs, or the Library photographs. The Amberson home abounded with photographs of the three children, gradeschool photographs, highschool photographs, college photographs, wedding photographs, even candid snapshots. Amberson's two dead sons jumped at him from everywhere, as did a young and forever pretty Florence.)

Amberson rubbed his chest. He said to himself: I have attended too many funerals. I am now at the point where I rejoice in them. Why? For the simple reason that I am not the attraction on display. I must write that down. I must write it in the ledger. It probably is rather important. (We sit and wait for the conclusion, and we will be better off when it finally comes, and yet my heart terrifies me. Anne complains of dust and old photographs, and her despair accelerates, but she cleans house every day, and she prepares all the meals, and she still takes pride in her garden and her rhubarb plants, and she carries on in the face of all her pain. I suppose we are, in a sense, indomitable. But to what purpose?)

Sinclair came into the room, jumped on the bed, flopped on Amberson's belly and took a bath. Anne was asleep now. Her hands were in fists, but her breath came regularly. Amberson scratched Sinclair under the chin. Amberson's teeth were so tightly shut it was as though he were biting down on a small reluctant seed.

Our mutual virginity had been, for the most part, a matter of choice. In those antique and preposterous days, of course, the retention of one's virginity had significant moral implications. It was a badge of virtue; it was somehow supposed to exalt the marriage bed.

This is not to say, however, that Anne and I were not tempted. Many were the times that we came within a breath and one more kiss of defying the sexual conventions. We were nothing if not human; we had blood and heat, and our juices were abundant. On a superficial level, judging from what I have so far written about Anne, one might fail to see any significant difference between her and the jettisoned Joanna Lyman. But there was a *profound* difference. On the surface, both girls were chattery and bright—but *Joanna's* chatter and brightness were, as she admitted, conscious products of her will. Anne, on the other hand, was chattery and bright because those qualities lay within her *nature*. She was not attempting to defend herself from a tribe of Brobdingnags. She was not trying to be heard over a roar. She interested me much more than poor Joanna, whose manner had been manufactured. The difference, then, was between the real and the artificial, and I have always preferred the real. For this reason, Anne was more of a strain on my virtue than Joanna ever had been. And it was more than a matter of Anne's breasts, which were considerably larger. She instinctively knew when to chatter and when not to chatter, and she did not bother to flatter or reassure me. She did not *have* to. She simply was *there,* and she *participated,* and I just about exploded. Not to make too fine a point of it, she drove me mad.

Still, we did remain virgins until our wedding night. Now, in retrospect, I see this as having been an astonishing accomplishment. At the time, though, I was too concerned with my pain. I simply tried to endure it—and the enduring was an ordeal, believe me.

Perhaps now is a good a time as any to describe the Famous Buick Incident. It has become a legendary topic of conversation with Anne, and it illustrates the extent of the ordeal. In addition, it represents the closest we came to having at one another without benefit of clergy. It took place in the early spring of 1921, about two months before we were married. We were in Lancaster on a weekend visit to Ed and Christine Wohl's place, and the Buick belonged to Ed. It was a 1919, and it had curtains.

There was an American Legion dance in Lancaster that Saturday night, and I was grateful to Ed for offering me the use of the car so I could take Anne to the affair in some sort of style. "Ah, bullwax," said Ed, "I was young myself a million years ago." Christine, who was sitting next to Ed at the supper table when he made that remark, laughed quite loudly, then affectionately tweaked one of the layers of fat that lined his neck. "And just what does that make *me,* you scoundrel you?" she asked him. And Ed Wohl said: "A miracle and a blessing." And then everyone smiled, even the children and even I.

The dance band was too loud. But the punch had been spiked, and my first drink of it brought a pleasant warmth to my cheeks. I am afraid my vision became a bit pink. Dancing with Anne, I held her closer than perhaps I should have. She was all soft and fragrant, and she wore a dark blue skirt and pale yellow shirtwaist. (The fragrance was lavender, I believe.) Her hair was pulled back with a blue ribbon, and I told her the ribbon went well with her eyes. I was able to feel the warmth passing into my chest and belly. I smiled at Anne and told her I loved her.

She stuck out her tongue at me. Then she kissed my chin and said: "I do believe the spiked punch has gone to your head."

"And elsewhere," I said.

"Is little mans a teensyweensy tipsy?"

"Yes. A teensyweensy tipsy. I'll ignore the little mans stuff."

"Good for you," said Anne.

"Teensyweensy tipsy," I said. "Sounds like a song. *He's a teen-syweensy tipsy, but I love him just the same. His eyes are red and bloodshot, but devotion is his name.*"

"Very *good,*" said Anne. "*Good* Howard. *Good* dog."

There were not many slow dances, and there were even fewer quiet ones, and so Anne and I made more trips to the punchbowl than we should have. It was against my nature, all that drinking, but for some reason I felt rather wickedly reckless, and I told Anne I did not care whether school kept, or the cows came home, or anything. And Anne, who also was a bit to the wind, squealed and hugged me, pressing her adorable breasts against me. We stood at the punchbowl and hugged one another, and the punch was a triumph. The band blared and tootled, and it became clear that these musicians were not specialists in the tango or the foxtrot, which were the only dances I could safely negotiate. Instead, the band concentrated on ragtime and other of the various hotcha steps that were all the rage, and the musicians all were sweating like field hands. They all wore straw hats, white shirts, enormous rubber bow ties and striped red and white trousers. They stamped and writhed with the music, and most of them had lost control of their shirttails. I watched them with a sort of apprehensiveness, and I told myself: Great God, the world certainly is speeding up. (I hoped I would be able to keep pace. I was just twentythree years old and completing my first year on the faculty at Paradise Falls High, but sometimes . . . especially when I heard fast music and saw other young people dancing with such athletic frenzy . . . I honestly felt like someone's doddering grandfather sipping buttermilk at the county home. But I suppose that was, and is, *my* nature. In all my life, the only times I truly freed myself from it were when I ran track. Not even sex ever really suppressed all of my reserve. I was, you see, always a gentleman—even on this night of the Famous Buick Incident.)

Finally, when I could abide the music no longer, I took Anne by an arm and escorted her outside for some fresh air. We stood on the front steps of the brandnew Legion Hall (the dance was in honor of its dedication, and a number of public officials had orated at some length earlier in the evening, summoning once again images of patriotism and doughboys and fields of poppies), and I remember turning to Anne and saying: "Sometimes I wish I'd been more than an ROTC cadet. What I mean is—the war didn't even interfere with a single class of mine. Two years in the ROTC and all I can remember from it is that I learned how to pound down a tent stake."

"I say you don't know how lucky you were," she told me. Her cheeks were flushed, and she was dabbing at them with a handkerchief.

"Because no one shot at me?"

"Yes."

"But so many other people were shot at. Why should I have been an exception?"

"To be a man, a fellow doesn't have to be shot at. And he doesn't have to be the one who *does* the shooting, either."

"Well, that's all very well and good for you to say, but—"

"Don't but *me* your buts, Mister," said Anne, holding up a hand. She finished dabbing at her cheeks. Carefully she folded her handkerchief and replaced it in her purse, which was tiny and beaded. She snapped shut the purse, then said: "It would have made you sick, and you know it. And you would have ended up calling yourself a coward. You wouldn't have known the difference between being sick and being afraid. I know *you*, and I know what you'd have *felt*, and I'm glad you didn't go to France. For *myself*, speaking of places to go, *I* want to go somewhere where we can kiss."

"What? Now?"

"How now, brown cow," said Anne, smiling. "Yes. Now. I want to go somewhere now. Somewhere nice and quiet where we can *kiss* and *hug* and do whatever *else* seems . . . appropriate. You see, you're not the only one who's enjoyed the punch."

"You're being very brazen."

"I am a bit tipsy too, and I'm sorry if it disturbs your great reverence for the proprieties, but tipsy people are seldom . . . ah, *oblique.*"

"I do believe you are making an indecent proposal," I said.

"That is correct," said Anne. She cast her eyes demurely downward, but I am afraid her mouth was twitching.

I cleared my throat. *"Really,* Miss Howell, is that any way for a proper young lady to talk?"

"Really, Mr. Amberson, since when have I told you I am proper? Have I ever produced any sort of certificate? You take a lot upon yourself when you blandly assume I am proper without full knowledge of the facts."

"I am to take it then that you are not proper?"

"You are to take it that I am *trying* to be not proper."

"Oh *my,* " I said, frowning at my lady love. "The way girls behave these days, I just don't know what the world is coming to."

Anne flung back her head and laughed. She went clattering down the Legion Hall's stone front steps. Still laughing, she looked up at me and hollered: "Last one to the machine is a *communist,* a flaming evil *bolshevik* with a big black *beard!*"

And so I raced my lady love to the car, which was parked a block away. I had run the middle distances at both Paradise Falls High and Ohio State, and so I loped easily, with Anne skittering along beside me. She giggled and shrieked, and her breasts bounced, and the scent of lavender reached high into my nostrils. She wore spindly black pumps, and her ankles were unsteady, but she stumbled along without complaining. We held hands the last twenty yards or so, and she told me she knew a fine place where we could go. I asked her how she knew about the fine place, and she told me never you mind *that;* I went to *high school* here, you silly tipsy *poop* you, and there were a *few* boys who liked to take me to dark quiet places. I'm not all that much of a face on the barroom floor, you know.

Laughing, I told Anne she was the world's absolute limit. I fetched the crank, and the Buick's engine caught on the second try. Anne clapped her hands. I helped her into the car. She told me I was a really splendid fellow with a crank. I thanked her, then scuttled around the car and got in on the driver's side. She gave the directions, and the Buick went stuttering off toward the end of town. "We'll go to the fairgrounds," said Anne. "It's full of places."

"That's just fine," I said. My temples were warm. I rubbed them and squeezed my forehead.

"Do you feel all right?" she asked me.

"I feel splendid," I said, and my hand came away from my head.

"You are an exception to the rule," said Anne.

"What rule?"

"A little while ago I said something about tipsy people seldom beating around the bush."

"So?"

"Well, *I* didn't beat around the bush. *You,* on the other hand, were very *pompous.* You accused me of making an indecent proposal, and I distinctly recall that you cleared your throat. And *you* are every bit as tipsy as *I* am. Probably more so. I just bet you sneaked to the punchbowl and had an extra cup or two of that stuff when I wasn't looking, when I was in the powder room or whatever."

"You could be right," I said. (And she was.)

"But why then are you so dignified?"

"You are one sort of person, and I am another. If I am really dignified, and my dignity displeases you, I'm sorry but I don't know what I can do about it."

"Sometimes I want to stick you with a hatpin and listen to the air rush out."

"It probably would be hot air," I said.

"Probably," said Anne. She covered her mouth and giggled.

I smiled. My hands were perspiring, but I managed not to let the wheel slip. Anne moved closer to me, and her odor of lavender (I am now certain that was what it was) made my eyes water. She hugged me, and the Buick swerved, but I said nothing. There was really nothing either of us needed to say. The words all had been said. I loved her, and I had told her I loved her. And she had told me she loved me. But I was not comforted. Well, perhaps the comfort would come later. Perhaps the comfort in love was reserved for old people. Some day, God willing, I would be an old person, and perhaps then I would know. But now was no time to be reflecting on the secrets of old age. There I was, a silly tipsy *poop* whose words contained too many syllables and whose manner was too avuncular and starched, and yet I was in love with the most glorious girl that any young man could imagine in his most feverish dreams, and by God *she* loved *me,* and it all was a *miracle.* And so, smiling, I draped an arm around Anne's shoulders, and she reached inside my jacket and began fingering my necktie and the buttons on my shirtfront. And my chest began to hurt, and I knew she was as far removed from Joanna Lyman as the moon. And my breath came damply, and I nearly sideswiped a horse and wagon, and it was clearer than ever that Joanna and I had never known anything approaching this. (It is interesting, though, and perhaps contradictory, that Joanna occupies so much space in this narrative. However, it must be pointed out that she was the first girl who ever was seriously interested in me, and one's ego just about demands that he treasure the memory of his first flame.) At any rate, the contrast between Anne and Joanna was, as far as I was concerned, astonishing. Joanna never had caused me to groan in the night (and Anne had), and Joanna never had been interested in that which was real (and Anne was), and Joanna never had been an adversary (and Anne *most certainly* was). Joanna had flattered me too enthusiastically, and the flattery had caused her to pay little attention to truth. Anne, on the other hand, saw truth as being some sort of ultimate goal of human behavior, and she gave it a great deal of her energy. It sat at the core of what she saw as being her love for me, and I have quite a vivid memory of how she explained it. The words came not long after we began seeing one another exclusively —on the night, in fact, we both blurted our first acknowledgment that we did indeed love one another. Anne had been hugging and kissing me, but abruptly she twisted away, wiped her mouth with the back of a hand, frowned at me and said: All right, Mr. Big Cheese, yes, all right, it's *love,* and it's all hunkered and flopped inside me like a big *lump,* and I suppose there's nothing I can do about it. Sometimes when I'm with you I feel as though I have swallowed a bag of *peach pits.* And that's all just hunkydory, isn't it? And it probably makes you feel very proud of yourself, doesn't it? Well, Mister, you're going to find out that it will affect more of you than your silly *vanity.* Seeing as how I *love* you, that means I am *interested* in you, and it means I will be *digging* at you a lot of the time. If you really love me and I really love you, it means we'll probably get married. All right. Fine. If you propose to me (and you'd *better* propose to me, you nincompoop), I'll accept. But be warned, Mister. My love for you means that there now exists on this earth a person who is interested in everything you do. Every hem and whipstitch. Every nub and eyelash. *Everything.* Now then, I don't mean to make it sound like a prison sentence, and I apologize if it does, but it's the way I *am,* and I'm pretty sure it has something to do with why you love me. After all, if you're not in love with what I *am,* what *are* you in love with? (To the best of my recollection, it was a Friday night in December of 1919 when Anne said all of the foregoing, and her voice was steady throughout. She and I were sitting on a divan in the front parlor of the Pi Phi house, and somewhere upstairs a girl was singing.) That conversation—or, more accurately, monologue—had taken place more than a year before the night of the Famous Buick Incident, but for some reason I thought back on it as Anne and I went clattering north over those nearly deserted Lancaster streets, north toward the fairgrounds and God knows what. Finally I made a small exasperated sound deep in my throat and impatiently told myself: There is a time to push aside *words* and *explanations* and *philosophy.* You are not Immanuel Kant, so kindly stop trying to reason it out. You are simply a young smalltown schoolteacher who perhaps . . . *perhaps* . . . is about to embark on that one adventure that has eluded him and vexed his serenity for more years than he cares to admit. So ride with it, old fellow. A dear sweet cheek rests against your shoulder, and now a knee is pressing against your knee, and the lovely moonlight dapples her shirtwaist and the outline of her breasts, and the scent of her hair has made your eyes smart, and where's the sense of rhetoric at a time like this?

Naturally, what with all that sort of thinking, I was just about beside myself by the time I parked the Buick (on Anne's instructions) behind a grove of trees not far from the fairgrounds grandstand. I felt as though someone had rubbed the inside of my mouth with gravel. I looked down at Anne.

She straightened, pulled back, smiled at me and said: "There are some things I like better than dancing."

"Yes," I said. I rubbed my palms against my knees.

"*I* am sitting *here,*" said Anne, "and *you* are sitting *there.* Which means one of us will have to sort of, ah, squiggle over a little . . ."

"Yes," I said, and I slid to her. I squiggled. At this point, it becomes necessary for me to write in explicit terms. If my wife ever reads the description that follows, she probably will be embarrassed and perhaps angry. But I cannot help this. If the Famous Buick Incident is to be described at all, it must be described fully. Otherwise, the reader will not be able to appreciate it. And so, with this in mind, I perforce, ahem, press on. And state that I kissed her. And state that she permitted me to open her mouth. I kissed her ears, and I placed a hand against her right breast. The shirtwaist crackled. Anne moaned a little, and I kissed the base of her throat. I told her I loved her, and she whispered yes, yes, she knew I did. I kissed her ears, and I kissed the downy places behind her ears. Her hands were clasped tightly around the back of my neck, and her palms were damp. I undid the ribbon from her hair. She had brown hair; it was soft; she shook her head, and her hair fluffed down, draping her shoulders. I blew gently on the downy places behind Anne's ears, and she whispered several words I did not catch. My hand stroked the front of her shirtwaist, and presently I was able to feel the outline of a nipple. Anne wriggled and moaned. She had been correct. There were *indeed* certain activities to be preferred over dancing. Grunting, I began unbuttoning the shirtwaist. Anne kissed my chin and my ears, and her hands rubbed the back of my neck. Then her hands parted, and her fingers traced the outline of my ears. The sensation was a bit ticklish, but I did not laugh, nor did I want to laugh. Instead, I began to wheeze, and my own fingers were slow and incompetent as they struggled with the buttons of the shirtwaist. Anne's legs had been tucked under the seat, and now she suddenly flung them out, and the Buick rocked a little. My face was pressed against her hair, and I breathed nothing but pure lavender, and those damnable buttons were driving my fingers mad. I could not understand what was happening. Damn me for a fool, but those buttons were *sweaty,* and who had ever heard of *sweaty buttons?* The entire idea was preposterous, but how come my fingers were fumbling so? Now Anne was breathing wetly, and I grimaced, bit my tongue and fell to my work with renewed vigor. This time five of the buttons finally gave way to my assault. I could just about have whooped for joy. Still grimacing, I reached inside the shirtwaist, and Anne whispered more words that I did not catch, and I reached inside her slip, and then my hand cupped her right breast and a hard warm little nipple. Again she spoke, and this time I was able to catch the words, and hooray for that. "Yes," she said, gasping, "yes, anything you . . . want . . ." Thus renewed, I bent over her dear breast, tugged at the shirtwaist and slip and exposed it. She lay back and held the breast for me, and I licked it. Using her free hand, she took one of my hands and kissed and licked the fingers. "Oh, *heavenly,*" she said, kissing and licking, "whatever . . . ah, you want, then . . . ah, *I* want it too." I seem to recall that I nodded at this, but I did not interrupt my licking. I had one hand remaining to me, though, and so it ventured down and disappeared under her skirt. I lifted her skirt, and never before had she permitted me to lift her skirt, but this time she did not resist, and my mouth moved in jubilant circles around her glorious nipple. My nose was pressed flat against her flesh, and I barely could breathe, but what did *that* matter? I had entered the grand principality of her *thighs,* and *that* was what mattered! (I fully realize that here I am yielding to melodrama and betraying my promise not to become florid, but I cannot help myself. If I am to be accurate in describing all this, I must be breathless.) At this point, however, Anne interrupted my happy breathless work, and for a moment I thought she had changed her mind. She twisted away from me, released my one hand and pulled the other out from under her skirt. Was the game over? Would the proprieties again prevail? I rubbed my face and listened to the sounds of her breathing, and finally she spoke, and her words astonished me. "Darling, there is more . . . oh *my,* I tell you, the things you *do* to me . . . ah, there is more room in the . . . in the, ah, back seat. I . . . well, *I* want to be comfortable, and I want *you* to be comfortable." Then, smiling, she unfastened the remaining shirtwaist buttons and shucked herself out of it. She pulled the slip over her head, and now both her breasts were in view, and this was the first time she ever had exposed them for me, and the smile still tugged bravely at the corners of her mouth, and she said: "Whatever . . . anything . . . I don't care . . ." She leaned forward and kissed me on the mouth, and I reached out and held both her breasts with both my hands. They were such very warm breasts, and the one I had been licking was a bit damp. She glanced down at them for a moment, then said: "Come on . . ." She slid over, opened the door on the passenger's side and slipped out of the car. Then she opened the rear door and climbed back inside. Grunting, rubbing my lips (my mouth was a trifle sore), I joined her in the back seat, which was indeed quite a bit more roomy. She was in a sort of sprawl, and her skirt was hiked up, and she said: "Pull the curtains." Nodding, I reached across her and pulled down a side curtain, then reached behind myself and pulled down the other side curtain. "I'm cold," said Anne, "and I want you to warm me up." Quickly I nodded, and then I flung myself atop my lady love, and this time I kissed and licked both her nipples, and she opened her legs, and my hand went scurrying up her thighs and inside her bloomers, and she was moist as a new morning. Her head went from side to side, and all her teeth were exposed. I nuzzled her breasts, and my hand explored all the strange (to me) furry magnificence of her. Then there was a sharp report, followed by a sort of flapping noise.

Anne shrieked.

My hand shot out of her bloomers

"What . . . what was it?" Anne wanted to know.

I shrugged. For all I knew, someone had taken a shot at us. I glanced out a window, and then of course I remembered. I had *pulled the curtains,* and yet now I was able to glance out a window—the window on my side. Its curtain had flown up; that was all. It was as simple as that. "This stupid curtain flew up," I said. I then tried to smile, but I do not believe I was particularly successful.

"Well," said Anne, "pull it *down.*"

I nodded. Quickly I reached back and pulled down the curtain.

"Thank you," said Anne. She reached for me, and I bent toward her, and the renewed darkness was a comfort and a thing of great beauty.

Then there was a second sharp report, followed by a repetition of the flapping noise. The *other* curtain had flown up—the one on her side.

Again Anne flinched, but this time she also giggled a little.

"Godalmighty," I said. I did not often curse, but this time I felt I was entitled. I reached past her and pulled down *that* curtain.

Anne looked at me. She was shaking a bit, and still was hunched over her naked breasts, but now one of her arms came away from them, and she held out a hand, and I was able to make out two crossed fingers.

I held my breath. My belly hurt, and my groin was swollen, and I saw nothing funny in the situation, nothing funny at all. My eyes flicked from one curtain to the other curtain. I began to breathe again, but at the same time my mind was sending the curtains an ultimatum: Now listen *here,* you stupid curtains you. I *will* you to stay down. I *will* you to stop interrupting and embarrassing us this way.

A few more moments passed, and then Anne said: "Well, ah, hooray . . ."

Again I tried to smile, and this time I believe I was more successful.

Anne uncradled her breasts and reached for me. Like a doughboy leaping from a trench and renewing some great furiously valiant assault, once again I flung myself atop my lady love, and again my mouth went traveling across her dark and fragrant breasts, and again my hand went scrabbling up her skirt and inside her dear damp bloomers. And Anne unbuttoned my coat and shirt, pulled off my necktie and began caressing my chest. And her other hand strayed to my poor distended groin, and then—abruptly—she squeezed it. I gave a sort of yelp.

"Sh," she said, patting me there. Then abruptly she gasped.

Neither of the curtains had flown up, and so what was the matter?

"Howard?"

"Yes. I'm . . . right here. No one else is here. Just . . . me."

"Don't be *smart.* I just *heard* something."

My breath was heavier than death, and I said: *"I* didn't hear anything."

"Well, *I* did," said Anne. "It was like a snort—you know, like a snort a horse makes."

"Oh, certainly. Of course. A horse."

"Yes, Mr. Poet-and-Don't-Know-It, a horse. I want you to find out where it is."

"Me?"

"Yes," said Anne, "and right now." Her hand came away from my groin. She seized me by the shoulders and pushed me back.

I was a bit off balance. My hand was forced out of her bloomers, and I flailed, and I bumped against the door, and the curtain flew up, bang and flap, and I looked out the window, and an eye was staring at me, and it was an immense and exceedingly mournful eye, and stars were reflected in it, and it was unquestionably the eye of a horse, and I said: "Oh, for God's sake."

This time Anne went ahead and laughed right out loud.

The horse gently sighed, flapping his lips.

Anne howled. Anne Howell howled. That she did.

I opened the door and climbed out of the car. The horse was a roan gelding, and a cluster of moist straw clung to its chin. It stood no more than five feet from the car, and it had gray lips. There were cramps in my belly, and I was unable to stand upright. I felt like Quasimodo. And probably looked worse.

Hugging my belly, I glared at the horse and said: "Go home. Your mother wants you."

(Inside the car, Anne Howell howled more loudly.)

I advanced perhaps three steps, and I looked squarely into one of the horse's eyes. "Now then," I said, "this is none of your concern, and I want you to go back where you came from."

The horse blinked at me.

I raised an arm.

Inside the car, Anne managed to interrupt her howling long enough to say: "Why don't you punch it in the nose?"

"It just might come to that," I said ominously.

The horse blinked at my upraised arm, then began to move toward me.

I quickly lowered the arm. I retreated a step, then another step, then a third, and then I bumped against the car. I was trapped. There was no place I could go, unless I scrambled back inside the car. And of course *that* would be cowardice in the face of the enemy, and my old ROTC instructors would not have been pleased with me. So I reluctantly stood my ground and hoped for the best.

The horse was not a particularly large one, but it was large enough for *me*, and that is a fact. It probably had wandered away from one of the barns at the fairgrounds. With that in mind, I inclined my head in the direction of the fairgrounds. "Ah, see here," I said, "home is where the heart is, and that's where I want you to go."

The horse whinnied quietly, then nuzzled my face, rubbing its soft gray lips against my cheek.

Now Anne was bleating and whooping. "You have . . . ah, you have made a friend . . ." she said, sputtering.

Speaking to no one in particular, I said: "First I am kissed by the glamorous and provocative Anne Howell, and then I am kissed by a horse. I am a very lucky fellow, yes indeed."

Anne then asked the inevitable question: "Could you tell the . . . ah, difference?"

"I think so," I said.

"Thank you very much," said Anne.

"You're quite welcome," I said. Then I felt the horse's lips once again against my cheek. I sidled along the car until I was out of range. The horse looked at me. "I'm sorry," I said to the horse, "but there have been too many kisses tonight, and I simply can't take any more." I moved away from the car, and I hoped the horse would follow me. And it did. It gave a quiet whinny, then moved toward me. I made kissing sounds. I walked backwards away from the car. The horse ambled after me. I had a plan. I had a fine plan. As soon as the horse was safely clear of the car, I would implement my fine plan, my glorious plan, this brilliant triumph of mind over horse. "Kissy kissy," I said, puckering. "Oh, kissy kissy kiss." And my amorous sounds made the horse's ears twitch. Then, when the horse was perhaps thirty feet from the car and facing squarely in the direction of the fairgrounds, I scurried around behind it and gave it a heroic swat on the rump. "All right now!" I shouted. "You just *skedaddle!*"

The horse did not budge. It looked back at me. There was enough light so I could see the reproach that lay all viscous and grieving in its great brown eyes.

(Inside the car, Anne was making thumping sounds—perhaps she was having some sort of stroke or fit or cardiac seizure.)

Grunting, I glowered at the horse. Then I began to jump up and down. I flapped my arms.

The horse's eyes narrowed. It nickered. It did not move.

I gave a great yell. I vaulted through the air and slammed a shoulder against the horse's obstinate rump.

Nothing. Not a move. Not a twitch.

My shoulder hurt. I rubbed it. I gasped. Again I gave a great yell, and again I slammed into the horse's rump, only this time with more vigor. Much more, in fact. Too much more, in fact. The impact sent me sprawling, and I landed on my coccyx, and a flash of pain shot up my spine. I made a sort of squealing noise, and my head was full of pins and bells and broken glass.

The horse bared its teeth and laughed.

(Inside the car, God knows what was happening.)

I stood up. I shook my head, rubbed my coccyx. My vision whirled, and I had to blink several times to bring it back into focus. Again I advanced on the horse. I would fight it out on this line if it took all summer.

The horse blinked, and I supposed it thought it was being coy.

Wincing, I again jumped up and down. And I again flapped my arms. And I again yelled—only this time the yell was more of a croak.

And *finally* . . . glory be to heaven . . . the horse began to move away. Apparently it at last recognized lunacy and wanted no more part of it. It ambled, and it kept looking back at me, and its eyes contained something that I rather suspect was apprehensiveness.

Still massaging my battered coccyx, I spoke quietly. "Yes sir, old steed," I said. "You just go back where you came from. Have yourself some nice oats. Lie down and dream of green pastures. Enjoy life."

"Hooray for our side," said a voice from the car.

I returned to the car in triumph. "Thank you," I said. "Thank you very much." Wincing, I bowed deeply, then reentered the back seat and drew the curtains. Anne was huddled in a corner, and now her hands were over her face, and her dear tummy was shaking with laughter. I slid across the seat and pulled her hands away from her face. She started to say something, but I kissed her, doing away with her words. I would not by God be denied, come curtains, come horses, come the end of the world, and so I kissed her throat, and then I kissed the deep place between her breasts, and my thumbs massaged her nipples. She kissed my ears and the top of my head, and her hands groped for my groin, and she lay back, and my own hands went scrambling up her thighs, and she spread her legs and opened the front of my trousers (Victory! Empire! Hallelujah!), and then . . . of course . . . naturally . . . predictably . . . the car made a gentle hissing sound and began to list.

When I finally spoke, I did so quietly, and this may have been one of the great signal accomplishments of my life. Rubbing my face, I said: "I do believe the air has gone out of one of the tires."

"I do believe you are correct," said Anne. Her voice was solemn and thoughtful.

It took me nearly an hour to change the tire. I buttoned my trousers, put on my shirt, rolled up my sleeves and fell to the task with what I can only describe as a kind of quiet desperation. In those days, the changing of a tire was no easy thing. One pried off the punctured tire with what was called a tire spoon, then filled the spare and its innertube with air from a hand pump, then somehow—with the aid, such as it was, of the tire spoon—fitted the spare to the rim. Fortunately, Ed Wohl was fond of his car, and all the necessary tools were on hand, plus the pump and a sturdy jack. Still, it was hard work. I have never been particularly good at that sort of thing.

While I labored (and there still was pain in my shoulder and coccyx), Anne sat on the grass and chatted quietly with me. She had combed her hair and put her clothing back in order, and I had spread a blanket for her. She told me she had no idea where the horse could have come from. "At this time of the year," she said, "I don't *think* there are any horses at the fairgrounds, and so maybe it came from *miles away.* Just imagine that, will you? A dear horse coming from *miles away* just to pay a call *on us.* Doesn't that make you feel proud?"

"No," I said, grunting over the tire spoon.

"Well," said Anne, "it makes *me* feel proud."

"Good for you," I said. "That's just . . . tremendous . . ."

Anne laughed quietly. Her hands were folded in her lap, and her legs were neatly tucked inside her skirt, and the laugh was very polite, like water in a clean crystal glass. And, needless to say, that was the end of the Famous Buick Incident. The engine caught on the first whirl of the crank, and I drove her home to Ed and Christine's place, and the following Monday I bought Ed a tire patch. It was three or four days before the pain left my shoulder and my coccyx (if you have ever fallen on your tailbone, you will understand why that particular pain lingered as long as it did), but my *memory* of the pain . . . and all the rest of it . . . has stayed with me vividly to this day. (And Anne insists it is one of the two or three loveliest memories she has. Certainly she brings it up often enough.) And, speaking for myself, I am not ashamed of it. One might ask: What sort of ridiculous old man would remember in such warm and meticulous detail an incident that occurred more than half a century ago? And naturally, if I were asked to respond, I would say: What sort of ridiculous old man would *not?*

In 1971, the Ambersons' only surviving child was their daughter, Florence, who was fortyone and married to a man named Earl Portman, who operated a chain of chicken carryout establishments in and around Cincinnati, Hamilton, Middletown and Dayton. The Portmans made their home in Dayton, and they had five daughters, ranging in age from fourteen down to six. Earl Portman was Florence's second husband. Back in 1951, just after her graduation from Ohio University, she had married a young assistant political science professor named Tom Rimers, but the fellow had been killed six months later in an automobile accident. Florence then went to Cincinnati, where she taught elementary art for four years. She met Earl Portman on a blind date, and they were married eleven days later. At one time, Florence had been quite pretty, in a frail and smallboned way. Now, at fortyone, she no longer was pretty, and she had gone to fat. Ah, but who cared about fat? Howard and Anne Amberson loved their daughter, and they loved their five granddaughters (and they even, in a way, loved Earl Portman, despite their belief that his mouth was too loud too often, and despite the fact that his fingers consistently gave off oily odors, probably of chicken batter). And so, because Howard and Anne Amberson felt the way they did, it was only right that they telephone Florence and tell her they were leaving on a little trip. Amberson dialed the number, and it was a bit complicated, what with the Area Code rigamarole and all, but even though it was Sunday evening the call went through the first time, and the telephone was answered by Florence's youngest, little Margaret Anne. The first thing Margaret Anne said was: "Who's this?"

Amberson smiled. "It's Grandpa Amberson," he said. "How are you, Margaret Anne?" He made a kissing sound. "We love you, Margaret Anne."

"Send her my love, too," said Anne Amberson, who was sitting next to her husband.

"Grandma Amberson and I," said Amberson into the receiver. He spoke too loudly, but he always spoke too loudly when he was calling longdistance. He had tried to reason himself out of the habit, but it had been no use. "Both of us," he said. "We love you."

"All right," said Margaret Anne. Then there was an abrupt sound, quite loud.

Amberson held the receiver away from his ear. He rubbed the side of his head. "I believe she dropped the telephone," he said to his wife.

"Has she gone to get Florence?"

"I hope so."

"Well, *I* just hope she didn't wander *off.*"

"We'll see," said Amberson. He placed the receiver tightly against his ear.

"Can you hear anything?" Anne asked him.

"Yes. Voices in the distance. Dishes. I think I just heard Florence ask Margaret Anne who that was on the telephone."

"*Was?*"

"Is."

"Oh. All right. I wouldn't want us just to be left *hanging* there."

"It will be all right. I think I hear footsteps."

"They're probably all in the family room," said Anne. "I bet you they're watching Walt Disney. I think it's time for Walt Disney."

"Yes," said Amberson. "I wouldn't be surprised."

"Florence has always liked Walt Disney. When she was a very little girl, we gave her a box of seven bars of soap, and each bar was in the shape of one of the seven dwarfs, you remember that?"

"Yes."

"And I can remember when we took her to see *Pinocchio.*"

"Yes. So can I."

"She ate too much candy, and she had terrible heartburn, and I think she threw up."

"Yes," said Amberson. "She did throw up."

Then Amberson heard his daughter's voice. He heard her say: "Oh, for God's sake." Then there was a metallic sound, and she apparently had picked up the receiver. "Ah, hello?" she said. "Daddy?"

"Hello, Florence," said Amberson. "How are you?"

"Very good, thank you. Alive and well in deepest Dayton. I'm sorry I was so long coming to the phone, but I was right in the middle of popping some pop corn, and I couldn't leave the popper. The girls are watching Walt Disney."

"Oh, that's perfectly—"

"And please excuse Margaret Anne's . . . ah, *cavalier* treatment of the receiver. I hope the noise didn't hurt your eardrums. It must have sounded like World War Three. How's Mother?"

"She's just fine. She's sitting right here."

"Give her my love," said Anne Amberson.

"She sends her love," said Amberson.

"Tell her the feeling is mutual," said Florence.

"She says I should tell you the feeling is mutual," said Amberson to his wife.

Florence lowered her voice. "Can Mother hear what I'm saying?"

"I don't believe so."

"Is she feeling any better?"

"Ah . . . no."

"What does Dr. Groh say?"

"Not much."

"Is she feeling any *worse?*"

"Sometimes. It all depends."

"What are you two *talking* about?" Anne Amberson wanted to know.

Amberson smiled at his wife and handed her the receiver. "Here," he said. "You do the talking for awhile."

Anne Amberson squeezed the receiver, and the tips of her fingers reddened. She said: "Hello, dear . . . yes . . . yes, as well as can be expected . . . no, the leaves are just now starting to change . . . the next two weekends should be the prettiest . . . she *what?* . . . well, did she *hurt* herself? . . . did you say *bounced?* . . . really? . . . just a minute . . . I, I have to tell your father." Anne Amberson placed a hand over the receiver and said to her husband: "Ruth fell out of the car this morning on the way to church, but all she did was *bounce.* They took her to the doctor, and he didn't even find a bruise on her. And not even a bump or a scratch." Then, uncovering the mouthpiece, Anne said: "Florence? You there? . . . well, she's lucky she's just nine years old and has a little, ah, baby fat. The car people ought to put some sort of safety device on the rear doors of cars, something the driver can control, something that will prevent children from fussing with the latches . . . yes . . . absolutely . . . I mean, if man can fly to the moon, why can't he invent a safety system for car doors? . . . yes . . . absolutely . . . I *know* it must have half frightened you to death . . . I understand . . . uh huh . . . say, how is your cold? . . . good . . . *me?* How am *I?* Well, I *told* you: I'm feeling as *well* as can be *expected,* for an old biddy with one of her boobies in the ashcan . . . hah, that's a very nice thing to say, but *you* don't have to go around all day with just one booby, and *you* don't have to go around all day on these old bones. It's too bad people can't turn in their old boobies and their old bones, like at a used car lot. But then they wouldn't have much value, would they? . . . now, no . . . no . . . I didn't mean to sound that way . . . you know me better than that . . . no . . . no . . . I am not—I definitely am *not* feeling sorry for myself . . . and *I* love *you,* too . . . and *I* worry about *you,*

too . . . well, I'll tell you something : I'm *glad* you worry about me
. . . all right . . . yes . . . here's your father . . ."

Amberson took the receiver from his wife.

"Daddy," said Florence. "My God . . ."

"How's that?"

"She sounds so *frightened* . . ."

"Well . . ." said Amberson. He glanced at his wife and decided there
was nothing more he could safely say.

"I know you can't talk, but . . . is it near?"

"I don't know. Perhaps soon. Perhaps not. I don't know."

"What's she asking you?" said Anne Amberson to her husband.

Amberson covered the mouthpiece. "She's asking me when we plan
to come visit her."

"Oh," said Anne. She folded her arms and began picking at an elbow.

Amberson uncovered the mouthpiece. "Florence? We, ah, the reason
we called is that—"

Florence interrupted. "I heard your little lie," she said, whispering.
"You didn't do a very efficient job of covering the mouthpiece. Do you
want me to come there? Is that it? I can be there in five hours. I'll leave
right now. I don't mind driving at night. I never have."

"No," said Amberson. "The reason we called is that we're taking a
little trip."

"Trip? Where?"

"We don't know."

"What?"

"We're leaving tomorrow morning, and we'll travel about in a more
or less footloose fashion. I've bought a movie camera, and I hope to
bring home lots of pretty color film."

Florence's voice had become louder, but now it again dropped to a
whisper. "Pretty color film? What are you talking about? Mother is
dying, and you can't—"

"Oh yes we can," said Amberson. "And we will." His palms were
damp. He felt a coldness come into his voice. His daughter should not
have said *dying.* It was an obscenity, and he would not tolerate it. "I
have made up my mind, young lady, and you might as well accept it."

". . . well, how . . . how long will you be gone?"

"We don't know."

"*You don't know?* Now, Daddy, for heaven's sake, you—"

"We're taking two thousand dollars' worth of Travelers' Cheques.
I'll keep half of them in one pocket and half in the other. When the first
pocket is empty, we'll turn around and head home."

"I never heard of anything so ridiculous in all my life," said Florence.

"Perhaps you're right," said Amberson. "But your mother and I want to understand some things."

"What things?"

"If we knew what they were, we wouldn't have to go, would we?"

"Daddy, please don't play at semantics with me. Please. Just give me a direct answer. Are you taking her off to *die,* is *that* it?"

Amberson closed his eyes for a moment. "I don't know," he said. He cradled the phone against his head and rubbed his palms on the knees of his trousers.

"Why can't she die in her own home?"

"I don't know."

"Don't be angry with me. Please. It's just that I want to understand. I love you, and I love Mother, and I don't mean any offense, but—"

"I'd answer if I could. All I can say is that it has something to do with what I call the apparatus. You mother and I need to examine it."

"Speak for yourself," said Anne, nudging her husband.

Amberson chuckled a little. He had no right to be angry with Florence, and he knew it. "Don't mind me," he said. "Your mother just told me I should speak for myself about this apparatus thing. I believe she thinks all the arteries have hardened in my brain, but then she's known for a long time that I can be strange."

"Amen," said Anne, picking at the elbow.

Florence's voice lightened. "Yes. Very strange. Like the time you put the Roosevelt sign in the front yard."

"Correct," said Amberson.

"I thought I would die of mortification."

"I know. I remember."

"She really doesn't have long at all, does she?"

"That is correct," said Amberson.

"And there's nothing I can do, nothing at all?"

"That is correct. But rest assured we love you."

"I know that," said Florence. "and how do *you* feel?"

"Pretty fair, all things considered."

"Will I hear from you? Will you call?"

Amberson scratched his chin. "Tell you what. We'll call every Sunday. From wherever we are, we'll call. But please don't look for any great cosmic reason for the trip. We simply want to—"

"Comic reason?"

"*Cosmic* reason," said Amberson. "Having to do with the cosmos. The heavens, matters of that sort."

"Oh. I beg your pardon. I thought you said comic."

Before Amberson could say anything more, Anne interrrupted. "Here," she said to him. "Give me that thing." She took the receiver from him and said: "Florence, I've gone along with him this long, so I might as well go along with him on this trip idea he has, whatever it means . . . yes, that's right; he calls it some sort of apparatus . . . well, at first I didn't know what he was talking about, but now . . . now I think I'm beginning to get the hang of it . . . and look, let's face it, whatever he wants to do, I want to do it too . . . yes . . . uh huh . . . of course . . . I'll take plenty of warm clothes . . . yes, I think that's it. I think he feels we have some sort of obligation to try to see what the country is. After all, we've lived in it for a long time, and I suppose we have a right . . . yes . . . naturally . . . and Mrs. Glanz will keep an eye on the house . . . I've already called the paper and the milk company . . . no, he's going with us . . . he likes to ride in the car . . . your father believes *he* needs to understand the apparatus too . . . no, I don't think many motels object to cats . . . just as long as you bring plenty of sand . . . yes, fifty pounds. He bought it yesterday at the Big Bear . . . no, I am *not* kidding you. *Fifty pounds.* It's in the car, and it's all ready to go. It's enough to take Sinclair to Timbuktu and back, but when your father gets an idea he leaves no stone unturned. Or grain of sand, for that matter . . . yes . . . well, thank you . . . I've always liked to think I had a sense of humor . . . yes . . . of course . . . no, I won't let your father drive more than six hours at a stretch . . . yes . . . all right . . . here he . . . yes, I love you too . . . ah, here he is . . ." Smiling, Anne handed the receiver back to her husband.

Florence's voice was girlish and splintered. "Daddy?"

"Yes?"

"You're sure you're doing the right thing? I mean, it isn't all some sort of aberration, is it?"

"Everything will be fine," said Amberson. "There will be no trouble."

"I guess I believe you."

"Thank you," said Amberson. "And, oh, I'm sorry about Ruth falling out of the car."

"She'll be fine," said Florence, "but I wouldn't be too sure about the pavement."

"How is that husband of yours?"

"Up to his you-know-what in thighs and legs," said Florence. "Alive and sassy and getting richer by the second."

"Well, give him our best."

"I'll do that. Thank you. And I'm sure he sends you *his* best. He's out right now. There was a grease fire in Middletown. He's gone to talk with the insurance people. First Ruth falls out of the car, and then a grease fire comes along. It's been quite a day. Well, if I know *him,* he'll make a profit out of it. I wouldn't want to be the insurance company."

"He works hard," said Amberson. "He does the best he can."

"Yes," said Florence. "And oh, by the way, I'm painting again. A little."

"That's fine," said Amberson. All right, if Florence wanted to move the subject away from her husband, he would let her. Her life was her own, which meant her attitudes were her own, and it was far too late to give her a lecture.

"The stuff's not very good," said Florence, "and it's terribly primitive. Big splashes of watercolor, childish, almost like cartoons."

"Well, you always have admired Disney. I seem to recall your saying a long time back that his techniques were a great deal more sophisticated than they ap—"

"This has nothing to do with *Disney.*"

"Oh?"

"I don't want *sophistication,*" said Florence. "I want *basics.*"

"Oh," said Amberson. "Well, very good."

"I want reality, not appearance, and reality begins with basics, with direct communication. So I'm just splashing on the color like mad, and nuts to technique."

"Does it gratify you?"

"Yes."

"Then it is good."

"I'm glad you think so," said Florence. "I really am."

"I don't mean to sound like some sort of sweaty hedonist, but it seems to me you don't get enough gratification."

"Daddy, no one's ever going to mistake you for a sweaty hedonist."

"I hope not," said Amberson. He smiled into the mouthpiece, then said: "This reference you have made to basics . . . ah, it interests me. If you really mean what you say, perhaps you can understand why your mother and I are going on our little trip."

"What do you mean?"

"We are looking for basics, too. When people are as old as we are, they wake up one fine morning to discover that their lives have become too clouded by events, by comings and goings, by history and technology and changing customs. They ask themselves: What is the real sense of the world today? What is its true schematic plan? And most of them do not have the vaguest idea how to answer those questions."

"So you and Mother are going off to try to find those answers?"

"Yes."

"You never will."

"Perhaps you are right—but isn't the search itself what is really important?"

"I don't know. I think maybe you've lost me."

"Not really," said Amberson. "Not if you mean what you say about your painting."

"You're really trying very hard to explain, aren't you?"

"Yes. I suppose I am."

"Daddy, there is a very peculiar tone to your words . . ."

"How do you mean?"

"It's as though you're trying to leave something behind that I can ponder . . ."

"Well, I hope I leave a lot of things behind when the time comes."

"I am being more specific. I am accusing you of giving me some sort of farewell lecture . . . oh my God, my . . . Daddy, you . . . I won't listen to any more of this . . ."

Amberson made a circle with his lips. His wife frowned at him. Rubbing his neck, Amberson said: "Shhh . . . now . . . you just shush, Florence . . . you're letting your imagination—"

"What's going on?" Anne wanted to know.

Amberson covered the mouthpiece. "Nothing," he said. "Florence is being a little melodramatic."

"Do you want me to talk to her?" Anne asked him.

"No," said Amberson. "It will be all right."

At the other end of the line, Florence was snuffling and trying to clear her throat. "You . . . shouldn't talk to me like . . . that. It scares me. I . . . can't cope with that sort of talk. I . . . *hate* . . . finality . . ."

"Nobody loves it. But you must learn to accept it. And I rather suspect it is one of those basics you seek. Wouldn't you say there is a good chance of that?"

"You . . . you sound like a schoolteacher . . ."

Amberson smiled. "Yes," he said. "And owls sound like owls."

"You old rascal," said Florence, snuffling.

"*Now* what are you talking about?" Anne wanted to know.

Amberson covered the mouthpiece and raised his eyebrows. "That's a good question," he said. Then, uncovering the mouthpiece: "Florence, whatever it is we must do, we must do it."

"Harrumph and ahem," said Anne.

"Your mother is giving me the old razz," said Amberson into the mouthpiece.

"Well," said Florence, "she loves you . . ."

"Do you?"

"Do I? Yes. Of course I do."

"And do you trust me not to do anything stupid?"

"Yes."

"Then trust me now."

"Yes, Daddy."

"You mean so much to us, and we would not hurt you if revolvers were pressed to our heads, and surely you know that."

"Yes. I know that."

"Keep after those basics," said Amberson.

"You, too," said Florence.

"Have trust and faith."

"Yes."

"Be good to your husband."

"All right."

"We shall be thinking of you."

"Thank you."

"Be a good girl."

"Yes."

"Goodbye," said Amberson.

"Good . . . goodbye," said Florence, her voice rising to a wail.

Amberson abruptly hung up. He smiled at his wife but said nothing. Anne coughed dryly but said nothing either. They sat silently for several minutes, and then he asked her what was on TV, and she fixed him a toasted cheese sandwich and a glass of root beer.

All my life, I have given much thought to love and death. As who doesn't? What is larger than love and death? The former, I have known firsthand. The latter, I have known because of loss. Sometimes it seems to me that I have spent half of all my waking hours attending funerals. Of the fortyone young persons who were graduated with me from Paradise Falls High School in June of 1915, all but twelve are dead. And my father is dead (1927), and my mother is dead (1923), and my two brothers are dead (Ernest in 1934 and Alvin Jr. in 1959), and my sister is dead (1922), and my two sons are dead (Henry in 1945 and Lewis in 1967), and I have outlived four house dogs and seven house cats, and now my wife soon will be dead, and I myself unquestionably also soon will be dead, and yet I persist in the perhaps absurd belief that it all somehow has been of value. And not untinged with gallantry.

This is not to say I value all the dying. I do not. Rather, I value all the living that preceded the dying. All the living and all the love.

Now and then, when I am unable to sleep, when I lie musing and remembering, I try to sort out the separate varieties of love that I have known. The love of son for father and mother. The love of brother for brother. The love of brother for sister. The love of father for child. The love of husband for wife. And I say to myself: The older you become, the more persons who are included—and the more who are taken away. Entrances and exits abound.

It may not reflect well on me to admit such a thing, but I find the remembering all very delicious. Obviously, it is better to look back fondly on the peripheral Joanna Lyman than to worry about the next heartbeat. Fred Boyd is of more value to me than terror. And so is, heaven spare us all, the magical and unduplicated Regina Ingersoll.

I have a technique for all this. I am able to edit away most of the embarrassments and the discomforts and the times of genuine pain. I still remember them, but distance has blurred them. And what is wrong with that? It is the way human beings make peace with their history, isn't it?

But why then, if it is all so blurred, do I find myself so often thinking of the past in the present tense?

Because I *do,* you know.

Is it all an avoidance of truth? What is the currently fashionable phrase? Cop-out?

Am I a copper-outer? Can I not face my history full and square and admit the finality?

So far, all I have done in this journal is laugh at myself. Well, there has been more to my life than the Famous Buick Incident. I have kissed many corpses, and I have known anguish, and isn't it about time I described *those* events? Either I am an honest man or I am not.

Now, just hold on. For heaven's sake, Amberson, stop flogging yourself.

Why should you feel so guilty about good things? You are not all that much of a terrible fellow. Stop belaboring yourself. So far you have lied about nothing. See it this way, Amberson: Acknowledge yourself to be an honest man but at the same time moderate and thoughtful and not afraid of sentiment, not afraid to embrace it here near the end of your life as your days leak away.

So take one last look, Amberson.

Monday

Anne Amberson prepared well for the trip, and they got off to a reasonably early start that Monday morning in October of 1971. She fixed leftover ham sandwiches and a thermos of coffee, gave all perishables to Mrs. Glanz next door and carefully loaded the car, a 1964 Pontiac twodoor, with suitcases full of clothing, toilet articles and even a selection of books. She also took along heavy coats for both of them, galoshes for herself and rubbers for her husband. "For all I know," she said, "we might not get home until after the snow starts flying."

"You could be right," said Amberson.

Anne spread newspapers on the back seat, and Amberson placed Sinclair's box on them. It was layered with clean sand. Anne telephoned the police and asked them to watch the house—for probably a week or two, she said. Then she checked all the windows and doors and asked Amberson did he have the Travelers' Cheques on him. He smiled, patted an inside breast pocket of his suitcoat and told her yes indeed, he was carrying them practically next to his heart.

She had packed the three George Vannice photographs of the children in one of the suitcases. Just before leaving, she walked from room to room in the house. She held Sinclair in her arms, and Amberson accompanied her. "When we return," she said, "the dust will be a mile thick. Whoo, it makes me want to *sneeze* just *thinking* about it." A small black cloth hat was perched on her head, and she was wearing her long winter coat. It was a dark plaid. Her tour of the rooms was leisurely, and Sinclair stared at her. She touched things. She rubbed a spot off a cherry endtable in the front room. She unplugged the television set and the refrigerator (which she had defrosted the night before). She said: "Mabel Glanz thinks we are crazy. When I talked to her this morning, I could tell she was trying to ask me whether I thought maybe you should be put away. But do you want to know something? I like her anyway. She has been a decent woman and a good neighbor. I won't ever see this place again, will I?"

They were standing in the front hall, and Amberson had been about to open the door. He turned and said: "That's not so. We're just going on a little trip."

"I knew that was what you would say."

"Well," said Amberson, "it's the truth."

"All right," said Anne. She rubbed her shoulder. Her eyes were dry, but moist sounds were coming from behind her teeth.

Amberson opened the door, and they went out. He closed the door firmly, then pulled it to make sure it was locked. He and Anne walked to the car, and she scratched Sinclair behind the ears. The car was parked in the driveway. Amberson stood at the car door and looked up at the sky. It was sunny to the east and north, gray to the west and south. There was a thin cold wind and a sound of leaves.

"What do you see up there?" Anne asked him.

"Looks like rain is coming in from the west."

"Which means we'll head east?"

"Yes. East and north."

"Well, I'm glad *that's* settled. I was about to die of suspense."

Amberson removed his spectacles and pinched the bridge of his nose.

Why the movie camera? Well, I need to define what it is I am leaving, what it is that has occupied my seventyfour years. To attempt to learn where the changes have taken place. I of course realize that the film will be obsolete as soon as it rolls past the lens, and this is what I believe to be the essense of the book Anne is reading. Nonetheless, I need to make the effort to record. I need to *freeze time* and announce to the world: All right. I was here for X number of years. I have a definite beginning and end, and here is the way things were at the end. Tomorrow is the stars, and I know nothing about the stars. My camera will examine the present as this journal examines the past. For the world's education, of course, but mainly for mine. (Change is immense and scarifying, but what else can we do beyond trying to understand it and fit ourselves into its pattern?)

How does the expression go? Am I out of my zonk?

Now, in 1971, only a few of my contemporaries still survive, and there is not a one (myself included, I suppose) who has not lost at least partial control of his zonk. This deficiency usually takes the form of cloudy reminiscence. We gather together, waxworks all, with our bony spotted hands and our dentured peppermint breath, at picnics and funerals and bridge tables and Thanksgiving dinners, and we muse endlessly on old scandals, old loves, old causes, old sunsets and hayfields and dogs and passenger trains and football games and steak dinners . . . anything at all, as long as it is *old*. And I listen to the words, and provide words of my own, with immense interest. In remembering, say, the year 1917, what is more important, the Great War or the shape of Joanna Lyman's lips? In 1921, Turks were slaughtering Greeks, and President Warren G. Harding was having at Nan Britton in the White House broom closet—but 1921 also was the year of my marriage to Anne Howell, and she wore forgetmenots in her hair. Obviously, the forgetmenots take precedence over slaughtered Greeks and the President's sexual activities. If the shape of my memory were anything but what it is, I would be a thoroughgoing misanthrope . . . and, what's more, probably a madman. Therefore, it is not such a terrible thing when Anne and I gather with our contemporaries and summon our sweetly edited past.

And the sweet memories exist in multitudes. I see large dollops of my history in terms that are placid. My boyhood may have vexed me at the time, but I remember little of such matters. Rather, I remember candy and blankets and the warm feel of my mother's cheerful White Shrine hands. And I remember the laughing zeal with which my brothers tormented all the Catholic children who lived in our neighborhood. And somehow my misty musings have made these tormentings unmalicious, or at least innocent. (And, in historical perspective, they are more than a little laughable, seeing as how Alvin Jr. eventually married a girl named Mary Frances O'Shea, and Ernest married one named Bernadette Walter. Both girls were as Catholic as the Holy Father's underdrawers, and all of Alvin Jr.'s and Ernest's children were reared strictly by the tenets and fragrant purring dogmas of their mothers' religion. They all wore gold crucifixes, and Ernest's youngest boy even studied briefly for the priesthood. His name was Peter, and thankfully he learned that the Lord's work could also be carried out by those who knew the flesh of women, and so he abandoned his somewhat shaky vocation, married a nicely fleshed girl of Italian extraction and became a social worker in Richmond, Virginia. I am quite fond of my nephew Peter, and two or three times a year we exchange long, garrulous letters. His hair is long, and he participates in peace demonstrations, and he greatly admires Corita Kent, and there is a possibility he knows something about the apparatus. Perhaps Anne and I will drive in the direction of Richmond. Perhaps a chat with Peter will do us some good. And why shouldn't we visit him? We are footloose, aren't we? Richmond is just as good a place to visit as any, isn't it?)

And so, as I write this, I find myself drifting away from my posture of bland serenity. I begin to be assaulted by complications, by relationships and intricacies, entrances and exits. In thinking of Peter, I think of the drawings of Corita Kent, and I think of the war, and I also think of my father; he becomes mixed together with politics and horror. His name was Alvin Amberson Sr., and he was a snappish little fellow with a good head for statistics and the financial rewards to be derived from the purchase of cemetery real estate, and he begat Ernest Amberson (among others), and Ernest Amberson begat Peter Amberson (among others), and Peter Amberson admires Corita Kent (as well as Daniel Ellsberg, Buffy Sainte-Marie and Muhammad Ali, among others), and it is all beyond statistics and reason. Sometimes I wish I had been born an orphan and without loins, constructed and plasticized, like an automobile fender or a frisbee. That way, I would be able to avoid all these damnable confusions. Great God, when one lives to be seventyfour, how can he truly sort out all the *people* he has known, all the *events,* all the *moving about,* all the *changes?* Where is the order? What is the schematic essense? Or is the question an absurdity? Perhaps so. Quite probably so.

And so I suppose I am incorrect in seeing my history as having been all that placid. Too many doors have been banged open and shut; there have been too many entrances and exits. And my brothers' tormenting of the Catholic children was not all that innocent. And what about Caroline and her sad talk of Magic Gas? And what about the way my brother Ernest died? And the way my son Henry died? There have been many tears, and I have an obligation to catalogue them and that is all there is to it.

Amberson was a slow and cautious driver, and he did not judge distances particularly well. Sometimes, when Anne was in a grouchy mood, she would accuse him of being a menace to traffic. But the fact was, in more than fifty years of driving he had never been involved in an accident. He liked to say that he didn't drive his own car as much as he drove everyone else's. The key, he was forever telling her, is *defensive* driving. Never take it for granted that the other fellow will do the right thing. Instead, anticipate that he will do the most stupid thing. That way, you will avoid accidents. That way, you will survive.

Over the years, Anne had had to put up with a great deal of that sort of talk, and Amberson supposed it was a wonder she hadn't taken after him with a cleaver. No one could be more schoolteacherish than he; no one could be more insufferably starchy. He had occasional epiphanies when he saw himself, warts and all, and the largest of the warts always seemed to be sprinkled with starch and polysyllabic rhetoric, and they just about made him laugh. Now, driving north on Mulberry Street a few blocks from his home, he smiled a little, but he kept his face averted from his wife.

Anne was staring out the window. Sinclair had jumped into the back seat, and he was scrabbling in his box.

"We going out Ninety-three?" Anne wanted to know.

"Yes," said Amberson. "We'll head up toward Logan and then maybe in the direction of Athens or Marietta or whatever."

"Please drive slowly."

"I always drive slowly."

"I want to look at Paradise Falls," said Anne. "It has nothing to do with how you drive. I want to look at the houses and the people."

"All right, my love," said Amberson, and the car crept past Hocking Street toward the Mulberry Street hill, close to the curb, in case anyone wanted to pass.

The Monday morning sounds of Paradise Falls were brisk and relentless. Doors slammed; dogs yipped; women stood in their back yards and grimly raked leaves. "The world really seems to be up and about," said Anne. A woman named Edith Kapper was walking on the sidewalk, and Anne waved at her. Edith Kapper frowned at the car and finally gave a tentative little wave in its direction. "Her eyes are very bad," said Anne. "I understand she is forever falling over things."

"Well," said Amberson, "she must be seventy."

"Easily," said Anne.

"Did her grandson ever get out of the penitentiary?"

"I don't think so. I think he still has about five years to go."

"What was it? Armed robbery?"

"Yes," said Anne. "A fillingstation. Seventeen dollars."

"God save us all," said Amberson. He glanced at the speedometer, and it registered 20.

"Thank you for driving slowly," said Anne.

"We aim to please," said Amberson.

Here in the north end, Paradise Falls was quite pretty. Mulberry and Cumberland and Hocking were three of the best streets in town, and they all were in the north end. Most of the houses were large and set well back from the street, with deep lawns and heavily substantial trees. In the days before automobiles, lovers walked along these streets and held hands and quietly spoke to one another of their devotion. The sidewalks were made of brick, and each brick had been engraved with the letters PFCP, for Paradise Falls Clay Products. They were sturdy sidewalks. They had been built in 1905, and Amberson seemed to recall that his father had had something to do with obtaining the purchase contract from the city. The streets themselves also had once been paved with brick, but along about 1960 the brick had been covered with asphalt. There had been little objection to this, seeing as how most people believed brick to be too slippery in bad weather, yet Amberson had mourned the passing of the brick (or, more properly, its burial); it had been to him a sort of finite symbol of Paradise Falls and his life there. But of course this sort of thinking was extremely silly. Brick was simply brick, and he chided himself for being such an arrant ninny. And now, as the Pontiac moved along the Mulberry Street curb, he watched Anne. Her mouth was open, and she was rubbing her shoulder. Her hat tipped forward a bit. An Omar truck clattered past, and the man at the wheel waved at the Ambersons. It was Walter Klopfer, and he had run track for Amberson. He had been the Ambersons' bread and baked goods man for years, and he liked to kid Amberson about all the ginger snaps they ordered. Amberson tooted his horn, and again Walter Klopfer waved. Amberson said: "Did you tell Walter we were going away?"

"Yes," said Anne, and she scratched her nose.

Sinclair crawled onto the shelf behind the back seat and began giving himself a bath. Outside, on the sidewalk, Mr. Hugo G. Underwood walked past. He was plump, and he was past sixty, and he had once been a member of the United States House of Representatives. He was said to be the richest man in town. He was a lawyer, and it was an open secret that his secretary was his mistress. When there was nothing else to do in Paradise Falls, one could always discuss Mr. Hugo G. Underwood.

"He doesn't look good," said Anne.

"I suppose not," said Amberson.

"His coloring is terrible, so pale and all. He ought to get outdoors more."

"Well, the practice of law is indoor work."

Anne nodded. She reached up and straightened her hat. "He didn't even *glance* at us," she said.

"Perhaps he was thinking of his lady friend."

"Or his money."

"We're not being very charitable."

"Well," said Anne, "I'm sure he couldn't care less what we think."

"Perhaps you're right," said Amberson.

The car began climbing the Mulberry Street hill, past the old high school where Amberson had taught. (It now was a junior high; a new high school, named after Paradise Falls' most famous citizen, William W. Ackerman, the noted World War I air ace, had been opened last year.) Amberson clicked his teeth together and glanced at the firstfloor window of his old homeroom. He told himself it would be better if he looked somewhere else, but of course he was not that strong. He said to himself: This is absurd. I am too reasonable to be feeling this way. He said to himself: Past is past, and grief accomplishes nothing. He said to himself: See it there, sagging now, the bricks so pale, washed by generations of rainstorms, with the words PARADISE FALLS HIGH SCHOOL still engraved on the cement arch over the main entrance, and what is it other than aging junk that will be replaced as soon as the voters of Paradise Falls, in their infinite wisdom, pass a bond issue that will provide the funds for the job? He said to himself: Then why do I want to reach out and touch it?

I have made a decision, and it is this:

If I am to describe the past in any meaningful way, I must do so in the present tense. At my age, there is no reality more vivid than the past. The present is beyond me, and (as I have said) the future is the stars, and I know nothing of stars. Therefore, I must stop hawing and fretting and admit right out that I cannot even begin to summon the past unless I see it as being still without resolution.

So here begins the catalogue, and I ask that we see now 1945. Can we do such a thing? I pray we can.

It is a gray morning in early April, 1945, speckled with a thin and reluctant rain, and Anne's daffs have begun to pop open. She and I and Florence are breakfasting, and she smiles and says: "The rain should do everything a world of good."

"The world is very pretty when it rains," says Florence.

Smiling, I say, "Good grief, what a romantic couple of women are sharing my roof."

My wife and daughter smile at me, and they both show their teeth. Florence is fifteen and luminous, and she is always showing her teeth. (She is a great help in distracting me from the absense of Henry and Lewis, who are both in the army. Henry is an infantry lieutenant with Patton's Third Army probably somewhere in Germany, and Lewis is a captain stationed at the arsenal in Ravenna, Ohio.) As for my wife, well, Anne is still plumply trim. Even at this hour of the morning, she is wearing all her foundation garments under her print dress. She is eating her Post Toasties with skimmed milk. Florence and I are having cream with ours.

"You and your skimmed milk," I say to Anne. "I don't know why you bother."

"Thank you," says Anne, patting her tummy.

"You look remarkably nifty for an old lady of fortysix," I tell her.

"Oh, *phooey,*" says Anne, "this damp weather will straighten my *hair* and make me *sweat* and look *awful.*"

Florence speaks up. She is at an age where she is much given to extravagant adjectives, and they delight me. Spooning her cereal, she says: "Mother, if *the world* looked as awful as you do, it'd be a *super delicious* world, and I don't want to hear any sass from you about it."

Making a face at Florence, Anne says: "That'll be just about enough out of you, Miss Snip." But Anne then smiles, reaches across the table and pats one of Florence's hands.

"Aw, garsh," says Florence, batting her eyes.

I snort, and Anne laughs out loud, and I am terribly pleased to be hearing it. Her daffs aside, this is a good spring for my wife. Everyone knows that the Germans are about to surrender, which means Henry will be coming home soon. Lewis probably will have to remain in Ravenna, Ohio, until the Japanese quit, but no one is worried about Lewis. As he himself often tells Anne and me, the casualty figures from Ravenna, Ohio, are, ha ha, remarkably light. No, it is *Henry* whose safety concerns his family—and especially his mother. It is no secret that he has always meant more to his mother than breath and laughter. He is her firstborn, and he did not come easily, and she has always called him her best beau. She also calls him her Always Boy, and by this she means: She always will love him no matter what; she always will be ready to nestle him; she always will defend him from any trolls and witches and dragons and villains that might foolishly try to get the best of him. Is this love excessive? Unquestionably, and she admits it. She and I have discussed it many times, and she can only defend herself by saying: I have no control over it. It sits in my blood, and who can live without blood?

This is not to say that she has less love for Lewis and Florence. She loves them deeply and without reservation, but there is a difference, and it has to do with the fact that they came easily, and their arrival was without pain. Henry, on the other hand, nearly killed her. He came awkwardly, he came choking and coughing, and she later told me that the pain even penetrated her unconsciousness, and his kicks and squirmings tore at her and made her gush redly. Which means he is much more a part of her than Lewis or Florence. Otherwise, he wouldn't have been so reluctant to leave.

But Anne has never neglected Lewis and Florence. She is not a stupid woman, and she knows that her incessant references to Henry as her Always Boy must somehow be diluted. And so she publicly laughs at her devotion. She describes herself as being a true Textbook Case, and oh *my,* she says, wouldn't some psychiatrist have a lot of fun with *me.* And, beyond the ridicule, she has even gone so far as to attempt to explain the devotion to Lewis and Florence, sitting them down with her and telling them: When I love him and hug him and kiss him, try to understand that I'm loving and hugging and kissing *you two* at the same time. You two. You, too. T-W-O and T-O-O. I *do* love you. You *know* that, don't you? Ah, listen to me. Methinks the lady doth blabbeth too much. Well, maybe she does, but she means what she says.

And, usually, at the conclusion of this sort of talk, she beckons Lewis and Florence to her, and hugs and kisses abound, and smiles flash, and warm hands touch and squeeze.

Florence never has questioned her mother's attempt at an explanation. Lewis perhaps has, but he has never permitted his doubts to emerge. He knows how to smile, does this Lewis. He is barely twenty years old, and he is already a *captain,* and it is clear to me that he is playing some sort of urgent and secret game. Whatever this game is, I think I deplore it. I am too aware of what seems to be a football stadium, and there are times when I believe I hear cheerleaders whooping in his skull. The game is as important to him as Henry, the Always Boy, is to my wife, and I do not doubt that he will win. The cheerleaders yip and leap, and his skull is a clamor of neatly relentless triumphs. He has curled himself around a precise and unwavering destiny. His eyes are blue, and his hair is wavy, and he is already a *captain,* and he measures his days with calipers and a sharp pencil. No amount of talk of an Always Boy will derail *Lewis Charles Amberson,* not on your grandmother's tintype. He is already a *captain,* and the calipers are held steadily, the pencil does not slip or smudge. He will fight. And he will win.

As for Florence, well, it is enough that her complexion is clear. It is enough that she already has good breasts. It is enough that boys whistle at her and buy her banana splits. She has been told she resembles Ann Blyth, and this delights her. And why *shouldn't* it? What is she supposed to do? Go around insisting she *really* resembles *Marjorie Main?*

And so there it is. Five lives, here in the spring of 1945, caught warmly plugging along, the sum total of thousands of days, of lunchboxes and tinted photographs and Christmas carols and the thrum and whir of Anne's 1938 Singer electric sewing machine, of Lewis winning election as president of the Paradise Falls High School 1942 graduating class, of Florence's saddle shoes and her dimpled knees, of June Allyson at the Ritz and Frankieboy singing on what Anne cheerfully calls the raddio (to aggravate my feelings about pronunciation, I expect), of secret times when an old gentleman of fortyeight (almost) crawls atop his nifty wife of fortysix (just) and they whisper and thresh and occasionally giggle over the great horsy shadeflapping memory of a legendary old Buick, of letters from Henry the Always Boy, of hollyhocks and rainbarrels and brave springtime daffs, of chalkdust and sweatsocks and the nearly brandnew Ohio Class A Track & Field championship trophy that stands resplendently under glass in the downstairs front hall of Paradise Falls High School, of aprons and pillowcases and soap and the grainy feel of my homeroom attendance book, of hands always willing to be squeezed (could they be called Always Hands?), of funerals and ration stamps and skinned elbows, of fugitive visions of a forever lost Regina Ingersoll and her outrageous question . . . ah, how it all piles together in such witless profusion, this multitude of warmly plugging days. And yet, for all that, I nonetheless see myself as being capable of understanding its general outline. At fortyeight, I am as neat as ever, and as deliberate, and I am able to grasp dimensions and ramifications. Or at least I think I am, and I suppose this is all that matters. I sense that the future (the world's, not mine) will become too complicated for rational analysis—but that is the world's problem, not mine. As of today, as of this damp springtime Post Toastied morning in 1945, my life has a place for everything, and everything is in its place. I always know how many clean shirts are in the dresser, and there are no missing entries in my homeroom attendance book, and my shoes are never untied nor my trousers unpressed. And I always check my fly before joining my wife and daughter for breakfast. (There is, after all, a place for everything.)

I walk to school with Florence this morning, as I have walked to school in the past with Henry and Lewis, and I am aware of the imminence of new leaves. Both Florence and I are carrying umbrellas, and she says: "Maybe I'm crazy or something, but I just *adore* this sort of a morning."

"It has promise," I tell her.

"You ain't just whistling the Battle Hymn of the Republic, my friend," says Florence.

I smile. My daughter seems to understand something of the uses of the language, and this delights me. The sidewalk is slick, and I am able to smell damp moss. Boys and girls go gibbling past, and a boy named Ralph Jackman accuses Florence of trying to applepolish old Mr. Amberson. Florence sticks out her tongue at this Ralph Jackman, and he flaps his arms and begins to guffaw. Old Mr. Amberson clears his throat, and Ralph Jackman (who is a hurdler for me) darts across the street and joins a shambling aimless clutch of hooting boys, some of whom are wearing PF letter sweaters.

"That moron," says Florence, giggling.

"Old Mr. Amberson indeed," I say.

"Now, now. Don't pout."

"I would consider it a great favor if you did not talk like your mother."

Florence laughs. "I should walk to school with you more often," she says. "You're a real card."

"Oh, yes," I say. "I really have a large reputation in that area." But I cannot help but smile. I enjoy my daughter a great deal, and that is a fact. Yet—seeing as how I am what I am (namely, a teacher) and she is what she is (namely, a pupil, albeit a teacher's daughter) —we seldom walk to school together. She has never said anything to me about this, but clearly she does not want to damage her standing with her peer group, as the educators say. And I cannot blame her for the attitude. If she felt any other way, she would be a strange girl indeed. And so, because of all this, she usually walks to school with a classmate named Sally Luebke, a narrow little redhaired girl with freckles. But Sally Luebke is staying home today because of a cold, and I have inherited her place. And I am rather pleased.

"That Ralph Jackman thinks *he's* a real card," says Florence. "Every time I walk to school with you, there's some jerk who comes up to me and makes with a bigdeal *joke* about it."

"There's practice tonight," I say. "I do believe he has earned himself an extra lap around the track."

"It'd serve him right."

"Well, just remember: Ralph Jackman belongs to a large club, the Dazzling Original Remark Club."

"*You* can call it that if you want to," says Florence. "*Me,* I'll call it the Dumb Club."

I smile, and raindrops slide down the front of my spectacles, softening my vision. And then Florence excuses herself. She has spied several of her girlfriends, and so she goes skittering toward them, and old Mr. Amberson is left behind. She waves and shrieks, and her friends wave and shriek, and she darts across the street, and their heads converge, and they giggle and whisper. And I am aware of my breath and my bones and the places where my flesh has begun to give way, and I say to myself: Yes, old Mr. Amberson indeed. And I watch my daughter and say to myself: She should put some of that energy in a masonjar and store it down cellar. Then, grimacing, I remove my spectacles and try to wipe away the moisture. But I cannot do this, seeing as how the rain is still falling. I replace my spectacles, and all I have succeeded in doing is smear the lenses even more, and so I give myself a scolding. I say to myself: Leave your spectacles *be.* Stop *fussing.* And leave Florence be. Let her be what she is. One cannot store one's youth in a masonjar. The thought is ridiculous. You should know better.

I slosh alone up the Mulberry Street hill to the school, and I breathe deeply of the green morning, and the masonjar thoughts drift away. Ducking my head against the rain and holding my umbrella at a slant, I smile at the pupils who scurry with me to the front door, and someone tells me it is a great morning for ducks, and the front hall echoes with shouts and a steady squishing sound of wet shoes and rubbers and galoshes, and I hear a barrage of slamming locker doors, and there is a counterpoint of squeals, whoops, squeaks, laughter and hollow restless snaps and clicks and sighings and even the thwuck and pound of tennis shoes, and faces pass in a sort of blind clamor, and my nostrils detect a regiment of dimestore scents, all green and leaky and aimed straight for the groin, and I say to myself: Ah, another day, another dollar, you clever coiner of phrases you.

My homeroom number is III. It has been my homeroom for more than twenty years, and I teach all my classes there as well. I fold my umbrella and shuck myself out of my raincoat. I hang them in the cloakroom and go to my desk. Several of my homeroom boys are already there, and one or two of them smile at me. I nod, seat myself and begin polishing my spectacles. More boys drift in. At Paradise

Falls High School, the homerooms are segregated by sexes. My boys are juniors this year, and today they are quite noisy, and their bodies seem to give off steam. I am able to remember how I felt when I was their age and full of a sort of sopping springtime tumescence, and I do not envy them, and I am almost grateful for my fortyeight years. The boys clutch and snigger, but I pay them no mind. The bell has not yet rung, and I am not the sort of teacher who requires silence when it is not necessary. I am vaguely aware of argyle socks and damply rancid shoes and wrinkled cotton trousers, and voices pick and scrape at the periphery of my brain, but these things are of no consequence to me, and so I enter the date in my homeroom attendance book and wait for the first bell to ring. A boy named Tom Kapper comes to me and asks to be excused from his fourthperiod studyhall so he can go home and help his father take his invalid mother to the doctor for some sort of checkup. I fill out a CLASS EXCUSE form for him, and he smiles and thanks me. He is a polite boy, quite small with immense brown eyes. He washes his own shirts, socks and underwear, and the story is that his poor mother does not have long to live. He carefully folds the CLASS EXCUSE form, slides it into his shirt pocket and returns to his seat. Then Mary Grandstaff comes into the room. Now, being what they are, my boys usually respond in various audible ways (with low whistles, for instance, and dry sniggers) when a girl comes into the room. But they do not respond when Mary Grandstaff enters, and I doubt that they ever will. She is a senior honors student who works in the school office and is one of my best pupils, a writer of rather sensitive and lovely verse. But she is quite fat, and her cheeks are pockmarked, and she has an unfortunate moustache. The boys have a word for her, and it is beast. And I have heard them call her Hairy Mary. Obviously, she is everyone's idea of an honors student, and I have been unable to suppress a small resentment of her . . . perhaps because she is such a dreary cliché. Sensitive poetry or no sensitive poetry, she is such a terrible lump of a girl that I have difficulty looking her straight in the face. But she is undaunted, and she comes directly to my desk and says: "Mr. Amberson, Mr. Busse wants to see you in the office right away. He says it is very important."

I stare at Mary Grandstaff for a moment. I stare her straight in the face. She has put on too much lipstick, and it is too dark, and she has done nothing about that damnable moustache. Aren't there creams available? Surely there is *some* step that can be taken. And then I say to myself: Why are you being so cruel?

Several of the boys look up at us.

I keep staring Mary Grandstaff straight in the face, and I am overtaken by a sense of some sort of small triumph. I smile at her and say: "All right, Mary, let us be about our business, you and I." I rise, and she precedes me out of the room. Her feet make large flapping sounds in the hallway. There is only about a minute or so until the first bell, and latecomers go scurrying past us, their books and notebooks clutched to their chests. I follow a step or so behind Mary. She is wearing a plaid skirt, and there is a flabby wobble to her buttocks. (It would do no good to ask her what this is all about. She does not know, and therefore the question would be a waste of time. I have never believed in wasting time, and I never will. I am, after all, the *track coach,* and what sort of track coach is it who seeks to waste time? One does not squander one's most precious commodity.) I follow Mary Grandstaff's gelatinous rump into the office, and I am walking briskly, but my belly feels a bit thick. I go straight to the principal's inner office, and I cannot remember when the last time was I have been pulled out of my room in such a manner, and it is at this point that I begin to suspect that the summons may have something to do with Henry.

Herman W. Busse, the principal of Paradise Falls High School, is standing behind his desk. He is a bright young fellow of thirtynine. He has red hair and a compact body, and he was wounded two years ago in Tunisia, and half of the Paradise Falls High School female population (both pupil and faculty) is wildly in love with him. He comes from a family of teachers, and here in 1945 there are four members of the scholarly Busse clan working in the Paradise Falls system. A sister and a brother teach at the South End Elementary School, and another sister teaches at the West End Elementary School.

Herman W. Busse tries to smile. He reaches up and scratches his scalp. He scratches busily. Then he points to a chair and says: "Please sit down."

I walk to the chair and seat myself. "All right now, Herman— what is it?" I ask him. (All the faculty members call him Herman. He has insisted on it. He has told us: Look, I hope I have your respect, but I'm not about to make you use my surname when addressing me. There are too many Busses in this system as it is. So please call me Herman. It isn't much of a name, but I do hope you'll use it.)

Now Herman Busse leans forward, pressing his palms against the surface of the desk. His hair is mussed from the scratching. "Karl Lutz just telephoned here," he says.

"You mean the Karl Lutz from Western Union?" I ask him. "He has a daughter named Paula who's in my sophomore World Literature class. She's a bright little thing."

"Yes," says Herman Busse. "That's the Karl Lutz I mean."

My cheeks are warm, and so are my eyes. My mouth is full of splinters, and I say: "Is it . . . ah, it has something to do with Henry, doesn't it?"

Herman Busse sits down heavily. His chair squeals. His voice clogged, he says: "Yes. Karl Lutz . . . well, the telegram is addressed to both you and your, ah, your wife, but he didn't want to, ah, telephone her at your home. He . . . it occurred to him that . . . ah, my God . . . that perhaps *you* would want to tell your—"

"Henry is dead, isn't he? He's not wounded or missing, is he? He's absolutely . . . outandout *dead,* isn't that correct?"

Herman Busse closes his eyes and nods.

I rush out of Herman Busse's office. I bump against the counter in the outer office, and I am moaning, and I cannot see, and then I collide with a soft warm body, and it belongs to Mary Grandstaff. I embrace her, and she wriggles. The collision has knocked my spectacles askew, and they dangle from my left ear. I weep into Mary Grandstaff's chest, and after a time she stops wriggling, and then she strokes my head. The other office people gather around us, and nothing is said, and presently I am led away. By this time, Mary Grandstaff also is weeping. My spectacles fall to the floor, and they are shattered.

Sinclair's bath was completed to his satisfaction. He tucked his forepaws under his chin, closed his eyes and went to sleep. The Ambersons' car moved past the high school and on up the Mulberry Street hill toward the two cemeteries, the "old" Oak Hill to the right and the "new" Oak Grove to the left. Cars whipped by, and several of the drivers waved at the Ambersons.

"They probably think there's something wrong with the engine," said Amberson.

"Well, I don't care what they think," said Anne.

"And neither do I," said Amberson. He smiled. The old high school was several hundred yards behind them now, and out of sight, out of mind.

"Did you see who that last driver was?" Anne asked him.

"No. It was just a shadowy form and an arm in a Ford station wagon."

"It was John Barnett."

"You mean old John Barnett who used to own the ice plant?"

"The same," said Anne.

"My Lord, I thought he was dead."

"No. You're thinking of his brother Pete, the one who drank so much."

"Oh yes. I suppose I am. Well, what's old John doing speeding along in a Ford station wagon? He must be eighty."

"If he's eighty, he's a young eighty."

"What do you mean?"

Anne sighed. "Howard, my goodness, don't you pay *any* attention to what's going *on* in this town? About a year ago old John Barnett married the Kuchmans' daughter Marie, the widow with the four children."

"Oh yes. Now I remember."

"And she can't be more than fortyfive."

"And that's why old John went speeding up the street?"

"It's as good a reason as any, isn't it?"

"I suppose so," said Amberson, grinning.

Now the car was approaching the top of the hill. On the right was the tall frame house that once had been owned by the spinster named Bagley. It was the house where Regina Ingersoll had roomed back in 1927 and part of 1928. Miss Bagley was long dead, and now the place was occupied by a family named McHenry, which consisted of a husband, wife and seven children. A small boy was embracing a puppy in the front yard. Amberson could see the puppy's eyes, and they appeared to be a bit apprehensive.

The cemetery entrances flanked Mulberry Street, and they were directly beyond the McHenry place. Anne Amberson touched her husband's arm and said: "Would it be all right if we drove through the cemetery?"

He looked at her. "The new one?"

"Yes."

"Why?"

"Just because I want to. I'd like to read the names and all. And anyway, we're footloose, aren't we? We don't have a schedule to keep, do we?"

"No," said Amberson. "Of course not." He twisted the wheel to the left, and the car turned into the Oak Grove Cemetery. He should have chosen some other direction this morning. It was stupid of him to have chosen a route that took them past the cemeteries.

Anne spoke quietly. "I just want to see it from this side," she said.

Then she coughed dryly, almost timidly, without passion or even grief.

Amberson nodded. "All right," he said. "All right. Fine."

"And *you* should want to see it too," said Anne.

"Yes," said Amberson. He removed his foot from the accelerator, and the car coasted through the cemetery gates and along a narrow asphalt roadway. It was cracked and gutted, and weeds slapped at the sides of the car.

"The eye of the bird as opposed to the eye of the worm," said Anne.

"All *right,*" said Amberson.

"Do you understand what I mean?" she asked him. She stared straight ahead, and her hands were folded in her lap.

"*Yes,*" said Amberson.

Anne was silent. Amberson tried to focus his eyes on the hood of the car. And the car was coasting more slowly. Gravestones marched off in every direction. They were white and gray, and some of them were cracked, and some of them had moss curling at their base. And Amberson's eyes were drawn away from the hood of the car by the names on the tombstones, and he became aware of his former colleague, that old pumpkinhead of a rascal of a

FREDERICK T. BOYD
1864–1936

and, next to that name, the name of

MARTHA W. BOYD
1868–1954

and quickly Amberson looked away, his gaze crossing to the other side of the roadway and encountering the likes of SOEDER and HOVING and BIRD and JONES and INGRAHAM and MCBRIDE and CORD and ERWINE and REPPLER, and now the car was coasting so slowly that he had to nudge the accelerator a bit, and the headstones were here and there spangled with early fall leaves (here on the hill, fall came sooner, what with all the cold and the night winds), and trees stood dark and heavy in rows and clusters, and the names included SLAUGHTER and PRES-COTT and CASTER and HILL and MASONBRINK and TUMULTY and LILLIS, and then the car rolled down an incline and came to the place where a number of people named AMBERSON were buried. It was shaded by several rigid tulip trees. Amberson braked the car to a stop, and he and Anne listened to the wind in the trees, and finally she said: "I'd like to get out."

"All right," said Amberson. He opened the door and slid out of the driver's seat. He was cold. He walked around the front of the car, and his joints were stiff. He helped Anne out of the car. They walked to where the gravestones were, and he held her by an elbow. They went first to Henry's grave, and she bent and plucked some weeds.

Perhaps this time the summoning of the past as the present will not be so difficult. Perhaps the paradox will become more acceptable once familiarity sets in.

So see now 1923, and it is the morning after the day of my mother's funeral, and the grieving Worthy High Priestesses all have entrained for home. It is a lovely and gentle morning, yellow and all atwitter, and I am first made aware of it when my wife begins to scream and shudder. Sunlight speckles the bedclothes, and Anne's face is oily and pale, slack with pain. I sit up, and her pelvis pumps, and the bed rocks. Springs resist noisily, and she beats her fists against the mattress. I lean over her and kiss her on the forehead, and my lips come away sticky. I turn from her and wipe my mouth with the back of a hand. She hollers something I cannot understand. I pat one of her hands, then jump from the bed and hurry downstairs to the telephone.

The doctor's name is Horace O. Button, and he assures me he will be right over. "You just hold on," he says. "Everything will be just fine."

"She seems to be in great pain," I say.

"Yes," says Dr. Button. "I'll be there before you can say Grover Cleveland Alexander. And don't worry about the pain. A little of it can be helpful. And anyway, I can take care of it." Then, abruptly, he hangs up.

I rush back upstairs to the bedroom.

Anne is drooling, but she is making no sounds. For the moment at least, she is neither screaming nor shuddering. She wipes her mouth with the corner of a sheet, then says (speaking quietly, the words a bit breathless but otherwise remarkably precise): "I am a baby when it comes to things like this."

"It doesn't matter," I tell her.

"Did you call the doctor?"

"Yes."

"First your mother dies, and now *this.*"

"The one has nothing to do with the other."

"Do you love me?" she wants to know.

"Of course I love you."

"I am such a . . . such a baby . . ."

"Well, soon there'll be another one to keep you company."

Anne starts to say something, but then her eyes erupt with tears. I smile at my wife. I bend over her and kiss her full on the lips. I smoothe back her hair, and she is so very pretty. I pat her enormous belly. She winces a little but does not speak. She squeezes her face, rubs away the tears, then tries to speak. I tell her shush. I seat myself on the edge of the bed and hold one of her hands in both of mine. She is lying flat on her back, and her legs have been flung apart. Her threshings have forced down the bedclothes, and her nightdress is open at the throat. I am able to see the outlines of her nipples. She has always enjoyed my kissing them. I unfasten the front of the nightdress, bend down and lick both nipples until they are hard. My hands again enclose her hand, and she sighs. She uses her free hand to stroke the back of my neck. I have an erection, and my penis pokes through the fly of my pajamas, and she sees it and laughs a little. She tells me I am the absolute limit, and I smile. Her nipples are warm. She is quite proud of her breasts. She considers them to be her best feature. She is just twentyfour, and there are no lines on her face. She scratches the nape of my neck, then begins to squeeze it, then begins to moan and writhe, and it is clear that the pain is returning, and so I pull away and tuck my penis back inside my pajamas. (And here I say to myself: Great God, what a strange time to have an erection. Ah, but then I've been living like a monk for quite a few months now, and I suppose it's only natural. Well, at least I haven't gone roaming in the park and molested any children.)

This time Anne roars and kicks, and her feet become entangled in the sheets. I pull the sheets free, but in so doing I twist one of her ankles. She shrieks. More tears sprout from her eyes, and I attempt to kiss them away, but her head jerks from side to side, and my lips only brush her ear, and I say something to the effect that I seem to be zagging every time she zigs. She does not reply. Her buttocks rise and fall, and I wonder if perhaps she would care for a glass of water. I try to ask her the question, but my words are blotted by her roarings and her rearings and the hard loud sound of the bedsprings.

I scurry to the closet and put on my bathrobe and slippers. Then I return to the bed and stand over my wife, and now the pain apparently is coming in waves. I want to press my hands over my ears, and perhaps even my eyes, but of course it would be unconscionably rude and cowardly of me to do either, and so I simply stand there, and after a time I say: "I'm right here." Which is all I can think of to say. I stand with my arms folded, and Anne's tongue is exposed, and her groans come in spasms.

I stand there for perhaps ten minutes, and then I hear footsteps on the porch and the sound of the front door being opened.

I go clattering down the stairs and greet Dr. Button, who is accompanied by his nurse, a Miss Emerald White.

These two people have provided as much good bonemarrow juicy Paradise Falls gossip as the human mind is capable of imagining. As topics of conversation, they are as mandatory as the weather and the tomato crop. They have become living legends, and I have no idea what the town would do without them. Emerald White is a neat little woman, svelte and pretty and blacker than the devil's hind leg. It is no particular secret that she is Dr. Button's mistress as well as his nurse, and neither of them has bothered to hide a thing. She came with him when he moved from Columbus to Paradise Falls in 1919, and no one has ever heard her call him anything other than Horace. Never Dr. Button. Never even Mr. Button. And never even sir. Her voice is soft, but it is not servile, and she is not reluctant to look the world squarely in its gossiping scandalized face. Her employer (and, obviously, lover) is a small man, bald as a parboiled wiener, and his practice is remarkably robust, all things considered. The Emerald White situation aside, he happens to be a good doctor, and nothing appears to ruffle him—which is as handy an indicator of a good doctor as any. When he and Emerald White came to Paradise Falls four years ago (for reasons that never have been made clear), there was a horrendous influenza outbreak tearing through the town. This gave his practice a splendid initial impetus. There were only three other doctors, and the sick could not afford to be choosy in that sort of emergency. So Dr. Button and the mysterious Emerald worked eighteen and twenty hours a day. He rented a large old house on North High Street and turned it into an emergency hospital. Two dozen folding cots were shipped in by Railway Express from Columbus, and his little impromptu hospital was filled within a day of its opening. (There was not—and still is not, here in 1923—a regular hospital in Paradise Falls.) And the thing about this Dr. Button was, he moved calmly. The town's other three doctors had become grumpy rumpled hulks, snappish from harassment and lack of sleep, but Dr. Button never even seemed particularly tired. He of course wore a mask when he moved among his crouping and feverish patients, but one was able to see his eyes, and they were steady, and eyes are always terribly important, and so within two weeks more than thirty families had transferred their business to him on a permanent basis. He never shouted, and his clothing always was neat, and Emerald White always was somewhere nearby, and his patients liked to comment on how warm his hands were, and of course hands also are always terribly important. Most people figured well, all right, so he probably does sleep with that pickaninny wench, but he still is a damned good doctor, and after all, isn't *that* what's really important? (Now, looking back on the arrival of Dr. Button and his companion, I hope he appreciates how luckily it was timed. Had they come to Paradise Falls when there had been no emergency, the town unquestionably would have been less tolerant of their indifference to the conventions. However, in *that* situation, it knew enough not to flog a gift horse, even though that gift horse cohabited with a zebra.) And finally, when the outbreak had run its course and the victims had been counted, it was learned that Dr. Button had lost not a single patient. And none of the town's other doctors could make that claim. In all, seventeen residents of Paradise County had died, but none of them had been under Dr. Button's care. And so he prospered. And still prospers, four years later. He belongs to no civic groups or fraternal organizations, and no one of any importance has anything to do with him socially (good Lord, suppose he were invited to a party and he brought along that dusky jewel of an Emerald White? who could afford to take such a risk?), but he prospers nonetheless, and he is never impolite. And he is never seen in the company of any woman other than Emerald White. They walk along the streets together, conspicuous and brazen as a couple of warts on a Poland China hog, and Dr. Button always tips his hat to passing ladies, and Emerald White always smiles a somewhat metallic smile, and they obviously do not give a whoop if the entire world clucks and gossips, and I for one am willing to credit them with something that just may be a kind of gallantry.

God knows what Dr. Button and Emerald White do when they are alone together—and, as the saying goes, He isn't telling. I rather suspect their activities are grand and exotic. At least I hope so. As long as they are creating such a scandal, they might as well be enjoying themselves. But one thing is for certain—she does live with him. There is a colony of Negroes in the south end (about forty families were imported from Alabama in 1916 to work at the Paradise Falls Clay Products Co. as strikebreakers . . . over my father's strenuous objections, by the way), but Emerald White has nothing to do with those people. I would not be surprised if she feels she is too good for them. Instead, she lives right smack with Dr. Button in that same rented house on North High Street, and she obviously is no servant. He has told me that she has a nursing degree from some Negro college down in Mississippi or Georgia or wherever, and he has also told me that she is the best nurse he has ever encountered. And I like them both. I wish Anne and I had the courage to invite them over for supper. But that much courage is as yet beyond us, and all we can do is admire them.

Even now, so early in this warm golden morning, Emerald White is turned out well. She is wearing a smart cloche hat and a neat black dress, and Dr. Button stands aside and lets her through the doorway first. She is carrying a small bag, and Dr. Button is carrying another that is even smaller. Anne's screams are clearly audible, and so Dr. Button says nothing, asks no useless questions. He and Emerald White hurry upstairs, and I scramble after them.

I usher Dr. Button into the bedroom. Emerald White heads for the bathroom. Dr. Button goes to Anne, and Anne still is screaming, and Dr. Button seizes her by the shoulders and shakes her until she is silent. She gasps, but the screams are gone, and he says: "All right now, Mrs. Amberson. We'll work at it, and everything will be fine." Then he turns to me and says: "You can go now. Please wait down-stairs." His voice is not unkind, but it has a flat and final quality that clearly does not leave room for any sort of dispute.

I nod, then go to the bed, bend over my wife and kiss her on the mouth. Tears have leaked down onto her lips, and their saltiness rubs against my tongue. I smile at her and say: "Be nice to the doctor and do what he says. I . . . I love you . . ."

Choking and blinking, Anne says: "Yes, I'll be . . . good. And I . . . I love you too." The sweat on her face has formed syrupy globs and rivulets. She reaches up and pats my cheek.

I rush out of the bedroom. I do not look back. I nearly bump into Emerald White in the hallway. She has changed into her nurse's uniform. She brushes past me, and she carries with her an odor of warm soap, and Anne again is screaming.

I go shambling downstairs to the kitchen and fix myself a pot of coffee. The kitchen is directly below the bedroom, and Anne's screams are quite distinct. I also hear footsteps marching to the bathroom and back. They are brisk, and they click, and I suppose they belong to Emerald White. I wonder if the time ever will come when Anne and I will have the courage to invite Dr. Button and Emerald White for supper. I have my doubts. This is a sad thing to be admitting, but it is nonetheless true.

The coffee is scalding hot. I fill a cup, blow on the coffee, seat myself at the kitchen table. It is Saturday, and I am able to hear automobiles, slamming doors, the shouts of children. Our cat, Pru-nella by name, comes up from the cellar and jumps on the table. Her tail brushes against my face, and so I go to the icebox and fill a bowl with shreds of leftover bacon. Prunella skitters across the floor and begins busily eating her breakfast. Her jaws are energetic, and the bacon crackles. When she is finished with it I let her out the back door. I listen to Anne's screams. I stand there at the back door, and my head hurts from the sound of them. I say to myself: Labor. I say to myself: Pain. I say to myself: Labor pains. I say to myself: Labor pains us all. I walk into the pantry and take a stub of pencil and a scratch pad from one of the drawers. I return to the kitchen table and write, in large capitals, the word LABOR. I have decided to find out how many other words I can make from it. I write:

OR . . . LAB (?) . . . ROB . . . BOAR . . . ORB . . . OAR . . . BAR . . . BRA (?) . . . LOB . . . I ponder the inclusion of LAB and BRA. They are little more than abbreviations, and perhaps they should be excluded. But, on the other hand, they *have* fallen into common usage, and so I decide to retain them. Then I write the word PAIN, and I come up with:

AN . . . NIP . . . PIN . . . PAN . . . NAP . . . IN . . . I study the list. I say to myself: BRA PAN. I shake my head, wad up the paper, sip at my coffee. It has cooled quite a bit. I say to myself: BRA NIP. I clear my throat, rub my eyes. My mother was buried yesterday, and now Anne is screaming, and I say to myself: Only an imbecile would play a stupid game at a time like this. I rub my cheeks and my chin. I scratch my chest and I sip at my lukewarm coffee.

The telephone rings. I hurry into the front room and snatch up the receiver. It is a Mrs. Zook from across the street. She has heard the screams, and she has seen the arrival of Dr. Button and Emerald White. She asks if there is anything she can do. I tell her no thank you, I think everything is perking along as well as can be expected. Mrs. Zook says something to the effect that she surely is terribly sorry about my mother. I tell Mrs. Zook I truly appreciated her attendance at the funeral yesterday. And Mrs. Zook tells me she is ready to be of assistance any time she is asked. I thank Mrs. Zook, but I assure her everything is just fine, fine yes, fine and dandy. After hanging up, I return to the kitchen, unwad the paper, press it flat and write the word NOSY, deriving from it the following:

YON . . . SON . . . ON . . . OS . . . SO . . . NO . . . SOY . . . Upstairs, Anne's screams rise and fall, subsiding for perhaps five minutes at a time, then resuming in a sort of shrill rhythm, and the sound of them has just about made me do some screaming of my own. I wipe my forehead with a sleeve of my bathrobe. I stare at all the inane words I have written, and I cannot see them too clearly. I glance around the kitchen, and it is neat, washed with sunshine, and there is a place for everything, and everything is in its place, and a warmth rises from my throat and floods into my eyes, and so I lay my head against the tabletop, and I close my eyes, and the screams penetrate the darkness, and quietly I weep, and there is no refuge for me, not even in darkness.

Then I hear a commotion at the front door. I open my eyes. I blink, and the tabletop is cool against my cheek, and why do I have to be bothered with more commotion? Hasn't there been enough commotion already? I sigh. I stand up. I hurry to the front door, and there stand my brother Alvin Jr. and his wife, the former Mary Frances O'Shea, a plump blond woman with a substantial overbite. "Mrs. Zook telephoned," says Alvin Jr., frowning.

I blink at him.

Alvin Jr. glances up the stairs. "The baby is on its way, right?"

I nod. Anne screams. I nod again. "Yes," I say. "It is my understanding that what we're presently hearing is the sound of labor pains."

"You don't have to be smart," says Alvin Jr.

"I'm sorry," I tell him. "I didn't mean to be."

"Mrs. Zook said you sounded peculiar."

"Well, I *feel* peculiar."

Alvin Jr. comes to me and claps me gently on a shoulder. "We all do," he says, "but life goes on—right, little brother? A death one day and a birth the next."

I nod. I do not know what to say. I turn away from my brother and look up the stairs and move one of my hands in time with the rhythm of my wife's screams.

"Now . . . now . . ." says Mary Frances.

I turn back to my brother and his wife. "There's coffee in the kitchen," I say. "Come on. I'll warm it up."

Alvin Jr. hesitates for a moment. He is pale, and his hands pluck at his coat, and he swallows before speaking. "That'd hit the spot just fine," he says.

Alvin Jr. and Mary Frances follow me into the kitchen. I warm up the coffee. Mary Frances fetches cream from the icebox for herself and her husband. We seat ourselves at the table, and I pour the coffee. Alvin Jr. and Mary Frances already have three children of their own, and she smiles and says: "The first one is the worst. After this, it will be like falling off the proverbial log." (She is wearing a bright yellow dress, and her teeth are glistening.)

"Well," I tell her, "I certainly am glad to hear that." (The dress is too tight, and her breasts are distended, and the color of the dress hurts my eyes.)

"Is Button up there with his colored woman?" Alvin Jr. asks me.

"That is correct."

"The consensus of opinion is that he's a good doctor. I'll give him credit for *that.*"

"How's that?"

"Never mind. I was just talking about Button."

"No. I was referring to the redundancy. You said 'consensus of opinion.' "

"You giving grammar lessons?" Alvin Jr. asks me. He leans forward, and one of his elbows bumps the edge of the table. "You being smart again?"

I shrug. I say nothing.

"A person would think you'd have enough on your mind without being so goddamned smart."

"I'm sorry," I say.

Alvin Jr. says nothing. Noisily he sucks on his coffee. He is florid and thirtyfour, but he still is trimly built. He is in the real estate business, and last year he branched out a bit—founding a cartage company that hauls coal from the smaller Paradise County mines up to the power plants in and around Columbus. The Chesapeake & Ohio, which took over the old Columbus, Paradise Valley & Marietta in 1914, is reportedly fit to be tied because of this development, and Alvin Jr. figures that in a year or two he'll get a good price from the C&O. He admits that his cartage company is a sort of blackmail, but what the hell; that's *business,* and anyway, it isn't as though he made the rules.

I try to smile at my brother, but he does not appear to notice. He is wearing the same black suit he wore at the funeral yesterday, and he keeps plucking at his coat.

Upstairs, the screams persist. I turn my smile (it is now fullfledged, with numerous teeth visible) to Mary Frances. "Sometimes I can behave like a lunatic," I tell her.

Mary Frances closes her lips, hiding the overbite. "All right," she says, "but you shouldn't make fun of Alvin."

"There's no reason for you to butt in," says Alvin Jr. to Mary Frances.

"But I *want* to butt in," says Mary Frances. "You're my *husband.*"

Alvin Jr. grunts, blows on his coffee.

Mary Frances shakes her head.

I am about to say something when I hear a renewed commotion at the front door. This time it is my brother Ernest, accompanied by his wife, the former Bernadette Walter. It turns out that Alvin Jr. has earlier telephoned Ernest, and perhaps, the next thing you know, someone will invite the mayor and all the members of the city council. Ernest shakes my hand and asks me how I am holding up. I tell him I am holding up like a veritable Jesse James, and he frowns, but Bernadette smiles widely. She is a tall angular girl with luxuriant dark hair, and I have always been quite fond of her. She married Ernest six years ago when she was seventeen, and they already have four children. (The first baby, in fact, kept him from being drafted.) At twentyseven, Ernest is only a year older than I, but he is considerably better fixed. He is a hairy and energetic fellow with a true and honest gift for understanding the workings of any sort of machinery one would care to name, and he owns and operates what is perhaps the most successful fillingstation in the county. Four years ago he borrowed two thousand dollars from the Paradise Falls State Bank and built the fillingstation near a little lowland village called Egypt, which is northwest of Paradise Falls on the Lancaster road, about eight miles up the valley. It is the only fillingstation in the entire stretch of eighteen miles from Paradise Falls to Lancaster, and it has prospered from the beginning, and Ernest paid off the bank loan in just nineteen months. He is heavier than either Alvin Jr. or I, and he drinks perhaps more than he should, but he surely does know crankshafts and sparkplugs, and this means that his place prospers for more reasons than its location. Here in 1923, there are not that many people who truly understand automobiles. Or, if there are, they do not live in Paradise County.

Everyone reassembles in the kitchen, and we all try to ignore the noises that still are coming from upstairs. Mary Frances asks me if I have had anything to eat. I tell her no, I have not. She smiles, whips out a skillet and sets to work fixing me bacon and eggs. Bernadette sets the table and rinses out the coffee cups.

Alvin Jr. speaks to me of our father, who has spent the night at Alvin Jr.'s place on Grainger Street. "I think it did him a world of good," says Alvin Jr., "and I liked the way he looked when he got up this morning. He had real good color in his face. Real good."

"That's fine," I say.

"And anyway," says Alvin Jr., "it wouldn't of been right to of left him all alone in that big place, with the smell of the flowers still in the air. Maybe we should of laid her out at the undertaker's place. Now it's going to take two or three days to air out the house, and you take *that,* plus all the memories of her that just *got* to be in every nook and cranny, and I tell you I'm real glad we took him in. And right now he's playing with the kids, and he seems happy as a clam, and honest to God, you ought to *see* his color."

"That's good news," I say.

"He's a good old boy," says Ernest. He is wearing coveralls, and there is a smudge of oil or grease on the back of his left hand.

I cock my head toward the ceiling and listen to the noise.

The table set, Bernadette seats herself across from me. She has a flat chest and pierced ears, and her mouth is quite large. "We know this is an ordeal," she says.

I nod. I say nothing, but I do manage to nod.

Alvin Jr. and Ernest are lounging against the counter, and Mary Frances is fussing at the stove. Grease pops, and warm odors nudge at me. Bernadette reaches across the table, and there is a piece of paper in her hand. "This was on the table," she says quietly.

I take the piece of paper from her, and it contains of course the list of words I derived from LABOR and PAIN and NOSY. I thrust the piece of paper in a pocket of my bathrobe.

"What's *that* all about?" Alvin Jr. wants to know.

"This wife of mine passing you love notes?" Ernest asks me.

Bernadette glares at her husband. "It's none of your business," she says.

"By God, she *is* passing him love notes," says Alvin Jr. to Ernest.

"I think maybe I got to see it," says Ernest, and he starts to move toward me.

My hand is still in the pocket. I close it around the piece of paper. "It . . . it has nothing to do with you," I tell Ernest.

Ernest grins. "Then why are you so nervous?" he asks me.

Bernadette stands up. *"Ernest,"* she says, "now you *stop* it. If I were passing him a love note, do you think I'd just *hand it to him at the kitchen table* with you standing right there? How stupid do you think I *am?"*

"I think this is all in very bad taste," says Mary Frances from the stove. Her lips have pulled back from her teeth, and my eyes are beginning to smart.

"Shut your trap," Alvin Jr. tells her.

Bernadette sighs and spreads her arms. "This is turning out to be a lovely family occasion, isn't it?"

Mary Frances faces away from the rest of us. She stirs the eggs.

Ernest advances until he is standing over me. "All right," he says, "give it to me."

"No," I tell him, "I don't believe I want to do that."

"I don't give a damn what you *want*. I'm *telling* you—give it to me."

"Howard, you'd better do like he says," Alvin Jr. tells me.

"Oh my *God* in *Heaven*," says Bernadette. "The Amberson family at its finest hour."

Ernest pays no attention to Bernadette's words. "I'm bigger than you," he says to me. "Whatever it is, I want it right now, and no sass."

"You're going to be awfully surprised."

"I got a real good heart," says Ernest, "and I expect I'll be able to stand it." He seizes my wrist and jerks the hand from the pocket. He pulls me off my chair, and I fall to my knees. Holding my wrist in one hand, he pries at my fingers with the other. "Come *on* now . . ." he says, grunting.

Upstairs, Anne delivers herself of an enormous scream.

Ernest hesitates. I jerk my hand free, then scrabble backwards on all fours, like an animal retreating from an adversary that is too formidable for it. I stand up and lean against the table, and I am gasping. "When Mama was alive," I say, "this sort of thing never was permitted to happen, isn't that right? Serenity was our watchword, wasn't it? Serenity forever." I stare at Ernest. Then I open my hand and carefully place the piece of paper on the table. I press down on the piece of paper, smoothing it. My eyes concentrate on a point just above Ernest's lips, and I say: "It is a list. A stupid list. A list of words that can be derived from other words. I drew it up this morning after the doctor arrived. You see, he banished me to the downstairs, and I didn't know how to pass the time. In case you've forgotten, my wife is having a baby, and it's apparently more than she bargained for. And there's nothing I can do about it. So I sat here and drew up the list, and Bernadette found it while she was setting the table. It was something to do, you know? But *you* had to go and breathe something dark and dirty into it, didn't you?" Here I hesitate, but Ernest says nothing. I have him now, and we both know it, and I continue: "Are you such a lunatic that you believe that Bernadette and I are lusting after one another? What *are* you? For all I know, my wife is dying, and so what do *you* do? You knock me down, and that proves a great deal, doesn't it? You've married a damned good woman, and you ought to have more respect for her, and you ought to have more respect for yourself, and you ought to have more respect for *me*. All right. You want to see what's on the piece of paper. Go ahead. Take a look. The only reason I wanted it kept hidden was that . . . well,

I didn't think you'd understand. But right now I don't care *what* you understand. I've had about all of—"

"All right, Howard," says Bernadette. She comes around the table and takes me by an arm. "All *right* now. All *right.*"

Ernest backs away a step. His face is crimson. Alvin Jr. leans against the counter and watches me. Mary Frances is facing me again, and the bacon and eggs are bubbling.

I shudder a little, and Bernadette pats my arm.

Ernest tries to smile, and it as though the corners of his mouth are being tugged at with threads. "I . . . well, Jesus Christ . . . I guess I was . . . well, you know, I guess I was wrong . . ."

"I guess you were," I tell him.

"My God," says Alvin Jr., "my little brother is a tiger."

I do not reply. I seat myself at the table. Bernadette stands over me for a moment, then returns to her place. Ernest walks to the cupboard, takes out a glass, fills it with water from the tap. He drinks. Then, staring out the back window, he says to no one in particular: "Sometimes I . . . well, the thing is, sometimes I get out of line." He turns and looks directly at me. "I'm really sorry. Honest to God."

I nod. "Forget it," I say to him.

"I don't know what the hell—"

"I said *forget it.*"

"All . . . ah, all right," says Ernest.

I wad up the piece of paper and drop it on the floor. Upstairs, Anne screams.

Alvin Jr. shakes his head. "My goodness," he says.

I breathe deeply, and no one speaks. I close my eyes and ponder my angry selfrighteousness, and I tell myself I should be ashamed. But I cannot *feel* ashamed. Instead I feel exhilarated. I am a tiger, and I want to growl. I open my eyes, and Mary Frances is filling a plate with bacon and eggs, and the eggs are scrambled, and they appear pasty, and I despise pasty scrambled eggs. Anne never makes them pasty. But Mary Frances is no Anne—and, say, perhaps it is time I told her that. Perhaps it is time to tell this prissy bucktoothed cow of a Mary Frances precisely what I think of her. As long as I am being such a beast of the jungle, I might as well rip some more flesh. And so I grimace at Mary Frances as she approaches with the plate. But, before I can speak, she says: "Howard, I hope this is all right. I am very sorry if we've upset you. I—well, you know . . ."

She places the plate before me. Her eyes are wet. I open my mouth, and I know that the tiger has decamped for parts unknown, and I say: "Thank you, Mary Frances. Thank you very much." And I eat every bit of the bacon, and I eat every last heavy glob of the pasty eggs. And gradually the tension subsides, even though Anne's terrible sounds still come from the bedroom. My brothers and their wives begin exchanging small talk—hesitantly at first, for fear the tiger will object, but then more and more confidently, as it becomes apparent that I have managed to, ah, pull myself together, as the saying goes. I am once again the quiet and fastidious Howard Amberson they all recognize, and so the small talk accelerates, and within ten minutes they are all behaving as though nothing has happened. (And, in a sense, nothing has. One incident cannot change a man, or at least not to any significant extent. A special stress had caused me to behave tigerishly, but I am not at heart a tiger at all, and I never will be. I am what I appear to be, and that is the truth, and it has nothing to do with growls or ripped flesh.) And the small talk centers itself on Dr. Button and Emerald White (as when *doesn't* it, whenever two or three are gathered in Paradise Falls?), and Mary Frances says: "One thing you have to admit about that colored woman, she surely does have an *ex*quisite figure."

"I wouldn't know," says Alvin Jr., grinning. "I've never noticed."

"Yes," says Mary Frances. "And the sun has never set in the west."

"Myself," says Ernest, "I like them lean and hungry."

"Thank you," says Bernadette. She speaks coldly, and several of her fingers briskly tap the surface of the table.

"A little old geezer like that Button," says Alvin Jr., "and look what he's got . . . all that delicious dark meat and him without a hair on his head. Great day in the morning."

"You are filthy," says Mary Frances.

"Absolutely," says Alvin Jr., "and you ought to know."

Ernest laughs at this, but the women do not join him, and so the subject is changed. It settles briefly on politics, then moves to the facilities provided by the Zimmerman Funeral Home and the presence (or lack of presence) of certain Paradise Falls residents at yesterday's last rites for Margaret Rossiter Amberson (1860–1923). Bernadette tells me I should try to pay no attention to Anne's cries. Bernadette smiles, and she does not have particularly good teeth, but I have always liked her, and I am willing for it to be enough that she means well. My brothers and their wives stay with me all day. Alvin Jr. ventures upstairs from time to time and returns with progress reports. "It's not an easy one," he tells us, "but Button says there's not a thing to worry about. And I believe him. I mean, there's just some women have a harder time than others." (I myself venture upstairs on three separate occasions, and each time I am met at the bedroom door by Emerald White, whose uniform has become smeared and damp. She tells me everything will be just fine, but she does not smile, and why won't she do that much for me? I peer past her each time, and each time I see Dr. Button bent over the bed with his hands pressed against Anne's knees. And, on each of those three occasions, I visit the bathroom and sit on the throne and struggle with an urge to vomit. I win the struggle each time, but just barely, and my belly muscles become knotted and sore.) The kitchen babble persists all day. Alvin Jr. and Ernest discuss baseball, and Bernadette fixes a platter of ham sandwiches, and Alvin Jr. allows as how he is really enjoying the C&O's resentment of what he calls his little itsybitsy cartage company, and Ernest says he doesn't expect the spring floods to amount to much this year, and Mary Frances seats herself next to me, leans forward and says: "Now Howard, some women go into labor for a full *day* or so before anything happens. It isn't unusual at *all.* I know that sounds *terrible,* but it *is* a *fact.*" I nod. I tell Mary Frances I appreciate her concern. I step out onto the back porch and breathe deeply. Prunella comes out from under the house, skitters up the steps and rubs against my legs. I seat myself on the stoop, then pick up Prunella and hug her. I scratch her under the chin. She yawns, purrs, folds her forepaws over my wrist. I stroke her and I scratch her, and then I place my mouth close to one of her ears, and I ask her a confidential question. "Tell me, Prunella," I whisper, "what did I deposit inside your mistress? Rocks and knives and blocks of cement?"

It is nearly 7:30 in the evening when the baby finally comes. It squalls and gurgles, and we in the kitchen hear it quite clearly. I am the first one up the stairs, and I negotiate them two at a time, and for no reason whatever I beat my arms across my chest—like someone who has just come in from a blizzard. I bolt into the bedroom, and Emerald White is standing at the foot of the bed, and she is grinning. She is wiping the baby with an enormous towel. It is a boy, a very large boy. It hollers and sucks, and its eyes are tightly shut. My brothers and their wives cluster behind me in the doorway, and Alvin Jr. says: "My God, that's what I call a *big* baby."

"He'll be a football player for sure," says Emerald White, blinking.

Anne is pale and motionless in the bed. Her eyes are open, however, and she is smiling. "Look," she says, "we've come through."

Emerald White takes the baby to Anne, and I follow along.

Dr. Button is slumped in a chair next to the bed. He glances up at me and says: "I'll sleep well tonight."

"So will I," I tell him.

"So will all of us," says Alvin Jr. from the doorway.

Anne cradles the baby so that its head rests against her upper arm. She strokes its forehead and its cheeks. "Baby . . ." she says. "Oh, dear little . . . baby . . ."

I bend down and kiss the baby on the forehead. Then I kiss my wife on the mouth. My eyes are awash, and my cheeks are dripping, and I cannot speak. I straighten and rub my eyes.

"Awww . . ." says MaryFrances from the doorway.

"He will be a great big fellow," says Emerald White to Anne.

Now the baby is quiet. Anne kisses the top of its head and says: "And he'll be a remarkable man." She speaks calmly. Her voice is hollow, and her throat sounds dry, but she is possessed of a fragile exhausted serenity that no doubt would have made my mother very proud of her. "Howard?" she says.

"Yes?"

"He came sideways," she says. "Sideways—or something like that. You can check with Dr. Button. Sideways or insideout or *something* like that."

I glance at Dr. Button, who nods.

"We've come through," says Anne.

"Yes. And I am very proud of you."

"I want you to be proud of both of us."

"I am proud of both of you."

"I hurt everywhere," says Anne, closing her eyes.

"Yes. I expect you do."

She opens her eyes, glances down at the baby. "He will be very remarkable. He is my best beau. Do you understand that?"

"Yes."

"I mean it."

"I know you do," I tell her.

"I am very happy. Nobody could be happier."

"So am I."

"And so are we," says Alvin Jr. from the doorway. And he and the others happily advance on the bed. And everyone chatters and laughs, even Anne and even Dr. Button. Emerald White fetches the bathroom scales and weighs the baby. The dial registers ten pounds, three ounces. We all gasp and shake our heads, and Alvin Jr. grins at me and calls me Kid Dynamite. The baby is named Henry, after Anne's late father, the victim of the interurban accident.

Anne worked at the weeds for a minute or so, then straightened and said: "You'd think they'd do a better job keeping up the grounds."

"I know," said Amberson.

"Well, you're a stockholder. You ought to do something about it yourself."

"I suppose I should."

"But you're too sedate, aren't you? You're too old to start a fuss over weeds in the cemetery, aren't you?"

"Well, there aren't that many weeds. Not really."

"There are *enough*," said Anne. "He was *your* son, too."

"It's just that the mowers can't get at the weeds that are that close to a headstone."

"Well then, why don't they trim *those* weeds by hand?"

"I don't—"

"Good old elbow grease," said Anne. "Good old hard work. All that's required is a little effort. What's happened to effort? Why don't people take pride any more in what they do?"

"Perhaps because they don't like what they do."

"Then they should find something they *do* like to do."

"It's not all that simple," said Amberson. "Everything is so plasticized, and things wear out so quickly, and it seems to me that human beings want more *substantial* things."

"Which means?"

"Which means that so much work nowadays is so empty. Nothing is *created* from it. Nothing real, I mean. Nothing a person can regard with pride."

"And that includes the cutting of weeds in a cemetery?"

"Perhaps."

"But it seems to me that the cutting of weeds is real enough," said Anne. "Especially in a cemetery. After all, when you cut weeds in a cemetery, you are cleaning house for the dead, and the dead are people, too. And anytime you do something for people, you are doing something constructive."

Amberson sighed. "Well," he said, "that's an interesting point."

"When you clean house for the dead, I say it is a creative act."

"All right, if you say so."

"And it is a loving act."

"Fine," said Amberson. "Good enough."

"You think I'm out of my mind, don't you?"

"Sometimes," said Amberson, shrugging.

"I am not out of my mind," said Anne. She began to cry.

Amberson, who was standing only a foot or so from his wife, went

to her and embraced her. "You are not out of your mind," he said. "No
. . . no . . . now . . . there's no reason to believe such a thing . . . shhh
. . . shhh . . . I love you . . . you are a good old girl . . ." He patted
her shoulderblades, and he kissed her cheek, and it was softly fragrant,
and its wrinkles were not unpleasant against his mouth, and then he
said: "You are the sanest person I have ever met . . ." He patted her,
and she trembled, and he said: "I miss him, too. I miss them all. But
please . . . ah, please now . . . you're, ah, you're tearing me apart, do
you know that?"

Anne snuffled. She shook her head and blinked. She pulled free of
the embrace, then rummaged in her purse for a handkerchief. She
wiped her eyes, blew her nose. She reached up and straightened her hat,
and then she said: "I . . . well, I shouldn't carry on like that. I'm
. . . sorry . . ."

Amberson said nothing. The clouds were darker to the west, and
there was a sound of thunder faroff. The wind was colder, and Amberson shivered. He did not like the wind, nor did he like the distant
thunder. It was too late in the year for that sort of thunder, and the
wind was too cold. It was summer thunder, and therefore an anachronism, and he did not like to think of anachronisms.

See now 1968 (hopefully, the paradox is becoming more acceptable), and my nephew Peter—Ernest's youngest boy, the one who
briefly studied for the priesthood and then became a social worker
in Richmond, Virginia—is visiting Paradise Falls with his wife, Carmela, and four children. Peter's children are named Timothy, Guido
(after Carmela's father), Linda and Kathy, and their ages range from
eleven down to five, and they have been whooping and flapping
through the house and out on the streets for the past three days now,
and I cannot recall when I have seen Anne appear happier. She fixes
them enormous meals, and she has taken them to the municipal pool,
and she has bought them numerous cones and sundaes at the Dip-O-
Freez, and she has shown more energy than I have seen from her in
years.

Peter and his family are on their way home from Chicago, where
he participated in the antiwar demonstrations. Peter is thirtyfive and
he insists he is no hippie, even though his hair is long and he does
not dress particularly well. He and I have gone for a walk, and now
we are sitting at the edge of the river near the mossy and powdered
ruins of a grist mill.

Peter grimaces in the direction of the nearby falls. He is wearing combat boots, and as he digs his heels into the earth, chunks of earth roll down the bank. He has chosen this moment to speak of Chicago. We have talked about everything else, but not Chicago.

"Have you wondered why?" he asks me.

"Yes."

"Well," says Peter, "it's because I don't really know what to make of it. I mean, I'm sure you watched television and saw for yourself. I feel like such an anachronism."

"Anachronism? How so?"

Peter rubs his mouth. "Because of the way I've always felt about things. I mean about basic goodness."

"And now?" I ask my nephew.

Peter swivels his heels into the dirt. "I think fear is larger than goodness," he says. "I think fear is larger than anything."

I ask him to try to explain what he means.

Peter shrugs. He is silent for a moment, then: "The Chicago thing was the ultimate triumph of fear, and I can't understand it. Why is everybody so afraid? I think I can understand the nature of fear, and I certainly know I've *experienced* it, but what sort of fear is it when *you* have clubs and guns and tear gas and the people who frighten you have no weapons whatever? Uncle Howard, you know me. I'm no radical. I'm only a liberal, with the prescribed soft center, the whole bit. Most of the people who came to Chicago were just kids, and all they sought to do was protest the war and carry some signs. I am thirtyfive, and believe me, next to *them* I felt like the old man of the mountain. But it was like we were a *terrible menace,* you know? And when the cops came at us, they . . . you really want to hear about it?"

I nod. "Yes," I say. "If you want to tell me, I want to hear."

"All right," says Peter. "All right. Good enough. *Now,* the cops. The day they came at us, I'd had enough presence of mind to leave Carmela and the kids at her brother's place. I've told you about him, haven't I? His name is Paul, and if I am a cliché liberal, then Paul DiSanto is the greatest *lumpen bourgeoisie* reactionary in the western world. Well, anyway, those cops were his kind of people. He lives on the north side, and he is some sort of salesman for a hardware wholesale firm, and he belongs to some outfit called the Fraternal Order of Police Associates, and he likes to say that Martin Luther King was a fag communist, just to get under my skin, you know? And the only reason he put us up was that he didn't want *his* sister and *his* nieces and nephews sleeping in the park with a bunch of spacedout pot freaks and hippie punks. He couldn't have cared less about *me,* and he told me so."

I say nothing. I want to smile, but I am not altogether sure it would be appropriate.

Peter resumes. "Anyway, that day in the park. I went there alone, and I arrived just as the thing began. They came at us, those cops. They came at us and they came at us, and it didn't matter who you were. You could have been a CPA out walking the dog, or you could have been a registered Republican and a financial contributor to the John Birch Society, and it wouldn't have mattered one lousy bit. If you'd been in the way of those cops and their clubs, it would have been your sweet ass. You see, it wasn't only *kids* who were worked over. No indeed. It was anybody who happened to be passing by." Peter shakes his head. He seizes a handful of earth and flings it down into the river. Then: "But you know the really horrible thing? I mean, why I am so upset, *really* why? Because that's where the anachronism thing comes in. I'll admit it—my entire life has been predicated on the belief that man has a nub of basic goodness. It goes back to the religious thing, when I was in the seminary. My favorite saints were the gentle ones, and I didn't care for the warriors at all. I carried a banner in those days, and the banner said LOVE. And even later, after I found out the seminary bit wasn't for me and I quit the place and went off and married Carmela, I still carried the ridiculous goddamned thing. The Jews had been gassed at Auschwitz, and somebody kept shooting at people from the Texas Tower, and every day there was some new refinement of horror, but good old Peter Amberson clung steadfastly to his banner, tra-la, and he firmly believed that any day now the basic goodness would burst out, all smiling and gay, tra-la, like buttercups in the meadows of Paradise, or whatever." Here Peter gives a short laugh. He beats his palms together. "The liberal intellectual unmasked," he says. "Now I ask you—doesn't that make me an anachronism? Because, you see, I *still* want to believe all that shit. But I can't. Either I believe what I see or I don't. And what I have seen has made me impotent. It has told me that fear is larger than anything, certainly larger than truth and obviously larger than goodness. You see, my banner has been shot out of my hands. I go through the motions, but to what purpose? I—"

At this point, I am able to take no more of my nephew's words. I interrupt, saying: "Peter, for heaven's sake, that's no way to talk. There's still a great deal of kindness in the world. And love, too, for that matter."

"Yes. They exist, but they don't govern."

"What?"

"Uncle Howard, kindness and love have to be more than *facts*. They have to be *governing principles*. And they *aren't* governing principles. And I have always believed they were, which is why I am such an anachronism. Or, at any rate, was."

"Was?"

"Yes. Was. Because I'm not an anachronism *now*. Or at least I won't be, once I accept it and don't have to talk about it."

"And then what will you be?"

"What I am right now," says Peter. "A walking testimonial to impotence. All I have to do is accept it."

I look at him.

My nephew glares at me. He has red hair and freckles, and his eyes are blue, and he says: "I mean that." The sunlight is too intense, and it ravages his face.

The Ambersons moved quietly among the graves and headstones there in that cluster of rigid tulip trees, and the leaves were golden, and the cold anachronistic thunder persisted to the west. Amberson and his wife did not walk together; they simply roamed, and Anne bent down now and then to pluck at more weeds and pick up scraps of paper. She stuffed the scraps of paper in a pocket of her coat. She was cleaning house for the dead, and Amberson supposed it was giving her pleasure, and so he said nothing to her. He walked slowly, and he paused often, and he thrust his hands into his pockets and cautiously made his way from grave to headstone to grave to headstone to grave, from

HENRY S. AMBERSON
1st Lt, US Infantry
May 12, 1923–April 5, 1945

up a slight incline to

AMBERSON

LEWIS C.   ALICE I.
1925–1967   1928–

and then, to the right and near one of the trees, an immense and imposing obelisk proclaiming

AMBERSON

Alvin A. Jr.

1889–1959

Mary F.

1892–1941

Laura H.

1913–1932

and Amberson said to himself: Dear Laura. When was the last time anyone has thought of her? And he moved beyond the trees to a small pair of headstones that announced

ERNEST B. AMBERSON

1896–1934

and

BERNADETTE W. AMBERSON

1900–1955

and he stared at Bernadette's headstone for perhaps a full minute or two, and he thought of the flour that had been on her hands that day in 1938 when she had stayed home from her job in order to bake a birthday cake for her precious little Peter, the last of her seven children and the most precious, oh yes, precious indeed, she told Amberson while reaching toward him and taking both his hands in both of hers and powdering them with the flour. And Amberson blinked, then moved away from Bernadette's grave and down the incline to his parents' modest

AMBERSON

Alvin A. Sr.   Margaret R.

1855–1927   1860–1923

but he did not think of his parents. He still was thinking of Bernadette, and her little house in the village of Egypt, that little house with its rusted sheetmetal roof and the begonias growing in the flower boxes. And the solemnity with which he and Bernadette had washed their hands at the kitchen sink, sponging away the flour in the cool clean water that came from the well his brother had dug. And now Amberson grunted. And pulled his hands from his pockets and rubbed his knuckles. And heard Bernadette say: Kindness, for God's sake. And then shuddered. And looked around for Anne. She was standing off by one of the trees. He went to her, and an enormous urgency was tearing at him, and he said: "Well old girl, shall we be off?"

"Who are you supposed to be? Ronald Colman?"

"Yes ma'am. That's right ma'am."

"Now you sound like Gary Cooper."

"Well, I never was very good at impersonations."

"I'm glad to hear that," said Anne, smiling.

Amberson took her by an arm. They returned to the car. Anne glanced back over her shoulder several times. After they both were back inside the car, Amberson started the engine and said: "It was a good idea, coming here. I thank you for having it."

"Are you sure you mean that?" she asked him.

"Yes," said Amberson.

"Are all your memories good?"

"Many of them. Most of them."

"So are mine. Most of them."

"Good enough," said Amberson. "Now, my ladyship, isn't it about time we embarked on our great adventure?"

"Yes, James," said Anne. "Drive on."

"Hip hip," said Amberson. The car coasted down an incline, around several curves, then out of the cemetery and out of Paradise Falls. Ohio 93 stretched ahead; north by northeast, twisted and splendid. Amberson kept the accelerator at 40.

See now, again, 1968. It is evening of the day Peter and I discussed Chicago. He and I have driven to the Broasted Chicken place to pick up a carryout order for supper. We sit in his station wagon and wait for the girl to bring us the stuff, and Peter says: "You know, that girl really gave me a peculiar look."

"Oh?"

"Yes," says Peter, "and I don't think it was because she wants my body."

"Do you have an alternate theory?"

"Yes. I think it was because of my hair. In Paradise Falls, people don't wear hair like mine. Especially people my age. She's probably in there right now telling the fry cook I look like an old Veronica Lake."

"She is too young to remember Veronica Lake."

"All right then, how about an old Goldie Hawn?"

"Very good. Much better."

Peter grins. "Perhaps I am undergoing a sexual identity crisis," he says.

"I doubt that very much," I tell him.

"Well, look at me," says Peter, still grinning. He shakes his head, and his hair moves in waves. It comes down nearly to his shoulders, and he constantly is shaking his head to keep his forelocks from covering his eyes. He probably does this five hundred times a day, and it is a wonder to me that he has not strained his neck. But so far there seems to be no damage, and now he is even laughing a little. "Remember what I was talking about this afternoon?" he asks me. "What I said about impotence?"

"I'm afraid I do."

"Well, if you carry the thing a step farther, you can even find an explanation for my hair."

"I don't think I follow you," I say.

"Uncle Howard, the hair is a disguise. It hides my impotence. Now since it is impossible for a woman to be impotent—only a man can be impotent—if I look womanish enough, then no one will make impossible demands on me."

I turn in my seat until I am facing my nephew squarely. "Would you like to know *my* theory about your hair?"

"I would be delighted to hear it," says Peter. He slaps me gently on a knee. "And I bet it'll be well thought out, too."

"Well," I tell him, "I wouldn't be too sure about *that,* but I'll give it a try."

He smiles. He brushes hair back from his eyes.

"Peter, all this talk of impotence is ridiculous," I say, measuring my words and speaking slowly. "What you *are* is—*angry.* Not discouraged. Not defeated. Certainly not impotent. Simply *angry.* And that banner with the strange device, the word LOVE. You say it has been destroyed. Well, I say that is nonsense. Your talk and your pain mean that you are angry, and anger means caring, and caring means being alive, and being alive has nothing to do with impotence. The banner is still there, and never mind about the snow and ice. Which means that *your* hair theory is, ah, all wet. Now, as to *my* hair theory, it is simply this: Peter Amberson is trying to secede from his generation. He sees it as being responsible for most of the ills of the world. That brotherinlaw of yours, that Paul Whatshisname in Chicago, the one with the hateful political opinions—*he* represents your generation to you, and you tell yourself: I must drop out; I must disassociate myself from those who say terrible things about Martin Luther King. So you adopt the hair style and mode of dress of a younger generation, a generation that considers you to be, as you say, the old man of the mountain, a generation that you consider to be blameless. It is comfortable for you. You enjoy it. So then *all right,* enjoy it. If it helps you get through your days, *fine.* I'm not quite so sure that your adoptive generation will remain as blameless as you think it is now, but that is something you will have to experience for yourself. All *I* ask is that you not sell yourself so short. I know you, Peter. I know what you *are*. And I know what you are *not*. And one of the things you are *not* is impotent."

Peter does not at first say anything. He leans forward, draping his arms on the steering wheel. The lot here at the Broasted Chicken place is crowded with automobiles, and children run and yip, and a smiling neon hen blinks from the roof of the place, and a balloon comes from her happy yellow mouth, and written inside the balloon are the words BR ASTED CHICK N OPEN DA & NITE, and I smell gasoline fumes and chicken grease, and for a moment I am reminded of Earl Portman, and then Peter turns to me and says: "My mother was right about you."

"I beg your pardon?"

"I've known about it for a long time."

"Known about what?" I ask him. There is no moisture in my mouth, and my hands squeeze my legs.

"She was very fond of you, and you were very fond of her."

"Yes. That is correct. Bernadette was a very, ah, fine lady."

"I mean more than that, Uncle Howard. It's all right. Don't worry about it. I approve."

"I don't know what you're talking about."

"She told me all about it. She was dying, and she said: 'Peter, your Uncle Howard is the finest man I've ever known. And the dearest and the gentlest.' "

"Well, I'm, ah, very flattered . . ."

"She was right, you know. So right. You *are* a dear and gentle man —and you see things very well. What you just said about me . . . the hair and all of it . . . you were absolutely on target. I, well, I see that . . . and, well, the rhetoric was pretty dreadful, wasn't it?"

"Yes."

"Well," says Peter, "wellnow, we . . . we are still friends, aren't we?" He rests his chin against the steering wheel for a moment, then leans back and smiles.

"Of course we are still friends," I tell him.

"She told me all about it. She told me and she told Father Westfall. You remember him, don't you?"

"Yes. He's . . . dead now."

"That's right," says Peter. "And oh, she didn't tell any of my brothers or sisters. She didn't even tell Jean, and they were pretty close, as you know."

"Am I supposed to be admitting something along about now?"

"No," says Peter. "The only reason I bring it up is because I want you to know I think you're a good man, Charlie Brown."

"Peter?"

"Yes?"

"You are the most contemporary person I know, and contemporary persons are said to speak their minds clearly and directly. Why don't you do that for me?"

"I *have* done that for you. I have told you I know about you and my mother, and I have told you I am pleased about it, and I have told you you're a good man. You are kind, and you have wisdom, and you have straightened out some of my thinking, and I hope you live forever."

"From your contemporary point of view, was what we did acceptable?"

"Absolutely," says Peter, speaking quickly. "When you stop to consider that my father was dead, and when you stop to consider *how* he died, and when you stop to consider that you, my Uncle Howard whom I shall always love, did what you did out of a feeling of kindness and mercy, then *of course* what you and Mother did was acceptable. Under the circumstances, it was *more* than acceptable. It was downright *necessary.*"

"I'd like to believe that."

"You can take my word on it," says Peter.

I cannot think of anything further to say, and apparently neither can Peter. I have admitted the thing, and he has absolved me, and why—after thirty years—can't I absolve myself? Was what I did really a kindness? Or was it something dark and foul and shameful? I close my eyes for a moment and think of my wife. This is intolerable, though, and I quickly open them, just in time to see the girl approaching with an enormous steaming carton of broasted chicken. The girl is dark and rather pretty, and she wears a badge that says IOLA. She passes the box through the window to Peter and tells him: "Here you are, sir. This should feed a regiment."

"Twenty pieces, right?" he asks her.

"Peter?" I say.

"Yes sir," says the girl, "twenty pieces, and nothing but breasts and legs, just like you ordered."

"Peter?" I say.

"There are eight of us," says Peter to the girl, "four adults and four children, and we're all of us very hungry."

"Peter, please?" I say. I am sitting bolt upright, and something has tied a chain around my chest.

"Well," says the girl, "this should hold you real good."

The bill comes to $4.25. Peter gives the girl five dollars and tells her to keep the change. The girl smiles, takes the money, then tells Peter he has real pretty hair, and that is a fact. She is wearing culottes and a tight white blouse, and she struts away from the car, and Peter tells me great God, the way some females can make their asses churn is enough to send sane men straight up the wall. I slump forward, and I bump my forehead against the dashboard, and the smell of the chicken is like a hot greasy washrag, and I am having the second of my heart attacks, and I say to myself: Is this any way to die? Awash in odors of broasted chicken?

The road was open and clear, and there were smears of red and gold in some of the far hills. Amberson glanced in the mirror and saw that Sinclair still was asleep on the rear shelf. Many of the Ambersons' friends, those who owned cats, called Sinclair a remarkable animal. As a general rule, cats were not fond of riding in automobiles, and Amberson had heard countless stories of cats that had vomited in automobiles, cats that had scratched and clawed in automobiles, cats that had urinated, mewled, gasped, howled and even hissed in automobiles. But Sinclair was, to coin a phrase, a special breed of cat. Whenever he rode in the Amberson car, all he did was purr and sleep. He was a good old cat, and the Ambersons loved him dearly. He enjoyed napping in the shade of the rhubarb plants that grew in the back yard. On a sunny day, when he sought warmth, he clambered to the roof of the back shed, but he seldom ventured off the Amberson property. And why should he have? Would the sunlight have been brighter elsewhere? The rhubarb plants friendlier? Sinclair was not stupid; he did not embark on risky adventures. If what the Egyptians said about cats was true, and if cats really were reincarnations of human beings, then Sinclair surely was a reincarnated Republican. His steps always were cautiously deliberate; he seemed to be forever testing the ground that lay before him; his sniffings were stately and fastidious; he always looked before he pounced, and then—more often than not—he did not pounce at all. Why pounce when one's dish in the kitchen always contained a generous ration of 9-Lives? When one lived in a warm house and had taken possession of an elderly couple, one acquired a certain complacency; one ate one's Super Supper with a sort of plumply arrogant serenity, and the urge to pounce was not as important as it might have been. He valued routine and sameness, and anyway, he needed to keep an eye on those old folks and, as they liked to tell their friends, remind them who was boss. Once twilight came, he never showed the least inclination to explore the outdoors. As a result of all this, Sinclair was what the Ambersons called a Day Cat; he did not roam at night. Instead, he slept toward the foot of the Ambersons' bed, pressing himself against their bodies so that his head rested against Anne's thigh and his rump against whatever portion of Amberson's anatomy happened to be handy. In the wintertime, Anne especially appreciated Sinclair. She said he was better than a hot water bottle, and he never turned to ice halfway through the night. If he went wandering off at night, perhaps he would be forced to return to the life he had led before taking over their household. And he was too old for that; his fat declining days were too delicious. And obviously his early days had not been a bit delicious. And he was not about to return to them. He had come to the Amberson home, tattered and bruised, four years ago, turning up on the back porch one morning about a week after the death of the Ambersons' younger son, Lewis. He was skinny and tufted, with patches of bare flesh showing at his haunches and around his eyes. He was a tom, and he growled at the Ambersons and would not permit them to come near him. They set a bowl of milk and a dish of raw liver on the back stoop, and he sneaked up and devoured it when no one was looking. But the milk and liver were too much for him, or too rich for him, and he vomited and collapsed. Amberson found him and took him to a veterinarian, Dr. George F. Westenheimer, a kindly and avuncular fat man who forever smelled of liniment and iodine and who told Amberson: My God, Howard, I think we'd better put this animal away. But Amberson was not so sure. He asked Dr. Westenheimer if there was a chance the cat could be saved. And Dr. Westenheimer said yes, if I really work at it I just might be able to bring this fellow back from the dead. But he looks like a ratty and mean old devil, and are you sure you want me to do it? If it's a cat you want, I can find you as many as you like. And Amberson said: The cat I want is *this* one. (There was some sort of point to be proved here, some sort of thought to be followed to some sort of reasonable conclusion.) Dr. Westenheimer shook his head and made a number of skeptical sounds, but he set to work patching up the Ambersons' mangy visitor. He estimated the cat's age to be about seven, and he recommended that it be castrated for its own good. This old boy, said Dr. Westenheimer, needs to be retired from combat. If he isn't, it'll be Katy-bar-the-door for sure. (And, with these words, Dr. Westenheimer pulled back the fur around the cat's eyes and showed a patchwork of scabs and welts. The cat howled and tried to bite Dr. Westenheimer's hand, and he frowned and gave it a vigorous shake, telling it there, there, you just settle down.) And so, under the conditions, Amberson agreed to the castration, albeit reluctantly. The cat was daubed, cleansed, combed, scraped, wormed, fed, watered and patched, and its testicles were removed, and two days later Amberson brought it home, carrying it in his arms all the way and whispering gentle comforting words into one of its torn ears. And the animal blinked at him and rewarded him with an uneven sequence of tentative purrings. The distance was seven blocks, and the cat's body warmed Amberson's chest, and its claws plucked contentedly at the sleeves of his coat. Yes, all right, said Amberson to the cat. Yes. Everything is fine. You have been brought back from the dead. Good old fellow. Milk and fish await. (As indeed they did, and the cat staggered to the bowl of milk and lapped at it with an exhausted frenzy, and Anne squatted next to it and scratched its back, bringing forth more purrings, and this time they were steady and not a bit tentative. And Amberson stood over his wife and the cat and said: For whatever it is worth, he has been brought back from the dead. And Anne looked up at Amberson and said: It is foolishness, and I know it is foolishness, but I don't think I care. And Amberson said: There are worse things than foolishness. And Anne said: Yes. Many.) And, from then on, Sinclair took possession of the household. As for his name, well, it evolved in something of a peculiar manner. At first the Ambersons simply called him Mister Cat, but Anne was not happy with such a passionless and impersonal name. Would you like it, she asked her husband, if people simply called you Mister Human Being? And Amberson said: No. I wouldn't. And Anne said: All right then, we must settle on something more appropriate and . . . *personal.* (She was holding Mister Cat on her lap, and he was nuzzling her wrists.) So the discussion began, and at first it centered on the animal's color, and such names as The Gray Ghost, Stormy, Robert E. Lee and Mister Pale were proposed—and quickly rejected. Then the Ambersons decided to concentrate on the animal's increasingly haughty personality, and they came up with Horatio, Percy, Jeeves, Bishop, Winston and even (from some shadowed memory of movies past) Arthur Treacher and Eric Blore. But these names provided little other than weak laughter, and so Amberson and his wife shifted the focus of the search to still another area . . . literature. Amberson immediately thought of Holy Scripture and proposed Lazarus, and the name at first met with much favor from Anne, and she allowed it was the best they had come up with so far. But then she snapped her fingers and said: *Sherwood!* We can call him Sherwood Amberson! And Amberson said: Hey, that's a fine idea. Sherwood Amberson, the literary cat for the hard of hearing. Do you think there would be any objections in Winesburg, Ohio? And Anne cupped her ear and said: I don't hear any. I always have liked Sherwood Anderson's work, and I bet he would be delighted. A man who wrote as well as *he* did just *had* to like cats. He had humanity in him, or compassion or whatever. And Amberson said: All right then, it's settled. The beast's name will be Sherwood . . . ah, just a minute. I think I . . . ah, I think I may have a better one. How does Sinclair strike your fancy? And Anne said: Sinclair? And Amberson, rubbing his hands together, said: Lewis is dead, but we have brought Sinclair back from the dead. We have lost a Lewis but gained a Sinclair. What do you think? And Anne said: Is that supposed to be a joke? And Amberson told her no, it was no joke at all. The cat's appearance on the back porch so shortly after the death of their son had a symbolism that was rather interesting. After all, a stray cat never had visited their home before in all the fortysix years they had lived there, and so why had *that* time been chosen? Could there be some sort of connection? What if the Egyptians were right? Couldn't the *possibility* at least be *acknowledged* by making the cat's name a sort of sign that yes, yes, there are mysteries that are beyond us? And Anne said: But *that* name would be a *reminder*. And Amberson said: Yes—but what do we propose to do? Forget? If Sinclair helps us remember Lewis, is his name a bad joke or is it a manifestation of loving charity? And of course Anne had no answer to this, and the animal was duly named Sinclair, and the discussion was closed. In the four years since then, Amberson occasionally questioned the choice, and he even occasionally felt a sort of shame, a lump in his belly that demanded to know why he had treated his son's memory in such a frivolous manner. But Amberson was able to dismiss the doubts. To him, it was more important that Sinclair represented some sort of point, perhaps some sort of proof of order, of giving and of taking and of balance. And, beyond that, wasn't the life that flowed in a cat just as profound as a human life? Had not God created cats? Could anyone explain the origin of *any* life, whether it be of a nuclear scientist or the most shabby and blundering beast of the field? Was selectivity all that important when it came to the miracle of creation?

Amberson grimaced, and Sinclair slept, and Anne stared straight ahead, and Amberson kept the accelerator at 40 and hoped to heaven he was not as childish as he sometimes suspected he was.

See now 1931 (the paradox returneth), and it is eight o'clock of a summer evening, and little Lewis, who is six, already has been put to bed for the night. But Henry, who is all of eight and as large as most boys of twelve, has leave now to stay up until nine, and he is keeping me company while I nudge and jostle the cheerful Baby Florence. She is trying to eat my thumb. Perhaps I should have salted it. (I have no idea how we have come to call her Baby Florence. No one consciously *thought up* this sticky itsypoo pejorative. It simply sneaked into our vocabulary, and its Fanny Brice implications annoy me no end.)

Henry has just suggested that we embark on a splendid adventure. He proposes that we take the last trolley ride on the Paradise Valley Traction Company interurban. Tomorrow night the owl local will make its final run at midnight from Paradise Falls to Lancaster. This will mark the end of interurban service for the PVT, which has gone into receivership.

"And how would we get back to Paradise Falls?" I ask him.

"I think I got a good idea on that," says Henry, nodding.

"Well, don't expect your mother to drive to Lancaster after dark. She's never cared for night driving."

"Yes sir, I know that. And so I went and talked to Mr. Pflug today."

"Charley Pflug from Cameo Taxi?"

"Yes sir. He said he'd do it for five dollars. Bring us back."

"All the way from Lancaster?" I ask my son. I jiggle Baby Florence on my lap, and she giggles.

"Yes sir," says Henry.

"You expect me to pay five dollars to have Charley Pflug drive us from Lancaster to Paradise Falls?"

"No sir. I'll pay the five dollars. I got nine dollars *Liberty* money. And I still got the dollar Uncle Alvin gave me last Christmas. That's ten dollars, so I'll still have five dollars after paying Mr. Pflug."

I lift Baby Florence and pat her bottom. I am fully aware that I will permit the adventure, but it is necessary that he first explain himself. Anne is working in the diningroom on her jigsaw puzzle, and she knows nothing of this, and I had better have some answers when she makes what I feel will be her inevitable protest. And protest she almost certainly will, even though all Henry really seeks to do is stay up until perhaps three in the morning because of a trolley ride. It is no wicked thing, this proposal of his. And, since he wants me to accompany him, there obviously is no boyish mischief involved. Still, before I tell him yes, I require the explanation. So I say to my son: "I still don't understand why this means so much to you."

"Well . . ." says Henry, and then he apparently can think of nothing further to say.

"Come on now," I tell him, "you've never been at a loss for words in your life."

He smiles at me and tries to shrug. Then: "I . . . well, I . . . I feel bad about it . . ."

"I wasn't aware you had stock in the company," I tell him—and, as soon as the words are out of my mouth, I regret them. I should not ridicule him. If he feels *bad,* as he puts it, then he feels *bad,* and I have no right to deride his emotions. And, beyond that, he is a remarkable person, and one does not belittle remarkable persons. One treasures them. I therefore smile at him and say: "Hey, old sport, I shouldn't have said that. But I'm afraid you're still going to have to explain yourself."

"That's all right," says Henry, rubbing his knuckles. "Well . . . like I said, I *feel* bad . . ."

"*As* I said," I tell him. I smile. "There I go with my relentless grammar again. And the knee bone connects to the thigh bone, and Dover is the capital of Maryland, if you follow me."

Henry grins, shakes his head. "Yes sir," says Henry. His face glistens. "Yes *sir.*" He folds his arms across his chest, and his trousers are about three sizes too short, and his tennis shoes, which we bought for him only three or four months ago, already are beginning to split at the sides.

I say to him: "Still, your father is going to have to put your sister to bed in a few minutes, and he'd like to hear some words from you before he leaves this room. You have the floor," so speak up. The gentleman from the north side of the room yields to the gentleman from the south side of the room."

"Yes sir. All right." Henry leans forward again. Then: "Papa, don't you ever feel sorry for things?"

"Things? You mean tie pins and shovels and tractors and old tin cans?"

"Papa, I been thinking about it ever since I read about it in the paper. I been thinking about all the people who rode those cars, all the places they went, and like the way the cars *click* and *hum,* you know?"

"Yes. They do click and hum."

"And them so big. And what I *want* is: I want to *show* something."

"What is it that you want to show?"

"That I'm sorry. That I love them. That I wish it shouldn't have to happen. I mean, I walk over to the barns and look at them a whole lot, and I listen to the clicking and the humming. Like when one of them is just sitting, and somewhere underneath the floor there's this thing going kick kick kick kick kick, like maybe it's tapping its fingers on the table because it's real, ah, *impatient.*"

I stare at my son.

He continues: "It's like *somebody* ought to feel *something,* you know?"

"Yes," I say.

"So can we go?"

"Yes."

Henry leaps to his feet, and the soles of his tennis shoes slap jubilantly against the floor. He opens his mouth to shout, but then he sees Baby Florence, who has now wrapped one of her hands around my thumb, and he apparently understands that she is just about asleep, so he grins and covers his mouth. "Hot dog," he says, keeping his voice down. "Oh, hot *spit.*" His hand comes away from his mouth, and he walks to me and strokes Baby Florence's hair. He looms. He is but eight years of age, and he *looms,* and he says: "Thank you, Papa. I thank you very much." He smiles down at Baby Florence and says: "She's real pretty, isn't she?"

"Yes," I say.

"I love her."

"All right. I'll buy that."

"I love the world, Papa. Frank Esterbrook thinks I'm crazy, but I *do.*"

"You probably *are* crazy, but it's the best way of being crazy I know."

Now Henry directs his smile at me, and he says: "I don't care what Frank Esterbrook thinks."

"I don't believe you do."

"Frank Esterbrook is full of beeswax," says Henry.

"That is correct,"I tell him.

"I don't care when people make fun."

"I know you don't."

Henry shifts his weight, stares down at his feet, wriggles his toes inside the tennis shoes. "They got a right," he says. "I mean, if *I* was like *them,* and I saw someone big as I am come flopping up the road, *I'd* make fun *too.*"

"I doubt that, but we'll let it go."

"I don't hurt nobody."

"Anybody."

"I don't hurt *anybody.*"

"That is correct," I say to my son. "You do not."

He bends over me and kisses me on a cheek. It is a loud kiss, and Baby Florence twitches in her sleep.

I smile at Henry and say: "Thank you, old sport. I appreciate that."

"Yes sir," he says. Shrugging and hunching, he goes out of the room, and I look down at Baby Florence and whisper: "Wellnow, what are we to make of this brother of yours?"

And this is a good question. It is perhaps the largest question in the Amberson household. I ponder it as I carry Baby Florence upstairs and deposit her in her bed. It has a fence around it, and its blankets are pink, and a large yellow stuffed doggie lies waiting next to the pillow. I carefully slide Baby Florence under the blankets, and she reaches in her sleep for the stuffed doggie, draping an arm across its neck. It has brown buttony eyes. The room's wallpaper is decorated with circus elephants and lions and trumpets and drums and clowns. It was Lewis's room before Florence was born, and it was Henry's room before Lewis was born. Anne and I still call it Henry's Old Room, even though he has not slept in it for more than six years.

I tuck the blankets around Baby Florence, then quietly slip out of the room. Henry's room—his New Room, if you will—is across the hall, and I hear him moving around, preparing for bed. I hesitate for a moment, and I have a strong desire to ask him if *he* would like to be tucked in, but the desire is absurd. We have already fully stated our feelings for one another; one does not garnish whipped cream with whipped cream. That sort of extravagance is deplorable, so, knowing all this, I quickly move to Henry's door and enter his room. "Would you, ah, would you like me to tuck you in?" I ask him.

He is standing next to the bed, and he is buttoning the tops of his pajamas. The pajama bottoms are too tight around the crotch and hips. The pajamas are green, and I seem to recall that Anne made them for him only two or three months ago. Good Lord, at this rate he soon will be outgrowing his clothing before their first laundering. He smiles at me and says: "I'm going to bed early. It's not even eight-thirty yet, but I want to get a whole lot of sleep tonight."

"So you won't fall asleep tomorrow night?"

"Yes sir," says Henry.

"So, would you like me to tuck you in? Or are you too big for that?"

"You can tuck me in," says Henry, fussing with the last of the buttons. "I think that'd be real nice."

"*Very* nice," I tell him.

"Very nice," says Henry. He finishes with the buttons and lies down. "I . . . yes sir, very real nice . . ."

"You are a rascal and a devil," I say. I go to the bed and pull up the covers. "Now. Have a nice sleep. We have a big trolley ride tomorrow night."

"Yes sir," says Henry. "You can tuck me in any time you want to."

"Thank you."

"Papa?"

"Yes?"

"I don't like to say this, but Dover is the capital of Delaware."

"How's that again?"

"Downstairs just now, when we were talking, you said Dover is the capital of Maryland."

"I did?"

"Yes sir," says Henry. He speaks solemnly. "I don't mean to be a smartypants, but that's what you said."

"Well, I stand corrected. And don't worry about being a smartypants. If I can correct your grammar, you can correct my geography."

"Thank you."

"Annapolis is the capital of Maryland, isn't it?"

"Yes sir," says Henry. "That's right."

"Don't ever be afraid to correct me when I'm wrong."

"Yes sir."

"Have a nice sleep. Don't let the bedbugs bite."

"I'll try not to," says Henry. He rolls on his side and closes his eyes. The bed creaks. It is a small bed, and I wonder how much longer it will be able to accommodate him. I sigh, and I glance around the room, and its walls are decorated with photographs of Babe Ruth, Lindbergh, Hoot Gibson and Tom Mix, and there is nothing here to indicate that he is in any way extraordinary, but I know differently, and I am astonished, and I am perhaps even frightened. I switch off the light and leave the room quietly. When one has three children, one learns to move stealthily in the night. I return downstairs, and Anne still is in the diningroom. Her jigsaw puzzle is nearly complete. It shows a quail in a sunny field. Part of the quail's head is missing, and so is a section of the sky, but otherwise the thing has been filled out, and I tell Anne I see she is on the old homestretch, to coin a phrase. She is wearing a brown and white print dress, and she has unfastened its two top buttons. She scratches her throat and nods. She is holding a piece of sky. Not looking up, she asks me what

Henry and I were discussing at such great and serious length. I do not reply. Instead, I stare at the outline of her breasts, which are pressed against the edge of the table. The unfastened buttons have enabled me to see the softly warm beginnings of what she likes to call her matronly bustworks (she usually summons up the phrase when we are in bed and I am grabbing for them), and at thirtytwo she still is plumply delicious; she still is able—at will—to make me steam and gasp and thresh. I tighten my lips, and a familiar warmth begins to rise. After ten years of marriage, this warmth has become a dear friend, and one does not confound or betray one's dear friends, no indeed. I seat myself next to Anne and pat her thigh. But she still is waiting for me to answer her question about the conversation with Henry. She looks at me. She taps the piece of sky against her teeth. She tells me to get my dirty lustful *hand* off her *thigh* and *answer* the *question*. I say nothing. Instead, I simply smile, then quickly lean to her ear and begin licking it. The piece of sky flies from her fingers, and she wriggles, and she tells me *stop* that, you randy old goat you. And, whispering, I tell her bushwah, I know advertising when I see it. She starts to ask me what I mean, but then I slide a hand inside the place where the buttons are unfastened, and now she knows what I mean. And she giggles. And we kiss. And I unfasten the remaining buttons. And she tells me for heaven's *sake,* this is the *diningroom,* you nitwit. And she tells me *now stop that, Howard,* the curtains are up, and we can be seen right through the front room window, and what will Cumberland Street say? And I tell her shhhhh, it will do Cumberland Street good. And I unsnap her brassiere. Shhhhh, I say to her, and I am grinning, and I begin kissing her, ah, matronly bustworks. And I reach up her dress, and she is wearing nothing there other than panties. Sometimes she wears a girdle and hose, but tonight she is not wearing a girdle and hose, and ah, ah, the Lord provides graciously for those who are steadfast and pure of heart. And Anne is responding. She already is damp, and she is kissing my neck and my ears. She whispers that we should be quiet. She whispers that she doesn't want the children to hear anything. I tell her everything is fine; the children will hear nothing. Our chairs bump, and our legs are entangled, and we begin to teeter, and then Esquire comes wandering into the room. He is our dog, a shambling and somewhat awkward dachshund of forlorn countenance. Anne sees him and gives an involuntary little shriek. She tells me *really,* Howard, this is the absolute . . . ah, ah, don't stop . . . limit. I tell her shhhhh, and Esquire comes sniffing. I kick at him. He whines, retreats into a corner and flops down under the stand that holds the goldfish bowl. Anne tells me no, no, Howard, not the *diningroom,* and I tell her shhhhh, I don't want to hear any more out of you. At the sound of the shhhh, Esquire struggles to his feet, bumping the stand. It wobbles, and the goldfish scurry, but it does not fall, and I would not care if it did. I am too far along in what I am doing, and Anne is traveling that happy road right at my side. Esquire comes sniffing, but Anne and I pay him no mind, and somehow my trousers have fallen. How could they have fallen when I am sitting down and have not stood up? This is an excellent question, and perhaps at some other time I shall give it my earnest and devoted attention. I press against Anne, and suddenly her chair slides out from under her. Esquire yips, hurries back to his place under the goldfish stand. Anne's arms fly out and slap the table and the jigsaw puzzle, and the puzzle begins to come apart. Her hands scrabble, and she is fighting for her balance, and the parts of the puzzle begin to bounce and rattle like corn in a popper. She becomes entangled in her dress and her undergarments, and she knocks loose the board that supports a leaf of the table, and the leaf slams down, and she slides to the floor, and I slide with her, and the shattered jigsaw puzzle rains down on us, and Esquire begins to growl, and Anne tells me oh all right, all right, yes my darling, and I am of course more than ready, and she whispers oh the diningroom, the diningroom, oh my dear God the *diningroom,* and I move quickly and jubilantly, easily penetrating all that fretful entangled dampness, and we are half on the rug and half under the table, and Anne moans, and she laughs as she moans, and an occasional stray fragment of the puzzle plunks down on us as we buck and rear. And then we are done. And there is a slice of the quail in her hair. And we lie quietly. And then Anne says: "Cumberland Street." And I say: "Never mind Cumberland Street." And Anne says: "We are animals." And I say: "Absolutely." And Esquire comes stumbling to us and sniffs at us, and his face is as melancholy as I have ever seen it. And Anne rubs his head and tells him: "Your master is more of an animal than you are. So is your mistress, for that matter." Then she plucks the slice of quail from her hair, scrootches out from under me and sits up. She glances around, and the floor is littered with fragments of the puzzle. "Well," she says, "we certainly did wonders for my puzzle." She is wearing nothing whatever, and so she reaches for her discarded dress and drapes it over the front of her body. "Now tell me," she says, "what were you and my Always Boy discussing at such length? You never *did* answer the question, you know."

And there, to be sure, is what I so often see as the essential Anne

Georgia Howell Amberson, the devoted and relentless mother of the Always Boy, and perhaps I should laugh, but somehow I cannot. (It is painful to admit, but from time to time I have trouble suppressing a sort of jealousy. I am no Freudian, and I do not like it when Anne jokes that she is a Textbook Case, but still . . . well, what do I have to do to divert her attention?)

I sit crosslegged on the floor with her, and I am naked except for my undershirt and socks and shoes, and my lips and belly are sore, and I idly pluck at pieces of the puzzle as I describe Henry's proposal. "It was really very interesting," I tell her. "He wants to go to Lancaster in the last interurban tomorrow night."

"What?"

"You heard me correctly. He wants to ride the last trolley out of here. He wants me to go with him. And he's arranged with Charley Pflug to bring us back. It will cost him five of the nine dollars he's saved from his *Liberty* money."

Anne's dress is knotted, and one of its sleeves has been pulled inside out. She reverses the sleeve, then slips into the dress. She does not bother with her undergarments. She is frowning.

"He feels sorry about it," I tell her.

"Please put some clothes on. You look ridiculous sitting there like that."

I nod. I retrieve my undershorts, my shirt and my trousers. I stand up, and I am a bit wobbly, but I manage to keep my balance. I struggle into my clothes. "I think . . . I, well, yes, I think I can . . . understand it . . ."

Anne stands up. Her brassiere and panties have been kicked under the table, but she makes no move to retrieve them.

Our chairs have been overturned. I place them on their feet. I collapse into one. "I don't know about *you*, my dear, but *I* am a little fagged out."

"Yes," says Anne. Her voice is remote. "Of course you are." She sits down. "Now, you say he feels sorry about it. Why is that? Things outlive their usefulness, and traction companies are going into receivership every day. It's this depression. And automobiles. The poor old interurbans just can't compete."

"Ah, you called them *poor old* interurbans. Doesn't that perhaps give you a *hint* of how he feels?"

"Oh. Well. Maybe so."

"He's not an ordinary boy."

"Don't you think *I* know that? It's what I *tell* you every day. Don't you listen?"

"Yes, Anne. I listen. Please don't be angry. I mean, it wasn't five minutes ago that we were—"

"I'm sorry," says Anne, reaching out and touching one of my hands.

"It's just that sometimes Henry seems to—"

"I know. You don't have to say it. I'm very, very sorry. I really am."

"It was ridiculous just now, but I enjoyed it very much."

"So did I . . ."

"And you weren't thinking about Henry?"

"No. Of course not. Not when it was happening. Maybe I was thinking about my jigsaw puzzle, but I wasn't thinking about *Henry.*"

"Well, as long as it was your jigsaw puzzle, that's all right."

Anne smiles. "You and your humor," she says. She pats my hand. "I love you, Howard. You are my *husband,* and you give me what no other man possibly could. Does that sound stupid and trite? Well, I'm sorry if it does, but it happens to be true. We are stuck with one another, and it's not so terrible, right?"

"Yes."

"But we do have to face one single extraordinary fact."

"That Henry is a remarkable boy?"

"Yes," says Anne. "And you know it goes beyond any excess of love I might have for him. You saw those test scores. You know what they mean. And we've talked with his teachers, and we know what they've been saying to us for the past two years. And we've watched him read, the way he can zip through one of his books in about fifteen minutes. He'll only be going into the third grade next month, but he already can do square roots. How many minutes did it take for you to teach it to him? Thirty? Now, Howard, I ask you: Fifteen minutes to read a book, thirty minutes to learn square roots—what do those things *mean?* Well, you know what they mean as well as I do."

I have listened to all this with what I hope is no expression on my face. I know I love my son, and I know I love him deeply, with whatever it is that passes for passion within me. But is there no way to divert my wife from him? So now I shake my head, and I say: "Darling, I just don't want to get into a contest with him. That's all I'm trying to say . . ."

"You are *not* in a contest with him. But I've never lived with a certified genius before, and you'll have to understand that I just can't pass it off, tra-la, as though it were the most ordinary thing in the world."

"But we have to remember to allow him to be a boy first. There's enough time later to be a genius."

Anne stares sharply at me. "Howard, why are we arguing?"

"How's that?"

"I don't want to argue any more. I'm full of you, and I want to enjoy it. And besides, it's all beginning to sound very artificial."

"What do you mean?" I ask her.

Anne bats her eyes in a way that reminds me of the Betty Boop comic character. "When you and I were finished down there on the floor and I asked the question about Henry, I was only trying to be funny."

"Really?"

"Yes, really. Oh, what a dumbbell I am."

"Does that mean your love for me is genuine and undistracted?"

"Yes, I swear it, by the Holy Mother."

"Very well then, my child. Go and sin no more."

Anne assumes a crestfallen look. "Awww, *shoot,*" she says.

I laugh aloud. Anne reaches for me, and we embrace. She pats my shoulders. I press my face against her neck, and I say: "You are right. We have no argument. You are my wife, and you are my love."

"An impure suspicion," says Anne, murmuring, "is a terrible thing."

I squeeze her. I kiss her neck. Her flesh is delicious. It exalts my tongue. "I have . . . no . . . suspicions," I say to her.

"Henry is one thing, and we are another," says Anne.

"Yes . . ."

Anne pulls away from me. She is smiling. "I mean you no harm. Please believe me."

"I do. Of course I do."

"And I hope you two enjoy yourselves tomorrow night. It sounds like great fun."

"You have no objections? I thought you might think it was silly."

"I *do* think that, but I am honestly *trying* not to smother him. As I've told you many times, his *nature* . . . the way he has compassion for just about everything and everybody in the whole world . . . impresses me as much as his brains do. And probably more. So, for heaven's sake, if he wants to be affectionate and silly about some old *trolleycars,* more power to him."

"Anne, I love you."

"Well, I should *hope* so—after the way you've just *ravished* me."

"Now, I'm being serious."

Anne nods. She still is smiling. She fans herself with the hem of her dress. "I know you are," she says. "You are a very serious man, and it's what makes you such an answer to a housewife's prayer. And I don't even care if you got me pregnant tonight. As my mother used to say: 'Anne, any child that is conceived under the diningroom table is bound to grow up to be President of the United States.'"

"And an expert at putting together jigsaw puzzles."

We laugh. The crisis . . . or whatever . . . has passed. We scramble about on the floor and gather up the pieces of the puzzle. (My mind has little truck with symbols, and so I do not anoint this activity with any particular importance.) I crawl under the table and retrieve the brassiere and the panties, and Anne tells me I am a true gentleman. We embrace, and Esquire sniffs at our feet, then waddles off to his "bed," an old clothes basket that Anne has lined with flannel and placed under the kitchen stove. He walks spreadlegged, and Anne and I watch him, and she smiles and says something to the effect that the poor creature looks as though he's got the worst case of hemorrhoids ever suffered by man or beast. I give a sort of professorial snort, then allow as how I agree. Anne checks the floor to make sure no stray puzzle fragments have been overlooked, and then we turn out the lights and creep upstairs to our room. No sounds come from the rooms where our children are sleeping. Keeping my voice at a whisper, I ask Anne whether she put anything in their food this evening. She makes a face at me and tells me they have clear consciences, and people with clear consciences are heavy sleepers, didn't I know that? And I tell her gosh, what a marvelously acute observation. We go into the bedroom and change into our nightclothes. Anne says she knows she really should take a bath, but somehow she has suddenly become awfully tired. I smile and tell her well, your sleepiness probably comes from a clear conscience. We lie down together. We do not even bother to go to the bathroom and brush our teeth. Our bodies touch, and we kiss, and she tells me I am a dear lovely man. I grin in the dark and inform her that the feeling is mutual. Our bodies separate, and we roll away from one another, settling on our sides for the night. Anne yawns. Her voice thick, she whispers: "My goodness . . . the diningroom . . ."

I chuckle, and a few minutes later she is asleep. I envy her. I am nowhere near sleep yet, and I know it. My mind feels as though it is being stretched on pins, and I am not sure I understand the essence of anything that has happened tonight. It is childish and absurd of me to be jealous of my own son, but the feeling persists, and what am I to do about it? Anne called our argument artificial, but is that really true? I *love* my wife, by God, and why does she have to be diverted by her relentless concern for Henry? Is *that* an artificial question? *Is* it? I say it is not, and I say it must be examined. All right then, where do we stand? She insists her love for me has not been diminished, and yet at the same time she admits that her love for Henry is excessive. How can the one be compatible with the other? And yet . . . just hold on. Perhaps her love for him is not as excessive as she believes it to be. She is making an honest *effort* not to smother him. So do I not owe it to her to honor that effort and acknowledge it? I must not be petty. I must not permit myself the obscene luxury of envying my own flesh. And besides, how can I know what *Anne* is experiencing? She is neither stupid nor insensitive, and she has been aware for several years that her devotion to Henry has given me discomfort. Which means, if she loves me (and I have no doubt of this), that the discomfort in *me* has created a discomfort in *her*. And what right do I have pecking and gouging her the way I do? It is important that I remember how Henry was born, how she screamed and whooped, how large he was and reluctant to come out and join the world. If Anne's love for Henry is larger than her love for our other two children, and if on occasion it gives me discomfort, I need to remind myself of the immense and apocalyptic event that created it. I need to remind myself of all those whooping hours. It was her event, not mine. She was there. I was not.

Now I relax a little, and some of the tension goes out of my body. I plump my pillow, and Anne sighs in her sleep. I think of my son Henry—*our* son Henry. I know that no one can doubt his special nature. He tries to hide it from the world, but he cannot do this. He is, after all, only eight years old, and he does not want to be seen as a freak. His life abounds with Frank Esterbrooks, and he values them, and he seeks to be at one with them. But he cannot. Except for his size, he does not appear to be extraordinary. He has blond hair, and his face is flat, and he moves heavily. But he is forever smiling. His unremarkable face hides nothing. Not when one sees the smile. And the Frank Esterbrooks all understand that he is more than they ever will be. And so they ridicule him; they call him crazy, a freak. This may be cruel, but it certainly is understandable. I am able to project myself inside them, and I know how they feel. I *have* been *there*. Oh yes *indeed*. For instance, Henry was three when I taught him to read. It took two days. Today, at the age of eight, he has already read all of Dickens, Poe, Stevenson and Sir Arthur Conan Doyle. When he was four, he was able to pick out tunes on the piano. At five, he drew a map of the United States from memory, filling in all the states and naming every one. At six, he was able to recite the complete player rosters of all sixteen major league baseball teams. At seven, he drew a map of Paradise Falls from memory, filling in all the streets and naming every one. He has inspected the cellar wiring, and he knows which circuits control which outlets, and he is able to replace a fuse more quickly than I can. He understands why Ivory Soap floats and others do not. (Do *I?* Well, ah, if the truth were known, no.) He plays chess and checkers so well that he no longer can find opponents. His teachers tell me they *know* he has to pinch himself in class so he does not fall asleep from boredom. His scores in all the intelligence tests are colossal, and the principal at the West End Elementary School has suggested that Anne and I consent to have him skipped ahead at least two grades and perhaps three. But we have resisted this. We want him to remain with his contemporaries. No one questions his brilliance, but he is still and all a *boy,* and right now, to Anne and me, his boyhood is a central issue, since *we* are the ones who *know* how young and vulnerable he really is. We know. We shall not harm him. And we shall not permit anyone else to harm him. And yet, for all our concern, there is a spirit within him that protects him even as it sets him apart. His contemporaries ridicule him, true enough, but at the same time they allow him to play in all their games, and they even look to him as a sort of mediator. See now a vacant lot, and Henry and his contemporaries are playing baseball. Here now is a close play at second base, and an argument begins, and everyone hollers at once. The shortstop angrily jumps up and down, and he waves the ball. The baserunner tells him he is full of baloney up to his eyeballs; I was safe and you know it. The players gather around menacingly, and then someone says oh what the heck, let's ask Hank Amberson. And once he is asked, Henry delivers the judgment . . . and, curiously, both sides abide by it (even his own teammates, should it be against them). I have seen him in this situation, and it is astonishing. He plays in all the games, and his size makes him the strongest and most skillful of them all, but he is still more of a *presence* than a *participant.* He hits many home runs, and he scores touchdowns galore (even though he moves heavily, he is not clumsy, and he is really quite a fine athlete), but nonetheless he is held away from the center of what is happening. His size and skill make him the first to be chosen, but at the same time he never is a chooser. Only those who truly *belong* are choosers, and Henry is obviously unlike the others, so how could he belong? (Lewis, on the other hand, is already a chooser and a belonger, and at six he runs his friends' lives like a drill sergeant.) But I have never once heard Henry complain about any of this. When he speaks of it (which is not often), he does so with a sort of resignation. He says: Hey, I scored five touchdowns today, and three of the guys clapped me on the back. *Three* of them. Honest. And so this then is our son Henry, enigmatic but not peculiar, contradictory but not illogical, a smiler and a mourner, a genius and a respected outcast. Surely Anne is right. Surely he is an Always Boy. And now there is this business of the interurbans, and surely it follows the pattern. When he was two years old, he came to me one summer evening. He pointed at the fading orange sunlight and, weeping, he asked me: Papa, Papa, what happens to all the dead days? And I looked at him, and all I could think to say was: God takes them. They are so beautiful, and they will stay with Him forever, and He will take care of them always. Now then, I ask most humbly, what sort of boy is it who would ask such a question? What sort of boy is it who would weep for dead days? (And at the same time he reads his schoolbooks in fifteen minutes, and he already has read everything ever written by Dickens, Poe, Stevenson and Sir Arthur Conan Doyle, and he even knows why Ivory Soap floats.) What sort of phenomenon have Anne and I produced? And how can he love us so much? And he does love us, and greatly. He loves us, and he loves his world, and he is forever displaying his love. There are so many examples, I hardly know where to begin. Perhaps a few recent ones will suffice, so let us begin then with a friend, young Master Magnificent. He came to us last winter, shortly after the death of our elderly cat, Prunella. He was an orange and white striped kitten of impeccable manners and disposition, and he was given to us by some friends, a couple named Jones. The name of course came from the Tarkington novel, *The Magnificent Ambersons.* We have for many years been the victims of that book (I have never read it, incidentally), and old Fred Boyd for one is fond of addressing me as O Magnificent One. It is a fate we share with all persons named Forsyte or Babbitt or Copperfield, and we have tried to bear up under it as well as we can, through all the bad jokes and hideous puns. So why then did we name the kitten Magnificent? Well, we sought to make the world aware that we *knew* about the novel, that we had *heard* all the jokes and puns, that we were taking it all in our stride and could laugh about our name as heartily as any stranger or chance acquaintance. Perhaps, in a certain sense, we were being cruel to poor little Magnificent, but I do not believe so. The puns aside, Magnificent is a splendid name . . . nay, a magnificent name. I would not mind being named Magnificent myself. When I think of Lorenzo the Magnificent, I envy him, and that is a fact. So therefore, as far as I was concerned, Magnificent was a fine name for our new kitten, and we all treasured it—even Lewis, despite the fact that his mastery of syllables was insufficient for an accurate pronunciation of it, a deficiency that resulted in his calling the animal Magnicent. But the rest of us (Baby Florence excluded, of course) had no trouble with the name, and it almost always made us smile. As for Magnificent himself, he was utterly delightful, forever purring and hopping on laps, nosing in the back yard, playing with string and a little soft yarn ball that Anne made for him. In addition, he was the only cat I ever knew who actually seemed to smile, and even Esquire—not a cat fancier by any manner or means—was disarmed. The relationship between Esquire and Prunella had been one of mutual wariness, but for some reason the dog seemed to trust Magnificent and even went so far as to allow him to share the "bed" under the kitchen stove. And so Magnificent thrived, in general conducting himself in a most magnificent manner, and there is no other word for it. Then, one morning in February of this year, after breakfasting on ham leftovers and milk, Magnificent was run down and killed by a coal truck in the alley behind our house. The driver, a tall homely fellow named Clarence Cockroft, brought Magnificent's torn and mangled body to me, and he was crying. He told me oh Goddamn, Goddamn, I just didn't see the poor little thing until it was too late. I'm real sorry, Mr. Amberson. I honest to God am. Me and the missus got three of our own, and we love them real good, you know what I mean? I nodded and told Clarence Cockroft yes, I knew what he meant. It was a Saturday, and I had planned to take Henry and Lewis sledding at Elysian Park. There were several inches of snow on the ground, and more was coming down, and it would indeed have been a fine day for sledding, but now I was standing on the back porch with this poor snuffling Clarence Cockroft, and I was holding the crumpled bloody body of dear Magnificent, and I am afraid I also wept. I told Clarence Cockroft all right, all right, I know you didn't mean to do it, and I thank you very much for owning up to it and bringing him to us instead of driving off and leaving him in the alley, where automobiles and other trucks probably would have squashed him beyond recognition. I said all right, *all right,* thank you very much; you are a good man, and I bear you no grudge. Then, after Clarence Cockroft had gone shambling back to his truck, I called for Henry, and he helped me prepare Magnificent's grave. We dug it in a shady place near the garage, not far from where we had buried Prunella. The earth was frozen, and we took turns digging, and snow got into

133

our eyes. Magnificent's body lay a few feet away, and it became sprinkled with snow, which softened the redness. Anne was back in the house, and I knew she was weeping. She had refused to come look at Magnificent, and she would not allow Lewis to come look. "Just bury Magnificent and get it *over* with," she told me. "I don't want to *think* about it." She wept—and so did Lewis, although for more reasons than simple grief. He jumped up and down, and he whimpered that he wanted to see what Magnicent looked like. "Magnicent was my kitty *too,*" said Lewis, whining, "and I want to see what the blood looks like, and his fur and his bones and all. His eyes, they open or shut?" And Anne went to Lewis and covered his mouth with her hand, and she told him: "That is enough out of you. I do not want to hear another peep out of you. One more word and you stay in your room until Monday." Her voice was metallic, and it astonished all of us, including Lewis, who promptly subsided. Henry and I grunted as we worked with the shovel. "It must be dug deep," I said, "so that no animal will be able to get at him." And Henry said: "Yes sir." And so we dug a narrow trench that was perhaps four feet deep, and snow spattered the raw earth at the bottom of the trench, and it was Henry who carefully placed poor Magnificent down there, straightening the body (it was partially frozen, and it crackled a bit) and adjusting it so that it lay on its left side, which had always been its favorite position for sleeping. Then Henry looked up at me, and I said: "God bless our cat." And Henry said: "Amen." Esquire came to investigate, and snow rubbed his belly, and he sat at the edge of the grave and licked his private parts. Henry reached for him and hugged him, and Esquire gave a short yip, and Henry looked at me and said: "That was Esquire's amen." And I said: "Good old Esquire." And then Henry and I filled the grave and returned to the house, and Anne fixed us some nice hot cocoa. Her eyes were damp, and Henry hugged her as he had hugged Esquire, and he said: "Poor little kitty. Yes, Mama. Yes." The following Tuesday, when I arrived home from school, Anne gave me a letter to read. It had arrived that day, and the writing was Henry's, and the envelope was addressed thusly:

MAGNIFICENT
K. H.

MRS. H. W. AMBERSON
120 CUMBERLAND ST.
PARADISE FALLS, O.

The letter itself contained these words:

DEAR MAMA,

JUST A NOTE TO LET YOU KNOW I AM
FEELING REAL GOOD HEAR IN KITTY
HEAVEN, AND GOD GIVES ME A WHOLE
LOT TO EAT. THERE ARE MANY KIT-
TIES HEAR WITH ME, AND WE RUN
AND SNIF AND PUR ALL THE DAY LONG.
HOW IS EVERYBODDY? I MISS YOU
BUT I AM REAL HAPPY THO, AND I
DOANT WANT YOU TO BAWL. I AM AL-
WAYS WARM AND I JUST PLAY AND I
JUST PLAY AND I JUST PLAY AND I
JUST PLAY. VERY TRULEY YOURS.
MAGNIFICENT AMBERSON.

The letter literally made me flop on the sofa, and I stared at Anne, and she said: "What do you suppose the K and the H on the envelope meant?" And I said: "Kitty Heaven." And then Anne tried to smile at me, but her mouth fell apart, and she began to weep, and she tried to speak, but she could not speak for the weeping, and finally she simply came to me and placed her head against my chest, and I told her: "I shall read this letter at the supper table tonight. It must be acknowledged." And I did. Lewis appeared astonished. Henry smiled. Anne cleared her throat. And Baby Florence dribbled pea soup onto her bib. And later, after everyone had gone upstairs, I spoke aloud to the empty parlor and the mantel clock and the antimacassars and the horsehair sofa, and I said: "My God, what have You sent down to us?" And perhaps, in a sense, I am as excessive toward Henry as Anne is, and perhaps my responses to him are too enthusiastic, but by heaven I *live* with him. I stand in awe. All I really can do is salute him. For instance, neither Anne nor I has ever in any way indicated knowing who wrote the Kitty Heaven letter. But of course Henry knows we know, and therefore he knows that by not saying anything to him we are displaying a large love. By this I mean: Anne and I would have behaved contemptibly if we had made a great gushy fuss over him and the letter. It would have shown an appalling condescension, and it would have done away with all the goodness of heart contained in the letter. Effusiveness would have meant indulgence, and indulgence would have destroyed the sentiment. And so

Anne and I never by word or deed indicated anything other than an absolute belief that the Kitty Heaven letter was a statement sent straight from poor Magnificent. Anne has saved the letter, and she says she always will keep it, and I certainly hope she does. Some day, when Henry's love conquers the world, she will be able to flourish it and shout: *See! See! We knew what was coming all the time!* But, until that day comes, all we can do is pay tribute to our son, and we try in every way we know, and he understands this, I am sure. In the meantime, his life abounds with his simple goodness (I know of no other way to put it), and it even extends to what he calls his "dumb old grammar." His talk is laced with grammatical errors, but Anne and I are convinced they mostly are deliberate. The same can be said for his spelling errors, such as those contained in the Kitty Heaven letter. The grammatical errors serve two purposes, I think. First, they enable him to talk like his contemporaries, and this is very important to him. As has already been shown, he seeks to be at one with them, and the grammatical errors help—or at least so he believes. The second reason for the grammatical errors is directly concerned with me, and I am convinced of this. By saying *like* instead of *as* and *bad* instead of *badly,* he is really saying to me: Papa, do your stuff. I am leaving myself open, and I want you to correct me. And this same reasoning probably is at the root of Henry's spelling errors. They are, to him, an act of kindness and of love. Anne agrees with me on all this, and she has pointed out to me that Henry has read too many books to be so careless with his grammar and spelling. And in our household, God knows, the emphasis always has been on language. With the exception of certain politicians, I surely must be the most polysyllabic man in Paradise Falls, and it is said that the influence of the home is a powerful factor in a child's development. Therefore, since Henry is as intelligent as he is, and as perceptive, his poor grammar and spelling *must* be deliberate. And kind. And loving. (By correcting him, I am given *something to do,* and I am made to feel that I am functioning as a father.) Does this all seem cynical? Perhaps it does, but truth is truth. And I lie awake when I should be sleeping. And I plump my pillow. And I think of the capital of Maryland. And tomorrow night perhaps something new will happen, perhaps some larger dimension will make itself known (a grief for things?), and I hope I am up to it. Tomorrow night the last car will run at midnight. And Henry will be on it. And so will I. And, unless I miss my guess, so will a great many other people. (How could I be jealous of him? I am *not* jealous of him. The very idea is preposterous. He has shown me nothing but love. One does not spit in the face of such splendor.

He is the Always Boy, and he already is legendary, but how much of this has he really *sought?* Can he help it if he makes the rest of us feel clumsy and stupid and insensitive? He comes flopping and grinning, does this Henry, and he loves and mourns the world simultaneously, and who can resist him? And why should anyone even want to *try?* I am *not* jealous of him. I love him. He is my flesh. I know him. I see him. No more need be said.) And finally then I am able to sleep. My plumped pillow is warm, and my cheeks sweat, but something has removed the pins that have been stretching my brain, so I drift off, and my dreams have no shape, and that is probably just as well.

Ohio 93 took the Ambersons past the farm homes of many families they had known, people whose names were Froelich and Tomlinson and Gifford and Trelawney and Zeller and Bachman. Utility poles made gentle whisking sounds, and Amberson whistled softly through the few real teeth he had remaining to him, and the strange thunder still rolled off to the west.

Anne cleared her throat. "What will we see on this trip?" she wanted to know.

"We shall see whatever we shall see," said Amberson.

"That's no answer. You should watch yourself about being pompous. You're still too much of a schoolteacher. You can take the old man out of schoolteaching, but you can't take the schoolteaching out of the old man."

"I didn't mean to be pompous," said Amberson. "If I sounded that way, I am very sorry."

"Then tell me what we'll be seeing on this trip."

Amberson sighed. "Mailboxes," he said.

"Mailboxes?"

"Yes. Look. Here comes a mailbox now. It says FREW."

"I remember a family named Frew from when I lived in Lancaster. I expect these people are related to the Lancaster Frews. After all, how many Frews are there in the world?"

"Not many, I expect," said Amberson.

A snort from Anne. "And so *that's* what we're going to do? Read names off mailboxes and talk about them?"

"Among other things."

"What other things?"

"Well, perhaps we'll talk about some of the towns we pass through. Perhaps we'll stop at a supermarket and compare food prices. Or perhaps we'll count the number of frozen custard stands we see. Or we could stop and look at the sky. Or we could ring someone's doorbell and pretend we are from the Bureau of the Census. Or . . . oh, I don't know . . . there is a possibility we could stop at a roadside saloon and sit at the bar and drink whiskey and ask the bartender why he voted for George Wallace. Or perhaps we could rescue a turtle from the middle of the road. It seems to me there are a great many—"

"You're trying to tell me that you don't know *what* we'll be doing, isn't that right?"

"Yes. That's absolutely right. When I said footloose, I meant footloose. And fancyfree and all that."

"Well, when will our first footloose and fancyfree thing happen?"

"I hope soon," said Amberson.

"So do I," said Anne.

They were silent again. The country became more hilly, and Ohio 93's curves less graceful. The farms faded behind them, and Amberson had to hang onto the wheel with both hands. The farmhouses were at an end, and now there began a succession of shacks and cabins, and here and there the hulk of an automobile, and tires hanging from trees, and tiny children scrabbling in the dirt. Ohio 93 was climbing into the mining country that was in and around the village of Blood, and here the great strip mine country began. There were those in Paradise County who called this area Moon Township, and the name was hideously appropriate, as far as Amberson was concerned. Here indeed was the moon. Here indeed was a place of rocks and gullies and immense gray mounds of ruined earth. The strippers had come, and they had gone, and they had pocked the land forever. And Ohio 93 was cautious and hesitant as it picked its way through this shattered place, and Amberson said: "My God, we have a lot to answer for."

"We?" said Anne.

"The human race," said Amberson. "It wasn't the dinosaurs or the squirrels or the brown bears who chewed up this land."

"You're right," said Anne.

"How do you feel?"

"I'm still breathing."

"Any pain?"

"Some."

"Perhaps you should take one of your pills."

"No," said Anne. "I don't want to be a *pill popper*. I want to be stronger than that. If I haven't developed strength of character by *this* time, when *will* I?"

"Fine," said Amberson. He smiled, rubbed his jaw. "Just as long as your enjoyment of the trip isn't impaired."

"I won't let that happen."

"Good," said Amberson.

"Any minute now the excitement will reach, ah, epic dimensions, won't it?"

"Absolutely," said Amberson.

"Be still, my heart," said Anne.

See now 1951, and I am fussing with pins and tissuepaper, extracting them from a new shirt. I mumble to myself, and my wife smiles. Her face is flushed, and she is—by her own happy admission—excited and anxious. The motel room is hot, and I am utterly nude, and Anne says: "It is remarkable that a man of your age still has such a flat belly."

"If I were fat, I would look ridiculous," I tell her. "I am too short to be fat. I would be Mister Five-by-Five."

"You have made an intellectual determination not to be fat?"

"I suppose I have."

"I wish *I* could," says Anne. She is sitting on the edge of the bed, and she is fastening her garterbelt to her hose. Her breasts are flabby and mottled. It has been more than six years since the death of Henry the Always Boy, and she has gained perhaps thirty pounds in that time. But today she is smiling, and her color is as full and healthy as I have seen it in I do not know how long.

I finish with my shirt. I spread it carefully on top of the dresser. Then I put on the underwear and socks that Anne has laid out for me on the bedspread. I am freshly shaved and powdered, and my motel shower has given me an odor of Ivory Soap. And this is as it should be. Today is my daughter Florence's wedding day, and it is necessary that I gleam.

Florence has turned out to be a pretty and slender little thing with a talent for painting and laughter. The groom is a man named Thomas E. Rimers, who is an assistant professor of political science at Ohio University. I rather like this Thomas E. Rimers, who is a large young fellow with a broad face and a cheerful manner. He does not appear to fit the conventional academic mold, and this pleases me —for Florence's sake. She is too lively for that sort of thing, and too much solemnity would wither her.

We have come, the four of us, to a town called Angola, Indiana, which is a wellknown marriage mill. (When I was a boy, such places were called Gretna Greens.) The motel room is not airconditioned, and I see that my wife is perspiring a little. She asks me to zip up her dress, which I do—but I say nothing to her about the tiny drops that already have gathered in a sort of chain across the back of her neck.

Anne squeezes her swollen feet into a pair of new blue pumps. She walks to the mirror, fluffs her hair, then tells me she is going nextdoor to help Florence finish getting ready. "Ah," says Anne to the mirror, "such beauty . . ." Then, grinning, she leaves our room, and a moment later I hear her knocking on Florence's door. Then I hear squeals and laughter, and, smiling, I finish dressing just as the telephone rings. It is Tom Rimers calling from the front desk. "I'm ready whenever you people are," he says. (The appointment with the minister is for 5:30, and it is now 5:15 by my watch. The four of us arrived in Angola early this morning after driving most of the night, and the blood tests and the license already have been attended to.)

I tell Tom we will be joining him in a shake. I go next door, open the door to Florence's room without bothering to knock, and she is dressed all in white, and her eyes are shining, and my heart gives a sort of clap. "Good gracious," I say, "what a beautiful girl . . ."

Florence and her mother are standing close together with their hands touching. They smile at me, but neither is able to speak.

"Tom is ready," I tell them.

It is Florence who finally speaks. "So . . . so am I," she says. She reaches for Anne, and they embrace.

It is time for me to intervene, to do something schoolteacherish that perhaps will change the mood. And so I clear my throat noisily, and I say: "Ah, my daughter is a beauty of the purest ray serene. To gaze upon her luminous countenance is to know and treasure the precious delights of the heavenly empyrean, to comprehend the magnificent—"

I am interrupted by Florence's laughter. She brushes away her tears, and now everything is all right. Anne chides me for being a frightful old windbag, and I say yes, yes, it's all true, anything you say, but let us get a wiggle on; time and the minister wait for no one. And so we scurry to the lobby, and the bride teeters on the new spiked white shoes we have bought her, and we all are laughing. Tom is standing at the front entrance, and he is grinning, and we hurry to the car. I insist on driving the car to the chapel, and Tom does not protest. He and Florence sit in the back, and Anne sits up front with me. Nobody says a word. Anne's face pops sweat, and she dabs at it with a lace handkerchief.

It is a clear July day, and there are no clouds to block the late afternoon heat. The pavement is sticky, and the car's tires hiss wetly. The chapel is a small white frame building, and it could use a fresh coat of paint. The old paint is blistered and shredded, and the white is really more of a gray. We enter a close and musty room that perhaps is a narthex of some sort. We are greeted by the minister. His name is Ralph F. Trueman. He is florid and rumpled, and veins squiggle across his nose in all directions. (Florence glances at Tom Rimers, and he squeezes her hand.) "I am no relation to the President," says the Rev. Mr. Trueman. "My name is spelled differently. It's T-R-U-E-M-A-N. Now, tell me, which one of us has the license?"

Tom Rimers produces the license, and it is signed by the Rev. Mr. Trueman with a purple ballpoint pen that he fishes from an inside pocket of his unpressed black frock coat. Then the Rev. Mr. Trueman ushers us into another small room, and this one has an altar and paper flowers. The ceremony is brief. I am best man, and Anne is matron of honor. The newlyweds kiss, and Tom Rimers' legs and arms are shaking. The Rev. Mr. Trueman smiles, and his teeth are not good. He receives ten dollars for his services, and we all troop out of the place. On the way, Florence nudges me and whispers: "This has to be one of the greatest weddings of all time." I smile, and then I cover my mouth, and Florence makes a quiet dry sound deep in her throat.

Outside, blinking in the sunlight, we encounter a young couple coming up the walk. The Rev. Mr. Trueman, standing in the doorway behind us, says: "Ah, just in time. This must be Mr. Keller and Miss Loomis." We all nod at Mr. Keller and Miss Loomis, but they do not acknowledge us. Miss Loomis is thin and blond, and she appears to be about eight months pregnant. She is wearing a yellow maternity dress, and there is a Band-Aid on her right knee. Mr. Keller is short, with a crewcut and acne, and he is walking a pace or two behind Miss Loomis. "Good luck to you," says Tom Rimers as he and Florence pass Miss Loomis. She does not reply, but Mr. Keller does manage a weak wounded look. Tom Rimers smiles, and so does Florence, and so do Anne and I. The Rev. Mr. Trueman ushers Mr. Keller and Miss Loomis into the chapel, and then a car comes careening up to the curb, and two women scramble out. They are plump and middleaged, and one says: "They just went inside. I saw them. Come on, Edna. Hurry." And the two women scuttle up the walk. They are wearing flowered print dresses, and their heavy shoes make frenzied clacking noises. They push past us as though we are made of straw. "Woops," says Florence, and her skirt swirls.

We manage to contain our laughter until we are inside the car.

Then, when it comes, it comes shrilly. I start the car, and we drive in search of a place where we can celebrate. (Florence is not pregnant, and I have her word on it. Last night, before we all set out on this trip to Angola, she told me: "Please don't get the wrong idea about any of this. It's not that I've been *dishonored* or anything like *that*. Tom and I just don't want a lot of *ceremony* and *fuss*. He doesn't believe in it, and I don't care much about it one way or the other.") We find a restaurant on US 20 at the eastern edge of town. I order champagne, and toasts are offered. Everyone smiles, and there is a great deal of happy discussion concerning Mr. Keller and Miss Loomis and their two clacking duennas or whatever.

I smile and I smile, and my eyes are warm, and everyone chatters at once, and I tell myself: Yes. It will be all right. The champagne tickles my nostrils, and I tell myself: They are old enough, and their lives are their own.

Still, it has been barely twentyfour hours since Florence brought her Tom Rimers to the house and told us they were on their way to Angola, and would we care to join them? Naturally, Anne and I were thunderstruck. I had met Tom Rimers precisely two times before last night, and I must admit I had a few questions to ask. But I also must admit Tom Rimers was forthright in answering them. "Mr. Amberson," he said, "these things sometimes just *happen*. I am thirty years of age, which makes me nine years older than your daughter, but I don't think that's a *prohibitive* difference, do you? And after all, the older we become, the less the difference will matter. When a man is eighty and his wife is seventyone, they're not exactly a case for Ripley, are they?"

"But why the haste?" I asked him.

Tom Rimers smiled. "Because I don't happen to believe in a lot of formal ritual," he said. "I have known your daughter for more than a year, and we have made up our minds about one another, and so why should we have to wait? I am not a difficult person, and I am not belligerent, but I do have blood in my veins, and I get all steamed up as often as the next fellow." Another smile. Tom Rimers was sitting next to my daughter on the sofa. He patted her hand, and she blushed a little. And my wife, who was sitting across the room from them, rubbed her cheeks and shook her head. But there was a sort of delight working at the corners of her mouth, and it pleased me. In the past six years, she had not known much delight. She had made herself unavailable to it. But now, as Tom Rimers spoke, she almost was smiling. "Florence and I aren't getting married because we *have* to," he said, "but because we *want* to."

"We are *impatient,*" said Florence, "but we haven't been *hasty.*"

"Exactly," said Tom Rimers.

"Which means I should not get the wrong idea?" I asked him.

"Exactly," said Tom Rimers. He leaned forward and rubbed his knees. He scratched his head, patted one of Florence's thighs. "There is a point beyond which one cannot wait, however." Then he laughed and gave Florence's thigh a joyous thwock. "Ah, listen to the obfuscating academic, will you!" Another thwock, and then he said: "We all know what I'm talking about, don't we? And so all right, there you have it. I am a human being. I love. I want."

Florence smiled, and so did Anne. I looked at them for a moment, and then I said to Tom Rimers: "Well, I expect I have lost a daughter but gained a talker."

And we all laughed. And Anne quickly packed our suitcases, and she and Florence chattered and giggled, and Anne said oh *my,* wait until Lewis hears about this, and Tom Rimers and I sat in the kitchen and drank cold buttermilk, and within an hour we were on our way to Angola in his car. And I said to myself: Yes, well, all right, if this is what Florence wants, this is what she shall have. And I draped a loose arm across Anne's shoulders, and she fell asleep with her head against my chest. Up front, Tom Rimers and Florence chatted all night long. At midmorning we went to a bridal shop and bought dresses and shoes for the ladies, and later Anne and I napped while Tom and Florence obtained the license and the blood test certificate. And now, as the toasts are exchanged, I grin fuzzily at my daughter and her husband, and finally I say to Tom: "She has always been a good daughter, a creature of infinite grace. My wife and I have faith in her good judgment, and therefore we have faith in you, and we wish you both the best of everything." (My vision is far too warm, and I suppose my rhetoric is far too inflated, but I can honestly say I do not give a whoop.)

The next morning, before we begin the return drive to Paradise Falls, we take turns photographing one another, singly and in pairs (Anne has brought along her Brownie). The session takes place in front of the motel, and the newlyweds hold hands. They smile and blink, and somehow they almost seem too vulnerable for survival. I think of love, and I think of our son Lewis (who will not approve of any of this), and I think of Bernadette and the flour and the cool clear spring water, and I see the brave thrusting grins that have been spread so warmly across the faces of my daughter and her husband, and I hope to God they will treasure this day as long as they live, and then I embrace my wife, and she says to me: "You are a nice man, Howard, and I love you very much." (She is in her fifties now, and the loss of the Always Boy has made her too fat, but she still *feels,* and she still *exists,* and I believe her words of love. She is a great many things, but she is not a liar.) And now a milk truck whips past, and the driver leans out his window and hollers: *"You'll be sorry!"* And Florence giggles, then kisses her husband flush on the mouth. And the driver gives his horn a series of jaunty toots. On Christmas Eve 1951, Tom Rimers is killed when his car skids off US 33 on a curve near Nelsonville. Florence is with him (they are on their way to Paradise Falls to spend the holiday with Anne and me), but she is thrown free and not injured.

The blasted and pallid Moon Township earthscape crowded at the edges of the village of Blood, which lay all ramshackle and dispirited in a sort of wide gully that had been formed by a creek called the Tuesday. Ohio 93 dropped abruptly down the south side of the gully, then turned sharply to the east and meandered along Tuesday Creek, which was muddy these days, muddy and foul, dotted with floating rubbish and shreds and lumps of what appeared to be either dead things or garbage. It was the backside of Moon Township—its urinary canal, to put it vulgarly but appropriately. The Ambersons were silent as they drove through the village of Blood. All one could do was experience it. The meandering Ohio 93 straightened briefly and became the village's Main Street. It was lined with buildings that carried signs that said COAL and EAT and LIQUOR and ICE and—rather astonishingly—PIZZA. The sidewalks were paved with powdered old bricks that had grass growing through them like hair, and the gutters were gummy with mud. There were great jagged cracks in the pavement of the street, and Amberson coasted the car down to 20. More than a century ago, before the discovery of coal, Blood had been a farming community, and the place had been much favored as a picnic spot. Amberson's father had remembered visiting Blood as a boy, and he had been fond of reminiscing on its beauties. (It was a botanist's delight, Alvin Amberson Sr. had told his family, and in the autumn the color of the leaves was enough to bring even the most insensitive person right up short in his tracks.) But that all changed in the 1870's, after the coal was found. A man named C. P. Wells bought up all the land where the deposits were; the Columbus, Paradise Valley & Marietta built a branch line from Paradise Falls; the shafts were dug, and it was not long before Blood became a roistering and scandalous mining town. Then, in 1884, the miners went out on strike against C. P. Wells; there were several murders, and finally the enraged men set several of the mines on fire. The mines never stopped burning (after all, what burns better than coal?), and the more they burned, the more Blood declined, and the more its population fell away. And finally, in 1946, just after the end of the Second World War, the last of the C. P. Wells mines was closed. And the strippers came and went. And by 1955 or so all the strippable coal had been dug. And yet, deep in the earth, the great mine fire persisted, and even now—here in the autumn of 1971—it still burned, and here and there thin spurts of smoke still rose from the ground. The hillsides were festooned with row upon claptrap row of company houses that dated back a century, sleazy little structures that now were owned by the county in default of taxes (they were administered by the Paradise County Welfare Department, which rented them for thirty dollars a month), but most of them were unoccupied, and some had fallen down altogether, and a few even had vanished into the earth, sucked away by immense holes created by the hellish and undefeated mine fires. In 1935 the WPA built a school in Blood, a fine structure of concrete and brick, two stories tall and containing all the best classroom equipment federal money could buy. One Sunday morning in January of 1936, less than a month after its dedication, the school made a great shuddering sound and began to sink from view. Its walls caved in, and then its roof came down, and all the concrete and all the brick gave way, and the entire shebang was devoured by what appeared to be a giant mouth, and within three hours there was nothing left of the place. It never was rebuilt, and the old school was restored to use. And now, driving along the rutted streets of this foul and pulverized place, Amberson asked himself: Is this part of the apparatus? If so, what is its function? Is it supposed to be some sort of monument? Sighing, he glanced at Anne, and she was rubbing her right shoulder. Her face was pinched, and it was obvious she was alone with something dreadful, and perhaps he should speak to her, perhaps utter some word of comfort. But he said nothing. Here, in this place, words of comfort were absurd. And so Amberson kept his peace, and a few minutes later Ohio 93 was climbing north out of the Tuesday Creek gully, and the village of Blood was gone, and Anne was the first to speak. Rubbing the shoulder, she said: "Did you notice anything strange back there?"

"No. Not really."

"There were no people."

"What?"

"There were no people out on the streets. I didn't see a single soul. And not even a dog or a cat."

"Perhaps it fits something I was just thinking," said Amberson.

"Which was?"

"I was thinking about the apparatus, and I was—"

"You and your apparatus," said Anne.

"Now hear me out," said Amberson. "If the essense of the apparatus is change, then Blood represents the end of the procedure. Or at least a *kind* of end. Perhaps we should keep that in mind."

"You and all your talk about this apparatus. You keep insisting on schemes and progressions, but what do they have to do with the way things happen?"

"I do not *insist* on the schemes and the progressions," said Amberson. "I am merely trying to determine if they exist."

"Forever the schoolteacher," said Anne.

"That is correct," said Amberson.

Ohio 93 curved to the northeast, climbing through rough scrub woods and rocky open places, then headed due north and crossed the line from Paradise County into Hocking County. Sinclair hopped down from his shelf and urinated in his box. Anne opened her window. Amberson still hung onto the wheel with both hands. Logan, the seat of Hocking County, was twenty miles ahead, and perhaps they would eat their lunch there.

See now 1922 (with a lingering examination of times past), and my sister has been married to a man named Delbert Zachary for twelve years. Caroline is thirtytwo, and Delbert Zachary is forty. It is more than a decade since she has talked with her dolls, and at thirtytwo she appears to be twenty. Her skin is fair, and her body is lean and rather elegant. She wears spectacles, and she is much taken with using the editorial We, *à la* the late Queen Victoria.

Delbert Zachary is from Logan, Ohio, and he met Caroline in 1909 at the funeral of his Aunt Lydia, who had been one of Caroline's teachers at Paradise Falls High School. The woman's full name had been Lydia Prentiss Corby, and she had never married. Her bosom had been like rocks and milk glass, and she had taught English, elocution, dramatics and music appreciation.

Caroline had revered Lydia Prentiss Corby. For her part, Lydia Prentiss Corby had been more than a little fond of Caroline. I can recall seeing them hold hands, and they were forever kissing and hugging one another. They made several visits together to Columbus to attend concerts and plays, riding white and crisp in the interurban cars, taking tea at the Neil House, chatting solemnly of Brahms and Molière. And on one golden occasion I went along with them. I wore a pinchback suit, a hard rubber bow tie and a tiny derby, and Lydia Prentiss Corby pronounced me absolutely *élégant,* and I blushed and stammered, and a smiling Caroline allowed as how most of the time I was just the most *adorable* little boy *imaginable.*

We had a light supper at the Neil House (coffee and small cheese sandwiches, as I recall), and we rode in a hansom cab to the concert hall. We were passed by a number of automobiles, and Lydia Prentiss Corby shuddered and said something to the effect that they were gross and obscene. The program was all-Beethoven, and it was performed by a touring orchestra from Philadelphia.

I glanced at Caroline from time to time after the music began, and her fingers were keeping time, and a smile nudged the corners of her mouth. First came the Coriolanus Overture, then the Fifth Symphony, then the Sixth Symphony, and the smile never went away. She worked her lips, and she bit at the smile, but it persisted, and I decided I loved her very much. Next to her, Lydia Prentiss Corby sat erectly, hands folded in lap, flushed and browneyed, with all shirtwaist folds in order, and now and again the woman opened her mouth a bit, permitting her tongue to move gently and lovingly across her lower lip. She stared straight ahead, and her eyes did not appear to blink, and nothing moved except her tongue.

Later, on the way home, as the great high swaying interurban car went aclattering over the uneven roadbed and across loose railjoints, the time came when Lydia Prentiss Corby and my sister held hands. The hands nestled in Lydia Prentiss Corby's lap, and both she and my sister smiled.

I was sitting facing them riding backwards, and I did not quite know what to make of the handholding, so I pressed my nose against the window and watched lights and the outline of distant hills. I hummed the opening bars of the *Pastorale,* kept my eyes on the lights and the hills, and I supposed the opening bars of the *Pastorale* were the prettiest music I had ever heard, and I told myself: I don't care if I *am* only ten. Maybe tonight, right now, I know what it means to be big and all that. And I told myself: There's nothing bad about holding hands. And so I drew my face back from the window, turned, smiled at my sister and her friend, gave a sort of dry little cough and said: "I thank you very much for the nice evening."

"*See!*" said Caroline to Lydia Prentiss Corby. "I *told* you he's adorable!"

"Yes, dear," said Lydia Prentiss Corby, patting one of Caroline's wrists.

That was 1907, and Lydia Prentiss Corby was dead less than two years later of intestinal cancer. She was just fortyfour. In her prime, she had been a large woman, quite blond, heavy of bust and thigh. When she died, she weighed perhaps ninety pounds. I accompanied Caroline to Logan for the funeral. We rode the interurban to Lancaster, then caught a train for Logan. She bought me a stick of licorice at the candystand in the Lancaster depot while we were waiting for the train. It was July, and the depot was stuffy, so we went outside and sat on a bench.

The train arrived, and the only available seats were in the smoker. Covering her mouth with her handkerchief, Caroline allowed me to sit next to the window. The coach was blue with smoke, and she asked me to open the window, but it would not budge, and I told her, well, now I could understand why these seats had been empty. She smiled briefly from behind the handkerchief, and then for some reason she got to talking about the fact that it was summertime, and she said: "Yes, yes, I *know* I am imposing on you, the weather being so gloriously warm and all, such a fine time for little boys to run and romp and play . . . but it's just that, well, Howard, you see, I just don't want to be *alone* today . . ."

"That's all right," I said, sucking on the licorice.

Caroline wiped her forehead, folded the handkerchief, closed a fist around it. "Miss Corby meant a lot to me; she really did. I could *talk* to her, do you understand? I could *talk* to her, and she *listened;* she was never bored. She made it so I didn't, ah, *languish* quite so much, if you get what I mean. She made it so I understood that there are other people in the world who feel the way I do. Certainly *you* can appreciate *that,* am I correct?"

"I don't know what you mean."

Caroline unfolded the handkerchief and wiped at her lips. "You do *too* know what I mean," she said. "Like the time you gave that talk about Judge Parker—it's not your ordinary runofthemill boy who does such a thing. And the way you're always trying to reason things out and put them in order. You're *different,* Howard, and you might as well look it straight in the face. You're twelve years old now, and it's about time you tried to understand yourself. And you're like me, which means maybe you're just a speck . . . well . . . peculiar . . ."

I smiled. I had to. Perversely, I felt flattered. After all, who wanted to be like everyone else?

Caroline continued: "I hope you find someone who does for you what Miss Corby did for me. I mean, someone who will not judge or make fun . . ."

I did not reply. There was nothing I knew to say. I figured *maybe* I knew what my sister was talking about, but then again maybe I did *not.* And maybe no one else understood Caroline either. Mama had objected to my accompanying Caroline on this trip, telling Caroline that it would put an unnecessarily morbid strain on me. But Caroline had wept a little, and Mama had relented. Sometimes it seemed that Caroline knew how to use her tears the way other people used their fists. It was her method of getting her way, and it had worked for as long as I could remember. They came quietly, those tears of Caroline's, and her shy fluted voice quavered, and her hands made hapless plucking movements, and the tears always were plump, and they coursed down her cheeks like blots of golden rainwater, and who could resist them? Her tearful timidity was a valuable weapon. Even though she seldom spoke unless spoken to, this implacably fey sister of mine, she exercised a sort of fragile tyranny over the household, and Papa and Mama usually let her do precisely what she pleased. Which at first consisted of sitting in her room and talking to her dolls. Which later consisted of long solitary walks (she flowed as she moved, and she had a sort of bareheaded windswept beauty that put one in mind of music and perhaps some sort of thinly graceful summer bird), of dubious battle with ornate Chopin miniatures on the piano, and finally (due to the influence of Lydia Prentiss Corby), of an exhaustive interest in books, and books and books and more books, covering regiments of subjects and authors from mythology to fashion to Hamlin Garland to Beethoven to the Greek Olympiads to Whitman to botany to Marie Antoinette to the theater to Poe to Byron to Keats to needlework to flower arrangements to Arthurian legend to a study of the deciduous foliage found in Paradise, Hocking, Athens and Vinton counties. Every three or four days she brought a new armful of books home from the library, and she always took one with her when she went off on her long solitary walks, and of course Mama had become most distressed. Why, my goodness, she said, that girl's *eyeballs* are going to fall out! What on earth is the *matter* with her? Here she is, nineteen already and not a single beau. And she's such a handsome girl, half the young men in this town would fall down in a swoon if she even gave them a sideways glance. But she doesn't seem to care about that. All she cares about is those *books,* and I tell you, it's a *terrible* situation. My stars, what are we going to do? (Mama always smiled a little when she expressed herself on the subject of Caroline, and it was as though she were trying to belittle her concern. But she was belittling nothing; she actually was being most urgent and serious.) And so there was a complexity within Caroline, and none of us understood it. Even then, riding in that train with her on that July afternoon in 1909, and I just twelve years old and innocent of the ways of the world, I sensed that there was more to her than the quiet buttercup face and manner that she cultivated. At nineteen, she was a paradox—who had gently intimidated all of us. There was more to her, and she was less vulnerable, than appearances revealed, and I was respectful of her. Not afraid—simply respectful. And at the same time I loved her. And so all right, if she wanted to be ethereal and a bit grandly tearful, that was her business, and none of it was about to make the planet slide off its axis. I saw her tyranny as benevolent, and I was quite sure she meant no harm. I had never known her to be malicious. And after all, I was just twelve, and had more things on my mind than my sister's attitudes and strategems. (I had never been to Logan, and perhaps Logan would be interesting.)

Lydia Prentiss Corby was laid out in the front room of an older sister's home, and Caroline shrieked when she saw the corpse. It was the first time I had ever heard Caroline shriek, and the sound made me flinch. A dark young man came forward and led her to a sofa. Now she was weeping, but they were not the usual soft Caroline tears. They were harsh and dry, and they made me grimace. My cheeks were warm, and I knew I could not just stand there in the middle of the room, so I walked to the coffin and stared down at Lydia Prentiss Corby.

She wore a maroon dress, and the undertaker had made her lips too red. Her mouth was tightly closed, and I could not see her tongue. (I was remembering the concert and the way her tongue had moved so lovingly across her lower lip.) Her left arm had been draped across her belly, and her right arm lay at her side. A book was nestled on the blanket just beyond her right hand. I squinted down at it, and of course it was a Bible. They were burying her with a Bible. Well, imagine that. It was all very interesting, and it made for a worthwhile trip. Caroline had spoken of running and romping and playing, but they could wait until tomorrow. After all, a person could run and romp and play *any* time.

Rubbing my tongue against the roof of my mouth and tasting sweet salivary vestiges of the licorice, I must have stood over the Lydia Prentiss Corby coffin for a quarter of an hour, and perhaps longer, and I had little trouble blotting away the sound of my sister's harshly uncharacteristic tears. People came and went, and they said nothing to me, nor I to them. Perhaps, for all some of them knew, I was a Member of the Family. I decided it would be interesting to be a Member of a Family that had suffered a death. I had attended few funerals in my twelve years, but I did know that a Member of the Family received preferential treatment. He was placed in the front row, and he got to participate in all sorts of whispered conferences. Unlike the casual funeral guest, he always knew What Was Going On and What Would Happen Next. And he was black and silent, and people looked at him, and he was more important than they.

When I finally turned away from the coffin and looked back toward the sofa where Caroline was sitting, I saw that one of her hands was sandwiched between both of the dark young man's hands. Her tears had subsided, and she was whispering to the fellow. I drifted toward them, and Caroline was saying (her voice dry and pinched): ". . . an inspiration, yes. Exactly. An inspiration."

"I loved her very much," whispered the young man. "She was so gentle, and she so enjoyed the finer things . . ."

"Yes, Mr. Zachary, yes indeed . . ."

"She spoke of you very often. She was quite fond of you. She said you were, ah, sensitive and, ah, intelligent and, ah, quite a beauty. Which of course, now that I have met you, goes without saying . . ."

"Well, thank you . . ."

Mr. Zachary leaned close to my sister. Patting her hand, he whispered: "One time, when I was about seven or eight, I came down with the, ah, mumps, and she came to my room every day and read Grimm's to me. And something that had to do with Marco Polo. And I think some of the Uncle Remus stories. She had such a *gift* for reading aloud. She made everything seem so *dramatic,* if you know what I mean . . ."

"Yes," whispered Caroline, "that is a fact. Nothing ever was boring to her. She never languished. She never felt sorry for herself . . ."

"She would not want us to feel sorry for her . . ."

"Yes. I know that . . ."

"There are other worlds," whispered Mr. Zachary, "other planes of existence where there is no death, where there is nothing but gentleness and, ah, lovely clouds and sweet laughter . . ."

"Yes," whispered Caroline, "oh yes indeed . . ."

Mr. Zachary squeezed Caroline's hand.

Caroline smiled.

I turned away from them. They had not even seen me. A woman came over and asked me would I care for a nice glass of milk. I nodded, and I told her thank you ma'am, and she led me back to the kitchen. She poured the milk from a tin pitcher and told me goodness, Sonny, what a sad time this is for all of us. I told her yes, I know it is. I sat at the kitchen table and sipped at the milk, while she bustled about, fussing with a tray and some glasses. She filled the glasses with something crimson that came from a large brown crock. Smiling, she told me it was nice homemade wine for the grownups. Then she scuttled out with the trayful of brimming glasses, leaving the crock on the table. I lifted the crock, and it was heavy, but I managed to pour some of the wine into my milk. I shook the glass, swirling the wine and the milk, mixing them together. I had read *Dr. Jekyll and Mr. Hyde,* and I smiled. The mixture was a smeary sort of pink. I grimaced, baring my upper teeth. Then I gave a quietly demonic little laugh and began to drink. The liquid tasted like wet candy. The liquid was warm going down, warm as cat fur, and I belched. Blinking, I said to myself: Maybe some day I'll be important. Maybe some day I'll get to sit in the front row. I drank down all of the mixture, and my cheeks and eyes became hot, and again I belched. Leaning against the surface of the table, I cautiously stood up. I took the glass to the sink and rinsed it in water from the tap, and the last traces of the pink mixture made flabby gurgling sounds as they went down the drain. I giggled. I wiped my forehead with the back of a hand.

I returned to the front room. Caroline and Mr. Zachary still were sitting on the sofa, and they still were whispering, and her hand still was locked in both of his. I stood next to the sofa, but they did not acknowledge me, and my breath tasted peculiar.

The funeral was held in a Presbyterian church, and a skinny woman sang hymns having to do with the love of a Benevolent Creator. Caroline and I sat *near* the front, but of course we did not sit in the *very* front. Dusty sunlight smeared the coffin and made it golden, and from time to time I belched, but I covered my mouth each time, and Caroline apparently heard nothing. She sat with her hands folded in her lap, and a corner of her forlorn little handkerchief protruded from between her fingers. Mr. Zachary, who was sitting two rows in front of us, glanced back at her a total of fourteen times —this according to my careful count. This Mr. Zachary obviously was a very important fellow. He was sitting in the absolute front row, and it was clear that he had a complete grasp of What Was Going On and What Would Happen Next. His face was coarse and quite dark, but he had a splendid moustache, and his cravat was neatly tied. He wore a gray suit, and a black band had been pinned on an arm of his suitcoat, and he smiled a little each time he glanced back at Caroline. Her eyes were pink, and her clasped fingers squirmed like insects, but she acknowledged each of the smiles with a wan little smile of her own, and it was as though she and Mr. Zachary were sending telegrams back and forth. And she talked to me all the way home . . . on the train to Lancaster and the interurban to Paradise Falls. She spoke of how deeply she would miss her friend Lydia Prentiss Corby, but mostly she spoke of her *new* friend Mr. Zachary. She said: "I really believe he understands how I feel about the world. And I really believe he understands gentle things and delicate emotions. There seems to be nothing *heavyhanded* about him, if you follow me. Most men are so, well, obvious and *impatient* and *loud* —but I don't believe *he's* that way hardly a bit. He has *read books*, and there is a *serenity* to him, and it's all very exciting, Howard. It really is. Very. He says he will come see me. Do you think he will? I hope so. I want him to. He has such a nice voice, and he knows how to smile without making it seem, well, *forward*, if you follow me. Ah, *listen* to me. Listen to your shy retiring sister. Listen to her blabber on. Oh, she really is *something*, isn't she? Well, I think I'm entitled. It's about time I stopped being such a terrible *stick*. It's about time I, ah, *opened my wings*, wouldn't you say? I am not such a ninny that I have to spend the rest of my life sitting all alone with no one to . . . ah, Howard, I feel that something *tremendous* and *scarifying* and *grand* is about to happen to me, and I can hardly wait. I mean that. And oh, by the way, what on *earth* is the matter with your breath? Did something crawl in your mouth and *die?* And, for heaven's sake, why have you been *belching* so much? Something wrong with your tummy?"

And so there came into existence a Caroline none of us had known, a garrulous Caroline, a Caroline who had been made excited by the serenity (and never mind the paradox) of a man named Delbert Donald Zachary. And he did indeed come see her. And so began the courtship of Delbert Donald Zachary and Caroline Louisa Amberson. It lasted a year, and then they were married. He lived in Lancaster, where he was a typesetter for a newspaper. He owned a 1905 Ford, and he drove it down to Paradise Falls every Saturday while he was courting Caroline. He was most gracious and polite, and he told us he did not propose to be a typesetter forever. "It may sound ridiculous for me to make this sort of confession," he said, "but there is something very large and clamorous within me. I honestly feel the approach of a Calling, something far more profound than the setting of type. It nudges at me, and it nips at my soul, and some day it will emerge, and it will lead to a substantial fulfillment, and I will have left my imprint on this globe."

We were all amused by Delbert Zachary and his rhetoric and his global imprints, but he and Caroline certainly were devoted to one another. Beyond that, printers made reasonably good wages, and there was really no reason to believe he would not be a good husband for her—and never mind the hyperbole and the silly intimations. And finally, as Mama pointed out, it wasn't as though the male population was breaking down the front door with a battering ram in its anxiety to get at Caroline. And so Mama welcomed Delbert Zachary, and she was more than willing to make any allowances that were necessary. And the rest of us took our cue from her, and my brother Alvin Jr. even grew a moustache that was the spit and image of the one worn by the saturnine and polysyllabic Del, as we came to call him. (It certainly is a short name, said Mama, for a fellow who uses such long words.)

The newlyweds honeymooned in French Lick, Indiana, and Caroline sent me a postcard showing a tinted montage of the place and its sundry attractions. Then they settled in Lancaster, renting a small white frame house on the south side of town. Numerous visits were exchanged, and Caroline promptly became pregnant. The baby, a girl, was born dead in the spring of 1911. It was in 1913, after a second baby, a boy, had been born dead, that Del Zachary began to drink. The exchange of visits became less and less frequent, and by 1914 they had stopped altogether. Del was dismissed from his newspaper job in 1915. He sold his car, borrowed five hundred dollars from an aunt and opened a small job printing shop on a side street not far from the Pennsy yards. The shop failed in 1917, and by that time he was sober perhaps one day in seven. And his moustache had become stringy, his hair unkempt. Caroline took a job clerking in a millinery establishment, and she read Holy Scripture a good deal. I was attending Ohio State in those days, and I occasionally journeyed down to Lancaster to visit my sister and her shambling husband. (But not too often, since that was the year I became involved with the delightful and enthusiastic Joanna Lyman, who took up almost all my free time.) Still, I did *occasionally* see the Zacharys, and the visits made me feel, well, helpless.

Caroline was having trouble with her teeth, and several of them had fallen out, but otherwise she appeared unchanged. The dead babies had not done noticeable harm to her figure, and her manner was just as elegant as ever. "Nothing is easy," she told me, "and we cannot permit ourselves to surrender. We must have faith, and then perhaps we shall—in the ultimate judgment—prevail." (It was at about this time that I first became aware of her fondness for the editorial We. It was too oratorical and distant for my taste, and I wanted to tell her to come *off* it, but I never did.)

As for Del Zachary, it was clear that the nature of his clamorous intimations never had revealed itself to him. He seldom left the house, and Caroline brought him whiskey every other night or so. He was unfailingly polite to me, and he always managed to smile, but at the same time I was aware that something had loosened his bones, and his movements all were flatfooted and flabby. He seldom wore anything other than pajamas, a robe and a pair of frayed gray slippers, and he neither shaved nor bathed as often as he should have. He spoke of an epic poem he was writing, but I never saw a sample of it, and I am not altogether sure it ever existed outside of whatever it was that passed for his mind. I once or twice asked Del for permission to read at least a fragment of his work-in-progress, but he refused, telling me that no one, not even Caroline, would be allowed to read a single line of it before it was completed. "Please indulge my kittenish attitude," he said, "but the creative process is, you see, exceedingly private, and it would make me immensely uncomfortable if anyone were to see my work before it was completed to my, ah, satisfaction." (Del scratched himself a great deal, and his breath almost always was foul. It smelled like eggs, and sometimes I almost was willing to swear I could see yellow clouds of it. And then there were his eyeballs, which were pink. And his fingernails, which were torn and split. He drank his whisky from a jellyglass, and now and then, when he was thinking, his tongue slid from his mouth and lapped and caressed the rim of the jellyglass.)

Caroline always was present when I talked with her husband. Perhaps she did not trust us alone together; I do not know. She and I usually were perched side by side on the sofa, and she invariably smiled at her husband, then turned to me and said something to this effect: "Ah, Howard, you see, we believe in our husband's abilities. He is no ordinary man. It would be unjust to apply conventional standards of accomplishment to an artist and a creator . . ."

And, after listening to this recitation, I invariably said to myself: Yes, that is correct. He is no ordinary man.

And Del invariably smiled at Caroline, and his teeth were as yellow as his breath. And the jellyglass rose defiantly to his lips.

It was clear to me that something should be done about the Del Zachary situation, and there were a number of family discussions on the subject, and my father said: "All she has to do is give the word, and I'll go up to Lancaster and fetch her home. But, until then, just what am I to do? She is an adult, and her life is her own, no matter how miserable. She knows how we feel, and she knows all she has to do is open her mouth one time. But I refuse to abduct her; I refuse to treat her as though she were a runaway child. Tell me, Howard, do you see that as being some sort of abdication on my part?"

"No," I said. "I do not."

"It would have been different if her babies had lived," said Mama.

"I expect so," said my father.

"Babies mean a great deal to a woman," said Mama.

"And perhaps they meant a great deal to Del," said my father. "His drinking dates from about the time they were born dead, and perhaps that is no coincidence."

"If one of *my* babies would have been born dead," said Mama, "I don't know what I'd have done. Just to *think* about it turns my stomach."

Ernest and Alvin Jr. were with us, and Alvin Jr. said: "I'm glad *I* wasn't born dead. It would have cramped my style for fair."

"That is a *terrible* thing to say!" said Mama, laughing.

"Yes, Mama," said Alvin Jr., snorting. "But you know *me,* Alvin the dumbbell." He covered his mouth and cast his eyes downward in what I supposed was an attempt at an expression of mock contrition. Meantime, Mama and my father were laughing, and so was Ernest. I glanced at the mantel, and the clock was ten minutes slow, so I went to it, set it, inserted the key and gave it a vigorous winding. The works squealed. It seemed to me that Alvin (the Dumbbell) always could make my parents laugh, while I (who everyone agreed certainly was no dumbbell) never had the knack. . . .

I remember one afternoon, when I was only six years old, Alvin Jr. had come slambanging and laughing across the back yard, flourishing Fred Suiter's britches. "Fat pig! Him and his Pope!" he yelled, exploding into the kitchen.

Mama had turned from the stove, her face had reddened and she had said: "You nasty boy you!"

Giggling, Alvin Jr. coyly covered his face with Fred Suiter's fat Papist britches. "I was doing the work of the Lord."

I was sitting at the kitchen table. I snickered. But Mama glared at me and said: "Sonny, I want you to leave this kitchen. Otherwise, you're going to share in the whipping."

I scooted from the kitchen and went slamming into the pantry, but I stood just inside the pantry door, waiting for the sound of blows. But Alvin Jr. continued to giggle, and then there was a low sound, and it came from Mama, and it was a chuckle. "If I die before my time," I heard her say to Alvin Jr., "you'll be responsible, you terrible little devil you."

"Heathens deserve what they get," said my brother.

"That's not a proper thing to say," I heard my mother answer.

"Then why don't you whip me?" he had asked her.

"I wouldn't dirty my hand."

Alvin Jr. laughed. He laughed out loud.

And my mother laughed, too. She laughed out loud.

I remember that my face had gone hot. I had always liked Fred Suiter.

I did not question my mother but went upstairs to my room and counted the rosettes that decorated the wallpaper. (Even though I was only six, I was able to count and do sums up into double and even triple numbers.) But I never learned how to make my parents laugh. . . .

It was in 1919 that I discontinued my visits to my sister and her husband. By then, I was courting Anne Howell, and I went to Lancaster quite often to call on her at Ed Wohl's place, but I never stopped in to see the Zacharys. I was beyond knowing what to do for them, and clearly they wanted their doom to remain private. (Doom? Yes. Doom. There was no other word. It had foul breath, and it nourished itself from a jellyglass, and it much favored the editorial We, and what other way was there to define what was happening?) Therefore, since they chose to reveal nothing, and since their only posture was one of pitiful smiles and ridiculous words having to do with the creative process and some sort of work-in-progress that probably had no existence in fact, and since I lacked the wit and the style to give them any sort of comfort or assistance, I chose not to call on them at all. And, for their part, they chose to disaffiliate themselves from the family. They did not even attend the gatherings at Christmas and the other holidays. Perhaps, for all I knew, they had given themselves an overdose of Caroline's legendary Magic Gas. (What was it that *happened* to people? Del Zachary had been eager and ambitious, a handsomely saturnine fellow with certain bookish pretentions and a nice little gift for polite discourse, but then some sort of cruel stinking joke had been played on him, some weakness or corruption revealing itself, depriving him of knowing the nature and extent of his alleged Calling, and it had transformed him into a foul hulk that uttered windbag words, a shuffling beslippered jellyglassed mound of unbathed human junk that mumbled platitudes having to with the creative process. Sometimes, when I thought too deeply on my wrecked brotherinlaw, I felt a colossal and quite uncharacteristic fury come all aboiling in my belly, and I had to remind myself: There is nothing you can do. Whatever has happened to him will forever elude you, and there is no point brooding about it. And yet, despite the reminder, I still wanted to know what it was that had *happened.* I could not avoid examining the question, and I could not avoid asking myself whether *I* would forever be immune to the wretched thing that had so thoroughly flattened Delbert Donald Zachary, who had not really been such a bad fellow at the beginning.)

And so see now 1922, and a resolution of sorts. Something is devouring my sister's bones, and she lies dying in the bedroom of that small white frame house on the south side of Lancaster (the neighborhood has gone to pot, and there is a loud ramshackle brothel directly across the street, and every night drunkards visit the place and holler loudly for their Muriels and their Coras and their Rosies), and Del Zachary is drunk in the front room, and my brother Ernest is trying to get him to drink some hot coffee, and the doctor has said there is no hope for Caroline. She has a cancer, and there is of course no way to prevent it from chewing her to shreds. "Cancer is cancer," the doctor has told us, "and what more can I say?" (He is a thin fellow, and his two upper front teeth seem to have been soldered together. They put me in mind of a rather pretentious tombstone.)

The doctor has left (there is nothing he can do, and so he has gone off to a hospital to see some patients for whom there still is hope— and I do not blame him for this), and I am standing alone at the foot of Caroline's bed. She is awake, and she smiles at me, and she motions with her eyes for me to come closer. I do not really want to come closer, but I obey. I have not seen her in more than a year. The last time we talked was just before I was married, and Anne and I bought her lunch in a hotel restaurant. I remember that Caroline wore a white flowered hat that day, and I also remember that its brim was frayed, with sad disheveled little threads hanging in droopy clusters here and there. And I remember that Anne was quiet and thoughtful after we had taken Caroline home. She said not a word about Caroline's hat, but she was a woman, and I was sure she had noticed it. She spoke just once, and all she said was: "My, how pretty your sister still is." I glanced sharply at Anne, and I was annoyed. Why had she said *still?* To me, the word was an acknowledgment of some final and permanent ruin. Oh yes, I believed my sister to be doomed, but somehow *Anne's* recognition of the doom was an outrage. By becoming obvious even to a stranger, it became certified, sealed, stamped and beyond hope of change. And therefore I was angry with my Anne, but of course I said nothing. That sort of naked behavior was beyond me, and all my life I had suppressed emotional words. Sometimes I wondered what had become of them. Were they strewn about on the floor of my belly like broken glass? Would they eventually fill it to its ceiling? What would happen then? Would my belly burst? And so now, as I lean over my smiling dying sister, and knowing that in any normal person this would indeed be a time for emotional words, I wonder how many more of them I will be able to abort before they begin scratching the ceiling. Outside the door, Ernest is arguing with Del Zachary, and my mother and father are sleeping in a room off the kitchen. They have been up all night with Caroline, and now it is my turn to be with her, and she wants to speak, and I am not at all sure I want to hear whatever it is she has to say. But I know my duty, and so I lean over her. Caroline moistens her lips with a gray tongue and whispers: "We know what they think . . ."

"How's that?" I ask her. I seat myself in a straightbacked cane chair that is next to the bed.

"They think the dead babies were . . . responsible. Well, they weren't . . ."

"We've always been very sorry about them," I tell her.

"Ah, it . . . it would have happened anyway . . ."

"What?"

Caroline's head lolls toward me. Her cheek rubs the pillow. "We have . . . fixed so . . . many *dinners*, and we have . . . smiled, oh yes indeed, *smiled* so nicely at all our customers, the blue is quite flattering to your eyes, Mrs. Schmitz, do you . . . ah, understand what we mean? We have your best interests at heart, really we do, and the dead babies had . . . nothing . . . to do with it, do you hear?"

I have no idea what to say, so I simply nod.

"We . . . feel . . . so . . . *exalted* . . ."

"Yes, Caroline."

"This is . . . Howard, isn't it?"

"Yes."

"Not afraid. Not grieving. Only exalted, and no one can . . . share it with us. A . . . private . . . ecstasy . . . beyond care or fear or . . . even praise God . . . sentiment . . ."

I rub my eyes, and my vision explodes.

Caroline continues: "There were many penetrations, but he hurt us in such a . . . oh my God such a delicious way. Please don't think he . . . betrayed . . . us. That would be . . . unfair."

"All right." My hands come away from my eyes.

"We like to talk . . ."

"Yes."

"We did not formerly like to talk, but that was . . . before we met . . . our dear Delbert. He made us talkative, didn't he?"

"Yes."

"I talk . . . and I talk . . . and I used to talk secretly a great deal, but tell me, how many have . . . listened? Whether secretly or . . . publicly, why has there been such a small . . . audience?"

"I don't know. Why don't you rest now? I don't think all this talk is the best—"

Caroline pays me no mind. She shakes her head and whispers: "Later is . . . time enough for . . . ah, silence; no, I like my dolls very much; they never sass me, and I keep their faces clean; yes, I will, always; if the love were not always there, how could I exist? Yes, but you're *always* making a botch of the inventory and turning around and blaming *me* for it, and I tell you it's not *fair* . . . what happens to the Lily Maid of Astelot when she lives across the street from a brothel? Oh . . . Howard . . . Howard . . . you are right here, aren't you?"

". . . yes."

"Don't blame my Delbert . . ."

"All right."

"I want to talk . . ."

"Yes," I tell her. "All right. You go ahead. Whatever it is, I am listening.

". . . please, my precious thoughtful brother, don't blame him, please oh please don't do that . . . he is not . . . deliberately . . . what he is. If he hurt me, please believe me when I tell you he hurt me in a delicious way, and this is a . . . fact . . . of . . . nature . . . Please, please be courteous to him. You don't *know*, you see, how many times he . . . lay his head against my chest and . . . wept . . ."

I hug myself. I rock from side to side, and the cane chair makes wrenching sounds.

Caroline's mouth is wet, and now she is whispering more thickly than before. ". . . oh yes, I believe there still is . . . room in the world . . . for polite discourse . . . whichever suits your fancy, although I must say I *do* prefer the cloche . . . Chopin was beyond me, but I fought bravely, didn't I? I, well, yes, there have been . . . so . . . many . . . books . . . to . . . read that Mama used to tease me and tell me I was on the . . . verge . . . of going blind . . . do I contradict myself? Very well, I contradict myself. See the vastness. Listen to the multitudes. Listen to the mockingbird. Listen to the mockingbird asinging all day long. Is that how it goes? I wish

I could remember. Howard, are you there?"

"Yes. I am . . . right here . . ."

". . . my Delbert, oh such a dapper fellow he was, and the way he could . . . ah, talk . . . I ask you to consider his feelings . . . his trumpet is real . . ."

"Trumpet?"

Now Caroline's eyes are closed, and I am barely able to hear her whispered words. I lean forward, and her breath is creamy and warm, and she resumes: "You see, my Delbert . . . hears . . . a trumpet, but he doesn't know where the sound is coming from. This is a sort of agony, isn't it? You see, he doesn't know . . . *why* . . . it sounds. Is it a warning or is it a summons? Can there be anything more . . . ah, frightening? Please answer me . . ."

"I don't know how to answer that," I tell her. I stroke her forehead and her cheeks.

Caroline's eyes pop open, and her tongue emerges, and she begins to die.

"Hello?" I say.

Her chin gives way, and more of her tongue is exposed. She stares at nothing.

"Caroline?" I say.

No movement. She is dead. I kiss her moist dead forehead. I weep. I press her eyes shut. Del Zachary is groaning in the front room. I think of Magic Gas, and it occurs to me that somewhere in our conversation Caroline abandoned the use of the editorial We. Perhaps this indicates some sort of pattern, a progression from the personal I of the young Caroline to the editorial We of the married Caroline and finally the personal I of the dying Caroline. Had her life been in the form of a sonata, moving from A to B and finally back to A in a sort of whispered incoherent coda? Oh God, what a thing to be thinking.

My mother and father come into the room, and my mother screams. Ernest comes into the room, and he has Del Zachary with him, but Del Zachary will not approach the bed. Mama and Papa kneel next to the bed, and they begin praying, and Del leans against the door. He is wearing his pajamas and robe and frayed slippers, and his fingers are laced across his belly, and now he is no longer moaning. His mouth is open, though, and he is breathing loudly. Ernest glares at him and starts to say something, but I hold up a hand. I go to Ernest and whisper: "Please. There's no sense talking to him."

"Jesus," says Ernest, turning away.

"I do believe," says Del Zachary, "I shall have a little snort."

Mama and Papa look up from their praying.

"What?" says Ernest. His back is to the rest of us, and his shoulders hunch.

"There's no sense . . . trying to explain . . . it's beyond that," says Del. He pushes himself through the doorway, and a moment later we hear a sound, a very quiet sound, of liquid being poured into a glass. And then a resumption of the groans, and they are louder than before.

Caroline is taken to Logan for burial in the Zachary family plot. Del's aunt, the one who loaned him the five hundred dollars to start the job printing business, pays for the funeral. I sit in the very front row, smack next to Del, who lo and behold is brighteyed and well-bathed, who smells of pomade, whose suit is crisp. He sits erect and calm, and his moustache is trimmed, his cheeks are shaved smooth as an egg, and his hair is combed just so. His hands are steady, and his breath has an odor of mint.

After that day, we never see him again.

He moves to Columbus, courts and marries a wealthy young widow, makes and loses at least three fortunes in grain speculation, then dies in 1938 of a stroke suffered while exercising with a barbell at the Columbus Athletic Club. He is buried next to Caroline, and the second wife joins them in 1961.

He died a successful man, the sort of man the world respects and admires. He was not destroyed. He should have been destroyed, but he was not. It is clear to me that nothing is clear to me. There are mysteries and there are mysteries, and I know I shall never understand what happened between Caroline and her husband, or why he first started to live the day she died (the obituaries used the word *zest*), and perhaps this is just as well. (Sonata form? Order out of chaos? Pardon me while I smile.)

The rest of the drive to Logan was graciously green and crimson. Ohio 93 rolled north through a country of small scrubby farms and deep woods, and the thunder diminished. Apparently the storm would move south of them. Amberson began to relax, and now his joints were not so stiff, and he was a bit hungry. He smiled at Anne and said: "There's a park at the south end of Logan. Kachelmacher Park. We can stop there and have a little picnic here in the car. Or maybe outside— if it's not too cold."

"Fine," said Anne.

"Kachelmacher was a mining man."

"Like C. P. Wells?"

"Yes."

"Well, that's very interesting."

"You sound excited."

"Yes," said Anne. "I am absolutely *bursting.*"

"Good," said Amberson. "I wouldn't want you to be bored."

Anne smiled. "You are the limit," she said.

Amberson chuckled. The car thrummed, and now he was steering it easily, and there was little discomfort in his bones or anywhere else. He removed one of his hands from the wheel, and he whistled silently through his dentures. The car passed a mailbox that said MIZE, and it slowed for the flashing *20 mph* light in front of a small country school, and children were running and leaping in the schoolyard, and he was aware of caps and mittens and heavy stockings, and perhaps it was colder outside than he realized (he had turned on the heater some miles back—at Anne's request), and the car passed a mailbox that said STROTHER, and a mailbox that said RUPLE, and the sky had been scraped clear of clouds (except to the west and now the south), and a rumpled chicken pecked disconsolately at the side of the road, and Amberson said: "Perhaps we should play a game."

"What sort of game?" Anne asked him.

"A things-we-are-seeing game."

"How is it played?"

"We take turns listing the things we are seeing. Right now, for example, I am seeing a double yellow line that I am prohibited to cross."

"A car is coming toward us," said Anne. "And now it has passed us."

"I see a wire fence, and there is a metal CLABBER GIRL sign attached to it," said Amberson.

"I see a brick house with smoke coming from its chimney," said Anne.

"I see telephone poles," said Amberson.

"I see a sign advertising a restaurant called BLOSSER'S," said Anne.

"To our left, I see cattle grazing in the shade of a large maple tree," said Amberson.

"They are Guernseys," said Anne.

"I see haystacks," said Amberson.

"I see the outline of distant hills," said Anne.

"I see a mailbox that says W. W. SHERIDAN," said Amberson.

"I see a truck approaching," said Anne.

"It is a coal truck," said Amberson, "a gypsy coal truck."

"It has now passed us," said Anne, "and its driver was wearing a moustache."

"I see a fillingstation," said Amberson.

"The sign says TEXACO," said Anne.

"A man is wiping the windshield of a Chevrolet," said Amberson.

"There is a large dog in the back seat of the Chevrolet," said Anne.

"It is better to have a small cat," said Amberson.

"Yes," said Anne.

"Are you enjoying this game?"

"Yes."

"Good," said Amberson. "Now then, I see a house trailer, and it sports a very tall television aerial."

"It is painted green," said Anne. "The trailer, that is, not the aerial."

"And whoever lives there has taken the trouble to mow the grass that surrounds the place," said Amberson.

"WHITNEY lives there," said Anne, "according to the mailbox."

"I regret to report that there is a dead raccoon in the road," said Amberson.

"The poor thing," said Anne.

"Yes," said Amberson.

"It is too bad we didn't take a blind person along with us," said Anne.

"Yes," said Amberson. "He would have appreciated all this."

"Or she."

"Am I a male chauvinist?"

"Perhaps."

"I see a cat," said Amberson.

"Where?"

"To the left. Sitting in front of those bushes. A yellow cat."

"Oh yes," said Anne. "I see it now."

"And now I see a sign that is in the shape of the state of Ohio, and the numeral 93 is written on it."

"Well, I'm glad we're not lost," said Anne.

"Ah, but when one is footloose, what difference does it make?"

Anne shrugged. "None, I suppose."

"I see a yellow car approaching," said Amberson.

"A woman is driving," said Anne.

"She has blond hair," said Amberson.

"It goes well with the car," said Anne.

"And now a red car is behind us," said Amberson.

"It wants to pass," said Anne.

"It is passing," said Amberson.

"It has passed," said Anne.

"Another milestone in the history of American motoring," said Amberson.

"Absolutely," said Anne.

"I see a curve, and a hill, and an oak tree, and a sign that says WARNING NO HUNTING ALLOWED."

"I see a crow in yonder field."

"I see *two* crows in yonder *other* field, the one to the left," said Amberson.

"My crow is larger than your crows," said Anne.

"If you say so," said Amberson.

"He seemed assertive."

"Good for him."

"He just flew off."

"Gone but not forgotten."

"I wish *I'd* said that."

"You have my permission to write it down for future use," said Amberson.

"Thank you," said Anne.

"I see a lovely lady," said Amberson.

"Where?"

"Right here in this car. Sitting next to me."

"Ah, and *I* see a handsome gentleman."

"Where?"

"Where do you think?"

"At my age, is it empty and ridiculous for me to say I love you?"

"No," said Anne.

"Well, I do love you," said Amberson.

"Rave on," said Anne.

"I mean it," said Amberson.

"Yes," said Anne. "I believe you do."

"Let me rave in peace."

"All right."

The highway curved sharply to the east just before entering Logan. It followed the south bank of the Hocking River for perhaps a mile, then came to the entrance of Kachelmacher Park. Amberson guided the car into the parking area and pulled up next to a picnic shelter. It was deserted, and it had a vague odor of damp wood. He opened his window part way, and the fresh air was cool.

"Don't open it all the way," said Anne. "We don't want Sinclair jumping out."

"Yes, I know. Would you like to get out?"

"Do those tables and benches look dry?"

"Yes," said Amberson.

"All right then, let's get out."

Sinclair hopped into the front seat, and Amberson stroked him. Then, grunting with the effort after sitting so long, he and Anne got out of the car, leaving Sinclair inside. It was unfortunate that Sinclair had to stay inside, but Amberson was in no condition to chase after him in case he strayed away. Anne carried the sandwiches and the thermos, and she picked a table where there was sunshine. Amberson breathed hollowly, and he was able to see his breath. He judged the temperature to be about fortyfive. Anne unwrapped a ham sandwich and gave it to him, then poured coffee into two plastic cups she had brought along. The coffee steamed busily. Amberson rubbed his hands together, then took a bite out of his sandwich. He glanced at her, and saw that she had unwrapped no sandwich for herself. "Aren't you eating?"

"I'm not hungry," said Anne. She fished a jar of Preem from the bag. She poured the Preem into her coffee, then stirred the mixture with a green plastic spoon. She sipped at the coffee. She blinked at Amberson. "It's all right," she said. "I'm just not hungry. We had a nice breakfast, remember? I had an egg and *two* pieces of toast."

"Well, we do want you to keep up your strength."

"For what? I am *dying.*"

Amberson carefully set down his sandwich. "Anne, we are all dying," he said.

"But I mean right *now* . . ."

"Please don't be moody. This is no time to be moody and sad. Please, Anne. Please don't."

"And why shouldn't I be? I don't understand *any* of this. I want to be in my own home when I die."

"This has nothing to do with dying. We're here because we *seek,* because we have a *purpose.*"

"The exploration and conquest of Kachelmachel Park. Very exciting."

"It is Kachelmach*er* Park."

"I never could pronounce the name of this place. But who *cares* how it's pronounced? Howard, I do love you very much, but I just don't know what you're *up* to."

"Is that so important?"

"Yes."

"Suppose I were to tell you I didn't *exactly* know *what* I was up to? Would you believe me?"

"Maybe."

"We have talked about it at some length, but it's still ambiguous—and maybe *that's* the purpose."

"What?"

"To get rid of the ambiguity. If a pattern can be found, then the ambiguity will be pushed away."

"Will it be found in Kachelmachel Park?"

"Kachelmach*er*. I don't know. If I did know, then the answer would be clear."

"The answer to what?"

"The answer to the question of what is happening," said Amberson, grunting. He picked up his sandwich and took another bite. He swallowed. He drank some of his coffee, and it was hot and strong. Anne had supplied him with a flowered paper napkin, and he wiped his mouth. "Please, Anne, *please,* all I ask is that you let this thing happen. We have two thousand dollars. As soon as half of it is spent, we shall head for home. Or perhaps even sooner, depending on whatever strikes our fancy. If we are overcome by an urge to return to our house and the rhubarb plants and all those photographs and our television set and all the rest of it, all right, fine, we shall do so. But, for the next few days at least, can't we be properly footloose?"

Anne spread her arms on the table, then opened her hands like a beggar seeking alms. She made a shrugging movement. "All right," she said. "All *right.*" She removed her arms from the table. "Tell you what I'll do."

"What's that?"

She opened the sandwich bag and reached inside. "You're right," she said. "I do have to keep up my strength. So I think I *will* have one of these things." She pulled out a sandwich, unwrapped it and began to eat. Smiling, her mouth bulging, she held out her coffee cup and mumbled: "Your gooh healt . . ."

Amberson touched his cup to his wife's. "Be brave, old girl," he said.

"Umpf," said Anne, "never you mine abow tha ol grl stuf . . ."

Amberson gave a great snort, and Anne batted her eyes at him, and he thought of Betty Boop, and his snort became an outright laugh.

See now 1911, and I am fourteen years of age, and I am running. It is autumn, and I am a freshman at Paradise Falls High School, and I wear spectacles and knickerbockers and knitted sweaters, and every afternoon I run, and I am laughing, and the running tears the laughter out of me in jets and gasps. I am running alone in a woods behind the school, a quiet woods where no one comes. I run in an easy openmouthed lope, and twigs snap, and the hardening earth stings my feet and my legs, and it all is mine, and no one need share it, and the sky is topped with suds, and not Mama, not Papa, not Alvin Jr., not Ernest, not Caroline and not even Del Zachary (whom I think I admire) knows even a hint of what happens to me here in this cool and leafy place every afternoon when school is out and I am free to test some final and impossible thing that roars within me and tells me yes, yes, some day by the grace of God you will *fly!*

The treetops clabber at the sky, and my lungs suck and shrink, suck and shrink, and my head and shoulders are scraped by low branches, and occasionally I stumble and fall, and occasionally my knees and face bleed, but I feel no pain, and because I *feel* no pain, there *is* no pain, and I lurch ahead, and my only opponent is myself (I need not abuse another, which delights me), and occasionally a small animal is frightened away by the ferocious blundering noise I make as I come laughing and pumping and thrashing over the leaves and the twigs and the reluctant earth, and my hands are in claws that *push* the air behind me, and my shoulders churn and knot, and my laughter comes as a series of squeals and wheezings, and I rejoice, and I shall of course live forever.

This is my first totally private thing. No one will learn of it. It is myself versus myself, but it is also myself in conjunction with myself. I am private, and I never have twitched at stereopticon shows, and I offer few opinions, and I am obedient in school, but none of this means I am subdued. I am *not* subdued! I *run!* I *test myself!* I laugh into the wind, and I suck the wind, and earth and leaf and sky whirl behind me, and so I flap, and I squeal, and my legs are tight as wires, and nothing will defeat me, and I shall of course live forever.

To bound, yes. To bound and thrash and churn. To whoop at God and challenge Him with lungs and legs and laughter. To press toward an ultimate defiance of His natural laws by some day leaping up, and up, twisting and sailing and then, with an enormous shout of jubilation, a great splintered caw of a cry that will seize His attention and perhaps cause Him to give some sort of profound celestial blink, to go *flying away!* Oh, yes, yes, praise God! (I am fourteen years of age, and I shall of course live forever.)

Anne ate half of her sandwich, and an accommodating Amberson finished it for her. He finished a second cup of coffee, and he and Anne gathered up the wrappers and deposited them in a trash barrel. Then they returned to the car, and Sinclair crawled on Anne's lap and began to purr. She had brought him a cup of water from a spigot in the picnic shelter, and he noisily lapped at it.

Amberson leaned against the steering wheel, but he did not start the engine. "There's something I'd like to ask you," he said.

"Go ahead," said Anne, scratching Sinclair behind the ears.

"As long as we're in Logan, do you suppose we could, ah, well—"

"Visit your sister's grave?"

". . . yes."

"Of course we can."

"Well," said Amberson, "we've already visited *one* cemetery today, and I'm trying very hard not to be morbid."

"One more grave won't kill us," said Anne. "I didn't know her very well. I didn't have the chance. But I know you loved her, and that's good enough for me."

Amberson started the car. "Well, I appreciate your indulging me."

"It was *you* who did the indulging *earlier.*"

"How's that?"

"Back in Paradise Falls this morning, who originated the idea of driving into the cemetery?"

"Oh," said Amberson.

"So don't put the burden of our madness all on *your* shoulders."

"Isn't 'madness' an extreme word?"

"We live in extreme times," said Anne.

"Is that a quotation from *Future Shock?*"

"No, sir. It is a quotation from Anne Howell Amberson."

Amberson drove across the city of Logan, and it was leafy, and a three-for-thirty-cents sale on Mounds bars was advertised in the window of a Rexall drugstore. Amberson told his wife he surely had enjoyed his sandwich and a half, and she told him he was getting to be quite a glutton in his old age. He told her that perhaps later he would stop someplace and buy them both some candy. The Logan cemetery also was on a hill. The Pontiac edged along another narrow roadway, rounded a curve, then came upon the immense

ZACHARY

Caroline L.	Delbert D.	Ruth P.
1890–1922	1882–1938	1902–1961

LORD, GRANT THEM PEACE

monument. It was white marble, and it was perhaps four feet high by fifteen feet wide, and a plump whitehaired woman was sitting atop it.

Her ankles were crossed daintily. She was eating a sandwich and drinking from a can of Rolling Rock.

See now 1937, a morning in early November, and a man named Elmer Carmichael, who is president and chief executive officer of the Paradise Falls Clay Products Co., is shouting at me. He and I and the other cemetery trustees have gathered in his front room to discuss the Horace O. Button lawsuit. There are seven of us, and I am the only one not in favor of fighting it. I have pointed out that we are about to let ourselves in for a great deal of unfavorable publicity, and to what purpose? The morality of the matter is clear, and we are on the wrong side. But Carmichael, never a moderate man, disputes this. "Goddamnit," he says, "people have a right to rest in peace."

"All people?" I ask him. "Or just white people?"

Elmer Carmichael is standing at the mantel, and I am seated a few feet away. He glares down at me and says: "People have a right to be with their own kind. We've never had trouble with niggers *before,* and now it's a goddamned *white man* who starts it. If he wants to fuck a pickaninny, that's *his* business, but he's not about to get her buried in Oak Grove."

"He has a lot, and it's paid for."

"Sure, but it's for *him.*"

"It is a double lot."

"Shit," says Elmer Carmichael. He is a large man with a flat face, and he is perhaps fiftyfive. He whacks the mantel with an open hand, and then he says: "It's . . . ah, it's *misrepresentation!*" He faces his soninlaw, a flabby and pallid young man named Hugo G. Underwood. "Well, Hugo, you're a lawyer—isn't that right?"

"Yes," says Hugo G. Underwood. He is slumped in a wing chair. "That is correct. I am a lawyer."

"I didn't mean *that,* you goddamned idiot! I'm asking you: Is it or is it not misrepresentation?"

Hugo G. Underwood shrugs. "I don't know. I would have to read through one of the contracts. Until I do, I shall have to remain a goddamned idiot."

"Oh, for Christ's sake," says Elmer Carmichael, "try to keep from bleeding all over the rug, will you?" Then, turning back to me: "Howard, I always knew you were one of those fairy Rosyfelt suckholes, but that doesn't mean you're going to make any trouble for *me.*"

My hands are in fists, and there is a gurgling in my throat, and I cannot remember ever having been so frightened, but I manage to say: "I don't want to cause any trouble, but there's a principle here, and I think it must be defended."

"What the fuck are you talking about?"

"Decency."

"What?"

"It would be indecent, and it would be cruel, not to permit the burial of Emerald White in Oak Grove Cemetery. I know of no more direct way to put the thought."

Elmer Carmichael shakes his head. "You know what I do with *my* niggers, don't you? Whenever one of them dies, I have him shipped back to wherever he came from—and at my expense. I pay for the box, and I pay for the ticket back to Mississippi or wherever, and I even pay for a preacher down there. Is that indecent?"

"If that's what *they* want, it's not, no."

"I've shipped seventeen dead niggers back home since 1916. Tell you what. I'll pay to have her packed off anywhere Button wants her to go. Anywhere at all."

"My God, that's not the point."

"Point? What point? I'll pay for it out of my own pocket."

A man named Ervin F. Truscott speaks up. He is the secretary and treasurer of the Paradise Falls Clay Products Co., the man who succeeded my late father at that position in 1920—for reasons that I never have been able to determine. For a man of sixty, he is handsome in a florid way. His voice is actorish and declamatory, and he says: "It all sounds very reasonable to *me.*"

"Attaboy, Erv," says Hugo G. Underwood.

It is my turn to speak, and I look directly at Elmer Carmichael and say: "I don't believe any purpose will be served by continuing this conversation." I stand up, and now I am facing Elmer Carmichael more squarely. My fists begin to shake, so I jam them into the pockets of my trousers. "I shall do whatever is necessary to open Oak Grove Cemetery to Emerald White," I tell Elmer Carmichael. "I don't like to lose my temper this way. It's ridiculous. But you have forced me into it. You have made me behave uncharacteristically. Well, by God, as long I am behaving uncharacteristically, I might as well stick by my guns. So hear me, Elmer. Hear me and believe me when I tell you that if you persist in preventing this burial, I shall join with Dr. Button in the suit. And, as a cemetery trustee, I am an interested party, wouldn't you say? I know little about the law, but it seems to me that my name on that document would carry some weight."

"He's right," says Hugo G. Underwood to Elmer Carmichael. "If he joins in the suit, it'll mean we won't have a united front—and, even if he and Button lose, his name on the paper will almost guarantee an appeal being heard. Which means it could go on and on. And you, as the chairman of the trustees, would receive a lot of publicity, and not much of it favorable. And remember, there are a great many liberals in this country, and some of them even buy brick and tile."

"Do you think I give a damn about *that?*" Elmer Carmichael asks his soninlaw.

"Yes," says Hugo G. Underwood, and he is perspiring.

"You sure are talking big," says Elmer Carmichael.

Hugo G. Underwood shrugs. He studies his lap, and sweat rolls down into his eyebrows. His face is pink. He flicks at the sweat.

It is again my turn to speak, and I say: "Elmer, I am not, ah, kidding. I mean every word of what I just said."

"But what the hell difference does it make to *you?*"

And now I begin to shout. "My God! Don't you ever *listen?* It's immoral, Elmer! *Immoral!* That's spelled I-M-M-O-R-A-L! It means lacking morality!"

"You sonofabitch! I can have your ass reamed from here to Circleville! What the fuck *are* you but a goddamned nearsighted shrimp *schoolteacher!* And just how long do you think you're going to hold on to your job?"

"You're not bullying *me,* Elmer!" I holler. "If you have me fired because of this, the *stink* will go all the way to Circleville—*and back again!* My God in Heaven, you ought to *see* yourself! You're acting like a . . . like a *villain* in a *melodrama!* Harriet Beecher Stowe would have paid a fortune to have met someone like you!"

Now Elmer Carmichael is leaning against the mantel. "I'm going to have your balls for this," he tells me. And he is not shouting. His voice is flat, and he is simply stating a fact.

I feel as though I am about to vomit, but I am able to lower my own voice, and I say: "Like hell you will."

Then I turn and walk out of the room and out of Elmer Carmichael's house. I am forty years old, and I am trembling like a sick dog, and my armpits have begun to drip. My shoes scuff at leaves, and my hands are clammy, and we have six hundred dollars in the savings account, and I suppose the Columbus school system will be my best bet. It has a fine track program. I wonder how I will be able to tell Anne of what has happened this morning. She knows I have planned to argue in favor of the burial of Emerald White in Oak Grove, but she has warned me to be careful, and of course I have not been careful at all. My footsteps feel remote, and it is as though I am walking encased in glass. In all the years since the birth of Henry the Always Boy, Anne and I never have invited Dr. Button and Emerald White to take supper with us, and so why then have I jeopardized myself for them? Is it guilt? Or am I really a champion of decency? I wish I knew. All I do know is that I have never thought much about Negroes one way or the other. I favor social justice, and I have voted twice for President Roosevelt and will vote for him again if he seeks a third term, and this is all very well and good—but isn't my feeling for social justice really an abstraction? What do I know of poverty and bigotry? Oh yes, we occasionally drive through the village of Blood, and the place's ramshackle squalor is enough to make one's belly growl, but we are nonetheless *outsiders;* we have *experienced* none of it. And yet, for all that, the exclusion of Emerald White from Oak Grove has angered me deeply, and it still angers me, and the devil take my job. Elmer Carmichael can curse and condemn me from here to Circleville to Timbuktu to the moon, and I do not give a damn. Right is right, and I will not back away. I am forty years old, and my world sees me as stiff and bookish and quietly thoughtful, but perhaps there is more to me than that. Ha, and perhaps there also is a tendency in me to inflate myself. Ha. Ha. Very amusing. (I think of my boyhood, and I think of my glorious ambition to run so fast that some day I would fly, and I think of all the squirrels and chipmunks that scattered in my urgent relentless path, and of course I have to smile, and now some of the tightness is drawn from my bones, and the glass casing is shattered, and gradually a distance is achieved, and I say to myself: Alvin Jr. once called me a tiger—but then the tiger decamped for parts unknown, and I was no longer a tiger. And then today the tiger returned, a fearsome prodigal come to smite the bigot. A tiger with spectacles. A fairy Rosyfelt suckhole tiger. My goodness.) I walk straight to school, and by the time I arrive, I am back to my normal self, whatever that is. I rinse my face in the faculty men's room; I comb my hair; I straighten my necktie. The mirror reveals an unvexed Howard W. Amberson, a neat little fellow, always calm and precise. Because of the cemetery trustees' meeting, my first two classes have been excused, but I meet as usual with my third class, and we have a lively discussion of Poe's House of Usher tale. (The amusing aspects of this do not escape me.) Late that afternoon, when I come home from school, Anne is waiting for me at the front door. She demands to know why I did not telephone her and tell her what happened at the meeting. I shrug. I tell her there was nothing significant to report. She frowns, asks me whether I am fibbing. I assure her I am not. I tell her the matter is still up in the air. I let it go at that. I try to change the subject, but Anne wants to know more. She asks me whether words were exchanged. I admit there were a few. She asks me if there were any bad feelings. I tell her oh, no, no indeed, we were all very gentlemanly. I smile, and I hope enough of my teeth are showing. Her curiosity abates somewhat, and then the children begin arriving home, and she has other matters to occupy her attention and I am of course relieved. Florence, who is seven, gets to crying over the fact that the roof of her doll house has caved in, and Lewis, who is twelve, complains because this is the third straight evening he has been conscripted to walk the dog, and Henry the Always Boy, who is fourteen, tootles vainly on his trumpet scales, and I sit alone in the front room and listen to all this sweet commotion, and I think of ruin and exile, and finally I can stand it no longer, so I go down cellar, fetch a hammer and nails and set to work trying to repair the doll house. After whacking away for an hour or so, I manage to restore the roof (after a fashion), and Florence rewards me with hugs and squeals and kisses. I briefly consider calling everyone together and telling the exact truth of what happened this morning, but I cannot do this. The tiger has again decamped, and all that remains is Howard W. Amberson, and he definitely is not the fellow for such a job. And so I let it go. I smile at the children. I am Papa, and nothing vexes Papa. I am in charge. I am in control of myself. I am the civilizing force. I am justice. I am mercy. Nothing frightens me. I eat my supper calmly, and I know when to smile and when to speak, and the room bubbles with the chatter of my wife and my children (down cellar, the furnace roars crisply, and the November chill has been banished, and I pity those hapless strangers and criminals and homeless who must endure it), and two portions of Anne's meatloaf move snugly into my belly, and oh what the devil, no matter what happens, the universe will not fall down, will it? Then, just as Anne is pouring my second cup of coffee, the telephone rings. I twitch a little, but Anne does not notice. The telephone is on a table in the front hall, and she hurries to answer it. She returns a moment later and tells me great balls of fire, it is none other than Mr. Elmer Carmichael *himself.* Henry grins at me and begins to applaud. Florence joins him. Anne shushes them. I shake my head, rise, wipe my mouth, leave the kitchen and walk down the front hall to the telephone. I walk slowly, and I feel like a condemned felon in a George Raft movie. I pick up the receiver. "Hello?"

"Hello, you miserable Rosyfelt-loving sonofabitch, this is Elmer Carmichael."

"Yes. I know it is."

"I've got news for you, hotshot."

I lean against a wall. I sigh. "Yes," I tell him. "I expect you do."

"It's not the news you're expecting, buddyboy."

"Oh?"

"We're going to go ahead and let that nigger whore be buried in Oak Grove. Hugo's just been talking with your friend Button, and he's agreed to drop the suit."

"Of course. And apple trees sprout walnuts in the spring."

Elmer Carmichael laughs. "Hey, that's a pretty good figure of speech—but I'm not lying to you. It's all over. All. Over. You and Button and the nigger whore have carried the day, my friend."

"How am I supposed to believe that?"

"Because I'm *telling* you, that's how."

"Excuse me, but is this the Elmer Carmichael with whom I, ah, exchanged, ah, imprecations this morning?"

"It's none other than," says Elmer Carmichael.

"Then you'll have to explain."

"All right," says Elmer Carmichael, "that I'll do. Now, we left it with you storming out of my place, right?"

"That is correct," I tell him. I have no idea what any of this conversation means, and I suspect I have gone mad, and it all is part of some fevered lunatic dream.

"Well," says Elmer Carmichael, "I was so goddamned pissed off it's a wonder I didn't poop prunes. And I hollered and raved at the other fellows like I was about to declare war on the fucking solar system. And nobody was going to tell me a thing. I was out to nail your ass to the flagpole, and that was all there was *to* it. So I set out to do just that."

"But you changed your mind?"

"That's right. I changed my mind because it isn't going to work."

"What do you mean?" I ask him.

Elmer Carmichael laughed again. "I got you guessing, haven't I?"

"Yes. That is absolutely true."

"I made some telephone calls, that's what I did. The other fellows were right there with me in my front room, and I called the superintendent of schools, and he said to me: 'Mr. Carmichael, it won't work. Howard Amberson is too well liked, and he is too good a teacher. The town won't sit still for it.' "

"Mr. Milligan said that? You talked to Mr. Milligan?"

"That I did, and that's what he said. So I called your principal—what the hell's his name? Everhart?"

"Eberhart. Mr. Eberhart."

"Yeah, that's it. Eberhart. And he told me what Milligan had told me. And so then I called old Pat Coughlin at the *Journal-Democrat,* and *he* just about had a stroke. He told me Jesus Christ, half the town knew you from the school and the track team and all that shit. And what's more, according to him, you got a way of making people listen to you. I spelled out for him what you said you would do, how you were threatening to join with Button in the lawsuit and all the rest of it, and old Pat damn near choked on his false teeth. He said to me: 'Elmer, I've known you for a long time, and I kind of even like you, you rotten skunk, so you better believe me when I tell you Howard Amberson means what he says.' Wellnow, I respect old Pat, so I sort of took his words to heart. I hung up the goddamned telephone, and I talked it over with the other fellows, even that fucking sissy of a soninlaw of mine. We thrashed it out for the best part of two hours. And we decided what the hell, that darky bitch can rot in Oak Grove for all we care. One of the reasons is that you're against us, and I guess you're stronger than I thought. But there are *other* reasons. Would you like to hear them?"

"Yes. Very much."

"All right. *Number One:* No dead nigger is worth the money we would have to spend to fight the goddamned thing through the courts. *Number Two:* The longer we fought it, the more sympathy we'd lose. And let's face it, the country is in the hands of Rosyfelt's bleedyhearts, and they got a way of twisting things to suit their own fucking niggerloving purposes. *Number Three:* There's no profit in it. Dollarwise and centwise, we don't make a nickel from it. *Number Four:* Hugo tells me we'd probably eventually lose the thing in court anyway. There are too many liberal judges, he says, and I sure as hell agree with him on *that.* So, if we're bound to lose, why go into the thing at all? And finally, *Number Five:* You stood up to me, you puling little niggerlicking sonofabitch you. You're just like your father. He was a mean little pisser too. And I like that in a man. I honest to God do. I'm forever surrounded by asskissers and fucking backbiters, so I *got* to respect a man who's carrying more between his legs than a thing he takes a leak out of. This making sense to you?"

I am rubbing my throat. My face is warm, and I very much want to laugh. Anne comes in from the kitchen and stands frowning at me. I place a finger to my lips, and then—keeping my voice steady—I say: "Yes. I understand what you're saying."

"We're going to raise a little hell about it, you understand."

"How's that?"

"We're going to make a show of not wanting Emerald White in Oak Grove. That way, the town'll think we've done our duty. I've given Pat Coughlin a lot of bullshit about how the law is tying our hands and all that sort of thing, we have no choice, blah blah blah . . ."

I nod. "All right. It's a minor point." I feel rather magnanimous, like General Grant at Appomattox.

"There's something else I want to talk to you about," says Elmer Carmichael.

"Oh? What's that?"

"You aren't making enough money to keep a frog in cold water, are you?"

"What?"

"If it wasn't for your cemetery money, you'd be on county poor relief, right?"

"Not exactly, but what's your interest in all that?"

"Well," says Elmer Carmichael, "in view of what's happened, it may sound crazier than a whore with her tit caught in a cement mixer, but how'd you like to come work for me?"

"I beg your pardon?"

"You heard me, you miserable little pisser you. I want you to come work for me. I'd start you off at twice what that goddamned school system pays you. What do you make? Two thousand a year? Hell, I'd give you five."

"And what would I do?"

"Jesus Christ, *I* don't know. We'd figure that out after you came aboard."

"This is the most ridiculous thing I've ever heard," I tell him. I raise my eyebrows and smile at Anne. Her face is wide, warm, astonished, even a bit stricken. "There's no way in the world I will entertain your proposal."

"*Entertain* my *proposal*? Shit, you sound like a goddamned virgin telling her boyfriend oh, Rodney, Rodney, get your hand off my twat, this is so sudden . . ."

I begin to laugh. "No . . . no," I tell him, "it's all just too absurd . . ."

"You think I'm being funny?"

"No . . . I, ah, I realize you're not *trying* to be, but it's just that . . . well, I appreciate the offer very much, but the thing is impossible . . ."

"You mean that?" he asks me.

"Yes. Absolutely."

"The offer surprised you, didn't it?"

"Yes. Of course it did."

"Well, you little cockface bastard you, you should never say 'of course' when you're dealing with people."

"I don't understand."

"When you're dealing with people, you never should expect the expected. You've always thought of old Elmer Carmichael as being the prize asshole of the western world, right? Well, shit, just what the hell do you *know* about Elmer Carmichael? Just what the hell does anybody know about anybody? Maybe, for all *you* know, I take a big fat teddybear to bed with me every night."

"Do you really?" I ask him.

The other end of the line explodes in a series of snorts and guffaws. I hold the receiver away from my ear. This day has been absolutely too much for human comprehension, and how have I been able to survive it? Finally Elmer Carmichael subsides enough to tell me to go take a flying shit in a soupbowl, and his laughter is rich, and I tell him I am very grateful for the suggestion and will treasure it forever, and then we hang up, and I press my forehead against the wall, and my laughter is rusted and cracked, and Anne anxiously plucks at my shirt and demands to know what has happened, and how in the name of God can I tell her so that she will understand?

But eventually I do tell her, although I do not tell her all of it. I edit down all the shouting and the threats. They would disturb her, and where would be the sense in that? The really important thing is that Emerald White and Dr. Button and I have won, and I do not seek to take upon myself any undue gallantry. If indeed it exists, it exists only when the tiger comes calling, and he is not what one would describe as a frequent visitor. Oh yes, it is comforting to find that there are those who like and respect me, and I am flattered and pleased, but I know I cannot permit that sort of thing too much freedom. The earning of affection and respect is an ongoing process; it must be renewed each day, and one cannot afford to be smug about it. (Still, I do wish I could go to Mr. Milligan and Mr. Eberhart and old Pat Coughlin and thank them for their kind words. But I cannot do this. It would reveal too much. It would call back Elmer Carmichael's anger—and my own—and what purpose would be achieved? The sooner the entire incident is forgotten, the better off we all shall be.) I wonder if I have learned anything from all this, and I think perhaps I have. From now on, I doubt that I shall rely so heavily on appearances and rhetoric. Elmer Carmichael has taught me this. Granted, he is a greedy bigot with the vocabulary of a whoremaster and the manners of an ape. But I have discovered a further dimension to him, and it is humorous and almost genial. In addition, it hints at a terrible huddled loneliness that whoops and shudders somewhere within him. His offer to me was genuine. I am certain of that. It came from the terrible huddled thing, and it reveals him to be not quite the dreadful loudmouthed monster most of us have always believed him to be. (He lives to the age of eightyseven, dying in the summer of 1970 of a liver ailment. Until the end, his only concession to age is a large knotted cane, and he remains loud and obscene up to his final breath. For years we smile at one another when we pass on the street, and he rags me mercilessly about what he calls my niggers. And yet I feel a sort of love for him, and I genuinely mourn his passing, and I doubt that Harriet Beecher Stowe would have known what to make of him.)

Anne and I attend the funeral of Emerald White, which is held in the front room of Dr. Button's house on North High Street. Only four other persons are present. One is Dr. Button, two are undertakers and one is a Negro clergyman imported from Columbus. The man becomes a trifle overwrought, and on two occasions rushes to the coffin and kisses the corpse while delivering the eulogy (he never met Emerald White), but the service is at least reasonably brief. Emerald White is fortyseven according to Dr. Button, but she still is remarkably handsome. She has died of an embolism that followed a stroke, and she appears utterly undamaged. (Perhaps this is why the minister kisses her. Perhaps he believes his kisses will work some sweetly magic spell and bring her back to life.) The minister and the two undertakers and I serve as pallbearers, and the coffin is heavy, and I say to myself: There should be some lesson here. A good woman dies, and this town cannot even supply a full complement of pallbearers for her. She was a mistress, and I know there are those—such as perhaps Elmer Carmichael—who honestly believe she was a whore, but she also performed an abundance of good works, and we all have witnessed them, so why doesn't this coffin have six men carrying it? What possible harm could there be in *that*? (I am perspiring freely by the time we slide the coffin into the hearse, and I am full of an enormous sadness that is larger than simple grief.) Anne and I ride with Dr. Button to the cemetery. He has become shrunken and wrinkled, and he tells me for perhaps the fiftieth time that he is extremely grateful for my help in opening Oak Grove to Emerald, and *I* tell *him* for perhaps the fiftieth time it was the least I could do. He does not weep. He does not speak of his feelings for Emerald. Anne pats his hands, and he says: "I thank you." Two sprays of flowers are left at the grave after the coffin is lowered. One of the sprays is from Dr. Button; the other is from Anne and me and the children. Dr. Button retires from active practice the following summer. His health deteriorates, and he finally dies in January of 1941. His estate, when probated, comes to nearly fortyseven thousand dollars. It is left in its entirety to a fund for the construction of a hospital in Paradise Falls. He must have loved Paradise Falls. It is all very strange. But then it must be pointed out that he and Emerald White have chosen to stay there forever. They lie close together, and the earth is Paradise Falls earth. Hopefully, the Lord has granted them peace.

"Well, for heaven's sake," said Anne, "look at *her,* will you?"

Amberson braked the car to a stop. Sinclair hopped into the front seat, and Amberson idly stroked him behind the ears and under the chin.

"Are we going to get out?" Anne wanted to know.

Amberson smiled. He switched off the engine. "Of course we're going to get out," he said. "That woman is a gift from God."

"Oh?"

Amberson gently lifted Sinclair and deposited him in the back seat. "She is part of the apparatus, I think. Perhaps she will be instructive." Then Amberson opened the door and stepped out of the car. He walked around the car and opened Anne's door. "Please, madam, won't you come outside into the sunshine?"

Up on the monument the woman was smiling at them. Her waist and torso were thick, but she had slender legs. Her white hair was in a sort of upsweep, and she appeared to be about fifty. She was wearing a gray coat that had white fur cuffs and collar.

"Hello there," said the woman, smiling.

"How do you do," said Amberson.

The woman's sandwich appeared to contain cheese. Still smiling, she ate the last of it, took a deep swallow from the can of Rolling Rock, then removed a handkerchief from her purse and wiped her hands.

Amberson and Anne advanced until they were standing within a few yards of the monument.

"Oh," said the woman. "Oh *dear.* Is someone you knew buried here?"

"Yes," said Amberson. "My sister was Caroline L., the one to your right."

"Goodness," said the woman. "Oh, this is terrible." Quickly she hopped down from the monument, then took away her purse and the beer can from its top. She cradled them in her arms, and then she said: "I can imagine what you must think of me."

Amberson started to say something, but Anne interrupted him. "It's all right," she said to the woman. "It really is."

"Yes," said Amberson. "That's absolutely correct."

"You think I'm crazy," said the woman. "And I can't say as I blame you."

"No," said Amberson. "Really. We don't think any such thing."

"Really we don't," said Anne.

"I dress well," said the woman, "and I don't *look* crazy, do I? Why, you know, people have always told me I have good legs, and in my day I was a fine figger of a girl, to say the least. The boys used to say hubba. Do you remember when boys said hubba?"

"Yes," said Amberson. "And sometimes they leaped about and scratched themselves like chimpanzees. It was their way of paying tribute to a pretty girl."

"That's right," said the woman, swallowing another mouthful of beer. "Right with Eversharp. Do you remember *that?*"

"Yes," said Amberson.

"I come here because of my husband, you know."

"Is he dead?" Amberson asked the woman.

"Well, if he *wasn't* dead, I wouldn't come *here*, would I?"

"No," said Amberson. "I suppose not."

Anne looked around. "Is he buried somewhere around here?"

"He's not buried here at all," said the woman. She took a last swallow of the beer, then walked to a nearby trash barrel and dropped the can into it. "He went down with the *Indianapolis*," she said.

Amberson frowned. "The *Indianapolis?*"

The woman advanced on him. She moved gracefully, and her hose whispered. "Yes," she said. "It was a cruiser, and it went down on July 30, 1945, at twelve-fourteen a.m. It was torpedoed by a Japanese submarine not far from Pelieu Island. Do you remember the incident?"

"No," said Amberson, "I'm afraid I don't."

"There were one thousand, one hundred ninetysix men aboard. Of that number, only three hundred sixteen survived. Of the eight hundred eighty men who died, a number were eaten by sharks. My husband was eaten by sharks. According to what I have learned, he survived the explosion in fine fettle. But his life raft collapsed, and the sharks ate him. It was three days before the navy even knew the ship had gone down. The captain's name was McVay, and he was courtmartialed. You don't remember any of this, do you?"

"No," said Amberson. "I'm very sorry, but I do not."

"And neither do I," said Anne.

"His name was Lewis Robinson," said the woman, "and he was a Seaman Second Class. Just a Seaman Second Class. Not an admiral or anything like that. Just a Seaman Second Class."

Anne smiled at the woman. "Was the Lewis spelled L-E-W-I-S?"

"Yes."

"We had a son named Lewis," said Anne. "He's dead now, too."

"I am very sorry to be hearing that," said the woman.

"Thank you," said Anne.

"It wasn't even three weeks later that the war was over," said the woman. "You'd think we'd have learned how to fight it by *then*. We were winning all the battles, but we lost the *Indianapolis*. Does that seem right to you?"

"No," said Anne.

The woman looked at Amberson. "To *you?*"

"No," said Amberson. "Not a bit right."

"Well, anyway," said the woman, "it's why I come here."

Amberson looked at her.

She smiled. "No," she said, "I'm not some sort of loopy. Maybe I behave that way, but appearances aren't everything, are they?"

"No," said Amberson. "Of course not."

"I come here because I think I am *entitled,*" said the woman.

"Oh?" said Amberson. "Entitled?"

"Yes. Please let me explain. I come here every day on my lunch hour, and somehow I am able to imagine my husband being here. He *deserves* to be *somewhere,* doesn't he? I mean, somewhere besides the belly of a shark. And, I mean, the shark is long dead now, too. And something probably ate *it.* And something probably ate the thing that ate the shark. And so forth and so on, like the House That Jack Built. So, anyhow, I have imagined for Lewis an existence within a grave in this place. Specifically, I have buried him here with these people named Zachary. I remember old Mrs. Ruth Zachary very well, and she was a nice lady, and she had a great deal of money. My brother Oliver buried her, as a matter of fact. She came here from Columbus right after her husband died in Thirtyeight, and she bought a big house on Hunter Street, and she visited this place day in and day out. She must have been really devoted to him. Did you know her?"

"No," said Amberson. "We never met her. We don't get up to Logan this often. We're from Paradise Falls."

"Yes. I know that."

"Oh? How?"

"Your car has Paradise County license plates."

"So it does," said Amberson.

"So anyhow," said the woman, "that's the story. I don't believe I am profaning this place, do you?"

"No," said Amberson.

"Not a bit," said Anne.

"I still take pride in my appearance," said the woman, "and I am not exactly the Madwoman of Chaillot, am I?"

"No," said Amberson.

"Not a bit," said Anne.

"Men still take me out to shows and parties," said the woman, "but I have never remarried. I am a truly monogamous female. Lewis Robinson was the only man I've ever loved. We were married in 1943, and we only had nine days together. Nine days *in toto,* as the saying goes. But I am willing to settle for those nine days. I am not a greedy person. He drove a bread truck, and he favored bow ties, and he looked a little like Donald O'Connor. You remember Donald O'Connor, I am sure. And I was the warm and bouncy Loretta Nelson, and we used to neck in the back seat of his father's Studebaker. I twirled batons in those days, and I trailed clouds of hubba behind me, if you know what I mean. Lewis considered himself to be a very lucky fellow, and he told me so many times. I was seventeen when we started going together, and I married him when I was nineteen, while he was home on leave. We spent seven of those nine days in the Poconos, and I tell you, sometimes the odor of pine needles still brings tears to my eyes. And so that's it. That's really it. There's nothing more to say. I am fortyseven, and perhaps my white hair makes me appear older, but I *do* try to keep myself looking as presentable as possible, and every day when I come here I sense that Lewis is somewhere near, smiling at me and fussing with his tie."

Anne took Amberson's arm, but neither of them said anything.

"The view here is lovely," said the woman. "Especially if you're sitting on top of that nice Zachary monument. You can see Logan, and you can see the Hocking River, and I like to watch the freight trains crawl past. I can think of no better place to spend a lunch hour."

"Do you work somewhere nearby?" Amberson asked the woman.

"I am the receptionist at my brother's funeral home. His name is Oliver T. Nelson, and he and I and his wife live on the second floor. It takes no more than five minutes to drive here." Here the woman pointed back over a shoulder. "My car is parked off beyond those trees."

Amberson nodded. He glanced at Anne. "Well," he said, "perhaps we should be on our way."

"Are you on your way home?" the woman asked him.

"No. We started out on a little trip this morning."

"Where are you going?"

Amberson smiled. "We don't know," he said. "We're trying to be genuinely footloose. We've lived a long time, and we simply—"

"We simply are crazy," said Anne, laughing.

The woman rubbed her chin. "You mean you've just gone wandering off with no idea of your destination?"

"Yes," said Amberson, and Anne nodded.

The woman grinned. "I think that's *wonderful,*" she said.

"You do?" said Anne.

"I *certainly do,*" said the woman. "Any time anyone does a free and open thing, it is good. I hope you have a good time. I think you will. I *know* you will."

"I appreciate your saying that," said Amberson. "My wife has had her doubts about all this."

The woman went to Anne and patted Anne's arm. "Have faith, baby," she said.

"Right on," said Anne.

They all three of them laughed, and the woman walked to the monument. "I still have nearly half an hour," she said, "so I believe I'll contemplate the world and think about my husband."

Amberson took a step toward her. "Would you like some help?"

"In what? Thinking about my husband?"

"No," said Amberson. "I meant getting back up there."

The woman smiled. "That won't be necessary. I'm very good at this. It's come with practice." She placed her hands on the monument, coiled herself, then jumped into a sitting position. She slid to the middle, dangling her slender legs over the H in ZACHARY. "Easy as pie," she said.

"Very nicely done," said Amberson. He and Anne started back toward the car.

"Have a nice trip," said the woman.

They turned and waved at her, and they both were smiling.

"Give my love to the world," said the woman.

"We'll do that," said Amberson.

Here I must briefly interrupt this catalogue of times past as time present. I have a sort of announcement to make.

I have turned back to the beginning of all this, and I have read every word that so far has been written. I have done this because I am seeking, as you know, some sort of pattern, some sort of logical progression that will explain my personal apparatus. There have been a great many words, correct? A great many births and deaths and comedies and collisions, correct? Caroline contained multitudes, and evidently so do I. But as yet there is no essence to be derived from all my words. The scheme still eludes me. Oh, there are obvious portions of the gridwork now visible, and the largest of them certainly is death. Or deaths. Or deaths upon deaths. It seems that every four or five pages I am describing someone keeling over, and perhaps to the casual reader (what casual reader? what reader at all?) this is absurd. However, in my defense I must point out that I am seventyfour years old—and when one is at such an age, one's history is punctuated by many deaths. They sit large. They rivet. They provide the measurement by which one can define one's survival. In addition, it is a bald fact of old age that death occupies more and more of the mind. One is surrounded by attrition. So kindly do not mock all these deaths. They exist in such abundance because I am so old, because nearly all those I have loved are gone. A death, like a mountain, is a large fact, and I shall not apologize for it. Still, death is not the pattern of all the words I have written. An element is not an explanation. And so now comes the announcement, namely and to wit: We must press on. The essence is not yet in sight. Therefore, more days must be examined . . . and even, yes, more deaths.

The Ambersons continued north and east on Ohio 93, passing through the old mining towns of New Straitsville and Shawnee (the landscape was similar to the landscape in and around Blood), and they discussed the woman they had met back in that Logan cemetery. Sinclair had returned to his perch behind the back seat. "Well, I'll tell you one thing," said Amberson, "for a woman of fortyseven, she certainly was handsome. And she had very fine legs."

"I wish you wouldn't use 'handsome' to describe a *woman*. It makes me think of *Clark Gable,* and I keep looking for a *moustache.*"

"You've been telling me that for fifty years. Some day I may learn."

"Some day in the sweet bye and bye, no doubt."

"Probably."

"And she'll come and sit on your tombstone."

"Good. The view of her thighs probably would be spectacular."

"She might spill beer on you," said Anne.

"I'd take the chance," said Amberson.

"She was crazy, you know."

"I'm not so sure."

Anne made a clucking sound. "Well, for heaven's sake, do *sane* people eat their lunches in cemeteries? Do *sane* people imagine their dead husbands fussing with bow ties?"

"*Unimaginative* people don't, but as for *sane* people, I can't say."

"In other words, as far as you're concerned, she was simply *imaginative* and nothing more?"

"Yes," said Amberson.

"Well, *I* say she was crazy. Pleasant enough, but crazy."

"A thought has occurred to me."

"And what might it be?" Anne asked her husband.

"If she is indeed crazy but at the same time pleasant enough, as you put it, then I believe I have gained a small insight. You see, I have always thought of crazy persons as being irascible and dangerous, with foamflecked lips and all that. But why should they all be that way? Isn't it possible for personality traits to be transferred from one state to the other? Isn't it possible for a gentle sane man to become a gentle lunatic? And, after all, aren't there graduations in the personalities of those who are sane? Don't we have crabby sane people, and trivial sane people, and happygolucky sane people, and sentimental sane people? If and when they go mad, do their *dispositions* necessarily change? Couldn't a trivial sane man become a trivial lunatic? Do I have a point or don't I?"

"I suppose you do, but you'll pardon me if I don't faint from the thrill of it all."

"Crazy people are people, Anne."

"I'll go along with that."

"For myself," said Amberson, "I thought that woman was rather gallant."

"In a crazy way."

"All right. In a crazy way. But at least she has a sort of governing *idea* going for her."

"What do you mean?"

"She has defined her life in terms of the nine days she had with her husband. She knows what is important to her. She knows where she stands."

"But she has wasted the years since then. All that peculiar business about having lunch in the cemetery and never marrying again is enough to make me want to shudder."

"If *I* had been eaten by a shark, would *you* have married again?"

"Absolutely—if anyone would have had me."

"You answered that very quickly."

"I didn't have to think about it. It's a logical and natural reflex. It shows the sort of person I am. Dead is dead, and the living should not sacrifice themselves."

"I should have said that to you when Henry was killed."

"Well," said Anne, "Henry was different. He was special."

"All those we love are special."

"But I never *ate lunch* at his *grave.*"

"I wouldn't have minded if you had. You're my wife, and whatever you do is important and proper."

"That is a sweet thing to say."

"I mean it," said Amberson.

"Yes," said Anne, nodding.

"I'll remember to stay away from sharks."

"I don't think you have to worry. We're in Perry County now, and there hasn't been a shark sighted in Perry County in years."

And then the Ambersons laughed, and the Pontiac followed Ohio 93 as it curved through Perry County, and the strippers had done their work here, too. New Lexington, the twin villages of Crooksville and Roseville, at one time quite famous for their potterymaking—now they were quiet. Amberson sighed. He supposed he should think of personal things, of the journal he was keeping, of Anne and the monstrous affliction that was devouring her, but his mind was drawn to the slag piles his eyes could not avoid, to the gray and brown mounds of dead earth that the strippers had left behind, to the desolate shops and factory buildings that stood boarded and shattered and silent. Here again was the apparatus (everything was the apparatus), but its function had been lost, and why had this been permitted? Why had this place been chosen to die? Had the people here committed some dreadful crime? No, such thoughts were nothing more than romantic postures; they did not move one toward any sort of mature answer. Brusquely he cleared his throat, and Anne glanced at him. He checked the speedometer, and it showed 40. She asked him did he feel all right, and he told her yes, I feel fine. He looked off to the west, and the distant grayness was gone, and it occurred to him that there had been no thunder for some time. He did not know precisely when it had stopped, but he was glad that it no longer was nicking at the edge of his consciousness, and he said to Anne: "Well, the day certainly has cleared up very nicely." And Anne said: "Yes indeed. That is a fact." They drove up Ohio 93 to a place called Moxahala Park, where it joined US 22 for a short stretch that led northeast into Zanesville. The highway was crowded now, lined with frozen custard stands and fillingstations and here and there a usedcar lot (tiny flags were strung in the usedcar lots, and they flapped busily, like trapped moths). Amberson slowed to 35, then 30, and he kept in the curb lane. Cars and trucks zipped around the Pontiac, and he said: "Everybody seems in a hurry to get to Zanesville. Perhaps someone is giving away free girls." And Anne said: "Humpf. Howard W. Amberson, the Dirty Old Man." And Amberson said: "Well at least if you smell an odor of goat, you'll know where it is coming from." And Anne said: "I can hardly wait." And then she and Amberson again laughed, and the sound of it was delicious to him. (Was laughter a part of the apparatus? Of course. Why not?) He cautiously steered the Pontiac through the Zanesville traffic, and he told Anne they might as well follow US 40 to the east; it was as good a direction as any. Anne shrugged. "You're the boss," she said. "You're the big footloose expert, and I am at your disposal." Amberson nodded and told his wife he surely did appreciate the generous spirit of cooperation she was displaying. The car edged through the crowded downtown section, and Anne glanced at the windows of dress shops and a department store, and she said: "When I lived with Ed and Christine, we knew some people who came from Zanesville. They were always talking about the famous Zanesville Y Bridge. To them it was as remarkable as the Hanging Gardens." And Amberson said: "Well, in its day it was really something." And Anne said: "Will we cross it?" And Amberson said: "No. We've already crossed the Muskingum. It was five or six blocks back. Didn't you notice it?" And Anne said: "Oh yes. So we did." And Amberson said: "We crossed on the famous Zanesville I Bridge." And Anne said: "Verry funnny." And Amberson said: "Thank you." East of Zanesville, US 40 paralleled the new Interstate 70, but Amberson wanted no part of Interstate 70. The speed limit there was seventy, and Amberson never had driven seventy miles an hour in his life. As a boy and a young man, he had been much taken with speed, and running had been one of the great golden things of his youth. And obviously it had led to his coaching of track for all those years at Paradise Falls High School. But his interest in speed had never carried over to mechanical contraptions. He had always been a slow driver, and a careful one (the qualities not necessarily being synonymous), and he had not even particularly cared to ride in fast trains. And he had never once been a passenger in an airplane. He had visited many parts of the United States, but always at his leisure, packing Anne and the children (when they still were young) into the car and taking off on loose and meandering motoring trips, as they were called in those days. And so he eschewed the gleaming Interstate 70 for the more anachronistic attractions of US 40. And here, east of Zanesville, the country was more placid, the farms more plump, and Amberson said to himself: Yes. A postcard America. They passed through the village of New Concord, which was the birthplace of John Glenn, the astronaut, and Amberson said: "A man from this little community goes whirling off into space, and meanwhile, right next door so to speak, Perry County is dying. I just don't understand it, and I don't suppose I ever will." And Anne said: "Then don't think about it." Sinclair had crawled onto her lap, and he was asleep with his forepaws covering his eyes.

It was barely 3:30 in the afternoon when Amberson decided to stop for the night, and Anne did not object. They checked into a motel just west of Cambridge, and Sinclair's box was the first thing Amberson carried to the room. He walked slowly, but he still was able to hear his heart. The sand had an odor of urine, but the odor was not yet particularly strong. Anne helped him with the suitcases, and within five minutes they were lying down, fullyclothed, on their double bed. Anne had carried Sinclair into the room, and he was sniffing in the bathroom, where Amberson had placed his box. "It's been an interesting day, but I am tired," said Amberson.

"So am I," said Anne.

"We went ninety miles today."

"A new alltime speed record. Barney Oldfield will whirl in his grave."

"Ah, but what difference does it make when one is footloose?"

"None, I suppose," said Anne. Her eyes were closed, and she was rubbing her right shoulder. She rolled on her left side, facing away from her husband. "I'm going to try to take a little nap."

"Do you want anything for your shoulder?"

"No."

Amberson nodded but did not say anything. He got out of bed and stripped down to his shorts and undershirt. He carefully hung his clothes in the closet, returned to the bed and again lay down. He was cold, so he slid under the covers. He listened to the sound of Anne's breathing. It was heavy and slow, and she already was asleep. Sinclair hopped on the bed and curled up at Anne's feet. Amberson reached down and stroked Sinclair behind the ears. Sinclair began to purr. Amberson smiled. "Good old fellow," he whispered. "Brave old Sinclair." Then Amberson closed his eyes and dozed off. He and Anne slept for perhaps two hours, and then they ate dinner in the motel restaurant and were back in the room in time to watch the NBC network news. They took baths, and watched television until perhaps nine o'clock, and then they went to bed. At ten, when he was certain

Anne was asleep again, Amberson crept out of bed, slipped into his clothes and went out to the car. The journal was hidden behind the spare tire in the trunk. He went into the motel lobby, smiled at the clerk, seated himself on a sofa and worked on the journal for more than an hour. At 11:15, by the lobby clock, he knew he was too tired to continue, so he returned to the car, hid the journal, then went back to the room. He undressed and crawled back into bed. Anne was snoring, and Sinclair was stretched out beside her, his belly and paws flat against the calf of her left leg. Amberson quickly fell asleep—but just before he did, it occurred to him that he had left the movie camera sitting on the table in the front hall back home. Ah, good God. Anne would slit his throat in the morning. Amberson placed a hand over his mouth so his laughter would not awaken his wife. He fell asleep with his hand still over his mouth.

Tuesday

See again 1931, and the night when I have promised Henry I will go with him on the last Paradise Valley Traction trolley from Paradise Falls to Lancaster. The line is converting to buses—and it is hoped that buses, with their ability to go anywhere business warrants, will attract new riders. In addition, abandonment of the interurban line (with its extensive private rightofway) will result in an annual saving of more than a quarter of a million dollars in real estate taxes. The PVT trustees say these economies *could* save the company, but there certainly is no optimism surrounding the possibility, and one of the trustees, a Lima banker with the somewhat inappropriate name of George P. Poore, has already accused several of the PVT's former executives of fraud and embezzlement. It is said that indictments are pending, but then the PVT has always been a colorful road, with a devious and rakish history. It was chartered in 1900, and for the first fifteen years of its existence called itself the Columbus & West Virginia. In view of the fact that the main line never extended farther southeast than Paradise Falls, this name was a bit pretentious, to say the least. And right from the start it was in trouble. In the first place, it paralleled an established steam road, the Columbus, Paradise Valley & Marietta. Second, construction costs were higher than the original owners had anticipated, and they had to borrow money to build the line even as far as Paradise Falls. Third, passenger revenues never reached the anticipated levels. Apparently no one at the C&WVa had bothered to examine the population figures for southeastern Ohio. Had they done so, they would have realized that this part of the state simply did not have enough people available for a healthy interurban business. But somehow the C&WVa did manage to stagger into existence, even though competition between the C&WVa and the CPV&M steam road was vicious and at times violent, especially after the C&WVa purchased fifty trailers and went into the freight business. There were numerous incidents of vandalism and deliberate derailings, and once there nearly was a murder. This struggle lasted for more than a decade, and it was not resolved until 1914, when the CPV&M was purchased by the Chesapeake & Ohio as distressed merchandise, and it was agreed that the C&WVa would get out of the freight business and the C&O would provide only as much passenger competition as the law demanded. And so the C&O lopped off four of the seven roundtrip passenger trains serving the area between Paradise Falls and Columbus, and the following year the C&WVa, facing facts, changed its name to Paradise Valley Traction. And yet, even after having most of the passenger business placed in its lap, the interurban line continued to be wobbly. The Great War was a slight help to revenues, but the slump of 1921 more than wiped out what little had been gained. And more and more flivvers were coming into use, and sometimes they were able to outrace the interurbans along the Lancaster road, and you could go anywhere you wanted in a flivver; it did not require tracks or wires or a motorman. The PVT tried all sorts of inducements (free rides for children under five, special holiday and excursion fares, group rates and the like), but nothing seemed to help. The trend had been established. In 1919, the annual report to the stockholders showed a loss. Since then, each annual report has shown a larger loss. And finally, less than six weeks ago, the road went into receivership. And then, last Friday afternoon, the trustees announced the last run at midnight tonight . . . the owl local from Paradise Falls to Lancaster. And it would pull along as many other cars as were remaining in the Paradise Falls barns. They had already been sold to a Columbus scrap firm, and a representative of the scrap firm, a Mr. Timmons by name, would be aboard to discourage possible thievery by those seeking souvenirs on the valedictory run. According to a statement published in the Paradise Falls *Journal,* the scrap firm's president was perfectly willing to part with bells, wicker seats, fareboxes, destination rolls and anything else wanted by sentimentalists—as long as they paid a reasonable market price for their treasures.

To make sure we will have plenty of time, Henry and I leave the house shortly after eleven o'clock. It is a night for insects, and there are no clouds, and Anne stands waving at the front door and tells us to be careful.

We will walk to the barns. The distance is seventeen blocks according to Henry, the map expert. The street is silent, and Henry says: "I sure do appreciate this, Papa."

"It should be very interesting," I tell him. "And an historical event, to boot."

"Listen to the bugs. When people are asleep, the bugs really set up a commotion, don't they?"

"Well, I suppose it is the only time they feel they can make their voices *heard*. The human race usually drowns them out, doesn't it? The human race usually drowns *everything* out, isn't that so?"

"Yes sir."

"Scurry and commotion are the order of the day."

"Yes sir."

In Paradise Falls, the blocks are short, and seventeen of them cover no more than a mile and a half, and Henry and I have plenty of time. Still, we walk briskly, and I begin to feel invigorated. I breathe in cadence with my steps, and I am reminded of the days when I ran track. I smile. I am silent. It is better to smile and be silent than to burden my son with any further portentous musings about the scurry and commotion of the human race. When it comes to platitudes, I yield to no one, not even politicians. Perhaps I have missed my calling. Perhaps I should have run for public office.

"I should get out and run more," I say to my son. "I am only thirtyfour, and this exercise still feels awfully good. I used to run a mile every day—but of course you know that, don't you?"

"Yes sir."

"I don't run enough with the fellows I coach. I should run right along with them. I should challenge them. Perhaps next year I'll do that."

"Yes sir. It sounds like a good idea."

"We had a better team than we showed," I say. "I shall have to work harder next year. There are two or three fellows, Tom Crider in the eight-eighty, for instance, and Bob Froelich in the mile, who ought to be able to qualify for Columbus. I shall have to work with them very hard. They are good boys."

"Yes sir," says Henry. He nods, and his footsteps slap and pound, and his head is bobbing, and perhaps he is hearing some secret music. Who knows?

The houses along Cumberland Street all are dark, and now and then a dog barks. I smell honeysuckle and tar and the high rich odors of grass. Here and there tree roots have created mounds in the brick sidewalk. The houses loom, but they do not frighten or astonish. I have been inside too many of them. I have lived here all my life, and I have eaten too many pieces of cherry pie in too many kitchens, and I have seen too many lithographs of the Blessed Savior, and my fingers have idly plucked pins from too many antimacassars, and I have stood at too many pianos and sung too many songs, and I have consumed too many helpings of fried chicken, and my familiarity with so many of these houses has done away with any fear or astonishment, and I know I am comfortable with this town, this Paradise Falls with its ponderously ironic name; I know I love the place, and I suspect I always shall love it. We turn right at Market Street and walk south to Main, then east on Main toward the barns. The PVT's single track runs straight down the center of Main, and all we have to do is follow it. Nothing is stirring. Henry and I see no one, and there are not even any automobiles parked at the curb. The Depression is just beginning to affect Paradise Falls, and old Frank Moore's newsstand went out of business a month or so ago, and the Ritz Dress Shoppe is rumored to be, ah, up to its hem in debt, and there are those who say that Ted Billingham's hardware store is about to go under. And now the PVT interurbans are leaving us forever, and I suspect that the situation will become a great deal worse. One of our newspapers, the *Democrat,* is also reported to be in trouble, and some pessimists are even speculating that the Paradise Falls Clay Products Co. may lay off as many as fifty men. And now, walking along Main Street with my son, I am aware of a sort of decrepitude. The buildings are too old. Some of them have reasonably new concrete fronts, but the buildings themselves all date from before 1900, and the concrete fronts cannot hide their sagging and withered aspect. And it occurs to me that not a one of them has been built in my lifetime—and I have been on this earth more than a third of a century. The buildings stand unevenly, and most of them are of brick, with immensely high arched Victorian windows, and there is something fragile about them, especially now in all this silence. It is strange to be experiencing Main Street at night, and the truth of Main Street rises up like a slap. And it is a truth of old age, and I am saddened. As surely as the old looming houses of Paradise Falls give me comfort, its dispirited business section does not. It is one thing for a place to be destroyed, but it is quite another for that place to sag and crumble simply from natural attrition. Surely something can be done about all this. Surely Paradise Falls will not fall down like an abandoned privy. And now I glance at my son as he hurries along beside me, and perhaps I am beginning to understand some of his grief for the interurban line that tonight will cease to exist. I say to him: "Are you really looking forward to this?"

"Yes sir," says Henry.

"But at the same time you're sad, isn't that so?"

"Yes sir."

"Then why are we doing this?"

"Ah," says Henry, "the thing is, sometimes the sad thing is the right thing. Somebody's got to be there, and somebody's got to say goodbye. That's the right thing—and sad don't matter."

"*Doesn't* matter," I tell him.

"Doesn't," says Henry. "Me and my dumb old grammar."

We cross Mulberry Street and Paradise Street and Morris Avenue, and now the stores and office buildings are behind us, and again we are in the presence of the old houses, and I begin to relax. "Well," I say, "it is more pleasant here, isn't it?" Henry does not reply. We cross Hill Street and Syria Street and Highland Avenue, and Henry is moving in a sort of trot. The houses are farther apart now, and then we come to Wells Street and the PVT barns. We see lights, and we hear voices, and a tall old interurban car stands on a siding that adjoins the barns. (Actually, these "barns" are more like sheds. They can accommodate perhaps six cars at the most. No shop work has ever been done here, and the sheds' only function has been the storage of layover cars. The PVT's main shops and barns are—or were—in Columbus.) Henry and I walk toward the lights and the voices, crossing the lot and scrambling over rails and ties and switches. Perhaps thirty persons are clustered around the tall old interurban car, and most of them are men. They are talking loudly, and some of them are laughing. The motorman is standing by the car's forward door, and I recognize him. His name is Caspar (Red) Bickerstaff, and one of his sons ran hurdles for me back in '27. He is a large man, and florid, and sometime shortly after the turn of the century he was a legendary football player at Paradise Falls High School—a fullback of remarkable attainments, I am told. His son, however, was a skinny little fellow, and I am afraid not much of a hurdler. The boy's legs were always bleeding from the hurdles they hit. Poor little Jack Bickerstaff, one of the great, ah, hurdlehitters of all time. I have not seen him in several years, and I get to wondering vaguely where he is and what he is doing. Perhaps, if the opportunity presents itself, I shall ask his father. But not right now, however. Caspar (Red) Bickerstaff is too busy talking with a stout rumpled man who is wearing a Palm Beach suit and a skimmer. The fellow has immense lips and poor teeth, and his complexion is yellowish. As Henry and I approach, the man points to the crowd and says: "They sheem lie a pree goo bunch of fellahs, Birstaff, buh you got to hel me if they may trouble. Your shtil an employee uh thish hear roah."

Caspar (Red) Bickerstaff grins. "Yessir, Mr. Timmons," he says, "you can count on me." He pushes his PVT cap to the back of his head and scratches a bald place above his forehead. He nods toward the car. "This here is your property now, and my folks taught me always to have respect for property. I come from a *good* family, Mr. Timmons, and that's a fact."

"Thangyew," says Mr. Timmons. He is swaying. "Thangyew vair muh."

Henry nudges me. "That the man from the scrap company?" he whispers.

"I wouldn't be surprised," I tell my son.

"He been drinking?"

"I wouldn't be surprised *a bit.*"

Henry smiles. "This here is going to be some ride," he says.

"I wouldn't be—"

"—surprised," says Henry, finishing it for me.

I laugh. I tell my son he is a devil. He laughs along with me. Now Mr. Timmons is clambering aboard the car. Several men hoot and whistle at him, and he grins. His skimmer slides forward, and apparently he does not have an overabundance of hair. He adjusts the skimmer. He teeters on the steps. More hoots and whistles, and he takes a little bow, which causes him to lose his balance, and he comes hurtling back down the steps, and Caspar (Red) Bickerstaff catches him. They embrace, and they do a brief dance, and everyone laughs, but Caspar (Red) Bickerstaff manages to keep Mr. Timmons from falling down. "Jesus H. Christ," says Caspar (Red) Bickerstaff, pulling away from his impromptu dance partner, "now you just take it easy, Mr. Timmons."

It is 11:55 by my watch, and people begin crowding aboard the car. Henry is among the first, and he grabs two seats just behind the motorman's little cubicle. Mr. Timmons, who has been helped aboard, is slumped across the aisle from us. The crowd comes tumbling and laughing into the car, and Caspar (Red) Bickerstaff is not bothering to collect fares. "Come on aboard!" he hollers. "Anybody who wants a free ride, come on!" He is laughing right along with everyone else, but I wonder how much of it he really means. Will he be able to drive a bus for the PVT? He has been a motorman all his adult life, but the driving of a bus is an altogether different proposition, and perhaps he will not be able to master it. Or perhaps he already has been told that his services no longer will be needed. At any rate, his laughter seems a bit too loud, his shouts a trifle forced, and his face too florid for a night that is not all that warm. I suspect that the trip will be even more interesting than I have anticipated, and I turn to Henry and say: "Well, I hope we get home all in one piece."

Henry nods. "Yes sir," he says.

"Madness," I say.

"Yes sir," says Henry. He looks away from me.

I know a great many of the passengers, and they nod and smile at me as they go pushing back to their seats. They include Patrick S. Coughlin, editor of the Paradise Falls *Journal,* who has brought a flashbulb camera and is busy popping away (the other paper, the *Democrat,* is not represented); David E. Faulhaber, the county auditor; Wes Scofield, who owns the local ice plant (which is in poor financial shape, I am told); old Bill Light, who owns a furniture store; Frank Partee, a deputy sheriff; Samuel D. Aspinwall, a foreman at the Paradise Falls Clay Products Co.; Lambert Graff, who operates a number of clay and gravel pits scattered through Paradise and Hocking counties; Bob Stulpnagel, a florist; and James N. (Jimmy) Jones, a salesman who is accompanied by his pretty wife, Elizabeth, and their son Walter, who is eleven or twelve. The Joneses crowd into the seats directly behind us, and Jimmy Jones leans forward and says to me: "This is the damnedest thing I've ever seen." I grin and nod, and Henry politely scrootches around and says hello to Mrs. Jones and Walter. Mrs. Jones smiles at him, and Walter squints out the window. (Even though he is three or four years older than Henry, Walter is a full head shorter than my son, and apparently this causes him some discomfort.)

The crowd also includes a number of men who are strangers to me. Many of them are wearing American Legion caps, and several appear to be as far down the road as the hapless Mr. Timmons, who now is lolling bonelessly and mumbling to himself. They come laughing and shambling, these Legionnaires, and several are brandishing bottles, and again Jimmy Jones leans forward, and this time he says: "They been over to Joe Masonbrink's place."

I nod. Joe Masonbrink is our most famous bootlegger, and he operates a speakeasy in the front room of his place on Wells Street. He owns several stills up near the old mining town of Blood. He is a scrofulously cheerful fellow, and everyone likes him, and he is fond of saying that Prohibition is the greatest thing that has happened to him since the night he first received pleasure from a woman.

"That's where the scrap man got drunk," says Jimmy Jones. "They took him with them. They'd all come down together on the nine-fifty-five, and they made a beeline straight for old Joe's place, and I guess this fellow's one of those men all he's got to do is smell the cork, you know?"

"It's probably his chemistry," says Mrs. Jones. She is in her late thirties, and she is perhaps fifteen years younger than her husband. She is brownhaired and slender, and she always has appeared to me to have great dignity. She was born and reared in Virginia, and she always speaks softly, and she always is called Elizabeth. Never Liz or Lizzie or Betty or Bess.

"Well, he certainly has a snootful," I tell them. I smile. I am quite fond of Jimmy and Elizabeth Jones. They are among our closest friends. (It was they who gave us poor Magnificent, our cat.)

"The Legion men from Columbus?" I ask.

"That's right," says Jimmy Jones. "I talked to a couple of them, and they told me they're just out having a good time. They said they want to give the old PVT a nice sendoff."

"I wonder why so many Paradise Falls people turned out."

"Same reason," says Jimmy Jones. "They want to say goodbye."

"It means that much to them?"

Jimmy Jones shrugs, smiles, spreads his hands. He is tall and knobbed, and he has gray hair and large teeth. "Suppose the court house was torn down. Wouldn't you go look?"

"Yes. I suppose I would."

"Well, Howard, this here's the same thing. These cars been going up and down Main Street for nearly thirty years. They're big, and they make a lot of noise, and it's hard to ignore them, right?"

"Yes."

"And year after year they sort of get more and more set in your mind, you know what I mean?"

"I think so."

"All *right* then," says Jimmy Jones. "So, when they *go*, the average person'll *feel* something. Me, I feel something. I been riding these cars all the thirty years, back and forth to Columbus, and I know every tie and switch and frog. You know I rode the first car to Columbus?"

"No. I didn't know that."

"Well, it's the truth. It was Nineteen and Two, and they served free beer and sandwiches on that first run, and I just about floated off, I tell you. I was in about as good a shape as this here fellow from the scrap company."

"*You,* an imbiber of alcoholic beverages?"

"Yessir," says Jimmy Jones. "I know that must come as a shock to you, but I cannot tell a lie."

And then we all laugh, even Henry and even the silent Walter. The last of the passengers comes tumbling aboard, and Caspar (Red) Bickerstaff climbs the steps and says: "Well, I expect this'll do her." He blinks at us, rubs his face, then slips into the cubicle and seats himself. He twists a crank, and the forward door slaps shut. The passengers applaud. Then, to louder applause, he pushes the control knob, and the car begins to move forward. It moves cautiously, clacking over switches, and Henry leans forward. The car slides past the sheds, and they are empty. Apparently all the stored cars already have been moved to Columbus, and so it will be this car—and this car alone—making the final run. There will be no trailers or dead-head cars sharing the journey, as announced, and somehow this seems most proper. The car's number, 404, is painted on the partition that stands just behind the motorman's cubicle. It is painted in what appears to be gold leaf, and the numerals are delicate and filigreed. The car has an odor of straw and sweat, but its motor hums comfortably, and there is a solid feel to its trucks as they clip over the railjoints. One of the Legionnaires is sitting across the aisle from me, smack next to the gelatinous Mr. Timmons. He grins at me and says: "This here is a good one, a Cincy."

I look at the man. I have no idea what his words mean.

The fellow is heavy, perhaps thirtyfive, and he is wearing spectacles. "The Cincinnati Car Company," he says, "rebuilt this here car in 1914 from an original Kuhlman of 1898. Changed it from wood to steel. Tell you something—with the right track and roadbed, it could rip along at eighty, and no strain."

"Well," I tell him, "you certainly seem to know a lot about it."

"They been my hobby since I was a boy. I got nearly a thousand photos in my home. I'm in the sporting goods business myself, but these here interurban cars been in my blood just about as long as I can remember. I'm the one who had the idea for this here ride. Got together with the boys Saturday night, and they thought it was a good idea. Why, even old *Fred Runyon* is here, and he's the post commander. He's the little one sitting in the back with the houndstooth coat on."

Henry leans across me. "You say eighty?" he asks the man.

"That's right, sonny. Eighty in a breeze."

"That's really something," says Henry.

"It surely is," says the man.

The car rumbles out of the yards, crosses Wells Street and begins its journey down Main Street. Caspar (Red) Bickerstaff is hunched over the control knob, and his head moves from side to side. I wonder if he is trying to memorize everything. I suppose he is. This is a large event for him, and he obviously wants to forget nothing. I glance out a window, and the homes and buildings seem different. I have been a passenger in these cars hundreds of times, but I never have noticed the difference until just now. The houses and buildings appear smaller, almost like decorations for a boy's toy train set. Henry and I have just walked along this same Main Street, but it was a familiar Main Street—it was in the proper proportion. This peculiar new Main Street has been diminished. We are riding so high above the pavement that we have by some magic of perspective been removed from reality. We are larger than reality, and somehow we are imperious and magisterial. A distance has been achieved, and it is not unpleasant. I glance back at all the laughing and jabbering passengers, and Bob Stulpnagel is nodding at something old Bill Light has said, and Lambert Graff is engaged in earnest discourse with one of the Legionnaires, and another of the Legionnaires is passing a bottle to Wes Scofield, and David E. Faulhaber is telling Samuel D. Aspinwall what appears to be a very long story, and the lights are too bright, and the laughter and jabber are too loud (a roisterous *trolleycar?* who ever heard of such a thing?), and I feel dislocated, and it is as though I am a stranger in my own world. I am encapsulated and alone, and what has happened to dimensions? Jimmy Jones grins at me, and I shrug, and then Caspar (Red) Bickerstaff pulls the bell cord and sets off a clamor. He grins back at us and hollers: *"What the hell!"* And the passengers begin to cheer. And Henry is cheering with the loudest of them. Caspar (Red) Bickerstaff pulls the cord and he pulls the cord and he pulls the cord, and the bell clangs and it clangs and it clangs, and someone in the back yells: *"Hallelujah!"* And someone else yells: *"Praise the Lord!"* And now, clanging and whooping, old 404 rocks from side to side, and Mr. Timmons makes flabbergasted sounds, and everyone laughs. Even I laugh. And even Walter Jones laughs. His mother hugs him, and their heads come together, and she tells him ohhh isn't this *fun?* And Walter Jones nods. And the bell clangs. And the silence of Main Street is torn away. Again Caspar (Red) Bickerstaff grins back at us, and this time he yells: *"All my life I've wanted to do this!"* His hand pumps the bell cord. *"The hell with the regulations! I don't give a damn if we wake up the whole town!"* His face is crimson. He has removed his cap, and his rustcolored hair is damp. He pumps, and the bell clangs. *"I'm in charge here!"* he hollers. *"If I want to ring the goddamned bell, I'll ring the goddamned bell!"* He laughs, and we all laugh with him. (And oh yes indeed, he is in charge. No one has ever been more in charge of anything. This is his apotheosis, and I almost envy him his desperately bewildered and grieving jubilation. He is saying: Let us go out bravely and proudly. Let us proclaim to the world that we have been here. Let the proclamation not be timid.) And I feel a great confidence in this Caspar (Red) Bickerstaff. He will never be a better man than he is tonight. Nothing larger ever will happen to him (there is no such thing as apotheosis beyond apotheosis). Three years ago, for economy reasons, the PVT abolished conductors and switched to oneman operation of its cars, and I am happy it did. Had a conductor been aboard this car, he would have been in charge, and Caspar (Red) Bickerstaff would have been denied the apotheosis, and this would have been an outrage. And so the car goes rollicking down the center of Main Street, and the night shudders, and the insects' clackings rise to a hollow roar, and Henry wriggles and grins, and I say to him: "Hey, this is a happy time—in a way." And Henry says: "Yes sir. In a way." And then, draping an arm around his shoulders, I say to him: "You are a good boy." And he says: "Thank you, Papa. That's what I want to be." And he smiles, and I embrace him, and everyone whoops and laughs. (He wants to be a good boy. He has never wanted to be anything else. Yet last night, with Anne, wasn't I jealous of him? How could anyone be jealous of him? Only a monster could be jealous of him.) Old 404 rolls past the Elysian Theater (Richard Dix and Irene Dunne are starring in *Cimarron*) and Steinfelder's Department Store and the Paradise County Court House and the F. W. Woolworth's and Vance's Drug Store and the Ritz Dress Shoppe, past a shuttered little structure called "POP" KORN'S POPCORN PALACE (it is my understanding that old Pop Korn is dying in a Lancaster hospital), past Al's Barber Shop and Penney's and Esterbrook's Men's Wear and the Olivia Pomeroy Beauty Boutique and Soeder's Restaurant and the Paradise Valley Monument Co., and the bell clangs and echoes, and the hand of Caspar (Red) Bickerstaff squeezes the rope and jerks it, and my Legionnaire friend grins at me and says: "This is the way to do her. Big and loud, and the world can go to hell, like the motorman says." I nod. I agree with the man. I agree with him most heartily. I only wish the noise would cause the heavens to split open and the dead to come whirling from their graves. My eyes are warmer than they should be, but who cares? The insects roar. Old 404 rumbles. The bell clangs, and voices rise, and somebody shouts: *"Let's have a great big hand for the motorman!"* And we all applaud. And, next to me, Henry cheers and whistles. He still is wriggling, and his hands are in fists. The car turns south onto High Street, then west onto Grainger Street, and now it is clanging and rumbling through a residential area, and lights come on in a number of the houses that line Grainger Street, and Elizabeth Jones shouts: *"Hey, how about that! We're starting to wake up the town!"* She nudges her son Walter, and he smiles. Now some of the passengers are leaning out the windows. *"Wake them all up, Goddamn it!"* someone shouts. Grinning, Henry leans out his window and whistles through his teeth, and I say nothing to him about it. Yes, it is about *time* the dead came whirling from their graves, and West Grainger Street is a good place to begin the process. By any standard, it is one of the most respectable streets in Paradise Falls, and many of the town's movers and shakers, including Mayor Dwight F. Estes and Elmer Carmichael, the president of the Paradise Falls Clay Products Co., live in its large comfortable houses, and it gives me enormous satisfaction to think that perhaps old 404 is disrupting their sleep. And the lights come on. And shapes appear at windows. And Caspar (Red) Bickerstaff clangs and whoops. He keeps grinning back at us, and he has undone his collar, and his eyes are wild. *"That's it, folks!"* he yells. *"You just holler all you want!"* And Jimmy Jones laughs and slaps one of my shoulders. And Henry squirms and whistles. And old Bill Light, the furniture man, shrieks wordlessly out a window. And the Legionnaires pummel one another. A man in pajamas appears on the front porch of the Estes home, and it is none other than His Honor himself. *"Happy New Year, your Eminence!"* shouts Wes Scofield, leaning out a window and giving Dwight F. Estes a loud wet raspberry. A number of the Legionnaires join Wes Scofield, adding to the serenade, even though they do not know Dwight F. Estes from a hill of beans. The mayor gesticulates toward old 404, and everyone laughs. His pajamas are purple, and one of the Legionnaires wonders aloud if maybe the old boy isn't some sort of fruiter. More laughter, and another of the Legionnaires says: "Well, Ralph, it takes one to know one, ain't that right?" And the pummeling resumes, and the Honorable Dwight F.

Estes is left gesticulating on his front porch, there to dwindle and vanish. And now old 404 is at the edge of town, and Grainger Street becomes US 33-A, and the track veers to the side of the road, and the houses and buildings of Paradise Falls fall behind, but Caspar (Red) Bickerstaff continues to ring the bell, and the passengers' clamor does not abate. The air is green and cool. Caspar (Red) Bickerstaff moves the control knob, and old 404 picks up speed. *"Hey!"* shouts the Legionnaire who is sitting across from me. *"That's more like it!"* Caspar (Red) Bickerstaff nods, gives the knob another push. Now old 404 is swaying, and Elizabeth Jones giggles, and my son Henry clambers over me before I can do anything about it, and he hurries to the motorman's cubicle and stands behind Caspar (Red) Bickerstaff and jumps up and down. *"Yes sir!"* he shouts. *"This is the way to do it! Yes sir!"* And Caspar (Red) Bickerstaff swivels around and winks at Henry and shouts: *"We going to do it right?"* And Henry shouts: *"Yes sir!"* And my Legionnaire friend claps and whistles. He stands up and faces the rest of us. *"You people got any objection to seeing how much she can do?"* he yells. And the passengers all holler: "NO!" Even Elizabeth Jones hollers: "NO!" Even her son Walter hollers: "NO!" And Jimmy Jones hugs them both, and several of the Legionnaires wave their caps. And Mr. Timmons flops and mumbles, his great lips moving wetly. His eyes flick open, then roll shut. His skimmer has dropped to the floor, and now its crown is crushed. My Legionnaire friend grins down at him. *"Don't you worry none about your property!"* he tells Mr. Timmons. *"We're just going to stretch her wings one last time so God and the world'll know what she can do when she's of a mind!"* Then, turning toward Caspar (Red) Bickerstaff and my son: "LET HER RIP!" And so old 404 begins to rip. Caspar (Red) Bickerstaff pushes the knob, and Henry is standing over him, and he hollers to Henry to take the bell cord and just keep pulling, boy, just keep pulling like hell. And Henry nods, seizes the cord and begins tugging on it, and the bell clangs, and the bell clangs, and the bell clangs. And old 404's comfortable hum is no longer comfortable; it is more of a loudly urgent throb. And now I am able to hear the wind. And now Caspar (Red) Bickerstaff has hold of the knob with both hands. And old 404's heavy trucks thump ominously over the weedgrown track, and the trolleypoles snap past in a quickening rhythm, and I know for a fact that these cars seldom exceed thirtyfive miles an hour, and I also know for a fact that old 404 must be doing at least forty right now, with more no doubt to come. And my Legionnaire friend happily lurches up and down the aisle. And Henry pumps away at the bell. And Caspar (Red) Bickerstaff is coiled over the knob, opening it a hair at a time and peering out into the rocketing valedictory night, hollering at Henry to ring that thing, boy, just ring it as good and as loud as you know how. And now everyone is swaying and jouncing, and for some reason I say to myself: Last night with Anne under the diningroom table with a puzzle in her hair. Tonight *this.* What will come *tomorrow* night? Armageddon? And I grip the sides of my seat with both hands, and the wicker is slick against my palms. And I say to myself: We are all demented. We are all going to die. And I want to pray, but I cannot seem to form the words. And old 404 bounces over railjoints with such velocity that the trucks seem to leave the rails, and it comes careening around a bend and enters the river hamlet of Egypt. My brother Ernest lives here with his wife Bernadette and their children, and perhaps Henry and I should get off (Ernest's fillingstation is the PVT ticket agency for Egypt), but how can we get off when I cannot even rise from my seat? So we flash past Ernest's fillingstation (no one is waiting there to come aboard, and so we do not even have to slow down, let alone stop, damn it all), and then Egypt promptly falls behind us, and Caspar (Red) Bickerstaff pushes the knob another hair and hollers back at us: *"Now we can REALLY do her! Next station stop is Lancaster, and it's FOURTEEN MILES!"* I rock from side to side, and my mouth tastes as though it is full of steel filings, and my hands slip off the wicker, and I nearly fall into the aisle. But my Legionnaire friend comes stumbling up and braces me. He pushes me back into my seat. *"Hold on, old buddy!"* he hollers, and the corners of his mouth are rimmed with saliva. I slump back, and the windowpanes are rattling, and Jimmy Jones leans to me and yells: *"Make way for the Pearly Gates Express!"* But I do not laugh. I do not even smile. A valedictory is one thing; lunacy is another. I cringe. I want to cover my eyes, and I cannot understand why I do not. I glance around. Some of the passengers are standing—or trying to stand—but most of them are flopping back and forth like dry beans in a sack. I see Pat Coughlin holding onto his camera with both hands, and I see old Bill Light still leaning out a window, and now the old fellow is grinning into the wind, and his wordless shrieks are made silent by the wind (it is stuffing the shrieks back down his throat, and that is the exact truth of the matter), and I see several of the Legionnaires crawling and bouncing in the aisle, and Wes Scofield trips over them and sprawls whooping, and Bob Stulpnagel pitches forward and back and forward and back as though he is rowing a skiff in a windstorm, and then Caspar (Red) Bickerstaff hollers: *"Sixty, by God! SIXTY!"* And my son Henry hollers: "WHOOPEE! HOORAY FOR THIS OLD

206

TROLLEYCAR!" And I finally yield to the urge: I press my hands to my face and cover my eyes. But not for long. A body slams down on me, and my eyes pop open, and I am entangled with none other than Mr. Timmons, who apparently has risen like Lazarus (in a manner of speaking). He blinks at me, and he is bouncing on my lap, and he licks his massive lips and says: "Ah, wha . . . whafug's goin on?" Behind me, all the Joneses laugh, even Elizabeth. I push at Mr. Timmons's chest, and he goes flapping into the aisle. He loses his balance and falls into a sitting position in the aisle. He looks around. "Where . . . where my haaa . . . my wife bough it for me an no sumbitch goin steal it . . . where my haaa . . . where my *hat?*" I glance toward the place on the floor where I last saw Mr. Timmons's skimmer, but it is gone. It apparently has gone bouncing off God knows where. The bell clangs. Henry leaps and chortles. Caspar (Red) Bickerstaff still pushes at the knob. The passengers moil and thresh, and just about all of them are laughing. Mr. Timmons sits on the floor and scratches his hatless head. Or, to be more accurate, his skimmerless head. His shoulders bang against the sides of the seats, but he does not appear to notice, and he certainly does not appear to be in any pain. Again Caspar (Red) Bickerstaff swivels around. "SEVENTY!" he hollers. "HONEST TO GOD! SEVENTY ON THE OLD NOSE, AND THIS BOY HERE IS MY WITNESS!" He points toward a dial, and Henry leans forward, examines the dial for a moment, then turns to the rest of us and shouts: "SEVENTY ON THE OLD NOSE!" Down on the floor, Mr. Timmons frowns at Henry. "How's . . . whafug *tha* mean?" Mr. Timmons wants to know. Another frown, and then he looks around. "I, ah . . . hey, how *fass* we goin? We goin too fass, huh? How come we goin so goddamn fass?" And now Mr. Timmons tries to brace himself and stand up. "This here piece uh . . . rollin stock . . . is the, ah, the proprt uh the uh R. T. Davis an Sons Iron an Steel Compny," he says, grunting, "an ain't no sumbitch goin to wreck it long's Fred Timmons is on tha job, by Jeez Cry . . ." Scrabbling at the sides of the seats, he pulls himself to his feet. "I the fuggn *controller,* an I gah job to do. You betcha." He moves toward the motorman's cubicle. Caspar (Red) Bickerstaff and Henry have their backs to him. "Hey now," says Mr. Timmons, "hey now, you juss . . ." But by this time I am out of my seat, and I have hold of Mr. Timmons, and I have pinned his arms behind him. We roll and bounce from side to side, and Henry's bell slams like doom and judgment, and the rhythm of the trolleypoles is now simply a mad whooshing blur, formless and unrelenting, and several of the Legionnaires come tottering toward us, and I say to Mr. Timmons: "No sir.

I'm terribly sorry but no. You have no right to interfere, so kindly just contain yourself." And, needless to say, I am astonished. I am behaving uncharacteristically. I have become a participant in all this demented nonsense. I am no better than the whoopers and the laughers. But my grip on Mr. Timmons does not relax, and I no longer want to cover my eyes. There is not enough money in the world to make me cover my eyes. The Pearly Gates Express must be allowed to proceed unvexed. One has one's duty, and one does one's duty as one sees fit. So Mr. Timmons and I dance and stagger, and his breath is as foul as the underside of a sheep pen, and then my son Henry turns around, sees what is happening and smiles at us. I smile back at him, and he yells: "YES SIR, PAPA! THAT'S THE WAY TO GO!" And I yell: "LET HER RIP!" And Henry tugs jubilantly, and the bell smacks and clamors, and old 404 goes ripping along, and the rails shout and rattle, and the Legionnaires help me drag a struggling Mr. Timmons to the rear of the swaying car, and he foams and wriggles, but we do not release him. We slam him down on one of the seats, and a fat Legionnaire sits on his lap, and veins bulge in his forehead, and the fat Legionnaire brays, bouncing on Mr. Timmons's lap and telling him: *"Old George Blewitt's got you now, Mister Junkman, and there ain't no sense trying to go* NOWHERE!" And everyone laughs, and I shake hands with the Legionnaires, then go lurching back to my seat, and Jimmy and Elizabeth Jones clap me on the shoulders, and I grin. I am all teeth and gums and tongue, and I grin like a man who has just had his first bowel movement in six weeks. (This is precisely the analogy that occurs to me, and I am fully aware of its tastelessness, but it is nonetheless most accurate, and I am really not ashamed of it at all.) And I relax. I permit myself to flop and bounce. It is the last night of the world, and there is no way I can amend the verdict, and so I wobble and bump like a sack of potatoes, and my grin has been pasted on my face like a badge, and old 404 whirls through the mad last night of the world, pealing and clattering, abrim with laughter and shouts. (Does my son love me? Of course my son loves me. He loves the world, and I am part of the world, and I have acknowledged its last night, and he cannot help but love me.) But this is not the last night of the world, except for old 404, and my thinking has all been a lot of romantic hyperbole. We come careening into the outskirts of Lancaster, and Caspar (Red) Bickerstaff pulls back the control knob, and we slow down, and he tells Henry to stop ringing the bell. "I'm sorry, sonny," he says, "but we got to bring this here thing back to normal. And besides, I might be wanting to get a job here as a motorman on the city railroad. No sense hurting my chances, is there?" Then, turning with a smile to the passengers, Caspar (Red) Bickerstaff says: "Well, folks, she got up to seventysix. Honest to God." And then we begin to applaud. And we stand (all of us except Mr. Timmons, who is sprawled flat in his new seat and apparently has passed out again). And we are grinning. And we clap until our palms are red. Even Pat Coughlin claps, and even old Bill Light, and even little Walter Jones. And Caspar (Red) Bickerstaff takes a bow. And he nudges Henry, and Henry takes a bow with him. And then I look at Henry, who has turned away. He presses his forehead against the cubicle wall, and Caspar (Red) Bickerstaff tells him all right, sonny, *all right now,* the world goes on. And Henry nods, but he has no words, and so I go to him and take him back to our seat. He sits silently next to me, and he stares straight ahead. Old 404 rumbles over the switchpoints that connect the PVT with the Lancaster city streetcar system, and gradually the applause dies away. And now the passengers sit down and talk quietly among themselves. Lancaster is black and silent, and there is not even any automobile traffic. Henry swipes at his nose with the back of a hand. He blinks, smiles, then says to me: "It was worth it, Papa." And I say to him: "Yes. It was indeed." And Henry says: "You understand, don't you, about going out good?" I do not bother to correct his grammar. Instead I simply say: "Yes. I do understand. Absolutely." And Henry nods. "I thought you did," he says. The PVT's Lancaster ticket office is in a shuttered hardware store on Broad Street. About twenty persons, mostly men, are clustered on the sidewalk outside the place. One of them is playing, of all things, a harmonica. Pat Coughlin leans out a window and takes several shots of the crowd. At the same time, several men in the crowd photograph old 404 as it approaches. Someone yells something to the effect that we are nine minutes early, and Caspar (Red) Bickerstaff laughs, and so do several of the passengers. Jimmy Jones leans forward and points to an automobile that is parked across the street and asks me do we have a ride back to Paradise Falls. His oldest son, Alan, a telegrapher for the C&O, works in Lancaster, and he has agreed to drive his mother and father and little brother back home. "I'm sure there's room for two more," says Jimmy Jones. I glance at Henry, and he nods toward a car that is parked in front of Alan's, and I recognize Charley Pflug's taxicab. I say to Jimmy Jones: "I thank you very much, but Henry already has made the arrangements." And Henry says: "Yes sir. Thank you very much." And Jimmy Jones smiles and says: "Ah, good old Henry." And I say: "Yes. That is correct." Old 404 comes to a stop, and the Lancaster passengers crowd toward the door. Mr.

Timmons now is flat on his back and snoring. Caspar (Red) Bicker-staff opens the door. One by one, the Lancaster passengers shake hands with him as they file out. Nothing much is said. Outside, some of the waiting crowd quietly applauds. The car's idling motor goes kick kick kick kick kick. Henry and I shake hands with Caspar (Red) Bickerstaff, but we say nothing, and neither does he. Henry and I cross the street to the taxicab, and Charley Pflug opens the door for us and tells us ah, wellnow, she's a little early, ain't she? We tell him yes, he is absolutely right. The old interurban car gives off a yellow smear of light, and the harmonica makes sentimental and preposter-ous sounds, and I turn my face away from my son. He says: "Yes . . . this was the right way . . ." He is eight years of age. Eight. I say to myself: My God. My God in Heaven. Henry and I and Charley Pflug talk quietly all the way home. It occurs to me that I never asked Caspar (Red) Bickerstaff about his son Jack, the erstwhile incompe-tent hurdler. Within a month, the PVT tracks are ripped up and sold for scrap. Caspar (Red) Bickerstaff and his family move to Spring-field, where he goes to work as a motorman for the Cincinnati & Lake Erie. That road is abandoned in 1939, and after that I lose track of him, no pun intended.

Amberson came awake in the motel bed at 7:30 Tuesday morning, and for a moment he did not know where he was. He came awake tentatively, and there was a pain somewhere in the region of his kid-neys. He blinked, rubbed the corners of his eyes, then said to himself: Ah yes, now I remember. It is Cambridge. (In his journal, he had written of what he called *tumblejumping optimism,* using the phrase to describe the way he felt on certain mornings when there actually seemed to be a reason to get up and attack the world as though the issue still were in doubt. But *this* was not one of those silly enthusiastic mornings. Instead, it was just another morning, and he would have to cope with it as best he could, considering how tired he was. And considering the pain he was feeling in his kidneys. And his gums. And his joints. And considering the ominous spasms and flutters of his heartbeat.)

Then he thought of the movie camera, and he decided now was as good a time as any to tell Anne he had forgotten it. He would catch her before she was fully awake. Yawning, he rolled over, but her side of the bed was empty. He sat up and looked around. There was a light on in the bathroom. "Anne?" he said. "You in there?"

Sinclair came out from under the dresser and hopped on the bed. He was purring, and Amberson stroked his ears.

"Anne?" said Amberson. He got out of bed and went to the bathroom door. It was open and he looked inside. Anne was seated on the toilet, leaning forward with her elbows resting on her knees; her hands covered her face, and she was slowly rocking forward and back. Her hands covered her face so tightly that it was impossible to see how she was able to breathe.

"Anne?" said Amberson. He leaned against the door frame.

She groaned.

"What is it?" he asked her.

Her hands came away from her face. She did not look at him. Instead she simply continued to rock forward and back. "I hurt," she said. She folded her arms over her waist. "That's all. Nothing special. I just *hurt.*"

"Did you take your medication last night?"

She shook her head.

"Why not?"

She glared at him, and her eyes were white. "Because I didn't *want* to. I don't want to be some sort of *dependent vegetable,* is *that* so hard to understand?"

"No. Of course not. But when you're in pain you really should face up to—"

"No," said Anne. "I thought we were supposed to be looking for truth."

"What?"

"Your apparatus. How will I be able to understand it if I'm doped up like some sort of, ah, heroin addict? Please, Howard, please just . . . I'll be all right. It'll pass. It always does."

Amberson said nothing. He rubbed his mouth, ran a finger along his sore gums. His finger was warm, it comforted his gums. He nodded. "All right," he said.

Anne closed her eyes. "Thank you," she said. "I've been up since seven. What is it now?"

"About half past."

"Well, the worst of it is over. It usually lasts about half an hour, sometimes forty minutes." She opened her eyes. "I've been thinking," she said.

"About what?"

"The Kitty Heaven letter. I was wondering. Tonight, when we get wherever it is we're going, would you read it to me? I've brought it along. It's in my suitcase."

"I'd be delighted to read it to you," said Amberson.

"We'll get in bed, and it'll be nice and warm, and Sinclair can get in bed with us if he wants, and then you can read me the letter. You're very good at reading things out loud."

"Thank you."

"Flattery will get me everywhere, correct?"

"Yes."

"It means so much to me," said Anne.

"Fine," said Amberson. "Consider it done."

See now 1906, and I am nine years old. I am sitting barefoot at the edge of the Paradise River with my friend Fred Suiter, a chunky boy who is interested in fishing, sleeping, telling stories and singing quiet songs. His people are Catholic, and my brothers love to torment him. They are particularly fond of divesting him of his britches. It is an afternoon in early fall, and he is munching on an apple, and he says to me: "Should of brought my pole today. Maybe they would of been biting."

"But this isn't *Friday*," I tell him. "No need to fish *today*."

"I like to fish, and it don't matter what the day is."

"My brothers say you snap for mackerel."

"I know what they say. Some day I'm going to be big, and then they won't say them things no more."

"I don't like the things they do to you. You got a right to be a mackrelsnapper or anything else you want to be."

"Damn right," says Fred Suiter.

"You going to talk to the fish today?"

"Maybe. We'll see."

I nod. Fred Suiter has been talking to fish and birds and animals as long as either of us can remember. And sometimes he sings to them. He says he has a calling for this sort of thing, and I do not dispute him. I have seen him talk to the fish and the birds and the animals, and I have seen how attentively they listen. His middle name is Francis, and he says he has been touched by some saint who had that name. He says he loves this saint, and he has shown me drawings of the fellow, and sure enough, the drawings show that old saint surrounded by fish and birds and animals. It is all very interesting, and I like Fred Suiter a great deal. He is my closest friend—and never mind the things my brothers do to him. And so now I wait to see what he will do. We are sitting downstream from the falls, and the river is white and noisy, full of large rocks that have been worn slick and green. Fred leans forward and spits into the water. He has finished his apple, all of it except the stem. He says he likes the seeds and the core best of all. His mother has warned him that some day an apple tree will sprout from his nose, but he does not appear to be too worried. And anyway, if it *does,* he figures he can make a lot of money showing himself at carnivals. Or at least this is what he has told me. (Sometimes I have trouble knowing when to believe my friend Fred, and that is for sure.) Again he spits, and this time he tries to force the spit through the opening between his two front teeth. He is not very successful, and most of the spit dribbles on his chin. He grimaces, snorts, wipes away the spit with the side of a finger. I wriggle my toes and look away. I sift sand through my fingers. "You see any yet?"

"No," says Fred, frowning at the water.

The sky is high and crisp, and I squint at the sun.

"Some day it's going to be different," says Fred.

The sun smacks at my eyes, and I blink.

"I'm going to grow up some day," says Fred, "and then they'll leave me alone."

"See any fish?"

"No."

"I don't like it when they take your britches."

"I know that," says Fred. "You don't have to keep telling me."

I stare at a backwash from the white water. It is small and calm, and Fred and I have seen fish there before. And an occasional frog. Fred talks to frogs, too. And they often talk back. They are among his very favorite friends. He much admires their mouths and their throats, and he is quite impressed by the distances they are able to leap. Perhaps, if no fish comes along, we shall see a frog.

"There's one," says Fred.

"A fish?"

"No. A *locomotive,* dumbbell." Fred is grinning, and he points toward a large green rock. "Looks like a cat to me," he says. "See him there, laying in the shadow?"

I narrow my eyes. I peer in the direction Fred is pointing. I see nothing but the shadow. Perhaps something is there, or perhaps nothing is there. I cannot tell. I glance at Fred. "You sure you see something?"

"I do," says Fred, "and it's a big old cat."

I shrug. "All right. You're better at this than I am."

Fred holds up a hand. "Be quiet. I want to hear what he's got to say for himself." Fred cups both hands over his mouth. "Hey there, Mister Catfish, can you hear me?"

The water roars, and my eyes are fixed on the shadow.

Fred waves at the shadow. "My name is Fred Suiter," he says. He hesitates, and now he obviously is listening to whatever it is the fish has to say. "Yes . . . yes, well, hey, that's real nice. Was it good? It was, huh? Well, I'm glad to hear it. Yes . . . ah, well, you see, me and Howard here we just sit here and talk to whoever happens to pass by. Or, anyhow, *I* talk. Howard, all *he* does is listen."

I nudge Fred. "What'd the fish say?" I ask him.

Fred ignores me. "Yes sir," he says to the shadow, "last week we had a nice little chat with a crow who's a Black Republican . . . swear to God we did, and all he wanted to talk about was Teddy Roosevelt, Teddy Roosevelt . . . like Teddy Roosevelt was the greatest man who ever walked the face of the earth . . . yes sir, I'm a Democrat too . . . thank you . . . it's nice to know we agree on politics . . ."

"Politics?" I say.

Fred glances at me. "He's a Democrat, and he had a spider for his breakfast today."

"A spider? Do catfish eat spiders?"

"Well, he's a *cat,* ain't he? And *real* cats eat spiders."

"They do?"

"Yes," says Fred. "Now you be quiet. I want to hear what else he has to say." Again Fred stares at the shadow, and then he says: "It's about sixty miles, I think. Straight downstream. You can't miss it. Yes . . . that's right . . . just, ah, follow your nose . . ."

"Where's he want to go?" I ask Fred.

"The Ohio River. He says he's got some aunts and uncles and cousins down there. He says they live somewhere near Pomeroy, or maybe Gallipolis."

"Oh?"

"Yeh. That's what he says, and he don't look like a fibber to me."

"Well, I'm glad to hear that."

Fred smiles at the shadow. "That's all right, Mister Catfish," he says. "I'm real glad to be of help . . . well, I appreciate your kind words . . . I really do . . . it was no trouble at all . . . thank you kindly . . . goodbye . . . have a nice trip . . . yes . . . all right . . . if I ever get down that way, I sure will try to look you up . . . thank you . . . thank you very much . . ." And Fred sits up straight, smiles, lifts an arm and waves.

"You want me to wave?" I ask Fred.

"That'd be real nice," says Fred, waving.

"All right," I say. I wave, and the water foams and hisses. I watch Fred from a corner of an eye. When he lowers his arm, I lower mine.

"Did you like him all right?" I want to know.

Fred shrugs. "Oh, he was good enough. Not much of a talker, but he seemed decent enough. I mean, your average catfish isn't one to pass the time of day in idle chitchat. He's too serious for that sort of thing. Things aren't all that easy for a catfish—what with people like me always after them with hooks."

"Yes. I can see where that would be a sort of trial."

"Uh huh," says Fred, nodding.

And then we are silent, and we listen to the river, and I think of catfish that eat spiders and vote Democrat. I really love Fred's stories. He has a mind for them. I suppose it is a special mind, and I suppose I am lucky to be the one who gets to hear all the things that come from it. The stories and the songs and the conversations and whatever. I yawn. The sunlight slams down. I stretch out my legs, and Fred is humming something, but I cannot make out the tune. "Was there really a fish down there?" I ask him.

"You calling me a liar?" says Fred, hugging his knees. He does not look at me.

"No."

"Then you believe I'm telling the truth?"

"Yes."

"All right then—why'd you ask the question?"

"I don't know."

"Well," says Fred, "just to put the record straight, I ain't no liar."

"All right," I tell him. "Good enough."

"We talked about the spider he ate, and we talked about Teddy Roosevelt, and we talked about the Ohio River. It wasn't the most exciting conversation I ever had, but then you shouldn't expect the world from a catfish."

"No. That's right. You shouldn't."

Fred is about to say something more, but he is interrupted by my brothers, who come stumbling down the riverbank. Fred and I scrootch back on our rear ends, but it is too late: we have no chance to stand and flee. Alvin Jr. and Ernest are upon us too quickly. Ignoring me, they seize Fred and drag him toward the water. I watch what is happening, and I do not move. Ernest is only ten, but Alvin Jr. is almost *seventeen,* and why is this so necessary for him? He is Mama's favorite, and we all know that, so what is he trying to prove? He and Ernest dance in a circle around Fred, who already has begun to tremble. Suddenly Alvin Jr. drops his britches. *"The Pope can kiss my ass!"* he shouts, bending over and displaying his bare rump. Laughing, Ernest kicks out at Alvin Jr.'s rump, and it is then that

Fred tries to get up and run. But Ernest tackles him, and they roll and thresh in the coarse riverbank sand. As this is happening, Alvin Jr. pulls up his britches and fastens them. He is seventeen, and Fred Suiter is nine, and what has Fred ever done to him? I scramble to my feet and holler at my brothers, but they pay me no mind. Ernest has rolled Fred on his back, and he is sitting on Fred's chest, and Fred is howling. Alvin Jr. scoops up a handful of sand and presses it into Fred's face. "The Pope is a sissy," says Alvin Jr., rubbing the sand back and forth. By this time Fred is bleating and sputtering, and he tries to squirm free. Alvin Jr. slaps him and says: "Don't you move, you Papist snotsucker shithead you." Then Alvin Jr. and Ernest remove Fred's britches and tear them to shreds. A picture of the Blessed Savior falls from one of the ripped pockets. "Sacrilege," says Alvin Jr. He wads up the picture, thinks for a moment, then shoves the wad against Fred's gasping mouth. "Eat it," says Alvin Jr., grinning. "Eat your Jesus." Fred's head moves from side to side, and so Alvin Jr. grabs his hair and gives it a great yank. Fred screams, and Alvin Jr. shoves the wad in his mouth before he can close it. "Now then," says Alvin Jr., "you just go ahead and eat it." Choking, Fred begins to work his jaws. "That's a good Papist," says Alvin Jr., nodding. And so Fred eats the wad, swallowing all of it. And my brothers remove his shirt and underdrawers, tearing them to shreds as they have torn his britches to shreds, and now Fred is utterly naked, and his body is pale and flabby. Alvin Jr. and Ernest rise and stand back from him. They both are laughing. Alvin Jr. gathers up the remains of Fred's clothing and throws them in the river. They whirl off, and they are lost in the white water. "Hey," says Alvin Jr., "he's got tits. And look at his littleteeny dingle. Poor Freddyweddy with his littleteeny dinglewingle. You know, he ain't going to grow up to be much of a man, and that's a fact. Maybe we can do him a favor. That water looks nice and cold, don't it? If we was to throw him in, his little dinglewingle would probably freeze right off, and then he'd never have to worry about being a man, now would he?" And Ernest says: "Sounds like a good idea to me." So Alvin Jr. bends over Fred, whose hands are cupped over his crotch. "Hey there, Mister Tits," says Alvin Jr., chucking Fred under the chin, "what you need is a nice little swim, yes indeed." He seizes Fred by the shoulders, and Ernest seizes Fred by the legs, and Fred is mewling, and I am weeping, and they carry Fred to the edge of the river. He is kicking weakly, and his hands still are cupped over his crotch. My brothers swing him back, forward, back, forward, back, forward, back. Now the proper momentum has been achieved, and they heave him out into the river, and his hands still are cupped over his crotch, and he hits the water with a flat despairing plash, and the current carries him thirty or forty yards downstream before he is able to stagger ashore. Alvin Jr. and Ernest laugh and dance. I run past them to Fred, who is kneeling in the sand. *"What are you going to do? Kiss him?"* Alvin Jr. shouts at me. He guffaws, and so does Ernest. Fred is weeping, and his face is cut, and his chest and back are bruised. I remove my shirt and hand it to him. He wraps it around his waist. He does not speak, and probably he cannot speak. He stands up, moves forward a few feet, then falls flat on his chest, and my brothers whoop. I move toward him, but he glares up and says: "Stay away." Then he vomits up the wad, and I begin to run, and my bladder feels as though it is about to explode, and my bare chest is cold, and I run all the way home. I scramble upstairs to the bathroom, and Mama calls after me and wants to know what has happened to my shirt, and I stand weeping over the toilet, and I make enough peepee to drown the world.

As Anne had predicted, her pain did relent, and within ten minutes she was washing her face and going through the rest of her morning routine. At the same time, Amberson went outside and cleaned out Sinclair's box, refilled it with sand from the bag in the trunk of the car and placed it on the newspapers in the back seat. He returned to the room and opened a can of 9-Lives Super Supper (sure enough, Anne *had* packed an opener) and placed it on the floor, and Sinclair came running. He filled a large hollow ashtray with water, and when Anne, who was combing her hair, asked him what on earth did he think he was doing, he told her: Now Sinclair has a water dish. He was gratified to see Sinclair lap it up. Male cats needed to drink plenty of water to avoid developing kidney trouble.

He and Anne carried the suitcases to the car, but decided to leave Sinclair in the room until they were ready to go. There was no sense cooping up the poor animal any more than necessary. Amberson cashed fifty dollars in Travelers' Cheques and paid the bill, which came to $21.50. The clerk was a plump girl with brilliant green eyes, and she wore a badge that said KATHY ERWINE. She asked Amberson whether he had had a pleasant night, and he told her oh yes indeed, thank you, a very pleasant night. He and Anne went into the coffee shop for breakfast, and their waitress was a plump girl with brilliant green eyes, and she wore a badge that said KAREN ERWINE. Amberson asked the inevitable question, and Karen Erwine smiled and said: "You know, you're the fourth person to ask me that already this morning, and it's barely eight o'clock."

"Well," said Amberson, "you *will* have to admit that there's a remarkable resemblance."

Karen Erwine nodded. She had given menus to the Ambersons, and now she was filling their glasses with ice water. "Would you believe me if I told you I never saw that woman before in my life?"

"Of course I would," said Amberson. "As long as *you* believe *me* when I tell you the moon is made of green cheese and tarpaper."

"Green cheese and *tarpaper?"* said Karen Erwine. "Why, that's *ridiculous."*

"It's a ridiculous world we live in," said Amberson.

"I wish *I'd* said that," said Anne.

And then they all laughed, and Karen Erwine said yes, yes, I cannot tell a lie; Kathy is my sister, and we are identical twins. Not fraternal but identical, and it's great fun when we're dating. Why, we even go on diets together, which is just about all the time, I'll tell *you.* Kathy's boyfriend can pick *her* three times out of four, but *my* boyfriend is utterly at a loss. Utterly. But then he says he doesn't really care; we're both of us such hot stuff, ha ha. And here Karen Erwine laughed again, and Amberson decided he liked her very much. She reminded him a bit of what Anne had been as a girl, and he hoped she would find someone who would appreciate her. He ordered bacon, scrambled eggs, toast and coffee. Anne ordered toast and coffee. He frowned at her, but she shook her head and told him no, no, really, don't nag me about it; it's all I want. And so Amberson said nothing, and Karen Erwine went away. He glanced around the coffee shop, and most of the customers were solitary men. Salesmen, he supposed. He wondered if they all were in the process of cranking up their smiles and their shoeshines. He smiled at Anne and said: "I'm glad I never was a salesman."

"What?"

"These men sitting in this place, I would say most of them are salesmen. And it got me to thinking about Willy Loman."

"From *Death of a Salesman?"*

"Yes. And that famous line about the smile and the shoeshine. I was wondering what happens to a salesman when he doesn't *feel* like smiling or shining his shoes."

"Well, I suppose he would be wise to find some other line of work."

"My senior Contemporary Literature classes always enjoyed that play."

Anne said she hadn't liked the movie.

"Oh? Why not?"

"You know why not. I've *told* you. I didn't like the movie because Fredric March was too *strong* and *dignified,* and I couldn't believe he would allow himself to get into such a fix."

"Oh yes," said Amberson. "I guess you have told me."

"Is my husband becoming forgetful in his old age?"

"Perhaps so," he said.

Anne smiled. There were enormous circles under her eyes, but her smile was strong. "Like with his movie camera, his great big elaborate window to the world or whatever?"

"Oh dear," said Amberson. "My secret is out. When did you think of it?"

"Yesterday afternoon. Somewhere around Zanesville. I didn't say anything because I didn't want you to drive off the road."

"I left it right on the table by the front door, didn't I?"

"Yes. I believe you did."

Amberson shook his head and sipped at his ice water. "All that money," he said.

"Well, it wasn't worth turning around and driving back such a distance."

Amberson nodded. "We don't need it," he said. "It was just a silly notion, a joke more than anything else. The church basement idea. 'Footloose with the Ambersons,' my foot. Tell me, would *you* attend an illustrated lecture called 'Footloose with the Ambersons'?"

"Not on your life."

"Well, neither would I. And besides, I don't believe I really knew how to operate the thing. The man at Heimrich's very patiently gave me instructions, but I'm afraid they were too much for me. If I'd brought the thing along, I probably would have aimed it the wrong way, and our record of this trip would have turned out to be one long closeup of my nose."

"When did you remember the camera?"

"Last night. Just before I fell asleep."

"Well, you shouldn't feel too badly. You're not the only forgetful one. First of all, as you already have deduced, *I* forgot Sinclair's food bowl *and* his water dish. Secondly, I also forgot my *Future Shock.* Please don't laugh."

"I had no intention of laughing," said Amberson.

"I *bet,*" said Anne.

Karen Erwine came bustling up with the breakfasts, and Amberson was pleased to note that his scrambled eggs were not gummy. Anne asked the girl whether she had any people in Paradise Falls. "That's where we're from," said Anne, "and there are several families named Erwine."

Pouring the coffee, Karen Erwine said: "Well, Kathy and I were *born* in *Blood.*" She smiled. "Sounds awful, doesn't it?"

"Probably to a stranger," said Amberson, "but we're used to the name."

"I suppose so," said Karen Erwine. "Well, at any rate, we were born in Blood, but Mama and Papa brought us here when we were about a year old. Papa loved Paradise County, but there just wasn't anything for him to *do* down in Blood. He had been a miner, but you know what happened to the mines. I guess Blood was a terrible place in those days."

"It still is," said Anne, buttering her toast.

"Oh?" said Karen Erwine. "I'm sorry to hear that."

"We know some people named Tom and Henrietta Erwine," said Anne. "Are they related to you?"

"He's my father's brother," said Karen.

Anne smiled and bit into her toast. "Well, goodness gracious," she said, "what a small world."

Karen filled out the check and placed it facedown on the table. "If you want more coffee, just holler," she said. "Refills are free." Another smile, then: "You're nice people, and it's been a pleasure serving you."

"Well," said Amberson, "thank you very much."

Karen nodded, then went off to wait on a man who had just seated himself in a corner booth.

Amberson buttered his own toast and then said: "I am open to suggestions."

"About what?"

"Where we should go today. We are footloose, and the world awaits."

"Well," said Anne, "how about Cleveland?"

"Cleveland? I thought you didn't like Cleveland."

"Something occurred to me yesterday, a family thing, and maybe we should take care of it. Alice's name is on Lewis's headstone, but does she still want to be buried there? I mean, she has a new husband and all, and I expect she might want to be buried with *him.*"

Amberson was genuinely astonished. "You mean you want to go to *Cleveland* and see *Alice?*"

"Well, it's not exactly *Cleveland.* It's *Shaker Heights.*"

"All right. Shaker Heights. But I didn't think you cared much for Alice."

"If you mean do I stay awake nights thinking how much I miss her, the answer is no. But, well, that headstone will look awfully ridiculous if she's never buried there."

"She'll be delighted," said Amberson. "Especially if we come traipsing into her place and sit down and say to her: 'Alice, have you firmed up your funeral arrangements yet? And, if so, what are your headstone plans?' "

Anne snickered, wiped her mouth. "Howard, I don't really dislike her. Why should I? She can't help being what she is, and I can make allowances. Ah, listen to me. Mrs. La-De-Dah, making allowances."

Amberson smiled. "Well," he said, "if we drive north, at least we won't be heading into the sun." He glanced out a window. "And it looks as though it's going to be a very clear day. Should we telephone and let her know we're coming?"

"Not on your tintype," said Anne. "I think we should give her a nice surprise."

"Well, it certainly will be a surprise. I don't know how nice, though." He cut a strip of bacon, then: "But all I ask is one thing."

"That Alice and I don't pick up our argument?"

"Yes."

Anne shrugged. "All right. But I still think she nourished the worst in him."

"I know you do. And I suppose I agree. But done is done."

"Yes," said Anne.

They finished breakfast, and Amberson left Karen a dollar tip on a check that came to only $1.44, including the tax. He looked around for her as he and Anne walked out of the place, but she was nowhere to be seen. He wondered if he and Anne ever would in truth become footloose. This morning, for instance, they already had encountered a girl who had people in Paradise Falls, and now they were on their way to visit their former daughterinlaw. The chains still were binding, and that was a fact. He and Anne crossed the lobby, and then he smiled at the other Erwine girl, Kathy, who was making change for a Negro man wearing a flowered summer shirt. Kathy Erwine spotted the Ambersons and waved at them just as they were going out the door. They waved back, and then the Negro man waved, and everyone smiled.

They pulled out of the motel parking lot, filled the tank at a Shell station, and Amberson wheeled the car out into the traffic. A few minutes later Cambridge was gone, and the car was headed northwest on Ohio 209. The country was rolling and golden, and Anne said: "The leaves are really a great deal further along up here."

"Fall is your favorite season, isn't it?"

"Yes. And it always has been. But you know that."

"I know I know it," said Amberson, nodding. "Please excuse the question."

"There's nothing to excuse. Everything we discuss we've discussed before. I mean, after fifty years, fresh topics do become a bit scarce. I'm sorry. I shouldn't have snapped at you back there. About Fredric March. That movie must be twenty years old, and you can't be expected to remember everything. Besides, I have a compliment for you."

"Fine. I'm waiting."

"It's about Sinclair's box. You remembered your promise to clean it and take care of it. I appreciate that."

"Oh, my Lord," said Amberson.

"What?"

"Would it be fair to say that our principal topic of conversation this morning has been forgetfulness?"

"I forget," said Anne, smiling.

Amberson slowed the car and turned into a side road.

"What are you doing?" Anne asked him.

Amberson braked the car, put it in reverse and backed onto Ohio 209, and now it was headed back toward Cambridge. "We forgot Sinclair," he said. "He's still in the room."

"Oh, dear," said Anne.

The drive back to Cambridge was silent. Anne sat stiffly, and Amberson said to himself: Sinclair is perfectly all right. This is no different than if we'd taken an extra half an hour or so for our breakfast. So kindly do not get yourself lathered up about it, you foolish old goat. The speedometer hit 50 several times, and Amberson grasped the wheel tightly. The steering felt a bit wobbly, and perhaps this was the car's way of saying: What's going on here? Why the unaccustomed rush? The car jerked to a stop in the motel lot, and the Ambersons scrambled out and hurried toward the room. Its door was open. A large middleaged woman was running a vacuum cleaner. The Ambersons rushed inside and the woman looked at them and said: "Was that *your* cat?"

"Yes," said Amberson. "Is he here?"

"No. He ran out soon as I opened the door. Whisk. Just like that."

"Where did he go?" Anne asked the woman.

"I got no idea," said the woman, shrugging.

"How long ago was it?" Anne wanted to know.

"Maybe five minutes," said the woman. "I ain't even made the bed yet, so it ain't been too long."

"All right," said Amberson. "Fine. Thank you very much." He and Anne turned and went out of the room, and Anne bumped into a cart that was standing outside the door. It had rubber wheels, and it contained linens and cleaning solvents, and Anne momentarily lost her balance. But Amberson grabbed her, and she did not fall.

The woman came to the door. "You all right?" she said.

Amberson nodded. "Yes. Fine." He took Anne by an arm, then said to the woman: "He didn't go toward the road, did he?"

"No," said the woman.

"If you see him, will you hold him for us?"

"All right—if I can catch him."

"Thank you," said Amberson.

"You drive off and forget him?"

"Yes."

The woman shook her head. "You must not care an awful lot about him."

"That's not true," said Anne. "What do *you* know about it?"

The woman snorted and went back inside and switched on the vacuum cleaner. Its sound seemed too loud, at least it did to Amberson.

"What does *she* know about it?" said Anne.

Amberson patted his wife's shoulder. "We can discuss all that after we find Sinclair," he said. "Now, let's get organized." He looked right and left; motel rooms and doors stretched off in both directions. "I'll go to the left," he said, "and you go to the right. If any rooms are open, go inside and take a look. There are more rooms in the back, and we'd better check them, too."

"If I know *him,* he's *hiding.*"

"I'm sure he hasn't gone very far at all, so let's find him."

"Yes," said Anne. She walked slowly. "Kitty kitty," she said, *"here kitty kitty kitty . . ."*

Amberson walked along the line of rooms to the left. "Sinclair?" he said. He rubbed his gums. "Come on, old fellow. Come on now. Where are you?" He looked back, but Anne was nowhere to be seen. Apparently she had gone inside an open room. He removed his spectacles, cleaned them with a handkerchief, then squatted and peered under parked cars. "Sinclair?" he said. "Hey now, where are you hiding yourself?" He straightened, and his knees popped. "Sinclair?" he said. "What's the matter? Don't you want to go to Shaker Heights and see nice Alice in her big splendid house?" He proceeded along the walkway in front of the rooms, his eyes moving from side to side and up and down. Yes, even up. Sometimes Sinclair liked to sun himself on top of a car. Obviously, nothing could be overlooked. And then Amberson came to a room that had an open door. He went inside but stopped just beyond the threshold. A darkhaired girl of about twenty was lying on the bed and reading *TV Guide*. She was wearing hornrimmed glasses and a pair of electric blue shorty pajamas, and she said: "Well, good morning. Are you the room service man?"

"No. I beg your pardon. I'm looking for a stray cat."

The girl grinned, pushed the glasses up on her forehead. "Well," she said, "I do believe you've found one."

Amberson cleared his throat. "No . . . I, ah . . . you, ah, haven't *seen* a cat, have you?"

"You mean the kind that has whiskers and claws and goes purr, purr, purr?"

"Yes."

"Well, no. I'm sorry, but I can't say as I have."

Amberson backed toward the door. "Well, I . . . I beg your pardon. I shouldn't have come blundering in here like this."

The girl stretched. She had immense breasts and very long legs. Her toenails were painted green. "Think nothing of it," she said. Then she abruptly sat up, and her breasts wobbled. "Would you like me to help you?"

"Oh . . . well . . . you . . ."

"No. I mean it. I'm just laying around this place trying to figure out what bus I should catch for home. It'd give me something to do."

"Well, my wife already is out there—"

The girl smiled. "Now, now," she said, "I'm not after your body. I just want to help. I bet your wife's a very nice lady, and I bet she wouldn't mind a bit."

"But what about the room service man? Aren't you expecting him?"

The girl scribbled a note on a piece of motel stationery, then rummaged in her purse and came up with a quarter and a dime. "He can leave the coffee right here. That's all it is—just coffee," she said. "And there's his tip. She slipped her feet into a pair of bunnyslippers. "All right," she said. "I'm ready if you are."

"You'd better wear a coat."

"Oh, *no*. I *love* cold weather. Why do you think the door was open? I'm a Svenska, you see. Duluth, Minnesota, and what do you think of that?"

"I think you'll catch pneumonia."

"Never," said the girl. "I have very warm blood." She took Amberson by an arm. "We have us a kittycat to find," she said. "Let us be about our business."

Amberson smiled. He did not know what else to do. The girl had a warm odor, and he supposed it was an odor of sex. He said: "All right, young lady. It's your pneumonia."

"What kind of a kittycat is it we're looking for?" she asked, as she steered Amberson out of the room.

"A gray male, neutered and rather fat. His name is Sinclair."

"Like Sinclair Lewis?"

"Yes."

"Sinclair Lewis was from Minnesota. Sauk Centre. We read *Elmer Gantry* in the eleventh grade. You ever been to Duluth?"

"No."

"Well, don't break your back getting there. It's not that much."

"All right," said Amberson. He peered back and forth, but he saw no sign of Sinclair.

"Does he answer when you call him?" the girl asked.

"No. He's a very independent fellow."

"I know all about very independent fellows," said the girl.

Amberson moved up the walkway, and the girl moved with him, and her electric blue pajamas glistened in the sunlight. Her slippered feet made soft sounds. "You're really not cold?" he asked her.

"Not a bit. You can't *imagine* how warm my blood is."

"If I were about twenty years younger, I surely would like to try."

"Thank you very much, sir," said the girl.

"Ah, to be fiftyfive again," said Amberson.

"You're a terrible flirt, you know that?"

Amberson chuckled. "It's most uncharacteristic of me."

"Well, in that case, I'm flattered. I've turned you on a little bit, haven't I? Wait . . . you don't have to answer that if you don't want to."

"Oh, I don't mind," said Amberson. "I am seventyfour years old, and I can afford candor. And, to answer your question, you *have* turned me on—or at least you've turned me on as much as a man my age *can* be turned on. Which isn't really much, I'm afraid. The spirit may be willing, but the flesh keeps getting weaker and weaker."

"I think we both ought to be arrested."

"So do I, I suppose."

"Here we are," said the girl, winking, "you seventyfour and me twentytwo, out here in all this bright sunshine and all, and we're coming on so strong it's about to make the pavement curl up."

"Really?"

"Yes. Absolutely. I know a sexy man when I see one."

They came to the end of the row of rooms. All during this ridiculous conversation with this ridiculous girl, Amberson had seen no sign of Sinclair. He took the girl's arm and steered her around the side of the building. He smiled at her and said: "That is the nicest compliment I've received in I don't know how long."

"I didn't mean it as a *compliment.* I meant it as a *fact.* I don't know much about much, but I do know something about sexy men. My name is Doris Lundgren. What's yours?"

"Howard Amberson."

She stuck out a hand. "Pleased to meet you, Mr. Amberson."

"My pleasure, Miss Lundgren," said Amberson. He squeezed the girl's hand, and it was warm.

Tears formed in the corners of Miss Lundgren's eyes.

"Hey," said Amberson, releasing her hand. Doris Lundgren hunched forward, and she pressed her hands against her mouth. "Now, now," said Amberson. He reached out and patted one of her shoulders.

She embraced him. She was taller than he, and she pressed his face against her collarbone. He closed his eyes, and he was able to hear his heart. Perhaps he was about to die. Well, he could think of worse ways. "I'm very . . . sorry . . ." said Doris Lundgren, snuffling. She pulled back from him. "It's just that . . . well, this has been the worst . . . ah, whoo, I *am* sorry . . . the worst night of my life . . ."

"Is there anything I can do?"

"Can you let me talk? We can still look for the cat, and maybe you can just let me talk. Would that be all right with you?"

"Of course," said Amberson.

Doris Lundgren took his arm, and they resumed walking toward the rear of the motel. "My friend brought me here all the way from Columbus last night," she said. "He wanted to come this far so he'd be *sure* he wasn't recognized. So he'd be *good* and sure. It's not that he's *ashamed* of me or anything like *that,* oh no *indeedy,* no *sir,* never. But every time we get together, he drives about halfway to the moon. One time we went all the way to *Anderson, Indiana.* Another time Cincinnati. And it's been going on for a year. He doesn't want his wife to find out, and he doesn't want the governor to find out, and he's oh just so careful it makes me want to—"

"Did you say the governor?"

"Yes. He works for the governor. He's a very important man."

Now they were in the parking lot behind the motel. Amberson squatted and peered under some more parked cars. No Sinclair. He straightened and looked around, and there was no sign of Anne either.

"Are you listening to me?" said Doris Lundgren.

"Yes," said Amberson. "I'm listening to every word. But I don't want to miss our cat in case he makes an appearance. We're very fond of him."

"I'm sorry. Of course you are. And you're worried too, I bet."

226

Amberson smiled at Doris Lundgren. "Please," he said. "Please go on."

"All right." Doris Lundgren fluffed her hair. "Do you know something? A lot of people, when they first see me, they think I'm in show biz. Good old show biz. They think I'm a chorus girl or something."

"Well, I certainly can understand why they would," said Amberson.

"That's what Larry thought. My *friend*. He met me at a party and he thought I was some real hot stuff heavy chorus girl."

"Heavy?"

"It means, ah, like *groovy* used to mean. Sort of like *bad,* you know?"

"Yes. I think so."

Doris Lundgren shrugged. She and Amberson had walked to the middle of the parking lot. She placed her hands on her hips and said: "You look to the right, and I'll look to the left. Now look *slow*. Don't let your eyes *skim.*"

"All right," said Amberson. He squinted, and his vision moved slowly along the wire fence that surrounded the parking lot on three sides. Sinclair could be crouched anywhere, and perhaps some small movement would reveal him.

"Can I talk?"

"Yes."

"Well, in spite of what Larry thought, I'm no *chorus girl.* You know what I do? I work for the telephone company, *that's* what I do. I'm a trouble operator. You know, if your telephone breaks down, you call the trouble operator. Anyhoo, Larry and I got this big *thing* going, and he says he loves me, but he won't *do* anything about it. He's got a wife and two little children, and he says it wouldn't be fair to them. And I don't think the governor would like it either, do you?"

"Well, I doubt that he would throw his hat in the air."

"Exactly. And that's all very fine—but where does it leave Doris, huh? I mean, I know what I got, and I know that men don't exactly want to *throw up* when they look at me, so why do I waste my time on Larry, will you tell me that?"

"I don't know."

"Right. You don't know. And *I* don't know. So last night, when Larry and I were finished doing you-know, I said to him: 'Larry, this is it. Either you get rid of that Sylvia of yours or it's Split City, if you know what I mean.' And that got us really going. And I mean *really* going. He told me I didn't understand. He told me I was a big dumb bitch with my mind in my crotch. He told me he was *sick* and *tired* of the way I was always after him about Sylvia. And, well, I got *my* licks in, too. I called him a cheater, and I called him gutless, and I said to him: 'Larry, if you had one more ball, that would give you a grand total of one and a half—maybe.' Oh, it was a *scene* and a half, let me tell you. And the upshot was that he gave me fifty dollars, like I was some cheap whore, and he went storming out of that room at three o'clock in the morning. And the next bus for Columbus comes through here at two-thirty this afternoon, and that concludes my sad tale of woe . . ."

Amberson turned to Doris Lundgren. "It doesn't sound so sad to me. He does not seem like a very impressive person, and you're better off without him. You can do better."

"Well, I know *that,*" said Doris Lundgren, and she began crying again. "He's a . . . a fat little jerk with a . . . a *pot* . . . and he . . . what am I going to *do* about him?"

Doris Lundgren hunched and wept, and there were goosebumps on her legs.

Amberson watched her. There was a knot in his belly, but it was reserved for Sinclair. He had no idea of anything further he could say to this girl. Perhaps she simply would have to work through her dilemma by herself. But, in the meantime, what had happened to Sinclair? What had happened to Anne? Amberson cleared his throat. "Now really," he said, "there's no reason for you to—"

Doris Lundgren looked up at Amberson. "If Billy had of lived, none of it would of happened." Again she wiped at her eyes.

"Who?"

"Billy. He was my husband. Billy Snead. He was an installer for the telephone company. It's because of him that I came to Columbus from Duluth. He was in the army with my brother, and Bud brought him home for Christmas four years ago, and Billy and I were married the next summer, soon as he got his discharge. And we came to Columbus, and he got me my job so I could help him save up some money because he wanted to go into the TV repair business, and we rented a nice little house down in Grove City, and we even kept a little vegetable garden out back, but he was a car freak, you know? Biggest car freak in the world. And Harry Maxwell and my Billy got themselves killed two years ago last May twentyninth when their car ran off the road just outside Greenfield, Indiana. They were on their way to the Indy Five Hundred, and I guess they were having a little Indy Five Hundred of their own, only all the pit stops were for whiskey. There was a third fellow in the car, old Dan Freeman, and *he* wasn't hurt even so much as a scratch, and he was the one told me about the pit stops. And Dan Freeman, *he* was the driver, and he got two years for vehicular manslaughter, and—hey, what's wrong?"

Amberson suddenly found himself go weak. His knees felt as if they would give way, and he wished he had something to lean against. He did not know why he was so affected. Oh, he knew *why*, but he could not understand why he was *giving way* to it. He was not the sort to give way.

"Now, please," said Doris Lundgren. "Please, Mr. Anderson . . ."

Amberson removed his spectacles. He looked around, and all dimensions were sharp and sunny, and everything—the fence, the motel, the parked cars—was touched with the most brilliant reality he had ever known. He tried to smile at Doris Lundgren, and finally he was able to say: "Excuse me—but we love our cat very much, and I just want to find him. He is a . . . a good cat . . . he really is . . . just the most affectionate cat one would want to . . . well, perhaps you know what I mean." The girl had moved toward him a step, but he shook his head and felt his feet steady under him once again. He shook his head, smiled a little and said: "No. No. I'm all right. Evidently the story about your husband touched me a great deal. I suppose, well, at my age I have heard so many such stories, and I have . . . well, I have been *involved* in so many of them . . . that I just . . . ah, perhaps it was one story too many. I'm very sorry. It's not very manly of me, I know."

Doris Lundgren smiled. "Mr. Anderson," she said, "you're the most manly man I've met since I don't know when. You are *heavy*, Mr. Anderson. You really are. To stand out here when you're worried half to death about your cat, to stand out here and listen to all my crap about my dumb personal life, that's being a *man*, Mr. Anderson, and don't you think otherwise. For all you know, I'm some dumb bitch with big boobies who hasn't got the sense God gave a pile of boards, and yet you *listen* to me and you *talk* to me. You *take the time*. You're a good man, Mr. Anderson, and I don't want to hear any argument from you." Then Doris Lundgren's smile became larger. "Ah *ha*," she said. "Maybe you ought to take a look behind you."

Amberson turned around. Anne was walking toward him, and she was smiling, and the Erwine twins were with her, and she was carrying Sinclair.

See now 1952, and it is election night, and Lewis sits grinning in front of his DuMont, and he is nibbling at his fingernails, and my daughterinlaw Alice is telling Anne oh you have no *idea* how hard he has worked for this. He's been up since 5:30 this morning, and he's visited every precinct in the county, *every single one*. Alice is redhaired and highbosomed and extraordinarily pretty, and she has a voice that is like steel filings in an old tin can, and I sit as far across the room from her as the walls permit.

Eisenhower is whaling the stuffing out of poor Adlai Stevenson, and Lewis shakes a plump jubilant fist at Edward R. Murrow and says: "Yeah, you New Deal creep you, you having a good time, huh?" And then Lewis sniggers. I glance away. It is not pleasant to watch one's own son snigger. One does not think of real persons as being sniggerers. It is too Dickensian. One thinks of Fagin, or perhaps even Scrooge, but never one's own *son.* And yet there Lewis is, hunched and absurdly sniggering, with a glass of Old Crow in his hand, and something has laid a cruel and smirking maliciousness across his face, and I suspect he never will change. He and his hoarsely luminous Alice (the former Alice Iverson of the Lakewood, Ohio, Iversons, and second runnerup in the voting for Ohio State University's 1949 homecoming queen) have gone too far down their personal road. He is twentyseven, and he was graduated three years ago from the Ohio State school of business, and in February of this year he opened the first Dodge-Plymouth dealership Paradise Falls ever has had. He calls it Paradise Plymouth, and its advertising symbol is a small grinning boy angel wearing a diaper. To his friends (and he has many), Lewis calls the angel Little PP . . . for Paradise Plymouth, of course. He is fond of saying that between the two of them, he and Little PP really know how to piss all over the unwary customer. He set himself up in business with a GI loan, plus money borrowed from both the Paradise Falls banks. Before taking this step, he had worked two years for a Chevrolet dealer named Sam Goettling, and Sam Goettling freely admits that when it came to selling a car, or a truck, or a wheelbarrow, or a sack of turtles, or anything else you would care to name, young Lew Amberson was an absolute crackerjack of a gogetter, and no mistake. And Sam Goettling has told us we shall be very proud of our Lewis. He has said to us: That boy will conquer the moon; he is the real stuff, and I honest to Christ feel sorry for anyone who tries to get in his way. Sam Goettling's words are admiring, and he means them as a compliment and a boost to our parental pride, but Anne and I are of course appalled by them. Have we created some sort of relentlessly grinning parody of George F. Babbitt? Have we shown him no values? And how is it possible to create a parody of a parody? Are Anne and I frauds? Do we know nothing? Does our love count for nothing? How can he *be* this way? Was our devotion to his brother Henry—the fabled Always Boy—all *that* overpowering? Well, perhaps so. Or at least this is what the evidence would seem to indicate. And if these conclusions are accurate, then I have no right to avert my eyes from Lewis and his sniggering jubilation; I have no right to disown what I have helped create. Either I am a father or I am not. It is as annihilatingly simple as that.

And so my head swivels back, and I contemplate him squarely. He is as handsome as ever, and his hair is just as wavy, and it is clear to me that the cheerleaders still leap and yip in his brain. (And he will fight. And he will win.) Tonight's gathering is a combined housewarming and election night party, and more than thirty persons have been invited. The house, which is a bit too angular and chilly for my taste, is among the first to be built in the new Hilltop Acres development, which is located on high ground west of the Oak Grove Cemetery. It has eleven rooms and two baths, and Lewis has had to borrow an additional ten thousand dollars for the down payment and the purchase of more furniture. Altogether, he must be at least thirty thousand dollars in debt, but he never has confided in us concerning such matters, and I expect he never will. (Is this because he feels we have betrayed him? Perhaps so. Ah, be honest and admit it: Probably so.) He and Alice were married in June of 1950. The wedding, which took place in a splendid Episcopal church in Lakewood, was most elaborate, and Alice's widowed mother (who paid for it all, rejecting my offer to share the cost) fluttered and clucked and kept telling us how happy she was that her Only Baby was marrying such a fine young man. But I do not believe Mrs. Iverson was happy at all. She sees herself as having a certain peripheral social status, but it is based on lineage and gentility rather than wealth. Her late husband was a vice president of a Cleveland bank, but that particular bank has at least fifty vice presidents, and Herbert C. Iverson was not the sort to emerge from the crowd—or so I have deduced from certain remarks that have been dropped by Alice and her mother. In addition, Lakewood is not a fashionable suburb of Cleveland, and Mrs. Iverson obviously is most embarrassingly aware of this. Therefore, Anne and I suspect quite strongly . . . and I think with good reason . . . that Mrs. Iverson was most disappointed by her Only Baby's choice of a husband. Clearly the woman had dreamed of marrying off Alice to someone with impeccable credentials whose family lived in one of the chic suburbs—Shaker Heights, for instance, or (better yet) Bratenahl or Gates Mills. It is a cliché, I know, but Mrs. Iverson's vision probably had created a pleasant enough but not too terribly bright young man with (a) an Ivy League diploma, (b) plenty of money, (c) an interest in horses, and (d) a family that was willing to accept ambitious outsiders. But this was not to be, especially for a woman from *Lakewood,* which was absolutely beyond the pale, as the saying goes. (I do not list an interest in Cleveland's social structure as being among the abiding passions of my life, but I do have a certain knowledge of the subject—gained first from Joanna Lyman more than thirty years ago and embellished more recently by Alice's constant references to it. I sometimes almost feel sorry for her. When she talks about the people who really *matter* in Cleveland, she sounds like a shopgirl gushing over Clark Gable and Marilyn Monroe. And I always have been saddened by unrequited love—especially when it is focused on the remote or the inaccessible or the patently unreal.) And so, because of all these factors, Alice evidently decided to make do with our son Lewis. She shares her mother's social aspirations, but there is a substantial pragmatism at work within our Alice, and she is not unaware of the rewards to be gained from being a large fish in a small creek. Better this than nothing, and so she has made do, and Lewis obviously is her enthusiastic accomplice. And that is of course the principal reason they bought so much new furniture when they moved into this house just last week. Ever since their marriage, they lived in a rented brick house on Spring Street (which is not chic *at all,* even by Paradise Falls standards), and Alice has told us that she never will set *foot* in that place again, not for *any* reason. "If there were *a million dollars* buried in the basement," she has said, "I absolutely would *not* go in to dig it up. Oh, I might *send* somebody in. I'm not *altogether* stupid. But as for going in there *myself,* no, no, not on your life, *ever.* " And now looking around the livingroom of this new house, I count seven pieces of new furniture—four chairs, two tables and a sofa. The basic pattern of the room is wrought iron, and to me it is all about as cheerful as a foundry. I wonder where Lewis goes when he wants to rest. Or is rest *necessary* to him? Perhaps, as far as he is concerned, rest is a waste of time. After all, how many Plymouths can one sell if one is lying flat on one's back?

Lewis is quite active in the Paradise County Republican party. He was an officer of the Young Republicans at Ohio State (and it was through this group, incidentally, that he met Alice), and this summer he was elected the youngest member of the county executive committee. He is talking of running for council next year, and I rather suspect he will. Today he has been in full charge of all the Republican precinct challengers throughout the county, and this evidently has made Alice quite proud. According to her (and if she has said it once, she has said it a dozen times), Lewis has visited each of the polling places at least once today, and she insists that he has logged a minimum of a hundred miles on his brandnew '53 club coupe—a Plymouth, of course.

The guest list, however, is reasonably bipartisan. Anne and I are both lifelong Democrats. Another guest, Hugo G. Underwood, the attorney, was a Democratic Congressman for two years, riding into office when Truman surprised Dewey in '48, but riding back out in '50 when our district reverted to its normal Republican voting pattern. He is a portly fellow, and it is said he is (or was) something of a philanderer. His wife, Jane, is a large horsefaced woman, girdled and ominous, and if he is indeed a philanderer, I for one certainly can understand why. Now she is sitting next to him on the sofa, and she is sitting bolt upright, and I would not be surprised if a ring of keys were hanging at her waist, attached to her dress with a leather thong. She is the daughter and only child of my old friend Elmer Carmichael, the president of the Paradise Falls Clay Products Co. and my adversary back in '37 during the Emerald White cemetery dispute. This is the man who called me a miserable little pisser and then in the next breath offered me a job. He is, as one might expect, a Republican, and he is quite friendly with a former governor, John W. Bricker, who is being reelected to the United States Senate tonight, easily defeating a man named Michael V. DiSalle. Carmichael is lounging in an easy chair (if there is such a thing as a wrought iron "easy" chair), and he is drinking beer from a bottle. Most of the other guests are milling and chatting and munching on snacks and drinking highballs, and Alice moves smoothly from group to group, the gracious hostess, smiling and brighteyed, her lush body neatly tucked and cinched in a long green dress cut low in the bosom and tight across the hips. (I say to myself: Ah, if only she did not possess the power of speech.) Most of these other guests are Republicans. The party may be bipartisan, but it is not too bipartisan, seeing as how the ratio is perhaps nine to one in favor of the Grand Old Party. These people include lawyers and businessmen and politicians and the like—and they are here of course with their wives, whose eyes are taking stern and meticulous inventory of the house and its furnishings. Tomorrow these women will telephone one another, and they will employ such adjectives as "nice" and "daring" and "tasteful" and "tacky," and a great clacking will rise, and many are the ears that will flap and twitch.

It is all very interesting, and I smile at everyone. Several of the male guests are former members of my track teams. They are prosperous now, and all barbered and fragrant, but I can remember when they had acne, and somehow this comforts me. I have voted for Stevenson today, and perhaps my candidate's defeat has made me a bit malicious, but I do not particularly care. If I choose to remember all these successful fellows as once having been pimply boys, that is my affair, and I need answer to no one. If I am petulant, I am petulant. Tomorrow will be another day.

Anne comes and seats herself in an empty chair next to mine. She is enormously fat, and she is wearing a red and white dress that has an unflattering pattern of checks and stripes. She has now gained perhaps forty pounds since the death of Henry the Always Boy seven and a half years ago. She is carrying a glass of Coca-Cola and a handful of tiny sandwiches spread with cream cheese. She offers me one of the sandwiches. I do not want it, but I take it anyway. If I eat it, then she will not, and I will have struck a blow for something or other. Ah, but she knows why she has gained so much weight, and she knows it is absurd and improper for one to express one's grief by eating too much. As a result, she is forever going on diets. And she is forever going off diets. I still love her very much, and I do not want her to burst. But I do not know what to do about the situation, and so I have let it go. My soul is curdled whenever I think about it, and I keep pushing it away, and why does she still have to talk so often about the Kitty Heaven letter?

Anne sighs, munches on one of the tiny sandwiches. "Well," she says, "this certainly is a grand affair."

"The elephant triumphant. A large grin and a little dog named Checkers will do it every time."

"Now, don't be *sarcastic*. Eisenhower is a nice man, and maybe he'll be a good President."

I swallow the last of my sandwich. *"Warren G. Harding* was a nice man, a *very* nice man—especially when he was in the broom closet with Nan Britton."

"Nobody loves a bad loser," says Anne.

"That is probably correct," I tell her. I still am smiling, and I hope my face is properly bland. That way, my expression will disguise what I am saying, and none of these multitudinous Republicans will suspect a thing. For some reason, I am quite tired tonight, and I do not want to become involved in any sort of political argument. With Anne, however, it is different. She is my *wife*, and we have been married more than thirty years, and she knows enough not to take me seriously when I become cynical and make sour references to broom closets.

More and more of the guests have clustered around the DuMont, and they are clapping and laughing. It is not yet ten o'clock, and Eisenhower is already nearly two million votes ahead. He has carried a number of southern states, and it is obvious he will sweep the country. Lewis has turned up the volume, and I am able to hear just about every word, despite the babble of the guests. Anne and I (she is munching energetically) are sitting against a far wall, and it is almost as though we have been cast adrift from the rest of the party. However, considering the nature of the party and the results of the balloting, this is not unpleasant. I have never made a secret of my Democratic sympathies, and the wonder is that none of these Republicans has come to hoot at me and, ah, give me the razz.

Lewis still is sitting in his chair, and he still holds the glass of Old Crow. Alice is standing behind the chair, and she is rubbing the back of his neck. He reaches behind his head and pats one of her wrists. She smiles down on him, and perhaps a photographer should be there: Loving Wife Comforts Tired Warrior. (I am reminded of that dreadful Nixon and his cardboard spunglass wife.)

Then, for some reason, Lewis grins at me and waves.

I wave back, and I still am smiling. I never have stopped smiling.

Munching, Anne also waves.

Lewis whispers something to Alice. She nods, bends over and helps him out of his chair. He leans against it for a moment, then straightens and starts toward me. He still has the glass of Old Crow, and Alice has hold of his free arm. He stops in front of the sofa for a moment, and he says something to Hugo G. Underwood, who stiffens for an instant, then shrugs and grins. But Elmer Carmichael, who obviously has heard the remark, laughs loudly, and several of the guests turn to stare. And Jane Underwood, who still is sitting rigidly next to her husband, also seems quite amused. Lewis claps Hugo G. Underwood on a shoulder and comes directly across the room to me. Alice still is at his side, and they both are grinning. By this time, *most* of the guests have turned to stare, and the babble and laughter diminish. It is clear to me that my time has come, that my son is about to embark on a journey to, ah, the Land of Gloat. Oh well, I suppose he is entitled, and I think I have enough grace to take it well. At least I hope so.

Lewis stands splayfooted in front of me. He places his hands on his hips. His grin has caused the corners of his eyes to crinkle. Next to him, Alice moistens her lips with her tongue. He leans forward, and now he is rocking on the balls of his feet, and he says: "Well, Pop, what do you think?"

"I expect you already know what I think," I tell him.

"The world has gone to hell in a handcart, right?"

"Well, perhaps not the world. Perhaps only the country."

"You'll miss old Hairy-Ass Truman, right?"

"Right."

"The jackals are loose in the palace grounds, right?"

"Right."

"The forces of darkness have taken over, right?"

"Right."

"But you're not going to fall on your sword, right?"

"Right."

"Maybe in Fiftysix the Democrats will win, right?"

"Right."

"It's always darkest before the dawn, right?"

"Right."

Lewis nudges his wife, takes a swallow of Old Crow, then: "That's what I like about old Pop—he's such a great talker. Such . . . ah, eloquence. I had a brother once who was the same way. So eloquent it was hard to believe. He's a . . . saint, you know." Now Lewis waggles a finger at Alice. "Don't laugh. He's a real *saint,* and he's off somewhere strumming a harp and playing with the angels and the lambypoos and all the little dead kittycats. He—"

"Lewis," says Anne. "Lewis, you be quiet now."

Now the place is silent except for the voices from the DuMont. Lewis is swaying over me, and finally, after twentyseven years, it all has been exposed, and I can think of absolutely nothing to say.

But Alice can. Trust Alice. She pats my son's arm and says: "Now, now, down, boy. Let's not get carried away." Then she looks at me and says: "I'm very sorry, Father Amberson, I know that must have hurt you." (She has always called me "Father Amberson." And Anne is always "Mother Amberson." And somehow her use of those ghastly names has always made a great deal of sense. Being what she is, one would hardly expect her to call us anything else. Am I being uncharitable? Of course I am being uncharitable. I am like everyone else. I am flawed. I cannot love the world. Only Henry could love the world—but he was flawed, too, else he never could have been a soldier.)

I stare at Alice. She is twentyfour years old, but at the same time she obviously is older than sin and corruption. By saying what she said, she underscored the scene for any witnesses who did not quite understand what was happening. I say to her (and my voice is steady): "Thank you, Alice. Thank you very much indeed."

And so it finally has emerged—after all those years. The guests clear their throats and begin talking loudly again, and Alice steers a grinning Lewis back to his chair. Anne and I go to the hall closet, fetch our hats and coats and leave that place of wassail and triumph.

Neither Lewis nor Alice even as much as glances in our direction. That way, they can always say well, for heaven's sake, we didn't even know you were gone. Anne and I walk slowly down the High Street hill, and she is crying, but the only way I know this is from the sound of her breath. Her throat makes no sound whatever. The night is clear and rather warm for this time of the year, and leaves crunch under our feet. I think of how Anne has tried to avoid all this. I call to mind all those times when she hugged and kissed Lewis and Florence and told them yes, yes, *yes,* she loved *them* too, and it was not only the Always Boy she loved. And I think Florence believed her and still does. But Lewis obviously never believed her. And still does not. And finally, after all these years and all his smiles and all the gogetter optimism, he has permitted his skepticism to emerge. And now his mother weeps. And I cannot think of a thing to say. No. That is not true. I could say to her: Anne, we allowed ourselves to be captured by an excessive and unnatural love, and because of it we neglected our other children. Therefore, we are to blame, and tonight we deserved Lewis's words. They have been long overdue. Ah, but how can I say such things to Anne? I may be flawed, but I am not cruel. At least not *that* cruel. And anyway, what of Lewis? *He* certainly behaved cruelly tonight. Granted, Anne and I may not have been perfect parents—in his view. But we never were *malicious* toward him, God knows. And we permitted him to go his own way, God knows. And we would have helped him if we had ever been asked, God knows. And perhaps *there,* as the fellow said, is the crux of the matter. He never sought our help, this Lewis . . . not once. He never relented, and he was elected to numerous offices in school, and he was a *captain* at twenty, and his Ravenna Arsenal superiors spoke highly of him, and he never even had pimples. And he was forever a participant. Unlike the Always Boy, he was never an outcast, and it always was necessary that he be with people. He always was a chooser and a belonger (and he still is). And it always has been necessary that he shape all conversations, games, excursions and social affairs to conform to his ideas of what they are supposed to accomplish. He is, in short, a sort of bully, and clearly he always has been. And clearly he will go far in the world. And it is *his* world, a world the Always Boy never would have been able to penetrate. And oh yes, there *indeed* is the crux of the matter, but can I discuss it with Anne? Can I say to her: We excluded Lewis, and now he is excluding us? No. This is beyond me, and so I say nothing. We walk home, and neither of us speaks, and we put on our nightclothes and brush our teeth and go to bed, and we do not sleep particularly well, and I have an idea of what will happen the next day, and it does. A haggard and redeyed Lewis visits us at breakfast, and he tries to smile, and he apologizes, and of course we both embrace him, and of course nothing has changed. He has coffee with us, and he speaks of crankshafts and dealer preparation fees and tinted windows, and he tells me: Don't worry, Pop; the Republicans won't be as bad as you think. (He may be haggard and redeyed, but every wavy hair is in place, and his suit is neatly pressed, and his tie is knotted just so.) He smiles and jokes. His teeth are brilliant. He tells us Alice gave him unshirted hell for his behavior. He says he is very sorry neither of them noticed us leave. He says Elmer Carmichael gave him the devil for speaking to his father that way. He says: Well, I hope you understand how sorry I am. And I say to him: Yes, I understand how sorry you are. And the subject never again comes up until the very last day of his life.

"Look who's here," said Anne.

Sinclair was curled in Anne's arms like an infant, and Amberson again felt a little wobbly in the legs, and he said: "Oh. Hey. You found him."

"He's a cutiepie," said Doris Lundgren, still grinning. "I can see why you were so worried."

Anne held up Sinclair and waggled a paw. Amberson began to laugh. "Ah," he said, "good old fellow. Good old Sinclair . . ."

"Surprise," said Karen Erwine, winking.

"Say hello to your lord and master," Anne told Sinclair, and again she waggled the paw. Sinclair looked up at her, yawned, then scratched himself behind an ear. Anne laughed, and so did the Erwine twins, and so did Doris Lundgren. Everyone was laughing at once, and Amberson scooped Sinclair from Anne's arms, and he hugged Sinclair, and he scratched Sinclair under the chin, and Sinclair purred, and everyone beamed at everyone else.

After a minute or so of this, Amberson got around to introducing Doris Lundgren. She apologized for appearing so, ah, informal, but she told Anne and the twins that she was a Svenska from Minnesota and enjoyed cold weather very much. The Erwine girls told how they had found Sinclair. The cat had gone wandering through an open door into the motel kitchen, probably attracted by odors of garbage. The Erwine twins had been there on a coffee and doughnut break, and Sinclair had promptly hopped on the lap of Karen. She had known right away that he was someone's loved pet; he was too plump and wellgroomed to be just a stray. She and Kathy had been discussing what to do with him

238

when Anne had suddenly appeared at the kitchen door. End of story.

As far as Amberson was concerned, this called for a celebration, or at least a cup of coffee. Doris Lundgren tried to beg off, but the others insisted, and so she ran to her room, fetched her coat and joined the Ambersons and the Erwine twins (and Sinclair) in the coffee shop. Animals were not allowed in the coffee shop, and so Anne was keeping Sinclair in her lap, and only his ears were visible over the edge of the table. While they were waiting for Doris, Amberson smiled at Anne and said: "Don't let appearances deceive you. She seems to be a very nice young woman. She was really quite helpful to me."

"Well," said Anne, "it must be nice being helped by a Playboy Bunny."

Kathy Erwine was sitting next to Anne, while Karen went off to get the coffee. Kathy grinned and said: "*I'd* like to be a Playboy Bunny, just for one day. I'd like to know what it *feels* like."

"You might catch cold," said Anne.

"I'd take that chance," she said. "But I'll never be a Playboy Bunny or anything else. I'm too *fat*. So is Karen. The Beef Trust Twins. I mean, back there in the kitchen when your cat came wandering in, what were we doing? We were having a coffee *and doughnut* break. We need doughnuts like Howard Hughes needs, ah, a dime for a telephone call."

"You and your sister are very attractive," said Amberson.

"And he's an expert on that sort of thing," said Anne.

"I mean it," said Amberson.

"He does," said Anne. "And he's right. You and your sister have lovely eyes and complexions, and you have warm dispositions."

"But I'd need two centerfolds," said Kathy, shaking her head.

Amberson chuckled, and Anne made a clucking sound of disapproval.

Doris Lundgren arrived and slid into the booth next to Amberson. She was wearing a long raincoat, and she had done up her hair. She smiled at Sinclair and said: "Ah, he looks like such a nice kitty."

Sinclair peeked over the edge of the table at Doris Lundgren.

"*I see you*," said Doris Lundgren, widening her eyes. "*I see you,* Mister Kitty. You and your big old whiskers." Her mouth made a number of kissing sounds, and Sinclair stared steadily at her. Her thigh rubbed against Amberson's, and he wished Karen would hurry with the coffee.

"I thank you for helping my husband," said Anne, not unpleasantly.

"It was my pleasure," said Doris Lundgren. "Mr. Anderson and I had a nice talk while we were walking around, and he—"

Amberson interrupted. "I'm sorry," he said, "but it's *Amberson*. A-M-B, not A-N-D."

"Oh, I *am* sorry. I thought it was Anderson. Up in Minnesota, we have lots of Andersons."

"But not a single Amberson," said Anne.

"No, I'm afraid not," said Doris Lundgren.

Anne smiled. "Well, don't let it bother you. People are forever calling us Anderson. We once belonged to the Book-of-the-Month Club, and it *insisted* our name was Anderson. And we almost got to believing it, too."

"I was a schoolteacher," said Amberson, "and about thirty years ago I got on some sucker list that had me down as H. W. Anderson. Sucker lists are bought and sold, you know, and I can't tell you how many textbook firms, athletic supply houses and magazine publishers sent me mail addressed to that mystery man, H. W. Anderson."

"You were a coach of some sort?" said Kathy.

"Yes. Track. At Paradise Falls High School. I wasn't all that much of a—"

"He's being modest," said Anne to Kathy. "His team won the state Class A championship in 1944, and it always had a fine winning tradition."

"Hey, that's wonderful," said Kathy.

"Yes indeed," said Doris Lundgren, and her thigh had become quite warm. She wriggled a bit, and Amberson cleared his throat. Anne smiled at them both.

Karen came with the coffee. She seated herself next to her sister and smiled at Doris Lundgren. "Thank you for helping this nice man."

"That's why I helped him," said Doris Lundgren. "Because he's a nice man."

"Stop it now, girls," said Amberson.

"And you're loving every golden moment of it," said Anne.

"Yes," said Amberson.

Everyone laughed, and Sinclair looked around. They drank coffee and the girls chatted of clothes and makeup and diets. Kathy and Karen told Doris Lundgren they envied her figure, and she grinned and allowed as how it was a battle. If I'm not on one diet, she said, I'm another. I can gain weight just by *looking* at food, and that is the plain truth. And then Karen smiled at Doris Lundgren and said: Maybe I shouldn't tell you this, but you are beautiful—do you know that? No. Don't shake your head. I mean it. Doris Lundgren began to sniffle. And Amberson looked at her and said: It is as I told you. There is nothing the matter with you, and you'll come out of it just fine. All you have to do is use your common sense. Doris Lundgren dabbed at her eyes with her napkin. Anne smiled at her and said: I don't know what my husband means, but I would advise you to believe him. He is not a bad sort of fellow for an old goat. And Doris Lundgren breathed deeply, wadded up her napkin, made a long shuddering sound, then said: You people come off the top shelf, you know what I mean? You really do, and I . . . well, I, ah, don't really deserve your attention, but do you want to *know* something? I don't *care* whether I deserve it. I'm, ah, I'm going to accept it. I thank you . . . oh yes. And then, without another word, Doris Lundgren stood up and hurried away. Amberson watched Doris Lundgren's legs and the movements of her hips, and then looked at the Erwine twins and shrugged. He did not know what he felt. He did not even know what he was supposed to feel. All he knew was that something had moved him, something desperate and loving and grateful. He asked himself: Can it be possible that we *helped* that girl? If this is true, then today we have made a contribution to the apparatus, which means we still are alive, which means we have not altogether yielded to our liverspots and our cancers and our aching gums. Kathy said something to the effect that perhaps that poor girl had a really bad problem. And Kathy said: I don't recall seeing the name Doris Lundgren in the register. And Amberson said: You didn't. And Kathy said: Is that the problem? And Amberson said: Of course. He finished his coffee. Anne finished hers. The Erwine twins told the Ambersons they surely had enjoyed making their acquaintance and walked the Ambersons to the car. Anne carried Sinclair clutched against her chest. Amberson started the engine and rolled down the window and thanked the Erwine twins. He rolled up the window and said to Anne: "Shall we?" And Anne said: "Let's." They pulled out of the parking lot, and the Erwine twins waved at them, and Sinclair scrambled into the back seat and baptized his box for the day.

See now 1936, a steaming and languid Wednesday afternoon in late August, and we are sprawled, the Ambersons recumbent, all five of us, on the thick mushy sand at the edge of Paradise Lake. Behind us are sounds of a calliope and of funhouse laughter, and an occasional child darts past us and goes plashing and whooping into the warm golden water, but today is not a loud day. There is a depression, and most people have neither the time nor the money for amusement park frivolity. Especially on a Wednesday.

We are all wearing swimsuits, and the cast on my left ankle has begun to itch. I did a stupid thing last week. I fell off the roof. There had been a rainstorm, and a tree branch had been torn loose and blown into the chimney, clogging it. And so, with great intrepidity and zeal, I borrowed a ladder from my friend Jimmy Jones and clambered up on the roof.

I do not quite know what happened. One moment I was tugging on the branch, and the next I was sliding and flailing, reaching for hooks in the sky. The roof of our home is on an extreme slant, and so I rolled as I slid, and the more I rolled, the more I slid, until I went crashing and bleating off the edge of the roof and landed smack on the front sidewalk, breaking the ankle and lacerating my hands, buttocks, elbows and back. Later, when Dr. Button treated me in his office, he told me: Mr. Amberson, it is a wonder of Almighty God that you didn't jam your coccyx up against your adamsapple. (Emerald White, busy bandaging my lacerations, turned away from me for a moment, and her hand covered her mouth, and I saw her shoulders move.)

At any rate, it was a ridiculous and brainless accident, a thing that would have made even Harold Lloyd blush, and I have received a good deal of ragging about it from Anne and the children, even little Florence, who is just six years old and really shouldn't be so hard on her dimwitted old papa. Now, as we loll and blink into the sun, and as we sip on the Cokes Lewis has fetched from a stand over by the funhouse, I rub my lacerated places, and I wince a little, and Anne says: "Who ever heard of a onelegged track coach?"

"He's about as useful as a onelegged tap dancer," says Lewis, who is eleven and sturdy and already handsomely blond.

I throw up my arms and shield my eyes. "Mercy," I say. "Have mercy on me. Please."

Florence has been scooping sand into a damp mound. She looks up and covers her mouth, and I am reminded of Emerald White. But when Florence's hand comes away from her mouth, her lips are encircled by sand, and it is my turn to smile, and Lewis tells her she looks like a goof. Florence blinks at him, then sets to work rubbing away the sand.

"You shouldn't call your sister a goof," Anne tells Lewis.

Lewis shrugs. "I hurt her feelings or something?"

"He didn't hurt my feelings," says Florence, rubbing.

"See? I didn't hurt her feelings," Lewis tells his mother.

Henry is sitting next to me, and he smiles at the world and says: "It's too nice a day for that." He is thirteen and enormous, and he is wearing nothing but a set of trunks, and his belly is flat.

Anne smiles at Henry, then turns to Lewis and says: "He's right."

"Sure," says Lewis, looking away. He jams the straw deeper into his Coke bottle and begins noisily sucking.

Henry lies back, places his Coke bottle on his flat belly and closes his eyes. The moisture from the sweating bottle spreads on his flesh.

Florence finishes rubbing off the sand. She licks her lips, spits away a final grain or two, then resumes building her mound. She hums, but I cannot make out the tune. She is quite pretty, and she is no bother, and Anne and I love her very much. She will be entering the first grade next month, but she already can read a little. Henry has taught her. He reads the comics to her every afternoon, and she is able to follow along quite nicely.

Ferociously sucking, Lewis glares over his straw and says to Anne: "He's always right."

"How's that?" says Anne. "What are you talking about?"

"Old Henry," says Lewis. "No matter what happens, he's the one who's always right. If I was to tell you water was wet, and he was to tell you it felt like fire, it'd turn out feeling like fire, wouldn't it?"

"Now you're being ridiculous," says Anne.

"Yeah," says Lewis, sucking.

Henry quickly finishes his Coke. His eyes still closed, he talks across me to his brother. "Hey now," he says, "nobody's right about *everything.*"

"Yeah," says Lewis. Abruptly he scrambles to his feet. He walks away.

Henry opens his eyes and sits up.

"It's all right, dear," says Anne to Henry.

He looks at her, and his eyes are soft, and then he rubs his palms against his knees.

Florence hums and digs.

We watch Lewis. He scuffs as he walks. He beats his arms across his chest, and he begins to run, and he goes scrambling off toward the funhouse. We lose sight of him, and then Anne says: "Sometimes I think he enjoys feeling sorry for himself." (She is speaking to no one, and perhaps she is not aware that she is speaking at all.)

"He's got no reason," says Henry.

Anne and I look at him.

"What do you mean?" I ask him.

"He's got no reason to hate me," says Henry. "I don't want him to hate me. I never gave him—"

Anne breaks in. "That's nonsense," she says. "He doesn't hate you. He loves you. You're his brother, and he loves you very much. You shouldn't talk about hate. You don't know anything about hate."

Henry's head moves from side to side, and then he smiles at his mother. "I . . . well, I got to do something about it."

Anne is wearing an orange swimsuit, and she fills it well. Her chest is freckled, and she is wearing smoked glasses. She pushes the smoked glasses down her nose and blinks over them at Henry. "There's *nothing* you have to *do*," she tells Henry. "That's a stupid thing to say, and you ought to know better."

Henry shrugs. "Okay," he says.

"He has little temper fits every so often," says Anne. "There's nothing more to it than that . . ."

"Okay," says Henry.

"Believe me," says Anne, "that's all it is."

"Fine," says Henry.

"We don't want to blow it up all out of proportion," says Anne. Then she looks sharply at me and says: "Isn't that right?"

"Of course," I tell her.

Anne nods. She lies back, folds her hands on her belly. "This is too nice a day for this kind of talk."

"Absolutely," I tell her. Then I smile at Henry and say: "Indulge him, old sport. He doesn't mean you any harm. Not really."

"Okay," says Henry and stands up. "I'll be back," he says. He walks toward the water and wades until the water is up to his neck, then gives a sort of shout and begins to swim. He cuts through the water with ease, and his arms are very long.

Anne sits up and watches him. She says nothing, and neither do I. In front of us, Florence hums over her mound of sand, and the sky is yellow and blank. Anne leans forward and hugs her knees. She watches Henry quite closely, and I suppose I have a reasonably good idea what she is thinking. She will personally see to it that no harm ever comes to him. She will personally see to it that no one ever hates him. And anyway, why would anyone hate Henry? He cannot help being special. She has tried and *tried* to explain all this to Lewis, but Lewis either cannot or will not understand. Oh, he knows enough to smile most of the time, and his little temper fits, as Anne calls them, do not really come so often, but something terribly urgent and proclamative is clawing at him, and I know this, and so does Anne, if she ever will admit it. He works so hard at everything. He is always in charge of his playmates. He is the captain and the leader, and I have no doubt but what he will succeed in whatever he attempts. And he must know this, too. Yet he is consumed by a drive to compete, and it is as though he is forever inadequate and attempting to pass some impossible test. His hands are often in fists, and I have seen him slam those fists against the earth, raging against some childish frustration. A fumbled football, or the inability to hold his breath for two minutes. Everything he does receives maximum effort, whether it be football or a spelling contest or a footrace or the devouring of pancakes. And he is forever looking to Anne and me and telling us: See how well I can throw a football. See how many pancakes I can devour. And Anne, knowing all this, is constantly taking him aside and trying to reassure him. She hugs him and kisses him and tells him: Yes, yes, you are a wonderful little boy, and we love you. And he always smiles at her. And his smile is tough and rigid. And he tells her: Yeah. Sure. I know that. And he never forgets to show her enough teeth. Sometimes little Florence is there, and sometimes he turns to little Florence and says: Mama loves us a whole lot, and don't you forget it. (But the tough and rigid smile always is there, and it has a way of frightening me, and I do not like to watch those little scenes.)

Anne looks at me. "How's your ankle?"

"It itches a little, but other than that it's fine."

"I . . . I wish Lewis wouldn't behave that way . . ."

"It doesn't happen very often, and anyway, it didn't amount to much."

"Will he ever understand?" Anne asks me.

"I have no idea."

"I can't help the way I feel about Henry, and all I'm asking Lewis to *do* is *accept* it . . ."

"Well, yes. That's all very well and good, but he feels that somehow the way you feel about Henry takes something away from *him.*"

"But I *love* him!"

Florence looks up from her mound of sand. "*I* love Lewis, too," she says. Her swimsuit is white, with green polkadots, and it is smeared with muddy sand. There was a rain last night. "Mary Woods is in love with him, and she's going to marry him when she and him grow up."

I smile. Mary Woods is perhaps seven, and her mouth is full of steel braces, and she talks with a salivary lisp. "Does Lewis know about all this?" I ask my daughter.

"No," says Florence. "It's a secret. She made me cross my heart and spit and everything."

"But you just told us," says Anne.

"You don't count," says Florence.

"That's a *terrible* thing to say," says Anne, smiling.

"Grownups don't count," says Florence, speaking solemnly, her voice calm and patient as she explains the rules to us. She pats the mounded sand, and then she says: "It's got nothing to do with mommies and daddies . . ."

"Oh," says Anne. "All right then."

Anne hunkers to where Florence is sitting. She hugs Florence, but she is careful not to disturb the mound. I grin at them, and my cast itches. Out in the lake, Henry moves efficiently. He is an excellent swimmer. He has been swimming since he was about five or six, and I recall that it took me about five or ten minutes to teach him the hang of it, as the saying goes. He did precisely what I told him to do, and he listened carefully, and that was that. Oh yes, he is remarkable, and his future is beyond imagining.

Anne and Florence giggle and snicker together, and Anne helps Florence with the mound. I look around for Lewis, but he is nowhere to be seen. I gave him a halfdollar this morning, and perhaps he is exploring the funhouse or riding on one of the rollercoasters. I have been leaning back on my elbows, and my arms have stiffened. I sit up and rub my arms and the lacerated places, especially the lacerated places on my elbows. I rub away sand, and I have a terrible urge to tear away the cast on my poor stupid left ankle. A crutch lies in the sand next to me, and I surely would like to beat the damned cast with the crutch. Just whack it and whack it, like Lewis when he is having one of his little temper fits, as Anne calls them.

I shake my head. I am ridiculous. I glare at the sun. I am not wearing smoked glasses, and so my eyes water.

Anne sees all this. She kisses Florence, then hunkers back to where I am sitting. "Are you all right?" she asks me.

"I am fine," I tell her. "Stupid and ridiculous, but all in all just fine and dandy."

"Why were you making a face at the sun?"

"Would you like to know the truth?"

"Yes. I always like to know the truth."

"Well, because my itch is driving me mad. I can no longer behave rationally."

Anne smiles. "Forgive me for smiling," she says, "but I just can't help it."

"Fine. You go ahead and smile. The more he suffers, the more she smiles."

Anne covers her mouth.

I reach out for her.

She squirms a little. "Florence . . . she's right over there and . . ."

"Never mind Florence," I tell my wife.

"Yes sir," says Anne. She hunkers closer to me, and then I am hugging her. She has an odor of sand and sun, all yellow and hot. Her breath is dry against my neck. "You hug good," she says.

"I hug *well*," I tell her. I kiss her hair. Her smoked glasses have slipped to the end of her nose.

Florence looks across at us and grins.

Anne blinks at me. "Can you do it with your ankle in a cast?" she asks me.

"That's the fourth time you've asked me that today."

"Well, the need for an answer is becoming more and more urgent."

"You're beginning to talk the way I talk."

"It's the force of your personality," says Anne. "But don't change the subject. Answer my question."

"Can I do what? Hug?"

"*No,* you ninny. Not *hug.* I meant *something else.*"

"Kiss your breasts?"

"No."

"Interpose my tongue in your ear?"

"No . . . but you're sort of on the right track . . ."

"Am I?"

"Yes."

"Is Florence watching us?"

"No."

"Suppose I were to put my hand . . . well, perhaps you—"

"That would be just grand . . ."

"The elastic is not all that tight, is it?"

"No . . . but it wouldn't matter if it were . . ."

"Is this the right track?"

"Yes . . . oh, yes . . ."

"Try to sit as quietly as you can."

"You must be . . . joking . . ."

I smile. I kiss Anne's ears. The elastic presses against my hand, but I still am able to move my finger. I move it as subtly as I can, and Anne gasps. "I see no reason why we cannot make an effort tonight," I tell her.

"I'm all wet. I don't swim a *stroke,* and here I *am* . . . all wet . . ."

"I'll start with your breasts. You have marvelous breasts. Freckles and all."

"They only have the freckles in the . . . summer. In the winter they're ah, *snowy* . . ."

"Your nipples are so dark and lovely."

"Thank . . . you . . ."

"In the morning . . ."

"In the evening . . ."

"Ain't we got fun?"

"Oh . . . oh, *yes,*" says Anne, murmuring.

I look away from Anne for a moment. Florence has abandoned her mound of sand, and now she is wading at the edge of the lake. Anne and I lie back, and I remove my hand from inside the elastic. Her mouth is open, and her smoked glasses are askew. "We'll find a way," I tell her. "Perhaps I can prop myself with the crutch."

"That would be nice . . ."

"Where there is a will, there is a way."

She lightly touches me.

"Yes ma'am," I tell her. "The will is there."

"Oh, hunkydory . . ." says Anne.

"Nothing like amusing oneself at an amusement park."

"Yes," says Anne. "You know, I think I came a little."

"Oh?"

"Yes—but only a little. What with God and the world so near, I had to . . . well, you know . . . "

"Suppress it?"

"Yes . . . as much as I could . . ."

"Did you enjoy it?"

"Yes . . . but I'll enjoy tonight more . . ."

I close my eyes. "Remember the jigsaw puzzle?"

"Of course I remember the jigsaw puzzle."

"Did you ever retrieve all the pieces?"

"I don't believe so . . ."

"I wonder if that indicates some sort of symbolism."

"Stop being so *academic* . . ."

"Yes ma'am."

"It was *terrible,* but it was *fun.*"

"Yes ma'am."

"We *rutted.* We went and *rutted* right there on the *floor,* and it was wonderful . . ."

"Yes ma'am."

"I came a little just now. I really did."

"So you said."

"I hate to repeat myself, but it was very nice."

"Repeat yourself all you like. I enjoy hearing it."

"You make me come so *quickly* . . ."

"Good."

Anne's hand still is resting on me. She squeezes me a little, and I cannot suppress a sort of moan. "Ah," she says, "the gander gives it to the goose . . ."

"In a manner of speaking . . ."

"Sometimes we're vulgar, aren't we?"

"A little . . ."

"Are you offended?"

"No."

"Good. And neither am I. Does that mean we are terrible?"

"Only moderately terrible. And next to some people, we're hardly terrible at all. Take that fellow Hitler, for instance."

"I don't want to talk about *Hitler*. This is no time to be talking about *current events.*"

"All right. I was simply trying to cite an example, that's all."

"Well, thank you very much, but no thanks."

"Yes ma'am," I say.

Then, for a time, we say nothing. My wife's hand does not move, but she is silent, and so am I. My eyes remain closed, and I listen to the sounds of the lake and a distant sound of children and music. It is tinny music, imprecise and lovely. I suppose there are those who might think Anne and I are a scandal, but I do not care. We love one another, and we have always preferred to talk openly. I rub my face. It is smeared with warmth from the sunlight. Anne pats me, and I smile, and then Florence begins to scream.

I open my eyes and sit up. So does Anne. Her hand comes away from me.

Florence has waded out too far in the water. She is thrashing and flailing, and her screams are wet.

Anne jumps up. "Oh my God!" she cries, and she starts running toward the water.

I struggle to my feet as best I can. Using my crutch, I hobble after her. I look around for Henry, but I do not see him. He is not in the water, and he is not on the beach, and neither is Lewis, and Anne cannot swim a stroke, and I am crippled like an injured dog, and Florence screams and flails. My mouth is full of bile, and my legs ache. Anne begins wading out into the water, but she will never get to Florence, who is out perhaps thirty or forty yards, where the water is at least fifteen feet deep. I should know. I have swum there many times. I follow Anne into the water, and the sand sucks at my crutch and my cast and my good foot. I look around, and Henry is running down a bank, followed by Lewis. They both are holding hot dogs.

They sprint to the water, but at the edge Henry hesitates. He looks back to Lewis. He is close enough so I can see he appears to be frowning a little. Lewis tosses away his hot dog and sprints past Henry and goes splashing out into the water. He is also an excellent swimmer, perhaps almost as expert as Henry, who stands watching him. Now Anne is weeping, and the water is up to her neck, and we cannot see Florence. Lewis dives under the surface, and I stumble and fall to my knees, and I lose my crutch, and it floats away, and my ankle stabs me with a pain that is so bright and hard I nearly faint, and then Lewis comes to the surface, and he has Florence, and she is gasping and whimpering. He pulls her behind him, and she kicks and screams, but he does not release her. "It's all right!" I shout to Anne. "He's bringing her back!" (I look over my shoulder, and Henry still is standing at the edge of the water, and he is smiling, and I know why he is smiling, and my God, my dear God, please forgive me, but I do know why he is smiling.)

Lewis brings Florence ashore, and Anne stumbles after them. Henry wades into the water, retrieves my crutch and helps me to my feet. He asks me whether I am all right. I tell him I am fine. I do not look at him. I look elsewhere. He tells me to lean my weight against him. I nod, and he steers me to the place where Florence is lying. Her eyes are open, and Anne is stroking her hair, and Lewis squats next to her. Anne sends Henry to fetch a towel. When he returns with the towel, she takes it from him without saying anything. She bends over Florence and wipes Florence's face and body. Florence is crying, but there appears to be nothing the matter with her. Anne hugs her, and I hug her, and Lewis squats and grins. Henry stands over us, and he says to Lewis: "Hey, that was real fine."

Lewis looks up at his brother. "No thanks to *you.*"

"I guess not," says Henry, but he is not angry, and I know why he is not angry. And he is not hurt, and I know why he is not hurt.

"She's going to be okay," Lewis tells Anne. "She only got a little water, and she's going to be just fine."

Anne looks at Lewis, and then she looks at Henry. Her smoked glasses are gone, and I have no idea whether she lost them in the water or what. She glances at me for a moment, then says to Lewis: "Thank you . . ."

"You're welcome," says Lewis. "She's going to be just fine and dandy."

And Florence is indeed fine and dandy. We fuss over her, and Anne scolds her for wandering out so far in the water, and she promises she won't ever, ever do it again. She coughs a little, and her eyes run, but no harm has been done, and her brother Lewis is this day a hero. She kisses him on the chin, and he says aw, shoot. Henry beams at them, and I give him money to go buy ice cream cones for one and all. I glance at Anne, and it is obvious she knows what I know, and it is equally obvious Lewis never will. She tells him he is a fine fellow, and *I* tell him he is a fine fellow, and perhaps he believes us. We have no way of knowing, at least not for certain. He smiles, and his smile is tough, and he appears to be biting down on something the world cannot see.

In bed that night, Anne says to me: "Henry wasn't gambling with her life. I mean not *really*. He knew Lewis would be able to save her."

"Yes."

"He loves Lewis very much."

"He loves the world."

Anne embraces me, and I am able to make love to her. We scrunch over, and my bad ankle hangs off the edge of the bed.

Now they were driving northwest of Cambridge, and the country was golden and splendid, and Anne rubbed her right shoulder and said: "Oh, *Lord.*"

"Does it hurt badly?"

"It'll be all right. It comes and goes."

"I still don't know why you are so reluctant to take your medication."

"I *told* you. I don't want to be a *vegetable.*"

"All right. All right."

"It is *my* pain, and I'll deal with it as *I* see fit."

"All right. Good enough."

"Just don't forget you promised to read me the Kitty Heaven letter tonight. It still makes me cry, and I'm not ashamed to admit it. Ah, but then I suppose we were lucky."

"How?"

"To have had him as long as we did."

"We shouldn't canonize him this way. We make him less real."

"Well," said Anne, "how real *was* he? If you want *real,* you can think about Lewis. *He* was *real.* He was the most real person I've ever known, if you think of real as meaning *specific* or *concrete.* He was real right down to the last centimeter and tenth of a second. He was always measurable, always exactly what he seemed to be."

"Was he? Why then did he fool us so many years? It wasn't until he was an adult that we learned *how* deeply he had resented Henry. That night he became drunk. That election night."

"I remember," said Anne.

"So how can you say he was exactly what he seemed to be?"

"Well, maybe he wasn't."

"We always talk of him as though he were the family villain," said Amberson, "and I don't think that's fair."

"It probably isn't. I've always thought a lot of it had to do with Alice."

"I know you have. And so does she."

"Well, *I* didn't start that argument."

"It never should have happened," said Amberson.

"Yes," said Anne. "I'll admit that."

"Then why do you still want to see her?"

"I've *told* you why. Her name is on his headstone, and now she has a new husband, and I expect she'll be wanting to be buried with—"

"That's a trivial reason," said Amberson. "There has to be more to it than that."

Anne snorted, squinted out her window. "Look at how yellow the sunlight makes the trees," she said.

"Yes, it does," said Amberson.

"I am trying to change the subject."

"Yes, I know."

"All *I* know is I want to *see* her."

"All right."

"Don't pout."

"I'm not pouting. I have no reason to pout. It is a lovely day, and I shall concentrate on it."

"We're a caution, the way we bicker all the time. Remember Don Ameche and who was it, Frances Langford?"

"I think it was *Jim* Ameche and Frances Langford."

"Well, anyway," said Anne, "whoever they were, they were the Bickersons, and they were always going at it hammer and tongs."

"We're not the *Bickersons,*" said Amberson. "We *discuss* things. We do not *bicker.*"

"Yes, dear," said Anne, smiling.

"How does your shoulder feel now?"

"A little better."

Amberson nodded. He checked the speedometer, and it read 40. There was a tension in his chest, and he did not feel a bit footloose. They came to the junction with Ohio 93 and turned right, to the northeast. "It's a gift, isn't it, this country. *Look* at it. The colors and all."

"Yes," said Amberson, "but the strip mines are practically over the last hill."

"Well, let's just not think about the strip mines for now." The countryside bellied up before them all brilliant and clear in the light from the unshaded sun, and Amberson supposed this probably was America as foreigners envisioned it to be, fatly barnyarded with neat homes and whitewashed rocks, with cattle clustered at the roots of shady trees, with odors of rich earth and dry leaves rising high in the nostrils and creating a sort of gentle Arcadian euphoria. And he supposed that this America was as valid as the stripmine America. One needed balance. The apparatus had many sides, and it could accommodate any frame of mind. The warm and hilly miles slid past with grace and a comforting feeling of *tradition* and *values* and a large genial stolidity. Anne hummed something, but Amberson was unable to make out the tune. He glanced in the mirror and saw that Sinclair was asleep, with his paws tucked under his chin. How could they have left the poor little fellow back in that motel room? Perhaps this forgetfulness was the most scarifying old age proclamation of them all. After all, liverspots and bad teeth did not create guilt. Nor did white hair or flabby skin; there was nothing one could do about them. But surely one *could* do something about one's forgetfulness. He had forgotten his movie camera, and Anne had forgotten the cat's dish and bowl *and* her copy of *Future Shock*—and they *both* had forgotten poor Sinclair. Were they really all that dotty? Well, Amberson for one did not *feel* dotty. A bit querulous and frightened perhaps, but dotty, no.

The colors deepened as the Pontiac made its stately way northeast, slowing for the gentle villages of Baltic and Sugarcreek and Strasburg, and it went through Amish country, passing spindly Amish buggies driven by bearded men in dark suits and large straw hats. The Amish farmhouses were neat and plain, stolidly utilitarian, and Amberson knew there no doubt were many things that could be said for the way these people lived. But he did not believe he ever could have adjusted to their way of life. He was afraid his own attitudes and interests were far too worldly. Still, it was comforting to know that these Amish somehow managed still to exist. Perhaps, in a sense, they were a sort of conscience for the worldly, a reminder that there was another way for human beings to seize their days.

A buggy came toward them, and a bonneted woman was sitting next to the bearded driver, and Anne waved at them, but they did not wave back. Perhaps they had not seen her wave. "I was only trying to be friendly," she said.

"Anne, I don't want to hurt your feelings, but isn't it possible that they see people who wave at them as being condescending?"

"You mean like children waving at the animals in their cages at some zoo?"

"Yes."

"All I know is what I felt. And it was simple friendship. I had no ulterior motives, and I wasn't trying to feel superior."

"I believe you, but *they* don't know you as well as *I* do."

He knew there was more to the Amish than this candified picturepostcard view. Wasn't it true that a great many of them had taken to driving tractors? Weren't their young people running off to the cities? How long could they last if this continued? Wasn't attrition the real overriding fact of their existence here in 1971? Wasn't it possible that the apparatus perhaps was, ah, phasing them out? Yet surely these gentle villages and stolid little farms had *some* worth—some function in the ultimate scheme. Amberson *had* to believe that the ultimate scheme was benevolent—otherwise this footloose trip would be a cruel absurdity. He grimaced into the coruscating afternoon light and glanced at his dear wife whom he had loved all these years, and he said to himself: Whatever we find, it is preferable to sitting at home and waiting to die, and Frank Groh's skepticism be damned. There are too many photographs. There are too many souvenirs. We need perspective, and for one last time we must free ourselves from all those static private reminders that persist in isolating us, especially at our age. (Is this a cruel attitude? How so?)

The Ambersons were silent. Ohio 93 slipped through the hills in a succession of wide curves and abrupt climbs and descents, and they saw mailboxes that said LANTZ and HAUSERMAN and VAN ZANDT and POHLING, and it was a little past two o'clock in the afternoon when they stopped for lunch. They were on US 21 now, south of Massillon near a town called Navarre, and they pulled into an Arthur Treacher's Fish & Chips place. Anne hurried to the ladies' room while Amberson placed the order. The fish had been treated with some sort of vinegar sauce, and they found it quite tasty. The man at the counter had told Amberson the sauce was a house specialty. Anne munched on her fish, and she used perhaps a dozen paper napkins to wipe her hands, and she allowed as how she probably would be awake half the night with heartburn. But Amberson disagreed. He told her he found the fish quite light and almost as tasty as broasted chicken. And then Anne reluctantly smiled and said something to the effect that oh yes, you really have a vested interest in broasted chicken, don't you? Ever since your heart attack it's really been preying on your mind, hasn't it? And Amberson told her well, you'd have had to experience it to know what I mean. There we were, Peter and I, minding our own business, and the

254

odor of broasted chicken was quite *pervasive,* I'll tell *you,* and then I went and keeled over, and my last thought was: Such a strange place for a heart attack. And, as you know, I thought I was a goner, and yet somehow I was almost amused, and that is no exaggeration. And Anne said: What a lot of bunk. And Amberson said: You'll get no argument from me.

They drove north through the city of Massillon, home of the famous Massillon High School Tigers, the almost perennial state football champions. The famous Paul Brown once had coached at Massillon, and he had developed a winning tradition that apparently would go forward until the final generation. Amberson had read that football was an obsession in Massillon, and he could believe it. All the world had become obsessive, and why should Massillon have been an exception? He and Anne had attended a number of Paradise Falls High School football and basketball games over the past few years, and they had become aware of a certain desperation that had seemed to spew from everyone—players, coaches and spectators alike. It was not enough any longer simply to *play* football or basketball. Now the team had to be Number One, and losing was not tolerated. In these times, the worst insult was to be called a "loser." At the football and basketball games, Amberson had noticed that incompetence had invariably created hatred. If So-and-So fumbled the ball, he *stank;* his transgression was an outrage, an offense against the community. In these times, if a boy chose to play football or basketball for his high school, he had to be prepared to undergo booing. On the other hand, if he and his team happened to be "winners," he had to be prepared to accept the most outlandishly excessive praise and adulation. In either case, how was he able to retain his humanity? And yet . . . and yet . . . the joy of winning was perhaps, for some people, an ultimate goal that gave them a reason for being alive. If one thought of his days in terms of adversaries to be defeated, no sacrifice was too large, as the fellow said. Amberson's son Lewis had been one of these people, and the cheerleaders had forever clamored. And he would fight. And he would win. And the cowbells and the horns had set up an unholy commotion, and Lewis had never faltered. And now, driving through the city of Massillon, Amberson shook his head, and Anne asked him what was the matter, and he said: "I was thinking about Massillon and football, and I was telling myself I am glad I was only a *track* coach. It never has been the most popular spectator sport, and I honestly don't know if I'd have been able to take spectators—at least not the way they are today, what with all their excesses. On Sunday afternoons, when I watch those professional football games, and the home team happens to be doing badly, and I hear all that booing . . . well, I'm just glad I'm not involved."

"But isn't booing a part of being alive? Don't we all have to be prepared to take it?"

"Yes, but it's the *frenzy* that bothers me these days. Perhaps my memory is distorted, but I don't believe booing was so vicious years ago."

"I suppose you're right, but people are so much *on edge* nowadays."

"Are *we* on edge?" Amberson wanted to know.

"Sometimes," said Anne, "because of our age, I suppose. It's why sometimes I snap at you for no real reason."

"But you have been snapping at me for fifty years."

"Have I been? Do you really mean that?"

Amberson supposed he had said too much—and anyway, it was not true. "No, no," he said, "I don't mean it. I was just joking."

"I would hate to think it's true," said Anne.

"It's not."

"I keep changing my mind about this trip."

"What do you mean?"

"One minute I'm against it. The next minute I'm for it. Right now I'm *for* it. It has given us a chance to talk, hasn't it?"

"Yes," said Amberson.

"And without distractions. We are alone in this car, and the telephone isn't about to ring, is it?"

"No," said Amberson. "I am not Aristotle Onassis. I do not have a telephone in my car."

"More's the pity."

"Would you like to be married to Aristotle Onassis?"

"Well, I don't know about *that,* but I wouldn't mind being Jacqueline Kennedy. I would get back thirty years."

"How would you spend them?"

Anne sighed. "Ah, I don't know," she said. "Probably by being married to a highschool track coach and English teacher. That shows you how much sense *I* have."

"It was a very nice thing to say."

"The funny thing is—I *mean* it."

Amberson shook his head. The damned sunlight was really a caution.

"Hey," said Anne, "did I get to you?"

Amberson nodded.

Anne leaned back and closed her eyes. Her left hand rubbed her right shoulder. "I may enjoy this trip after all," she said.

Cautiously Amberson edged the Pontiac through the Massillon traffic, which was considerable. He squinted, and he kept the car in the slow lane, and he ran no caution lights, nor did he attempt to pass any trucks or other cars. Sinclair hopped into the front seat and climbed on Anne's lap. She stroked him, and his claws went in and out. An occasional sound of an automobile horn made him flatten his ears, but otherwise he appeared perfectly calm. He was with the Ambersons, and he trusted them, and he knew they would keep him away from harm. Amberson reached over and scratched Sinclair behind the ears, and Sinclair looked up at him with placid curiosity. Amberson was aware of children skittering along the sidewalks, and some of them ran, their lips pulled back from their teeth, and he remembered the joy that running always had created within him, and he felt a sweet nostalgia flood into his mouth, and it was *palpable,* like syrup, and he swallowed hard several times, but it would not go away. Here then was another of the hazards of old age, this overpowering nostalgia, this foolishly urgent desire to recreate the past, and Amberson knew this was why he had labored so many secret hours over his journal and why he had finally chosen to write most of it in the present tense. The sections having to do with Regina Ingersoll and the Famous Buick Incident had been described in the past tense, but the past tense had made him uncomfortable, and so he had shifted literary gears, so to speak (*literary* gears? well, why not? to *him* the journal was literature, and who else would read it anyway? therefore, couldn't he call it whatever he wanted to call it?), moving from the remote past to the immediate present, and somehow this change had renewed him, and by God he would finish the thing or die in the attempt. Yes. Die in the attempt. Ha. And ha.

North of Massillon, US 21 was a divided highway, and the traffic was even heavier. It was past 3:30, and Anne sat up, opened her eyes and said: "Will we get to Cleveland before dark?"

"Yes. I believe so."

"Do you remember how to get to her place?"

"Yes."

"She may faint when she sees us. Would that upset you?"

"Well," said Amberson, "I wouldn't dance around and flap my arms, if that's what you mean. But, on the other hand, I believe I would be able to restrain any excessive consternation and somehow muddle along, my aplomb undisturbed, so to speak."

"Yes," said Anne. "So to speak."

The speed limit was 60 on this divided highway, but Amberson kept the car at 40. His back ached a bit, but otherwise he felt reasonably alert. For once, his gums had relented. Cars and trucks whipped around the Pontiac, passing it, one after the other, in a series of heavy and almost rhythmic roars and whooshes. West of Akron, US 21 joined with

Interstate 77, and the speed limit became 70, but Amberson still kept the car at 40. The country was hilly and wooded, and the traffic was a good deal heavier than it had been even back in Massillon. And billboards sprang up, proclaiming motels and restaurants and fillingstations. And Anne said: "I don't want to stay too long. We'll just take care of our business and then leave. What with those dogs of hers, Sinclair will have to stay in the car, and I don't want to keep him cooped up any longer than we have to."

"What if she invites us to spend the night?"

"I doubt that she will."

"But what if she does?"

"We'll politely decline. But I don't think you'll have to worry about it."

"And our only business is the headstone?"

"Yes."

"There'll be no arguments this time?"

"She won't hear a single nasty peep out of me. That I promise."

"Fine," said Amberson. "Now if only I could learn why you want to see her at all . . ."

"All right, I'll tell you," said Anne. "Not to make too fine a point of it, I want to see her because I'm nosy."

"Ah . . ." said Amberson.

"I just want to see how she is *doing,* what with her fine house and her husband's four children and all. After all these years, she's finally made it to Shaker Heights, and I'm curious to see how it's all affected her."

"I bet you a nickel she is flourishing," said Amberson.

"I wouldn't be a bit surprised," said Anne. "She has always been a good flourisher. She flourished all the time she was married to Lewis. She flourished like an army with banners. But how happy was she?"

"I think she loved him."

"So do I. But I *also* think she was a bad influence on him."

"Yes," said Amberson. "I know you do."

"She catered to his ambition, and he didn't need anyone to cater to his ambition. He catered to it enough himself. More than enough."

"Well, perhaps that was her way of showing him her love."

"Oh, I'm sure it *was,*" said Anne, "but that doesn't mean it was *good.*"

"But if she *thought* it was good, doesn't that make it worth something?"

"The road to hell is paved with you-know-what," said Anne.

"I'm sorry," said Amberson, "but I simply cannot think of her as
258

some sort of Lady Macbeth of Paradise Falls."

"And neither can I. I've never once seen her wring her hands."

"But if you had?"

"But if I had," said Anne, smiling, "well . . ."

"Enough, woman."

"Yes, o sire."

"Methinks thou casteth aspersions on the fair and beauteous Alice."

"O sire, pray not think ill of me for my poor wretched meanness of spirit, for I am but a young girl and unversed in the subtleties of artful discourse . . ."

"Silence, o fawning wench. Thy flaccid apologies ring vainly in the catacombs of my noble aural canal."

"Thy perception is exceeded, o grand and glorious master, only by thy good looks."

"The plenteous Alice is of high and imperious blood, and keep thy remarks to thineself, thou illborn frumpet."

"*Frumpet?*" said Anne.

"It just came to me," said Amberson, "in a flash of inspiration too dazzling to describe."

"How nice," said Anne.

And then the Ambersons both laughed, and there was more color in Anne's face than Amberson had seen in weeks. And she had stopped rubbing her shoulder. He reached across the seat and patted one of her hands, and she winked at him, and he told her he appreciated it when she went along with his little games. The Shakespeare game had been one of his favorites for years, and she always had been quite good at it. And, for some peculiar reason, the game had helped him keep himself reasonably fresh for teaching Shakespeare at Paradise Falls High School. It had made the old beleaguered Bard a great deal more human. And anything that accomplished *that* was welcomed. Now Amberson told his wife she really was a splendid person. And she giggled coyly and said: Oh, you're just saying that because it's true.

Amberson supposed he was like most men. He supposed he was afraid of women, or did not understand them, or both. And, to use the currently fashionable phrase, perhaps he was even a mild sort of male chauvinist pig. But he did believe he *knew* a few things about women, especially their pragmatism. Oh, there had been exceptions, such as Caroline and the fabled Regina Ingersoll, but most of the women Amberson had known had been sensible and never reckless. They always had been able to keep romance and idealism within *reasonable* bounds (even Bernadette, who had sought from Amberson a specific *function* that had answered a specific *need*). With most women, Amberson always was aware of cause and effect, with no eccentric deviations. For each man who sought to battle the heavens, there was a woman calculating the odds. For women, romance was a *diversion,* not a planned *life style,* as it was called these days. Romance was all right *in its place,* but it never would supersede reality. Women could weep at sentimental movies, and their hearts were splintered by crippled animals and starving orphans, but there was always the grocery list to face; there was always the stuff of homely days to occupy their attention. What was more important to most women, existentialism or canned peas? Oh, there were exceptions—the Zelda Fitzgeralds and the Edna St. Vincent Millays and even, he supposed, the Gloria Steinems. But Amberson's life had seldom been visited by such women, and anyway, he was too old to concern himself with exceptions. And so, as far as he was concerned, the canned peas represented the essential female concern, with the exceptions duly noted and acknowledged. As for his own wife, well, she was no exception. He loved her dearly, but she had never been one to lose sight of the canned peas. In all her life (as far as Amberson knew), there had been only one time when she had lost at least partial control of her realistic attitudes, and that had come in the days of Henry the Always Boy. He had been her one eccentric deviation, her one surrender to romance. But, even then, she had *recognized* the problem and had tried to do something about it. So how could it have represented a *total* surrender? (When there is a total surrender, how can one even know that a problem exists?) And so, if there was one characteristic that had governed Anne's life, it was her pragmatism. And Henry the Always Boy had not damaged it, not really. Still, despite all this, Anne was not (in Amberson's view) an ordinary woman. She was (in Amberson's view) an outstanding woman. There were many reasons for this, but he saw the largest as being her sense of humor. She was no literalminded stick who missed the point of jokes. Far from it. As the saying went, she gave as good as she got, and she did more than tolerate Amberson's little games; she *participated* in them, and her participation was enthusiastic. For decades she had enjoyed his Shakespeare game. Those ridiculous moments when he passed beyond the avuncular pomp of his rhetoric and entered the treacherous domain of the Bard had always been—for her—times of delight, and she had said so more than once. And she always gave as good as she got. One's mind had to be nimble to keep up with hers. Which meant she was outstanding, and Amberson would brook no argument on the matter. Humor sat at the center of her pragmatism, and he treasured it, and it was one of the largest reasons his love for her never had faltered. It is splendid when a woman loves a man. It is splendid when she gives him children.

But it is a golden blessing when she gives him humor. A golden blessing, and rare. Today the Ambersons would be visiting Alice, and Alice did not possess that blessing and never would. She still called them "Mother Amberson" and "Father Amberson," and she had never seen anything funny in the names. And never would. She smiled and laughed a great deal, but nothing ever came from below her throat; if she had viscera, she was not about to admit it. Her smiles and her laughter came from some cold little box in her brain, with a frozen door that was opened by force of will. She was no doubt still quite beautiful, and her body was no doubt as curved as ever, and her voice no doubt still sounded like rocks and shredded twigs, and the relentlessness never had gone out of her (she no doubt had her own insistent cheerleaders), and at fortythree she no doubt appeared to be perhaps thirty, and to Amberson she was—and always had been—the most contradictory female he had ever known. The beauty and the curves were exquisite, and he was the first to admit this, but what relationship did they have to her voice and the relentlessness? He believed her to be enormously flawed and cold, and yet nothing *showed*. Why was God so negligent that He had not shown the world some sign to serve as a warning? If Alice had had a club foot or a cluster of moles or even a missing finger, any of these imperfections would have given the rest of the human race a fair chance to pause and say: Well, perhaps she's not so much. Perhaps the club foot . . . or the moles, or the missing finger, or whatever . . . indicates some weakness. But Alice's feet were fine, and she had no moles and all ten of her fingers, and the unwary never had a chance with her. Despite her dreadful voice, she was able to charm the butter off a slice of toast and even the Ambersons (who had known her very well indeed for more than twenty years) were sometimes taken in by her. For instance, two years ago she had personally telephoned them to invite them to her wedding to her new husband, a man named Francis S. Ginn II, a widowed member of what she said was Cleveland's finest social set. This Francis S. Ginn II was the father of four teenaged children (the oldest, a girl of nineteen, was doing some sort of work with Ralph Nader in Washington), and the fellow had met Alice at a party given by mutual friends. Alice, who was childless, had moved back to Cleveland in 1967 shortly after Lewis's death. Lewis had left her more than one hundred thousand dollars in cash, plus one hundred fifty thousand dollars in securities, and she had taken an apartment in Bratenahl, which was one of the very chic Cleveland suburbs. With the help of her mother, Mrs. Iverson, who was still alive and thriving, she gradually began to infiltrate the right circles, and she soon left her mother behind, seeing as the poor woman still had the bad luck to live in Lakewood.

Francis S. Ginn II was grayhaired, about fifty, and his wife had been dead seven years—and, as Alice admitted on the telephone that night she called to invite the Ambersons to the wedding, he was utterly ripe for the, ah, plucking. And Alice promptly plucked him, and the Ambersons drove up to Cleveland to attend the wedding. It was held in Fairmount Presbyterian Church in Cleveland Heights, and perhaps four hundred persons attended the service (most of them, of course, Friends of the Groom—with the notable exception, of course, of Alice's mother, who that day unquestionably reached the apogee of her life), and Alice was smilingly radiant in a long blue gown, and Francis S. Ginn II was erect and distinguished, and Alice's mother sat with her chin poking triumphantly upward (she died of an embolism nine days later, and so there really was no doubt of the apogee), and all four of the Ginn children sat quietly with polite smiles glued on their faces like crooked and incompetent party masks, and the Ambersons even were invited to the reception. Even the reception. It was held in the spacious Ginn home on South Park Boulevard in Shaker Heights, and Alice's mother came up to the Ambersons, and she was holding a glass of champagne, and she told them today was the happiest day of her life, no offense intended. And the Ambersons smiled at her, and perhaps now they were wearing party masks of their own. Mrs. Iverson moved away in a sort of gelatinous shuffle, and her free hand happily patted and stroked her hair, which was blue and tightly coiffed. She looks like a Martian, whispered Anne, and Amberson smiled. A little later, Alice came to them with her new husband, and she introduced them as "Mother" and "Father" Amberson. Francis S. Ginn II gravely shook hands with both the Ambersons, and he told them well, Alice here is a real fan of yours. She says she has missed you a great deal. And then Alice smiled, squeezed her husband's arm and said: Francis my love, they are the dearest people in the world, and I don't know what I would have done without them. Then, to the Ambersons: I am *so* glad you were able to come. And Amberson said: It was our pleasure. And then the newlyweds were enveloped by two elderly women, both of whom were wearing small gold watches attached to their bodices. And shrieks and hugs abounded. And the Ambersons backed away. Francis S. Ginn II was the president of a real estate firm he had inherited from his father, and many of his business associates were on hand, and a man named Grizzard got to talking with Amberson about property values in Paradise Falls, at least you have none of the colored to worry about, am I right? And Amberson told Grizzard well, there *are* some, but they more or less stay in their own section of town, if you know what I mean. And Grizzard said: Oh yes. I know what you mean. But God help us if the Democrats get back in. We couldn't stand that, could we? And Amberson said: That would be a catastrophe. And Grizzard said: Right you are, brother. And Amberson said: Thank you very much. (This Grizzard was perhaps eighty, and he stood with the aid of a cane, and what would have been the sense of arguing with him?) The Ambersons stayed at the reception for perhaps half an hour, standing near a cluster of potted ferns in what apparently was some sort of solarium. They munched on canapés and they each drank two glasses of champagne, and then they said goodbye to Alice, who hugged them both and told them how *moved* she was that they had attended. And then, lowering her voice, she said to Anne: I hope there are no more hard feelings. And Anne said: No. There are none. And Alice said: I was carried away. And Anne said: So was I. And Alice said: I'll never forget your son. I loved him. I really did. And Anne said: Yes. I know that. And Alice said: Please come see us. And Anne said: Thank you. And Alice said: I *mean* that. And Anne said: Fine. And the Ambersons returned to their motel, and the next day they drove back down to Paradise Falls. The distance was perhaps two hundred miles, and Amberson covered it in six hours. And in the more than two years since then they had not heard from Alice except at Christmastime, when she sent them a plain black-and-white card with the words *Happy Holidays* written inside a wreath, the letters wavery and vague, as though from an old woodcut. The Ambersons had received the same card both Christmases, and the envelope had been stamped by a postage meter. The names—*Alice, Francis, Cornelia, Donald, Harlowe and Beth Ginn*—were printed, not signed, and Anne had told Amberson that the card was about as cheerful and intimate as a formal announcement of the opening of a new undertaking parlor. And yet now she wanted to visit Alice, whom she scarcely could abide. Ah, but then who understood women (those devious pragmatists)? Perhaps, as Anne had said, she wanted to see Alice again just out of simple nosiness. Or perhaps her dispute with Alice still was unfinished. It was all very strange, but at the same time it was all very interesting, and there was a chance that tonight's confrontation (if it could be called that) would provide some excitement and add a bit of conflict to these footloose wanderings. And there were worse things than conflict. Lies, for instance. And hypocrisy. And laughter that came from a cold little box.

Now the Ambersons were just south of Cleveland, and US 21 veered off to the right, and Amberson was grateful to be shut of Interstate 77 and all its urgent whooshing traffic. He slowed the Pontiac to the limit, which was 35, and he kept it in the slow lane. It passed a sign that said BRECKSVILLE CORPORATION LIMIT, then a number of motels and fillingstations. The road was wide and reasonably clear, and it entered a succession of low rolling hills, and here and there were the entrances to housing tracts, and Anne pointed out a sign that said GINN REALTY. "There's something I can't remember," she said.

"What's that?" Amberson asked her.

"The G in Alice's husband's name—is it hard or soft?"

"Hard, like the textbook publishing house. If it were soft, the name would sound too alcoholic and therefore undignified. Bad for the image and all that."

"Yes," said Anne. "I can see where it would be." Sinclair had fallen asleep on her lap. She scratched his rump and the base of his tail. She blinked, and her eyes appeared to be quite bright, and yes, perhaps she was beginning to enjoy the trip after all.

"Ginn as in next-of-Ginn," said Amberson.

"Not Ginn as in fix-me-a-whatchamacallit, a martini," said Anne.

"Precisely," said Amberson.

"I hope we surprise her."

"I wouldn't worry about *that.*"

"Mother Amberson and Father Amberson, descending like a plague of locusts."

"We are not a plague of locusts," said Amberson. "We are Mother Amberson and Father Amberson, and we are as sweet and lovable as the day is long, and she probably will swoon from the joy of it all."

"Yes indeed," said Anne.

"I wish you'd answer a question for me."

"I'll try," said Anne.

Amberson frowned. He rubbed his mouth and chin, and the warmth of his hand felt pleasant against his jaw. "I've been thinking back on her wedding," he said, "and I still can't understand why we were invited. After Lewis died, she couldn't wait to get out of Paradise Falls, and you know as well as I that she never thought any of us were good enough for her. And then there was that scene we had with her. So why did she ask us? She wasn't seeking a *reminder,* was she?"

"No," said Anne. "Of course not."

"Then what was it? Why were we invited? Do you know?"

"We were invited because she wanted to gloat."

"You really think so?"

"I certainly do. Why else would she have *telephoned* and told us *personally?* She wanted to gloat so badly she could *taste* it. She wanted to tell us well, la-de-dah, look what *I've* done. And of course a *written* invitation would have meant no chance to gloat. So she telephoned, and it was her idea of rubbing it in."

"Rubbing what in? Did she think we cared?"

"Maybe not. But *she* cared, and still does. And to *her* it was some sort of victory over her dear friends the sainted Mother and Father Whoozis. She is very much like Lewis in that respect; she enjoys victories. Even if she is the only player, and even if we don't care a hog's belch about the game . . ."

"A hog's belch?"

"That's what I said."

"It is a very vivid figure of speech."

"Do you approve of it?"

"I believe I do."

"Thank you," said Anne.

"You're quite welcome," said Amberson.

"Does the explanation satisfy you?"

"I believe it does."

"She is not my favorite person."

"Yes. I know that."

"But I won't make a scene. I just want to see her. I'm curious—that's all."

Amberson nodded. It was past four o'clock now, and the evening rush hour was getting under way. Cars were beginning to stream out of Cleveland, and Amberson was unable to time the Pontiac's speed to the traffic lights, and so he was forced to make numerous stops. US 21 still was four lanes but after a time the traffic became heavy and slow in both directions. He drove cautiously through the villages of Brecksville and Independence, then turned right on Ohio 17 at the base of a long hill that led into a sort of industrial valley. The traffic on Ohio 17 was even worse, and it narrowed to one lane in each direction. The Ambersons found themselves behind an enormous truck that had the word ROADWAY painted on the trailer door, and they were unable to pass it for perhaps three or four miles. Ohio 17 was called Libby Road, and it passed through the suburbs of Garfield Heights and Maple Heights, tidy little middleclass communities with row upon row of small neat houses, most of them freshly painted. If Amberson's memory served him correctly, Garfield Heights and Maple Heights were populated largely by the descendants of middle European immigrants. They were called "ethnics" these days, and they were said to be quite fond of Spiro Agnew and George C. Wallace, and the newspaper and magazine columnists insisted they represented as conservative a bloc of voters as the nation had known in years, and this all probably was true. Still, Amberson could not help but wonder if these people were as ignorant and benighted as the evidence suggested. Now, driving along

Libby Road, past shrines and churches and statues of the Blessed Mother, past signs that said LEWANDOWSKI and RZEPKA and PAV-LETICH, past all these little homes with their impeccable lawns and their blue slate roofs and their inevitable television aerials, Amberson saw small children riding tricycles, and he saw elderly women, their heads wrapped in kerchiefs, shuffling along the sidewalks, and somehow he sensed a stolid gallantry, and never mind Spiro Agnew and George C. Wallace. Perhaps these people *were* sinful unreconstructed bigots, and perhaps they *were* frightened by the prospect of any sort of change that might endanger their new and undoubtedly hardearned prosperity, but did this mean that they should be held in contempt and treated as though they were a tribe of vulgar barbarians? Surely, if they kept up their homes this well, there was some sensitivity within them. Surely they were not without hope. And surely they were human. Was it not human to fear change, especially after one's status had been gained so dearly? In a very real sense, these people still were strangers in a strange land, and its Anglo-Saxon culture was not yet all that familiar to them, and yet hadn't they helped build this country? Didn't they deserve tolerance, too? These were interesting questions, and Amberson wondered if they ever would be resolved. He surely hoped so. All this orderliness had great value, and it would be a pity if it were ignored or scorned.

"These people take great pride in their land, their properties, don't they?" said Anne.

"Yes. I was just thinking the same thing."

"Perhaps some people would call it selfishness, but I don't think it's all that bad."

"Neither do I," said Amberson.

"Especially when you consider their origins. This must really be a land of milk and honey to them."

"Or at least it was to their parents or grandparents. I'd venture to say that by now most of these people are nativeborn."

"Ah, but attitudes persist. What was important to the parents and the grandparents is probably just as important to the children and the grandchildren. Judging from the appearance of their homes, I expect they hold family life in high regard, which probably means a kind of isolation."

"Isolation?" said Amberson.

"Yes," said Anne. "And the isolation prevents the old ideas from leaking out."

"That's very interesting."

"I think so too," said Anne. "And you know what *else* I think?"

266

"What might that be?"

"I think this is a remarkable country."

"How so?" Amberson asked his wife.

"Well, take today, for instance. Take the *differences* we have seen. First the Amish and all they represent. Then Massillon and its football fever. Then that pretty suburb with its housing tracts, that Brecksville. And now these streets and these people and their homes. And let's face it, Howard. You're not a Barney Oldfield when it comes to driving a car. We didn't exactly *jet* up here, did we? And still, even though we haven't covered much mileage, think of all the *contrasts* we've experienced. They're fascinating, aren't they?"

"Yes. They are. And just think, if I were a faster driver, we might not have been able to savor them."

"Now, now. I'm not fussing at your driving. I like the way you drive. And anyway, why should *we* be in a hurry?"

Amberson nodded. "Exactly," he said. He paused for a moment, then: "I'm happy you find the apparatus as interesting as I do. The contrasts and all the rest of it."

"Oh, I *do,*" said Anne. "I really do."

"Never underestimate the educational power of the tortoise."

"I wouldn't *think* of it," said Anne.

Amberson smiled. He turned north at a street called Lee Road, and a few blocks later they were in southeast Cleveland, and now most of the faces they saw were black. Lee Road was wide and busy, but many of its storefronts were either shabby or boarded up, and the sidewalks and pavement were littered with trash. Anne reached over and pressed down the button that locked her door. Amberson said not a word. Sinclair awakened, yawned, hopped into the back seat and scrabbled in his box, then jumped up on his shelf and began taking a bath. Amberson glanced in the mirror and saw a Negro man grinning at Sinclair from the car behind them. The Negro man waved at Sinclair, but of course Sinclair paid him no mind. At the next traffic light, the Negro man changed lanes and pulled up next to Amberson. He leaned across the front seat, rolled down the window on the passenger's side and shouted something. Amberson rolled down his own window and said: "How's that? I didn't hear you."

"He's a beauty," said the Negro man. "We got four of our own, an I know what I'm talkin about."

"Oh, thank you."

"What you call him? Smoky? Foggy?"

"We call him Sinclair."

"Sinclair? Hey, that's some kind of name. I never would have thought of a name like that for no cat."

"Well," said Amberson, "we didn't want him to be—"

Then the light changed, and at the same time Sinclair came down from his shelf, hopped on Amberson's shoulder, then jumped out the open window. He skidded between the cars, cut in front of the Pontiac, crossed the sidewalk and entered a place called the LEE ROAD HOUSE OF RIBS.

"Oh, no," said Anne.

"I'm afraid so," said Amberson.

Still grinning, the Negro man cut his car in front of the Ambersons, pulled to the curb, wrenched open his door and quickly got out. Amberson parked behind him, then joined him on the sidewalk. The Negro man was perhaps fifty, stout and bald, with enormous ears, eyes and lips. He and Amberson hurried inside the LEE ROAD HOUSE OF RIBS just in time to see Sinclair hop over the counter where the carryout orders were filled. A girl of perhaps twenty was behind the counter, and she shrieked when Sinclair came at her. The place had a heavy odor of pork and chicken and tomatoes and peppers, and two customers, both teenaged boys, were leaning against the counter and laughing. The girl backed to one side, and Sinclair began sniffing at the door that apparently opened to the kitchen. "Hey now," said the Negro man, "hey now, little kitty, little St. Clair." He came around the counter and pounced on Sinclair before Sinclair knew what was happening. At the same time, Anne came scurrying into the place.

"Well, my *God,*" said the girl behind the counter.

"Looky there," said one of the boys. He was wearing what appeared to be a sort of tamoshanter. It was purple.

The Negro man carried Sinclair around the counter. He scratched Sinclair under the chin, and Sinclair closed his eyes. He handed Sinclair to Anne and said: "I'm real sorry."

Anne hugged Sinclair. "No harm done," she said, smiling. Then, to Sinclair: "You are a naughty cat."

"Naughty, naughty," said the boy in the tamoshanter. "Bad old cat."

"*Bad,*" said the other boy.

"*Real* bad," said the first. Chuckling, he and his companion faced one another. He held out his hands, palms up. His friend slapped them. Then he slapped his friend's palms. "Bad old mother," he said, and they both guffawed.

The girl was thin, and her hair grew in a halo, and Amberson believed the style was called an Afro. She leaned against a wall and said: "My God, he came in here like he was shot from a gun . . ."

"You goin to have to send out for rubber panties?" the tamoshantered boy asked her.

"You hush that, Bobby," said the girl. "That a tacky thing to say."

Amberson spoke up. "Well," he said, "I'm very sorry. Our cat here just . . . well, he just hopped out of the car."

"Yes," said Anne. "That's right."

"Right on," said the tamoshantered boy's companion.

The girl managed a smile. "Ah well," she said, "it put some life in my day. No sweat."

"You want *me* to put some life in your day?" the tamoshantered boy asked her.

She glared at him. "I said *hush* that."

The tamoshantered boy grinned at the Ambersons and said: "I keep tryin, but I ain't even got to the batter's box yet, seems like. Some dudes got it, an I guess I ain't."

The Negro man ushered the Ambersons to the door.

"Hey, man," said the tamoshantered boy to his friend, "who is that dude goin out with them folks there?"

The friend jammed his thumbs in the pockets of his trousers and assumed a cowboy pose. "Wellnow, Bobby," he said, "that be the Lone Ranger . . ."

"Rightin wrongs," said Bobby.

"An protectin the innocent," said Bobby's friend, sniggering.

The Negro man threw up his arms. "Come on," he said to the Ambersons, and laughter trailed behind them, and even the girl was taking part in it. The Negro man and the Ambersons went outside, and he turned to them and said: "I sure am sorry if I gave you a fright."

The Ambersons both smiled, and Anne said: "Thank you for helping us, and don't worry about any fright. We got him back so quickly there was no time for fright."

"That is correct," said Amberson.

The Negro man was wearing a business suit that appeared to be perhaps ten years old. "I'm a police officer," he said, "an this here rib place ain't exactly the garden spot of Lee Road, if you follow me."

"Well . . ." said Amberson, and then he did not know what to say, and so he said nothing.

The Negro man jerked a thumb back toward the door. "Me an them are good friends," he said. "When the weather's good, old Dorothy hustles on Carnegie Avenue an Chester Avenue, an then—when the leaves start fallin—she goes to work at the rib place. I guess she don't like cold weather much. And them two boys, Bobby an Greg, they sort of her *agents,* you know what I mean?"

"Oh," said Amberson, "I thought they were customers."

"*Customers?*" said the Negro man, smiling.

"Well, I had no way of knowing."

"Sure enough," said the Negro man. "But you can take my word for it—they ain't *customers*. The day they *customers* be the day old Richard Burton he got to *pay* for it, you know what I mean?"

"I only meant I thought they were buying ribs," said Amberson, smiling.

"Ribs . . ." said the Negro man, chuckling. "Yeah, they sure do dig ribs . . ." And then he exploded with laughter, and his chest and belly wobbled, and the Ambersons also laughed, but with more restraint. And Sinclair stared at all of them as though they had lost their minds. Then the Ambersons again thanked the Negro man for his help, and hands were shaken all around. He told them his name was Flonnoy, and he said he hoped they would enjoy their stay in Cleveland. When Amberson asked him how he knew they were from out of town, he pointed at the license plate and told them he read license plates the way other people read Holy Scripture. "Ever time I see a car," he said, "I got this reflex action where I just naturally check out the license number. I was in the black-an-whites for fourteen years, an I sort of got in the habit." And then the Negro man went to his car, waved at the Ambersons and drove away. They climbed back into their own car, and Amberson rolled up his window, and Anne gently scolded Sinclair, who sat on her lap and yawned and then washed himself behind the ears. The journey up Lee Road resumed, and twilight had begun to seep in from the east, and Amberson turned on the Pontiac's lights. It was past five o'clock, and the sun had turned a coruscating orange, and Amberson swiveled the sun visor so that it shaded the left side of his face. The warmth was pleasant, but the strain on his eyes was not. Anne asked him did he feel tired and he told her yes, a little. "This cat of ours has given me a couple of bad turns today," he said.

"I wonder what it was that made him jump out," said Anne. "The windows have been open many times when he's been with us, but he's never jumped out before."

"Well, perhaps he smelled the ribs."

"Perhaps," said Anne. "Or perhaps he knows something."

"Knows something? Knows what?"

"I couldn't say."

"You make it sound very dire," said Amberson.

"I'm sorry. I don't know what I'm saying. Pay no attention to me."

Amberson reached over and stroked Sinclair. "You're not getting away from us, old fellow. Not just yet."

Anne cleared her throat, rubbed her right shoulder. "From the Amish to those colored people in one day. The differences certainly do exist, don't they?"

"They do indeed."

"I didn't quite catch the gist of the things that man said. Was he telling us the girl is a prostitute?"

"Yes—and those two young men are her procurers. When the weather is warm, that is."

"They must not take their work very seriously."

Amberson smiled. "Yes," he said. "You might say that."

Now Lee Road crossed into the suburb of Shaker Heights, and within a few blocks the black faces were gone, and Anne told Amberson yes, yes, you are really something; I recognize the houses along here, and you've remembered the way *exactly*. And Amberson told his wife he wished he could remember other things, such as his movie camera, as well as he had remembered the route to Alice's place. And Anne told him, well, you always did have a peculiar mind. And Amberson said yes, that I cannot deny.

The homes were spacious and comfortable here in Shaker Heights, and leaves swirled, and the orange sunlight caught at them, and Amberson blinked at the traffic and kept his right foot poised to slam on the brake, and now the sound of all the cars and buses and trucks was an unrelenting rumble, and they whisked around him as he kept the Pontiac at a sedate 35, and occasionally someone honked at him, but by now he was used to that. He had read in some magazine that slow drivers were supposed to be a menace on the road, but he could not for the life of him understand why. He envied the Amish and their buggies, and that was the truth. He grimaced at the traffic, and Anne apparently sensed that something was troubling him. She reached over and patted his knee, and then she told him he was doing fine, and she was very proud of him. He nodded, but his tongue was pressed tightly against his dentures, and his hands were a bit clammy. He supposed he was perhaps more tired than he had thought. He glanced at the spacious homes and wished he could walk into one of them and lie down on the sofa, preferably in front of a fire in the hearth. The homes were splendidly shaded, and they appeared to be so terribly restful. Then he turned off Lee Road onto South Park Boulevard, and the gentle Shaker Lakes were off to the left, and Anne pointed out some gray ducks. And now the homes were enormous, and many of them were of a Tudor style, with great sweeping driveways and immense porticos, and Amberson said: "It won't be long now. If I remember correctly, the place is just around the next curve." And it was.

See now 1961, a morning in early December, and it is a day of unalloyed triumph for our son Lewis. He has been elected mayor of the city of Paradise Falls, and this morning he will take the oath of office. Anne has bought a new dress for the occasion, and it is my understanding that Alice has spent at least five hundred dollars (and with more no doubt to come) in refurbishing *her* wardrobe. But after all, she is about to become the First Lady of Paradise Falls, and obviously she has to look the part.

Lewis has been a councilman nearly eight years, and last month he defeated the incumbent mayor, one James K. Froelich, by a margin of fourteen votes out of 2,868 that were cast. Anne voted for Froelich; I voted for our son. She has told me she voted for Froelich because (a) he had not been a bad mayor, and (b) Lewis had enough irons in the fire, and she did not want him to destroy his health. But I did not accept these arguments, even though I could sympathize with them. To me, knowing for years now that Lewis still was competing with Henry the Always Boy, it was necessary that Lewis succeed in every way. Perhaps some day, if he kept succeeding and succeeding and succeeding, his cheerleaders would be satisfied, and he would find some sort of peace. Perhaps this was an illogical attitude on my part, but it did cause me to vote for our son, and I am not ashamed to admit it.

The Paradise Falls City Hall is an inconspicuous brick and tile building that faces the Paradise County Court House across a small square in the center of town. The ceremony is scheduled for 11:30 a.m., and a large crowd has been invited. Anne has me check her hair and her buttons and her zipper, and she takes a pair of tweezers and removes several hairs from my nostrils. We are making lastminute preparations in the bedroom of our home, and my fingernails are immaculate, and my cheeks smell of Aqua Velva. I am sixtyfour years of age, and my teeth have been giving me trouble, but this morning I feel rather splendid and magisterial. If Alice is about to become the First Lady of Paradise Falls, does it not follow that I am about to become the First Father? Perhaps now I can understand how Joseph Kennedy must feel (if he can feel anything at all, what with the stroke that has immobilized him).

Our daughter Florence and her husband, Earl Portman, have come from Dayton to be on hand, and we have put them up in Florence's old bedroom, and we are able to hear their talk and laughter. Their three small daughters have been left with Portman's mother, who lives in the Dayton suburb of Kettering, and Florence is saying that she surely does hope Nancy's cold is better, the poor frail little thing. I rather suspect that Florence will have more babies. She apparently has a real gift for motherhood, and I have always found her three girls to be utterly charming. They are not afraid to speak up, but at the same time they do not appear to be spoiled, and I have never seen any of them pout, whimper, whine or have a tantrum. Anne and I naturally dote on them. They are our only grandchildren, and we have just about given up hope for Lewis and Alice. According to Alice, her pelvis cannot accommodate a baby. This may or may not be true, I do not know. But this is no time to be having such bleak thoughts. If Lewis and Alice never have children, the planet will not dissolve. Dogs will still chase cats, and cats will still chase mice, and mice will still make old maids lift their skirts, and so I say to myself: Come on now. Keep it in perspective. This is your son's largest day, and kindly do not spoil the enjoyment of it. God knows, you owe him that much.

My two surviving children have created ambivalent feelings within me. I am proud of them, of course, but at the same time I wonder if perhaps I could do more to comfort and support them. I wonder how well—or badly—they remember Henry the Always Boy. Florence loved him (that I know), and Lewis did not love him (that I also know), but how do they *remember* him? Is there any truth involved? Or do they simply look back on him as though he were an *accident,* a brilliant and gentle and immense freak of nature? Did they ever really know him as well as Anne and I did? Did they ever really appreciate him? Somehow it is very important to me that he not be squeezed from their minds. But how can the preservation be accomplished? And why is it so desirable? As a justification? As a way of saying to them: Look, you two, if we did neglect you, it was in a good cause?

I adjust the knot of my necktie. I tell myself I shall never resolve the situation, so why do I have to keep nibbling at it?

Anne is sitting at her dressing table and powdering her nose. "I expect Alice will be dressed to the nines," she says.

"Oh, yes. She'll be spectacular. You can count on it."

"I dream of the day when she loses a button, or the wind knocks her hair all gollywhockered this way and that."

"It is a vain dream," I tell my wife.

"Yes," she says. "I'm sure it is." She is sixtytwo now, and she weighs one hundred seventy pounds. Dr. Groh has told her that she is putting an undue strain on her heart, but so far she has paid no attention to his warnings. Henry the Always Boy has been dead more than sixteen years, and her grief still balloons her. She knows this.

We have discussed it many times, but nothing has been resolved.

We join Florence and her husband in the front room, and Earl Portman tells us we look real nifty. There is a rumpled spaniel look to him, but he is a successful businessman, and he is not at all as casual and loosejointed as he would appear. He and Florence have been married more than five years, and in that time he has increased the number of his chicken carryout restaurants from two to five. Florence, meanwhile, has become a bit plump, and her three pregnancies have taken a great deal of the definition from her figure. She is only thirtyone, but her somewhat amorphous shape makes her appear older. She has become *matronly;* she no longer is the bright thrusting girl who married the unfortunate Tom Rimers ten years ago in Angola, Indiana; she has obviously made some sort of large *accommo-dation* that is comfortable enough but perhaps not terribly exciting. It is centered on diapers and soap operas and tuberous begonias and casserole recipes, and its days are carefully measured, and it has little room for whims or impulses or romance or even much passion—other than that which is assigned a definite *place* in a definite *schedule.* And yet I must keep reminding myself that she still laughs, that her love for her little girls is very real, that she has a right to move through her life in any way she sees fit. At thirtyone, and already once widowed, she is not exactly a strayed lamb, and the accommodation is *her* business, based on *her* experience and *her* attitudes, and I have no right to interfere. Not that I would. It is not my nature.

We ride to the city hall in Earl Portman's brandnew '62 Mercury, and a thin screen of snow is falling, but the earth is still warm, and so the snow promptly melts. Florence says something to the effect that the old town certainly doesn't change much, and she goes on to say that this is a comfort to her. "I don't know about *other* people," she says, "but it's very necessary to me that I have a sort of *home base,* an *anchor* or a *starting point* or whatever you'd like to call it."

Earl Portman grins. "Just in case your husband doesn't shape up, huh?"

"How's that again?" says Florence.

"Well, if old Earl flops on his face, you can always come back to the home base, right? You can just pack up the girls, and that's it. Whisko, bango, back to good old Paradise Falls . . ."

"Earl, my *parents* are in this car. What must they be *thinking?*"

"I'm not even listening," says Anne.

"Nor I," I tell them.

"My ears may be flapping," says Anne, "but it doesn't mean a thing."

Florence, who is up in the front seat with Earl, squiggles around, smiles at us and says: "Can I count on you to be discreet? I mean, I would hate to have it get out that I am about to take a powder on my noble and longsuffering husband."

"We'll be as silent as the, ah, tomb of King Tut," says Anne.

"Good," says Florence.

" 'Noble and longsuffering,' huh?" says Earl Portman, turning off Cumberland Street onto Market. "Well, I'll say amen to that."

Florence snickers. "Wait until he finds out about the vacuum cleaner salesman," she says to us, in a mock whisper.

"I'd welcome him," says Earl Portman. "I could be Whitey Ford, and he could be Luis Arroyo."

"Who?" says Florence.

"Whitey Ford is a pitcher for the New York Yankees," I tell her, "and Luis Arroyo is a relief pitcher who comes into the games from time to time to bail him out."

"Right you are," says Earl. "And *you* know, what with all these babies, don't you think *I* need help?"

"I'd prefer not to answer that," I say.

"He is a *beautiful* vacuum cleaner salesman," says Florence, girlishly batting her eyes and sighing heavily.

"She means he sells beautiful vacuum cleaners," says Earl.

"I do *not*," says Florence, punching her husband's shoulder.

Earl glances at us in the mirror. "See how she treats me? It's a good thing I have a strong constitution and a weak mind."

"Amen," says Florence. "Escpecially to that part about the weak mind."

Anne and I chuckle, and the Mercury glides into the city hall parking lot. We get out of the car and scurry across the lot, and snow spatters our faces, and we enter the city hall through a side door. The mayor's office is on the second floor, and it already is crowded with friends and wellwishers and a great many political persons—clerks and councilmen and the like. Lewis and Alice have not yet arrived, but it is only 11:20, and Lewis always has been almost frighteningly punctual. It is a compulsion with him the way personal neatness is a compulsion with me, and I suppose there really is not that much difference between them. Both represent a desire for orderliness, an insistence that loose ends be tucked in place. He and Alice will arrive here on time, and of that I have no doubt. The office is small, and the overflow has spilled out into the hall. Mayor James K. Froelich, who still has ten minutes or so before his term expires, is among those who are milling in the hall. He is smiling, but his eyes are blank. He is a tall man of fifty or so, and he is utterly bald, and he always wears a suit and vest and polkadotted bow tie, no matter the weather. The final official vote count was Amberson 1,441, Froelich 1,427, and it is generally agreed that the election was more of a popularity contest than anything else. Lewis was chosen president of council four years ago, and since then it was simply a matter of time before he challenged Froelich. Actually, they are rather close friends, and Froelich was one of those who engineered Lewis's first successful council campaign. They are both Republicans, and they were instrumental in carrying the county for Nixon last year, holding the Kennedy vote to less than 42 percent, and Lewis has often said to me that it is a tragedy that the rest of the GOP did not work as hard for the national ticket as he and old Jim Froelich did. (People just don't seem to understand the meaning of effort, my son has told me. In this life, if you really *want* something, you have to *work* for it, and the hell with sleeping and eating and all that jazz.) And certainly my son's attitudes governed his own campaigns, especially the one he waged this fall against his old friend Froelich. No club or lodge or veterans' meeting was too small, and he always arrived precisely when he said he would. There were no real issues in the campaign, and so he made sure his hair was always trimly wavy, and he hammered at the point that it was time for a younger and more vigorous man to serve the people as their mayor. Jim Froelich has been in office four terms, he told his audiences, and I think it's time we gave the old boy a rest. At his age, he could use it, believe me. (These remarks were always accompanied by a grin. Lewis was too smart not to realize that he could be taken for a brash whippersnapper if he did not temper his statements with a sort of humorous offhand approach.) And Alice always accompanied Lewis to the meetings, and her smile glittered, and she always listened carefully to anything anyone had to say to her, cocking her head and nodding, concentrating, narrowing her eyes. She was quite skillful at this, and she said she had learned the technique from watching Pat Nixon on television. The secret, she said, is to make the person think his problem is the most important problem in the world, that his words contain such wisdom as would take the breath away. That's all you really have to do—make them feel important. And so, because she has refined her techniques over the years, and because she is a beautiful woman with a smile that can scorch paint off the walls, Alice has been one of my son's principal campaign assets. And her childlessness apparently has not mattered. In Paradise Falls, childless women are usually held suspect, and most of them are thought to harbor some dreadful inadequacy or perhaps a sort of coldness, but Alice is an exception, and the town apparently is willing to make allowances. I suppose her vivaciousness is responsible. That and her appearance. She dresses so well, and she is such an acknowledged stunner, that she occupies a special place that is beyond the reach of the ordinary childbearing woman. In addition, our Alice has always tried to be as *contemporary* as possible. Therefore, I believe she has become a sort of surrogate for the childbearers. As long as she is contemporary, somehow the town is keeping in touch with the times, and she is defending it from accusations of provincialism. And the childbearers are able to say: This place is no backwater—not as long as Alice Amberson stays here. (Do I project too much? Very well, I project too much. But it is what I believe.) As a result of all this (assuming my theories are accurate), Alice has been most valuable to my son, and her energy has been every bit as unfettered as his. But this is not to say that she is the *principal* reason for his success. Any success that has been achieved by Lewis C. Amberson is directly attributable to *Lewis C. Amberson* and no one else. He could have married a gorilla and his destiny would have been the same. He simply would have had to work harder. Paradise Plymouth is the most successful Dodge-Plymouth agency in our part of the state, and customers come from as far away as Columbus. This is at least partially because he is so effective on television, where his wavy hair comes across very well indeed. He has been doing his own commercials on Columbus television for nearly five years, and his smile is unrelenting. COME TO PARADISE PLYMOUTH FOR A HEAVENLY DEAL, he tells the television audience, and he always concludes with this measured, straightforward phrase: FRIENDS, I REALLY MEAN IT—I . . . WANT . . . TO . . . SELL . . . YOU . . . A GOOD CAR . . . TODAY! The campaign, based in part on a Cleveland dealer's similar folksy approach, has been immensely successful, and Lewis is recognized wherever he goes. And Little PP still smiles angelically from all his advertising posters. If David Brinkley were to walk down Main Street, says Lewis, his recognition factor wouldn't be as large as mine. After all, *he* only appears on the *news,* and *I* appear everywhere—and all the time. The T and V is the greatest invention since the automobile, take my word for it. (And always, when Lewis speaks to me of his beloved T and V, as he calls it, he remembers to grin.) And, as might be expected, the T and V was a great help to Lewis in his campaign against Jim Froelich. This factor, together with his energy and his good looks and the eager assistance of the fair Alice, enabled him to squeeze past Froelich in an election that was characterized by smiles rather than heat. There was something almost illusory about it, as though it were an election held by elves to determine who would be king of some magic forest or whatever, with the winner getting to ride in a pumpkin to a castle in a shoe, where the investiture would be conducted by Queen Mab. Perhaps the T and V has something to do with my attitude. Perhaps I no longer know what is real. And perhaps, in a very urgent and terrible sense, I am somehow trying to denature my son's latest accomplishment. If this is true, I should be ashamed of myself. Therefore, the least I can do this happy morning is keep my own counsel and not mock. And so, my face solemn, I nod at Jim Froelich, and something narrows at the corners of his eyes, and he returns the nod, and then people come to us and begin shaking our hands, and I replace my solemnity with what I hope is a dignified smile. Numerous county officials are also on hand—and even our only elected Democrat, Sheriff Ralph Y. Timmons, has made an appearance. Lewis has sold automobiles to a great many of these people, and there is no one here whom he does not know on what he likes to call a "firstname basis." Then a large commotion arises, and Lewis and Alice come bounding up the stairs, and their faces are flushed, and they are buoyant, and Alice is wearing a white dress that brilliantly sets off her spectacular red hair, and she smiles and laughs like a virgin bride, and the crowd clusters around her and my son, and Florence nudges me and whispers into my ear: "Oh, wake me early, dear Father, for I am to be Queen of the May." The crowd edges forward, but Sheriff Ralph Y. Timmons clears a path for us (we have the status of Honored Guests, which is almost as important as a place in the front row at a funeral), and so Anne, Florence, Earl and I stand directly behind Lewis when he takes the oath of office. Alice is of course standing next to him, and she is breathing in happy gasps. The oath is administered by Paradise County Common Pleas Judge Thomas W. Brashear, a portly fellow who is county Republican chairman and another old political crony of my son's. (Jim Froelich, incidentally, stands near the door, and his arms are folded across his vest, and his bow tie is a bit askew. Lewis and Alice have already made a point of going to him and smiling and shaking his hand, and Lewis has said: Jim my friend, we'll need your help and your wisdom. You know that, don't you? And Jim Froelich, mustering a smile, has already muttered some sort of reply, but I have no idea what it was.) Lewis is wearing a dark suit, and there is a white carnation in his lapel, and I feel like the Father of the Groom. Anne squeezes my hand, and I smile at her. Florence gives me a wink, and I purse my lips. The ceremony is brief, and Lewis speaks clearly, and his voice carries well. He presses his left hand firmly against Judge Brashear's Bible, squeezing it. I am able to see the words PARADISE COUNTY COURT OF COMMON PLEAS stamped on faded blue ink on the edges of the Bible's pages, and for some reason my memory leaps back to the days when little old ladies were fond of producing what were called fore-edge paintings, and I wonder if the words PARADISE COUNTY COURT OF COMMON PLEAS would change to perhaps a sylvan scene if the Bible's pages were not so tightly pressed under my son's hand . . . a sylvan scene, yes, with deer and happy forest birds . . . a pleasant thought indeed. But then the ceremony is over, and I am roused from my witless nostalgia. Lewis shakes hands with Judge Brashear, and then he kisses Alice on the mouth, and everyone applauds, and then he kisses Anne on a cheek, and she hugs him and tells him how proud she is of him, and then he shakes my hand, and his palm is slippery (and something very anxious is nudging at his eyes and his mouth), and so I say to him: "This is a great day." And Lewis says: "You mean that, don't you?" And I say: "I certainly do." And Lewis nods briefly, then moves on to Florence, whom he also kisses on a cheek. He asks her how his wonderful nieces are doing, and she tells him oh fine, just fine; they're as mean and sassy as ever. And Lewis grins and tells her she is the biggest fibber he has ever met in his whole life. And he laughs, and at the same time he glances back at me, and I know he has not believed my words either, but then neither have I.

The Ginn home was white and enormous, with black shutters, high windows and a great red front door. Amberson turned onto a curved driveway. It was gravel, and the Pontiac's tires made a heavy comfortable sound.

"First the Lee Road House of Ribs, and now this," said Anne. "What a world."

Amberson nodded. He parked the car near the front steps, switched off the engine and started to open his door.

"Wait a minute," said Anne. "Is my hat on straight?"

He looked at her. "It's just fine."

"My hair all right?"

"It couldn't be better."

She patted her hair and adjusted her hat. She leaned to the left and studied herself in the rearview mirror. "I *do* feel sort of *tacky* after sitting in this car all day."

"You look splendid," said Amberson.

"Of course I do," said Anne. "Alice will expire of envy."

"That wouldn't surprise me a bit," said Amberson.

"You are a dear man," said Anne, patting her hair. Smiling a little, she said: "All right. I'm as ready as I'll ever be."

Amberson got out of the car, opened Anne's door for her. She took his hand and got out, and she was breathing with her mouth open. He was tempted to ask her how she felt, but perhaps now was not the time, and so he remained silent. He held her arm loosely. It was her right arm, and he did not want to hurt it. They climbed a sequence of low steps that was guarded by two rampant stone lions.

"I feel as though we are calling on royalty," said Anne. "Perhaps Prince Philip will open the door for us."

"Well, you never can tell," said Amberson.

He pressed the doorbell button, and the great red door was opened not by Prince Philip, but by the incandescent Alice herself, and she made a rusted sound that perhaps was a squeal, and then she said: "Well, my *God* in *Heaven* . . ."

"Hello, Alice," said Amberson. "We thought we would surprise you."

"Yes," said Anne, and her hands fluttered. "That's right."

Alice laughed. She rushed to them and hugged them both. "Oh my *goodness!*" she rasped. "What a *marvelous* surprise it *is!*" She kissed Amberson on a cheek, and she kissed Anne on the nose, then ushered the Ambersons into the house. The great red door slammed behind them, and then she said: "You *will* stay for dinner, of course. I want Francis and the children to have a chance to talk with you . . . a *real* chance, I mean. We haven't seen you since the wedding and—"

"No," said Anne. "No thank you. It's very nice of you to make the offer, but we were passing through, and we just thought we'd stop to see how you're doing."

"Nonsense," said Alice. She steered the Ambersons into an enormous front room. The carpet was thick under their feet. She helped them out of their coats and hung the coats and their hats in a closet next to an immense stone fireplace. "This is an adorable place for a closet," she said. "On a winter night, the guests' coats are warm for the journey home. I've never heard of putting a coat closet next to a fireplace, but it certainly is a good idea. Now, you two, don't just stand there. Please sit down." She pointed acorss the room. "Try that sofa over there. It's so comfortable it's almost *seductive* . . ."

Smiling, the Ambersons went to the sofa and seated themselves.

Alice walked to a door and shouted: "Cornelia! You'll never guess who's here! Come and bring Ted with you!" She leaned out the opening, and Amberson was afforded a fine view of her legs.

A voice sounded faintly somewhere in the back of the house. Alice crossed the room and perched on a chair near the sofa. "Cornelia's here with her fiancé. You remember Cornelia, don't you?"

"She's your husband's oldest child, isn't she?" said Amberson.

"Yes," said Alice. "And she's a grownup woman now." Then, smiling, Alice adjusted her skirt. "And Ted Frost is a fine young man. He's only twentyfour, but he's had a novel accepted for publication, and that's really something, wouldn't you say?"

"Yes," said Amberson. Next to him, Anne nodded. She patted her hair.

Again Alice adjusted her skirt. She wore a short blue dress, and her red hair curved against her cheeks, and she did indeed appear to be about thirty. The dress was cut low in front, and the outline of her breasts was round and full. Actually, the dress was cut so low in front that all the flesh of her breasts, down to just above the nipples, was in full view. Amberson kept his eyes averted. Four years ago, on the day Lewis died, Alice had made a terrible accusation, and it had been directed at Amberson, and so he did not look at her breasts. (Was he filthy? Was he lustful and diseased? Alice apparently had thought so, and she had said as much. And he was positive she remembered what she had said that day. The words had not been the sort to vanish with time.)

A girl and a young man came into the room. Cornelia was tall and blond with lank hair and long legs. She wore blue jeans, a khaki blouse and a sort of shawl. She was barefoot. The young man was rather stout, with large ears and a pinched little face. He blinked a great deal, and his teeth were uneven. He wore a blue suit and a white turtleneck sweater, and his feet were in sandals. Taken together, the suit and the sandals probably represented some sort of concession to the amenities. Or at least Amberson thought so.

Alice made the introductions, and handshakes were exchanged. Cornelia smiled and said oh yes, she remembered the Ambersons quite well from the wedding. Then she and Ted seated themselves on the floor. We like to sit on the floor, Cornelia told the Ambersons. I don't know *why* we do, but we *do*. And Ted Frost said: Perhaps one sits on the floor in order to be more *real*, which is very chic these days. The Ambersons smiled, and Alice said something to the effect that today's chic was tomorrow's leftover mashed potatoes, the way the world kept changing so rapidly. And Amberson said yes, that surely was true enough. He remembered Cornelia now. She was the one who had worked for Ralph Nader, and he recalled that he had rather liked her. They had had a brief but interesting conversation at her father's wedding reception two years ago, and Cornelia had spoken rather heatedly of the rights of the individual, using such words as *dehumanization* and *plastic* and *fragmented*. And yet, as Amberson remembered the conversation, she had seemed to him to be a sensible and reasonable girl and in no way a really foaming radical. Her eyes had been too steady, and she had laughed too often. (In Amberson's view, radicals . . . or at least foaming radicals . . . did not have steady eyes, and they did not laugh at all.)

Now Alice was speaking again. "Francis will be home any moment now, and he certainly will be delighted to see you two. And so will Donnie and Harlowe and Beth as soon as *they* get home . . ."

"There is a slew of us," said Cornelia, grinning.

"Ginns to the right of us," said Ted Frost. "Ginns to the left of us."

"We're up to our asses in Ginns," said Cornelia, picking at a toe and still grinning.

Alice laughed, and this surprised Amberson a little. "What will Mother and Father Amberson think of us?" she said to Cornelia. She reached out and patted Cornelia's hair. "They'll go away thinking we're *vulgar* and *awful* . . ."

Cornelia smiled up at her stepmother. "I'm sorry." Then, to the Ambersons: "Sometimes I'm too verbal."

"I believe we'll survive," said Amberson.

"No doubt about it," said Anne.

Alice leaned forward. "And *so*. Tell us. What brings you to our neck of the woods?"

"We're on a little motor trip," said Amberson.

"Oh? Where are you going?" Alice asked him.

"We don't quite know."

"Oh?"

Anne patted Amberson's knee. "He's having one of his notions," she said to Alice. "And so yesterday we just packed up our old kit bag, and away we went . . ."

"Hey," said Cornelia. "That's terrific."

"That's Father Amberson for you," said Alice. "A free and independent spirit. An adventurer at heart. Well, good enough. The world could use a few more such people . . ."

"A stickinthemud who is stuck in the mud comes up with nothing but mud," said Ted Frost.

Everyone looked at him.

"Ah, excuse me," he said, shrugging.

Then everyone laughed.

"You wouldn't know it," said Cornelia, nudging Ted Frost, "but he does have literary talent." Then she told the Ambersons that he was studying at Harvard for his doctorate in twentieth-century American literature, and his novel was scheduled to be published in the summer of 1972 by Doubleday. "He's from Bergen, New Jersey," she said, "and the book is about a man whose devotion to professional football destroys his life. This man is the Super Fan Number One of the New York Jets, and he . . . well, I don't want to tell too much, but the book is *important,* and it has something to say about the way we live, and I *love* it . . ."

"An unsolicited testimonial from an impartial source," said Ted.

"Now, don't go putting yourself *down,* " said Cornelia. "You're good, and you know it. People who are good always do."

"Okay. If you say so," said Ted.

Cornelia grinned at the Ambersons. She smoothed back her hair and then she said: "He really does have talent. Maybe I'm being *girlish* and *dumb,* but when I read the book . . . oh, I don't know . . . I just . . . well, how does it grab you if I say I'm proud?"

"Forgive her," said Ted, rolling his eyes.

Alice spoke up. "Father Amberson was an English teacher," she told Ted. "And he was a *good* one, too. So I just bet he can understand why Cornelia is proud. And anyway, we're *all* proud."

"That's telling him," said Cornelia.

Ted smiled at the Ambersons. "Pay no attention to the enthusiastic Cornelia," he told them. Then, to Amberson: "Did you teach around here? I have some friends on the faculty at Kent State, and—"

Amberson held up a hand. "No. I'm afraid I was only a highschool teacher. At, ah, Paradise Falls, which is a town in southeastern Ohio. It —"

"Oh, I've heard of the place," said Ted. "The rather heavy irony of the name has always interested me."

"It was not intended," said Amberson, "but it just so happens that a river called the Paradise flows through the town, and it just so happens that there is a, ah, waterfall. Hence, the name of the town."

"Then Milton doesn't enter into it?"

"No. I'm afraid not."

"That's too bad," said Ted. He leaned back on his elbows. "I mean, it would be nice to believe that a poetic intelligence had been at work. Some pre-Revolutionary pioneer scholar, alone in the wilderness with his books and his flintlock, sitting in a cabin and musing on sin or whatever . . ."

Amberson nodded. "I know what you mean, but poetry had nothing to do with it."

Alice cleared her throat. She stood up. "Well," she said, "this is all getting too deep for little old Alice. If you'll excuse me, I want to run back to the kitchen and tell Ethel there'll be two more for dinner."

"Now, really, Alice," said Amberson, "we didn't come here for a handout. We just wanted to see how you were doing. We'll be on our way very shortly."

"Yes," said Anne, leaning forward and rubbing her right arm. "We don't want to put you out."

"Nonsense," said Alice. "You'll join us for dinner, and that's all there is *to* it." She went out, and her skirts swirled, and her legs still were miraculous.

Amberson looked at Anne and shrugged.

Now Ted and Cornelia were holding hands. He was leaning forward again, and they both were sitting crosslegged. "There's something I don't understand," he said to Amberson. "Why did Mrs. Ginn call you Father Amberson? The name makes you sound like some sort of priest."

Cornelia answered before Amberson could say anything. "The Ambersons were her first husband's parents," she said. "To her, he's Father Amberson, and Mrs. Amberson is Mother Amberson."

"Oh," said Ted. "Well, what do you know about that. A sort of euphemistic way of saying inlaws, I suppose."

"Yes," said Amberson.

Cornelia smiled at the Ambersons. "It's all a lot of dreary bullshit, isn't it?" she said.

Amberson could think of nothing appropriate to say. He glanced at Anne.

Anne grinned. *"Yes,"* she said. "You're absolutely right."

And then they laughed—all four of them. And Cornelia told the Ambersons she hoped she had not shocked them. And Amberson told her well, perhaps you did, at least a little, but I honestly do not believe the world will fall down. There was more laughter, and everyone got to talking at once, and Cornelia told of the apartment she shared with Ted in good old Cambridge, Mass, and she said she hoped the Ambersons were not offended at learning that she and Ted *lived together.* And Amberson told her no, he was not offended; he was a faithful reader of *Time* magazine, and he knew all about such things. And then, still rubbing her arm, Anne told Cornelia she envied the young people these days, and that was a fact. "I'm as moral a woman as you'd ever hope to meet," said Anne, "and as Methodist as John Wesley himself, and very familiar with the Do's and Don't's and the Commandments and whatall. But at the same time I've never had much use for hypoc-
284

risy. What was the word you used?"

"I believe it was bullshit," said Cornelia.

"Yes," said Anne. "That's the word. And it represents a whatchama-callit, a *commodity* that seems to be taking over the world."

"But you don't know all the facts," said Cornelia.

Anne blinked at her. "What facts?"

Cornelia squeezed Ted's hand. "We're frauds, Ted and I."

"I'm afraid I don't understand," said Anne.

"Oh, it's no big thing," said Cornelia. "It's just that we aren't what we seem to be. We've talked it all out, and I suppose it's kind of amusing, but I don't think Daddy or Alice or anyone in this family would understand. You see, we're participating in a sort of charade, and it's *expected* of us, you know?"

"Charade?" said Anne.

"I worked for Ralph Nader. Did you know that?"

"Yes," said Anne. "You talked about him at the wedding."

"That's right," said Amberson. "And you seemed very determined to do something for the world."

"Well," said Cornelia, "I don't want to belabor the word, but it was all bullshit. Or crap. Or whatever you want to call it."

Ted Frost nodded but said nothing.

"You mean Ralph Nader is a fraud?" Amberson wanted to know.

"No," said Cornelia. "He's not a fraud. He's sincere, and the work he does is good. But I don't work for him any more. You see, I never did *relate* to any of it. It was all a lot of *rhetoric* to me. I mean, who am I anyway? I'm just a rich girl from Shaker Heights, that's all. I've never been downtrodden in my life. And so I was just going through the motions. It was all fake . . ."

"It just so happens that we like Doris Day movies," said Ted.

"I beg your pardon?" said Amberson.

"We're reactionaries," said Cornelia. "We really are. Oh, we're *bright* and we're *aware* and all *that,* but we keep wishing it was 1953. Honest to God we do. What we *appear* to be is just a lot of window-dressing. Like living together in mortal sin or whatever and screwing like chipmunks in a bed that has a lumpy mattress . . . and then *bragging* about it so we can show the world how *hip* we are. So like *cool* and *heavy,* you know? You see, we've always liked to believe that we were into everything, participating in relevant activities and all that. But we're not really into *anything.* You know something? I don't give a damn whether Ford makes safe cars or the world's worst death traps. When I worked for Ralph Nader, I was absolutely *bored* to *death.* Those people were all so serious and glum, like missionaries, you know?

And, well, I just never related to *any* of it. And that's why Ted and I are getting married. We don't *like* living in sin. It makes us feel *guilty*, so help me God. We want to *get married*, and he wants to be *successful* and *make money* from his books, and okay, if he has something to say, all very well and good, but he's just not all that into the social awareness thing, and neither am I. His book is good. It's very good, and it has something to say about the way people live today. But it's also *entertaining*, you know? And *amusing*. There's this scene where his hero is in Shea Stadium, and the Jets have just defeated the Green Bay Packers, and the—"

"The Cleveland Browns," said Ted.

"Oh?" said Cornelia. "I thought it was the Green Bay Packers. *Well*, at *any* rate, the poor man has managed to worm his way into the dressing room so he can get Joe Namath's autograph, but at the same time he has to *go to the bathroom* in the *worst possible way*, but he knows if he goes to the bathroom he won't have a chance to talk to Joe Namath, and so he steps into this dark hallway and tries to relieve himself, only a policeman sees him exposed and all, and, well, you can *imagine* what happens *then*. Maybe it all sounds vulgar, the way I tell it, but it's really very *funny*. Ted is a real writer, and you *must* get his book when it comes out. But that's not the *point*. The *point* is—Ted doesn't stay up nights trying to figure out ways to save the world. He's no *missionary* . . . and neither am *I* . . ."

"We'll never save a single soul," said Ted.

Cornelia went on. "We want to have a little *fun*, you know? Seeing movies and playing records and having babies and watching Dick Cavett. I . . . well, now look, I've marched in peace demonstrations and I've smoked pot and I've spent hours rapping with all sorts of people in encounter groups, and last year I even did up my hair so I looked like Viva, or maybe a cross between Viva and Gale Sondergaard . . . but I couldn't really stand any of it. I keep wishing it was 1953. I really do. I don't *remember* 1953 or anything like *that*, but so what? It's what I *want*. And so does Ted."

"Absolutely," said Ted.

Cornelia shook her head. She smiled at the Ambersons again. "Daddy and Alice will have a fit when they find out," she said.

"How so?" Amberson asked her.

"Because they're trying so hard to be hip. Both of them. They know that Ted and I have been living together, and they've been so *understanding* it just about makes my skin break out. Here we are, two guilty children looking for a spanking, and all we get is indulgent kindness. And when they find out we are reactionary, they'll just about fall down dead. They see themselves as being terribly *au courant,* don't you know, hip hip, old boy, jolly good show, eh wot?"

"Isn't that being a little harsh?" said Anne.

"I suppose so," said Cornelia. "But reactionaries are not gentle people."

Anne rubbed the arm. "Do you like Alice?"

"Yes," said Cornelia. "More than I thought I would."

"Why?"

"Well," said Cornelia, looking around. She lowered her voice. "For one thing, she's having the time of her life—and she's making no bones about it. She *enjoys* being the richbitch Shaker Heights matron, and she's so *honest* about her enjoyment. I mean, how could I possibly resent her? She's having a ball, and that's all there is *to* it."

Anne nodded. "Do your brothers and sisters like her?"

"I think so," said Cornelia. "Don is a jock, and I'm sure she's all right with him as long as she doesn't keep him from playing football at Hawken. And Harlowe is too busy with his chemicals and his electric trains and his chess books. As for *Beth,* well, she's only fifteen but she's built like Aunt Jane's cement privy, and so you can *imagine* what occupies all *her* attention."

"So then you would say Alice is happy?" Anne asked Cornelia.

"Yes," said Cornelia. "Very."

"And well enough liked by the children?"

"Yes."

"And not unkind to them?"

"Not a bit."

Anne looked at Amberson. "That's too bad," she said, rubbing the arm.

Amberson looked away.

"I beg your pardon?" said Cornelia.

"I don't like her," said Anne. "I never have."

Amberson placed his hands on his knees. His hands were warm, and they were a little damp. "Now, Anne," he said, not looking at her. "Please."

"If they're being honest with us," said Anne, "why can't we be honest with them?"

Amberson looked at his wife. He did not want to look at her, but he did. He adjusted his spectacles, and then he said: "They don't have to know about it. It doesn't concern them."

Anne's face was tight, and her lips were pressed against her teeth. "We shouldn't even *be* here," she said. "I don't want to sit down to dinner with her, and I don't want to talk with her. I want to go." She stood up, and she still was rubbing the arm.

Amberson looked up at her.

Cornelia and Ted quickly got to their feet. Cornelia walked to where Anne stood. She placed a hand on Anne's arm. "Is there something the matter? Does your arm hurt?"

"Yes," said Anne. "My arm hurts. I had a radical mastectomy last year, and the doctors cut out the lymph nodes, and they were in my arm, and it *hurts.*"

"Oh," said Cornelia. She withdrew the hand.

"We didn't mean to upset you," said Ted.

"You didn't upset me," said Anne. "I don't know why you told me the things you did. After all, who are we to you? But you didn't upset me. You didn't upset me a bit. As a mattter of fact, you've done me good. You really have."

Amberson stood up.

Anne glared at him. "I *hurt* . . ." she said.

Amberson nodded.

Cornelia looked at Ted. "Why *did* we tell them all this?" she asked him.

"You're the one who did the telling," said Ted.

"All right, then why did *I* do the telling?"

Ted shrugged. "They seem gentle, and sooner or later you would have had to tell *someone,* and it's always easier to confess to strangers. They pass out of your life, and they don't haunt you."

"Yes," said Cornelia. "I see." Then, to Anne: "Is that why you're telling *us* you don't like Alice?"

Anne nodded. Her flesh was waxy, and she was blinking, and she plucked and fussed with the arm. "She has too much ambition. It killed our son. She—"

"Bullshit," said Alice from the doorway. .

They all looked at her.

She came into the room. Her hands were in fists. "Cornelia," she said, "you'll pardon me if I borrow your favorite word, but these people are full of bullshit up to their eyebrows, and now I'm going to ask them to get out of my house."

"Now, Alice," said Amberson, "she didn't mean—"

"I did too," said Anne.

"She knows she meant it," Alice told Amberson. "She's always meant it. I thought we established that when Lewis died."

"We shouldn't talk like this," said Amberson. "It accomplishes nothing."

"Oh my God," said Alice. She looked at Cornelia and Ted. She opened a fist, pointed at Amberson and said: "He has an image of himself, and he has an image of his wife, and it's all goodness and honey. But it's also bullshit."

"I don't want to hear any more of this," said Anne. She started to move toward the closet where the coats and hats were.

"Just hold on," said Alice.

Anne hesitated.

Alice moved until she was standing directly in front of Amberson. Her lipstick was moist. "I want you to know something," she said. "I want you to know that today I was really making an effort. But this old harpy of yours couldn't hold her tongue, could she?"

"Really, Alice," said Cornelia, "there's nothing to be—"

Alice turned to Anne. "You even named a cat after him, didn't you? He was always slightly disreputable, wasn't he? His *values* weren't the same as yours, and so you found an old *cat,* and you named the old cat *Sinclair,* and—"

"We meant no harm by that," said Amberson. His chest was tight.

Alice turned to Cornelia and Ted. "You see, my husband's name was *Lewis,* and they named the cat *Sinclair,* and they figured stupid Alice would never catch the significance. Well, Alice may be stupid, but she's not *that* stupid."

"We had better go," said Amberson. He went to Anne and took her by an arm. She was shaking.

Alice followed him and tapped him on a shoulder.

He turned and faced her. So did Anne.

Alice tried to grin. She folded her arms over her bosom, and the grin was uneven, and she said: "I have news for you two. Remember the day Lewis died? Remember the things I said that day? Well, they're just as true now as they ever were. So get this, folks. You're going to have to make your way down Life's Highway with the full and certain knowledge that you're not universally admired, that there exists in this world one person—namely, myself—who cannot abide the sight or even the thought of you. You see yourselves as being sweet and kindly, don't you? The gentle schoolmaster and his darling wife. Well, that's all bullshit. Lewis was your son for a hell of a lot more years than he was my husband, but you never were able to figure him out, and you *never even made the effort.* You didn't care, did you? He wasn't worth worrying about, was he? There was always the sainted Henry, and *he—*"

Now Anne was weeping. "What . . . what do *you* know about it?"

"What do *I* know about it?" said Alice, snorting. "My God, I know more about it than *you* ever have or ever will. I *slept* with him, remember? He understood your contempt. To you, he was always some sort of clod, but you were wrong. He understood you very well, and—"

"That's enough of this," said Amberson. He pulled Anne toward the closet. "I don't want to hear any more." He wrenched open the closet door. "We'll . . . we'll just get our coats . . ." He blinked into the closet. Perhaps two dozen coats were on hangers, and he was unable to recognize which were his and Anne's. He blinked at all the coats. He tugged at one, and it fell to the floor. He tugged at another, and it also fell to the floor. "I can't seem to . . . which one of these is Anne's? Which one is mine? They all look . . ."

Alice came up behind them. Cornelia and Ted followed her. Cornelia tugged at Alice's arm, but Alice would not budge. "Have I upset you?" she said to the Ambersons. "Have I really actually managed to *get through?*"

Anne stood wailing. She pressed her hands over her face.

"Alice," said Cornelia, "all right now, please leave them alone . . ."

Alice jerked her arm free of Cornelia's grasp. "You find your coats," she told the Ambersons, "and you get the fuck out of my house."

"Jesus . . ." said Ted.

Amberson began rummaging desperately through the coats. He finally found Anne's, and then he found his own. He jerked the coats off their hangers, and the hangers clattered to the floor. He helped Anne into her coat. Their hats were on a shelf. He grabbed them. His own coat was draped over an arm, and he did not bother to put it on. Behind him, Alice was gasping. He turned to her, and her face was flushed, and her eyes were leaking. "You just get out," she said. "You just get out of here."

Amberson and his wife moved toward the door. Anne was hunched over, and she still was wailing. He put an arm around her and patted her shoulder, the sore one. She gave a little shriek and twisted away from him. Alice followed them. Her tongue made wet sounds.

The Ambersons retreated into the hall and made their way toward the front door. Alice skittered in front of them and pulled open the door. She bowed deeply from the waist, and Amberson was able to see all of her breasts. (Cornelia and Ted also came out into the hall, but they said nothing.)

The Ambersons pushed past Alice, and she said: "Good riddance."

Amberson shuddered. He and Anne stumbled out past the rampant stone lions.

The door was slammed shut behind them.

Wednesday

See now 1942, and we have been told that the world has exploded, but this is almost impossible to imagine. It is a Sunday afternoon in early January, and Henry is coming home today from Gambier for a brief visit. I spoke with him on the telephone last night, and he told me he has made up his mind to enlist in the army. He is not yet even nineteen, and Anne and I are both quite disturbed by his decision. We cannot really see him involving himself in hatred and violence. He has never prepared himself for hatred and violence, and he does not understand them.

Anne and I are sitting alone in the front room. Florence, who is nearly twelve now, has gone across the street to help her friend Wanda Crowley build a snowman. And Lewis, who is sixteen, is off at the Ritz with some friends. The featured attraction is a film called *Belle Starr*, with Randolph Scott and Gene Tierney, a lovely young newcomer whose photographs reveal a thoughtful face with an oriental cast to it, plus a large mouth that has a slight overbite. I would have liked to see the movie myself, but today's meeting with Henry is too important. (The girl's face has intrigued me ever since I first saw it in a newspaper photograph, and I tell myself I must make it a point to take Anne to the Ritz later this week before the feature changes.) Outside, snow has been falling since dawn. It is a soft snow, the sort that sticks and drifts and splatters, and I am glad I do not have to be out in an automobile today. I suppose I am the most timid motorist in Paradise County, and at fortyfour I know I am too old to change. I am still trim, though, and every spring I run laps with my track boys, and last year, on a dare, I did the mile in 4:57. The boys had goaded me into it, telling me I was too long in the tooth to break five minutes. Earl Potter, a dash man, held the stopwatch, and several of the other boys accused him of trying to butter me up by fibbing about the time. As a result, he became a bit angry, and I had to step between him and a boy named Jack Zeller. I still was puffing from my glorious 4:57 mile, and I told them for God's sake, boys, give me a chance to get my breath before you go at it— otherwise, I won't be able to enjoy it. This relieved the tension somewhat, and Earl Potter and Jack Zeller backed away from each other, and I took the watch from Earl and showed it to Jack, and there the time was: 4:57 flat. And I said: How could anyone be so cruel as to want to deprive an old man of his little victory? And if you think I'm trying to play on your sympathies, you're absolutely correct. And then someone laughed, and the crisis passed, and Jack Zeller grinned and told me my *Lord,* Mr. Amberson, you should of seen yourself on that last lap. You looked like you were running uphill on all fours, like it was a mountain and you'd never get to the top. And I gave Jack Zeller a sort of gasping laugh and told him he was not far from the truth, sad as it was to admit. Still, I *did* break five minutes, and I am as proud of that accomplishment (at my age) as I am of anything I ever did when I ran track at Paradise Falls High School and then Ohio State, back in that time when my hotly romantic imaginings had promised me that some day I would fly up into the sky on glorious winged feet. But now I know I shall never sprout the glorious winged feet, and so I happily settle for the 4:57 and I am proud of it. And I am proud of my flat belly and my more or less firm flesh. I never slouch or lollygag, and I still am able to feel tone in my muscles. My eyesight is acute, and Anne and I still have at each other regularly in bed, and sometimes she tells me my energy just about takes her breath away, and this pleases me enormously, as why shouldn't it? In the meantime, there are other matters to be considered; bills must be paid, and noses must be wiped, and wars must be faced, and one must come to terms with one's exploding world. This quiet Sunday afternoon is a lie, and so is the silent snow, and so are snowmen and the Ritz Theater and the foolish vanity of a middleaged schoolteacher who admires his flat belly. And Anne and I seem to have no words for one another. We have been sitting in the front room for perhaps half an hour, and we have said nothing. We listen to the clock, and we glance outside at the great splattering globs of snow that have pasted themselves over the streets and the yards and the houses, dimming rooftops and blending them against a tall vacant sky, and from time to time Anne plucks at one of the doilies that are pinned on the arms of the sofa where she is sitting, but where are our words? Shouldn't we begin to try to understand, and *right now,* so that we will be prepared for him when he arrives? I have treasured words all my life, and now I have none. I sigh, cross my legs. Perhaps I should turn on the radio. It is on a table next to me. Perhaps music would help. I twist my neck and glare at the radio as though it were some sort of vile enemy. He is driving down from Gambier with a boy named Ralph Griswold, his roommate. Ralph Griswold is the son of an Episcopal priest in Jackson, and he has his own car. Even by Kenyon standards, he is a rather grand fellow, with an immensely resonant voice and a large bony ecclesiastical frame, and he has told me he intends to do graduate work at Bexley Hall. I like Ralph Griswold well enough; he prays a great deal, and perhaps he represents some sort of test for my son, who still is the Always Boy, and make no mistake of that. Henry was graduated from Paradise Falls High School in 1940 just after his seventeenth birthday. (We had permitted him to skip one grade—the tenth.) He was of course the class valedictorian; he also was its historian. He had reached his full growth—six feet four inches and approximately two hundred fifteen pounds—at the age of fifteen, but he never went out for any of the athletic teams. I asked him about this on a number of occasions, and his answer always was the same. According to him, he was too clumsy, too much of a clodhopper. But this was—and is—untrue. He is not at all a clodhopper. He is an excellent athlete, and he always has been. His coordination is superb for a boy of such great size, and he has excellent instincts. I have often watched him play football and baseball and basketball with his friends (acquaintances, rather, since he has never had any real friends), and I can say for a fact that he could excel at any sport he would choose. But he refused to go out for any of the teams, including my track team. And God knows, I tried to get him. I told him he had the stuff to be an excellent 880 man or miler or perhaps a shotputter, but he smilingly declined. No sir, he said, I'm sorry, but I'm a clodhopper. And so, all through his days at Paradise Falls High School, he tried to remain as inconspicuous as possible. Still, he could not help but be the valedictorian of his class, even though he never consciously *sought* that honor. To have been anything else would have been a betrayal of his intelligence, and clearly he was unwilling to tolerate such a thing. The academic honors rolled into his lap as easily as marbles dropping off a tabletop, and therefore in the final judgment it did not really matter that he had refused to go out for the teams. He *still* was set apart from his contemporaries. Although he was not an athletic star he was an *academic* star, and his isolation was even worse than if he had won ten letters and led Paradise Falls High to, say, the state basketball championship. I suspect he sees excellence as being destructive, or at least terribly painful. All his life it has kept him under glass, and his world has held him at a respectful distance. But he is, after all, only a boy, and to see him shuffling alone to school every morning, smiling at his world that had no time for him because it lacked the capacity to understand him, was enough to break my heart, and I eventually found myself taking a different route, just so I would not have to encounter his large forlorn grin. All the time he attended Paradise Falls High School, he never went out with a girl. As far as I know, he never has gone out with a girl to this day. His features are a bit narrow, but he is not a badlooking boy, and his size makes him quite physically impressive, but the girls have had nothing to do with him. I suppose they are like everyone else. I suppose he makes them feel inadequate. But as far as I know no girl has ever let Henry know how she feels about him, and my God, the pain he must endure. (It is imperative that I keep reminding myself he is still only a *boy*, with a boy's energies and ambitions and warm fluids.) But I have seldom heard him complain about any of this. He still loves his world, even though it has respectfully banished him. He even loves his younger brother Lewis, a handsome and popular fellow who last fall, as a junior at Paradise Falls High, was a starting halfback on the football team and scored eleven touchdowns in nine games and was chosen as Paradise Falls' only member of the Hocking-Paradise Conference all-league team. Lewis often refers to Henry as Old Goofy, and he says Henry really ought to go buy a house on the moon, so he can sit all day and grin at the sky and pluck daffodils from his hair. Sometimes Anne and I take Lewis to task for that sort of talk, and then he invariably tells us he is sorry; he meant no offense. And he invariably grins, and the grin is relentless and irresistible, and it does away with our anger. Grinning and scuffing, he says: I talk too much. I know it. I'm sorry. One of these days I'm going to have to do something about my tongue. And then he kisses his mother, and his face is remorseful, and he has won, and we know it, and there is absolutely nothing we can do. (So see then these days. See me, still trim at fortyfour, still delighting in my wife, who is still plumply attractive at fortytwo, who still dotes on Henry the Always Boy, who is lonely and isolated and vainly seeking acceptance, whose younger brother is seeking to compete with him and perhaps defeat him, and see Florence too, a pretty girl who at eleven has a fragile sweetness that would disarm an artillery sergeant, a lovely child whose days are measured in candy and hairribbons. See then all of us, and listen to our voices and the words we speak, and say then yes, all right, this is a family; this is what we so far have made of our lives, and its sum is a sum of complexities, and the doors forever open and close, and it is a great life if you can stand the strain, yes indeed.) I clear my throat and Anne smiles at me. Perhaps I *should* turn on the radio, but I do not particurly enjoy the radio these days. Not even my two favorites, Jack Benny and Fred Allen, can do much to amuse me. The exploding world has provided too much horror. The Japanese have obviously gained a great victory in the Pacific, and everything west of Hawaii has either fallen to them or will shortly fall to them and this obviously will be a long war, and where is it written that we absolutely shall win? Justice apparently is on our side, but then it also apparently was on the side of the Poles and the French and the Marines who defended Wake Island, and look what happened to *them.* The President has announced that our factories are being geared to produce sixty thousand airplanes this year and one hundred twentyfive thousand more of them in 1943, and it seems that half the male population of Paradise Falls High School has enlisted in the armed forces, and at fortyfour I have registered for the draft and am at least technically eligible to be conscripted. San Francisco has been blacked out, and the President has met with Prime Minister Churchill in Washington, and automobile tires are under ration restrictions, with automobiles themselves (and gasoline) rumored soon to follow. The attack on Pearl Harbor has seriously emasculated our naval power, and it is said that General MacArthur's forces in the Philippines cannot hold out more than a few weeks more. The British navy also has been hacked to pieces in the Pacific, which has already been transformed into a Japanese duck pond. General MacArthur's army has been cut off from supplies and reinforcements, and each day we read the war news with increasing despair. And so why would I want to turn on the radio? It is better that I squint out the window and watch Florence and her friend Wanda Crowley put together the parts of their snowman. I watch the girls flap and tumble, and I note the care with which they construct the snowman's mouth and eyes, and Florence has taken along a bubble pipe, and she plunges it in the mouth at a rakish angle, and Wanda Crowley claps her mittened hands together in silent delight. What do Florence and Wanda know of horror? What do they know of a world that has exploded? It is lovely to watch them play this way, but what bearing does any of this have on all the wretched history that has been thrust upon us? In Russia, hundreds of thousands of men are killing one another in snow that is precisely like this snow that has so calmly drifted over our little town, and why *them* and not *us?* How does God determine who is sacrificed and who is spared? Surely there must be some sort of scheme. Surely the Lord has spared us for a purpose. If so, there is a responsibility we must confront, an obligation we must meet in exchange for all our peaceful days and our rakish snowmen. Perhaps Henry the Always Boy senses this, and perhaps it is why he wants to enlist, despite the fact that violence is an affront to his nature. Oh yes, he still weeps for dead animals, and he hugs stray kittens to his chest. And he undoubtedly will be what he is forever. I have seen him play checkers with the old men who sit and lounge on the courthouse steps, and I have seen him deliberately lose game after game to some tedious old rip who has tobacco juice leaking from a toothless mouth, and I have gone shambling across leafy autumn hills with him, and he has told me: Papa, it is not easy to be alive. There is so much to do, isn't there? Is it wrong for me to love them all? Why can't I be like everyone else? What happened? Did you put something in my food when I was a little boy? And then Henry the Always Boy laughs, and he says: Ah, listen to the dumb clodhopper. And then of course I try to reassure him that it is right for him to question his world. And I tell him: Whatever your nature is, you should not try to change it. Perhaps you're tired of hearing me say that, but it is the truth, and it will not run off and hide just because you are made uncomfortable by it. (And I think of the tedious old rips, and I know that for years now Henry has been the best checkers player in Paradise Falls, and he has often humiliated my friends, and I love my son beyond the poor power of any words to describe, and so why should he have to participate in all this corruption? Why does he feel it is so necessary? It could destroy him, and his benevolence would vanish forever, even out of memory.) On the telephone last night, Henry told me he would be home by noon—weather permitting. But obviously the roads are in bad shape, and there really is no knowing when he will arrive. He told me he would stay with us a day or two before going to Columbus to enlist. He also told me he doubted there was anything I could say that would change his mind. He was an honors student at Kenyon in his freshman year, and Ralph Griswold has told me that he

(Henry) has the highest point average in the sophomore class. Ralph Griswold, incidentally, is not a bad student himself, and his grades are in the B and B+ range—but he is as nothing compared with Henry. They both are history majors, and Henry has spoken vaguely of perhaps some day going into teaching. He is attending Kenyon on a partial scholarship, and the rest of the money has come from the Oak Grove Cemetery Association stock that was left to me by my father. Henry earns extra money by working in a dining hall, and from time to time he insists on giving me twenty dollars or so, telling me: I have no use for it, and I don't want to be a burden to you and Mama. That wouldn't be fair. (I always try to refuse the money, but he will not permit this, and his eyes assume such a wounded cast that I have no choice but to accept.) There is a draft somewhere and I rub my knees. I stand up and walk to the front window and peer up the street, and now the snow is horizontal, and the sky has been obscured, and I am unable to see the house three doors up toward High Street. I lean forward, and my forehead touches the cool pane, and I say to myself: He can beat anyone at checkers, and he is able to draw a map of Paradise Falls from memory. And I say to myself: I wish he would go out for one of the teams at Kenyon. And I say to myself: He always will lose to the old rips. He loves them that much. He loves the world that much. Why then does not the world have the capacity to love him? Must he ultimately be forced to vanish so it will understand? I turn away from the window, and return to my chair and seat myself. "Florence and Wanda seem to be having great fun," I say to Anne.

"I loved snow when I was a child," she says. "I had a sled, and sometimes the snow squeaked under the runners, and it delighted me, you know?"

"We have to talk him out of it, don't we?"

"Yes," says Anne. "I think so."

"How can we do that?" I ask her.

"I don't know."

"He wants to enlist because he thinks it will gain him some sort of acceptance, and at his age acceptance is very important."

"It is very important at *any* age," says Anne. "Or at least to *most* people."

"All right, if it's that important, perhaps we should not try to talk him out of it."

"But it's the wrong *kind* of acceptance," says Anne. "Or at least the *circumstances* are wrong. If a great many people get together and do a lot of killing, I suppose they build up a kind of *comradeship,* but is it the *right* kind of comradeship? And what will it *do* to Henry?"

"I don't know."

"And what will it do to Lewis?" says Anne. "What if Henry goes away and wins a medal or something, won't that bother him even more?"

I sigh, spread my hands. "I don't know," I say. "Lewis seems too sensible for that. What he has now is only jealousy, I think, and he is working it off by being competitive . . . the football and all that. I think he loves Henry. I really do."

"None of it seems to bother Florence."

"Well, Florence is Florence."

"Nicely put," says Anne, smiling.

"Thank you."

"Do you think we'll be able to talk Henry out of it?" my wife asks me.

"I don't believe so."

"But how can he be a soldier? Doesn't a soldier have to hate his enemy? And when has Henry ever hated anyone?"

"I do not think it is too difficult to hate the Nazis."

"Yes," says Anne, "for *you* it wouldn't be. And for *me* it wouldn't be. I mean, we hate them *now,* don't we? But for *Henry* maybe it'll be impossible."

"The Nazis are cruel. They kill people. Henry disapproves of killing."

"Of course," says Anne, "but does he disapprove of killing enough so that he can kill the people who do the killing?"

"He will have to discover that for himself."

". . . which is a very pompous and callous thing to say."

"Anne, that's not fair."

"Oh? And why *isn't* it fair? I suppose next thing you'll be saying *I'm* the one who's being unfair. Well, I happen to love him, and I just don't want him to get involved in something that could—"

"Do you think *I* don't love him?"

"I didn't say that."

I lean forward, and my face is warm, and I say to my wife: "We can't *smother* him, don't you understand that? If we really love him the way we *say* we do, then we'll have to allow him to make his own mistakes! And anyway, isn't this all really moot? He'll be drafted sooner or later anyway!"

"You don't have to shout!"

"Neither do you!"

Anne hesitates. She hugs herself, and I am aware of her breasts, and I do not want to shout at her, and I do not want her to shout at me, and I am about to tell her this, but she beats me to it. "I'm sorry . . ." she says. She stands up. She glares at the doily she has been plucking. She walks to the window. She is wearing house slippers, and her feet make soft sounds, and she looks out the window and says: "I'll worry about him a lot . . ."

"I know you will. And so will I."

"We should not shout at one another. We're not the sort."

"No. We're not."

"You don't shout at your students, do you?"

"Not very often."

Anne turns away from the window. She comes to my chair and stands over me and says: "I want to sit on your lap."

"That would be my pleasure," I tell her.

Smiling, Anne eases herself down onto my lap, arranging her legs and buttocks so that her weight is more or less evenly distributed. "Big old thing like me," she says. "I hope I'm not crushing you . . ."

I kiss a cheek and an ear. "Do you hear me complaining?"

She closes her eyes and embraces me. "What will we do without him?"

"We'll miss him. And we'll pray that he comes back safely. And we'll try to be . . . well, brave."

Anne's face is pressed against mine, and I can feel her nod.

There is more I must say. She needs more words of comfort. I stroke her hair, and then I say: "We must learn not to breathe down his neck. He is a human being; he is not a *pet*. Chains are cruel. If he is extraordinary, then we must permit him to be extraordinary in his own way. Anne . . . my God, Anne . . . he'll be all right. He is not a hothouse flower." Again I stroke her hair, and then I kiss it, and then I say: "I am trying to comfort you, and I suppose I am making a botch of it. I suppose I am lecturing you instead of comforting you. But, *believe* me, I *know* how you feel, and I feel the same things myself, and I—"

I am interrupted by a commotion at the front door, and Anne quickly comes off my lap. "I bet that's Henry," she says. She hesitates for a moment, and then she smiles at me and says: "Thank you. I understand what you're saying. I really do." Then she scurries out into the front hall, and I follow, and she pushes open the front door, and there stands Henry, grinning and hatless, and his hair is blotted with the silvery snow, and Florence is standing with him, and she says: "Hey, look what the snow just blew in!"

Henry turns and waves at Ralph Griswold, whose '38 Ford is pulling away from the curb across the street, and Ralph Griswold gives the horn several jaunty toots, and the Ford goes slithering away, its wipers flapping and its rear wheels throwing up a spray of snow. Henry and Florence come stamping into the house, and the door is slammed shut behind them, and Henry bends down and kisses his mother on a cheek, and she squeals and rubs the cheek and tells him he has cold lips. He grins and assures her that he has a warm heart, though . . . and we all laugh . . . and galoshes are unbuckled . . . and Florence hugs Henry and kisses him . . . and he tells her hey, that's some snowman you and Wanda built . . . and Florence tells her brother *whoo,* it was hard work . . . and coats are removed . . . and Henry lowers his head so his mother can brush melting snow from his hair . . . and then we go trooping back to the kitchen, where Anne fixes cocoa for all of us, and Henry seats himself at the table and says to me: "I've really made up my mind about it."

"About what?" says Florence, flopping down next to him.

"Your brother is enlisting in the army," I tell her.

"Hey!" says Florence. "That's great! Down with the dirty Japanazis, right?" She punches Henry's shoulder. "Good for you! Now I can tell Wanda what she can do with her old *cousin* in the *Marines!*"

Anne turns from the stove. "It's not a *game,*" she says to Florence, "and stop behaving like such a *flibbertygibbet.*"

Florence slumps back in her chair. She studies her knuckles. "I didn't mean anything by it," she tells her mother.

"Well, it's a *war,*" says Anne. "It's not a *football game* or some sort of *party.* You ought to *think* before you speak."

"It's all right, Mama," says Henry. He smiles. "There's no sense making a big thing out of it."

Anne blinks at her son. "Hasn't it occurred to you that it *is* a big thing?"

"Please," says Henry, and he still is smiling. "I don't want to argue."

"You come in here, and you sit yourself down, and first crack you tell us you've made up your mind about it, and I'm not even supposed to argue with you, is that it?"

Henry's smile has not diminished. He rubs his hands together. He says: "I have to go. I don't really *want* to, I suppose, but I *have* to."

Anne nods. "When you got to go, you got to go, is that it?"

"Yes," says Henry.

"Mama," says Florence, "I'm real sorry if I—"

"Oh, never mind," says Anne. She turns back to the stove, and the cocoa has begun to bubble, and so she stirs it, and her shoulders are hunched.

Florence looks at me.

I place a finger to my lips, then smile at my daughter. I nod toward Anne, whose back is still turned, and my mouth carefully forms the words: Don't worry about it.

Florence's hands are folded on the table, and Henry pats them. He focuses his smile on her, and his own mouth forms the words: Let it pass.

Florence nods, and she even manages a sort of smile of her own.

Anne wheels around from the stove. Cocoa drips from the spoon onto the floor. She is breathing thickly, and she opens her mouth to say something, but then she hesitates. I glance at Henry, and his smile persists, and she has seen his smile, and here at this instant . . . right now, in this bright kitchen with its immaculate oilcloth and its thickening odor of chocolate, with The Peaceable Kingdom (and Anne has always loved The Peaceable Kingdom) staring placidly down from a cheap tinted reproduction that features the 1942 edition of the CHARLES PALMER LIGHT HOUSE OF REST calendar that is hanging on the wall next to a timidly humming electric clock, with the cocoa fatly bubbling and the spoon warmly dripping, with Florence leaning forward and Henry smiling (and his smile is like the world's last hope of beating back the night) . . . Anne abruptly decides to surrender. Her anger has been pulled away by his great undefeated smile. She was about to shout at us, but now we know she will not. Her surrender shows itself in her mouth and her eyes, and her face becomes as soft as the faces of the dear animals who populate The Peaceable Kingdom. She makes a vague flapping gesture, then shrugs, looks down at the spoon and says to Henry: "Ah, would you . . . I mean, when I'm finished with this spoon, would you, ah, care to lick it?"

"Absolutely," says Henry.

"Ah, Florence?" says Anne, blinking.

Florence looks at her mother.

"Here," says Anne to Florence, "I want you to stir this cocoa for me." She holds out the spoon.

Florence stands up and goes to Anne and takes the spoon.

"When you're done, he gets it to lick," says Anne to Florence.

"Fine," says Florence, smiling.

Anne runs to Henry and hugs him. She kisses his cheeks and his forehead. I smile, and so does Florence, who resumes the stirring.

Henry nods, pats his mother, then tells her: "Hey, this is much better. Thank you, Mama. Thank you." And Anne nods, but she cannot speak. She keeps blinking. And Henry says: "Just . . . just try to be patient with me . . ."

And so there never really is a scene between mother and son over his decision to enlist. Later, after Henry has licked the spoon and we all are sitting at the kitchen table and our current dog Jasper (a sort of beagle) has come in yipping from the snow and Henry has scratched his ears (we also have a kitten named Gus, but Gus sleeps a great deal, and he has not bothered to stir from his bed under the stove), the son and the mother touch hands, and Florence beams at them, and I arrange my face in a smile of what I hope is equal benevolence, and Henry says to his mother: "This is all separate from the war, and we know that, don't we? I don't think the sergeant will give me any spoons to lick. Ha. Not likely. And I don't think I'll like it an awful lot. But, Mama, you see, I just don't have any choice. All my life I've had to sort of *stand back,* you know? Well, this time I *won't* stand back. I'm going to take part, and I mean *really* take part. Does this make sense?"

"Yes," says Anne, nodding.

"There's this war, and it's important. The world's bleeding, Mama. We don't know about it *here,* but it's happening, and that's important. So are the snowmen and the chocolate spoons, but sometimes first things have to come first, you know?"

"Yes," says Anne.

"Mama, is it all right if I ask you something?"

"Of course it is."

"All right. Now. Tell me. Do you think I am a good person?"

"Henry, you know better than to ask me that. You know I do."

"Does that mean you have faith in my judgment?"

"Yes."

"Then you have to have faith that I am doing the right thing," says Henry. He pats Anne's hand. "If I stayed home, it would be like *hiding.* And all my life I've been hiding. Either that, or I've been standing off to one side. You've fussed over me, and most of my teachers have fussed over me, but the rest of the world has said go peddle your fish, Henry Amberson, you're a crackpot. You and your clodhopping . . ."

"You're no *crackpot,*" says Anne. "Or *clodhopper* either."

"Fine. *You* know that, and *I* know it. But I want the rest of the world to know it, too. How would *you* like it if *you* were always being held off at arm's length?"

Anne does not reply. She sucks her lower lip, but she says nothing.

"I'm not talking about *you,*" says Henry. "And I'm not talking about Papa or Florence or Lewis. I'm talking about *the world.*"

"Yes," says Anne. "I know what you're talking about." She speaks quickly, and she punctuates her words with abrupt little nods. "All right. I think I understand. I really do."

"I don't want you to be angry."

"I'm not angry."

"Honest to God?" says Henry, grinning.

"Honest to God," says Anne, crossing her heart. "Hope to die," she says.

Florence speaks up. *"I'm* not angry at *anybody,*" she says.

We all laugh. Anne tells Florence she is a scamp and a troublemaker, and we all laugh some more. For once in my life, I say very little. Any sententious lecture from me would be absurd. I pray to heaven that the President and Prime Minister Churchill know what they are doing. I have little doubt that the war will be a long one, and it already has occurred to me that Henry will be a large target. Lewis comes home for supper, and his wavy hair is neat, and he shakes Henry's hand and tells him: Yes sir, kiddo, go get those dirty rats. And then Lewis says: No kidding. And Henry says: All right, we'll give it a try. And then Lewis grins and says: My turn will be coming soon, so save some of them for your little brother. Anne glances sharply at Lewis, so I speak up, asking him whether *Belle Starr* was a good movie. He tells me yeah, and that Gene Tierney is the, ah, real merchandise, Pop, and you better believe it. I mean, she's got a mouth on her that like to made old Bill Sanderson howl like a dog. He was sitting next to me, and he got to thrashing around like a bag of termites had crawled up his you-know-what. And again we all laugh—even Anne. And Lewis allows as how for a dumb *fullback,* old Bill Sanderson got deep *feelings,* if you know what I mean. And Anne hushes Lewis, telling him that will be just enough of *that* sort of talk, young man, and Lewis bows his head in mock dejection. We have a fine supper of steak, mashed potatoes, peas and mince pie, and Lewis talks about his newest girlfriend, whose name is Henrietta Loomis and whose father is the Paradise Falls fire chief. The thing I like about her, he says, is that she's quiet and she lets *me* do all the talking. Then Lewis grins at Henry and says: You know what I mean, don't you? And Henry looks up from his food and says: Yes. Absolutely. Keep Them Quiet—that's always been *my* motto, too. And Lewis says: I bet the girls in Gambier and Mount Vernon are absolutely *falling down,* right? And Henry says: Right. And some of them even fall down in the *streets,* which creates a little bit of a traffic hazard, you know? And Lewis says: Well, what can a fellow do when he's *got* it, right? And Henry says: Right. And then I decide it is again time to change the subject, so I ask Henry whether he will be able to retain any of the sophomore credits he has so far earned, and he tells me he really does not know; when he went to the dean's office and officially resigned, he did not think to ask. He stays with us for two days, and in those two days he does not leave the house. He spends most of the time sitting with his mother, and they chat quietly, and Jasper and Gus nuzzle at his feet. He bends to stroke and scratch them, and they keep nuzzling for more, and I am reminded of my poor tormented boyhood friend, Fred Suiter, the unfortunate Papist. In the mornings, when Florence and Lewis and I go off to school, we leave Henry and his mother sitting at the kitchen table. In the afternoons, when we return, they are still sitting at the kitchen table, and for all we know they have not moved. (I never ask my wife what she and Henry have discussed at such length. And she never tells me. I suppose most of their words have had to do with the reasons he is leaving, but this is only speculation. Perhaps, for all I know, they simply have been talking over his boyhood, summoning all the sweet times and the times of pain. Or perhaps they have been discussing dead animals and an abandoned interurban line. All I do know is that Henry and his mother seem at peace with one another, and their quiet talk has obviously done them good. And I do not resent any of this. God knows, quiet talk is needed in these times, and when will there be a chance for it again? So they sit there in the kitchen, my wife and my son, and perhaps they occasionally touch each other, and The Peaceable Kingdom casts its anachronistic benevolence down on them, and the bright proclamative snow is reflected whitely against the kitchen's crisp clean walls, and there are worse things than this; there are worse ways for a son and his mother to try to come together and understand what is happening, and I suspect they are perhaps achieving a great deal, and so I do them the courtesy of neither eavesdropping nor asking them questions.) And then, on a slushy Wednesday morning, we take Henry to the C&O depot, where he catches the morning train for Columbus, and Anne does not weep—which perhaps should surprise me but does not. All the talk has prepared her, and she simply stands there and smiles, and she hugs Henry fiercely when he comes to her, but there are no tears, and I decide I am very proud of her. The depot platform is lumpy and runny with melting snow, and our feet squish as we wait for the train to arrive, and Florence is all pink and sparkling in a bright plaid coat, and Lewis jumps up and down and moves his arms like pinwheels, tightening his muscles and breathing whitely (he is always the athlete, this Lewis, and he never misses an opportunity to keep himself fit), and Henry smiles at me and thanks me for arranging to take the time off from school—*and* for arranging that Florence and Lewis be excused. He says something to the effect that I am very thoughtful . . . and then, for some abrupt reason, I want to huddle there and rub my face against my hands, but I do no such thing. If Anne can resist that sort of behavior, then so by heaven can I. I clear my throat. I look around, and I am aware of boxcars and a snuffling yardengine, and a skinny young sparrow sits puffing its feathers on a baggage cart at the end of the platform, and I again clear my throat, and the moment passes, and then the train arrives, and it is roaring, and the locomotive's boiler appears to be sweating, and the sparrow flies away, and Henry smiles at all of us, and airbrakes hiss, and hugs and kisses and handshakes are exchanged, and then he jumps aboard one of the coaches, and his grin does not diminish, and then the train pulls out of the station, and he is gone, and then I swear to you: The sparrow returns to its perch on the baggage cart, and again it puffs its feathers. And my wife says: Well. *Wellnow.* Goodness.

The next morning was cloudy and windy, and the Ambersons were up early and about their footloose business. Amberson attended with dispatch to the cat's box, and Anne told him she had had an excellent night's sleep, the best in quite awhile, which rather surprised him. They had stopped for the night at a motel on Chagrin Boulevard. They had eaten dinner in the motel restaurant—Anne had lamb chops, Amberson roast beef—but neither of them had eaten particularly well. He had cashed a Travelers' Cheque for fifty dollars and bought a Cleveland *Press* and they had retired early.

Amberson opened another can of 9-Lives Super Supper for Sinclair, who went at it with gusto and great smacking of lips. "We must remember to buy him a dish for his food and a bowl for his water," said Anne when she saw Amberson give Sinclair fresh water in an ashtray. Amberson told her they would stop at the first dimestore they saw. The Ambersons had their breakfast in the motel coffee shop; he paid the bill, and then he and Anne carried their suitcases to the car, and this time they remembered Sinclair. They decided to drive east on US 422. The clouds had done away with any morning sun glare, and besides, if they drove in any other direction, they would have to contend with the

Cleveland morning rush hour traffic, and Amberson did not care for rush hour traffic—in Cleveland or anywhere else. "If my memory serves me correctly," he told Anne, "this 422 goes to Warren and Youngstown. I don't believe there will be much traffic, and I think we'll be passing through more Amish country." And Anne said: "Fine. The less traffic, the better." And she smiled and there was color in her face, and could Dr. Groh and the surgeon in Columbus have been wrong about her? Had the operation been successful after all? No. There was no sense thinking such a thing, and Amberson silently scolded himself and told himself it was cruel to think such a thing, and he told himself only a coward would think such a thing, and he told himself: You must not flinch from it. You must not flinch from the central fact of these days. And he settled behind the wheel, and Sinclair curled up on Anne's lap, and Anne continued to smile, and Amberson adjusted his spectacles, switched on the ignition and started the car. He asked Anne whether she wanted him to turn on the heater, but she told him no, she felt fine; the cool air was very refreshing so early in the morning. So the car moved out onto US 422 and headed east. The highway dipped into a valley, then climbed a succession of hills and passed through a town called Chagrin Falls, a pretty place with a gazebo in a small triangular park at the center of its business district. Most of the houses were built of wood, and most were painted white, and Amberson told Anne he understood the residents of the town paid the highest school taxes in the state. "I understand this is quite a wealthy place," he said.

"It reminds me of New England," said Anne.

"Well, we are in the Western Reserve, and most of the original settlers came from Connecticut I believe it was."

"Doesn't 'chagrin' mean something like shame?"

"Yes. One is chagrined when one falls on one's face while attempting some great deed."

"Like what happened with Alice yesterday," she said.

"I suppose you could put it that way," he said, pleased that she was able to view the episode with Alice with some humor now, the morning after.

Last night, in the motel room, they had watched part of the ABC Movie of the Week on Channel 5. But they could not concentrate on the movie, and so Amberson switched off the set. He had tried to read the Cleveland *Press,* but could not concentrate on it either. And so then, finally, he looked at his wife and said: "Have we learned anything today?"

Anne was sitting up in bed. She was doing nothing, simply sitting there. "What?"

"Did Alice teach us anything?"

"Nothing we didn't already know. What are you doing? Giving me a little examination?"

Amberson was sitting erect in an easy chair that had cushions made of some sort of plastic. Then: "Perhaps we're not as benevolent as we've always believed ourselves to be. There's a possibility she is right."

"I don't want to talk about it," said Anne.

"We never have talked about it."

"Well, Lewis is dead and gone. Nothing can change, even if we wanted it to."

"But I think we should look into what she said. Either admit it as truth or dismiss it as a lie."

"I *told* you. I don't want to *talk* about it."

"All right," said Amberson. He picked up the newspaper, unfolded it, adjusted his spectacles and began reading an article having to do with the Administration's controls on inflation.

Anne gave a sort of moan.

Amberson put aside the newspaper and looked at his wife.

Anne's head had rolled to one side, and she was rubbing her arm.

Amberson quickly went to the bed and lay down next to his wife. He embraced her, and she allowed him to stroke her arm. She smelled papery and very old. He kissed her neck and cheek, and her skin was soft and loose. He said to her: "At least we know it was not deliberate. At least we know that."

Anne nodded. Her eyes were closed. She swallowed several times.

"If we never understood him," said Amberson, "it was because of stupidity, not malice. It wasn't that we didn't *care* for him . . ."

Again Anne nodded.

"And so in that respect she was wrong," said Amberson.

Anne opened her eyes and blinked at her husband. "We never did ask her about the tombstone . . ."

Amberson did not know whether to laugh, and so instead he said: "I love you, and I know the truth about you, and Alice is full of baloney . . ."

"Thank you," said Anne.

Amberson pressed his face tightly against her neck, and it was her turn to embrace him. Anne patted him and kissed him. Had he been all that evil? Had she? Great God, what a question, and what a time to be asking it. Was this the ultimate purpose of their footloose wanderings? Was it the ultimate resolution of all their years? Amberson shook his head, opened his eyes, covered his mouth, then cleared his throat.

"No," he said aloud. "Not on your tintype."

"What?" said Anne.

He kissed her on the mouth. "I want us to forget Alice," he said.

"All right," said Anne.

"We may be flawed, but we are not evil."

"Yes. All right. I go along with that."

"We have never claimed perfection."

"That's right."

"There are good things we can remember."

"Yes."

"I love you. You are the best thing of all."

"Thank you," said Anne. She smiled. "Now, will you read me the Kitty Heaven letter?"

Amberson nodded. Anne fetched the letter from her suitcase and with Sinclair curled up at their feet, Amberson read the letter aloud.

Now, the next morning, Anne grinned at her husband in the car. "It's going to be a nice day," she said.

"You took your medication last night, didn't you?"

"Yes. Is there anything wrong with that?"

"No. Not a thing. I'm happy you did."

"Well," said Anne, "yesterday turned out to be awful, what with Alice and all that ugliness, so last night I popped the old pills, and today I'm just as loose as a goose."

"I beg your pardon?"

"I said: *Loose* as a *goose.*"

"That's what I thought you said."

Anne laughed. She patted Amberson's knee. "Today nothing matters," she said. "Today all that matters is that we enjoy ourselves."

Amberson glanced at his wife. Her tongue was rubbing her dentures. He said to her: "If you enjoy yourself, I enjoy myself. If you don't, I don't. That may sound fatuous, but it's true."

"It does not sound fatuous. I appreciate it very much. Isn't 'fatuous' a funny word? It sounds like maybe it should be used to describe Jackie Gleason, or President Taft."

"Do you remember President Taft?"

"Very well. He gave a speech once in Columbus, and my parents took me to hear him. I was about nine or ten at the time, and he made me think of St. Nicholas. He may not have been fatuous, but he certainly was fat."

"He was our fattest president. And I believe James Madison was the skinniest. Either Madison or Monroe, but I believe it was Madison."

"Can you name them in order? I believe Henry could."

"Yes," said Amberson. "He could. But I can't. I can name them from the Civil War on, but all those antebellum people—Tyler, Polk, Fillmore and the rest of them—have never arranged themselves properly in my mind."

"All right. Forget Tyler and Polk and Fillmore. Name the ones from the Civil War on."

"Lincoln," said Amberson. "Then Andrew Johnson. Then, ah, Grant. Then Hayes. Then Garfield. Then Arthur. Then Grover Cleveland. Then Benjamin Harrison. Then Grover Cleveland again. Then McKinley. Then Teddy Roosevelt. Then your friend Taft. Then Wilson. Then Warren G. Harding. Then Coolidge. Then Hoover. Then FDR. Then Truman. Then Eisenhower. Then Kennedy. Then Lyndon Johnson. Then Nixon."

"That's very good. Congratulations."

"Thank you," said Amberson. "I only wish Henry had been here to help me with Polk and Tyler and Fillmore and the rest of—"

"Howard, I'm sorry. I shouldn't have brought him into it."

"It doesn't matter," said Amberson. The car bounced across railroad tracks and began ascending another long hill, and then Chagrin Falls was behind them, and Amberson said: "Really. I'm not angry a bit. Why should I be angry? Because he was remarkable? That would mean I envied him, and I did not. I only loved him, and any time you want to talk about him, that's perfectly all right with me."

"Thank you for reading the letter to me last night."

"I enjoyed it."

"The medication was working, and the Alice thing was drifting away, you know? And the words were so lovely, and Sinclair was so warm down there at my feet, and I don't care if I *am* sentimental. At my age, I have a right to be whatever I want to be."

"Yes," said Amberson.

"I still remember the day he was born."

"So do I."

"You do?"

"Yes. Alvin Junior and Ernest and Mary Frances and Bernadette sat with me in the kitchen. You know all that. They sat with me all day long, and Emerald White kept giving me reassurances. And I had a silly argument with Ernest."

"Poor Ernest," said Anne.

"Well, poor *all* of them. They're all gone now."

"And we just keep on chugging or whatever."

"These days," said Amberson, "it's mostly the whatever."

Anne nodded, and then she was silent, and the countryside opened up in a sequence of low golden hills, and perhaps she was thinking of all the dead ones, or perhaps she was ordering her mind in such a way that Alice's words would not matter. Or perhaps she simply was looking at the scenery. Amberson sensed that a resolution would not be long in coming. Which meant that he did not have much time remaining for his journal. Which meant that he would have to understand the apparatus as soon as possible, or sooner than possible, or clearly not at all. He kept the Pontiac at 40, and other cars whipped around them, and this was their third day on the road, and what had they discovered? Was there anything *to* discover that they had not discovered in all the years they had lived? Why this compulsion to round off all the edges? Why this mad craving for a logical conclusion? Wasn't it enough simply to have lived and endured? Who but a fool would try to make sense from all of it? Who but a sentimental smalltown schoolteacher whose heart was failing and whose wife was being devoured by pain? And just precisely what had happened during the first two days of this absurd footless meander? What did strip mines have to do with Alice's contempt? How was Doris Lundgren connected to the Lee Road House of Ribs? All right, so the apparatus apparently still had room for diversity. What an exciting bit of information. Here the Ambersons were, traipsing all over Creation, learning something they already had known from reading *Time* magazine. Or from watching television. Or from simply sitting on their front porch and observing their own small world. And now Amberson was glaring, but he did not realize he was glaring, not until Anne said to him: "Stop frowning like that. Don't go acting like Alice on me. You look as though you hate the world, and I know that's not so." And then, chuckling a little, Amberson relaxed. His hands had been too tight on the wheel, and so he let the tension drain from his fingers, and then he said: "I'm sorry. You know how the old saying goes —the more one lives, the less one understands. And I'm at the point where I understand so little it almost makes me want to blush." And Anne nudged him and said: "Now, let's not talk about all *that*. Next thing you know, we'll be talking about your precious *apparatus,* and it's too early in the day for that. Let's just enjoy the things we see, all right? Maybe we can figure out a game to play." And Amberson said: "Yes. Of course. Excuse me for being so sour." And Anne said: "Come on now. The world hates a grouch. I mean, as an old established grouch, I know whereof I speak." And Amberson said: "The day you are a grouch will be the day the sky rains frogs." And Anne said: "Ah, such a smooth one with a compliment you are." And then the Ambersons laughed, and it was somewhere east of a place called Auburn Corners that the right front tire went flat. Amberson's heart was too treacherous to permit him to change it, and so he tied a white handkerchief to the radio aerial, and he and Anne and Sinclair sat in the car at the side of the road and waited for help. Anne smiled and said: "I feel as though we have surrendered."

See now 1967, and Anne and Alice and I are sitting on a sofa in the reception area at the brandnew Paradise Valley Memorial Hospital. The carpet is a dark green, and the walls have been painted a lighter green, and copies of *Fortune* and *Time* and *Newsweek* litter the coffee table in front of us. It is a boiling hot August afternoon, and Alice says: "This weather certainly didn't help."

"No, I'm sure it didn't," says Anne.

"If it hadn't been this hot," says Alice, "probably nothing would have happened." She is still wearing her golfing outfit. It consists of a yellow kerchief, yellow blouse and yellow shorts, and it hugs her body exquisitely. Her hair is pinned up in a bun, and her summer tan is deep and smooth. She reaches up and pats her hair, and then she says: "But it was a *challenge,* you know?"

Anne and I nod.

"All his life he never has been able to resist them," says Alice.

"Yes," says Anne. "We know that." She is hatless and coatless, and she is wearing a blue print dress. Alice's telephone call came an hour ago, and Anne and I simply picked up and hurried to this hospital without bothering to change. In an emergency, one did not change one's clothes.

Myself, I am wearing a plaid shirt and a frayed pair of wash pants. I was clearing junk from the attic when the call came. I am quite sweaty. The attic was very close, and I really do not know why I chose such a dreadfully hot day to go up there. I should have more sense, especially when one takes into account the heart attack I suffered two years ago.

A large bony nurse is sitting behind the reception desk. Dr. Groh has promised to telephone down as soon as he knows something definite. The nurse is aware of all this, and so from time to time she smiles at us from the reception desk. The airconditioning hums, and my legs and arms are clammy.

"I warned him," says Alice.

"Yes," says Anne.

"I *told* him: 'Lewis,' I said, 'you're no longer in the first flush of youth, and you're just going to have to ease up.' But you know Lewis.

He doesn't know what it means to ease up, and he never has."

"I hope they'll let us see him," says Anne.

"The Hoover boy telephoned the hospital. *He* wants to see him too."

I lean forward and glance down the sofa at Alice. Anne is between us. "Oh? How did you find out about that?"

"Frank Groh told me," says Alice. "The call came before you and Mother Amberson arrived here."

"We cannot blame the Hoover boy," says Anne. "That would not be fair."

"I have no intention of blaming him for anything," says Alice.

"That's fine," says Anne.

I lean back. I think of Lewis, and I mean I *really* think of him, and I do not permit my mind to dismiss him the way it usually does. It has been more than two decades since Henry the Always Boy was killed in Germany, but the Hoover lad was his proxy, and there can be little doubt of that. Some day Anne and I will have to do a great deal of answering, and there can be little doubt of *that* either. And now Lewis probably will die, and nothing ever had been resolved between us. The cheerleaders are as loud today as they ever were. They have never stopped leaping and yipping and imploring. And not a single wave has gone out of his hair. And I say to myself: All right, this wait may be a long one, so try to place it all in a logical sequence, try to make some sense out of it.

And so my thoughts again turn to the chronology, sliding back to 1942 and Henry's departure for the war. He received his basic training at Ft. Benning, Georgia, then served for six months on the post cadre before entering Officers Candidate School. (The army may have been stupid, but it was not so stupid that it did not understand his value.) Naturally, he was graduated at the head of his class, and in 1943, shortly before his twentieth birthday, the brandnew 2nd Lt. Henry S. Amberson was shipped overseas to Sicily, where he became a platoon leader in an infantry company. (His last visit home was in the spring of that year, but for some reason I do not remember too terribly much about it. As I recall, he and Anne had several more of their lengthy private conversations, the nature of which she never revealed to me. But that is just about all I do remember. I have often wondered about this, and I have decided that I have blotted from my memory most of his last visit home because that way I do not feel as much pain. My earlier memories of Henry are much clearer, and obviously this is because *then* he still had a *future,* with options and possibilities. But this last visit home was just that. It was the last, and therefore it marked an end, and I still cannot bear to bring it back.) He turned out to be a good soldier and officer. He earned a Bronze Star in Sicily and a Silver Star in France, where he was promoted to first lieutenant. He died while leading an attack against a roadblock defended by a company of young German troops newly recruited from the Hitler Jugend. He died instantly, we were told, and was the only casualty.

And somehow, perhaps paradoxically, I think I understand Henry. But what of my other son? What of the relentless Lewis and his wavy hair and his tireless cheerleaders? Is there more to him than competition born out of envy? Are there subtleties and complexities that I shall never know? All I can do is list the external evidence. All I can do is report that he was an outstanding football player at Paradise Falls High School, that he enlisted in the army just after his graduation in June of 1943, that within less than two years he had attained the rank of captain, that he never lost an election (first for senior class president, then for councilman, then for mayor), that Paradise Plymouth has thrived beyond the imaginings of the most fervent optimist, that he is the only resident of Paradise Falls who truly can be called a Television Personality (his commercials abound on the three Columbus stations like rabbits in a field of gentle clover), and that—ultimately—I never really have been able to penetrate him. All I understand is the obvious drive and energy, but surely there must be more to him than *that*. Surely his personality is not all that orderly and obvious. But how am I to discover the rest of him? When have any doors ever been opened? Oh, I *see* him often enough, and he is forever grinning at me from the TV as he tells the world to COME TO PARADISE PLYMOUTH FOR A HEAVENLY DEAL, and Anne and I exchange dinner visits with Lewis and Alice twice a month or so, and Lewis obviously enjoys being mayor and making speeches and signing documents and all that sort of thing—but what do I really *know* of him? When was the last time anything *real* emerged from all the dinner visits and the cheerful chitchat we are forever exchanging? Alice always flutters and smiles, and Lewis is obsessed with the notion that Nixon is the only Republican on the horizon who can dislodge LBJ from the White House next year, and he insists that the peace demonstrations are actually a help to the President. When the average American sees those longhaired creeps on the tube, and he watches them burning the flag and shouting all their treason, says Lewis, it's enough to make his blood boil, and so he winds up on Johnson's side. I don't give doodly squat *what* the polls say, says Lewis. If these demonstrations keep up, we'll have a hard time beating him next year—even with Nixon. And then Lewis says: It'll be a tough one, make no mistake of *that*. And from time to time I try to argue with my son. I try to indicate to him that I do not believe the war is moral, that it is a waste, that the government has lied to us, that citizens in a democracy have a perfect right to demonstrate against government policies they find obnoxious. And Lewis always tells me: Sure, I'll go along with that. This is a free country. But since when do those punks and creeps have a right to destroy property and disrupt the lives of other people? Is *that* democracy? You say *you* are against the war, but would *you* do that? Aw come on now, not old Pop, right? And then, shaking my head, I say to my son: I am seventy years of age. *Of course* I would not destroy property. But if I were nineteen, perhaps I would feel differently. And then, grinning, Lewis gives a kind of snort and tells me I am beyond hope, that I ought to grow long hair and a beard and go kiss the foot of that goddamned Wayne Morse and the rest of those lousy peaceniks. And I blink at my son and tell him: Peace is the dirtiest word in your vocabulary, isn't it? And a redness floods into my son's face, and at this point either Anne or Alice breaks in to try to call a truce, and they remind us that we are not about to change the course of history, no matter how much we argue. And Lewis shrugs and says well, it'll all come out in the wash anyway, once the American people make up their minds. And Alice goes to him and hugs him and tells him *hush* now, we don't see Mother and Father Amberson enough as it *is*, and we don't want to spoil the occasion with a lot of silly talk that won't solve a thing—am I right or am I right? (And she flattens her splendid breasts against his chest. And she kisses him. And she is thirtynine years old, but she appears to be about thirty, and sometimes I almost wonder whether there is more to her than I ever have suspected. Something indomitable perhaps. Something hugely loyal.) And so gradually the cheerful chitchat returns, and Alice shows off a new dress she has bought in Columbus, and Lewis speaks of taxes and paving contracts and bonded indebtedness, and I try to ignore the color that still sits ominously behind the taut skin that is stretched across his cheeks. And I ask myself: Why do I keep wanting to make him a villain? Why can't I allow him to be himself? Is it so terrible? Has he ever ordered human beings boiled down into soap? Was he responsible for the Rape of Nanking? Great God, try to place him in perspective. And so I smile at my son, and I listen very carefully to his talk (and it is knowing talk; I'll give him that) of the taxes and the paving contracts and the bonded indebtedness, and I know he has been a good mayor (I'll give him *that*, too), and so all right, perhaps he *did* hate Henry. But then perhaps he had reason—not because of anything Henry did but simply because of circumstance, because of the accident of Henry's intelligence and enormous size and overpowering love. (Does he suspect what Henry did for him that day at Paradise Lake?) As the vaudevillians might say, Henry was no doubt a tough act to follow. And I must keep this in mind. And I must look at Lewis on *his* terms. And what do I see beyond the ambition and the relentlessness? Well, for one thing, he truly has been a good mayor. He was easily reelected in '63 and '65, and he probably will not even have an opponent this year. (His '65 challenger, a man named Porter, did not even attract 25 percent of the vote—a statistic that is probably most discouraging to anyone who might be considering running against my son.) But, beyond his political popularity, it is a demonstrable fact that Lewis has been the most energetic and efficient mayor Paradise Falls has had in decades. Yet, at the same time, he has leavened the efficiency with what I believe is a genuine concern for the town. He has made numerous trips . . . at his own expense, I might add . . . to Chicago and Detroit and New York City, where he has gone to corporations with proposals that they move some facility or other to Paradise Falls. As a result, the past five years have seen one major electrical parts supplier open a warehouse in Paradise Falls, a hubcap and chrome plating concern build one of its major factories in Paradise Falls, and three trucking companies establish large terminal facilities in Paradise Falls. As a result of all this industrious proselytizing, hundreds of jobs have been created—and the tax base has been raised at no cost to the individual homeowner. Oh, all right, yes, politics enters into all this (after all, economic progress is an excellent tool for a mayor who seeks to perpetuate himself in office), but I think my son's motives are a bit deeper than that. I think he honestly loves the town —after his fashion. His love probably is the love of the big frog for the little pond, but it is better than no love at all, and whom really does it harm? He *enjoys* what he is, and he *enjoys* what he does, and he *enjoys* being called Mister Mayor, and he *enjoys* delivering speeches and presiding at ribboncuttings and grappling with the council over the annual budget, and his enjoyment is obvious and sincere, and surely it has to be preferred over the bored cynicism that characterizes so many politicians these days. And here perhaps the cheerleaders are not all that harmful. Or at least I like to think so. And I like to think that my son Lewis, the Honorable Mayor of our honorable city, is genuinely concerned with its welfare and its future. He once said to me: Pop, I rush around a lot like a chicken with its head cut off, and if it isn't a Rotary meeting it's a Legion meeting or a council meeting or a gettogether with my old buddies in the good old Paradise County Republican Executive Committee, or it's a trip up to Columbus to make another commercial tape, or it's selling old Elmer Carmichael another car he doesn't need, or it's getting on the telephone and talking to my sharp broker in New York, or it's taking on old Alice for a game of tennis at the club, or it's answering my mail or telling our boozer of a police chief to keep his drunken hands off the county auditor's wife, or it's patting some rotten little kid on the head and telling his mother *my, my, my,* what a *handsome* little guy he is, and sure, I get tired, but it's a *good* kind of tired, you know? It's the kind of tired that tells me: Lew old boy, you are *participating;* you are *alive.* And that doesn't make me much different from the rest of the human race, does it? I mean, I am no weirdo contemplating my navel and pulling out fuzz, no indeed. I hang in there, Pop, and I try to do the best I can. Honest to God. (I remember that there was a look of almost desperate intensity on his face when he told me all this, and I remember that I very much wanted to believe him. And perhaps I did. And perhaps I do.) But I still am not comfortable with Lewis. He is still handsome, and he has kept his flesh firm, and at fortytwo he still moves boyishly, lurching along with a sort of spraddled grace that is somehow almost endearing, and yet there is something within him—something beyond the cliché Babbittry—that causes me to ache if I am with him too long, that causes me to rub my joints and jiggle a foot and become curiously impatient. But *why?* All right, so I have known now for a long time that he resented Henry far more than Anne and I ever suspected back in the days when he was a boy and he referred to Henry as Old Goofy. All right, we *know* that. And we have lived with the knowledge for many years. But why then, after all those many years, do I have to keep *worrying* it? And why do I have this dreadful feeling that Lewis is parading his accomplishments before me as though they were precious burnished offerings? It is as though he seeks to overwhelm me, to make me stand up and say, clearly and for once and for all: Yes, Lewis. Yes. Yes. Yes. You have worth. Your accomplishments are enough to stagger the heavens. I love you, Lewis. I really do. So help me.

And now, as I sit with my wife and the luminous Alice in this biliously greenish reception area at the Paradise County Memorial Hospital, as I rub my clammy arms and stare through my spectacles at the bony nurse as she fusses with some papers at the reception desk, I begin to feel an enormous anguish, and I say to myself: We could have done more. *I* could have done more. And why have I judged him? What *right* do I have? *Judge not, lest ye be judged.* Ah, my God, the terrible truth of obvious thoughts. No wonder we forever seek subtleties. We do not want to be hammered to death by the clear and the simple.

Lewis was brought to the hospital from the Valley Country Club early this afternoon. It is a Wednesday, and he and Alice almost always spend their Wednesday afternoons at the Valley Country Club. They are both excellent golfers and tennis players, and Lewis is one of the club's founding members. The country club was a success from the start. It is the only legitimate country club between Columbus and Marietta, and there are those who say it gives our area some sort of special panache. Well, perhaps so. I would not know. All I do know is that Lewis and Alice have just about adopted the place as a second home, and they both are members of its board, and Lewis has twice served as the board's president. He and Alice had lunch there today, and then Alice and a woman named June Heinz went out to shoot nine holes. Lewis, in the meantime, had a light scotch and water, changed into his tennis clothes and began a game with a young man named Kevin Hoover, who was either Number 3 or 4 on the Ohio University team this spring. (I get all this from Alice, who gave us the details when we arrived at the hospital.) It is generally acknowledged that Kevin Hoover is the best tennis player at the Valley Country Club. He has won the club championship three years running, and in each of those three years Lewis has been the runnerup. This has vexed Lewis no end, especially since Kevin Hoover's father, Ralph P., is a member of the council and takes great delight in standing up at council meetings and delivering himself of remarks concerning the Honorable Mayor's, ah, penchant for being a perennial runnerup. Ralph P. Hoover is a large and hearty man, and I am sure he means no offense by his remarks, but they have annoyed Lewis for quite some time now, and so Lewis has been working on his game all summer long, and today was the day he chose to have his first match of the year with young Kevin—and, as I understand it, it was quite a match. It went, Alice tells us, to 6–5 Kevin, then 6–6, then 7–6 Lewis, then 7–7, then 8–7 Lewis, then 8–8, then 9–8 Lewis, then 9–9, then 10–9 Kevin, then 10–10, then 11–10 Kevin, then 11–11, then 12–11 Lewis, then 12–12, then 13–12 Kevin before Kevin finally won, 14–12. A goodsized crowd had gathered to watch, according to Alice, and Kevin's winning shot was a towering lob that eluded Lewis when he apparently stumbled and fell on his back. But he stood up quickly enough, and I understand the spectators applauded, and it was then that something went wrong. Or at least so we have been told by Alice. After getting to his feet, Lewis grinned and began moving toward the net to congratulate the Hoover boy. He was of course dripping sweat, and his face was crimson. And we are told that the Hoover boy was applauding him right along with the spectators. But then Lewis began to stagger, and it is our understanding that he flopped and stumbled like a drunkard on his last legs, and then—just as he made it to the net—he collapsed, falling forward into the net and swaying there like a harpooned fish. Someone summoned Alice from the golf course, and an ambulance was called, and Lewis was rushed here to the Paradise Valley Memorial Hospital, and Dr. Groh has so far only told us that it was a severe heart attack (and I remember my own heart attack, and my belly contracts, and I am very aware of my breathing), and that is where the matter stands at this moment, and I rub my arms and legs, and Alice is saying something to Anne, and perhaps I should try to listen. I lean forward and look at Alice, and she is saying (her voice forever a croak): ". . . no, not at all. I had *no idea*. When I left him, he only told me he was going to work a little on his baseline game and maybe have a few volleys with the Hoover boy. If I'd known he was going to have a regular match, I certainly wouldn't have gone off and played *golf*. And I certainly would have stopped that match when it got out of hand. I mean, for a man of his age to be involved in a match like *that*, why, it's *criminal*. The Hoover boy should have had more *sense*."

"Well," says Anne, "he's only a boy—and besides, I'm sure Lewis wouldn't have allowed him to stop. Lewis is not the sort to ask an opponent to ease up."

"He's over the worst part of it," I tell Alice.

She looks at me. "What?"

"When I had mine, Frank Groh told me that those who survived the first minute or so usually came through it—damaged of course, but still alive."

"Well," says Alice, "he *is* in good physical condition for a man his age."

Anne pats one of Alice's hands. "I bet he'll make it."

"I don't like the word 'damaged,' " says Alice.

"I'm afraid he'll have to adjust his style of living," I tell her.

"I don't know whether he'll be *able* to," she says.

"We'll have to help him," says Anne.

"How?" says Alice.

Anne shrugs. "I expect it'll be a day to day proposition. I expect we'll just have to find out what he *can* do and what he *can not* do and then sort of play it off the top of our heads." She looks at me. *"You've* made the adjustment, haven't you?"

"Yes," I say.

"But Father Amberson is *seventy,* " says Alice to Anne. "There's a *difference.* I don't mean any offense, but he's not exactly in the prime of life, is he? He's not *fortytwo,* and he's not *the mayor,* and he's not *running around* all the time and *playing tennis* and *making TV commercials* and all the rest of it. He can *afford* to sit back and relax. He doesn't have *the world* to contend with."

Anne nods. "That's all true," she says, "but we're just going to have to make Lewis understand. If necessary, we'll have to tie him to a chair, won't we?"

"That's easier said than done," says Alice. She inspects her fingernails. "You don't have to live with him. You don't know how he is. Every day it's some *plan* or other, some *idea* or *challenge* or whatever. When he gets up in the morning, he's like a boy, and he can't *wait* for the day to get rolling, as he puts it. To tie him to a chair would be like breaking the wings of a bird."

"If it has to be done," says Anne, "it has to be done."

"It seems to me that broken wings are preferable to death," I tell Alice.

She glares at me. "You want him to surrender, don't you?"

"How's that?"

"It's what you've always wanted, isn't it? You want him to give up and admit that nothing he can ever do will satisfy you. You've been grading him, haven't you? How is he doing? Has he made it up to a C-plus yet?"

"Now, Alice, that's ridiculous. I haven't been—"

Frank Groh comes hurrying into the reception area, and my words are cut off, and we all stand in unison. He comes directly to us. He is all in white, and his bald head is glistening, and he says: "I'm glad you're all here . . ." He hesitates, rubs the side of his jaw with a thumb.

"Yes?" says Alice. She is breathing thickly, and now she leans forward a bit, and I am able to see the outlines of her nipples through her yellow blouse. Her chest appears to be damp.

Frank Groh's thumb comes away from his jaw. He locks his fingers at his waist, lacing them over his belt buckle. "He . . . well, I think you should all go see him. He is conscious, and he says he wants to see you . . ."

"Is he *dying?*" Alice asks Frank Groh.

"Well, that's hard to say . . ."

"Say it anyway," says Alice.

"All right then," says Frank Groh, "yes, I think he is."

Anne seizes my arm and squeezes it, and I feel as though I have been electrocuted.

"Oh, my God," says Alice. She straightens. She clears her rusty throat. "Oh, dear sweet heaven . . ."

Frank Groh ushers us out of the reception area and down a hall. My legs feel numb, and it is all I can do to keep from stumbling. Frank has hold of Alice's arm, and she is almost shambling, which is not typical of her at all. "The damage was considerable," says Frank Groh to Alice. "We've given him external heart massage and oxygen, and you can rest assured we're doing everything we can."

"Oh, I'm resting assured just fine," says Alice. She is still wearing her golfing shoes, and their cleats make uneven sounds as she stumbles along. The sounds are loud in this tiled hall, and they bring pain to the top of my skull. And I say to myself: *Surrender?* Who ever said anything about any sort of *surrender?*

Frank Groh shows us into a room at the end of the hall, and Lewis is lying in a large white bed, and a skinny little nurse is standing over him. The shades are up, and the bed is splattered with sunlight, and the nurse turns to Frank Groh and says: "Mr. Amberson wanted the shades raised."

"Right you are, my dear . . ." says Lewis from the bed. His voice is papery, and we barely are able to hear it.

We hurry to the bed, and Alice bends over her husband and kisses him on the mouth, and he smiles at her.

Alice sits down next to the bed and holds one of Lewis's hands. Anne and I stand at the foot of the bed, and Anne leans forward, seizes the railing and rests her weight against it. The nurse retreats to the doorway and stands there with Frank Groh. "It was all right, wasn't it?" she says. "Raising the shades I mean."

"Yes," says Frank Groh, "of course it was."

"Sunshine is a *forward* thing . . ." says Lewis.

"What?" says Alice.

"It's an *optimistic* thing . . ." says Lewis.

"Oh," says Alice, "yes it is."

"How you doing there, Sexy?"

"Just fine," says Alice. "I had a fortyone on the front nine."

"Excellent . . ."

"It was my best score this year."

"Fortyone . . . it'd be a hell of a bra size, right?"

"Now you *stop* that," says Alice to her husband. "You're supposed to be *sick.*"

Next to me, Anne is weeping, but as yet she is making no sounds. Tears are squirting from the corners of her eyes, though, and her mouth has begun to give way.

"We need forward things . . ." says Lewis to his wife.

"Yes," says Alice, patting his hand.

"It was a real pisscutter . . ."

"Shhh . . ."

"I played the best tennis I've ever played in my life . . ."

"Yes," says Alice. "So I understand."

"Did Kevin tell you?"

"No. I haven't spoken with him yet. But George Hoaglin was there, and he told me you were something else."

"A regular dynamo . . ."

"Well," says Alice, "you've always been a dynamic man."

"I'm going to beat this . . ."

"Of course you are."

"Jesus, I never knew what pain *was* . . ."

"Shhh . . . you be quiet now."

"A pisscutter . . ."

"Yes."

"Frank Groh will get me out of this . . ."

"You bet," says Frank Groh from the doorway.

"I'd bet my life on it . . ." says Lewis, smiling.

"That's very funny," says Frank Groh.

"To know me is to laugh a lot . . ." says Lewis. His eyes are white, and he blinks at me, and then he says: "Right, Pop?"

"Absolutely," I tell him.

"When you had yours, it hurt, didn't it?"

"Yes."

"It's all over, isn't it?"

"No."

"Don't lie to me . . ."

"I am not lying," I tell my son. At the same time, I am telling myself: Liar. I rub my palms across my shirtfront, and the roof of my mouth is dusty.

"You . . . you will be all right," says Anne, coughing a little.

"Yes," says Alice, "everything will be just fine . . ."

Lewis smiles at his wife. "You think old Lew Amberson is a goner, but he's going to show you different . . ."

Alice can say nothing. She looks away from Lewis for a moment, and then a sort of smile pulls itself across her face, and she looks back at him and says: "You are a real fighter, and I am very proud of you . . ."

Again Lewis blinks at me. "I don't give up, Pop . . ."

I nod. "I know that," I tell him.

"Henry knew that. He used to say to me: 'You don't give up, do you?' And he grinned that grin of his, you know what I mean?"

"Yes. I remember it."

"There's always been two sides to it . . ."

"Yes."

"If you don't come to me, I don't come to you, and vice versa, you understand what I'm trying to say?"

I nod. I clear my throat. I nod again.

"It takes two to tango . . ."

I move around the bed until I am standing next to the place where Alice is sitting and holding my son's hand. Down at the foot of the bed, Anne is coughing. I place a hand against my son's cheek, and then I say to him: "We must, ah, learn to talk . . ."

He nods.

I stroke his face. I bend over him and kiss him on the forehead.

"We have to . . . get . . . together . . ." says Lewis.

I straighten. "Yes," I say. "That's just what we have to do."

"I'm not done. You may think I am, but I'm not. It's not over. I'm not giving up . . ."

Frank Groh comes to the bed. "I think now you should get some rest," he says.

"Just a second . . ." says Lewis. He slowly raises an arm and motions to Anne. "Mama?"

Anne comes to him. She pushes me aside. Alice frowns at her as she bends over Lewis and kisses him on the nose and then on the eyes.

"We really got to get together and thrash it all out . . ." says Lewis to his mother.

"Yes," says Anne. She seats herself on the edge of the bed and smoothes back Lewis's hair, restoring it to its usual neatly waved condition.

"All right now," says Frank Groh to Anne. "*Please.*"

Anne strokes her son's forehead, and Alice still is clinging to his hand.

"I believe Frank wants us to leave," I say to Anne.

She says nothing. She smiles at Lewis. She strokes his forehead, and the great ravishing sunlight is golden against the back of her neck. She says to him: "The first order of business is to get you better. Then we'll just sit down and talk and talk and talk."

"The way you used to talk and talk and talk with Henry?"

"Yes," says Anne, stroking. She has forced back her tears, but her voice is tight, and she is hiding nothing—at least from me.

"I remember Henry like it was yesterday I talked with him . . ." says Lewis.

"I know you do," says Anne. "We all do."

"I never hated him. Honest to God, I never did . . ."

Anne places a hand over her son's mouth. She looks up at me, and her eyes are glistening.

"I . . . well, we have to go now," I say to Lewis.

"That's a fact," says Frank Groh.

"I want to stay," says Alice. She makes a fist with her free hand.

Frank Groh looks at her. He shrugs. "All right," he says. "It'll be all right if one of you stays. But just *one.*"

"And I'm that one," says Alice, glancing at Anne and me.

"Yes, Alice," says Anne. "Of course you are." Again she kisses Lewis on the nose and the eyes, and then she stands up. "We know you're not done," she says to Lewis. "We know you're a fighter."

"That's the . . . God's truth . . ." says Lewis. "I got too much to *do* yet, and no goddamned pain in my chest is going to—"

"Shhh," says Alice to her husband.

"Yeah . . ." says Lewis. "All right . . ."

I take my wife by an arm and walk her out of the room and back down the hall to the reception area with its green carpeting and its green walls. We seat ourselves on that same sofa, and she says: "It, it was like he was a little boy again."

Anne's neck is so fat that some of her flesh spills over the collar of her dress. She reaches up, rubs away a drop of sweat, then says: "He'll die without ever believing it can happen."

"That's his nature," I say.

"I suppose we're all that way."

"I suppose so."

"Sometimes I feel that a girl of twenty is living inside me."

"I know what you mean."

"You always know what I mean."

"Well, I've lived with you for a long time."

"Women are supposed to be mysterious, but every time I say something, you tell me you know what I mean."

"You never worked at being mysterious. You never had the time for it."

"Regina Ingersoll was mysterious, wasn't she?"

"Very."

"And she sits in your memory to this day, doesn't she?"

I shrug. "Sometimes. Not always, but sometimes."

"We shouldn't be talking about *her*. We should be talking about *Lewis*."

"Yes."

"We'll have to have a long talk with him. It's not right that I should bring up Regina Ingersoll at a time like this. He wants the talk. He wants some sort of understanding. And don't *we* want an understanding, too?"

"Yes."

Anne nods. "Lord knows, it's long overdue."

"I only hope there is time for it."

"What did you say?" Anne asks me.

"You heard what Frank Groh said."

"I don't believe it."

"But if what he says is true, it will be left this way, and we'll have to face up to it."

"I don't believe what Frank Groh said. He's wrong."

"I hope so."

"Frank Groh is a human being, and he can make a mistake," says Anne. "All human beings make mistakes."

"Yes."

Anne begins to weep. I fold my hands in my lap. She bends forward, makes fists, then presses the fists against her eyes. I suppose I should pat Anne's head and tell her there, there, but how would it help to intrude on her grief? I cover my mouth. I cough. My eyes sting. I turn to my wife, and my hands unlock, and I tell myself ah, the devil with it, and I embrace my wife, and I pat her head, and I say to her: "There, there . . ." And now I also am weeping, and Anne presses her face against my shoulder. Lewis dies within the hour. His heart simply gives out. Frank Groh rips open his chest and massages his heart, but the damage has been too great, and it is Alice who comes into the reception area and tells us. Frank Groh is with her, and her damp nipples are dark, and she moves in a sort of crouch, and she lurches up to us and says: "Well, you won't have to worry about Lewis any more." Her voice is steady and dry.

Anne and I have stood up. We look at one another.

"He's gone," says Alice.

Anne coughs, rubs her throat.

"Did you *hear* me?" says Alice.

I nod. My belly feels as though it is full of gas. I am afraid to speak, lest I belch.

Alice straightens. She places her hands on her hips. She sucks mucous out of her nose, swallows, then says: "He never stopped. He just kept *at* it and *at* it. Do you understand?"

Anne embraces me.

"*Listen* to me," says Alice.

"All right, Alice," says Frank Groh, "you don't have to—"

"Stay out of this," says Alice to Frank Groh. "This is family business."

Frank Groh shrugs. He rubs his hands together. He tries to smile at me, but he cannot manage it.

Alice comes forward until she is quite close to us. I am able to smell her body. Anne's eyes are shut, and her face is averted from Alice, and she is trembling. "Oh yes," says Alice, "oh yes, that's it. Make sure your grief is appropriate for the occasion."

I blink at Alice. I pat Anne's shoulders.

"Very *touching*," says Alice. "You never understood him, and now you weep for him. That's just terrific."

Anne says something, but the words are indistinct.

"You know what I think of you two?" says Alice. "I think you never cared a damn about him. You created him, and then you made him what he was, and then you disapproved of what he was, but you never disapproved of *yourselves* for *making* him what he was. Now *that's* what I call *hypocrisy*."

Anne abruptly pulls away from me. She coughs. She clears her throat. "How *dare* you talk to us that way? How do *you* know what we feel? What *are* you anyway?"

"I am a *human being*," says Alice, and now her voice is crumbling. "Does that surprise you? I *loved* him, and I only wanted whatever it was *he* wanted . . . and I, I suppose that just surprises you beyond *words,* doesn't it? I know what you think of me. I know what—"

"You played off the worst in him . . ." says Anne.

"How would *you* know?" says Alice. "When did you ever take the time to find out anything about him?"

"You . . . you *phony,*" says Anne.

"Look who's talking . . ." says Alice, weeping.

Anne glares at me, and her face is wet, and she says: "Are you going to let her talk to us this way?"

"Come on, Alice," says Frank Groh, taking her by an arm.

She spins away from him. She folds her arms over her chest. "Stop looking at my breasts . . ." she says to me.

"I'm not looking at your damned breasts," I tell her. "And I want you to stop making these stupid accusations."

"About my breasts?" says Alice, grinning a lopsided grin that comes through clenched teeth.

"About *Lewis,*" I tell her. "We loved our son, and it is . . . *indecent* of you to say those things. Don't you have any sense of values?"

"Sense of *values?* What are you *talking* about?" Then, wailing, Alice turns to Frank Groh and hugs him. Shrugging, he leads her away. The nurse is leaning on the reception desk, and I glance at her, and she steps back and begins straightening some papers. Anne and I stand there weeping, and we listen to Alice's wailings, and I say to myself: I was not looking at her breasts. I was *not.*

Lewis's funeral is as grand and ornate as Alice can make it, and I never saw so many flowers in my life. Hundreds of persons attend, including Kevin Hoover, and Lewis glows pinkly in his coffin. We do not speak to Alice, nor she to us. We nod, yes, but we do not speak. She is spectacular in a tight black dress. A week or so later, we are adopted by a stray tomcat, and we name him Sinclair, after Lewis. Perhaps the propriety of this is questionable, but somehow to us it seems apt. Perhaps we are demented. Perhaps we are ridiculing our late son. But we do not *believe* we are demented. We see Alice from time to time, and we manage to speak to her, and she to us. We tell her about the cat, and the name we have chosen, but she apparently does not make the connection. Are we desecrating our son's memory? No! We simply are keeping it alive. We are not cruel. We never have been cruel. We even smile at Kevin Hoover when we see him on the street. Frank Groh tells me to take it easy and remember my heart. I tell him yes, I understand. Anne puts on more weight. We receive five thousand dollars from our son's will, and Alice receives the balance. We begrudge her nothing. We are not cruel. We never have been cruel. She leaves town as soon as the will is probated, and we do not hear from her again until she telephones to tell us of her approaching marriage to Francis S. Ginn II. (We *loved* our son. We did. Alice was wrong. To admit anything else would be a surrender, a shredding of memory and image.)

A grove of trees, maples mostly, lay across the highway from the Ambersons' parked and listing car. Leaves skidded in gusts over the pavement, and they made golden hissing sounds. The white handkerchief flapped and curled, and Amberson said: "I hope General Grant gives us generous terms."

"I hear he is a very generous man," said Anne.

"You don't mind this at all, do you?"

"Not a bit," said Anne. "It's not as though we were stuck in the middle of the Gobi Desert."

"Years ago, you'd have had a fit."

"Well, this is not years ago," said Anne. "This is now. A flat tire is only a flat tire, but a good man is hard to find."

Amberson smiled. "I choose to take that as a compliment."

"Well, you go right ahead and take it as whatever you want," said Anne.

"Ah . . . this looks to be pretty country."

Sinclair hopped onto the dashboard and began giving himself a bath. From time to time he nibbled at his claws. "I wonder if we'll have to wait long," said Anne, reaching out and stroking the busy Sinclair behind his ears. A car went past, but it neither stopped nor slowed. "Where *are* we anyway?" she said.

"Somewhere east of a place called Auburn Corners."

A truck rumbled past, but it did not slow down. "The same to *you*, Mister," said Anne.

"That's telling him," said Amberson.

"I always was a quick one with a quip."

"Quick quip," said Amberson. "It sounds like a brand name for a glue invented by Elmer Fudd."

"Who?"

"The little chap in the cartoons. The one that talks like a . . . ah, sissy. His product's motto would be: Get a Quick Grip with Quick Quip."

"You've lost me," said Anne.

"I'm stelabulating again."

"You know I can't stand it when you stelabulate. And besides, it is very injurious to your oscadental canal."

"That's easy for *you* to say."

"Well," said Anne, "I *mean* it. You know what your zoomentologist said. He was very specific."

"Ah," said Amberson, "but he is a *wilfong* zoomentologist, not a *particulate* zoomentologist, and I've been told that the wilfongs do not have the extensive training enjoyed by the particulates."

"Some of our *best friends* are wilfongs," said Anne. "How can you *talk* this way?"

Amberson rubbed his mouth. "I'm sorry," he said, "but sometimes I can't seem to control my brammerhoffenstein impulses."

"Well, at your age you ought to be *ashamed* of yourself."

"Oh, I am," said Amberson. "I surely am."

The Ambersons looked away from each other. They stared out their respective windows. This was their doubletalk game, and they loved it

just as much as they loved their Shakespeare game. They had been
playing it for years, and one of its cardinal rules was that they not laugh.
Amberson watched the leaves, and he watched a great fat cloud come
tumbling in from the northwest. It spread, fingered, dissolved into
trails.

A dozen more cars went past, and several of them slowed, but none
stopped. Sinclair finished his bath, rolled himself into a ball, tucked his
tail under his chin and narrowed his eyes. Anne sat with her arms
folded across her chest, and she breathed with her mouth open. Perhaps
she was in pain, but Amberson did not know for sure. "How are you
feeling?" he asked her.

"All right."

"You have pain, don't you?"

"A little . . ."

"Did you take your medication this morning?"

"No."

"Oh. Well. Perhaps you should have."

"It's not *that* pain," said Anne.

"How's that?"

"Well, if you must know, I am exhaustipated."

"Exhaustipated?"

"Yes. Exhausted and constipated. An hour ago, I was full of pep. But
not now. I can never travel without becoming constipated. You know
that."

"Would you like to lie down in the back?"

"With my head in Sinclair's box?"

"No, I can remove it."

"My head?"

"Sinclair's box."

"Oh," said Anne, smiling a little. "Well, *that's* a relief."

"There you go abusing my poor little pronouns. All right now. Tell
me—would you like to lie down in the back?"

"No thank you."

"Did you pack the enema bag?"

"Yes."

"Well then, tonight we'll take care of you."

"Thank you."

" 'Exhaustipated' is a good word," said Amberson.

"Well," said Anne, "it says what it means."

"I am a great one for saying things like that. Making up words.
Doubletalk."

"You are indeed," said Anne, smiling.

"It could be worse. I could be a drunkard or a dope fiend."

"At your age, you'd look ridiculous with holes in your arms. I'd have to buy you nothing but longsleeved shirts."

"Anne, I love you very much . . ."

"I love you too, Howard. I always have."

Amberson blinked. He rubbed his mouth with the back of a hand. He said: "This is all foolish, isn't it?"

"Isn't what?"

"This trip. This footloose nonsense."

"Not if you don't think it is. You are not a foolish man, and you don't do foolish things. Whatever this trip is, a sort of summation or whatever, it's important to you, and that's good enough for me. That's your nature. You're forever looking for order."

"Is that wrong?"

"It's neither *wrong* nor *right*. It's simply *you.*"

"And you don't mind?"

Anne grinned at her husband. "At this late date, what choice do I have? What could I *do* about it even if I *did* mind? Run off to Las Vegas with Frank Sinatra?"

"I expect he would be delighted."

"Oh *yes,*" said Anne. "He would be just absolutely *beside himself.* A wild weekend with Whistler's Mother is just what he wants. Especially seeing as how she has only one breast."

"But it is a very lovely breast."

"Oh, *very.*"

"You could regale him with stories of Buicks and jigsaw puzzles."

"Jigsaw puzzles?"

"Yes. Remember that night in Thirtyone when I became a little carried away and—"

"Did you say *Thirtyone?*"

"Yes."

"And you expect me to remember something that happened *then?*"

"Yes," said Amberson. "So tell me—do you?"

Anne covered her mouth. "Yes," she said. "I remember the night very well. And, as I recall, I was furious with you because we knocked the puzzle all gollywhockered—what with the way you *seized* me and all."

"Yes," said Amberson, "I'm afraid that's true."

Anne's hand came away from her mouth. "Is it bad of me to remember it as being a very sweet thing?"

"No. Of course not."

"I remember it as being very funny and beautiful all at once, do you know what I mean?"

"I certainly do," said Amberson.

"Ah, I tell you—listen to the senility talking . . ."

"No," said Amberson. His voice was sharp. "It is simply a loving memory, and loving memories have nothing to do with senility."

"You want to know something? You make me feel less exhaustipated. You still are willing to take the time to cheer up your poor decrepit old singlebreasted wife."

"We shouldn't feel sorry for ourselves," said Amberson. "We have lived a long time, and it's not been as bad as all that."

"Well, you know how I feel. I've told you often enough. I feel as though I'm not quite human any more. I feel as though I should list to one side, like this car."

"That's ridiculous," said Amberson. "You're exactly the same person you've always been."

"And that's what you always say," said Anne. She stared out her window, and now she was speaking softly. She said: "Even when I was so fat, I prided myself on my breasts. My *breasts.* Plural. And what I feel now, it's not unusual. Frank Groh has told me most women feel the same way after that operation. Breasts are important to women. You lose one, you're half of what you were before. Even at my age, breasts are important. Nobody wants to be lopsided and all cut up, like some sort of freak. And I know what it's done to me . . ."

"How's that?"

"It's maimed me, but to no purpose."

"What?"

"The thing wasn't stopped. It's still there. I can feel it. Why do you think I have all this pain? Do you think it's *neuralgia?* No. You don't think any such thing. You know as well as I do what's happening to me. It's like I'm being *chewed on,* with little teeth going nibble nibble. Yum, yum, isn't Anne delicious? We'll just nibble her down to the bone, and then the worms can have her, and . . . oh my Lord, my dear God . . . I . . . why is it we none of us ever believe we are going to die some day? I . . . I still like it here, Howard . . . I really do . . ., and I don't care *how* much Alice hates me . . . I don't want to have to go away from the birds and all the warm days . . . and what about Sinclair? I love Sinclair, and I'll miss him . . . I don't want to . . ." And now Anne pressed her hands over her face, and she bent forward, and she was sobbing loudly. "God help me, I don't want to die . . . I . . . no, it's . . . too much . . ."

Amberson slid across the seat and embraced his wife. Her cheeks were softly wattled, and her breath had an odor of breakfast egg, and he hugged her tightly, and now (and it came to him with a sickeningly abrupt crunch of awareness) he felt terribly, terribly old and querulous and alone. His gums hurt, and his heart ballooned ominously, and for a moment he thought his chest would burst, and he very much wanted to sob right along with his dear wife. And now Sinclair was staring at them, and Sinclair's eyes were enormous, and clearly they sought some understanding of what was happening, and Amberson wanted to say something to Sinclair, to tell him: Look at us, old friend, and mark well the impermanence of all things, a fact of nature that you too will have to face soon enough. See the dying, old friend. See the approach of terminations. We can barely face it. Will you be able to face it? Or do you have some wisdom about which we know nothing, some knowledge of balance and inevitability that we are incapable of accepting? And now Amberson snuffled, and Anne moaned into his chest, and he kissed her, but he had no words for her. And then the sun came from behind the crisply gray autumn clouds, and it came in an explosion of gold that slammed down on the car roof and streaked the windows and made Amberson squint, and it was a few minutes later that finally he spoke (the light was more or less permanent, and it deserved to be acknowledged). And he said: "The sun is with us." And he said: "It is the same good sun, and we should enjoy it." And he said: "All right, Anne. Yes. Dear Anne. Yes. Anne is my love. Yes. All right, dear Anne. The sun is a friend. Think of laughter, Anne. And remember how awful Henry was on his trumpet. We spent a lot of money on his lessons, but it was one thing he could not master. And remember how he used to laugh about it. He'd come clodhopping down from his room and his face would be red and he would tell us folks, I have about as much musical talent as a tonedeaf lizard. Now, Anne. Yes. Remember him. Shh. Shh now. Think of our Florence and her girls. They will be lovely young ladies. We can be proud of them. We cannot permit ourselves to dissolve. That is not our style. Shh. There. Yes. Ah, my love. For as long as we have, we must go on—not because we'll necessarily *find* anything but simply because it is all we know to do, and that should be good enough. Shh. You'll feel better. I'll help you tonight. We'll try to make it so you're not so exhaustipated. We'll—"

Anne pulled away from him. She nodded. "Yes . . ." she said. She fumbled in her purse and came up with a handkerchief. She blew her nose. She smiled crookedly at Amberson. She blinked and wiped at her eyes with her fingers. "Yes . . ." she said. "You're right . . ." Again she blew her nose. She wadded the handkerchief and returned it to her purse, and the snap of the purse's catch was quite loud. She glanced out a window. "It *is* a good sun." She cleared her throat. "I'm sorry. I really am. I suppose I just needed a few comforting words."

"We all do."

"Even you?"

"Even I," said Amberson.

"Would you like *me* to comfort *you?* Would you like some comforting words right now, some comforting words of your own?"

"Yes. Tell me a car will stop."

"A car will stop."

"Are you sure?"

"Yes," said Anne. "I am sure. I have a feeling."

"Ah, you have comforted me."

"I've always tried to, Howard. I've always tried to be on your side and do the best I can for you."

"I know that."

"You know what I was thinking about the other day?"

"What were you thinking about the other day?" Amberson asked his wife.

"I was thinking about the time you went to bat for Emerald White after she died and Elmer Carmichael and that bunch didn't want her to be buried in the cemetery. And I said to myself: Anne, your husband was a man ahead of his time, which meant he showed more courage than you'll ever be able to imagine. I said to myself: Anne, your husband is a real man, and he always has been."

"It wasn't that much."

"*At the time* it was."

"Well, you're nice to say so."

"You were just a little old schoolteacher, but you stood up to them, and you won out. I call *that* being a *man,* and I'm not being *nice* when I say so. I'm just speaking the truth."

Amberson said nothing. He squinted at the sun and watched another cloud dissolve.

Anne reached across and patted her husband's knee. "You've always had worth," she said. "And plenty of it. There's always been something about you that creates respect, or *commands* respect, or however the saying goes. I've talked with a lot of people who were in your classes, and a lot of people who ran track for you, and they've all said the same thing. They've all said: There's something about Mister Amberson that made most of us try to do better than we ordinarily would have done. One man—I can't remember who it was—said it maybe had something to do with *trust.* It was a long time ago when whoever it was said that, but I've always remembered it. And I think I know what he meant ... or *she,* or whoever it was. I think he or she meant: Mister Amberson *trusted* us to do our best. He didn't *demand* it ... he only *trusted* it.

And I guess they felt anything less than their best would have been a kind of . . . oh I don't know, a kind of *betrayal,* I suppose . . ."

Amberson smiled at his wife. It was a tight smile, and it hurt his gums. He said: "I wonder if Lewis felt that way. Alice seems to think he did."

"*I'm* sure he did," said Anne.

"As though perhaps I were a force looking over his shoulder."

"Yes," said Anne.

"Was that *good?*"

"Of course it was *good.* A father who serves as an inspiration is a good father. That ought to go without saying."

"But what if I was nothing more than a goad or an irritant?"

"That's silly," said Anne. "You know better than to say a thing like that. Now you're sounding like Alice."

"I suppose I am."

"She didn't know what she was talking about. We both of us loved Lewis, and you know that. You said so yourself just last night."

"Of course we did. But that really has nothing to do with the point she was trying to make."

"She wasn't trying to make a *point.* She doesn't like us, and she was only trying to make an *accusation.*"

"All right," said Amberson. "Call it whatever you like, but the fact remains—I never really thought enough of him to seek him out and try to understand *his* point of view. I never really took the time. I accepted all the surface things at face value. I—"

Anne broke in. "Stop *picking* at it," she said. "Done is done, for heaven's *sake.* If *I* can accept it, so can *you* . . ."

Amberson stared down at his lap. He rubbed his fingers together. He rubbed his face, and it was as softly wattled as Anne's. He said: "Yes. That's absolutely true. Done is done. I . . . well, I only wish I had done more . . . I do believe there was more that *could* have been done . . . from her point of view, Alice was speaking a kind of truth . . ."

"That we are, well, a little less than perfect? But we already knew that."

"We are what we are. Perhaps Alice does hate us. Certainly she's angry enough with us, but at my age anger is a terrible waste of time and perhaps even a menace to my health."

"Fifty years it's been, and I've seldom seen you angry, you know that?"

"I suppose you're right," said Amberson. "I wonder—have you missed something?"

"How's that?"

"Maybe I should have argued with you more. There is a possibility that my lack of, ah, *combativeness* has taken an element out of our marriage. A certain amount of spice perhaps."

"No," said Anne. "That's ridiculous. I have lived with you all these years because of what you *are,* not because of any old *quotas.*"

"Quotas?"

"Yes. A quota for anger. A quota for laughter. A quota for the bed thing. You're talking as though you should have *presented more anger,* and I'm saying that's ridiculous. I'm saying that honest emotions can't be *presented.* They simply happen."

Amberson nodded. "Natural is best," he said.

"Exactly," said Anne.

"The beer commercial about the Natural Man is what you mean."

"Exactly," said Anne.

"Never underestimate the power of a beer commercial," said Amberson.

"Yes *sir,*" said Anne.

Amberson smiled.

A yellow pickup truck, sputtering and rattling, came churning past them, pulled off on the shoulder and stopped a few feet away from the car. The words FRANK SCALISI LANDSCAPE GARDENER WARREN, O. were lettered on its sides. "Hey," said Anne, "look at this." A man and a boy got out of the truck. The boy was no more than twelve or thirteen, but he was fat, with small eyes, thick lips and an underslung jaw. The man was wiry and grayhaired, and there was a purple birthmark on his right cheek. Both the man and the boy were wearing suits and neckties, and their shoes were shined. Amberson got out of the car and went to them.

The man smiled at Amberson. "You got trouble?" he said.

"Yes," said Amberson. He nodded toward the flat tire. "I'm afraid I am unable to change it. I . . . well, not to make too fine a point of it, I have a heart condition."

The man smiled at the boy. "You think we can help this fellow?" he asked the boy.

"Me?" said the boy. "Me do it?"

The man nodded.

"*Me,*" said the boy, grinning.

Anne got out of the car. She appeared to be wheezing. She smiled at the boy. Sinclair sat up and looked out at all of them. He licked a paw. Anne moved up until she was standing next to Amberson.

The boy had seen Sinclair. He nudged the man and said: "Kitty."

"Yes," said the man. "A nice kitty." Then he draped an arm across

336

the boy's shoulders and said to the Ambersons: "This is my son Mike. My name is Frank Scalisi. He knows all about how to change a tire."

"Me. Yes," said the boy, still grinning.

The Ambersons introduced themselves, and hands were shaken. The boy said to Anne: "Kitty."

"Yes," said Anne. "A nice kitty. His name is Sinclair."

"Sclair?"

"*Sin*clair," said Anne, smiling at the boy.

". . . I pet him?" said the boy.

"Change the tire first," said the man. "Then you can pet him."

The boy nodded. He still was grinning. He went to the trunk of the Pontiac, opened it and removed the tools and the spare tire. He moved flatfooted, and humming sounds came from his throat. The air felt cold to Amberson, and he blew on his hands. He said to the man: "Ah, you're really sure he can do it?"

"Absolutely," said Frank Scalisi. "My exwife sends him to a good school, and they teach things like that. From what they say, he'll be able to take his rightful place in society. I think those are the words they use."

"He seems like a very nice boy," said Anne.

"He *is* a very nice boy," said Frank Scalisi, nodding. "They're all of them very nice. My God, you go to that school and take a look at them, it's enough to break your heart. All they want is for someone to love them, you know what I mean?"

"Yes," said Anne.

"It okay if he pets the cat when he's done with the tire?"

"Yes," said Anne. "Of course."

"I should of asked first. I'm sorry."

Anne smiled. "Oh, for heaven's sake," she said, "we're grateful for the help."

"He's good at it. You'll see. That's some school he goes to."

The boy worked slowly, but his movements were not tentative, and he seemed to know what he was doing. He squatted with the jack, pumped it, fixed it squarely to the car's undercarriage, then put his weight on the handle and jacked up the car. He kept grinning, and the humming sounds became louder. Amberson and Anne smiled at him.

"He doesn't need any help at all, does he?" said Amberson to Frank Scalisi.

"Not a bit," said Frank Scalisi, leaning against the truck door. "I mean, maybe it sounds funny, but for a retarded kid, he catches on fast."

"I think I know what you mean," said Amberson.

"I get him five days a month. I'll have him today, tomorrow, Friday, Saturday and Sunday. He's a good boy."

"We can see that," said Anne.

"You folks from around here?" Frank Scalisi asked them.

"No," said Amberson. "We're from southern Ohio, Paradise County. We're on a little vacation."

"Paradise County—that's near Athens somewhere, right?"

"Yes," said Amberson.

"Where you headed?"

"We don't really know," said Amberson.

"What?"

"We're just wandering around," said Anne. "Every morning we just point the car in some direction or other, and away we go. We call it being footloose."

"Sounds like maybe it's a good way to take a vacation," said Frank Scalisi, rubbing the birthmark.

"It's just a notion of my husband's," said Anne. "He has notions now and then, and there's not much I can do about them."

"You don't seem too worked up about it," said Scalisi.

"I'm not," said Anne. "I've been married to this man for fifty years, and I'm used to his notions."

The boy began removing the wheel bolts. He smiled at his father, and Frank Scalisi said: "You're doing great, pal. Keep up the good work."

"Know it. Me," said the boy. He grimaced as he untwisted the bolts.

"Bet you didn't think a retarded kid could change a tire," said Scalisi to Anne.

"No," said Anne. "I suppose I didn't." She leaned her weight against one of the Pontiac's fenders. "I . . . well, I think it's remarkable."

"Olympia can't get over it," said Scalisi. He hesitated, then: "Olympia is my exwife's name. That's some name, isn't it? She lives in Garfield Heights, and I get him five days a month. I guess I already told you that, didn't I? Maybe I'm getting old."

"It doesn't matter," said Anne.

Frank Scalisi blinked at Anne, and then he blinked at Amberson. "I . . . hey, you know, what would you say if I was to tell you . . . ah, never mind . . ."

The boy looked up. "Papa," he said. "Bolts done."

Scalisi nodded. "You know what to do now," he said to the boy.

"Wheel go off," said the boy.

"Right," said Scalisi.

The boy pulled off the wheel. His tongue was exposed, and he grunted. He rolled the wheel to one side, then dragged the spare and
338

its wheel to the axle. He fitted it to the axle. "Kitty," he said. "See kitty."

"Jesus Christ," said Frank Scalisi.

The Ambersons looked at him.

"Excuse me," he said, "but this here boy is the only kid I got, and I think I love him better than if he was all right. You mind if I say that?"

"Of course not," said Amberson.

Scalisi looked at Anne. His face was flushed. "I go see Olympia once a month, when I pick up the boy. She's married to a guy named Ferrone who owns a bar, and she's real fat now, you know what I mean? But once a month, on this particular same Wednesday, and it's usually in the morning, once a month when I go see her she keeps telling me she wants to . . . ah, whatchacallit, ah, *have relations* with me—and her husband's upstairs sleeping in the bedroom, and she says we can do it on the, ah, the davenport or the floor or whatever. She says Frank, we can put the boy in his room for half an hour or so. He won't be any trouble. He'll just sit in there and sing songs to himself. She says Frank, I miss you and I want you. That's what she says—honest to God it is."

The Ambersons said nothing. Amberson glanced at Anne, and there was a soft look to her face. It had gathered in her eyes, and it was compassionate; it had no room for her own pain; it bestowed; it was unselfish; it opened her face and made it vulnerable.

"I shouldn't of told you that," said Scalisi, shaking his head. "I don't know why I told you that. I don't know you people from a sack of coal, and what right I got?"

"You breathe air, don't you?" said Anne.

"What?" said Scalisi, and his hands made loose confused choppy movements. They plucked at the lapels of his jacket. "You're asking me what? You're asking me do I breathe air? Sure I breathe air. Everybody breathes air."

"And sometimes you feel as though your bones are being pulled out of your skin, don't you?"

"Yeah. All right. Ah, maybe so . . ."

Anne nodded. "Of course you do. Everyone does. So it just means you're human, that's all. It just means that sometimes you have to . . . ah, I suppose the best word for it is *holler*. And my husband and I happen to be the ones who are within range." Here Anne hesitated. She smiled. "And anyway, you ought to be flattered."

"Huh?"

"Your exwife knows she made a mistake. That should make you feel a little better about the situation."

Scalisi smiled. He folded his arms across his chest. He said: "You think so? No sh—kidding?"

"Yes," said Anne. "No kidding."

"Missus, you want to know something?"

"Yes?"

"I feel better. Honest to God I do."

Amberson spoke up. "My wife has that facility," he said.

"How's that?" said Scalisi.

"That's a schoolteacher's way of saying she has a talent for making people feel better," Amberson told Scalisi.

Scalisi's shoulders jerked. He rubbed his nose. He still was smiling. "I . . . well, this is all real crazy, isn't it? I don't know what to . . . I mean, she is *serious* about it, and sometimes I damn near want to *laugh,* you know? Once a month and there I am, come to her place to pick up Mike for the five days, and she's like a *girl,* and it's been going on for maybe a year now and maybe more, and I don't know whether to eat prunes or wind my watch . . . I mean, how come she got to act that way?"

"I don't believe there's much sense even asking the question," said Anne.

Scalisi stared at his shined shoes. He blinked. He said: "I'm fifty, and she's fortyeight, and sometimes I almost got to laugh. I mean, she's like a *girl* . . ."

"We have children inside us," said Amberson.

"What?"

"Children trying to come to the surface. Some vestige of youth. Something that has never admitted the *aging process,* as it's called. Something that keeps insisting we still have a *future* and *capacity* and *possibilities* and all that."

"In other words," said Scalisi, "something that won't face facts."

"Yes," said Amberson, "I suppose so. That phrase I just used—the *aging process*—is a very cruel phrase, so cold and inevitable. The child inside us is a protection, a necessary escape."

"But Olympia's no *girl.* She's *fortyeight years old.* She ought to face up to it and stop acting so stupid."

Anne frowned at Scalisi. "I'm sure she does. I'm sure she's aware of it night and day. But she's a human being, and she needs illusions, no matter how false. All human beings need illusions. You. I. My husband. Your boy. Your former wife. Everybody."

Scalisi nodded. "Maybe so," he said. "She always was of a real imaginative cast of mind." He nodded toward the boy, who was busy tightening the bolts on the wheel. "She was thirtyseven when she had Mike, and we'd been married nineteen years. When she was carrying him, she told me he kicked like a *president.* I asked her what she meant, and she said some people when they kick, they kick with *authority,* you know, like they were *in charge,* you get that? Like they *meant business.* And I said to her maybe *he* was a *she* and would grow up to be a chorus girl, a Radio City Rockette, you know? But she told me hell, no; the kicks were too *strong,* and no *girl* would kick so strong like that. And she was right, and when he came he was a big one, nine pounds four ounces, a big one and he took his time. He—"

"I had a big baby once," said Anne.

"Oh?" said Scalisi. "That so? Did it take its time?"

"Yes."

"Wellthen, okay. You know what I mean. And like, it had been *nineteen years,* and my brothers Guido and Johnny and their wives they'd been after us and *after* us all those years, asking how come we had none of the old pizzazz, you know? And what do you think? You think we were proud, Olympia and me? Hell, we weren't *proud.* We were fit to *burst.* It was like we had *invented* proud. Me, I walked so big it was like I was Wilt Chamberlain, and Olympia she fed the boy from her breasts, and it was like she always wanted his flesh touching hers, you understand? But then, later on, after we found out there was something wrong with him, some blank thing or whatever in his head, she turned on me and started talking all the time about how we had sinned, about how God had judged us badly. And she just about drove me out of the house, and that's a fact. And, Church or no Church, she divorced me, and three four years later she met Ferrone, and she married him, and she moved from Warren to Garfield Heights, and she took Mike with her, and Ferrone tells me *he* loves Mike too. Ferrone tells me Mike is enough to tear him apart, like there's some sweet thing sitting inside retarded people that makes them more lovable than the rest of us, the *straights* and the *sanes,* you understand what I mean?"

"Yes," said Amberson.

"I believe so," said Anne.

Scalisi continued. The words came quickly, and he leaned forward a little, and he said: "I shouldn't of said it that way. Mike's as sane as anybody. Retarded people aren't crazy. Maybe the world thinks they are, but the world's wrong, you understand? I mean, this kid can sit for hours and talk to *goldfish* and tell them how pretty they are. And sure, you and I know they're pretty, but do we *appreciate* them like Mike does? Do we really *concentrate* on watching them? Hell, no—they're like the wallpaper, right? The more I see of the kid, the more I watch him, the more I'm like Ferrone, the more I get torn apart, you know? I mean, look at him over there. He hums while he works. To him, it's fun; it's like a game, the change-the-tire game. You could starve that kid; you could beat him with a chain; it wouldn't make a bit of difference. He'd still love you, and he'd still hum while he works, hum and grin like it's all a game and the world's a toy. So like what's retarded, huh? There's something in him that's beyond my knowing a thing about it, so who's *really* retarded, huh? I making any sense, Missus?"

"Yes," said Anne, smiling.

Scalisi nodded. "All right," he said. "All right. *Now.* Look at him there. He's eleven, and he knows how to change a tire. He can change a tire faster than anybody I've ever seen. But he can't read a goddamned book. He can't even read his own name, let alone write it. So what's it mean? The thing is, Olympia and Yours Truly never were out to set the world on fire, or fly to the damn moon, or conquer anything. All we wanted was a baby, and so we got one, and look at him. Nineteen years, and then he came. What was it? An accident? A mistake? A tube get twisted wrong? How come *us?* I'd just like to know why we got—"

Amberson held up a hand. "Excuse me," he said.

"What?" said Scalisi, and his wet flustered face twitched. Anger nipped at his voice. He balled his hands.

"Excuse me," said Amberson, "I don't mean to interrupt, but speaking for myself, I was unable to change a tire until I was past twenty."

"That is absolutely true," said Anne to Scalisi.

"That supposed to make me fell better?" Scalisi asked them.

"I hope so," said Amberson. "Think about it for a moment."

"All right," said Scalisi. "I'm thinking about it. Maybe I know what you mean, and maybe I don't. I guess you're trying to make me feel better. Okay. Great. I appreciate that. You're good people."

"Yes," said Mike, squatting by the wheel.

They all looked at him.

He grinned at them. "Good," he said. "Yes. Kitty." He replaced the hubcap and slammed it tight. "Done. Flat. No more."

"Yes," said Scalisi to his son. "Hey, how about that?"

"Excellent," said Amberson, smiling.

"Kitty?" said Mike, blinking at Anne.

"Absolutely," said Anne.

Mike pumped the jack and lowered the car. He slid the jack out from under the car and returned it to the trunk. Then he rolled the flat tire to the rear of the car and lifted it into the trunk. Amberson walked to the trunk and said: "A fine job."

"Thank you," said Mike, humming. He grimaced as he lifted the tire and wheel and slid them into the trunk. The ledger was on the floor of the trunk, and the tire rolled over it, leaving a smear of dirt across the

342

cover. Amberson quickly reached into the trunk and shoved the ledger behind the tire.

"Book," said Mike.

"Yes," said Amberson. He glanced at Anne, but she seemed to be paying no attention. He hastily slammed down the trunk lid.

"Big book," said Mike.

"Yes," said Amberson. "Ah . . . you want to see the kitty now?"

"Yes," said Mike. "Pet kitty. Mike pet kitty?"

Anne came to them. "What's all this talk about a book?" she wanted to know.

"The . . . ah, service manual," said Amberson. "It's in the trunk."

"Oh," said Anne. "I didn't know that."

"Well, it *is*."

"I *believe* you," said Anne. She frowned at Amberson. "It's all right. I really do."

Amberson felt his face become warm. "Excuse me," he said. "I . . . ah, well, I didn't have to be so peevish about it."

"That's right," said Anne, grinning. Then she turned to Mike and said: "*Now* then, let's you and I go pay a little visit to the kitty."

"Yes," said Mike.

Anne glanced at Mike's hands. "We have Kleenex in the car, and you can wipe off your hands. We'll sit in the car and pet the kitty, all right?"

"Yes," said Mike.

Anne and the boy climbed inside the car. Amberson and Scalisi stood outside and watched them. Anne wiped the boy's hands with Kleenex, then scooped Sinclair off the dashboard and handed him to the boy. Mike smiled. He stroked Sinclair's fur the wrong way. Anne said something to him, and then he stroked Sinclair's fur the right way. He held Sinclair against his chest, and Sinclair wriggled a little, but Anne reached over and scratched Sinclair behind the ears, and he settled down. Amberson and Scalisi stood silently, and Scalisi was breathing with his mouth open. The leaves snapped and whirled, and the wind cooled Amberson's face. The boy kissed Sinclair on a cheek, and then the boy giggled and said something to Anne, who smiled at him and patted one of his shoulders. The windows were rolled up, and so her words could not be heard.

Scalisi cleared his throat. "You see what I mean?" he asked Amberson. "Goddamn, I'm glad we stopped."

"Thank you—and so are we."

"It's like I'm forever learning from him. Just to stand here and look at them, you know?"

"Yes."

"I'm soft, right?"

"There are worse things," said Amberson.

"It's a hell of a world if you can stand the strain, right?"

"Right," said Amberson.

Scalisi grunted. He went to the car, leaned across the hood and tapped the windshield. Anne and the boy and Sinclair looked out at him. "Come on, pal," he said to the boy. "We got to be on our way."

Inside the car, the boy looked at Anne. She smiled. He said something to Sinclair. By this time, Sinclair's paws were wrapped around the boy's forearm, and it was with some difficulty that the boy handed him back to Anne. She scratched Sinclair's rump, and he arched his back. Then the boy got out of the car, grinned at his father and said: "Nice. Yes. Kitty. Good pussy."

"Yeah," said Scalisi. "Right." Then, to Amberson: "Thanks a lot, okay?"

"And I thank *you*," said Amberson.

"Right," said Scalisi. He led the boy to the truck.

"Thank you very much, Mike," said Amberson to the boy's back. The father and son turned. Mike nodded. "Right," he said. Amberson smiled.

Scalisi and the boy climbed into the truck. Doors were slammed, and the truck went clattering off down the road. The boy turned around and waved through the window on his side. Amberson returned the wave. The truck went banging around a curve, and that was that. Amberson rubbed his hands together. Perhaps he should have felt cold, but he did not. He walked back to the car and got inside. Sinclair had returned to his perch on the dashboard, and Anne sat with her hands folded in her lap. Amberson started the car and eased it out onto the highway. "I am thinking the strangest thought," said Anne.

"And what might that be?" Amberson asked her.

"Just now, being with that boy, it reminded me of being with Henry."

"Oh?"

"Yes," said Anne. She unfolded her hands and rubbed her cheeks. "There was, ah, such a *kindness* to him . . ."

"There was indeed," said Amberson.

"Isn't that silly?"

"What?"

"Well, that boy is *retarded*. Henry wasn't retarded. Far *from* it. He was the most—"

"Kindness has nothing to do with retardation. Love has nothing to do with retardation. Compassion does not require a Stanford-Binet."

"I know that, but . . ."

"But what?" Amberson asked his wife.

"Oh, I don't know. It's just that . . . well, I've always had it steady in my mind that Henry was special, and now here comes along a *retarded* boy who's just as kind and loving as Henry ever was, and so maybe Henry wasn't so special after all."

"I disagree," said Amberson. "You are laboring under the assumption that the boy we saw just now is ordinary. Well, *I* say he is *special*. Therefore, if he is special, and if he somehow reminds us of Henry, then Henry also was special."

"You are a dear man," said Anne.

"Thank you very much," said Amberson.

Sinclair hopped into the back seat and used his box. Then he sat on the back shelf and stared out the window, and several motorists, jockeying for position to pass the Ambersons' car, grinned and waved at Sinclair. The Pontiac remained at 40, and the country spread in a succession of low brownish hills. The highway widened to four lanes, and the Pontiac passed an Amish buggy, and Anne said: "Well, they seem to be everywhere." Then, after a hesitation: "Say, just exactly where did you say this road goes, anyway?"

"Warren," said Amberson. "Then Youngstown. Then Pittsburgh. Then I don't know where."

"Are we going to Pittsburgh?"

"I don't think so."

"Then where *are* we going?"

"I'm not altogether certain."

"I had an idea this morning."

"About what?" Amberson asked his wife.

"About where we can go."

"Oh? All right, tell me—where?"

"How about if we were to go visit Peter and his family . . ."

"Peter?"

"Yes. You like him, don't you? I certainly know *I* do. And I bet he knows a great deal about the apparatus. He seems to be so much in touch with everything. And after all, we haven't seen him since Sixty-eight."

"I remember the occasion very well," said Amberson. "That attack of mine at the Broasted Chicken place isn't something that is easily forgotten."

"And he knew what to do. He got you to the hospital right away."

"Yes, he did," said Amberson. "He reminds you of Henry, doesn't he?"

Anne looked at her husband. The look was steady and flat. "Yes," she said.

"All right," said Amberson. "When we stop for lunch, I'll get out the road map and we'll head south. We should arrive there some time day after tomorrow, even with my slow driving."

"We'll surprise them," said Anne.

"Yes," said Amberson. "I expect so."

"I was thinking about Bernadette for some strange reason, and then my thoughts seemed to slide over to Peter. He is gentle the way his mother was. I have always been fond of him. I was fond of Bernadette, too."

"Yes," said Amberson.

"You were fond of her yourself, weren't you?"

"Yes," said Amberson. He squinted. The sunlight was back, and there was a glare on the windshield. It was warm and not as comforting as perhaps it should have been.

"Did you ever have an itch for her?"

"What?"

"Bernadette. I sometimes thought you may have entertained notions."

"Notions?"

"Yes. *Notions.* Stop playing Little Sir Echo."

"If you're trying to say did I entertain notions about Bernadette, that's silly."

"Silly? Silly like ha-ha, how funny?"

"Yes. Ha-ha, how funny."

"Well, I was just asking . . ."

"And you have your answer," said Amberson. He swallowed saliva. His hands were tight on the wheel.

"I didn't mean to get you upset," said Anne.

"I am not upset," said Amberson.

"Well, you could have fooled *me,*" said Anne, smiling.

Amberson shook his head. "Oh Lord," he said. He glanced down at the backs of his hands, and he would not have been surprised had they been streaked with flour, but of course they were not, and the very thought was absurd.

"I'm sorry," said Anne. "At my age, that sort of accusation is stupid."

Amberson said nothing.

"Now, don't be *angry."*

"You just finished saying I don't get angry. Very well, I am not angry," said Amberson, speaking tightly. And he was not, at least with his wife. He said to himself: Bernadette has been dead for sixteen years, and that one afternoon disrupted nothing, so why should it vex and confound me? Why am I so reluctant to acknowledge how trivial it has been made by time? That was *1938,* for God's sake, and there were no demands, and nothing evil followed from it, so kindly let it *go,* you fraudulent old man.

"That the truth?" Anne wanted to know.

"Yes," said Amberson, grunting.

"Fine," said Anne. She folded her arms across her chest.

Amberson was silent for a time. The Pontiac glided down a long hill and passed through a town called Parkman, which straddled a broad curve of US 422. It passed several more Amish buggies, and a small blond boy waved to the Ambersons from one of them. Anne smiled and returned the wave. Still smiling, she looked at Amberson, but his face apparently was too bleak, and so she said nothing. Finally he spoke, and he said: "Anne, you've lived with me for fifty years, and you should know what I am, and you should know how I behave. If I was, well, ah, a little angry, it was because I thought you were showing a kind of ignorance, and you're too bright for that sort of thing."

"Is . . . is that supposed to be a compliment?"

"Yes."

"Well, it was just an idle question—about Bernadette, I mean. I expect it sounded worse than I meant it to sound. I didn't mean to accuse you of *rolling* in the *hay* with her. I was just talking about a little bitty itch, that's all. I mean, I know *she* liked *you* a great deal. She certainly *told* me often enough."

"She did?"

"Yes. And sometimes there was a sort of light in her eyes, you know? We'd sit in the kitchen and drink coffee, and it was Howard this, Howard that, Howard the other thing. Howard, Howard, Howard, blah, blah, blah. And I used to make fun of her about it, and then we'd laugh."

"Laugh?"

"Yes, Little Sir Echo. *Laugh.*"

"Well, I'm happy I provided so much enjoyment for the two of you."

"Now, don't sulk. You ought to be flattered. She was a good woman, and you ought to be glad she talked so much about you, how *dignified* you were, and what a good *coach* and kindly *person* you were, and all that sort of thing, blah, blah, blah."

"I am delighted," said Amberson.

"Oh *yes,*" said Anne. "I can *tell.*"

Again Amberson fell silent. There was no sense pursuing any of this. And there certainly was no sense jumping down Anne's throat. If he reacted too strenuously, she would know without his having to say a word. And what would *that* be? A gift of a confessed betrayal as she prepared to die? What sort of gift was *that?*

"I really didn't mean to upset you," said Anne.

Amberson glanced at his wife.

She had opened her purse, and she was wiping her cheeks and eyes with a Kleenex. "I was just trying to make conversation, that's all . . ."

"I'm not upset," said Amberson. "Not really. Why should I be?"

Anne nodded.She snapped shut the purse and balled the Kleenex in her hand. She blinked, grimaced. Then she swiveled her head to the right, looked out her window and said: "I see a mailbox that says HUGHES."

"I see a cloud that is shaped like the train of some great lady's formal gown," said Amberson.

"I see a cow," said Anne.

"It is a black and white cow," said Amberson.

"I see a dead elm tree," said Anne.

"Here comes a Ford," said Amberson. "It is either a 1959 or a 1960."

"I see a billboard advertising Sunkist oranges," said Anne.

"We are about to pass an empty coal truck," said Amberson.

"We now have passed that empty coal truck," said Anne.

"We shall prevail," said Amberson.

"Absolutely. Hey," said Anne, "look at this."

Amberson hit the brake, and the car slowed. Scalisi's truck was parked on the berm up ahead, and Scalisi and the boy were standing by a fence, and the boy was busily talking to a brown pig that had stuck its snout through the fence. Amberson honked the horn. Scalisi and the boy turned, recognized the car and waved. Amberson tootled shave-and-a-haircut on the horn, and he and Anne waved at Scalisi and the boy. The boy clapped his hands together, and most of his teeth were visible. Sinclair sat up and looked around, then yawned, licked a foot and settled back to sleep. Scalisi and the boy dropped back out of sight, and Amberson nudged the car's speed back to 40, and Anne said: "Perhaps a lot of people will prevail."

"It would be nice to think so," said Amberson.

The Ambersons stopped for lunch at a Howard Johnson's southeast of Warren. He asked Anne if she still felt exhaustipated, and she told him yes, a little, and she was glad she had brought along the enema bag. Amberson smiled and allowed as how he would be happy to do the honors tonight before they retired. Anne looked up from her ice cream, winked and told him greater love had no man. Driving into Youngs-

348

town, they stopped at a place called the Mahoning Pet & Garden Shop, and Anne bought a bowl for Sinclair's food and a dish for his water. The Youngstown traffic was heavy, and the air hung like a gray scrim. Amberson turned on the radio, but all he could find was rock music, and neither Anne nor he understood rock music, and so he turned off the radio. Amberson and his wife never had been able to get the hang of it. Still, as he had heard a comedian say the other night on television, there were different strokes for different folks, and those who liked rock music had a right to listen to whatever they chose. Grasping the wheel tightly, Amberson mused on his splendid liberalism and looked around. There was a huddled quality to Youngstown, as though its buildings had to lean against each other for support. It was a city of automobile graveyards and immense steel mills, and the people on the sidewalks moved with a sort of hunched and grimy enervation. Many of them had flat faces with narrow Slavic eyes, and Amberson felt sorry for them. At the same time, though, he chided himself for again being so conde-scending. Perhaps, for all he knew, they loved Youngstown, and per-haps they would be terribly unhappy if they lived anywhere else. He said to himself: We do not all live under the same set of conditions. What is good to me may not be good to these people. Perhaps the rural delights of Paradise County would bore them to death. I should concen-trate on driving this automobile, and I should leave the philosophy to the philosophers.

They drove due south on Ohio 7 to Martins Ferry, then along the west bank of the Ohio River to Steubenville. There were barges on the river, and they appeared to move sluggishly. Amberson had a curious feeling that he and Anne had come to a place where time was sus-pended; there was a flavor of, say, 1940 to this area, and it was not even disturbed by all the clustering tall television aerials he saw. The houses and buildings seemed so terribly *old;* it was Crooksville all over again, or Roseville, or Blood. There were too many broken windows, too many listing abandoned buildings. Ambition had built those buildings, but attrition had knocked them all gollywhockered, as Anne would say. The Pontiac finally crossed the Ohio River on a high bridge, and the water below was green and brown, and the Ambersons drove across the extreme northern tip of West Virginia, and then they were in Pennsyl-vania, headed southeast, and the countryside spread a bit, and the hills were less jumbled and crowded, but there appeared to be no wealth here, and the towns were just as scruffy. The Ambersons did not say ten words to one another all the way to Washington, Pennsylvania, where they arrived at about four o'clock in the afternoon. The sun had fled, but Amberson's eyes were warm, and so he glanced at his wife and said: "I believe I've had it for today." And Anne said: "Yes. Fine. Let's stop someplace for the night." And Amberson said: "Good enough." They pulled into a Holiday Inn parking lot, and Amberson went inside, asked for a room on the first floor, signed the register, then was told by the clerk that the only available rooms, sorry sir, were on the second floor. He sighed, told the clerk all right, fine, may I have the key please? He returned to the car and told Anne he was sorry; he had tried to get a room on the first floor, but none was available. She said well, even though she was old and decrepit, she supposed she would be able to negotiate one piddling little flight of steps. She carried Sinclair up to the room, and Amberson struggled with the suitcases and Sinclair's box. Anne filled Sinclair's new water dish for him, and he lapped at it eagerly. Then she took off her coat and dress and lay down. Amberson carefully undressed and lay down next to his wife in his underclothes. He reached for her hand; he squeezed it and she smiled. Sinclair hopped onto the bed, seated himself at Anne's feet and took a bath. Then he lay down, pressing his head against Anne's feet and his hindquarters against Amberson's feet. Amberson closed his eyes and dozed off, but he was aware of traffic sounds, and he vaguely heard someone operating a soft drink machine somewhere. It made heavy clunking sounds. He summoned up the faces of Scalisi and the boy Mike. And he summoned up the glimpse he had had of the scene by the road when the boy had been talking to the brown pig. And he thought back to those ancient prehistoric days of Fred Suiter and the gregarious fish. And he thought of Alice. Loud Alice, with her breasts and her truth. And he snorted, gave a little cough. And then he was fully asleep, but his hand still lay in his wife's. The next thing he knew it was 6:30 and Anne was nudging him and telling him she was hungry. The waitress in the motel restaurant was a slight girl, with long dark hair, and she told the Ambersons that the roast beef seemed very good tonight. Amberson looked at Anne, and she said yes, that sounds just fine, and please make mine medium. And Amberson nodded at the waitress and told her make it two orders, both medium, and if he (Amberson) could have an end cut, he would be enormously pleased. The waitress smiled and said she would see what she could do. She asked the Ambersons would they like the baked potato and the tossed salad, and they told her yes, the baked potato and the tossed salad sounded just scrumptious. The girl nodded and went away, and Anne made amused sounds in her throat and then said: "In the past few years, have you noticed how careful we are when we order our meals out? And maybe 'careful' isn't even the word for it. Maybe I ought to just come out and say 'fussy' and be done with it. I mean, it is as though the *future* of the

350

world depends on whether the food is properly prepared."

"All I said was I wanted an end cut."

"No. No. I don't mean *that.* I'm talking about the way that girl spoke to us. It was almost as though she was trying to *guide* us, so we wouldn't *agonize* too long, as though she was trying to *help* us, to keep us from becoming *confused.* "

"I do not feel confused," said Amberson. He fiddled with his knife and fork, aligning them on each side of his plate.

Anne shook her head. "Perhaps I'm putting it badly," she said, "but it seems to me that we *do* take forever these days."

"Take forever? How so? In what?"

"In *everything.* Look, we have been driving for *three days,* and we're only in *Washington, Pennsylvania.* Doesn't that prove my point? I mean, *footloose* is *one* thing, but *slow* is *another* . . ."

Amberson smiled. "Well, we're not exactly the youngest chickens in the henhouse, and things simply take us more time."

"Ah," said Anne. "Don't mind me. It's just that I'm exhaustipated."

"We'll try to take care of that."

"You don't mind?"

"No," said Amberson, "but I do rather mind contemplating it just before the arrival of my fussily ordered end cut."

Now the amused sounds came from Anne's nostrils, and she said: "I beg your pardon, O noble and squeamish sire. I have rudely forsaken my delicate manner, and I humbly pray that thou not castigate me, unworthy wretch that I am, too strenuously. I wouldst then fain swoon from dire and blushing mortification . . ."

"Have no fear, fair maiden. My anger is like the morning dew; it fadeth quickly in the golden blossoming light of thy gracious wit."

"Great God Almighty," said Anne, and then she laughed aloud.

The roast beef was quite tasty and filling, and Amberson did indeed receive an end cut. He cashed another Travelers' Cheque, this one for twenty dollars, and he left the girl a tip of three dollars. Anne frowned at him but said nothing. They returned to their room, and Sinclair was asleep on the dresser. It was barely eight o'clock, but Anne told Amberson she was awfully tired. She smiled and asked him would he please do the honors now. He told her of course. She fetched the enema bag from a suitcase, and he went into the bathroom and began running warm water in the basin. He unwrapped a bar of Ivory Soap and swished it in the water, and he took off his jacket, rolled up a shirtsleeve and tested the water with an elbow. It was important that the water not be too hot. Then he spread all the bathtowels on the floor and filled the enema bag with lukewarm soapy water. Anne came into the bathroom, and she was wearing her nightgown. She smiled. She lay down on the towels. Amberson's fingers were closed tightly over the enema bag's tube. Anne rolled on her side and lifted the nightgown above her hips. She was facing away from Amberson, and she said: "I'm ready whenever you are." Amberson nodded, squatted behind her, inserted the tube, held up the bag and permitted the water to flow. "Oh, *my,*" said Anne. "Just hold fast," said Amberson. "Yes," said Anne. She writhed a little, and her buttocks contracted. Amberson was able to smell Ivory Soap. "Relax," he said, patting Anne's buttocks. Some of the tension went out of them. "That's a good girl," he said. "Hooray for me," said Anne, her voice muffled. Amberson smiled. "Things are . . . ah, happening," said Anne. "I wouldn't be surprised," said Amberson. Now Anne's legs were twitching and she said something to the effect that she did not know how much more of it she would be able to hold. He told her it was best if she waited as long as she could. She grunted. Her bare feet contracted. Then, wheezing heavily, she reached behind herself, removed the tube, got to her feet and hurried to the toilet. She seated herself heavily, and the explosion came, and she smiled. He went out of the bathroom. He seated himself in a heavy leather chair. She called after him that she was sorry, and he told her not to be ridiculous. She came to bed ten minutes later. She told him the enema had been a gratifying success, and she thanked him, and he kissed her on the forehead and told her shh, for heaven's sake, it was nothing. He tried to talk her into taking her medication, but she refused. She told him all she wanted was to sleep. He smiled, nodded. She closed her eyes. "Enemas make me drowsy," she said. He bent over her and kissed her eyes. Then he seated himself in a chair across the room and waited for her to fall asleep. This took perhaps fifteen minutes, and then she was breathing heavily, with an arm curled around her head. He quietly left the room, walked to the car, retrieved the ledger from the trunk, went to the lobby and worked on the ledger for nearly three hours. Then he returned the ledger to the car and went back to the room, undressed, brushed his teeth, put on his pajamas and crawled into bed next to Anne, who still was sleeping heavily. It was not quite midnight. He did not sleep well.

Thursday

See now 1921, and Anne and I have been married less than six hours. Fully clothed, we stand embracing at the foot of the bed in the bridal suite of the Acterhof House, which is generally acknowledged to be Paradise Falls's only "respectable" hotel. It is eight o'clock in the evening, and the windows are open, and we are able to hear a clamor of Saturdaynight sounds. As long as I can remember, Paradise Falls has been a Saturdaynight town, and the sounds are a loud agglutination of voices, laughter, music and clattering automobiles. But I am not really paying much mind to them. (I may be *somewhat* foolish, but I am not *altogether* foolish.) Anne and I giggle and sway—my brother Alvin Jr. has extravagantly spiked the reception punch with bootleg champagne. The room is smaller than I expected it to be, and it occurs to me that I am the third Amberson who will spend his wedding night here. I glance at the bed, and I briefly think of Alvin Jr. and Ernest and their wives, but then I tell myself I am being a damned imbecile, and my attention returns to my bride and the work at hand.

"Oh my *gooness*," whispers Anne. "I feel like such a naughty person . . ."

I kiss away a drop of moisture that has formed at a corner of her mouth. "Yes," I say, "and so do I."

Her voice is wet. "We're *terrible,* aren we?" she whispers.

"Yes—and ain't it grand?"

"Doan say *ain.* You got to member you a *schoolteacher.*"

"Oh yes. We don't want to forget that."

"Abslutely."

I clear my throat. I kiss Anne's ears and hair and neck. The forgetmenots still are in her hair. I remove them and drop them on the bedspread. She stands in a sort of slump. The room is dark, and its furnishings are heavy and warm. The Acterhof House dates back to the Civil War, and its windows are high and arched, and the bridal bed is enormous. I can wait no longer. I am twentyfour years old, and I have waited far too long as it is. Anne's slump is warmly submissive, and I know she will do whatever I want, and God bless Alvin Jr. and his spiked punch. The wallpaper is decorated with what appear to be purple roses and golden cherubs, and the dresser is massive, with squat bowed legs and a great shimmering horizontal mirror. I kiss my bride's throat, and my trousers are too tight. Several pictures are grouped on the wall at the head of the bed. They are reproductions of pastoral scenes. I am aware of barns and meadows and clusters of cattle. Now Anne is trembling. She is wearing a white dress that has little pink felt buttons marching down its front. I begin to breathe through my nostrils. "Oh my God," I say to my wife, "Mrs. Amberson, I love you . . ." I kiss Anne full on the lips, and she opens her mouth, and our tongues touch. Outside is a sound of flivvers, and a PVT interurban rumbles past, and it makes crackling noises, and for a moment the room is lighted by the reflection of its sparks. I fumble at the marching buttons, and I am able to feel the warmth of Anne's breasts. Lights reflect against the mirror over the dresser. They reflect pink and blue, and Anne's face is streaked with their shadows. I look around. I do not want the world to see any of this. I hurry to the windows and pull down the shades. Covering her mouth, Anne giggles. I return to her and hug her, and she whispers: "If that sisser of mine could only see me *now* . . . ah, that Chrissine, how she'd laugh an carry on . . . her an old Ed *both* of them . . ."

I nod. I kiss my bride. My attention returns to the buttons, and now I am in earnest, and Anne whispers: "Oh *my* . . . how *fresh* . . ."

"Yes indeed," I tell her.

"Well . . . two can can play at *that* game . . . an it makes it a better game, if ha you know what I mean . . ."

"What?"

Anne snickers. Her hands tug at the buckle of my belt.

Anne's snickering is softly laced with saliva. She has undone my belt, and now she unbuttons my fly. I unfasten all of her buttons, and the dress falls away. At the same time, my trousers drop to the floor, and Anne tugs my penis free of my underdrawers, and I suppose I am about to explode. "Oh dear," she whispers, "Anne is a hussy . . ." Gently she squeezes my penis, and I groan. I do hope the shades will not act up, and I do hope no horse will come calling. Now, her hands moving quickly, Anne unsnaps her brassiere, flings it away, then slips out of her shoes, hose and panties. "Lots of flesh for my husban," she whispers. "Lots of nice warm *flesh* . . ." She places both my hands on her breasts, and my thumbs manipulate her nipples, and she chuckles. Then, abruptly, she drops to her knees and helps me out of my shoes, stockings and garters. Her lips make kissing sounds, and she whispers: "Tonigh we see everything. Tonigh there will be no inneruptions. I love my husban. I love him oh dear a whole worl's worth . . ." Then, rising, pressing her crotch against my great quivering enthusiastic penis, she undoes my tie, unbuttons my shirt and unlocks my cufflinks. She helps me out of my shirt and undershirt and underdrawers, and now we both are as naked as we were the first day we saw light, and she presses her face against my neck and whispers: "I feel you. I feel you real good, an it's nice . . ." Her face is warm, and the floor is littered with our clothing, and our feet become entangled in it as we stumble to the bed. The blinds are behaving with splendid discretion, and there is not a horse in sight. We lie down side by side, and one of my hands cups her crotch, and I roll her to me, and I kiss her, and then I lick her breasts, and she whispers: "I'm . . . ah, I'm not afraid . . ." And I finger her, and she whispers: "Oh touch the lil bumpy place . . . the lil bumpy place, yes . . . I . . . oh my dear God . . . yes . . . *yes* . . ." And now she is stroking my penis, pulling back the foreskin and rubbing her thumb against the head, and then I utter a great shout and roll atop her, and she is damp and easy, and her breasts wobble and slap, and she claws my shoulders, and so I do not hesitate. I do not exactly know what I am doing, but whatever it is, I do not hesitate. I am twentyfour years of age and as virginal as a snowy morning, and by God it is about *time*. I pull her hand away from my penis. Then, grunting like the world's last great triumphant stallion and the savior of all fleshy delight, I shove inside her, and I pierce her in an instant, and she gushes, and I pump, and Anne pumps, and her nails rip the back of my neck, and now we are discovering bumpy places she never knew she had, and my breath is tight (it rubs the roof of my mouth and emerges from my nostrils, which are flared and twitching and most abundantly stallionish), and Anne's legs rise and lock themselves around the small of my back, and the great old bed roars and shudders, and oh yes, there are interurbans outside the windows; there are flivvers and lights and cats and straw hats and perfume and parents and brothers and silk stockings and oratory and nestling birds and telegrams and music and the wind and God's lovely abiding universe, *but who cares about those things? Who cares about any of it?* Now, right *now,* here within this glorious speck of finite time, I am working toward . . . toward . . . toward, ah sweet swaddled Christ . . . *toward* and *within* and *beyond* (unstopped and unstoppable and unstoppered), passing through in one immense burst that drenches my beloved's secret bloody chambers . . . *toward* and *within* and *beyond* the ultimate delicious agony of love, all of it clamorous and pompous and unutterably unique (after all these years of anticipation, I have a right to bathe in rhetoric and prolixity, don't I?), and so Anne and I are joined; our fluids mingle; we flop and swoon and laugh and gasp. The devil take all the interurban cars and all the nestling birds. We embrace and sprawl and investigate and stroke and kiss, and after a time she licks my ear and whispers: "This will last forever . . ."

"Yes . . ."

"We are different from other people . . ."

"Yes . . ."

"I don't feel tipsy any more . . . you sobered me up . . ."

"Good . . ."

"It didn't hurt . . ."

"I'm glad . . ."

Anne stares at me. "We will not wear out . . . maybe the rest of the world will wear out, but *we* won't . . ."

"Well," I tell her, "I'm game if you are . . ."

He had ugly dreams. He was with a doctor, and the doctor wore a mask, and he asked the doctor: What do they do with it? Throw it in the garbage? And the doctor said: Would you like it enshrined at Lourdes? And Amberson said: But it is more than *meat.* And the doctor said: Not any more it isn't. And Amberson said: But I kissed it and loved it. And the doctor said: But we had to remove it so we could save the rest of her. At her age, she had no particular use for it anyway. And Amberson said: That is a very cruel thing to say. And the doctor said: This is a cruel world, and after all, a breast is only a breast. Or, to use your word, it is only *meat.* And now Amberson was weeping, and he moved forward and tried to strike the doctor, but the doctor vanished, and then Amberson was running, and his throat was flooded, and he told himself: Fly, damn your eyes. *Fly.* Lose your feet. Lose this earth. Be footloose in the purest sense. See, by God, the sky, and the trees are like stilts that keep it from coming down, as Chicken Little has warned. No. Please. I do not really care for broasted chicken. The word sounds as though too much culinary fuss has been made over the poor fowl. (I shall awaken from all this totally unrefreshed. I am too old to be tormented in such a manner. What offense have I given?) And Amberson leaned over and rubbed his legs and feet, and Mr. Drummond from the Ohio High School Athletic Association smiled at him and told him he had every right to be proud as, ah, punch, and raindrops squiggled down Mr. Drummond's face. We are excellent mudders, said Amberson to his boys, and they all laughed, and Anne told him: For today, the world is yours, and I love you very much. And Amberson said: What about tomorrow? And, smiling, Anne said: Tomorrow, too. (She still had her figure, and Henry the Always Boy wrote regularly from overseas. She still created tightness in Amberson's belly, and men still looked at her admiringly at parties.) And Amberson saw Alice's breasts. He was on his hands and knees, and he was looking through the keyhole of her bedroom door, and she turned and smiled at the keyhole and cupped her breasts in her hands and waggled them at him. She was nude, and her pubic area was reddish. Would you like to come inside and chew on them a little? she said, winking at the keyhole, and so Amberson moaned, and Fred Suiter said to him: I'm going to grow up some day, and then they'll leave me alone, and you can write about the whole thing in that book of yours, and we'll both laugh. And Amberson embraced his friend Fred Suiter, but Fred Suiter was wearing no britches, and his rump was pink, and so Amberson ran away, and Lewis grinned handsomely at him and said: You didn't like what I *was,* but you never told me what I was *supposed* to be, and isn't that funny, huh? But, hell, that's all right. You're my father, and I love you, and if you want to speculate on Alice's breasts, be my guest. Be my breast guest, you might say, ha-ha. And the doctor said: It won't do any good to hit me. Done is done. And Amberson said: Just tell me what happened to it. Did it wind up in the garbage with the orange peels and the coffee grounds? And the doctor said: Correct. And again Amberson moaned, and someone was shouting at him something having to do with Arm A in Fig. I, and the warm rain had fogged his spectacles, and he had to keep swallowing so that his heart would not pop through his lips like an egg from a reluctant goose. And the Krapf boy grimaced into the speckled raindrop wind, and Anne said: I shall forever be lopsided.

See now 1944, and it all depends on a boy named Henry Krapf, who is running anchor for the Paradise Falls High School mile relay team. There is a misty rain in Columbus this June day, and the Allies landed in Normandy last week, and Frank Sinatra has the girls all agasp and aswoon, and the three top teams in the state meet are Columbus Northwest, with 38½ points, followed by Piqua, with 36, followed by Paradise Falls, with 32½, and a victory in the mile relay will win the championship for Paradise Falls, which once was a basketball stronghold but never has been known for its track teams.

I lean against a low wire fence, and I watch Henry Krapf as he takes the baton from a boy named Bobby Ganzenmueller, and the exchange is clean, with neither runner breaking stride (it is the sort of exchange one can find diagramed in the track & field manuals, with Arm A in Fig. 1 extended lefthanded, holding the baton tightly as shown in Fig. 2, firmly passing it to the backthrust Arm B shown in Fig. 3, with both runners moving in stride as per Fig. 4), and I never have seen a more precise baton exchange in all the years I have been coaching track, and so—even though I am normally quite impassive—on this particular occasion I forget myself and pound my palms together in one short frenzied burst. And my assistant, Bill Franks, who is standing next to me, claps me warmly on the back.

But Henry Krapf is beginning his anchor quartermile a good twelve or fifteen yards behind a tall Negro boy, the anchorman for Cleveland East Tech, traditionally a track powerhouse. I think of musculature, of timing and rhythm and stride, and I tell myself ah, God, no, this will not be the year. I glance at Bill Franks and I shake my head.

But Bill Franks will have none of it. Rain smears his face, and he wipes away some of the moisture, and he hollers: *"We're going to make it! By God, there's no doubt about it!"*

"I think you're wrong," I tell him, and I try to keep my voice down.

Bill Franks is about to say something, but then Bobby Ganzenmueller comes stumbling up to me (he lost perhaps ten yards for us), and I drape an arm around his shoulders. "You did a fine job," I say to him.

Bobby Ganzenmueller cannot look at me. His mouth is twisted, and he is hunched and gasping. "I . . . I did *shit,*" he says.

"Don't talk that way, young man," I tell him.

Choking, Bobby Ganzenmueller pulls away from me. He stumbles forward a few feet, then flops down on the wet grass.

"Hey!" hollers Bill Franks. *"Look at that!"* He points toward the runners.

Henry Krapf has begun to gain a little on the tall Negro. And Henry Krapf is churning. My tongue nudges a corner of my mouth, and my spectacles are fogged, and I am having difficulty with my breath. The tall Negro appears to be in some sort of trouble, and his stride is uneven. It is as though perhaps he has stumbled. And Henry Krapf keeps churning. But now the Negro boy regains his stride, and Henry Krapf is still a good three or four yards behind him. There is less than an eighth of a mile to go. Bobby Ganzenmueller gets to his feet and begins loping toward the finish line, his cleats kicking up clods of mud. He is making moaning sounds. Bill Franks and I trot behind him. My eyes are on Henry Krapf, and now he is nearly even with the Negro. "WOWEE!" yells Bill Franks, and Bobby Ganzenmueller's arms are flapping. There is now a little more than a hundred yards to go, and Henry Krapf's hands clutch at air, and he is even with the Negro, and yes, yes, all right, I know we shall win. It is obvious now, and only an act of the Almighty will deny it. And I slow to a walk, and I want to tell Bobby Ganzenmueller and Bill Franks and all the rest of my people all right, we have it; we have accomplished what we set out to do. And now Henry Krapf is flat even with the Negro, and they come pounding side by side toward the finish line, and their mouths are distended, and their arms are taut, and their legs are knotted (great God Almighty, how I love this sport!), and now Bobby Ganzenmueller and Bill Froelich and I and the rest of the Paradise Falls contingent are clustered at the finish line, and I see the East Tech coach beckoning to his boy, moving an arm in a grand and mighty scooping arched gesture and shouting to him: "All right now, Kenny! All right! ALL RIGHT!" But the man's gesture and his shouts are futile, and I know this, and it is now apparent that Henry Krapf has taken the lead. And so I, of all people, most uncharacteristically begin jumping up and down, and I do believe I am howling, and I do believe all the boys are howling, and I do believe Bill Franks is howling, and I see that some sort of moisture is leaking from Bobby Ganzenmueller's nostrils. And Henry Krapf is widening his lead, and he comes pumping toward the finish line, God save us all, with his eyes closed, hair streaming and shirttail wetly flapping, and he wins by five yards, and we swarm over him, and I say: "Yes. Yes indeed. Oh my."

The ugly lopsided dreams persisted, and Caroline said: It is better to talk to dolls than talk to nothing. We have made that determination, and we are convinced we are right. And please, the next time you go to the store, would you pick up some more Magic Gas? (She was smiling. Why was she smiling? Was she smiling because she had been resting in her grave for nearly fifty years while Amberson had been tormented by the affairs of the world? Was she mocking his survival? He wanted to ask her these questions, but a string had been drawn over his throat, and no words emerged.) Then came another masked doctor, and he said: Mr. Amberson, you must walk as though you are stepping on eggshells, and you must *never* under *any* circumstances do any *running*. And anyway, a man your age should have better sense. So relax. Look back on your life. Sum it up. Clear away the messy edges. Come to an understanding of why you have been here. And then the masked doctor removed his mask, and his face was vaguely familiar (was it somehow reminiscent of Henry's?), and he smiled, and he uttered a number of kindly benedictions, but Amberson never had heard of any of them. Be forever drewing, and may the lamplight of changeraps bless the porterfield of your quillums, said the doctor, holding up a benevolent hand and describing a number of circles, triangles, trapezoids and the like, not to mention trapeziums, arcs, squares, rectangles and whatnot. And now Amberson sniggered into his pillow, and Lewis threw a tennis ball at him, and the tennis ball struck his forehead, and Lewis laughed and said: Judge not, lest ye be judged. And Bernadette said: I am making no judgments. And Regina Ingersoll said: I am only asking a simple *question.* And Alvin Jr. said: I huffed and puffed a lot, didn't I? And Henry said: Who wants to stand outside and press his nose against a window all his life? And a large black man came belching out of the LEE ROAD HOUSE OF RIBS and said: You got to always watch out for the whores, or they'll come an take away your sacred honor, an that'd be a shame, right? And Alice said: Think of me as a chuckhole in the Highway of Life. And now came golden fields, and Amberson's legs were supple, and he ran with his brothers, and Caroline smiled at them, and it must have been the summer of perhaps 1912, and Amberson laughed, and his groin was full to bursting, and some day he would ride the great interurbans to the end of the world. Or perhaps he would run alongside them. Or perhaps he would pass them, scattering astonished motormen in his jubilant wake. Ah, how was it possible to live without such visions? He was no grub. He was no worm. He had visions, and he would not be destroyed. Some night, he told himself, Regina Ingersoll will ask me a terrible and profound question, and I must be prepared to answer it. I must cultivate my visions; I must not permit my ambition to wither. Great events are in store for me. I must be ready for them. (O hear the child within me! I must feed him! One day he will fly, and he must be strong!) Yes, said Scalisi, the child is there all right.

I won't deny it. He is a forever child, right? He never dies, right? (And Alice laughed.)

See now 1965, and I am sitting on a bench in the Elysian Park, and for some reason I am thinking of Barry Goldwater. It is a cloudy afternoon in late June, and I am thinking nothing *specific* about the man. I am simply conjuring his face and trying to remember the timbre of his voice—which is, as I recall, somewhat sharp but not highpitched. Somehow, when I saw him on television last fall and heard him give campaign speeches, I detected a vulnerability in his voice, and perhaps almost a kindliness. This is no doubt an absurd notion (after all, his warloving reputation certainly seems founded in a great deal of fact), but I have not been able to rid myself of it. And, beyond that, I am convinced I would like the man if I knew him. But of course I did not vote for him. I may be sentimental, but there are limits.

It is more than a mile from our place on Cumberland Street to the Elysian Park, and I walk here two or three times a week, when the weather is decent. (And occasionally, if I am sure no one is looking, I jog a bit. I have read that jogging is supposed to be good for one's heart, and at sixtyeight I am quite overpoweringly aware of my health. I am forever reading the medical-advice columns in the newspapers, and they all stress fitness and urge "programs of moderate exercise." Our physician, Frank Groh, is not altogether convinced that "programs of moderate exercise" will cure the ills of the world, but on the other hand he does not believe they are harmful—or at least too harmful. As he puts it, they are only "moderately" harmful, and then he laughs, claps me on the back and says: What the hell, Howard, how could we stand ourselves if we lived forever?)

This is Anne's day to shampoo and vacuum the carpeting, and she has thrown me out of the house. (Or is it vacuum and shampoo? Perhaps I have the order reversed.) I am wearing a dark suit, a white shirt and a narrow black tie that has gray polkadots. My shoes are shined, and my trousers are splendidly creased, and I am freshly bathed, and I glance at my hands folded in my lap, and they do not move (they have nothing to do, and so why should they move?), and I say to myself: It's a wonder you can stand the excitement.

It has been three years now since I retired, and I find that I am a great deal more interested in, say, Anne's garden than I ever was before. And the medical-advice columns in the newspapers. And gossip. And the weather. And gentle reminiscence. And television—

363

especially soap operas, to which I have become slavishly addicted. Yes, the admission must be made. One cannot deny the truth of one's vacant hours with Mike Karr and the other people who writhe, succumb, love and triumph on *The Edge of Night.* (Channel 10, 3:30 p.m., Monday through Friday.)

I like to think that I am waiting for something to happen. But what? And, at my age, to what purpose? At my age, shouldn't *Love of Life* (Channel 10, noon, Monday through Friday) and *The Doctors* (Channel 4, 2:30 p.m., Monday through Friday) provide enough, ah, thrills?

I sigh and look around. A little girl is sitting under a tree a few yards away. She has red hair, and she is perhaps ten, and she has plump pink legs. Her dress is white, decorated with processions of leaping brown monkeys. Their hands are joined. I can see that much. I really can. When I watch television, I sit clear across the room, and I see everything quite clearly. The heroine of *Love of Life,* whose character name is Vanessa Sterling, is a lovely blond woman named Audrey Peters, with a soft and subtle face, and I miss not a nuance. With each year, I become increasingly farsighted, and next thing you know, I shall have to sit out on the sidewalk in order to admire the splendid Miss Peters.

The little girl is reading a book. She looks up.

I look away from her. I did not mean to attract her attention. I remove my spectacles, fish a handkerchief from a pocket and begin to polish the lenses. I do not mean to attract anyone's attention. What could I have to say that would be of any earthly use to *anyone,* let alone a quiet little girl who probably only wants to read her book in peace?

She closes the book and comes toward me. "Hi," she says. "I know you."

I blink at her. "You do?"

"Yes," she says. She is not smiling. She seats herself next to me on the bench. She places the book on her lap, and she folds her hands over its cover. "You are the Mayor's daddy," she says.

"That's absolutely correct—but how do you know?"

Now the little girl smiles. "That's for me to know and you to find out," she says.

I finish polishing the lenses and return the spectacles to my nose. I decide I might as well smile, too. "I bet you like to play games, don't you?"

"Yes," she says.

"Which ones?"

"Jacks. Hopscotch. Basketball. Makebelieve."

"Basketball?"

"Yes," she says. She still is smiling. Her teeth are tiny. I have forgotten how tiny are the teeth of children. I suppose I have forgotten most things about children. Well, perhaps she will refresh my memory. "I can shoot baskets better than anyone in my gym class. I can shoot them from fifteen feet away. Miss Mannering says I am a regular Jerry West."

"Well, good for you."

"But I like makebelieve better. I like makebelieve best of all."

"A great many people do."

"If I want to be Jerry West, I can be Jerry West. If I want to be, uh, Jackie Kennedy, I can be Jackie Kennedy. That's makebelieve, and it's the best fun of all."

"Do you have a favorite makebelieve person?"

"Yes—but I won't tell you who it is."

"Please. I wish you would. Won't you reconsider?"

"If I told you, then you'd laugh," says the girl, frowning.

"No. I won't," I tell her. "I promise I won't."

"Lick a nigger's ass if you do?"

"What did you say, young lady?"

She turns her face away. "I shouldn't of said that. My mama gets mad at me when I talk like that." She unfolds her hands, plucks at her skirt. "I . . . well, I heard it from my brother. His name is Jimmy, and he talks real bad all the time. He taught me to say it when I was a real little girl and didn't know better. He was being funny, I guess. I keep trying to stop. Honest. I keep trying and trying. And I'm a whole lot better now than I used to be. I mean, used to be I'd say lick a nigger's ass ten twenty zillion times a day."

"It is a very nasty thing to say."

"Yes," says the girl.

"You seem strong enough to break yourself of the habit. All you have to do is concentrate on not letting the words slip out. And anyway, that's what life *is*, to a large extent."

The girl looks at me. "What?"

"Life is concentration," I tell her. I fold my arms across my midsection. I feel more than a little oracular and pompous, but the feeling is not unpleasant. God strike me dead, it is not unpleasant at all. "We cannot always do exactly what we *want* to do," I say to the girl. "Instead, we must do what is *right*, and even when the right thing is not easy. This sort of behavior is known as *discipline*, and it requires great concentration. And it means we cannot blurt out dirty hurtful things that add to the hatred and misery in the world."

"Mister?"

"Yes?"

"Do you talk like that all the time?"

"Yes. I'm afraid so."

"Doesn't it make you tired?"

I smile, and now I do not have to force it. "No," I say. "It makes the people who *listen* to me tired, but it does not make *me* tired."

"I think you talk nice."

"Thank you."

"You a teacher?"

"I was. I'm retired now."

"What's 'retired' mean?"

"It means you've stopped doing what you've always done. It means you're old and the world says go take a rest, go sit on a bench in the Elysian Park and talk with a nice little girl who has monkeys on her dress."

"It mean like you're worn out?"

"Well, yes . . . not to make too fine a point of it . . ."

"You feel worn out?"

"Sometimes."

"You don't *look* worn out. You look sort of nice."

"I do?"

"Yes," says the girl. She blinks at me. "You look like you wouldn't hurt a thing. I bet you were a good teacher in your day."

"Well, perhaps I was. In my day."

"I didn't mean that to sound bad. If it did, I'm sorry."

"That's all right," I tell the girl. "No harm done."

"If you want to know who my favorite makebelieve person is, I'll tell you."

"You trust me now?" I ask her.

"Yes," she says, nodding.

"All right then, I'd like to know."

"It's . . . ah, well . . . Ringo Starr, that's who it is . . ."

"Ringo Starr? Really?"

"You know who Ringo Starr is?"

"Of course I know who Ringo Starr is. I have seen him on the Ed Sullivan Show. He is the drummer with the Beatles. Now, tell me, why is he your favorite makebelieve person?"

"Guess."

"I can't—unless perhaps because he is so loved by so many people."

The girl's eyes widen. "That's it," she says.

"Oh?"

"Yes," says the girl. "You're the first person who's ever guessed it right."

"Really? The first person?"

"The first person in the whole world."

"Would you like to tell me how you arrived at Ringo Starr?"

"I love all the Beatles, but he's the homeliest, so I love him best."

"Oh. I see."

"You do?" the girl asks me.

"Yes," I tell her. "Absolutely."

"He's the homeliest, but everybody loves him anyway, so he's my favorite makebelive person. Every day he says to the world: Look at me, I'm homely, but you love me anyway, and I deserve it."

"He does?"

"Sure he does. He ever kill anybody?"

"No."

"He just beats on the drums, that's all he does. He doesn't hurt anybody, and like I said, he doesn't kill anybody. So . . . well, what I do is, sometimes I close my eyes, and I hear the whole world screaming happy screams, you know?"

"Happy screams?"

"Yes," says the girl. She closes her eyes. She smiles. "Like now. Like now, auld chap, I'm Ringo Stahh, don't you know, hip hip, and I say to you be happy, and go ahead and scream all the happy screams you want to scream, auld sock, because if they make you feel better, how can they be bad? I want to hold your hand . . . boo, boo . . . hold your hand . . ." She opens her eyes. The smile remains. "Just now I was Ringo Starr, you know that?"

"Yes. And I could almost hear the happy screams."

"You think I'm crazy?"

"If you are, then more people should be crazy."

She glances down. "My book is crazy," she says. "I love it, but it's crazy." She holds the book, and I see that it is a copy of *The Wizard of Oz*.

"That book isn't crazy," I tell her. "It's fun." I like this little girl very much. She reminds me of Florence at that age.

The girl appears to be pondering all the topics touched in our conversation. She wriggles a bit, hugs the book to her chest and finally says: "You want to know what my name is?"

"Yes, please. If it's not a secret."

"It's not a secret. My name is Patty Spire. Spire like on a church.

S-P-I-R-E. We live on High Street, and my daddy works at the plating company. We used to live in Zanesville, the home of the famous Y bridge. You ever seen the famous Y bridge?"

I nod. "I've seen it."

"You like it?"

I nod. "I think it is grand."

"You don't think it's dumb?"

"No. Of course not."

The girl nods. "Neither do I." She times her nodding with mine. She giggles. "We'll give ourselves headaches," she says.

"Well, if we do, it will be in a good cause."

"You like talking to me?" the girl wants to know. Now she is not nodding; she is squinting a little, and she has placed a hand on my arm.

"I like it just fine," I tell her. "You are a splendid conversational companion."

"Thank you."

"You're very welcome."

She squeezes my arm. "You look nice."

"I do?"

"Yes. Your suit's real neat, and you smell like you took a bath this morning."

"Well, as a matter of fact, I did."

"I wish my daddy looked so neat."

"Now, I don't think you should criticize your father. You must remember that *I* am retired, and therefore I have more time for baths and such things. Your father is no doubt a very busy man."

"Does busy mean you have to smell funny all the time?"

I do not have the vaguest idea what to say.

The girl removes her hand from my arm. "I love him and all that, but sometimes he smells funny."

"Sometimes all of us smell funny. Especially if we've been working hard so we can have the money to buy monkey dresses for our little girls."

"Oh," says the girl. She looks down at her dress. "Okay. Maybe you're right."

"Thank you."

She hugs her book. She begins swinging her legs back and forth. They dangle plumply over the edge of the bench. Finally she says: "It's my mama who told me about you. We saw you one day on Main Street, and she said: 'Patty, that's the Mayor's father.' And she told me she knew you, and she said you were a nice man."

"She knows me?"

"Yes. She was born in Paradise Falls. That's why we're living here now. She wanted to come home. My daddy is from Zanesville, but Mama wanted to come home, so here we are. He sold real estate in Zanesville, but now he's working for the plating company, and I don't think he likes it too much. But Mama came down hard on him. It was two years ago, and she told him she was homesick, and so, like I said, here we are."

"Paradise Falls isn't really all that bad, is it?"

"No. To tell you the truth, it makes me think of Zanesville."

I smile. "That's a good answer," I tell her.

"Direct and to the point—that's me," she says. She still swings her legs.

"How does your mother know me?"

"She's never said."

"What was her name before she was married?"

"Soeder. Ruth Soeder."

I nod. "Ruth Soeder. I remember a Ruth Soeder. Tall, with dark hair, am I correct?"

"Yes."

"She was a pupil of mine. About fifteen years ago."

"Maybe so."

"There are a great many Soeders in Paradise Falls, and I had a great many of them as pupils, but I do remember Ruth Soeder. When you see her, please give her my regards."

"All right."

"She was quite pretty, as I recall."

"She's still pretty. Everybody says so. And she's still tall, and her hair's still dark. She's not homely like me."

"You're not homely," I tell the girl. "You're pretty."

"My brother says I'm homely. He says my hair looks like something a baboon threw up."

"Well, don't you believe him. You have very pretty hair."

"Would a baboon throw up hair?"

"I doubt it."

"So do I," says the girl. "But then Jimmy likes to lay it on with a spoon, you know what I mean?"

"Yes, I believe I do."

Now the girl's legs have stopped swinging. She glares at me. "I don't like it when people lie to me," she says. "My hair looks like something a baboon threw up."

"Young lady, you are not homely, and that's all there is to it. Don't keep feeling sorry for yourself that way. If you do, you are only creating a problem where none exists. I know what pretty is, and when I say you are pretty, then *you are pretty,* and I'll thank you not to contradict me. Now then, let's talk about something else."

"You're not lying to me?"

"I'm not lying to you."

"How does a person go about measuring pretty?"

I link my fingers over my belly. "Well, ah, pretty is a general impression one person has of another. You look at someone and you say to yourself: My goodness, there is a pretty person. It comes to you in a flash, and it's not as though you have to take a ruler and a compass and measure it. It is either there or it is not there, and you can see it right away."

"Okay. You say I'm pretty. Did it come to you in a flash?"

"Yes. I looked at you while you were sitting over there by that tree; I looked at you and I said to myself: My goodness, there is a pretty person. And those are the exact words that went through my mind."

"Honest?" says the girl, her voice dubious.

"Yes."

"Hope to die?"

"Hope to die."

She tugs at her lower lip. She stares at me, frowns. "You feel yourself starting to die?"

"No."

"You don't feel sick?"

"Not a bit."

"Not even a little teeny bit?"

"Not even a little teeny bit. What are you trying to do? Talk me into it?"

She smiles. "No," she says. "I just wanted to make sure you were telling the truth. You really honest mean it, don't you?"

I sigh. My hands unlace. I rub my face. "Yes," I say. "I honest mean it, and I hope you finally understand that."

"I do . . . and I thank you . . ."

"Think nothing of it."

She slides closer to me and kisses me on a cheek. Her lips are moist and warm. "Thank you a whole lot," she says.

I look away from her for a moment or two. I rub my cheek, and finally I am able to say: "That felt good. I appreciate it."

"I meant it. I always mean it when I kiss someone. You want another one?"

"Yes—if you're of a mind."

"I'm of a mind," says the girl, giggling. This time the kiss is more firm, and it is quite loud. She pulls back from me and she says: "That was an extra special one."

"I know. I could tell."

"My loud ones are my extra special ones. The louder they are, the more extra special they are. And if they hurt my ears, they're the most extra special of them all."

"Did that one hurt your ears?"

"Yes."

"I am very flattered."

"Well," says the girl, "you ought to be." Her voice is solemn.

I look directly at her. I chuckle and lean forward. I press my hands against my legs and I say: "You're the nicest thing that has happened to me since I-don't-know-when. Are you always nice to people? I hope so. If you are, then you are much nicer than the ordinary person one meets in a park."

"I don't want to be an ordinary person."

"Well, you're not."

"Did you like it when you were a kid?"

I study her, and her face is as solemn as her voice. The question has come from nowhere, but apparently it means something to her, and perhaps it means a great deal to her. There is something further she wants from me, something beyond the simple reassurances that she is indeed pretty, that she has a nice kiss, and that she is perhaps more than an ordinary person. It is a serious question, and therefore I must give it a serious answer. I must not belittle it. I think for a moment. I breathe deeply, and I try to remember how the air tasted when I was a child, and then I say: "Yes, I do believe I did. And very much."

"I thought so."

"You did?"

"Yes," she says. "You talk to me like you don't hold it against me because I'm a kid. And you talk to me like you're not trying to spell out things on your fingers. Some grownups, *most* grownups, when they talk to me, it's one, two, three, do you follow me, Patty? Is it too complicated, Patty? Do you want me to make it simple, like it's pie maybe? How you doing, Patty? You following along okay? You get the drift of it, Patty?" Here she hesitates. She holds up a hand with the fingers open. She squeezes them one by one and she says: "Tick. One. Tick. Two. Tick, tick, tick. Three and four and five. When most grownups talk to me, it's like I'm so dumb I got to have everything ticked for me." Another hesitation. This time she smiles.

"But you're different," she says. "And so tell me, when you were a little kid, what was the favorite thing you liked to do? Was it talk? Was it sit and blab with the other kids?"

I chuckle again. "No," I say, "the sit-and-blab came later."

"Then what was it? I want to know the favorite thing you liked to do. The most favorite thing of them all. Was it read books?"

"No, it was not sit-and-blab, and it was not the reading of books. It was running."

"Like running a race?"

"Yes."

"How come?"

"You mean how come I liked it?"

"Yes," says the girl. "That's what I mean, right on the bean. And I'm a poet and don't know it."

"You are indeed," I tell her.

"So tell me. Why was running your favorite thing?"

"Well, because I was good at it, quick on my feet if I do say so myself. Quick and nimble. And because it made me feel important —at least to myself."

The girl squints. "What?"

"It made me feel very large. I actually thought that some day my feet would sprout wings and I would take off like a zeppelin."

"Like a what?"

"Like a zeppelin, which is a big bag of gas. Have you ever heard of the Goodyear blimp?"

"I think so. Don't they show the Goodyear blimp sometimes when there's a football game on TV?"

"Yes. That is the Goodyear blimp. And it's rather like a zeppelin, which was named after a German aristocrat, if I remember my history correctly. Well, *anyway,* I used to run and run and run, and it made me feel *grand* and *free* and *large* . . ."

"But you don't run any more?"

"I'm afraid I'm too old."

She motions toward a grassy field that spreads in front of us. It leads to the river. "Would you like me to run for you?"

I look at the girl.

"I mean it," she says, nodding. "When it comes to athletics, I can do more than shoot baskets. I'm a pretty good runner, too."

I do not know what to say. How does one respond to this sort of thing? I smile at the girl, and my mind is vacant. And then, like a slap, a sort of notion comes to me. It is ridiculous and probably dangerous, but I know immediately that I shall yield to it, and the devil take the absurdity and the danger. This little girl has made a splendid gesture, and I cannot remember when I last encountered such gallantry. I must respond to it in kind. And so, understanding all this, I say to her: "Perhaps we can run together."

"You mean it?" she asks me. Her eyes are immense, and she claps her hands. They make a dry brisk sound, like a pair of small flat stones.

"Yes," I say. "If you promise not to run too fast, perhaps I can trot along with you. I have been led to believe that moderate exercise is good for people my age." I stand up. I flex my knees a bit. They do not feel particularly stiff. I smile down at the girl.

She comes down off the bench. "The field out there?" she asks me. She points.

"The field looks fine," I say to her.

"Can I hold your hand?"

"I would be delighted."

She comes to me and squeezes my left hand with her right hand. I return the squeeze, and then we begin to trot forward, this little girl and I. She holds her book with her other hand, and we move easily, and I try to time my breathing with my stride. My knees and legs feel more resilient than I have any right to expect. The girl scuttles beside me, and she is laughing a little. I say to myself: Who is old other than those who seek to be old? Old is a state of mind. Old is nothing.

My mouth is open, and the air is damp, and the grass is a green smear, and my vision is awash in it. I am wearing my spectacles, and they are a bit loose, which makes them bounce against the bridge of my nose, and so I remove them and stuff them in a pocket without even bothering to slide them in their case, which is in an inside pocket of my jacket and far too unimportant to occupy even a corner of my attention at this particular time, what with this girl and her splendid gesture, what with the fine green air that curls around me and parts itself, making way for my stride, and so we move smartly along, this gallant little girl and I, and I smile at her, and I pick up the pace, and she flings back her head, and her hair flaps and bounces, and she laughs, and I laugh (her soprano nicking and edging my uneven baritone), and the grass is springy and damp, and now my free hand is in a fist, and wouldn't it be something if at this late date God reached down and finally affixed the wings to my feet? Would I or would I not be the rage of Paradise Falls? An old geezer of sixtyeight coming up with winged feet—goodness!

And now this is more than the desultory jogging that I have recently been trying. And it is more than "moderate exercise." It is at once a quest and a challenge, and this little girl and I have come together in a way that is terrific and profound and shatteringly joyous, and so vex not my thoughts with talk of silliness and romantic posturing. This little girl has asked me a question. She has asked me what I was. And I am showing her. And her laughter tells me she understands what she is seeing. I may not be the rage of Paradise Falls, but right now I am perhaps the rage of her spirit, and I know it to be a gallant spirit, and so I rejoice.

The little girl's hand is tight in mine, and her laughter whirls and swoops, and the grass and the sky bounce against one another, and now my mouth hangs open and my tongue is exposed, and now we are not *jogging,* and we are not *trotting;* we are *running,* and would Henry Krapf be proud of me or would he not be proud of me? Perhaps I shall yet be the rage of Paradise Falls—goodness! I stumble and flail, but the little girl's tight hand keeps me from losing my balance, and the monkeys dance and flap, and her laughter sends me forward (now it is a whistling sort of laughter, and much of it comes from her nostrils, and I wonder whether Ringo Starr can laugh that freely and well), and now, yes, when it comes, when the great hammer comes (and I know it surely must come), when it smites my chest and makes my eyes feel as though they have been drowned in blood, I almost welcome it. I groan deliriously, and I fall as though I have been struck on the head by the trunk of a tree (I see briefly Ernest and his bizarre death), and I roll on my back, and my legs twitch. My hands jerk and pluck, and the little girl kneels next to me and tells me she will run to get someone to help, and the pain is as pure and crisp as ice cream against a bad tooth. (It is the first of my heart attacks, and Frank Groh does not hesitate to call me a lunatic. He saves me, but he tells me he does not know how he did it. He says something to the effect that God must love small children and old fools. I tell him he is absolutely correct. I am in the hospital two weeks, and Anne forever fusses over me, and it is all quite pleasant. Patty Spire and her mother visit me, and Patty gives me a bouquet of flowers she has picked herself. Her mother, a striking woman with dark hair, appears to have aged little since the days when she was Ruth Soeder and a pupil of mine. She tells me she is sorry her daughter put me up to the running. I smile and assure her it was a good thing. She frowns but does not pursue the matter. Patty kisses me on a cheek when they leave. It is a splendidly loud kiss, and I am flattered. I still see Patty Spire from time to time. She is sixteen now,

374

and her figure is full, and her hair is brilliant, and she just may be the prettiest girl in Paradise Falls.)

That day, a Thursday, began brightly, with no clouds. Amberson had forgotten to draw the shades, and so the sunlight awakened him, and it was nearly nine in the morning, and his first thought was: My Lord, what do I want to do? Sleep my life away?

He rubbed his cheeks and his forehead. The dreams had tired him, as he had known they would, even when he was dreaming them. He only vaguely remembered what they had been about, but he did remember that most of them had frightened him, and so he did not try to bring them back. He glanced at Anne, and she was awake. She was staring at the ceiling. "Well," he said, "good morning."

She did not reply. Her arms were folded across her stomach, and Sinclair lay across her knees.

"Hello?" said Amberson.

"Hello," said Anne.

"Are you all right?"

"No. I'm not all right."

"Is it the pain?"

"Yes."

"You should have taken your medication last night."

"I knew you would say that. I knew you would wake up and say just that. I would have bet my life on it."

"Do you want your medication now?"

"No."

"Then what can I do for you?" he asked her.

"Just talk to me. You were dreaming last night, weren't you?"

"Yes."

"What about?"

"All sorts of things. Fragments. I don't remember them exactly."

"Was I in them?"

"Yes."

"Was I young or old or happy or sad or what?"

"I can't remember," said Amberson.

Anne glanced at him. Her face was gray. "I don't want to frighten you, but I believe I'm dying." She spoke easily, casually, and she reached toward him and squeezed his wrist, and then she said: "My Lord, I really don't want it to happen. I have no courage, do you know that? None whatever. Can you imagine? After all these years, still no courage. I . . ." And then Anne wept, and her husband embraced her, and the sound of her grief and fear was fragile, like broken sticks.

See now 1947, a warmly green and spangled afternoon in early May, and my classroom windows are all open, and a boy named Ralph Jewitt has allowed as how all the dying in *Hamlet* is plain silly. "Just absolutely dumb," he says, glancing defiantly around the room.

"What do you mean?" I ask him.

Ralph Jewitt is a heavyset boy with poor teeth. He is somewhat nearsighted, and he wears corduroy trousers that whistle when his thighs rub together. He says: "Everybody dies except Horatio. That's not true to life. It's not true to anything. Shakespeare didn't know what to do with all his people, so he killed them off. It's real simple that way, and it gets you out of a . . . of a whatchamacallit . . . a predicament . . ."

"Does anyone have an answer for Ralph?" I am leaning against my desk, and my arms are folded, and I smile at the pupils. This is a group of juniors, and a rather good group. It is perhaps the best English 302 class I have had in ten years. Its members actually seem to enjoy asking questions, which is quite unusual in this earnest and humorless postwar age. (Sometimes I wish there were more dissatisfaction. I really do. Or at least more of a willingness to question values. But the war obviously was fought to preserve and protect things as they are, and most of these kids seem completely committed to the blandly unquestioning rhythm of their times. But not this particular group. Perhaps a lively discussion will come from Ralph Jewitt's complaint. I certainly hope so.)

Charlotte Krapf (a younger sister of my legendary anchor runner, Henry Krapf) raises her hand. She is a sharpfeatured blond girl with beautiful long legs and a fine curved bosom, but she always sits with her knees pressed together, and her mouth is forever too tight. She has few friends, and she seldom says a word, and so I am surprised that she has raised her hand.

Quickly, before she changes her mind, I smile at her and say: "Yes, Charlotte. What is it?"

She speaks softly. "Mister Amberson, Ralph talks about . . ."

"I'm sorry, Charlotte. We can't hear you. Could you speak up a little?"

She scratches a shoulder, and I hear someone whisper, and I am able to make out one of the words, and it is Tits. I look around the room, but it is impossible to tell who did the whispering. All faces are blank. If Charlotte heard the word, she gives no indication.

Clearing her throat, she starts again, and now she is speaking more loudly, and she says: "Mister Amberson, Ralph talks about *Hamlet* not being true to life. Well, does it *have* to be? I mean, does it have to be *measured out* like a . . . well, like a formula in chemistry?"

"I'm sorry," I tell Charlotte, "but I'm afraid I don't quite follow you."

Quickly she nods. "Yes. All right. I know that." Her lips are pressed tightly against her teeth, and then she says: "I mean, it all came out of Shakespeare's *imagination,* didn't it? So why does it have to be true to life? I mean, is a *symphony* true to life?"

I look at Ralph Jewitt. "Can you answer that?"

He shrugs. "No," he says. "I don't even know what she's talking about."

Laughter. Charlotte blushes. A boy named Jimmy Van Zandt scratches his crotch and makes a flapping horsy sound with his lips.

I smile at Jimmy Van Zandt. "You apparently have some sort of opinion. Please share it with us."

Jimmy has been lounging at his desk. Now he sits up straight. "Ah, well, no," he says, "I . . . ah, I got no opinion."

"I'm afraid I don't believe that," I tell him. "When one flaps one's lips, it means one has an opinion. Either that, or one is losing his grip."

More laughter. Jimmy Van Zandt is a skinny little chap with red hair, and he is considered to be something of the class clown. But he certainly is harmless enough. He never has been more than a mild disciplinary problem, and I rather like him. Now, grinning a little, he folds his hands on his desk and says: "No, Mister Amberson, I got no opinion at all. I guess that means I'm losing my grip, but it's the God's truth."

"You have no opinion on death?"

"No."

"Do you ever think about it?"

"No."

Still smiling, I look around the room. "Does anybody here think about it?"

They all stare back at me.

"Well?" I ask them.

Not a hand is raised. Not Ralph Jewitt's. Not Charlotte Krapf's. Not anyone's.

"We'll all live forever, correct?" I say to them.

Smiles. Frowns. Here and there a look of vague apprehension. A boy named Donald Chappell picks at some loose skin on a thumb. Charlotte Krapf presses her palms against her cheeks.

"What is the main theme of *Hamlet?*" I ask them. "Is it death?"

Ralph Jewitt shakes his head no.

"All right, Ralph," I say to him, "then what is it?"

He looks at me. "Revenge?"

"Anyone else have any other ideas?" I ask the class.

Charlotte Krapf raises her hand.

"Yes, Charlotte?"

"Love?" she says. "He loved his father so much that maybe it made him go a little bit off his, ah, trolley?"

"In other words, first was the love, then came the desire for revenge, and then came all the dying?"

"Yes," says Charlotte.

"Which makes dying third in the order of importance?"

"Yes," says Charlotte.

I look at Ralph Jewitt. "Do you have anything to say to that?"

Ralph Jewitt frowns. He rubs his front teeth with the side of a finger. "I, ah, I never said the play was about dying. All I said was, the dying wasn't true to life."

"True to life dying. Is that something like true to death living?"

Mild laughter. Ralph Jewitt squirms a little.

I smile. "Ralph, I'm not trying to embarrass you. I'm only trying to make the same point Charlotte was trying to make. And she did a good job of it, incidentally. Do you have any idea what that point is?"

Ralph Jewitt's head slowly moves from side to side. He squints at me.

"Does the word 'emotions' give you any sort of clue?" I ask him.

Ralph Jewitt's squinting persists, and he still says nothing.

I glance at Charlotte. "Would you say that Shakespeare was interested in facts the way a journalist is interested in facts?"

"No," says Charlotte, speaking quickly.

"Would you say then he was interested in emotions?"

"Yes."

Now I again look at Ralph. "Do you agree?"

"Me?"

"Yes. You."

He folds his arms across his chest. "Yeah. I guess so."

"Then it follows, doesn't it, that he didn't care about being true to life?"

Ralph rubs his mouth. "But if he's not true to life, how are we supposed to believe any of it? If there's nothing in it we can, ah, recognize, why should we care?"

I smile. "Because it all comes to us through the sensibility of a genius." I hesitate for a moment, and Ralph is blinking at me, and then I say: "After all, if we want to know the *facts* of death, we can consult a medical journal, isn't that so? But *those things* didn't interest our friend Mister Shakespeare. It was the human heart that interested him, the agony of one man whose weakness was that he thought too much, that he weighed alternatives too long and therefore let his dilemma get out of hand. So all right. I'll grant you that all the dying is unrealistic and even a little silly, but what difference does it make? And anyway, to get back to your original point, what do any of us know of death? We have just admitted that we almost never consider it. Therefore, if we are ignorant of it, how can we accuse Shakespeare of not being realistic? Where do we get our expert knowledge? But, on the other hand, we *have* known love, correct? And the desire for revenge, correct? And so does Hamlet. And I believe in the character Shakespeare has created. I believe Hamlet to be a very human and very real man. And so, in that sense, I see him as being very true to life. And so are most of the other characters, including his mother and even Polonius. And it seems to me that if the people are real, then the play is real. So what I ask is—consider *Hamlet* in terms of those emotions we all recognize. And allow the play simply to *happen* to you. As Charlotte has pointed out, it is not a chemistry formula, and if we think of it that way, we are missing the point."

Ralph Jewitt has raised his hand.

I nod at him. (I am a bit breathless. Perhaps I have talked too much. It is a not uncommon occurrence with me.)

"All right, Mister Amberson," says Ralph, nodding. "All right, so maybe there are some things we can recognize, but if the . . . ah, the *framework* is dumb, doesn't that take away some of the truth? If the *people* are true but the *things they do* are silly, doesn't that take away some of the . . . ah, some of the value?"

"A good point," I say.

"Ah," says Ralph, grinning a little.

"However . . ." I say.

Laughter. Ralph squirms.

I hold up a hand. "Now everybody please calm down," I say to the class. "I was not trying to belittle Ralph. I simply want to add a point of my own. Now then, as you know, I am an extremely elderly sort of fellow, and that means I have experienced a great deal—or at least I *think* I have. And if there's one thing I feel I know, it is the absolutely aimless nature of most human behavior.

Or, to put it another way, the absolutely aimless nature of most human events. So who is really to say that none of the events could have happened? Has anyone here ever heard of a man named Gavrilo Princip?"

Jimmy Van Zandt grins, raises his hand. "Yeah," he says.

"All right," I tell him, "let's have a little information about the man."

"A little is all you're going to get," says Jimmy.

More laughter. "Well," I say, "a little is better than none at all, so kindly proceed."

"Well," says Jimmy, "I think he was the guy who killed Archduke Ferdinand and started the First World War."

I am impressed. "That is absolutely correct," I tell him. "Sometimes you honestly surprise me."

Jimmy beams. Applause. Laughter. He clenches his hands together and holds them over his head, like a prizefighter.

I hold up my hands for silence, and the noise dies away. I turn to Ralph Jewitt. "Do you have any idea why I brought up that name?"

He hesitates. Then, frowning, he says: "I think so . . ."

"All right. Tell me."

"Ah," says Ralph, "from what the guy did, a big war came. He kills the Archduke, and Austria declares war on Serbia, and Russia declares war on Austria, and Germany declares war on Russia, and France declares war on Germany, and away we go. I had the same history course with Jimmy, and it was only last year, and I remember it pretty good. And the reason you bring up the guy is because you're trying to show that history can be just as silly as all the dying that takes place in *Hamlet.*"

I smile. I am genuinely pleased. "Excellent," I say. "Excellent."

Ralph continues. "A little guy nobody heard of kills someone, and then millions of people die, and he's the one who started it, and it doesn't make a bit of sense . . ."

"Exactly."

"And that's supposed to be a way of . . . ah, *accepting* the way the people die in *Hamlet?*"

"Yes. And now can you?"

"No," says Ralph.

I laugh. I cannot help it. And everyone else laughs with me. I throw up my arms. It is hopeless and foolish, this discussion, and we all know it. This splendid spring afternoon is a green and spangled glory, and what else really is important? I let them laugh for a time, then I hold up my hands, silence them and finally say to them: "All right. All right. I surrender. I suppose all I'm really asking is that you try to examine the play with something approaching an open mind. That's called 'suspension of disbelief.' It's a longwinded and pompous way of saying: Let it happen. Let it take you along. Some of you are able to do this, and others are not. But, if you *are* able to do it, perhaps somehow you will be enriched; perhaps you will gain some sort of knowledge that might be helpful some day. And that's *really* what this conversation has been all about—suspension of disbelief."

Ralph Jewitt raises his hand. "That mean forgetting the grain of salt?"

"Yes. Exactly."

"And that's what you got to do when you read a book or see a play or a movie or whatever?"

"Yes. Do you think you are able to do that—or at least in this case, as a favor to Mister Shakespeare?"

"That means forgetting about all the dumb dying?" Ralph asks me.

"Yes."

"Oh," he says. "Okay."

"Does the 'okay' mean you'll try?"

Smiling a little, Ralph Jewitt nods.

In 1952, Ralph Jewitt is graduated from Ohio University with honors in English. Today, in 1971, he is a full professor of English at Northwestern University, and he drops in on us whenever he comes home to visit his parents. He insists on telling me I am responsible for his career as an academic. His specialty is the Bloomsbury Group, and he is said to be a distinguished authority on Virginia Woolf. He has written three books having to do with that lady. I have not read them, nor have I read Virginia Woolf. But then I have never climbed the Matterhorn either. Nor have I ever played defensive tackle for the Chicago Bears. One life can only encompass so much, and those particular manifestations of the apparatus I must leave for others to explore. Still, it is rather pleasant to know that Ralph Jewitt insists on giving me credit for propelling him into a scholarly career. He is a nice fellow, even though he does smoke too much and his breath is often quite foul. He has been married, incidentally, three times, and so there must be more energy to him than his somewhat avuncular academic manner reveals at, ah, first blush. (Do I have any choice but to call him *nice*? After all, he *likes* me. What should I do? Despise him? Call him a pompous fraud? No sir. Not on your sweet life. If he wants to clasp my hand warmly and tell me what a fine specimen of the human race I am, I say let him. And may he flourish until the sky falls down.)

As for the mildly obstreperous Jimmy Van Zandt, I have no idea what has happened to him. The last I heard (which was about 1961 or '62), he was operating a chain of drycleaning establishments somewhere up around Newark or Mount Vernon. At the time, it was my understanding that they were not doing too well. If this is true, it certainly is understandable . . . to me, at least. I simply cannot summon the image of Jimmy Van Zandt and a steam mangle.

I do see Charlotte Krapf quite often. She is married to a man named Henry Haskins, who works at the Western Electric store. She is much lovelier than she was as a young girl, even though she has put on a great deal of weight. She has been a mother nine times, but only four of her children are still alive here in 1971. The other five were killed in 1963 near Latrobe, Pennsylvania. They were passengers in a bus that was taking them to a Lutheran youth camp. The road was slippery from a summer rain, and the bus missed a curve and rolled over an embankment. It exploded, and twentyfour children, plus the driver, were killed. Only three children survived, and I seem to recall that they all were severely maimed. But today, when one meets Charlotte Krapf Haskins, she is charming. Do you understand that? Charming. There is a warm and motherly panache to her, and one always is aware of her teeth, which are still quite fine. It is said that she has had many love affairs since 1963, but I would not know about that. All I do know is that somehow she frightens me. She does not even object to discussing her five dead children. The last time I saw her, she sat with me on a bench in front of the court house and she told me all about the new headstones for which she and her husband were saving their money. "They will be simple," she said. "Simple but impressive, if you know what I mean. The thing is, we want the world to know that we were loving parents. This is very important to us. It makes it all worthwhile, if you know what I mean." And, as Charlotte spoke, she patted me on a knee with a warm hand. And her eyes were creamy. I suppose I can believe the love affairs. I suppose I can believe anything. There is a word for the way she is behaving these days. Perhaps the word is dysfunction. Or, at the very least, retreat. And now, whenever I see her, I mourn— as much for her as for those five dead children. If she has lovers, what do you suppose she discusses with them? Tombstones and rightness? The corruption of death into some vile and pious proclamation? Oh, my God. She is plump, yes, but she is very beautiful, and she is oh so terribly charming. Do you understand that? Charming.

But I prefer to remember her when she was not particularly charming. I prefer to remember her when she was shy and silent, the Charlotte Krapf of virginal antiquity who was serious about death and treated it with a fearful and curious respect, the sharpbreasted girl who did not look upon existence as a formula in chemistry, a dear child who was not afraid to suspend disbelief. For, you see, there is an addendum to that glorious spring day in 1947 when we all discussed the Melancholy Dane at such length. The bell has sounded, and I have dismissed the class. On his way out, Jimmy Van Zandt grins at me and says something to the effect that he will shortly be visiting the Charles Palmer Light House of Rest (our "best" undertaking establishment in 1947) so that the people there can measure him for his coffin. I smile at Jimmy Van Zandt and tell him yes, that is a good idea; those with big mouths usually die early. Whereupon Jimmy Van Zandt guffaws and goes lurching out of the room. I wearily shake my head and start to gather up my books and papers, and then I am aware that Charlotte is standing in front of my desk. She is hugging her books and notebooks to her bosom, and I notice some sort of spot, or blot, on her red and green plaid skirt. We are alone now, Charlotte and I, and I have not even heard her approach the desk. I am a bit annoyed, and I wish I knew why. I look up at her and I say: "You move very quietly."

Charlotte nods. "Yes," she says, and she is almost whispering. She does something with her tongue, rubbing it against the inside of a cheek, and it makes thin salivary sounds. "I . . . ah, I always try to stay out of the way," she says, swallowing the moisture or whatever it was.

I clear my throat, and it is almost as though I am providing a counterpoint for her saliva. My inexplicable annoyance persists, and I speak brusquely. "Well, is there some question you want to ask?

"Yes."

"About what?"

"Dying."

"Dying?"

"Yes, Mister Amberson. Dying. How come nobody thinks about it?" Now Charlotte's voice is quite distinct. She is leaning forward, and her eyes are enormous.

I pull back a bit. My chair is on casters, and they squeal. I shrug and then I say: "We try not to think about it because we are afraid of it."

"Then I must be funny," says Charlotte, frowning.

"Funny?"

"I'm the other way around. I'm afraid of it, so I think about it all the time. I . . . well, I wish there was something I could do so it would —no, that's . . . ahh, that's dumb . . ."

More noise from my chair's casters. "What's dumb?"

"Mister Amberson, is there anything I can do for death so it will stay . . . so it will, ah, stay away? I mean, what I want is to go to it and, ah, *kiss* it, you know?"

"Charlotte, for heaven's sake. What are you talking about?"

"I'm talking about death, Mister Amberson. I'm saying I want to be, ah, nice to it. Then maybe it won't come for me."

I stand up. This is definitely not a charming girl. The chair rolls back. "There's nothing I can say to you about any of this," I tell her.

"Yes, Mister Amberson. Yes. Do you think I'm crazy?"

"No. Of course not. But you shouldn't brood about something over which you have no—"

"I should be like all the rest of them? I should ignore death?"

"Well, I didn't say precisely—ah, wait a minute. All right. Exactly. You should be like the rest of them. You're too young to clutter your mind with such thoughts."

Charlotte nods, but she is paying my words no mind. She says: "I've given death a name." She smiles. "It's a dumb name. I call it Mister End-of-It-All. I see Mister End-of-It-All as maybe being a colored man. I would lie down for him, you know what I mean? Don Albrecht wants me to lie down for *him,* but I won't lie down for him. I'd lie down for Mister End-of-It-All, though. Any time he wanted. Just to keep him from taking me away. I'd make myself as pretty as I could. I'd—"

I move around the desk. I go to Charlotte and touch her shoulder, and it is warm. "That will be absolutely enough of that," I tell her.

"But I want to *do* something," she says.

"There is nothing you *can* do."

"I'm a virgin. Maybe he doesn't lie down with too many virgins."

I turn away from her. "I . . . wellnow, Charlotte, I have a teachers' meeting and, ah, I don't think this conversation is really—"

"All right, Mister Amberson," says Charlotte. She taps me on a shoulder, and I flinch a little. I turn so that I am facing her again, and she says: "I didn't mean to scare you. I just thought maybe you'd be somebody who'd tell me what to do about him." She smiles a little. "It's all right. I go my own way. Don Albrecht says he loves me, but what does he know, right? So it's all right, Mister Amberson. Don't fuss yourself. I'm sorry if I—"

"Charlotte, would you please leave this room?"

Her smile enlarges itself. I have never seen her smile so widely. She nods. She taps her forehead. "Weird," she says. And then she almost chuckles. She moves slowly, with immense dignity, and the heels of her saddle shoes hit the floor crisply and evenly. She walks out of the room, and I watch her, and her socks have flopped down over her ankles, and the back of her neck is pink and downy, and I want to shriek.

Yes, shriek. Like an impaled rabbit.

Sinclair hopped on the bed and gathered himself in a ball on Anne's lap. She scratched him behind the ears, and gradually her weeping subsided, and finally she blinked at Amberson and said: "Well, I . . . I think the best thing is that we keep moving. Don't you?"

"Yes," said Amberson. His own eyes were moist, and he wiped at them with his fingers, like a child.

Anne scratched Sinclair under the chin. He looked up at her, and his eyes narrowed, and he purred. "There are other things we can discuss, aren't there?" she said.

"That is correct," said Amberson.

Anne lifted Sinclair from her lap and embraced him. "He's a good cat," she said. "The best cat ever."

"That is correct," said Amberson.

"You're right about the medication. The other, I'll try not to talk about it. It's nothing we either of us can afford, is it?"

"That is correct."

"Thank you, Teacher."

"Think nothing of it."

"The Great God Jehovah performed a miracle, sire, when He reached in the brain pot and came up with your most esteemed, ah, cranial apparatus."

"Yes. That is correct."

Anne smiled. She still was hugging the cat. She pressed its face against her neck and said: "Ah, such a glory it is to be the humble recipient of all my lord and master's wisdom."

"It is enough to overemphasize the buscadilloes and make weak the yardleys, for such, such are the glories of my avinabulous intellect."

"Well put, " said Anne.

"Yes," said Amberson. "I rather thought so myself."

Anne handed her husband the cat, then went into the bathroom and took her medication. Amberson fed the cat while Anne was washing her hands and face and brushing her teeth. She was proud that a great many of her teeth remained, and he was proud for her. When Anne emerged from the bathroom, she went to the window and pulled the curtains open an inch or so. She peered outside, then told her husband it looked like rain. "An autumn rain can be pleasant," she said.

Amberson nodded and went into the bathroom. He washed himself carefully; he took his time. He cleaned his dentures carefully; he took his time. He shaved carefully; he took his time. He watched himself in the mirror, and he said to himself: I see it all as being very precious, every movement, every wrinkling of a knuckle, every smooth stroke of the razor. It has all become writ so large.

After dressing, Amberson went outside and did the honors with Sinclair's box. The rain appeared to be approaching from the hills to the west. He escorted Anne to the motel's coffee shop. They ordered oatmeal, toast, coffee and real cream. Most of the pain now was gone from her face. She asked him whether he had reached any conclusions concerning the apparatus. He smiled a little and told her he had not. She told him he was a fine man. He told her ah, bushwah. She smiled, and they chatted quietly, and the oatmeal was delicious, and he did not speak to her of his dreams.

Now again, briefly, I must interrupt this disjointed narrative of times past. Several hundred pages back, I did the same thing, and at that time I wrote the following:

. . . it is a bald fact of old age that death occupies more and more of the mind. One is surrounded by attrition. So kindly do not mock all these deaths. They exist in such abundance because I am so old, because nearly all those I have loved are gone. A death, like a mountain, is a large fact, and I shall not apologize for it. Still, death is not the pattern of all the words I have written. An element is not an explanation. . . .

I went on to say that we had to press on, that the *essence* of my life (or, at any rate, of my *words*) was not yet in sight. Well, the more of this I write, the more I wonder. Perhaps death *is* the essence of all this. Perhaps my precious apparatus is only a sort of scaffolding from which we leap into death. Perhaps the leap is the ultimate meaning—not the adventures we have along the way. The fact of death, and never mind salvation; never mind order; never mind my ceaseless (and quite probably foolish) search for a pattern.

But am I not entitled to an explanation?

If I am made in God's image, do not I have worth?

Surely He is good. Surely He would not betray me—and Himself

—by placing me within an apparatus that is hollow and illogical. I seek more than scaffolding. I demand more than scaffolding. I have little time remaining to me, and there are more deaths to record, and there is the incident with Bernadette to record, and perhaps such a lengthy catalogue of deaths is ridiculous, and perhaps the incident with Bernadette also is ridiculous, but I must get it all down. If I am to be freed of this world, I must free myself of my confusion (such being my nature), and these words represent the only way I know to attack the problem.

Therefore, the dying and the talk of dying must continue a bit longer. And the incident with Bernadette must be described. Logic must be served. I must be thorough (such being my nature). At least, if there are no answers, the questions can be posed neatly.

The rain pursued the Ambersons all that morning until just before noon. It was a thin rain, and it felt almost warm to Amberson, and he kept his vent window open a crack. He held the accelerator at a steady 40, and outside were mountains and trees, and he thought of death, and he thought of his dreams, but he said nothing to Anne about them. The Pontiac glided along US 40 as the old federal road slid southeast toward Maryland, and the rain pasted fallen leaves to the pavement, streaking it with gold and crimson, and Anne said something to the effect that wet fallen leaves were so terribly, terribly pretty. She held Sinclair on her lap, and he yawned a great deal. The mountains and trees were hazy, and the sky lay gray and blank.

"The rain is pretty, too," said Anne. She was slumped back, and her mouth hung open a bit, and apparently the medication was working as well as it had in a long time. She stroked Sinclair's rump, and he licked his forepaws. "I've always been fond of a morning mist . . ."

"Yes," said Amberson.

"You like morning mist? I never knew that."

"Well, I do."

"Tell me about it."

"I beg pardon?"

"Tell me about your fondness for morning mist. I want to hear you talk. I want to hear you describe your feelings. You speak well, and I enjoy listening to you . . ."

Amberson glanced at his wife, and now she was smiling.

"Please," she said. Her mouth seemed wobbly. She looked down at Sinclair. "All right now, Mister Cat," she said. "You listen, too. Your daddy has a gift for words, and I want you to pay attention."

Amberson nodded. "Thank you," he said to his wife. "It is pleasant to have the undivided attention of every creature in this automobile."

"We creatures are all ears," said Anne.

Amberson smiled. "All right, creatures," he said, "I hardly know where to begin. I was a schoolteacher for many, many years, and I walked to school on many and many a misty morning, misty spring mornings and misty autumn mornings, and there was of course a difference between the misty spring mornings and the misty autumn mornings. Or at least to *me* there was. I suppose the difference was governed by a third season—summer. Was summer approaching or had it taken its leave? If it was approaching, then the morning mist was a cool and most abundantly fragrant promise, and to me all the gray had overtones of a glorious green that soon would come. And my sap ran. Do you understand that? My sap. My body called my attention to my secret fluids. And I savored them. Good Lord, yes. I walked slowly, and I walked with what I hoped was a certain amount of dignity . . . after all, I *was* a *teacher* . . . but within me was a regiment of devils, and they all had deliciously hot breath, and they were gathered around an immense kettle, and flames snapped at the kettle, and all my juices bubbled oh so merrily and with such vigor as to make my belly churn. Now then, you creatures might think this is all a lot of foolish rhetoric, but I assure you it is not. When my sap ran, it *ran*—and perhaps at least one of you can attest to that."

Anne giggled. "Now, now," she said, "don't get dirty . . ."

"Ah," said Amberson, "I only wish I could."

Anne's giggling became a series of snorts. Sputtering a little, she finally said: "I want to hear about the morning mist. The *morning mist,* if you please, kind sir, and try not to get yourself into a state . . ."

"Ah," said Amberson "again I say to you: I only wish I could."

"The *morning mist,* if you *please.*"

Amberson nodded. "Yes," he said. "Of course. The morning mist." His hands were damp against the steering wheel. "All right, so much for the springtime morning mist, for all that coolness with its implied heat. The serenely promenading lecher and all that. I hope you have the vision pressed firmly in your mind."

"Very much so," said Anne.

"Then let us turn our attention to the morning mist of autumn. And again let us consider summer, but now it is a memory and not a promise. And so, to me, the morning mist of autumn has always been a bit mournful, and in my salad days I could feel the sap freeze, and it was as though all my devils were wearing earmuffs. And if it had not been for my knowledge of the wheel of the seasons, I would have been

depressed beyond measure. The morning mist of autumn is more fragile; the odors all soon will be destroyed. Oh yes, I know that in six
months' time they will be resurrected again, but this knowledge does
little to temper my grief. I believe it to be a sweet grief, but it is
nonetheless very much a sad thing. All right, so how was that for
rhetoric?"

"I would give you about a B-plus," said Anne.

"And a C-minus for originality," said Amberson.

"I thank you for your little speech."

"You are quite welcome."

Anne looked down at Sinclair. "He has a booger in his left eye." She
bent over Sinclair and wiped it away. "His eyes seem to tear a great deal
more than they used to."

"Perhaps he was reacting to my rhetoric."

Anne smiled down at Sinclair. "Are you a sentimental cat? Do you
remember how it was when your sap ran?"

Sinclair closed his eyes and rested his chin on his forepaws.

Then the Ambersons laughed a little, and for a time they both were
silent. The highway curved and swooped, and Amberson supposed they
would arrive in Richmond sometime tomorrow, perhaps around noon.
He knew they could cover the entire distance today, but that would
require more driving than he felt he was ready to undertake. He was
not that keen on driving, and he never had been. *This* sort of driving
was fine (strangely enough, he was invigorated by its leisureliness,
which made little sense but was nonetheless true), but he had never
cared for the sort of dawn-to-dark driving marathons that so many of
his friends and acquaintances had considered to be so enjoyable. He had
nothing against tests of endurance, but it seemed to him that there were
more meaningful ways to accomplish them. Such as running, for instance. And besides, why should one test oneself against a *machine?*
Amberson shook his head, grunted a little.

"Something wrong?" Anne asked him.

"No," said Amberson. "Not really. I was only . . . well, I was only
thinking about the rat race, about how the world never seems to slow
down."

"That is an autumnal thought if I ever heard one."

"Autumnal?"

"Yes. A little while ago you were talking about autumn, and conclusions, and devils with earmuffs and whatnot. Frozen sap and whatever.
You said all those things had to do with autumn. Well, don't they all
mean slowing down?"

"I suppose so," said Amberson.

"And the way we fuss when we order our food. The way you drive. Everything for us is very slow, wouldn't you say?"

"Yes, but is that so bad? And anyway, I've never been exactly what one would call impetuous. Even when I was young, I was deliberate."

"True," said Anne. "True enough. But when you were young you had a *choice.*"

"Ouch," said Amberson.

Sinclair hopped off Anne's lap and clambered into the back seat. She wiped some stray hairs off her lap. Then she said: "I . . . ah, when God created the seasons, He knew what He was doing."

Amberson's gums were beginning to give him pain again. "What do you mean?" he asked his wife.

"Spring is the beginning," said Anne, "and I'll give *myself* a C-minus for originality for *that.* The sap freely flowing and so forth. Youth. Heat. Promise. Then comes summer, and summer is the prime of life. Then the autumn, the harvest, the summing up. And finally the winter, which is cold and silent and final."

"Would you call them God's natural symbols for our lives?"

"Yes," said Anne, choking.

Amberson looked at her.

"I can't understand . . . I can't understand why I don't feel colder . . ."

"Now, now."

"By rights I should feel much colder. Why . . . I mean, why *don't* I? This is my winter, Howard. You know it and I know it. Don't tell me now, now. That . . . that doesn't do anything for me . . ."

Amberson said nothing. He looked away from his wife.

"Think of all the babies that are being born," said Anne, weeping. "Think of all the . . . oh, I don't know, the laughter and the smiles and . . ."

"Yes," said Amberson, barking out the word.

"What? What . . . did you say?"

Amberson did not look at his wife. He knew better than to do such a thing. If he looked at his wife, he would weep, and it would not be right for him to weep. Someone had to retain control. Someone had to say what needed to be said. And so, grimacing, peering through the rainspotted windshield, Amberson spoke briskly, and he said: "Anne, I shall *also* miss all the laughter and all the smiles. But don't you see? There is no sense railing against the inevitable. You speak of babies being born. So perhaps *think* about them. *Really* think. And, if you do, what do you find? You find a continuation, and I honestly believe it lessens the pain. At least we can face the inevitable with the knowledge

390

that we have carried our share of the burden, that the apparatus continues. Remember when Henry was born? It was the day after my mother's funeral, remember? And so I rejoiced as I mourned. I—"

"Are you trying to tell me I shouldn't be afraid?" Anne wanted to know. She had removed a Kleenex from her purse, and she was dabbing at her eyes and nostrils.

"I am not trying to tell you anything," said Amberson. "I am simply telling you how I feel."

"And that is?"

"I love you. We have lived a long time. If the book is to be closed, it is to be closed. It is not as though we are being cut down in the prime of our lives."

"Do you really believe all that, all what you just said?"

"No," said Amberson, and he began to weep.

Again, let us resume the catalogue. See now 1923, and my mother has died of a sugar condition. Eastern Star and White Shrine ladies have come to the funeral from as far away as Flint, Michigan. Pigeonbreasted and flowerhatted, with cameos clinging to their throats like great plump eggs, they sit along the walls in the front parlor of my parents' home, and they chat briskly, and from time to time one of them quietly laughs.

My mother's favorite color was yellow, and so a yellow corsage has been pinned to her dead bosom. She is wearing a dark blue dress, and her flesh glows pinkly. Taken together, the yellow corsage and the blue dress and the pink flesh present a quite blindingly colorful aspect, and I have overheard several of the Eastern Star and White Shrine ladies murmuring: "Lovely . . . lovely . . ."

My brothers and I take turns standing by the coffin and shaking hands with visitors, who include the Worthy High Priestesses of three states. I remember my mother's laughter and her lap and her good food. I also remember that she was not amused when my brothers became involved with Catholic girls. I remember how she said to my father: Alvin, land's sake, are you just going to *sit* there and do *nothing* and let it *happen?* Don't you understand the terrible *consequences?*

My brothers' wives stay in the background. They stand and are silent in a corner of the parlor. They watch the visiting ladies, and now and then one of them whispers something behind the back of a hand. But their words do not carry.

I stand erect, a blackly gleaming little fellow, and the Masonic ladies all have soft flabby palms. A great number of these ladies smell of heliotrope and lavender. Last year, barely fifty persons attended my sister Caroline's funeral. This year, more than five hundred sign the Guest Book provided by the undertaker. There are, in fact, two funerals for my mother. One is conducted by the Masonic ladies, and I am unable to attend. Anne, who is quite mountainously pregnant, becomes sick to her stomach, and I take her home and put her to bed.

We both do attend the church funeral, however. I sit between Anne and my father. He grasps my arm tightly and mutters dry snappish words that I cannot make out; a decline has laid its hand across him. (Late last year Mr. Elmer Carmichael, the president of the Paradise Falls Clay Products Co., retired him on a reasonably generous pension, telling him: It's no reflection on you, but—well, Goddamnit, Alvin, it's time for you to relax a little, laze in the sun as they say, read some books and let your old bones flop, if you know what I mean. Maybe I'm out of bounds for saying this, but I think your daughter's death took more out of you than you want to admit. And besides, we're none of us getting any younger, right? The years whack away at us, don't they?) And now, sitting in the crowded church, his face flatly white in the quick speckled sunlight that washes in through the pale painted windows, my father mutters a succession of crisply meaningless litanies, and his hand is too tight on my arm, but I do have the good grace not to say anything about it. (The conversation with Mr. Elmer Carmichael was later quoted by my father to me and my brothers—at a family gathering preceding the small retirement party Mr. Carmichael gave at the Carmichael home. And my father said: But it's all right. He knows what he's doing. I hold no grudge. These things happen. Sentiment is a waste of time.) But now my father apparently has decided to waste his time. When my mother died, he threw himself on her corpse and wept and screamed like a child. It took the combined efforts of all three of us —myself, Ernest and Alvin Jr.—to drag him away. He flopped and kicked like a skeleton connected with loose fragile wires. But now at least he is not flopping. He is simply muttering. Mr. Elmer Carmichael has not attended the funeral, and this is probably just as well. (To me it is apparent that my father and Mr. Elmer Carmichael share some sort of scandalously dreadful secret, and it is equally apparent that I shall never know what that secret is. And I suppose this is also just as well.) I shake my head. I smell a foul odor, and it is my father's breath. Again I shake my head. Anne frowns at me. Her face is a bit fat, and she has been listening with great care to the minister's prayers and benedictions. I smile at her and pat one of her hands.

The coffin gleams. Flowers are piled abundantly, and their odor mingles pleasantly with an odor of fresh shellac, providing some relief from my father's breath. The Masonic ladies quietly whisper. The day is warm, and most of the Masonic ladies have fans, and the fans shuck and caress, and I am abruptly aware of something quite profound, and I say to myself: My God, I am sitting in the very front row.

Amberson's weeping caused him to pull over to the side of the road and switch off the ignition, set the emergency brake, lean back, remove his spectacles and rub his eyes with the palms of his hands. Anne slid next to him and embraced him, and he snuffled into her hair, which was dry and quite soft. He closed his eyes, and she breathed against his chest, and his throat felt full of sand. He swallowed thickly, and then, gasping a little, he said: "I . . . ah, well, I only . . . you see, I only thought that . . . well, someone had to, ah, stay under . . . ah, control . . ."

Anne embraced him more tightly. "What . . . what difference does it make?" she asked her husband. "Do we have an . . . an *audience?*"

Amberson shook his head no, but he was unable to speak.

"It's not right for us to try to . . . fight off the truth," said Anne, patting Amberson's back and shoulders. "I'm . . . dying, and you're dying, and *that's* the truth . . ."

"Yes," said Amberson. "All right."

"And we are both of us . . . frightened . . ."

"Yes," said Amberson.

"Would we be human if we were anything else?"

"No."

"So what does *control* matter? What good does it do to, ah, *control* truth?"

"I can't think of . . . any . . ."

"So if we want to weep, we should weep . . ."

"Yes," said Amberson.

"But we should think of the nice things, too."

"The nice things?" said Amberson, opening his eyes.

Anne looked up at him, and she was smiling. She kissed the base of his throat. "The children," she said. "Picnics. Morning mist."

"We should think of Henry," said Amberson.

"Lewis, too. With or without Alice."

"And Florence. And her husband. And her girls."

"Yes," said Anne. "Exactly."

Amberson fumbled for his handkerchief. He pulled back from Anne and wiped his eyes and blew his nose. "Great God Almighty," he said, and he managed to work his mouth into a smile. "The apparatus surely does a job of work on us."

"How so?" Anne asked him.

"It makes us so reluctant to leave it. We don't know anything else, and so we become . . . ah, *dumbfounded* when we have to go away . . ."

"I don't feel dumbfounded," said Anne. "I only feel tired. And a lot of the time I hurt. I don't seem to have the time to feel dumbfounded."

"Well," said Amberson, "I'm sorry, but *I* feel *dumbfounded.*"

"Well," said Anne, "to each his own."

Amberson nodded. It was nearly 11 o'clock, and the warm rain persisted. He leaned against the steering wheel and stared out the windshield. He was silent for a time. He listened to the sound of his heart; it was thick in his ears. Finally he said: "You're right. Of course you're right. Truth only has value when it is exposed."

"Is that a schoolteacher's way of saying good old Anne still has a brain or two in her poor shrunken head?"

"Yes," said Amberson.

"That is very good news."

"We are forgetful," said Amberson, "and we move too slowly, and we are too fussy when we order our food, but we still do have *some* capacity for thought."

"And feeling."

"Yes."

Anne folded her arms across her chest. "When the world talks about people like us, it calls us 'golden agers,' and you want to know something? Those words make me want to throw up. I am not a '*golden* ager'; I am an '*olden* ager.' I am *old*. I am simply *elderly*. Why does your apparatus have to spread so much sugar over what people are?"

"Perhaps someone who says he is a 'golden ager' feels more useful than someone who simply says he is old."

"Useful? Useful for what? Remember that time Lewis talked you into going to the Rotary meeting with him?"

"Rotary meeting?"

"Yes. You know the one. It was 1956 or 1957, sometime around then, and some man gave a talk on what he called grief something-or-other. When you came home, you were just about beside yourself."

"Oh," said Amberson. "Yes. I do remember. And I even remember the man's name. At least I *think* I do. It was Thorberg, I believe. Something like Lars or Sven Thorberg, and he represented some undertaking group, and he spoke of the *responsibility* of the undertaker to

394

make sorrow as painless as possible. According to him, anything that provided an understanding of death was excessively morbid, and he and his group were manning the trenches against all things morbid."

"And what did he call what they were doing? It was grief something, but I can't remember what."

"Grief therapy," said Amberson.

"*Yes,*" said Anne. "*That's* it. Grief therapy. Isn't that the most sickening phrase you've ever heard?"

"Just about."

"If I die first, I want you to mourn me. I don't want anyone massaging your skull with any *therapy.*"

"I promise you I won't let anyone touch my skull."

"Bill Newhall's place has a nursery, and the wallpaper is decorated with pink ducks and blue giraffes. I remember that from your brother Alvin's funeral. His grandchildren were in there, and they were playing with dolls and blocks and even a little train on a string."

"I never liked Bill Newhall's place," said Amberson.

"You won't bury me out of there?"

"Of course not. I'll bury you out of Zimmerman's."

"Thank you. I don't like thinking about those ducks and giraffes."

"Neither do I," said Amberson.

"And please mourn me," said Anne.

"Yes," said Amberson.

See now 1959, an unseasonably warm day in late March, and my brother Alvin Jr., who has recently turned seventy, has taken me out onto his screened back porch, and we are lounging in canvas chairs, and he says: "Does anyone ever think about Laura? Does anyone ever bother to remember her?"

"I do," I tell him.

"I was punished for some goddamned thing or other, wasn't I?"

"That's ridiculous."

"It's not ridiculous if you have to live with it."

"All right," I tell him, "whatever you want to believe, you believe it. No words from me will change your mind, so I'm just not going to bother."

It is late on a Sunday afternoon. Anne is in the kitchen, and she is chatting with my brother's housekeeper, a Mrs. Kirchenbaum. Alvin Jr. has been a widower since the day in 1941 when his wife, the former Mary Frances O'Shea, succumbed to the ravages of an intestinal cancer. The last of his children left home for good about three or four years after Mary Frances's death, and since then he has lived alone with Mrs. Kirchenbaum in this large comfortable house on Grainger Street. She is a small woman of about sixty; she has dyed red hair and an enormous mouth, and at one time she was considered to be something of a hot ticket, or however the saying goes. At any rate, it is pretty well accepted that she and Alvin Jr. were lovers, and perhaps—for all I know—they still are. Perhaps Alvin Jr. is another Stokowski or Chaplin. The thought interests me, and I wish I had the nerve to ask him how he is doing in that particular department. (I am only eight years younger than he, and my own activity in that department has dwindled to nearly nil, and when it does take place, Anne and I behave awkwardly and with quite a bit of embarrassment. This is a shame, I know, but I do not see how I can do anything about it. Flesh is flesh, and enough said.)

Alvin Jr. holds a can of Rolling Rock in both hands. He rubs it against his cheeks. They are puffy, and his mouth has receded, and he is almost entirely bald. He is wearing a T-shirt that his daughter Mary gave him for his seventieth birthday. Written on it are the words OLYMPIC DRINKING TEAM. His two sons and his daughter visited him last month and helped him celebrate the birthday. The older son, John, is partner in a public relations firm in Toledo; the younger, Alvin III, is an attorney with offices in Columbus; and the daughter, Mary, is the wife of a police inspector in Indianapolis. John has four children; Alvin III has three and Mary has six, which I suppose represents a quite eloquent testimonial to their late mother's Catholicism, which was quite intense and of course aggravated *my* mother no end.

But now, as he sits fatly on this porch and rubs the cool beer can against his cheeks, my brother is not thinking of John or Alvin III or Mary or his grandchildren. He is thinking of Laura, who was his oldest child, who was not quite nineteen when she died, whose existence has been the one thing that has touched him beyond his capacity to understand it or cope with it. (He likes to call himself a *winner*, and surely his bank balance, which is substantial, underscores the many victories he has achieved. But Laura was not a victory. Laura was a calamity, and his tragedy is that he keeps trying to understand why.)

He leans forward. The canvas makes a quietly taut sound. "It never bothered Mary Frances as much as it did me," he says. "She liked to say that it was the price we had to pay for living. That's why the others came so quickly. She wanted to *show* me that there was nothing *wrong* with us, nothing in our blood or in my jism or whatever."

"It sounds to me as though she made a lot of sense."

"Oh, sure. What the hell, *you* can say that. There was nothing wrong with any of *your* kids. And Lewis is going to be the goddamned *mayor* some day, just you wait and see . . ."

"I have no idea what that has to do with—"

"Bull *shit*," says Alvin Jr., swallowing some of the beer and wiping his mouth with the back of a hand. "Howard, all your life you've been like some sort of neat little guardian of *logic* and *reason* and all the rest of it. But you can't explain Laura any more than I can. And don't talk to me about chemistry and accidents. Why don't you talk to me about God, about Him looking down on me and saying: Why, there is one miserable greedy sonofabitch, and I'm going to fix *him*. I'll just ruin his daughter—that's what I'll do."

"You don't believe that."

"How do *you* know what I don't believe?"

"If you really believed that, you would have *changed* after Laura was born. Your life would have been transformed by this heavenly judgment you keep insisting was passed on you. You would have been too afraid *not* to change, and too remorseful as well. But you didn't change by one whit. You made your pile, and you did whatever was necessary to achieve it, but you weren't all *that* evil, and you know it. You are a talented and intelligent man, Alvin. You are no monster and you should stop flogging yourself to death. *Laura was born the way she was born because that was the way she was born.* Period. End of thought. There is no more."

"You believe that?"

"Yes."

Alvin Jr. says nothing. He swallows more of the beer. He wipes his mouth. He is hunched over, and his hands squeeze the beer can, and his breath comes heavily through his nostrils.

I look away from him. He is my brother, and I wish I liked him more than I do. I wish I could do more to dispel this guilt he will not relinquish. But he never really has given me an opportunity to like him. He is too loud for my taste, and he proclaims himself with an excess of passion that is, to my way of thinking, downright vulgar. I love him (he is, after all, my brother), but I cannot honestly say that I like him, and I cannot honestly say that I ever have. I still remember the days of our boyhood and those times when he and Ernest tormented Fred Suiter, and I still remember the raucous whoop and clamor of them when they bragged about some deviltry or other, some scheme, some act that usually caused pain. Oh, yes indeed, I am fully aware that I am straightlaced and excessively conservative;

I know I never created a fuss at stereopticon shows; I know I was a wonder and a delight to my teachers; I know all these things and I acknowledge them . . . but still I think I have a right, prissy as I am, to criticize my brothers, to think of them as having been on occasion brutish beyond reason. Would Mama have loved them less if they had not made off with Fred Suiter's britches? Would the world have expelled them if they had been more quiet and reserved? I suppose it is unfair of me to impose my personal standards on them, but I cannot help doing so. I suppose I am a prig and an ass, but I am too old to change, and perhaps I was too old the day I was born.

Now Alvin Jr. sits hunched, older than seventy, older than the world, and his OLYMPIC DRINKING TEAM T-shirt has gathered itself in tight folds around his belly, and he mourns his dead ruined daughter. His voice has changed over the years. At one time it was an impressive baritone, but now it is tenorish and splintered. And now he is shrunken and wattled, and veins run narrow and blue, like cracks in an egg, across his naked gray skull. Here is a man who still walks to work every morning, whose real estate business has placed his net worth in excess of half a million dollars, a man who has been a *winner* since time out of mind, and yet I feel only a dry pity for him. Nearly everything he has touched has turned to gold; the Depression affected him not at all (he sold his coal cartage company to the C&O in April of '29 after years of negotiations, thus realizing his announced intent to screw the railroad to a faretheewell and make a lot of money in the process), and he has always had a gift for thinking ahead and anticipating trends. There have been two new housing developments built in Paradise Falls since the close of World War II, and he has been in on both of them. There have been three new major industries that have located in Paradise Falls since 1954, and he has sold the land for all three properties. He understands the value of high ground in Paradise Falls, seeing as how the river floods so often. In short, his life has been a poem to shrewdness, to the intelligent realization of what the world knows as the American Dream. And yet I do not particularly like him, and I never have. I love him, yes, but there is a difference . . .

"Ah, Jesus . . ." says Alvin Jr., lifting the can and finishing its contents. He tries to grin at me. "The worst sort of old fart is a sentimental old fart." He leans back and drops the can to the floor. "We should enjoy the day, for Christ's sake. We haven't got that many left . . ."

"Well, it *is* very unseasonable."

My brother cups a hand over his eyes. "This is about my fourth beer today," he says. "I never could handle beer. Remember that green beer old Alf Froelich used to sell back in Prohibition? It tasted like grasshopper piss."

"It was said that Joe Masonbrink provided a higher quality."

"That is absolutely correct, but I liked old Alf better. I used to run with his daughter Helen, and he let us screw in the front room. I had a pretty good cock on me in my day, you know that?"

"That must have been after you were married to Mary Frances."

"Hell, yes. Sometimes Mary Frances could be a pain in the ass, you know?"

"No. I don't. But I'll take your word for it."

"Yeah. You do that."

I have nothing to say, and so I keep my mouth shut. Perhaps Alvin Jr. will follow my example. I do not really care to hear any more of his beery confessions.

But he does not follow my example. His eyes are closed now, and he is breathing with his mouth open. "She was just so goddamned pretty," he says.

I seem to recall that Helen Froelich was rather a plain girl who married a C&O brakeman and moved to Columbus. "I remember her as being a little too horsy," I say to my brother.

"What?" says Alvin Jr., opening his eyes.

"Helen Froelich. I remember her as being a little too horsy."

"I wasn't talking about *Helen Froelich*, for Christ's sake. I was talking about *Laura*. I want to talk about Laura."

"All right."

"I want to talk about my little girl."

"Fine."

Alvin Jr. links his fingers over his belly. "You never heard a word from her—an angry word, I mean. She never complained. I fed her more times than Mary Frances did, you know that? I took my time with her, gave her a chance to chew her food. I remember that for a year or so, Twentyseven or Twentyeight I think it was, I had a little moustache. You remember it?"

"Yes."

"Well, she liked to have me tickle her nose with it. It was a reward for her. If she ate all her food, I would tickle her nose with my moustache. It made her giggle, and she would kick her legs against the chair. And I would go mew like a pussycat, mew, mew, and I would say to her: Mew, mew, here comes a pussycat taking a little walk across your nose."

"She enjoyed laughter. I remember that very distinctly."

"Yes," says my brother. "And she was bright, too. Just because she was the way she was, that doesn't mean she was some sort of moron."

"I don't recall that anyone ever said she was."

"Almost every morning I was the one who helped her get dressed. And I picked out most of her clothes for her."

"Yes. I know that. I know all of it."

"After Mama died, when Papa came to live with us, he was a little soft in the head, you know? Remember how we had to pull him off Mama after she died, that day in the hospital room?"

"Yes. Of course I remember it."

"You and me and old Ernie—all three of us."

"Yes."

"So anyway, when Papa came to live with us, he liked to play with the kids, and Laura spent more time with him than the other three put together. They played word games, and he helped her with her arithmetic, and sometimes I'd catch him hugging her and sort of groaning, you know?"

"*Yes.* I know *all* of that."

"And she would have patted his head if she could have. It was almost like she was his mother. He was one gone old goose, I tell you."

"*Yes.* My God, I *know.*"

Alvin Jr. averts his face. He presses his hands against his knees. "Well, *Jesus,*" he says.

I shift my weight. Perhaps I should go into the kitchen and see what the ladies are up to.

His face still averted, Alvin Jr. says: "The first time I saw her, I thought I was going to have a goddamned heart attack. It was when we lived over on Mulberry Street, and old Cora Hooper was the midwife, and she handed the baby to me and she said: 'Alvin, the Lord works in mysterious ways.' Honest to God, that is exactly what she said. And I looked at the baby, and Mary Frances was bawling in the bedroom, but the baby wasn't making any sounds whatsoever, and as a matter of fact it was smiling. That was August, the summer of 1913, and it was a hot afternoon, and I sort of pulled back the little blanket from its sweet face, and then I looked it up and down, and I *saw,* and I thank God old Cora was standing close by. Because, you see, I damn near dropped that baby. It was like a hammer had hit me across the chest, and I sort of *staggered,* you know? And old Cora scooped it away from me before I could do it harm. And I sat down.

And I don't think I said a word to anyone for maybe four or five hours. I just sat there in an old wicker rocker, and people came and went, and I didn't know what the hell was going on. I kept seeing that face, and by God it was such a *pretty* face. I mean, we *all* saw the prettiness—and right from the start, too. Those green eyes. You remember how green they were? Green and clear, like agates, the kind we used to play with when we were little kids. And you remember how fair her complexion was? And her blond hair, how soft it was? My God, she was a beauty . . ." And now Alvin Jr. is rubbing his head, and finally he manages to say: "It's like my whole world sat down in that chair and never got up . . ."

I stand up. I go over to where he is sitting and place a hand on his shoulder. He is a vulgar, frightened man, but he is my brother, and I do love him, and I know I love him, and I also know his deficiencies do not really matter, and so I say to him: "She was a beauty. She was precious. You have a right to feel whatever you like."

Alvin Jr. blinks up at me and nods. "I . . . I thank you for that," he says.

I turn away from him. I return to my chair and flop down.

My brother stares at nothing in particular.

I close my eyes, and I am able to see Laura. Perhaps not as clearly as Alvin Jr. sees her, but clearly enough. She was born with both hands horribly deformed, and it was bone cancer that destroyed her. She was, as I have said, not quite nineteen. I never saw her when she was not cheerful, and her face and body were indeed quite lovely. She was able to recite poetry from memory and had a fine little singing voice, soprano and quite accurate. She reminded me in many ways of my sister Caroline, even though she was much more open and gregarious than Caroline ever had been. (One could not, for instance, imagine Laura wishing for Magic Gas.) She once asked me whether I thought she was pretty. I told her I thought she was very pretty. And then she said to me: Coming from *you,* that means something.

Her death was not unexpected. It had been implicit at the time of her birth. So she went through her days with what I always saw as a remarkable serenity, and she uttered no recriminations when she died. Actually, according to her father and mother, she died smiling, and I have no reason not to believe them. She told us she loved us, said Mary Frances, and she told us we were the best Mama and Papa a girl could have.

Laura died in July of 1932. I recall that she had allowed her hair to grow long, and it curved around her face in gentle swirls in her coffin. She looked like some sort of legendary sleeping princess, and she even was smiling a little. (The undertaker, Zimmerman, some-how had retained her dying smile.) The church was crowded for the funeral, and Alvin Jr. wept throughout the service.

I open my eyes.

My brother is looking at me.

"I was just thinking about her," I tell him.

"I figured that."

"You have a right to believe whatever you like."

"You mean that? You're not just feeling sorry for me?"

"I mean it. If you want to see it as a punishment, then that's your privilege. She was *your* daughter."

"It'll be twentyseven years in July."

"Yes. So it will be."

"To me," says Alvin Jr., "1932 is like the day before yesterday. The older I get, the more I remember. You'd think I'd forget, but I don't."

"I am getting that way myself."

"You remember a boy named Fred Suiter?" Alvin Jr. asks me.

"Yes. I remember him very well."

"And you remember how Ernie and I treated him?"

"Yes."

"You think that had something to do with Laura?"

"I don't know."

"Maybe she was my punishment for treating him the way I did. Maybe God was keeping score."

"Laura was not a *punishment.* She was a sweet and precious *human being.*"

Alvin Jr. pays no attention to my words. Frowning, he says: "I kept expecting him to come back—Fred Suiter, I mean. I kept ex-pecting him to come back and take out some sort of revenge, but it never happened. When Fred Suiter and his people moved away from this town, they moved away for good, and that was the end of it. Except then came Laura, and I've always wondered whether . . . oh, *you* know, whether there was a *connection* . . ."

"Alvin, I have a logical mind, and it says you're talking a lot of nonsense, but I'm not going to make any hard and fast statements. As I said, you have a right to believe whatever you want to believe."

"Have I been that much of a sonofabitch?"

"No."

My brother shakes his head. "I am just one befuddled old geezer," he says. "It's like my head is full of cotton. I just can't *think* any more."

"I know the feeling," I tell him.

"You do?"

"Yes. Absolutely."

Alvin Jr. shudders. Again he shakes his head. "Well, at least I'm not alone."

"You're not," I tell him, "and you never have been."

"You're a good little prick, you know that?"

"Well, I've always tried to be."

This is the last time Alvin Jr. and I really talk to one another. He dies of a stroke in July of this year, 1959, and I have no way of knowing whether he ever came to terms with his grief and his guilt. I doubt it, though. After all those years, they probably were chiseled too deeply within him. But I do love him, and I do mourn his passing, and I try to remember Laura as often as I can. I try to remember her smile, and I try to remember all his quaking, pitiable, remorseful love. He was not so bad. There are worse.

The mountains steamed. The car was parked overlooking a narrow craggy valley slashed with sumac and evergreens and large moist rocks. Amberson rubbed his eyes. He rolled down his window. "I think perhaps we need air," he said.

Sinclair came out of the back seat and tried to leap out the open window, but Amberson caught him. "Whoops," said Amberson. "No, you don't, old fellow." He scratched Sinclair behind the ears. "You wouldn't last an hour out here. The bears would get you. Or the mountain lions."

"I don't believe there are mountain lions in this part of the country," said Anne, smiling.

Amberson scratched Sinclair vigorously, and Sinclair began to purr. "Well," said Amberson, "if there aren't, there ought to be." He opened his mouth and breathed deeply. The air stung Amberson's gums, but somehow the pain was not unpleasant. Or perhaps he had passed beyond caring. "Ahh," he said, "it makes these old lungs grateful . . ."

Anne nodded. She took several deep breaths of her own. "There is a real flavor to it today," she said. "Maybe the truth has helped. Alice and what she said. The whole thing."

"Maybe so."

"It certainly didn't *hurt*."

"No. Not a bit."

"Howard, we are only human, nothing more."

Amberson looked at his wife. Her hair was gray, but it never had become altogether white, and her face was not as wrinkled as one might have expected in a woman of seventytwo. "Can you imagine?" he said. "It's been more than fifty years."

"No. It doesn't seem that long. It doesn't seem half that long."

"How have you been able to put up with me?" he asked her.

"I might ask you the same question," said Anne.

"I asked the question first."

Anne shrugged and rubbed her right shoulder. "The only answer I have is that you have always been important. Important to *me,* I mean. I have always wanted to please you. I've always tried to cook your food the way you like it, and I try not to argue with you over what program we watch on the TV, and I go along with you when you start talking like Shakespeare or you go into your act about diseffluvinizing the wurraflaps or whatever. And what happens when I put all these things together? They say to me: Howard is important, and I love him, old bag that I am; I love him more than anything I've ever run across. And that even includes Henry. It includes everything."

Amberson massaged his right wrist with his left hand. He rolled up his window and handed the cat to his wife. "Ah . . . please don't make me bawl again," he said. "I . . . well, once is enough . . ."

Anne shook her head. "It doesn't *matter,*" she said. "Not *now.* Not any *more.*"

Amberson released the emergency brake and switched on the engine. He eased the car back out onto the highway, and then he said: "Can you imagine? Here I am, driving along in this automobile, and I become terribly moved, and so I weep, and my weeping forces me to pull over to the side of the road and stop the automobile, and yet I remember to *apply the emergency brake.* What do you think of *that?*"

"I think it means you didn't lose all control. I think it means you really are what you believe yourself to be. And I think maybe it means you're wonderful."

Warmth came into Amberson's eyes, and he could not speak. He rubbed his tongue against his dentures, and his gums hurt, but he said to himself: I never knew truth had a flavor. He pressed down on the accelerator, and the Pontiac returned to its customary 40. Amberson pointed out a 7-Up sign to Anne, and she pointed out a Stuckey's sign to him, and for the next half an hour or so they played their little game with spirit and delight. They talked gaily, and he rolled the truth on his tongue, and his fear slammed in his ears, but for some reason he felt rather gallant and blessed, and he knew the fear was not as important as the truth. He and Anne catalogued signs and sumac and trucks and leaves and raindrops and dogs and woodpeckers and even a mailbox that said SMACKERS, which they agreed was the most amusing name they had encountered on this entire footloose devilmaycare journey. And then, shortly after they crossed into Maryland, they saw a girl standing at the side of the highway. She was slender, and she had long black hair, and she was waving a large pistol at them.

See now 1938, a scalding summer day, and I am driving to the hamlet of Egypt to visit my brother Ernest's widow, Bernadette, who has stayed home from work today. Egypt is upriver from Paradise Falls about eight miles, and it was there that Ernest operated his fillingstation for thirteen years before going broke in 1932. It was taken over by Standard Oil in that year, and Ernest was retained as "manager" until his death in 1934. But he was not the same Ernest after losing ownership of the place, and his treatment of Bernadette and their children became downright miserable, and eventually he was literally destroyed by his foul temper—and in a most spectacularly thunderous way.

But that was four years ago this spring, and hopefully Bernadette and the children have begun to forget Ernest's clamorous death. And certainly the youngest child, Peter, remembers nothing of it at all. He was not even a year old when his father was killed; he was the last of seven children, and Bernadette has always insisted he was a great surprise. (Today is his birthday, incidentally, which is why I am visiting his mother.)

She and the children still live in a little frame house that Ernest bought in 1926 but had to relinquish to the Paradise Falls State Bank in '32. She rents it now for fifteen dollars a month, and she supports herself and the children by working as a clerk at Steinfelder's, which is Paradise Falls's only "good" drygoods store. She commutes by PVT bus, leaving the younger children each day in the care of a neighbor woman. Alvin Jr. and I have tried to help her financially, but she has refused all our offers. I have a strong back, she has told us, and there's nothing wrong with me. I'll not go on any old dole, whether it be from you two or the government. So thank you very much, but no thanks.

I like Bernadette, and I always have. There has been a sort of delicate kinship between us that has gone beyond the simple fact that my brother was her husband. And I must be honest—it has included a kind of flirtatiousness. She almost always takes my side when there is some sort of family argument, and we tacitly see ourselves as being defenders of reason and sensitivity. And our tastes seem parallel. We see the same things as being pretty and the same things as being ugly. We both prefer vanilla ice cream over chocolate, and we both think Greta Garbo is more beautiful than the late Jean Harlow. We are rather snobbish about our preferences, and we roll our eyes heavenward whenever people behave in what we consider to be a vulgar manner. Bernadette comes from a family of lawyers and petty politicians (and Democrats as well) and she also has refused their offers of financial assistance. Actually, it has been years since she has been close to her parents or her brothers and sisters, and she once told me: Oh, I know they all think I'm just too la-de-dah, but I can't help it —maybe I am. All they want to talk about is their KofC meetings and their communion breakfasts and what a shame it was that Al Smith lost the election. Well, I am as good a Catholic as they are, but there *are* other things. So, if that makes me la-de-dah, then that's me—Mrs. Bernadette W. La-De-Dah. I can't help what I feel. You understand, don't you, Howard? I mean, if anyone understood, it would be you.

And yes, I did understand, and I still do. Bernadette is thirtyeight now, and she is too tall and angular to be called pretty, but her hair is dark and rich, her mouth is large and warm, and there has been a definite communication between us, and I shall not be foolish enough to deny it. And it has more than vanilla and Garbo working in its behalf.

I am driving to Egypt to deliver Peter's birthday present—a set of building blocks. Anne was to have accompanied me, but Florence is sick in bed with a summer cold, and Anne has stayed home to take care of her. And so now, as I drive northwest on Ohio US 33-A, I begin to feel a sort of excitement. As far as I can remember, I have never spent any time alone with Bernadette, and the prospect fills me with a sort of glandular anxiety that is not altogether unpleasant. Of course her children will be running in and out of the house . . . but still, perhaps we *will* have a chance to talk, and the prospect interests me probably more than it should. (Occasionally I dream about her, and they are reasonably embarrassing dreams, but not so embarrassing that I do not enjoy them.)

There is a thermometer attached to the shed in our back yard, and at 10 o'clock this morning that thermometer registered 92 degrees. It is now about 1:30 in the afternoon, and the temperature must be at least 100. I seldom perspire, but today I do, and I have removed my jacket, necktie and hat. All the car windows are open, and my body everywhere feels sticky, and I would not be surprised if I came down with a summer cold like Florence's. (She has to sweat it out, Anne told me this morning. She needs a lot of bed rest so she can get the poisons out of her system. So I think I'll stay here to make sure she gets whatever she needs—and to make sure she stays in bed. You know our Florence. She's a lively one and then some. So please tell Bernadette I'm sorry I couldn't come.) I swipe at my forehead with the back of a hand. Sunlight shimmers against the river and the green lowlands. The highway passes straight as a rod through these lowlands, and they are acknowledged to be the best farm acreage in Paradise County—as long as there are no floods. My car is a '36 Studebaker, and its tires whine against the brick pavement, and the sack of building blocks bounces and joggles on the seat next to me. This is what Anne would call *hot* hot, even for July, and I wipe perspiration out of my eyes. I lick my fingers, and the salty taste burns my tongue.

Bernadette's house is set back about thirty or forty yards from 33-A, and it is directly across the highway from the fillingstation Ernest once owned. It is only a few feet from her back door to the edge of the river, and she and the children have been flooded out twice in the past three years. But she refuses to move—not until, as she puts it, she can do so without going into debt. And anyway, she is used to the floods. After moving into the house in '26, she and Ernest were routed by floods a total of five times in eight years, and she learned from him how to move furniture to the second floor in quick time. It's a challenge, she once told me, and I think challenges can be kind of fun—if you look at them the right way.

I think of this as I turn into Bernadette's driveway. I sigh and shake my head. The house stands in a cluster of willows, but the sun has penetrated the willows, and its light cooks the house's rusted sheetmetal roof. I pull up next to the house and switch off the engine, and the willows are silent, and I cannot even hear the river. I glance behind the house and I see that the river is as motionless as the trees. Today it is a pond rather than a river, and the sunlight has streaked it golden and blue.

I climb out of the car, taking my bag of building blocks with me. I look around, and it occurs to me that I see none of Bernadette's children. Usually, at this time of the year, at least two or three of them can be found out front scrabbling in the dirt, or running and whooping, or otherwise making their presence known. But today not a one of them is to be seen, and I am a bit puzzled. Shrugging, I knock on the door. While I wait, I inspect Bernadette's front windowboxes. They contain begonias, but the begonias are wilted, and the dirt is powdery. Obviously, the poor things are as much victims of the heat as the rest of us.

Bernadette opens the door. She is wearing a blue housedress, and its front is covered by a pink apron decorated with what appear to be daisies. She smiles at me and says: "I saw you looking at my begonias. I peeked out at you and I *saw.*"

"Caught in the act," I tell her.

"Would you like to do something about it?"

"About the begonias?"

"Yes. There's a bucket out back next to the cellar door. You could take that bucket and fill it with some of our nice riverwater and give my poor begonias a big drink."

"Oh. All right."

"I'm a poor working girl, and sometimes I just don't get around to my begonias."

I smile. "Well, that's perfectly understandable," I tell her.

"Here," she says, "give me that, whatever it is." She takes the bag from me. "Now, be about your business. I have some nice iced tea waiting for you when you come inside."

"Yes ma'am," I say. "To hear is to obey." I bow deeply from the waist, then hurry around the house and fetch the bucket, and her laughter follows me. I run down to the river and fill the bucket, then come lurching back to the windowboxes and give the begonias more than a drink; I give them a bath; I inflict upon them a torrent. And Bernadette stands with her hands on her hips, and she smiles, and her tongue rubs her lower lip, and she says: "Mmmm. Very good. An excellent job."

Again I bow deeply. "It was my pleasure," I tell her.

"You are a very gallant sort of fellow, you know that?"

"Thank you," I say, smiling. I put down the bucket and follow Bernadette into the house. All the windows are open, but the place still is quite stuffy. She leads me through the front room, and the floor is littered with toys, and she says something to the effect that seven kids just make it *impossible* for a person to keep a house neat and picked up. I tell her it's not such an easy job even when there are only three.

We walk into the kitchen, which is quite small. There are no windowshades, and the sunlight smears the table and the stove and the sink. A Zimmerman Funeral Home calendar hangs on the wall next to the back door, and it is decorated with a painting of shepherds and angels. "Sit," says Bernadette, pointing to the table. She sets down the bag of blocks, then goes to the icebox (she does not own a refrigerator) and fetches a pitcher of iced tea.

Bernadette fills two glasses with iced tea and brings them to the table. She hands me one, then sits down across from me. She lifts her glass. "Your very good health," she says.

"Thank you," I tell her, "and the same to you." I drink. The iced tea is so cold it hurts my teeth. "Ahhh, good Lord, that tastes good . . ."

"Yes," says Bernadette, sipping. Then: "Where's Anne? I thought she was coming out with you . . . I mean, I even made a little bit of an effort to pick up the house . . ."

"Florence has one of those summer colds, and Anne decided to stay home with her."

"Oh, the poor child. They can be nasty."

"Speaking of children, what happened to *your* brood?"

"My *brood,*" says Bernadette, "has been scattered to the four winds." She lifts a hand and begins ticking them off on her fingers. "Beth and Jean are off at Mrs. Pfister's place helping her put up some jam. Billy and Charley are playing baseball. Nancy and Bobby are visiting my sister Kathleen's place over by Sugar Grove. And Peter's upstairs taking his nap. The place is so quiet it almost scares me. I haven't been home on a Wednesday in *ages,* and it's a strange feeling."

"Did you have any trouble getting the day off?"

"I've never told you about Mister Wolf?" George Wolf is the owner of Steinfelder's Department Store, an astigmatic little man who married the last surviving Steinfelder daughter and came into ownership of the place back in '24 after old Otto Steinfelder was killed by a runaway Ford on Main Street just outside the store. "George Wolf is, ah, very fond of my behind," says Bernadette.

"I beg your pardon?"

"You heard me correctly. He likes to brush his hand against it, and he is forever jostling me and giving me a little pittypat—and with his *palm open,* at that."

"Well, I've always admired it, too."

"*Howard Amberson,* what a thing to *say!* I am very flattered."

(I do not know why I am talking this way. Such ridiculous banter is not my style. Ah well, perhaps it is the weather.)

"Well, *anyway,*" says Bernadette, "our friend George Wolf sees me as being The Hot Young Widow, and I'm bright enough to let him think whatever he likes. Not that I'm so Young any more, and not that I'm so Hot, but as long as he wants to believe that, I go ahead and let him. I smile at him often enough, and I compliment him often enough, that I'm sure he's thinking oh *boy,* she's really out *after* me. And so he doesn't fuss too much when I take a day off now and then. You should have seen me this time. You would have fallen down laughing. I went to him oh so sweet and ickypoo, and I said: 'Mister Wolf, Wednesday is my littlest boy's birthday, and I'd like to stay home and bake him a cake and fix up a little party for him. He will be five years of age, and it's about time he had a cake and a party of his very own.' And, while I was talking to good old George Wolf, I sort of *leaned forward* and *squeezed* one of his *wrists,* you know? Well, it was as though the poor man had received some sort of electrical shock. Now, I know I'm not exactly hot stuff when it comes to what I have out front, but that particular day I took care to wear a blouse that was scooped a little below the neck—which was why I leaned over. Well, his beady little eyes sort of *opened wide,* you know? And they sort of *danced,* you know? My terrific physical charms had just about done him in, if you can *believe* such a thing. And he said to me well, ah, er, um, harrumph, yes, of course, my dear, you may of course have the day off, harrumph. The poor little tyke. We do want him to have a nice birthday, ahem, harrumph, don't we?" And now Bernadette is laughing, and she has thrown back her head. *"My Lord!"* she hollers. *"I wonder what he would say if he saw my stretch marks!"*

I laugh right along with her. I rub my eyes. "You are something," I tell her. "A strange and crazy woman if I ever knew one."

Bernadette takes a large swallow of her iced tea. She shakes her head. "I've never had much experience at being a *femme fatale,"* she says, "and I must say: It's kind of fun. But can you imagine *me* carrying on with *George Wolf?* Why, he's so nearsighted he probably wouldn't even *find* it . . ." And now comes more laughter from Bernadette, and her laughter has a plump and desperate sound.

I lift my glass and try to drink some of my iced tea, but my concentration is disrupted by a terribly amusing vision. I see a naked and groping George Wolf, and a naked Bernadette is with him, and she is saying: Yes. Yes. Very good. You are getting warm. The thought makes me splutter into my iced tea, and some of it runs down the front of my shirt, and now I am laughing as loudly as Bernadette.

Bernadette gasps, swallows. Her eyes are wet. She takes a large shuddery breath, then says: "It would be like . . . ah, it would be like playing, ah, hah, yes, Pin-the-Tail-on-the-Donkey . . ." And she explodes again, and so do I. The iced tea is cold against my chest, and my arms move witlessly, like the wings of some great stupid bird that has forgotten how to fly. Finally I hug myself, and I am giggling weakly. Bernadette takes a handkerchief from an apron pocket, dabs at her eyes, blows her nose, then says: "Oh, we are *terrible . . .*"

"Yes," I tell her. "Just terrible."

"You spilled iced tea on your shirt."

"I know, but don't bother yourself about it. It's rather refreshing. It cools my chest."

"Good," says Bernadette. "I wouldn't want to be entertaining a gentleman who had a *hot chest.* I mean, what would the neighbors say?"

I smile. "You really are something," I tell her.

"You're prejudiced."

"I suppose I am. I suppose I always have been."

Bernadette fusses with the handkerchief, wads it in a ball and returns it to the apron pocket. "Remember the time Ernie accused you of passing me some sort of mash note?"

"Yes. It was the day Henry was born. Only it was the other way around. You found a piece of paper on which I had been doodling some words. You handed it to me, and then Ernest became angry, and *I* became angry, and there were a great many loud words. I was as angry as I've ever been in my life."

Bernadette nods. "And I got into it, too. I asked him did he think I was such a dumbbell that I would hand you a note right there in front of everyone?"

"Yes."

"Funny I had it the other way around."

"Well, it was a long time ago."

"Are you really prejudiced when it comes to me?"

"Yes."

"That's a very sweet thing to say."

"I mean it."

"Yes," says Bernadette. "I believe you do." She looks away from me. She looks at the wall behind my head. She presses her hands against the surface of the table, and the oilcloth squeaks. "This is the first time we've ever been alone together, isn't it?"

"I believe so."

She nods. She says nothing, simply nods.

Perhaps she cannot look at me, but I can look at her. Her forehead is lined, and her cheeks are too bony, and her wrists and hands are red, and her body is narrow and sharp. But her hair is as lush as it ever has been, and moisture has laid itself across her mouth, and something wild and frightened sits behind her eyes. She is breathing a bit noisily, and she keeps trying to smile. I clear my throat. I stare at my hands and press my fingers together. "I . . . ah, that's right," I say. "We've never really been—"

She interrupts me. "Would you like to watch me bake the cake? It should be very exciting. Especially on a day like this when I light the oven. Hades Junction, next stop. Come visit Bernadette Amberson, ladies and gentlemen, and get a preview of your final destination. So, tell me—doesn't that sound like fun?"

"Bernadette, whatever you want is—"

"Whatever I want," says Bernadette, "is not something to be wanting." She smiles, shakes her head, stands up. "It is in no way right," she says. "So, well, let's talk about Peter, okay?" She makes a vague distracted movement with a hand, and she still is not quite looking directly at me. "He will have a nice cake today, and at five-thirty this afternoon a dozen of the neighbors' brats will come descending on this place, and they'll have a little party, with cake and soda pop and I don't know what all. I've cut out a whole bunch of paper streamers, and I'll string them on the front porch this afternoon, and I've made some paper hats too, and they'll all wear the paper hats, and Mabel Ordway has promised to send over some of those little tin New Year's horns with her little girl, and I just bet you a good time will be had by one and all, don't you think so?"

"Yes."

Bernadette has moved to the stove, and she has removed a flour sack from a cupboard above the stove. She bends over and takes a pan and the flour sifter from a drawer next to the stove. Her dress gathers tightly over her buttocks. She straightens, glances briefly back at me and says: "The excitement is about to reach fever pitch, as they say."

I smile at her, but I can think of nothing appropriate to say. I am warmer now, but the weather has nothing to do with it. The spilled iced tea is no longer cold against my chest.

Bernadette speaks quickly. "It must really be a scorcher," she says. "I think this is the first time I've ever seen you without your coat and tie." She turns to the flour and the sifter and the pan, and she begins pouring flour through the sifter. Her hands whiten, and she says: "He is a precious little boy . . . the, ah, the most, ah, precious of them all . . ." She hesitates, then slams down the strainer and the bag of flour. Flour rises in a silent explosion. She holds out her arms and says: "He . . . today . . . I mean, today I'd set aside for him. He, ah, is the youngest, and he's so very precious to me . . ."

I come around the table to where she is standing. I take both her hands in both of mine, and now my hands also are white from the flour. I say nothing. My mouth is without flavor or moisture.

"We'll have to wash off the flour," says Bernadette, blinking.

I nod.

She leads me to the sink and turns on the tap. The water is cool and clear and quite hard. It comes from a well Ernest dug in '26. I clean the flour off my hands, and Bernadette does the same. She is shaking, and all her breath seems to be coming from her nostrils. We dry our hands, and then we face one another, and she shakes her head no, and then I kiss her, and I kiss her softly, and our mouths are open, and she is taller than I, and her arms curl around me, and I know there is no longer any choice but to go ahead.

We stand there I do not know how long, and our mouths are gentle and wet, and finally, still hugging me, she whispers: "The children could come home . . ."

"They won't . . ."

"I'll never get the cake baked . . ."

"Yes you will . . ."

She kisses my ear. Her body is pressed against mine, and her sweat is blending with mine, and she whispers: "You're ready, aren't you?"

"Yes . . ."

"So am I. God help me, so am I . . ."

We walk to her bedroom, which is downstairs. I help her untie the apron, and I help her pull the dress over her head. She is wearing a slip but no brassiere or panties. "It's too hot for all that stuff," she tells me. She helps me out of my shoes and socks, kneeling in front of me, hugging my waist, pressing a cheek against the front of my trousers. Then she helps me out of my shirt and trousers and underwear, and we totter to the bed, and she lies down, and I pull up the slip, and then I am on top of her, and she says: "Kindness, for God's sake . . . please . . . please give me that . . ."

There are doilies in this bedroom, and a tinted photograph of Ernest grins from atop the dresser, and Bernadette wraps her legs around the small of my back, and I enter her easily, and we pump and thresh, and she kisses me, and she moans, and she scratches me, and our sweat mingles and blots as it goes dribbling down our bodies, and she makes fists, and she flings her arms apart, and her face is knotted, and she tells me she is coming, and at that moment I begin to gush and spurt, and our rhythm is perfect, and it as though we have been here on this bed for years, and I come steadily, sweetly, transfixed in what is almost a sort of despair, and Bernadette grimaces, and she pounds her fists against the sides of the bed, and her mouth hangs open, and she tells me yes, and so I continue to pump

413

(there is enough of me remaining for that), and finally she gives one last shuddering upward thrust of her pelvis, and then she flops back, and she is groaning and licking her lips, and she tells me yes, yes; it happened; it really did.

I roll on my back and close my eyes. I wrap my arms around my chest, and I am wheezing. There is a faint grief within me, and I do not know why. It has gathered itself in my chest, and it rubs my throat, and there is a sweetness to it, and it is not a bit carnal. Have I fallen in love? I do not believe so. Do I feel sorry for Bernadette? No, not a bit. She is strong, and she is humorous, and there is no need to feel sorry for her.

Bernadette's hair is spread on the pillow in snarls and great loose waves. She shakes her head, brushes back her hair, sighs, then smiles at me and says: "You don't have to worry about it . . ."

I turn to her and kiss her throat and her breasts. "Worry about what?" I ask her.

"About me. I won't make any trouble."

"Trouble?"

"I won't *talk* or *fuss* or anything like *that,*" says Bernadette. Her hands are linked over her belly, and it is as though she is trying to hide her stretch marks, and she looks down and says: "And anyway, I'm not that much of a bargain."

"Don't talk foolishness. I have never cared much for people who talk foolishness. It's not like you, and you know that."

She shrugs. "Well, I just wanted you to understand that you don't have to endanger anything." She unlinks her hands and places one of them on my penis. She touches it lightly, and her thumb moves in a gentle circular motion, and then she says: "You've done a dear thing."

"Bernadette, I *care* about you. I wasn't doing you any sort of favor. I'm here with you because I *want* to be here with you."

"I care about you, too, Howard. I have for a long time."

"A long time?"

"Yes. Tell me, do you feel sad?"

"A little."

"Why?" she asks me, smiling, and the pain is reflected mostly in her eyes.

"I don't know," I tell her.

"Because this can go noplace?"

"Perhaps."

"How old are you? Thirtynine? Forty?"

"Fortyone."

Bernadette nods. "And I'm thirtyeight. It's a little late in the game to be falling in love, isn't it?"

"Is there a time limit?" I ask her.

"I have seven children, and you have three. That makes ten. And when there are ten children involved, plus one wife, then yes, there *is* a time limit."

I say nothing. There is no way to answer her argument, and I know it.

"I have a need," says Bernadette. "You're the first man I've been with since Ernie was killed. Even though I'm a skinny old bag of bones, I could have had some others, but I didn't. And you want to know why? It was because I've always insisted on some *feeling,* and I didn't *feel* anything. Not with them. But, with *you,* yes, there *is* a feeling, and I knew that the time would come some day. Which is why I've dreamed about you for so many years. Even when Ernie was alive, I dreamed about you."

I smile. "And *I've* dreamed about *you.* Very warm dreams, too."

"Good," says Bernadette. She still is holding my penis. "My dreams were warm, too. But there's one thing you have to understand." She rubs my penis. "You dear man," she says, "you dear, dear man, we have to go away from it now. You have helped me, and maybe somehow I have helped you, but there can't be anything more. You know we're both going to feel badly about it starting about a minute from now. And you know we're not going to tear apart our families by running off together or anything as dumb as that. And anyway, that's not the way we *are.* We have too much good sense. And we pay attention to our obligations. Well, am I right or am I right?"

"You are right . . ."

"You are the second man for me in my entire life."

"And you are the second woman."

"Really?"

"Really."

"Well," says Bernadette, "what do you know about that . . ."

We lie there and talk for perhaps half an hour all told. Then, by a sort of mutual consent, we get up and dress ourselves, and I kiss her, and we return to the kitchen. I am sleepy, and I am too warm, and I wash my hands and face in the cold water from the tap. Bernadette returns to the stove and her pan and her flour and the sifter. She allows as how her schedule has fallen apart. Peter will be awakening from his nap any time now, and she wants the cake to be in the oven before he comes downstairs. She begins working with the flour again, and I watch her for a moment, and I glance at the shepherds and the angels, and then I go to her, seize her by the waist, spin her around and kiss her full on the lips. Our hands touch, and the flour spreads from hers to mine, just as it did earlier, and she laughs and bends down and tries to kiss the flour off my hands, and now her mouth is white, and she smiles crookedly at me and says: "Thank you. God bless you. I'll be no trouble for you. That I promise."

And so, after again rinsing my hands, I leave that place. Bernadette accompanies me to the door, and she uses the hem of the apron to wipe the flour off her mouth and hands. "Thank you for giving the begonias a drink," she says.

We are at the front door. I turn to her.

"Don't say anything," she says. Her face begins to give way, and she draws back, and it is almost as though she expects me to hit her.

She is right, of course. I go out the door. I pick up the bucket and return it to its place out back by the cellar door. I walk to the Studebaker and climb inside. I glance toward the house, and she has closed the front door. I try to start the car, but it stalls. I tell myself for God's sake don't flood the engine. The second time I am more careful, and the engine catches. I carefully back out the driveway onto 33-A. It occurs to me that I have forgotten to show Bernadette the contents of the bag of building blocks, but I know I cannot go back inside that house with its sheetmetal roof and its foundering begonias. I trust Bernadette will open the bag and deduce that the blocks are a birthday present for Peter. I sigh, and my body odors are enough to set the heavens to exploding, and I drive very slowly all the way back to Paradise Falls. The lowlands shimmer, and the highway shimmers, and the river is a blinding gold. Today I have behaved most uncharacteristically, and I suppose I will carry my transgression for years. I blink through the windshield, and I am almost ready to believe that I can see Bernadette's angular humorous face blinking back at me. When I walk into the house, Anne takes one look at me and tells me *my,* the heat really got to you, didn't it? She is wearing a white dress and her face is open and plumply sweet, and I say something to the effect that the heat in Egypt is really terrible. I ask her how Florence is coming along. Fine, says Anne, just fine. She seems to be sweating very nicely.

I go upstairs and take a bath. Anne sits in the bathroom and watches me, and we talk a little about Henry the Always Boy (she tells me she sat on the front porch this afternoon and once again read the Kitty Heaven letter), and then she asks me how Bernadette is getting along, and I allow as how Bernadette is getting along just splendidly. Good, says Anne. I've always liked Bernadette.

The next day I come down with a perfectly dreadful summer cold. It takes up residence in my chest and sinuses, and I am laid up the better part of a week.

Amberson was so startled he slammed on the brakes without thinking. The Pontiac went into a skid on the wet pavement. Anne was thrown forward against the dashboard, and Sinclair gave a great howl. The skid took the Pontiac straight toward the spot where the girl was standing. Amberson fought the wheel, and he remembered something to the effect that one should steer in the direction of a skid, and he did so, and the car went bouncing onto the berm, and the girl screamed and jumped aside. There was an immense crunch and splatter of gravel, and Amberson's mouth was full of what tasted like blood. The car bumped over the gravel and headed straight toward a sign that said MARYLAND US 40, and again Amberson grappled with the wheel, and the car brushed past the sign, touching it just enough to make it give forth a sort of echoing metallic noise as it bent back and then madly began to wobble and moan. Amberson pressed the brake pedal to the floor, and the car finally came to a stop, and it was sideways on the berm, and Sinclair was standing on one of Amberson's shoulders, and Anne was shaking like something frail in a strong wind. Amberson leaned forward, pressed his forehead against the steering wheel and closed his eyes. He heard the girl's footsteps come crunching toward the car, but there was nothing he could do about it. He brushed Sinclair off his shoulder, but he did not open his eyes.

Then the back door was opened, and Anne gave a little shriek.

Amberson opened his eyes and looked around.

The girl climbed into the back seat. She had gray eyes, and she was wearing Levis and a heavy brown jacket, and there was an olivedrab pack on her back. She held the pistol loosely, and it was quite large. She was gasping, and her face was wet. She slammed shut the door, and then she said: "My God, I'm sorry . . . I didn't mean to . . . ahhh . . . ohhh . . . it's been a bad day, and you'll have to excuse me . . ."

Amberson simply looked at her.

"Thank you," said the girl. "Thank you very much. I mean, I just had to get somebody to stop. For all I know, he might, ah, come back . . ."

Anne's hands were over her face, and she apparently could not keep from trembling. Her shoulders moved in spasms, and her breath came in a sort of hiss.

"He might *really* be angry now," said the girl. "He might come back to, ah, reassert his *machismo*. People, people like him place great store in their *machismo* . . ."

"What?" said Amberson.

The girl looked down at the pistol. She breathed in a sort of shudder, and she brushed her hair back from her eyes. She smiled a little at Amberson, and her teeth were tiny and bright. "Don't . . . ah, don't let the gun scare you," she said. "I only use it to scare *them* when they get a bad case of the hands . . ."

Anne's hands came away from her face. "Young lady, just what are you talking about?" she wanted to know. Her voice was thin and shattered, and it was pitched too high.

The girl settled back. She swallowed air. "Just a second . . . I, ah, just let me get my breath . . ."

Amberson looked at Anne.

Anne had twisted around in her seat, and she was rubbing her right shoulder. "Are you holding us up or what?" she asked the girl.

The girl breathed deeply through her mouth. Her head moved from side to side. She was sitting next to Sinclair's box, and she glanced down at it, and then she smiled at Sinclair, who was lying on the back shelf and staring at her over his forepaws. "It looks like a nice kitty," said the girl. "I love kittycats."

"I asked you a question," said Anne.

Again the girl's head moved from side to side. "It's not even loaded," she said. "I carry it because my daddy gave it to me. I do a lot of hitchhiking . . . and, well, you never know . . ."

Anne looked at Amberson. "What do you think?" she asked him.

Amberson spread his hands. "I don't know what to think. Are you all right? Did you hurt your head against the dashboard?"

"No," said Anne. "I'm fine." Then, to the girl: "You could have killed us, waving that thing at the car the way you did."

"I'm sorry . . ." said the girl. "It's just that I was scared he'd come back."

"Who?" said Anne. "What are you talking about?"

The girl smiled. "All right now, friends, taking it from the top. My name is Sherry Muller, and I'm from Garrettsburg, Maryland, and I am a student at Oberlin College, in Ohio, where I major in dramatics and the trumpet. I am on my way home to see my brother Art, who was cut this week by the Buffalo Braves. This morning, on the Ohio Turnpike near Youngstown, I was picked up by a fellow in a red

418

Toyota. He was on his way to Washington, D.C., and I talked him into getting off the Pennsylvania Turnpike near Washington, Pennsylvania, and driving to Washington, D.C., by way of this US 40 that passes through Garrettsburg. Well, along about Washington, Pennsylvania, my friend in the red Toyota began to get friendly. He was about forty, and he was big and fat, and he told me his wife had died last year of sugar diabetes, and he got to talking about how sometimes all the *amenities* and the *maneuvers* just seemed like such a *waste* of *time* and prevented *true communication,* heh, heh, my dear, the whole W. C. Fields thing, if you know what I mean. And then his hands got to living a life of their own, and I swear to you every time his fingers touched my leg they felt like *worms.* Not that I'm some sort of blushing virgin, but *really,* the man was not exactly the answer to a maiden's prayer. So, one thing led to another, and finally I suggested he pull off to the side of the road, and it was then—after he stopped the car—that I pulled the gun out from under my jacket. And so I got out of the car. And he yelled at me. Called me all sorts of names. But he didn't come after me. I waved the gun at the car, and he drove off, and he was yelling all the way. And then you came along, and I was sort of uptight, you know? And it didn't occur to me that the gun would scare you, and that's the end of my sad story. So, tell me—would you mind taking me to Garrettsburg? It's only about twentyfive miles up the road . . ."

"You say that thing isn't loaded?" Anne wanted to know.

"No," said the girl. "Look." She lifted the pistol and placed the barrel in her mouth. She pulled the trigger, and there was a clicking sound. She again pulled the trigger. Another clicking sound.

"Stop that," said Amberson.

The girl removed the barrel from her mouth. She licked her lips. "Well, I *am* a dramatics major," she said. "Dramatics and trumpet." She opened her jacket. She was wearing a man's shirt under the jacket. It was yellow, and it was frayed. She had small pointed breasts. She tucked the pistol inside the waist of her Levis, then rebuttoned her jacket. She smiled. "Out of sight, out of mind," she said.

Sinclair came down off the shelf and climbed on the girl's lap.

Anne looked at Amberson, and again she rubbed her right shoulder.

He shrugged, grunted, moistened his tongue and shook his head.

The girl stroked Sinclair's spine, and his claws went in and out. She smiled at Amberson again, and she said: "Well, do I have a ride? It's cold and wet out there . . ."

He nodded. He put the car in gear. His gums hurt.

See now 1934, a grim and thunderous night in late March, and I am returning from Lancaster after attending a regional meeting of the state track coaches' association. My car is a '29 Chevrolet, and it pokes uneasily along a rainspattered 33-A northwest of Egypt. Its headlights are barely able to penetrate the heavy and stormy darkness, and I am driving the road more by memory than by vision. Frankly, I can barely see anything, and I am grateful that these valley lowlands are so flat. The wipers bang and clatter, and I am leaning forward so far that my nose and chin are just about touching the windshield. Here and there the road dips, and every dip means a pond, and the Chevrolet goes plashing through the ponds like a speedboat in a newsreel. I grimace. I hold my breath. I keep expecting the water to stall the engine. If this happens, I do not have the vaguest idea what I shall do. I know nothing about automobiles, and I never have.

Wind buffets the Chevrolet, and I am gripping the wheel with both hands. The car is too fragile for this sort of weather, too fragile and too old. Ernest keeps the engine in tune for me, but for more than a year now he has been telling me that what I *really* need is a new car, or at least a newer used car. But I cannot afford anything better, and who in this impoverished nation can? Certainly not a smalltown schoolteacher whose income . . . before taxes . . . is $1,500 a year. I must make do with this sputtering little machine, and that is all there is to it.

The highway parallels the river, but I cannot make out how high the river is. This is, to be sure, the flood season, and I wonder if Ernest and Bernadette are moving their furniture to the second floor. I am now about two or three miles northwest of their place, and if worse comes to worst I can always spend the night there—provided they are not flooded out. Still, the situation does not appear that critical, at least not yet. If it were, the Chevrolet would have been inundated by now, and I probably would be sitting on its roof or huddling in some farmer's attic. The Chevrolet is moving forward at about 15 miles an hour, and I dare not go any slower. If I did, it might stall. So I keep my foot steady on the accelerator, and I think loving thoughts about Our Lord, and I tell Him I shall forever be His humble and obedient servant if only He sees me through this soggy and wind-blasted ordeal. My feet are damp, and so are my armpits. I snuffle, and I wipe moisture from my eyes, and a great golden crack of lightning spreads across the sky, and I cringe a little.

In my time, I have known elderly ladies who hide in closets when there is such a storm as this. When I was a boy, I thought those elderly ladies were ridiculous. Now, I am not so sure. I say to myself: There is a frightened elderly lady living within you, and she is quaking like an angel that has stumbled upon Armageddon, and if she is ridiculous, then most assuredly so are you.

A car comes toward me, and I suck my lips. It is to my left, but is it far enough to my left? I edge to my right. The car's headlights are a smear of yellow, and it meets me at the bottom of a dip, and we exchange geysers, and my engine misfires, and I feel a sort of clap deep inside my chest, and I press down on the accelerator, and the engine dies for a moment (and the clap becomes a series of claps), but then it catches again, and I am out of the dip, and the other car is behind me, and I make a small triumphant squealing noise, and most of it comes from my nose.

Now the Chevrolet is doing 20 miles an hour, and its tires are hissing more loudly against the drenched bricks of 33-A, and I tell myself I have to stop sucking my lips and being such a ninny. I am thirtyseven years old, a grown man, and all I have to do is concentrate and everything will be fine. I tell the quaking elderly ladies to go away. I am a *man,* and I shall *prevail.*

I decide to play a little game with myself. Perhaps it will help me retain my manliness. I tell myself I am John Dillinger, and I have just robbed a bank, and my life depends on my successful escape. I ask myself: Would John Dillinger mewl like a cat and suck his lips? The answer is obvious, and so I bare my teeth and give a sort of snarl. So rage on, ye elements; John Dillinger is not afraid of you; he spits at you, and you are nothing. (Under normal circumstances, I deplore John Dillinger and the folk hero status he has attained. He is nothing but a cheap criminal, and the public is stupid for holding him in such adulation. And yet there is a sort of style to the man; he does possess a certain witty rakishness that is not altogether unattractive. And so, for perhaps that reason, I am John Dillinger, and the elements are to me what the police are to him, and it is necessary that I laugh at them.)

So here he sits, tiny and bespectacled, this nervously gnashing John Dillinger, cloaked in the foolproof disguise of a teacher and track coach, and the Chevrolet splashes through the urgent onrushing night, and he speaks aloud, and he says: "All right, boys. If they start to gain on us, aim for their tires. And remember—they're all a bunch of dirty rats." And then this shrunken John Dillinger grins a lopsided devilmaycare grin, and his eyes narrow, and he says: "If we got to go, we're going to take some of them with us, and don't you forget it."

A rush of thunder comes directly at the car, and it cracks overhead, and the car trembles, and John Dillinger has vanished, and his place has been taken by a fellow named Howard W. Amberson, and I wish I had two more hands so I could cover my ears. The game is finished, and I do not have the time to summon the illusions necessary for another one (I could perhaps be Buck Jones, and I could order the homesteaders to form a circle with their wagons), and so I have to be content to be Howard W. Amberson, stormtossed and bemused, with an elderly lady curled pitifully in his belly. I shake my head. I tell myself I am a lunatic. What has possessed me to talk aloud and play at makebelieve at a time like this? Great God, don't I understand the *seriousness* of the situation? I could *drown!* I could *ram a tree!* The car could *skid off the road and overturn!* And so I grimace. I gnaw. I squint. The interior of the Chevrolet is terribly warm, and the air is stale, but at least I am not drowning, and that is a decided plus. Suppose I were a field mouse tonight. Or a lost kitten. I undoubtedly would be dead by now, a soggy lump in someone's flooded cornfield. But I am a *human being.* I am a *man.* I have *intelligence.* I shall *prevail.*

Rain splatters the window next to my head, and occasionally I am able to make out the vague outline of trees, and the trees are bending, and sticks and shards and flapping pieces of cloth go flying across the road, impaled for a moment in the glow of the headlights, and I keep looking for Egypt . . . Egypt . . . just ahead *must* be Egypt. I know now that I will stop at Ernest's place. Perhaps I'll not spend the night there, but at least I will be able to rest before completing this hectic and fretful journey. Surely Bernadette will give me a cup of coffee, and surely Ernest will look at the car to make sure it is able to continue. His bankruptcy has affected him badly, and no one disputes that, but he still does take pride in his skill as a mechanic, and I am sure he will not mind checking over the Chevrolet.

I smile. I tell myself I have been behaving like a silly nincompoop. I have allowed my rhetoric and my sense of absurdity to distort the reality of the situation. There have been severe rainstorms before, and there will be severe rainstorms again, and it is stupid of me to embellish them with games and deceptions and flat little jests. (Do I have some sort of artistic temperament? Is that why I am so prone to distort the reality of all this? Great weeping God, an artistic temperament at $1,500 a year . . . before taxes . . .)

Again I smile. I try not to blink too often, lest my vision be blurred.

I concentrate on the pavement. As long as I can see the pavement, I am all right, and I shall be in Egypt before I know it. Just a little more concentration, and . . .

Then comes Egypt.

Glory be to God!

Rain smacks the windshield, and the wipers flap, and the headlights are hazy and vague, but this indeed is Egypt. No saint or zealot ever will see it as heaven, and no tablets ever will be struck in its honor, but to me *Egypt* is the Promised Land, and if I have thrown Scripture into reverse gear, so be it. My heart is full, and I want to sing Hallelujah. I see the spire of the EUB church; I see the Coca-Cola sign that hangs in front of Frank Auker's little store; I see the low sheetmetal roofs of the houses that line 33-A, and I rejoice. It is past eleven o'clock, and I slow down the Chevrolet, and it creeps through the puddles and the pools and over the shattered treebranches. There is no other traffic, and I see not a soul, but what does this matter? I have been *saved*. I have *prevailed*.

"Oh boy, oh boy," I say aloud as I guide the Chevrolet into Ernest's driveway. Its ruts are filled with water, and so I park out near the highway. Across the road, the fillingstation he "manages" is shuttered and dark. I get out of the car and start to sprint toward the house, and the rain catches me broadside, and I stumble and fall to my knees. The rain has smeared my spectacles so I cannot see. I remove my spectacles, and the rain comes into my eyes like pins, but at least *now* I can see a *little*, and I stand up and bend into the wind and the rain, and I begin to run again, and mud sucks at my shoes, but this time—even though I stagger and flail—I manage to make it to the front door, and I pound on the front door, and I am gasping and wheezing, but I have *made it;* I have *prevailed*.

The door is opened by Beth, who is Ernest's oldest child. She blinks out at me, and she starts to say something, but she is interrupted by an immense clap of thunder that causes the house to tremble. The clap of thunder is followed by a sort of surly menacing grumble, and then comes lightning, and Beth's face becomes abruptly gray and then blue. She gives a little shriek, places a hand over her mouth, then beckons me inside. I hurry across the threshold and slam the door behind me. Beth is fifteen . . . almost sixteen, in fact . . . and rather plump, but she has her mother's dark hair and coloring. She says to me my goodness, Uncle Howard, where did you come from? You look like a drowned rat. She leads me through the darkened front room and into the kitchen, and the rest of the family is there—all except Ernest. Bernadette, who is sitting at the table and holding the baby, Peter, smiles up at me and says *well,* for heaven's sake. The next oldest daughter, Jean, who is thirteen, is sitting next to her. The twin boys, Billy and Charley, are lounging on the floor, and the two next youngest children, Nancy and Bobby, are playing with a calico kitten that is trying to crawl under the stove. (I believe the twins are eleven or twelve, and I think Nancy is eight and Bobby six, although I would not want to wager my life on those statistics. It has always been difficult for me to keep all those ages straight, which I certainly believe is understandable, considering the size of this family. So kindly consider the ages to be only an approximation.) Smiling, Bernadette hands the baby to Jean and comes to me and helps me out of my coat and tells me to kick off my dirty wet shoes. She tells Beth to take a towel and clean off the shoes—but don't use a *good* towel; find a clean rag. Beth rummages in a drawer for a clean rag, and Bernadette takes me to the table, and we sit down side by side across from Jean and the baby, who apparently is quite soundly asleep. Its little hands are in fists, and its face is squeezed tight as a grape. Bernadette is wearing a frayed bathrobe over a pink flannel nightgown, and the lines on her forehead are deeper than I have remembered them. All the children also are wearing nightclothes (Beth's are too tight, and Jean's soon will be), and from time to time the younger ones yawn and rub fists in their eyes. Bernadette asks me if I would like a cup of coffee. I tell her yes, that would be just fine. She asks me do I mind leftover. I tell her no, of course not. She reaches across the table, takes the baby from Jean, then tells Jean to light the stove and warm up the coffee. By this time, Beth has found a rag, and she is vigorously wiping the mud and dirt off my shoes. She is standing at the sink, and holds the shoes over the sink while she works on them (she knows enough not to make a mess on the floor). Bernadette has always exercised a genial yet strong discipline over her children, and I do not believe I have ever seen any of them question her or give her any serious backtalk. Now she looks at me, and the baby presses its face against her arm, and she asks me what on *earth* am I doing *out* on a night like *this.* I explain to her about the coaches' meeting and my troubles on 33-A. She smiles and says well, this storm is a corker all right, and if it lasts much longer we'll probably have to start moving our stuff upstairs again. I nod and tell her I would be glad to help, and then she asks me will I be staying the night. I say to her no, I don't think so; Anne would worry. She tells me there is a pay telephone in the fillingstation, if I want to call Anne so she doesn't worry. I tell Bernadette let me drink my coffee first; then I'll make some sort of determination. She says fine, would you like to have it in the front room without all these kids underfoot? The twins look up at me and grin, and Beth giggles from the sink. Jean brings me my cup of coffee, and Bernadette gives her the baby. Bernadette and I go into the front room, and she switches on a table lamp. She seats herself on the sofa, and I sit down in the only easy chair. It is heavy and lumpy, and doilies are pinned to its arms. I sigh, settle back, stretch my legs. Bernadette gives me a narrow look, then says: "I bet your soaks are socked."

"How's that again?" I ask her, sipping my coffee.

"I say something wrong?"

"You said you bet my soaks were socked."

Bernadette grins. "I did?"

"You did indeed."

Now she laughs outright. "Well," she says, "it's been that kind of a night. What I *meant* to say was: I bet your socks are soaked."

"They're a little damp."

"Would you like to take them off so they can dry?"

"No. Thank you just the same, but they're fine. Really."

"Are your feet dirty?"

"Now, Bernadette, don't be naughty."

"Well, I was only *wondering* . . ."

"Ah, that's our Bernadette . . ."

Her laughter has subsided, but it still hangs at the edges of her mouth. "Socked soaks," she says. "Dear *me* . . ."

"Those were the words you used. By the way, where is my brother?"

"As long as we're speaking about socked soaks, where's Ernie, right?"

"Now, you know I didn't mean it that way," I tell her. I sip more coffee.

Bernadette shrugs. "Well, it's no secret," she says. She nods toward the door to the downstairs bedroom. "He's asleep in there. Passed out, if you want to know the truth. Today was payday, and he stopped at Frank Auker's place and bought fifteen bottles of beer, and he came home and down they went, down the hatch. He'll sleep through this whole storm, if I'm any judge. The noise has been enough to wake up the dead, but it didn't wake up *him,* no indeed. And it wasn't only the noise of the storm. The kids got to hollering and moving around upstairs, and Nancy went and started screaming that the world was coming to an end, so I went up there and brought them all down to the kitchen and turned on all the lights so they wouldn't be scared. And I've been sitting with them now for about an hour, maybe an hour and a half."

"May I ask you the obvious question?"

"Go ahead."

"Is he . . . ah, is he treating you any better?"

"No. The kids either."

"I thought he was reconciling himself."

"No. Not true. Tonight he hit Jean because she didn't fetch him his church key quick enough. He hit her across the mouth, and you know Jean; she hurt like the blazes but she didn't let on. She stood there and she rubbed her mouth and then she sort of dropped the church key in his lap. And he took the church key and he opened his bottle with such force that the cap went flying and Jean caught it before it hit the floor. She caught it and she looked at it, and then she went back into the kitchen, and there wasn't a peep out of her the whole time. That's Jean for you. A lot of the time I think maybe I like her the best of all of them. But then it's stupid to make that kind of comparison, and I usually wind up calling myself a lot of dumb names."

"She is a good child, but they all are good children. You should be proud."

"I am. I really honest-to-God am."

"Is Ernest drinking more?"

"He's always drinking more."

"And so he's not reconciled himself at all?"

"Not at all," says Bernadette. She stares down at her hands. She rubs her palms together. She rubs them slowly, and the sound of the rain makes them inaudible. "He . . . well, there was a keystone sitting in the middle of his life, and then that keystone was pulled out, and all the other stones came tumbling down. And now he doesn't even *wash* as often as he ought to. And his *breath* is bad all the time, you know? And then there are the times when he cries."

"You've told me about them," I tell her. I finish the coffee.

"They're coming more often."

"He just has to get through it as best he can, the way we all are trying to do."

"He tells me he's not a man any more," says Bernadette.

"That's nonsense."

"Tell *him* that."

"All he has to do is pick up a newspaper and he can see that—"

"We can't afford a newspaper."

I hesitate. I set down my empty cup on an end table. I have not known that my brother and his wife cannot afford a newspaper.

Then, lamely, I say: "But the *Journal-Democrat* is only twelve cents a week. And he does have a salary and a commission from Standard Oil."

"Twelve cents buys two loaves of dayold bread," says Bernadette, "and in a good week he makes twentyfive dollars. I'm not fooling you, Howard. Twentyfive dollars. Why do you think we've had the telephone taken out? Why do you think we sold the fridge? Why do you think the bank took this house away from us?"

"I'm sorry. I didn't mean to get you upset."

Bernadette sighs. "No," she says, and she leans forward and tries to smile, *"I'm* the one who ought to be sorry." She settles back, and now her hands again are motionless in her lap. She turns her head and briefly looks out the front window. She puffs out her cheeks, then again looks at me, exhales and says: "It's this stupid weather. Every spring it turns me into something I don't really like an awful lot." She hesitates, and there is a crack of lightning, followed by a distant echoing roll of thunder. "You see, with Ernie the thing is, it wasn't anything *he* did. I mean, I think he would be all right if it'd been something where he could say to himself: All right, I didn't know what I was doing, and so I failed. I was a dumbbell, and so the keystone was pulled out. But he *wasn't* a dumbbell; he was knocked down because people he doesn't even *know* somehow somehow *somehow* threw the *entire country* into this mess. And so now he sits around and drinks beer, and now and then he hits one of the kids, or he hits *me,* and I don't . . . I just can't really *blame* him. His whole life was that station and this house and his family, and now all he has left is the family part of it, and he can't do for his family what he *wants* to do for his family, and so *all right,* he *hits* us now and then, and we'll just have to take it. I mean, either we love him or we don't—*and,* if we *do,* we have to understand him. It's what I tell the kids after he's been mean to them. Which is the only way I've got of explaining it . . . " Another hesitation. "I want to be fair," she says. She gathers the bathrobe more tightly around her. "I'm his wife, and I try to take it seriously."

"Yes," I tell her. "I know you do." I have an impulse to go to her and embrace her, but I do not follow through on it. I have seldom followed through on impulses. That is not my nature.

"You have mud on the knees of your britches," she tells me.

"I fell down."

"It's been a terrible evening for you, hasn't it?"

"Until now. I am beginning to relax a little."

"Good," says Bernadette.

"It was something of an ordeal, driving through this storm."

"I can imagine."

"I was frightened. I really was."

"Is Thirtythree-A in bad shape?"

"Yes," I say. "The car should have had pontoons. Why, I even played a little game with myself. In order to give myself more courage, I tried to imagine I was John Dillinger."

"John who? John *Dillinger?*"

I nod. "He is a man who has to face a great many emergencies, and I tried to imagine myself in *his* shoes, and I tried to imagine what *his* attitude would be. I wanted to work myself into a state where I would be able to share his reckless and brave attitude. But it was all a lot of trivial nonsense. Who am I to say what John Dillinger's attitude is? I have never *met* the man. All I know about him is what I have read in the newspapers, and perhaps the image of him is untrue. Perhaps, for all *I* know, he is a blubbering coward. And anyway, what right did I have to play a silly *game* at a time like *that?* Instead of concentrating on the problem at hand, I was making up a false identity for myself, and it was pointless and foolish. So I just . . . well, I abandoned the game . . ."

Bernadette smiles. "Well, I don't think you're exactly the John Dillinger *type* . . ."

"Neither do I."

"Ernie could be, though."

"What's that?"

Bernadette's smile is gone. "If worse came to worst, I think he'd . . . well, *you* know . . ."

"What? Rob a bank?"

"Does it sound too farfetched? You think he really *wouldn't* if it was a question of keeping us out of the county home? I'm not saying he's about to go galloping into Paradise Falls with a *gun,* but I *am* saying he *could*—if it came down to that some day. As long as I've known him, he's had faith that he could, ah, make his own way and, ah, create his own luck. And he's had faith that the world would, ah, reward an honest day's work with an honest day's wages. But that feeling's gone now. Why, he's even talked to me about your John Dillinger. He's told me he doesn't see what's so terrible about John Dillinger. If the banks steal, and Standard Oil steals, why all the fuss about a little old holdup man? In a world of big thieves, why make such a commotion about a little thief?"

"Has Ernest *talked* about robbing a bank?"

"Not in so many words. But you never can tell."

"He's no John Dillinger. That's ridiculous."

Bernadette folds her arms over her belly. "*I* know that," she says, "and *you* know it, but I don't think *he* knows it. The thought keeps pushing around at the back of his mind."

"Well, that's just—"

The bedroom door opens, and my brother Ernest comes splaying into the room. He is wearing only his shorts and undershirt, and his hands and arms are layered with what appears to be grease. "Jesus H. Christ," he says, and his mouth is full of spittle. He swallows, blinks at me and says: "Well, looky here who came in out of the rain . . ."

Bernadette and I have both been startled—so much so that we both flinched when he so abruptly came into the room. I get to my feet. "Evening," I say to my brother.

"What the hell *you* doing here?"

"The storm is very bad," says Bernadette. "Howard was on his way back from Lancaster and he—"

"A coaches' meeting," I tell my brother, "and the driving was so difficult I thought I'd just stop awhile and rest. You know I'm not much of a driver, even when the weather is good . . ."

"All right," says Ernest. "Good for you." Then, to Bernadette: "Any more beer?"

"No," says Bernadette. "You drank it all." She draws up her legs under her body. Her arms have not come away from her belly, and so now she appears knotted, taut, exposing as little of herself as she can.

"Shit," says Ernest. He leans back against the door and closes his eyes. His body is hairy, and there are slabs of gray fat on his arms. He is not yet thirtyeight but he appears to be about fifty. "The kids all right?"

"Yes. They're in the kitchen. They were restless, and so I brought them downstairs."

"Any water coming in?"

"Not yet."

"I hit Beth, didn't I?"

"You hit *Jean.*"

Ernest opens his eyes. "I could of sworn it was Beth."

"It was Jean, and she didn't say a word. Not a peep."

Ernest looks at me. He comes a step or two away from the door. "Howard, honest to God I don't mean to hit them."

"I know that," I tell him.

He nods toward Bernadette. "Look at the way she's sitting. She thinks I'm going to hit *her.* She's getting ready for it."

"I think no such thing," says Bernadette. Her arms unfold. She stretches out her legs. "I'm not afraid. Not of *you.* You're my *husband.*"

Ernest still is looking at me. "I love her, and I love the kids, and I got no right hitting them." He shakes his head. "Jesus, I am like a piece of shit on a hot henhouse roof . . . I *stink* . . ."

"There's no need to talk that way," says Bernadette. "It's *common,* and it's *dumb,* and it doesn't *prove* anything."

Ernest tries to grin at me. He still is looking directly at me. It is as though some terrible pain awaits him if he looks at his wife. "She's still trying to make me into a gentleman," he says. He shakes his head. He rubs his forehead and his temples, streaking them. "My God," he says, "I don't know . . . I just . . . well, the thing is . . . the thing is, not even the goddamned beer tastes the way it used to . . . Mister Baker comes today with my pay, and we figure out my commission, and the whole shooting match comes to twentytwo dollars and sixty cents, and I go see Frank Auker and buy fifteen bottles at fifteen cents each, which comes to two dollars and twentyfive cents, and I bring home those fifteen bottles, and I drink down all the beer from all the bottles, and the rain starts to come, and I sit here and wait for the beer to do something for me like it used to when I'd be with my buddies and we'd get ourselves all *sloshed* and *loud* and *horny* or whatever . . . but now, I don't know . . . any more . . . any more all it does is twist my gut and make me piss a lot . . . and maybe hit Bernadette or one of the kids . . . you think something's been done to all the beer in the country? You think maybe that's one more thing the world's doing so it can crack my balls? Yeah, let's really split open old Ernie Amberson's balls. Let's make his beer taste like piss, and let's get him good and sick, and let's keep him dirty all the time, and let's see to it that he beats on his wife and his kids . . ." Then, grimacing, Ernest looks directly at his wife. "How can you put up with all this?" he asks her. He goes to the sofa and flops down next to her. He snuffles. He coughs. "You . . . you trying to be a saint or something?"

Bernadette smiles at him and touches one of his grimy hands. "I'm trying to be a wife," she says.

"I don't make it easy . . ."

"That's true."

Ernest grunts. "You don't lie much, do you?"

"I try not to."

Ernest looks at me. "Sit down," he says. "Christ's sake, I'm not going to hit her. Sit down and enjoy the hospitality of our house . . ."

"All right," I say. I return to the chair and seat myself. Outside, the rain slams against the windowpanes, and the thunder and lightning persist. I press my palms against the arms of the chair, and I am perspiring, but there is nothing healthy about my perspiration. It is too cold to be of any use. It itches and it vexes, and I want to scratch myself in a number of impolite places. I have no privacy, and so I shall have to wait.

"You want to hear a story?" Ernest asks me. Then, to Bernadette: "It's about the little bird, the robin, the one I saw today. I told you about it, didn't I? I mean, *before,* when I came home with the beer . . ."

"Yes," says Bernadette to her husband, "you told me. It was the excuse you gave for buying the beer, remember?"

"Oh," says Ernest, "yeah, I guess so."

"But tell him," says Bernadette. "Go ahead, Ernie. Let him hear all of it. If it makes you feel better . . . I mean, that's important . . ."

My brother nods. He rubs his jaw. "It was really something," he says to me. "It happened this morning about nine o'clock. I was over at the station, and I was just sitting there on the bench, the one outside the door. You know the bench I mean. The little green one. There wasn't a goddamned speck of business, and so I was just sitting there and watching the cars go by. And working with a toothpick, cleaning dirt out from under my fingernails. I do that sometimes to pass the time of day. It beats pissing in the wind, right?"

"Now, Ernie," says Bernadette, "just stick to the—"

"All right," he says. He blinks at Bernadette, and again he tries to grin. "Excuse me all to hell," he says. Again he looks at me, and he leans forward and resumes: "So then came this little bird, this robin, the first robin I've seen this spring. For a robin, it wasn't very big, and it landed on top of the ethyl pump and stared at me, brave as the daylights. And so I looked back at it. And then the little sonofabitch he hopped down right in front of me, and he went peep, peep, just like that, just like maybe he was nothing more than a baby. Peep, peep, sort of weak, and I wondered if there was something wrong with him. And then he hopped forward, one hop, two hops, three hops, four hops, maybe five, and then he gave another peep and sort of fell back on his ass. Honest to God. One second he was hopping, and the next second he just went blahhh, and he lay there

on his back with his feet in the air and by Jesus Christ he was *dead.*
The wind fluffed his feathers, but he didn't move. And he never *did*
move. He was deader than hell. I mean, what he *did* was, he came
up to me and he died. A heart attack or some goddamned thing. He
looked at good old Ernie Amberson and that was the end of him. And
all good old Ernie Amberson did was just sit there. I sat there maybe
fifteen or twenty minutes and I looked at my dead little friend, and
all that time I kept asking myself: Godalmighty, do I give off some
sort of poison gas?"

"That's ridiculous," I tell my brother.

Ernest waves a hand. "Shut up," he tells me. "It didn't happen to
you. No little bird came up to *you* and went blahhh. The kind of man
you are, if a little bird came up to you it'd probably hop on your
shoulder and sing grand opera. But *this particular bird* came up to
me and it *died.* And that's about the size of the story, except that
after the fifteen or twenty minutes George Quist's tomcat, the gray
one, came along, saw the bird, went to it and started to bat at it. And
you should of seen the look on that old cat's face when the bird didn't
move or flutter or anything else. The old cat, his eyes got big, and
then he ran like hell. And myself, I picked up the bird . . . it was
bleeding a little from where the cat had batted at it . . . and it was
cold already, even after that short a time, . . . and I got to bawling
. . . I don't know why . . . I just, well, Jesus, why was *I* the one he
had to come to? The world's full of people, and why'd he pick *me?*
So, well, I bawled. I held him in one hand, and he didn't weigh a
thing, and a little of his blood ran down my hand and out between
my fingers, and so *then* what do you think I did? Huh, Howard? You
got any idea? You want to guess?"

"No."

"I couldn't guess either when he told *me* the story," Bernadette
says to me.

"No," says Ernest, "she couldn't. For all I know, maybe she
thought I *ate* it. Maybe she—"

"Ernie," says Bernadette, seizing her husband by an arm, "that's
an awful thing to say. You keep saying you love me, and then you
accuse me of having that kind of a thought."

Ernest begins to weep. His eyes tighten, and his weeping is gut-
tural, almost a grunt. He embraces Bernadette, smearing her robe,
but she does not draw back. She pats his head and his neck, and she
kisses his eyes and his forehead. He gulps, snorts, shakes his head and
pulls away from her. He glares at me. He snuffles, and now Bernadette is plucking at him and making small comforting sounds. "I

. . . well, I stepped on him," he says. "I dropped him and I *stepped* on him, and he . . . ah, well, he squirted a little, you know? I was aggravated with him. Real aggravated. He had no right to do what he did. I hadn't ever done anything to *him,* had I?"

"Am I supposed to comment on that?" I ask my brother.

"You're supposed to shut up," says Ernest. "There's more."

"Now, now," says Bernadette to her husband, "that's enough . . ."

"I got to tell him the good part," says Ernest. He speaks hoarsely, but he is no longer weeping. He rubs his eyes with his fingers. He snuffles. Then: "An hour or so later, Mister Baker came along, him and his *vest* and his *clean fingernails* and his *nice new Buick.* My little friend has been laying there all the time, laying there all squashed and bloody with his little bones sticking out, laying there on that concrete right in front of my green bench, and the wind has been fluffing him now and then, you know? So, anyhow, Mister Baker gives me my money, and then he says excuse me, I got to use the rest room. And while he's in there, I pick up my little friend, and I carry my little friend to the nice new Buick, and I open the door, and I drop my little friend on the floor in the back. And then I go back inside the station, and Mister Baker comes out of the rest room, and he tells me *my goodness gracious,* Amberson, you ought to *clean up* that place; it's enough to make a person want to *puke;* it *smells* so bad and it's so *filthy* and all. And I tell Mister Baker yessir, I know it and I'm sorry, and I'll get to work on it right away. And he says yes, Amberson, that would be a good idea; you're a good fellow and I'm not going to report you, but *please,* try to do something about that place. And then, smiling like he's Christ on a crutch and like he's bestowed some kind of goddamned *blessing* on me, old Mister Baker goes sashaying out of the place and gets in his nice new Buick and drives away. And, as soon as he was out of earshot, I flopped down on the green bench and I just laughed fit to be tied. So he doesn't care much for stinks, huh? Well, he should just wait a day or two. He'll get into his nice new Buick some fine morning not so long from now, and my little friend will be stinking up the thing to a farethewell, and it's all very right and fitting and proper, wouldn't you say so? Huh? Wouldn't you say that's the truth?"

I shrug. I tuck my feet under the chair. "It was your way of getting back at Standard Oil, wasn't it?"

"Yeah. And it was right and fitting and proper. A stink for a stink."

"If that's the way you see it, fine. I'm not about to argue with you."

"Go ahead, you little prick. Argue with me."

433

"No," I tell my brother.

Ernest looks at his wife. "He's always so goddamned calm. It's like he's got cement in his veins, you know?"

"He's different from you," says Bernadette. "Different people are different, and you shouldn't call him dirty names . . ."

"You like him a whole lot, don't you?" says Ernest.

"Of course I do. You know that."

Ernest taps his teeth with his tongue. He swallows, then says to me: "You're not only *calm* all the time, you little prick. You're *clean* and you're *neat,* and you're just another goddamned Mister Baker, am I right or am I right?"

"I couldn't say. I have never met the man."

"You can take my word for it . . ."

"Ernie, you leave him be," says Bernadette.

"He's looking at me like he knows I stink," says Ernest. "I can see his little eyes behind his specs, and they're giving me the onceover like I was something hanging from a dog's ass . . ."

"All right now," I tell my brother. "That'll be enough of that. If you want to feel sorry for yourself, that's your right—but you have *no* right to accuse me of not caring about you." My face is warm, and my eyes sting. I lean forward, and my palms press heavily on the arms of the chair.

Ernest smiles lopsidedly. He nods toward Bernadette. "You care for *her*—that's who you care for."

Bernadette glares at Ernest. "What are you talking about?"

He turns to her. "The two of you, you think your shit smells like a field full of buttercups. Whenever you're together, you sort of sit off in a corner and you *chat,* la-de-dah, and the rest of us just aren't good enough for the two of you, seeing as how you're so *delicate* and *highminded* and all . . ."

Bernadette leans back and guffaws, and I for one am astonished. "Oh, my God!" she whoops. "*Delicate* and *highminded!* Seven kids and no money and a husband who pounds me like I'm a drum! That's the funniest thing I've heard in I don't know how long!" Then, as suddenly as it began, her guffawing ceases. She exhales, swipes at her forehead with the back of a hand, fluffs her hair a bit, then says: "Oh, Lord, Ernie, why do you have to behave like a chicken with its head cut off? Why can't you just try to make the best of it and let it go at that?"

Grunting, Ernest stands up. His arms hang loosely, and he sways.

Bernadette looks at him, and her eyes have enlarged themselves.

I open my mouth to speak.

"Shut up, Howard," says Ernest. "Just shut up. I'm not going to hit her."

I link my fingers together. I stare at them. The warmth in my face is too much warmth. My fingers are linked so tightly that I am able to feel the action of my pulse.

Ernest looks down at his wife. "I'm filthy and I stink, right?"

"I'm not complaining," says Bernadette.

"You never complain. You're a goddamned saint. You just sit there, and you take it, and you say to yourself: Poor Ernie. Too bad he feels sorry for himself and stinks all the time."

"If I do feel sorry for you, it's because you make it so I haven't got much choice," says Bernadette, blinking up at her husband. She pushes back her hair, sighs and tells him: "You had some sort of schedule, and it was interrupted. All right, I *know* that. But what *you* don't know is that an interruption doesn't have to be forever. My God, Ernie, where is it written that the Lord promised us nothing but milk and honey all the days we drew breath?"

Ernest looks at me. "What's she talking about? Who said anything about milk and honey? What *I* want to know is, do I stink or do I stink? I didn't ask her to tell me anything about *milk* and goddamned *honey* . . ."

"You really want me to answer your question?" I ask him.

"Yeah."

"All right then, you do indeed stink. You should take a bath."

Ernest turns to his wife. "You think I should take a bath?"

"Well," says Bernadette, "it wouldn't hurt."

"Okay," says Ernest, and his voice is tight, "I'll take a goddamned bath." He turns away from us and lurches across the room to the front window. The wind is rattling the pane, and the rain curls down in splatters and streaks. Then comes lightning, and he is outlined in gray and blue. "A bath," he says. "Yeah. Why not? I got to make myself more la-de-dah. Then maybe I can *talk* to them and they'll tell me what a good little boy I am . . ."

"No," says Bernadette, twisting around and half getting to her feet. "You've *done* that little trick. Three times last summer you did it, and it's a wonder you weren't arrested. The rest of your life, every time there's a big storm, you can't go—"

"You telling me what I can't do?"

"No," says Bernadette. "I was only—"

"I got to get clean," says Ernest. "The hell with milk and honey. I go to get *clean.*"

"What are you two talking about?" I ask them.

"I am going to take a goddamned bath," says Ernest. "A *big* goddamned bath. The biggest goddamned bath in the world. And all this grease and shit will go away, and I'll come back to you two, and you'll say: *My,* how *clean* he is . . ."

"I haven't the slightest idea what you're talking about," I tell Ernest.

"I'm talking about *this,* you cold little bastard," says Ernest, unfastening his shorts. They drop to the floor. His belly and genitals are flabby and pendulous.

"Oh *Lord,*" Bernadette says wearily.

Ernest shucks himself out of his undershirt.

"My goodness," says Bernadette, "what a beautiful sight . . ."

"If you don't like it," Ernest asks her, "how come you been sleeping with it all these years?" He walks to the front door. He turns and faces us. His body glistens, and his dirty arms are slick with the grease or whatever it is. His arms and chest are slabbed with fat. He rubs his chest and belly. "I may be the first fat starving man in history," he says.

Bernadette stands up. "Please don't do it. What'll happen if you catch cold and have to take off work?"

Ernest shakes his head no. "You want me to get clean. You want the fat starving man to smell like a field full of buttercups. All right. Fine. He'll do you that little favor. God'll give him a *real* bath . . ." He wrenches open the door, and the wind makes an enormous sucking sound, and the rain comes spattering through the screen door. "The hell with both of you!" he shouts. "The hell with you and your funny looks and your goddamned disapproval! I'm going out there, and God is going to wash me clean, and then I'll be the cleanest person in this whole house! You ever have a little bird come up to you and *die,* huh? I mean, just keel over like he's seen the worst thing in the world, and it's so ugly it makes his little heart give out? You think it's *fun* to see him flop on his ass? You think I *like* stinking the way I do? Does a piece of shit *want* to be a piece of shit, huh? WHAT THE GODDAMNED HELL AM I, ANYWAY?" He is weeping and howling now. He pushes open the screen door and goes whooping out into the rain and the wind, and his God welcomes him with a great raw smear of lightning that causes him to throw his arms in the air. Bernadette and I hurry to the doorway, and I start to go after him, but she touches my arm. I look at her.

"No," she says. "Let him do it. Maybe it'll make him feel better."

"He's done it before, hasn't he?"

"Yes."

"Has it made him feel better?"

"For a little while."

"But he could catch pneumonia."

"I know that, but bringing him in now would be worse."

"You're sure of that?" I ask her.

"Yes," says Bernadette.

I shrug. I do not know what else to do. Her hand still is touching my arm. We stare out into the roaring darkness, and now Ernest is floundering palely in the front yard, and he is flapping his arms, and he is laughing and leaping, and his feet send up sprays of water and mud. Or perhaps he is not laughing. Perhaps he still is howling. The sound of the storm has wrapped itself around him, and Bernadette and I cannot make out precisely what sort of noises are coming from my brother's throat. But we can make out his movements, and they are jerky, and it is almost as though he is trying to dance. He splays and waddles, and his legs move at crooked angles. He throws back his head, and for a moment we can hear a sort of hooting sound, like an owl. He splashes through puddles, and his buttocks joggle, and his arms move in urgent arcs and circles. Sticks and branches fly at him, and he bats them away. He bends over, and then he places a hand over his mouth, and again he hoots, and at the same time he dances, and the hand flutters, and now we see that he is playing at being an Indian, and he dances in a circle, and his torso bends forward and back, forward and back, and Bernadette's hand tightens on my arm. And Ernest drifts farther out into the yard, out toward the deserted and nearly inundated 33-A. And he abandons his Indian dance. And begins now to leap and flail. And then he begins to do a sort of jig, and he is kicking shoots of water from a puddle, and now and then he is illuminated by lightning, but we can no longer hear him. Then comes a crack of lightning that carries with it a great snapping golden flash. Then comes thunder, tumbling after the lightning and ripping open the sky with an enormous proclamation that makes my brother hesitate and look up. (We can see him. We really can. I do not know how this is possible, but it *is* possible. My brother is not an illusion. He *exists,* and we *are* seeing him.) And now Ernest jumps up and down, first on one leg and then on the other, and now he beats himself across the chest, and I think of what it will be like for the last man in the last night of the last deluge when the world has washed away and he has nothing remaining to him but his flesh and his posturing and his witless jiggling, and under other circumstances I suppose I would be amused. But now, here, it would be improper to be amused, and this is precisely what I am thinking when a second golden explosion comes tearing across the sky and points straight for the earth. And strikes the earth. And is accompanied by a shuddering smack of thunder. And a streak of flame comes sparking along the utility wires out there on 33-A. And a utility pole splits and teeters. And Ernest sees it and begins to run. And the pole falls toward him. And my brother runs. And he runs out from under it. But he does not run out from under the wires, and they are squirting fire, and the children come erupting out of the kitchen, and they all are screaming, and Jean is hugging the baby to her breast, and Bernadette gives a great sighing groan, and now she is squeezing my arm so tightly that I am squealing from the pain of it. My brother is dead, and I know it. When the wires came down, they struck him, and they struck him while his feet were in a puddle. In point of fact, they wrapped themselves around him. In further point of fact, they scourged his flesh.

Mottled and heavy, the mountains came shouldering down on US 40, laying mist across the pavement. Sherry Muller sat chattering in the back seat, and Amberson rubbed his jaw and his aching gums. Sinclair was curled on Sherry Muller's lap, and his eyes were closed, and his claws were moving in and out. Sherry Muller's voice was light, and a blind man would have thought she was a small child. "I am really *very* sorry about scaring you," she said. "But I was so scared *myself*, I just didn't think."

"It's over now," said Amberson. "No harm was done."

"But I just wanted you to *know*," said Sherry Muller.

"Fine," said Amberson.

Anne was silent. Amberson glanced at her and decided that her medication had begun to wear off. She turned her head away from him.

"It came from my daddy—the gun, I mean," said Sherry Muller. "He knows I hitch rides a lot, and he gave it to me so I could protect myself . . . or at least *try* to protect myself. You see, I've never had any bullets for it. He wouldn't buy me any, and I've never gotten around to buying any for myself. He thinks if I had bullets I'd shoot myself, and I think maybe he's right. He's a pharmacist, and he's a crack shot, and he belongs to, ugh, the National Rifle Association . . . ."

Amberson felt ridiculous. He had been angry with this Sherry Muller, but the anger had worn away, so why was he barely speaking to her? So far, Sinclair was the only friend she had in this automobile, and this was absurd.

"It's all right," said Sherry Muller.

"What?" said Amberson.

"If you don't want to talk, I'll shut up."

"No. You go ahead and talk. You have a pleasant voice."

"Really?"

"Yes. And our name is Amberson, by the way, and we are from Paradise Falls, Ohio. We're on our way to Richmond to visit a nephew."

"I'm sorry, did you say Anderson or Amberson?"

"Amberson."

"Well, I'm pleased to meet you. And I'm very grateful."

Anne spoke up. "I'm sorry if we seemed to be rude," she said. She twisted her neck and looked back at Sherry Muller, and she tried to smile, and then she said: "You apparently have made a friend."

Sherry Muller scratched Sinclair's spine. "I've always gotten along well with kittycats. The people who say kittycats aren't affectionate just don't know what they're talking about."

"He has always been a very affectionate fellow," said Amberson.

"What's his name?" Sherry Muller wanted to know.

"Sinclair."

"Hey, that's a *good* name for a gentleman cat. Very *dignified.*"

Amberson smiled. "Well, he is a very dignified cat."

"Yes," said Sherry Muller. She looked down at Sinclair and said to him: "Mister Sinclair, you look absolutely *senatorial,* you realize that? You and your fat cheeks and your big old whiskers . . ."

"That's a fine adjective," said Amberson.

"Thank you," said Sherry Muller. "I've always been sort of a verbal person—big surprise, right?" She grinned. "I shouldn't have bothered with dramatics and the trumpet. I should have majored in *talk.*"

"Dramatics and the trumpet is a strange combination," said Amberson.

"So I'm told," said Sherry Muller. Then she laughed a little. "Well, maybe I'm crazy. But, you want to know something? I don't *care.* I happen to *like* dramatics and the trumpet . . ."

"Then that's all that matters," said Anne, rubbing her right shoulder.

"I wish I'd brought my trumpet with me," said Sherry Muller. "I'd play something for you—if my friend Sinclair here didn't object. I'm not bad on it. I'm really not. But this Art thing came up allofasudden, and I just threw my stuff together, and I didn't want to have to lug my trumpet case."

"Art thing?" Amberson asked the girl.

"Yes," said Sherry Muller. "My brother Art, the one who was cut by the Buffalo Braves. Daddy telephoned me yesterday afternoon and told me Art was home and sort of moping around the house. You see, Art's been into this basketball thing since I don't know when, and he isn't able to take the idea that he isn't wanted."

"I'm very sorry," said Amberson, "but I'm afraid I don't quite follow you. The Buffalo Braves are a basketball team, aren't they? Was your brother released by them?"

"Yes," said Sherry Muller. "Exactly. Dolph Schayes, who's the coach, ah, weeded him out the day before yesterday. According to what Daddy said, Dolph Schayes told Art he wasn't fast enough. And poor Art, well, Daddy says he came home in a sort of daze. And I can understand that, can't you?"

"Yes," said Amberson, "of course I can."

"He's six feet nine inches tall, and he was one of the best basketball players Penn State ever had, and he works so very hard. Every day he works three and four hours on his jump shot. And for years now he's talked to me about playing professionally. He was drafted seventh by the Braves, and that night he came to me and he *hugged* me, and he sort of waltzed me around the room, and he told me seventh schmeventh, he'd make the team anyway. He said to me: 'Sherry, I'm going to be the second Muller in the National Basketball Association, and they won't call me the *other* Muller either. I'll be *the* Muller.' You see, there's another Muller in the league. His name is *Erwin* Mueller, and he spells it with an E after the U, even though it's pronounced the same. He's with the Detroit Pistons, and he's no relation. But, *anyway,* my brother didn't make it, and if I know *him,* he's pretty well done in by what happened. So that's why I'm going home. I want to talk to him; I want to see if maybe I can help him get his head straight. He doesn't talk much to people, not even to Daddy and Mommy, but he does talk to *me.* I don't know why, but I can relate to his jock attitudes. He knows I won't laugh or make fun."

"You care for him a great deal, don't you?" said Anne, turning her head again and smiling back at the girl.

"Yes," said Sherry Muller. "All he wants to do is play basketball." She paused for a moment, and Amberson glanced at her in the mirror. She tightened her mouth, reached up, smoothed back her hair and said: "But I don't think he's good enough. I think he's *almost* good enough, but I think Dolph Schayes was right. He's not quick enough, and he never has been. He can shoot and he can rebound, but he doesn't *move,* if you know what I mean . . ."

"I think we do," said Amberson.

"And somebody's going to have to make him understand that," said Sherry Muller. "And I think *I'm* elected. And I do love him, so I suppose I'll just have to tell him right out: Arthur dear, you're not good enough. I don't *want* to do it, but he's going to have to understand what's real . . ."

"I believe you will do it well," Amberson told the girl.

"You do?"

"Yes. You seem to have a good heart."

"Thank you," said Sherry Muller, smiling. "That's a very nice thing to say." Her smile was brilliant, toothy, quite theatrical. She looked down at Sinclair and said: "You have a nice daddy and mommy, Mister Senator Sinclair. I hope you appreciate them."

"He does—when it's feeding time," said Anne.

"Does he run your house?" the girl wanted to know.

"Absolutely," said Anne. "Like a tyrant."

"When he joins us in the morning," said Amberson, "he doesn't really *join* us. He calls us to order."

Sherry Muller laughed. "That's an interesting way to put it," she said.

"You say you do a lot of hitchhiking?" Anne asked her.

"Yes," said Sherry Muller. "Quite a bit. I suppose you want to know if it scares me."

"That's right," said Anne.

"Well, sometimes it does and sometimes it doesn't. But so many kids are hitchhiking these days, and kids will stop to pick up kids, and it's not as bad as you might think. Most people aren't as bad as my *friend* from today. But there's another thing about hitchhiking that I really like . . ."

"Which is?" Amberson wanted to know.

"The people you get to meet," said Sherry Muller. "I've been picked up by priests, salesmen, black people, college kids and once even a man who went from town to town selling little tin monkeys that dance when you wind them up. And sometimes, when I have my trumpet with me, I play it for them, and they seem to like it quite a bit. I usually play Purcell or Bach, and they tell me the high notes are really something. I dig the high clear notes the best, the purity or whatever it is. I want to be an actress some day, but I also wouldn't mind being a trumpet player, and sometimes I wish I had two lives, or six, or however many are necessary . . ."

"The world has prospects for you, doesn't it?" said Amberson.

"Yes," said Sherry Muller.

"Are you at home in it?"

"At home in it? Well, I suppose I am. Or at least as much as anyone can be, what with the war and the kids at Kent State and Nixon and his pal Doctor Strangelove Kissinger. I mean, it's the only world I know, and so I try to do the best I can."

Anne spoke up. "My husband sees the world as being some kind of apparatus. Do you see it that way?"

Sherry Muller shrugged. "If he means there is a connection between everything, then sure I do. Doesn't everybody?"

"But do you understand the nature of the connection?" Amberson wanted to know. "Do you understand how it functions?"

Another shrug. "I . . . well, I don't suppose I've ever thought about it. I mean, it's *there,* and I'll just have to function as well as I can within all the cogwheels and conveyor belts and whatever."

Amberson cleared his throat. "My wife and I have lived a long time, and we still do not know what to make of it. Which is one of the reasons we're taking this little journey. I think we have a right to try to acquaint ourselves with it."

Sherry Muller nodded. "Terrific," she said. "I think that's marvelous."

"You do?" said Amberson.

"Absolutely. I don't mean to sound like some sort of propagandist for the, ah, generation gap, but it's nice to know that some people can live a long time and still be human enough to admit they don't know all the answers. You see, that's what bugs so many kids—all these older people who are so *smug* and dump on you about the, ahem, Eternal Verities. It's as though God is all the time whispering in their ear. I believe in God, but I do not *necessarily* believe that He spends His time whispering in the ear of some automobile salesman, aged sixty, from Dubuque. Do you . . . do you understand what I mean?"

"Yes," said Amberson.

"You bet," said Anne, smiling.

"Take my father, for instance," said Sherry Muller. "I *adore* him, but he can be so *rigid.* According to him, the cities are full of rampaging, ah, blackamoors who rape and murder at will, and some day they'll join forces with the dirty pinko fag liberal commies and do away with all the *good, decent, Godfearing* people who have made this country what it is today. And, mind you, this is the sort of man who cries when a dog dies, who takes candy and little toys to the crippled children in the county hospital. And he is a *nice* man. The only thing is, he has all these *rigid answers* that I don't think are true at all. But, what the heck, if he wants me to tote a gun, I tote the gun, and it *has* given me a certain notoriety. Sometimes I take it with me when I go out with some guy for the first time. I stash it in my purse, and then—if he makes a pass and I'm not exactly turned on by him—I whip out the old persuader and, believe me, consternation reigns supreme . . ."

Amberson grinned. "Yes," he said, "I can understand why."

Sherry Muller fumbled at her waist, and Sinclair looked at her. She patted him, then hefted the pistol, squinted at it and said: "This here, folks, is a .38 caliber Smith and Wesson automatic pistol, and at short range it would blow you all this way and that like a pile of sticks. And believe me, ladies and gentlemen, it is guaranteed to reduce incipient horniness by such a percentage as would boggle the mind." Chuckling, she returned the pistol to her waist. "At *Oberlin College,*" she said, "I am something of a tourist attraction, believe me."

"I expect you are," said Amberson.

"But, anyway," said Sherry Muller, "everybody knows I'm harmless. After all, I *am* a dramatics major. But that's not really facing the issue of the apparatus, is it? I'm sorry, sometimes I get carried off the track . . ."

"It doesn't matter," said Amberson.

"All I can say is that I don't have the slightest idea how to define it."

"Neither can we," said Amberson, "but we do think the question is interesting."

"Or at least *he* does," Anne told the girl. "Myself, I've always worried more about daytoday things—meatloaves and my rhubarb plants and our children and whatever . . ."

"Well," said Sherry Muller, "we can't be philosophers all the time." She made a hapless motion with a hand. "I mean . . . well, if you talk too long about the state of the world, all you get from it is a headache, right?"

"And a feeling of insignificance," said Amberson.

"Absolutely," said Sherry Muller, grinning.

Then they all were silent for a time. Amberson kept the Pontiac at 40, and the highway curled through the mountains. In the back seat, Sherry Muller made small comforting sounds over Sinclair. She was sitting smack next to his box, but this did not seem to bother her. She stroked Sinclair, and he embraced one of her wrists with his forepaws. Up in the front seat, Anne squinted out at the mountains, and her hands were folded in her lap, and she breathed with her mouth open. Amberson concentrated on the driving. He concentrated on the center line. He concentrated on mailboxes and signs. He concentrated on the relentless hissing sound of the tires. The rain had begun to diminish, and now some of the mist was going away. Cool air came sucking through his open vent. He asked the ladies whether they were cold, but they assured him they were not. Leaves spun across the highway. Caught in an updraft from the car, they whirled over the hood, and some of them pasted themselves briefly to the windshield, there to cling until they were knocked away by the wipers. Amberson tapped his tongue against the roof of his mouth in rhythm with the wipers. He glanced at Anne from time to time, and he wondered if perhaps she wanted to lie down and rest. He thought of Sherry Muller, and he decided she had a great deal of dimension as a human being. Her entrance into their lives had been a bit melodramatic, to be sure, but she obviously had a good heart, and she surely was not afraid to speak her mind. The highway descended into a sort of valley, and here and there were small houses set close to the road, and he saw an old tire suspended from a tree, and he saw flowerbeds and a junked Volkswagen, and he saw a fat woman kneeling and clipping grass with a pair of shears. He rubbed his gums with a forefinger, but his tongue continued to tap away. He saw a NEHI sign, and he saw a NIXON-AGNEW sign, and he saw a sign that said JESUS DIED FOR OUR SINS. Cars and trucks whisked past in the other direction, splattering the windshield, but the clouds had begun to open, and a trickle of sunlight was leaking through them. Amberson thought back on the tears he had shed this morning, and he told himself he was not ashamed of them. If an occasion called for mourning, why not mourn? Why suppress the obvious and the true? Amberson was dying, and his wife was dying, and what was the sense of not making an acknowledgment? There was no sense whatever, and—

"It won't be long now," said Sherry Muller. "We are now approaching good old Garrettsburg, Maryland, and the fabled and romantic Muller mansion . . ."

"Well," said Amberson, "you just tell us where you want us to let you off."

"It's on Main Street," said Sherry Muller. "You'll go right past it. A nice big brick house with a nice big porch, and *vines,* and there are flowerbeds in the front yard."

"We have a brick house," said Anne.

"Do you like it?" Sherry Muller asked her.

"Yes," said Anne. "Very much."

"And *I* like *our* house, too," said Sherry Muller. "I've never known it to be cold, and Mama keeps everything spic as a pin. And there's an electric organ in the front room, and both Mama and Daddy know how to play it. It's quite an electric organ, if you have a thing about electric organs. Me, I can take an electric organ or leave it alone. It reminds me too much of *funeral homes,* if you know what I mean."

"I believe so," said Amberson.

444

"But, other than the electric organ, I like our house just fine. Andy Hardy could have lived there very comfortably, and he could have courted Ann Rutherford under the vines."

"How do you know about Andy Hardy?" Amberson wanted to know.

"Television," said Sherry Muller. "Dan and I adore watching old flicks. He's my boyfriend. He goes to the U of Maryland, and he says he wants to be a film director. He calls film the novel of the future, and I think he may have a point."

"Do girls still have boyfriends?" Anne asked the girl. "I thought that sort of thing was passé."

Sherry Muller smiled. "There are still some of us who are that oldfashioned. Only the thing is, a boy doesn't give a girl his fraternity pin any more; he gives her a box of pills."

"Oh, really now," said Anne.

Amberson glanced at his wife, and he saw that she was quietly laughing. He clucked at her and said: "You shouldn't even understand that—let alone laugh . . ."

"Did I say something wrong?" the girl asked Amberson.

"No . . ." said Anne. "Don't mind him . . ."

"My goodness," said Amberson, "what is this world coming to?"

Then Sherry Muller laughed aloud, and so did Amberson. Sinclair looked up at Sherry Muller, and she patted his rump. Now the rain had stopped, and so Amberson turned off the wipers. He chuckled in cadence with Sherry Muller, and she told him oh *dear,* sometimes she blurted out just the most *outrageous* things, and she was heartily ashamed of herself. But Amberson quickly assured her that a little shock now and then was good for his circulation and his bloodpressure, and it did not harm his wife either. The highway widened, and they passed a sign that said GARRETTSBURG POP. 5639 A NICE PLACE TO LIVE, and they passed brick houses and frame houses, and nearly all of these houses had a comfortable and settled look about them, and the mountains curved out beyond the town, and housewives with shopping baskets moved briskly on stout legs, and Sherry Muller allowed as how the old town hadn't changed by so much as a jot as long as she had lived there, and she told the Ambersons yes, maybe that dumb sign was true; maybe Garrettsburg *was* a nice place to live. And now, holding Sinclair with one hand and pushing back her hair with the other, she grinned out the window and told the Ambersons *yes,* by heck and by gum and by cracky, the smalltown girl thing still sat snugly somewhere within her. She shook her head and laughed and called herself a silly *poop,* but she couldn't help what she *was,* could she? The Pontiac moved slowly along this residential street, then edged its way through the two or three blocks that constituted the Garrettsburg business section. The sidewalks were crowded, but no one seemed in any particular hurry. A great many elderly men and women were poking along the sidewalks, and Sherry Muller pointed this out to the Ambersons, and she told them she supposed there was something in the mountain air that helped so many residents of Garrettsburg live such a long time. Then the business section was replaced by more of the brick and frame houses, and Sherry Muller told Amberson to stop up there on the right, the third house from now, and sure enough, it was large, and it had a large porch, and the porch had vines. Amberson pulled to a stop in front of the house, and Sherry Muller handed Sinclair to Anne and told the Ambersons oh *my,* thank you so much, and again, excuse me for giving you such a scare. She shook hands with both the Ambersons, wished them a happy trip, then clambered from the car. She ran up the walk and took the porch steps two at a time, and her long hair flapped and swayed. She pressed the doorbell button, then turned and waved at the Ambersons. She was grinning. The Ambersons waved back. Somebody opened the front door just as they drove away.

See now 1970. It is early February, and the day is crisp and blue. There is no snow, but the thermometer has been around zero all week long, and the Columbus streets have been streaked white from frost. The cancer man's offices are in a tall new building on North High Street, not far from the university hospital where Anne has been confined for surgery and postoperative care. His name is D. Walter Montgomery, and he is heavily dewlapped, and he has a slightly salivary lisp. Frank Groh and I are sitting in front of his desk, and he is standing at a window. The desktop holds a telephone, a blotter, one of those pen and pencil gimmicks and a framed color photograph of a boy, a woman and a Weimaraner, and nothing else. To me it appears to have been sterilized, like a pair of rubber gloves.

D. Walter Montgomery, MD, coughs gently and turns from the window. He says: "Some day the medical schools will give advice on this sort of conversation. I certainly can tell you I've never really known how to handle it."

"I only want the truth," I tell him.

"They all say that," says Dr. Montgomery.

"Walt, I *know* this man," says Frank Groh. "If he tells you he wants the truth, that's exactly what he wants."

It is late in the afternoon. Dr. Montgomery removed Anne's right breast early yesterday morning, but this is the first chance Frank Groh and I have had to speak with him. He comes to the desk, leans on the blotter and says to me: "All right, Mister Amberson, the plain truth of the matter is that the mastectomy has come too late . . . by at least a year and probably longer."

I have known this all along. I have known it. I have known it. I remove my spectacles and begin polishing them with a handkerchief. I blow on the lenses, and I take my time. Now the words have been spoken, and the acknowledgment has been made, but I will *not* lose control of myself in the presence of a stranger. That would not be proper. It would be indecent. My lips press against my dentures, but I speak quite distinctly. "She does not have much time, does she?"

The hard blue February light frames Dr. Montgomery's head. His features are shadowed. He shrugs. "There is no way of knowing," he says, "not with any *exactitude* . . ."

"Please don't bother yourself about *exactitude,*" I tell him. "Just try to give me a reasonably intelligent guess."

"Howard, that's very difficult for him to do," says Frank Groh.

I finish with my spectacles. I fold the handkerchief and replace it in my breast pocket. I put on the spectacles and look at Frank Groh, my dear friend for so many years, and I say to him: "I have to know. There are preparations that must be made. I need to have some sort of calendar in my mind, some sort of schedule. Can't you understand that?"

"But it's not that—"

Dr. Montgomery interrupts my friend. "We'll put her on medication," he says, "and it will do away with most of the pain. It will *cure* nothing, of course, but at least the pain will not be much of a factor. The debility will increase, though, along with a need for more and more rest. So, taking these factors into account, plus her general physical condition as it does *not* relate to the cancer, she may have as many as three or four years . . ."

"But that's a very rough estimate, isn't it?" Frank Groh wants to know.

"Yes," says Dr. Montgomery.

"She is a good woman," I say to Dr. Montgomery.

"Yes," he says. "She has a very sweet disposition indeed. She asked me this morning whether she would walk leaning to the left and unable to straighten. I assured her she would not."

"She has qualities," I say.

"Yes," says Dr. Montgomery.

"She still has things to say that are worthwhile."

"Yes," says Dr. Montgomery.

"She is an excellent cook."

"Yes."

"I shall never understand any of this."

"It is difficult," says Dr. Montgomery.

"There are no words," says Frank Groh. "No one has words."

I look at Dr. Montgomery. I want to ask him what they did with the breast, but such a question would not be proper. It would be indecent. My mind's eye sees a white garbage pail with a pedal that opens the lid. "You will try the cobalt treatments, won't you?" I ask him.

"Of course," says Dr. Montgomery.

"We have talked about that," Frank Groh tells me, "and the treatments will continue indefinitely—or at least until there is no reason for them to continue. Is that all right with you?"

"Yes," I tell my friend.

The light is quite harsh, and Dr. Montgomery seats himself behind the desk and swivels his chair so that he is facing away from the light. "Is there anything else you would like to know?"

"You *do* understand what a good woman she is?"

"Yes. I do."

"I have never known a better one."

"Yes."

"I am not making much sense. I apologize."

"That's not necessary."

"Are you telling me what is necessary?"

"I didn't mean to—"

Frank Groh breaks in on his colleague. He stands up, extends a hand to me and says: "I think we'd better be on our way."

I look up at him. I take his hand. "All right."

He hauls me to my feet. "Do you want to see her again today?"

I balance my weight evenly on both feet. My chest hurts. I visited Anne this morning, and she was a bit groggy, but otherwise she appeared in good spirits. Her face was too pink, however, and there was a white dryness in her fingers and knuckles that I have never noticed before. "Yes," I say to my friend, "of course I want to see her again today."

Dr. Montgomery gets to his feet. "I'm very sorry," he says.

"Yes," I tell him. "Of course you are."

Frank Groh steers me out of the cancer man's office, and I am choking, and my spectacles pinch my nose too tightly, and the hallway has an astringent odor that gathers itself in my nose and makes me sneeze. He leads me to the place where his car is parked. We climb inside, and he says: "My God, I wish I knew what to say."

"So do I," I tell him.

The Pontiac was barely a block away from Sherry Muller's home when Anne smiled at Amberson and said: "I . . . excuse me, I'm sorry, but I'm very tired. Do you suppose we could stop someplace around here?"

"It's not even quite noon yet. Do you hurt?"

"I don't hurt as much as I'm tired. Maybe that girl's spectacular gun display did me in. She is a nice enough young lady, but she surely did give me a turn."

Sinclair was sitting upright on Anne's lap. She rubbed him under the chin. "So is it all right with you if we stop?"

"Of course," said Amberson. "Being footloose the way we are, we have no schedule. If we did, then our feet would not be loose, correct?"

"Correct," said Anne.

Amberson smiled. If the truth were known, he felt a bit tired himself. And perhaps he felt more than tired. And perhaps Anne did, too. After a few more blocks, he came to another shopping area, a pizza stand, several fillingstations and a motel. It was called the CUMBERLAND MOUNTAIN INN. Amberson went inside, and yes, the clerk at the desk did have a nice room on the first floor—Room Number One, as a matter of fact, if the gentleman did not object to a double bed. Amberson told the clerk he had no objection whatever to a double bed. He drove to Room Number One, gave Anne the key and told her to go right inside and lie down. He brought in the luggage and Sinclair's box. Anne had taken off her dress, and she was lying down in her slip, the covers pulled up to her neck. Amberson asked if she wanted to put on a nightgown. She shook her head no. Her eyes were closed, but she still was breathing with her mouth open. Amberson seated himself in a chair next to the bed. Sinclair came to him and hopped on his lap, and he scratched the old cat's belly. Then Anne began to snore, and after a time Amberson dozed off in the chair, his hand firmly planted under Sinclair's belly. He slept for perhaps an hour, and when he awakened, Sinclair was curled at Anne's feet. Amberson's legs had fallen asleep. He shook his legs, gently stamped them on the floor, then took off his clothes and lay down in his underwear next to Anne, who still was snoring.

Amberson lay there for several hours, and he became cold, but he was too tired to do anything about it. He rolled on his side and stared at Anne's face. Skin hung in flaps from her chin, and all the muscles had given way in her cheeks. He reached out and gently touched her cheek with a forefinger. Smiling a little, he traced the word LOVE with the finger. Then he felt a sort of groan begin to build within him. He rolled away from his wife and covered his eyes with a forearm.

Anne came awake at about five o'clock. She came awake gradually, and she licked her lips. Sinclair stirred, stood up, stretched, then settled down again. Amberson uncovered his eyes and smiled at his wife. She blinked at him and told him oh *my,* that nap certainly had felt *good.* She had slept nearly five hours, and she was surprised when Amberson told her what time it was. She asked him if he had been able to sleep, and he told her oh yes, and it had been very relaxing. She went into the bathroom and then returned and seated herself heavily in the chair. She told him she was hungry, but she didn't really want to go out to eat. He said it was no particular problem; they could order from room service. Anne smiled and told him thank you, I was hoping you would say that. She got unsteadily to her feet, took her robe and a nightgown from a suitcase, then went back into the bathroom to change. Amberson dialed room service and ordered steaks, medium; hashed brown potatoes, not too crispy; asparagus; bread and butter, fruit cup and a large pot of coffee. Anne came out of the bathroom. She wore her nightgown and robe. They were pink, and the robe had a tasseled belt. She seated herself on the edge of the bed, then asked Amberson whether he would object if she lay down again. He told her for heaven's sake *no,* and so she lay down again. Amberson put on his trousers and shirt and waited for the food. He looked at his wife, and terror tore at his throat. And grief tore at his throat. Her mouth was open again, and she was rubbing her right shoulder. The food was brought by one of the motel's restaurant waitresses. She was a plump woman, perhaps forty, and she had frosted hair and a large mouth. She said to them *well,* folks, has it been a hard day of driving today? These here mountain roads can really be something, can't they? Amberson nodded and told the woman yes, it has been a hard day. The food was under a towel. The woman lifted the towel, smiled and told the Ambersons *my,* it surely smells *good,* doesn't it? She gave Amberson the bill, and it came to $13.52. He signed it and added a tip of two dollars. She told him she thanked him very much, and if there was anything else he wanted, all he had to do was call room service and ask for Bettye, Bettye with an E, that is, B-E-T-T-Y-E. Amberson smiled and told the woman yes, he would remember the name, Bettye it was, Bettye with an E. The woman left, and he took Anne's plate to her. She sat up, grinned thinly and said: My name is Anne, Anne with an E, that is, A-N-N-E.

The Ambersons ate well. They both were able to finish their steaks, which were tasty if a bit tough, and they did very well with their potatoes and asparagus, even though they agreed that the asparagus was far too rubbery. They drank coffee, and they touched hands from time to time, and now and then they yawned. It was not quite seven o'clock when Amberson put on his pajamas and crawled under the covers with his wife. Sinclair sat at their feet, and his face was smug. The Ambersons each had given him scraps from their steaks. He yawned, then lay down, pressing his head against Anne's feet and his hindquarters against Amberson's. Anne smiled down at him and said: "Good old Sinclair. He tries to show no favoritism."

"He just doesn't believe in taking chances," said Amberson. Then, after a short hesitation: "You know what I did this afternoon while you were asleep? I . . . ah, lay down beside you, and I . . . ah, I reached out, and I touched your face with a finger, and I traced a word on your cheek . . . and the word was simply *love* . . ."

"You did what? You wrote a word on my cheek, and the word was *love?*"

"Yes. With a finger. I simply felt like doing it, and so I did it. I . . . well, there were no traces. The moving finger, having writ, moved on."

"Don't make fun of it . . ."

"All right."

Anne blinked. "You . . . are . . . a . . . ninny," she said, drawing out the words slowly and blinking all the while. She shook her head. "You . . . ah, such a sweet thing to do . . ."

"I love you," said Amberson.

"Yes," said Anne.

"How do you feel?"

"Physically?"

"No," said Amberson. "I mean—how do you feel in your heart? Are you afraid right now?"

"Well, I am not afraid, and maybe I am not *not* afraid. I'm just . . . well, I'm just waiting for whatever it is will happen next . . ."

"And you have achieved something from the fifty years?"

"Yes."

"We were never quite fair to Henry. We idealized him too much."

"Yes," said Anne.

"And we never accepted all the gifts Lewis tried to bestow on us."

"Gifts?"

"Yes. His accomplishments. Being mayor and all the rest of it, Paradise Plymouth and all. He wanted us to understand what a resourceful and energetic fellow he was. Alice was right in that respect; we never understood. Or at least we never let him know we did."

"All right," said Anne. "Maybe that's true."

"And I never loved my brothers the way I should have."

"I don't know about that. Don't be so harsh on yourself."

"Well," said Amberson, "*I* know it."

"All right. If that's what you want to believe, go ahead."

"And I was fonder of Bernadettte than I should have been."

"I know that," said Anne.

"I . . . what?"

"She told me. It was a year or so before she died. She told me all about it, and she told me it happened just once . . ."

Amberson closed his eyes.

"It's all right," said Anne.

Amberson's mouth was pressed tightly shut. His gums hurt, and he was aware of blood in his cheeks and ears.

Anne touched Amberson's arm. "Really," she said. "And I mean that. Why would I lie at this late date?"

Amberson opened his eyes. He did not look at his wife. "I do believe I was on the brink of telling you," he said.

"Yes," said Anne. "I do believe you were."

Amberson turned his head and looked at his wife. "At least we are unscrambling our personal apparatus," he said. "The *real* world may elude us, but *our* world does not."

Anne kissed Amberson's cheek. "You asked me how I felt in my heart," she said. "It is not fear, and now I know it is not the *not* fear. And it is not resignation either. It's simply love. Ah, you and your funny questions. So you really think the heart is where the emotions are? I usually feel *mine* in my *stomach*. Why do we always speak of the heart when we speak of emotions?"

"Because your ninny of a husband has a weakness for romantic clichés. Because he could think of no other way to put the question."

"How dare you call my husband a ninny? My husband is a dear man, kind sir. Oh, he has had faults, but at the same time he has had the courage to admit they exist. And, because of this, he has tried to correct them. He has been kind and generous and loving. Howard . . . my God, Howard, I love you, and I have always loved you. You are a *strong* and *lovable* person, don't you understand that? And you have such *patience*. You've always known how I felt about Henry, for instance, but you never criticized me, and you never even said anything when I became so fat after he was killed. You have indulged my anger and my fussy ways, and you indulged my big belly, and you indulged all those photographs of the children we have all over the house. You are a dear, sweet,

452

lovely man, and I don't want to hear anything more about your romantic clichés or whatever. I'm about to *die,* Howard, and we both know that, but I will not go until I've made you understand that . . . well, that it all has been . . . worthwhile—and beyond my wildest girlhood dreams, pardon the romantic cliché. I just want to set the record straight for once and for all . . . I want you to understand that all your *thinking* and all your *concepts* and all your *logic* are fine—in their place. But you mustn't let them get in the way of the things that are basic. And the biggest of them is the fact that I love you . . . oh, look at me . . . a woman *my* age talking about *love,* as though maybe I expect someone to come serenade me with a ukulele . . . but I don't *care* . . . I need for you to know that it has been *good,* that dying isn't all *that* terrible because I've lived a long time *experiencing* the goodness . . . what am I, some spring flower that is being cut down before even the dew has left its first bloom? I am an *old woman,* and I *know* what I *know,* and please . . . *please* don't aggravate this old woman . . ."

Amberson plucked at his throat. He did not know what to say.

Anne had not spoken loudly. Her arms came out from under the covers, and she rubbed her right shoulder, and then she smiled at her husband and said: "Well, did any of that make sense?"

"Yes," said Amberson, and he could say no more. His eyes stung.

"I said it all very calmly, didn't I?"

"Yes."

"I maybe could have hit you with my fists, but I didn't."

"No. You didn't."

"Or I could have bawled, but I didn't."

'No. You didn't."

"So tell me—what do *you* think?"

"I think my beloved apparatus really doesn't matter."

"Really?"

"Yes. If I have experienced the *basic* thing, as you put it, why do I have to go clambering about in a lot of machinery?"

"I'm sorry," said Anne, "but I don't quite understand what you mean."

Amberson snuffled, cleared his throat. Then: "This little journey of ours . . . it came about because *I* wanted it, because *I* wanted to define whatever it is we are leaving. Now then, that is a very complicated definition, but could it be that love and respect and loyalty, although simple, are at the same time much more profound than all this machinery that has fascinated me so much? Does it sound too stupid of me to say that a warm hand and a loving heart are more important?"

"No," said Anne. "It's not stupid at all."

"And just what have we found on this trip? We have found a poor woman eating her lunch on Caroline's tombstone. We have met a girl whose lover deserted her but who still had the warmth and decency to help us look for our lost cat. We have visited Alice, and now we know there never will be any resolution of that particular ugly situation. We have encountered a nice Italian man who had a sweet retarded son. And we have had a sort of adventure with a rather interesting young girl who goes around toting a pistol. And we have seen Amish people, and we have read mailboxes, and we have crossed the famous I bridge, and we have been pursued by rain and mist, and we have been slow in ordering our food, and we have even spoken with Negroes. And hasn't there been a sort of benevolence to most of it? And hasn't the benevolence been the basic truth of almost everything we have seen and experienced? And what does the apparatus matter next to *that?*"

"Not much," said Anne.

"You know," said Amberson, "I am glad I forgot the movie camera."

"Oh?"

"It would have recorded the wrong apparatus, the *outside* apparatus, the one that is inexplicable and not profound."

"The one that caused our little friend to put the barrel of the gun in her mouth?"

"Yes."

"That was a terrible thing to do, wasn't it?"

"Yes. It fits into nothing we know. Therefore, it frightens us. When was it, two weeks ago that we went to see John Dietz in the hospital?"

"I guess. Something like that."

"And remember how he said to us he enjoyed the hospital because it kept disgusting people out of his sight?"

"Yes."

"Do you know what he meant by disgusting people?"

"I think so," said Anne. "I think he meant maybe young people with long hair, people like our girl with the pistol . . ."

"He was frightened, wasn't he?"

"Yes. Of course he was."

"Why was he frightened?"

"I don't know. Unless maybe it was because the times had gotten away from him. He is too old to . . . take in more information . . ."

"Why aren't we like John Dietz?"

"I don't know."

"How many people our age would have let that girl stay in the car after the fright she gave us?"

"Not many. But it frightened us for *her* sake, not our own."

"Yes," said Amberson. "Which means that perhaps we have been too sheltered. After all, what wars have we experienced? Have we ever experienced genuine hunger or been the victims of racial prejudice? We have been very lucky, Anne. Our generation eluded two wars, and we have kept a certain serenity."

"Now, Howard, don't start *that* all over again. So you never experienced a war. What's so terrible about that? You probably would have shot off your foot anyway. Your foot or Lord knows what."

"Probably my Lord knows what."

"Probably," said Anne.

"I wouldn't have been much of a husband without my Lord knows what."

"That is absolutely true," said Anne.

"It was faithful and steadfast for many years."

"Yes."

"I always have had a mildly salacious streak within me, do you know that?"

"Of course I do. After all, who has been its . . . principal beneficiary?"

"Anne?"

"Yes?"

"Please put your hand on it. Please do that."

"Yes," said Anne. She reached under the covers, opened his pajamas and touched him. She touched him gently, cupping her hand.

"Oh my God," said Amberson.

"It's all right," said Anne. "Everything is fine."

"I wanted to tell you about her. I've carried it with me for so many years."

"I know that, but I've been afraid to talk about it."

"It was just . . . well . . ."

"You don't have to talk about it."

"You forgive me?"

"Yes. That's why yesterday, or whenever it was, I brought up the subject of whether you'd ever had an itch for her. But you brushed it away. I expect you weren't ready."

"No. I wasn't. Ah, thank you."

"Yes," said Anne.

"It just *happened.* I never *expected* it to happen."

"Don't talk about it. It's done. It's . . . what's the word lawyers use?"

"Moot," he said.

"Yes. That's the word. It's moot. Such a peculiar word."

"There never was anyone else for you, was there?"

"No. Not a soul."

"Do you mind that I asked the question?"

"No. If there had ever been someone, I'd have told you. But there wasn't. You were always enough for me."

Amberson turned his head away. He pressed his hands over his face.

"Are you all right?" Anne asked him.

Amberson wrenched his hands away from his face. He reached down and touched Anne's cupped hand. He pulled it out from under the covers. He kissed her hand and her wrist. "Whatever it . . . whatever it is that's . . . coming, perhaps it will be something that'll . . . ah, make us, what I mean to say is, make us . . . I don't know . . . make us so we have a freedom . . . so the tiredness will go away . . . do you think so?"

"I don't know what I think," said Anne, smiling, "but I surely do hope so . . ."

"From Cumberland to Cumberland . . ."

"What?"

"From our house on Cumberland Street to the Cumberland Mountain Inn—a long journey. We are not the footloose Ambersons. We are the footsore Ambersons."

"Yes," said Anne, smiling again.

"We are strangers in this place, and we were strangers when we were born."

"Yes. Right you are. It makes everything neat, doesn't it?"

"I've always appreciated neatness."

"I know."

Amberson stared at the ceiling. "You have put up with so much."

"And so have you."

"I love you."

"Yes."

"Which is the essence," said Amberson.

"Yes," said Anne.

Amberson smiled at his wife.

Anne's eyes were closed, and her hands were clasped over her stomach.

"I love you," said Amberson.

"Always?" said Anne, not opening her eyes.

"Always," said Amberson.

"Will death do us part?"

"No," said Amberson.

"Thank . . . thank . . . you," said Anne, and now her voice was sluggish, clogged with drowsiness. She still was breathing with her mouth open.

"Nothing can pull apart an essence," said Amberson, whispering.

Anne did not reply. Her hands relaxed. Her jaw sagged. She began to snore. Amberson leaned to her and kissed her cheek. Then he lay quite still for perhaps half an hour. Anne's snoring gradually became heavier, and finally he carefully slipped out of the bed, put on his clothes and went out to the car. It was past eight o'clock, and the night was clamorous. The air was chilly and still damp, and the traffic noises were loud. He fetched the journal from the trunk of the car, then began walking toward the motel lobby. He glanced across the highway and saw a large building. It appeared to be made of brick and concrete, and it looked like a school of some sort. He had not seen it earlier. He had been looking for a motel; he had not been looking for a school. Frowning, he crossed the highway, and he was able to make out a large white sign. The sign had red lettering and it said GARRETTSBURG HIGH SCHOOL HOME OF THE RED DEVILS. Amberson hesitated and looked around. There was a football field behind the school and to its right. He walked toward the field. He walked across damp grass, and some of the moisture leaked into his shoes. He grimaced, and he hugged the journal to his chest. The field was surrounded by a low wire fence, but there was a gate, and the gate was unlocked. He walked past a line of shadowed bleachers, and then he was standing on the cinder track that encircled the football field. He glanced up, and he saw light towers poking at the sky, which was without stars. Still grimacing, he squatted. His joints cracked. He scooped up a handful of cinders. He straightened. He blinked at the cinders. He shook his head. He threw the cinders away. He surely was a ninny, and that was the truth. He had work to do; there were conclusions to be reached. Perhaps later he could indulge this witless romantic fancy, but now was not the time. Snorting, he walked back to the motel and seated himself at a desk in the lobby and went to work on the journal. He worked for perhaps an hour, and he grunted over his pen, and then he was interrupted by Bettye, the waitress. She was wearing a coat and hat. She told him it was closing time, but she would bring him a cup of coffee if he cared for one. Amberson smiled at her and said yes, thank you, a cup of coffee was a fine idea. Bettye went away and a few moments later returned with the cup of coffee. She asked him was he keeping some sort of record of his trip, and he told her yes, he was indeed. She grinned and asked him was writing a hobby of his. He told her yes indeed, it surely was. She told him she honest to God did admire people who wrote— even if it was only a hobby. Then she briefly touched his shoulder and wished him a good night. He nodded, but for some reason he could think of nothing to say. Still smiling, Bettye walked across the lobby, paused at the door for a moment, waved at him, then went out. Amberson sipped at his coffee as he worked. He paused from time to time and sucked at the butt of his Japanese pen. He wished he had said something to that Bettye. There must have been something appropriate he could have said. Finally, though, he was able to push Bettye away and concentrate on the conversation he had had tonight with his wife. He tried to keep his mind focused on essences. He worked until nearly midnight, returned to the car, hid the journal in the trunk, then let himself back into Room Number One.

He took a warm leisurely shower, put on clean pajamas and crawled into bed. Anne still was snoring, but this did not affect his sleep. He slept soundly, and he did not dream.

Friday

About two weeks ago, Anne and I went to the Paradise Valley Memorial Hospital and visited an old man named John Dietz, who had fallen and broken his hip. He is nearly eighty, and perhaps he will not recover. (Hip injuries can be quite dangerous at that age, I am told.) He is a former geography teacher and football coach at Paradise Falls High School, and he has been retired since 1956 or so. I have never particularly liked him (he has always been too loud and crass for my taste), but he *is* all alone, and he always has been all alone. A bachelor, he lives in a small frame house on Roundhouse Street not far from the C&O yards, and nothing shares that house with him, not a dog or a cat or even a bowl of goldfish. In the summertime, however, his house is quite pretty. He is fond of roses and honeysuckle and pansies and iris and daisies, and he labors over the earth ten and twelve hours a day, and his tiny yard explodes with the color of them. But he has no relatives other than some cousins who live in Granville, and he has told me that he seldom communicates with them. I am *informed,* though, that he has been overheard talking to his flowers (Caroline, do you hear that?). He curses a great deal when he talks to his flowers, or at least so I have been led to believe. Perhaps he is trying to intimidate them into becoming more beautiful, like a coach trying to goad a football team. (Actually, he was not a bad coach in his day, and his Paradise Falls teams almost always won more games than they lost.)

John Dietz lay in a bed in a small ward. We visited him on a sunny Saturday morning, and Anne had baked him an apple pie. (We visit the sick and the injured quite a lot. At our age, nearly everyone we know is sick or injured, or both.) The apple pie was warm, and Anne brought it to John in a tin pieplate covered with waxed paper. He looked at Anne, and then he looked at the pie, and then he smiled. "Well," he said, "my God, look at that."

The man in the next bed, a thin fellow with protruding eyes, covered his mouth and coughed into his pillow.

"Don't mind him," said John. "He's got the croup or some goddamned thing."

"Would he like a piece?" Anne wanted to know.

"He'd probably spit it up," said John Dietz, "but I'll ask him." Then John reached out and tapped the side of the thin fellow's bed. "Hey, Wrightson, you want a piece of homemade apple pie?"

The thin fellow groaned, coughed again.

John Dietz looked at us. "He's too far gone. The hell with him."

Anne and I exchanged glances. I seated myself at the foot of John's bed, and Anne sat down in a chair on the other side of the bed from the thin fellow. "I brought a knife and forks and some paper plates," she said to John. She rummaged in her purse, which was really more of a basket. She came up with the knife and the forks and the plates and began to cut the pie.

"Make mine a big one," said John.

"Of course," said Anne. "It's your pie." She cut a large slab of the pie, and the odor of the apples was spicy and warm. She scooped the slab onto a plate, gave John a fork, then handed him his plate.

"*Yeah,*" he said. "All *right.*" He began to eat. He sucked as he ate, and some of the juices leaked from a corner of his mouth. He wiped them away with a finger, then sucked the finger. He was half sitting up, and so he rested the plate on his belly. He was a large man, or at least he was the hulk of a large man, and his head was altogether bald. His mouth had caved in over his dentures, and his nose and cheeks were gray. His fingernails were split, and the backs of his hands were lumpy with veins. He ate quickly, and he snuffled, and his finger kept wiping away the leaky juices, and he kept sucking the finger.

Anne cut me a smaller piece, and she cut herself a piece that was even smaller than that.

When he was finished with his slab of pie, John handed the fork and the dirty plate to Anne. *"Yeah,"* he said. "God*damn* . . ."

Anne dropped the fork and the plate into a wastebasket under the stand next to the bed.

"How are you feeling?" I asked John. The pie was quite delicious, and my words came out plump and juicy.

"I'm getting there," said John. "Just because I fell down, that doesn't mean I'm going to die."

"Of course not."

"Wrightson's going to die before *I* do."

I chewed. I swallowed.

"But he's not so bad," said John. "God knows, I've known worse. There are a lot of disgusting people in the world, you know what I mean?"

"Well, I don't know whether it's—"

"It's all gotten away from me, you know that? Hell, I don't even mind this hospital that much. It keeps me away from the disgusting people, and I got a little money saved up, and if it wasn't for my flowers, I wouldn't mind staying here *forever*. What do you think of *that*, huh?"

"Well, I'm not quite sure I know what you mean by disgusting people."

"You do too know who I mean. I see them all the time. How come they don't take baths? How come the girls don't cover themselves? How come it's all gotten away from me, can you tell me that?"

I shrugged. I finished my piece and handed the plate and fork to Anne. She dropped them into the wastebasket. She rubbed her right shoulder, and she was not eating her own tiny piece of pie as much as she was pushing it around the plate.

"I work hard," said John Dietz, blinking at us. "And all I want is to be left be. But I keep *seeing* them. They walk around all over the place, and one day this summer three of them came along and picked my best roses. I went after them with my spade, but it was too late. God damn it all, what had I ever *done* to them? Huh? You tell me."

"I don't know."

"They just snapped off the stems. I went after them with my spade, but they just ran away. And they laughed."

"That's too bad," said Anne. "It's a terrible thing."

"Yeah," said John Dietz. He closed his eyes. "Shit," he said. "Everywhere a man looks, nothing but disgusting people . . ."

Anne tossed her plate and fork into the wastebasket. She glanced at me. "Well, Howard, maybe we should be running along . . ."

I stood up. "All right."

John Dietz opened his eyes. "Maybe if they could explain to me," he said.

"Goodbye, John," said Anne. "Enjoy the rest of your pie." She touched his arm. She was standing now.

"If they would come up to me and say: Look, we're going to kick you in the ass, and here's why. But they don't do that, do they?"

"No," said Anne. "They don't." She went to me, and she took my arm, and we walked out of that place, and Wrightson acknowledged our departure with a cough. We went outside to the car, and Anne was shuddering. On the way home, she said to me: "I don't believe he knew who we were."

"Neither do I," I said.

"He didn't say hello, and he didn't say goodbye. All he did was slobber over my pie."

"Yes. That's true."

"Why does it have to be that way?"

"I don't know."

And I did not. And I do not. All I *do* know is that I shall not participate in that sort of behavior. Granted, John Dietz is afraid, but why must he also be so *querulous?* I myself am querulous at times, but I do not believe I have permitted it to govern all of my final days. I do believe I have resisted it, and I know I shall *continue* to resist it. We are dying, Anne and I, and from time to time we weep. But we are also willing to make acknowledgments, to accept the termination without hating those who will survive us, and without gloating over those few who will not. The deaths and the cancers exist, yes, but there is such a thing as style; there is such a thing as gratitude; there is such a thing as benevolence. It has not been all that dreadful, and *there* is the essence of the situation.

That morning, a Friday, Amberson came awake crisply at about eight o'clock, and he felt enormously refreshed. He grinned, tapped his dentures. He had forgotten to take them out last night for their soak. The curtains were open, and today there was a dry hard sunlight and no mist. Blinking now and still grinning, he rolled over and started to say something to his wife, but her side of the bed was empty. Then he became aware of water running in the bathroom, and he sat up in bed and said: "It looks to be a fine morning, doesn't it?"

There was no reply. Apparently she was unable to hear over the water.

Amberson got out of bed and put on his robe and slippers. He went into the bathroom, and Anne lay on the floor. She lay flat on her back, and her tongue lolled from a corner of her mouth. Hot water was running in the sink.

"Anne?" he said.

She did not appear to be breathing.

He knelt beside her and touched her chest, and yes, she still was breathing. He straightened, hurried out of the bathroom and went to the telephone. He dialed the motel operator. The receiver was slippery in his hand.

"Good morning," said a girl's voice. "At your service."

"Miss, this is Mister Amberson in Room Number One. My . . . ah, my wife is very ill. Would you please call for a doctor and an ambulance?"

"Ill, sir?"

"Yes. Ill. My name is Amberson, and we are in Room Number One."

"Anderson?"

"Yes. All right. Anderson. Fine. Please call for the doctor and the ambulance."

"Is she injured, sir? Does she require first aid?"

"She is *ill*. She requires a doctor and an ambulance."

"Yes sir. We'll take care of it."

"Thank you," said Amberson. He hung up. He took a pillow and a blanket from the bed. He carried them into the bathroom, propped Anne's head on the pillow and covered her with the blanket. He turned off the water and seated himself on the toilet. His chest hurt. He hugged himself. Sinclair came in and started to use his box, which was perhaps a foot from Anne's head. "Oh my God," said Amberson. He came off the toilet, picked up the box and Sinclair and carried them to the coat closet just outside the bathroom door. He placed Sinclair and the box in the back of the closet. Weh, said Sinclair, looking at Amberson reproachfully. Amberson shook his head, returned to the bathroom for a moment, looked at Anne, then hurried back into the bedroom and got dressed. His hands shook as he tied his shoes, and now his chest was hurting like fire. He unlatched the outside door, then went stumbling back into the bathroom. He again sat on the toilet. He stared at Anne. Spittle bubbled out from under her protruding tongue. He took a washrag, knelt next to her and wiped away the spittle. His joints cracked. He kissed Anne's eyes, and they were warm. Her nightgown was open at the throat, and one button was undone. He fastened the button, then gathered the nightgown as close to her throat as he could. "Anne?" he said.

There was no reply.

"Anne? Can you hear me at all? Can you nod if you do?"

She did not move. More of the spittle began to bubble.

Amberson groaned. He stood up and went back into the bedroom. He pressed his fists against his eyes. Sinclair came up to him and rubbed against his legs. Groaning again, Amberson stumbled to one of the suitcases and rummaged about for a can of the 9-Lives. He came up with a can of Super Supper, and then he had to fumble for the opener. He finally found it. He opened the can and emptied it into Sinclair's dish, which he placed in a corner of the closet next to the box. Sinclair began to eat, and his tongue and jaws worked noisily.

There was a knock at the door, and Amberson went to answer it. His legs felt loose and flabby. He opened the door, and a neat young man in a houndstooth jacket smiled at him and said: "Mister Anderson?"

"Amberson. Come in. She's in the bathroom, Doctor."

The young man followed Amberson into the room. "I'm afraid I'm not a doctor," he said. "My name is Ralph Foster. I'm the assistant manager. Helen told me you had called her, and I—"

"She's in here," said Amberson, pointing toward the bathroom.

Ralph Foster followed Amberson into the bathroom. Anne still had not stirred. Ralph Foster looked down at her and said: "Ah. Oh, I see. Did she faint?"

"I don't know what happened. She was lying there when I woke up."

"Yes," said Ralph Foster. He shook his head.

"Can't you do something for her?"

"I'm sorry, sir. I'm not a doctor."

"You're not?"

"No sir. I told you that. My name is Ralph Foster, and I am the assistant manager of this motel. I . . . uh, well, I guess we'll just have to wait. I'm very sorry about this, but —"

Amberson went to the telephone and dialed the operator.

She came on immediately. "Good morning," she said. "At your service."

"This is Mister Amberson in Room Number One. Are the doctor and the ambulance on their way? Some man is here, and he says he is the assistant manager. Do you have an assistant manager? If so, what is his name?"

"His name is Mister Ralph Foster, sir."

Amberson hung up. He turned and faced Ralph Foster, who was straightening the knot in his tie. "How long will it be?" he asked the young man.

Ralph Foster shrugged. "Benbow's is pretty good. About a year ago, a man had a stroke here, and Benbow's ambulance came within, oh, fifteen or twenty minutes . . ."

"What about the doctor?"

"Oh, I'm very sorry. There are no doctors in Garrettsburg who make this sort of call."

"What?"

"I'm very sorry."

"My God," said Amberson. He lurched back into the bathroom. He dropped to his knees next to his wife. "The water was running," he said. "I expect she was getting ready for another day, starting to wash her face and hands. I . . . ah, I don't know what happened. When I came in here, she was lying like this. I brought the pillow and the blanket, but otherwise she was lying just like this . . ."

Ralph Foster stood in the doorway behind Amberson. "Does she . . . well, does she seem to be breathing?"

"Yes . . ."

"That's good."

"Yes . . ."

"The men from Benbow's will be here before you know it, Mister Anderson."

Amberson looked back at Ralph Foster. "Could you please get my name right? It is *Amberson.* Could you please do me that small favor?"

Ralph Foster thrust his hands in the pockets of his trousers. "I'm very sorry, sir. I must have misunderstood Helen when she gave me the name."

"She *did* call, didn't she?"

"Yes sir. Absolutely. The ambulance is definitely on its way, believe me."

"Does it have to come far?"

"Not too far."

"And how far is the hospital from here?"

"About five miles, Mister Amberson. It is the county hospital. It has fine doctors. My wife had a baby there just last month. A boy. It was our third baby, and they all have been born in the county hospital. She was cared for very well."

"I don't believe my wife is having a baby," said Amberson.

"No sir . . . I . . . well, I guess not . . ."

Amberson shook his head. Again he hugged himself. He still was on his knees next to Anne, and he was swaying. "Please ignore that remark," he said.

"Yes sir," said Ralph Foster. He was not tall; he had red hair and an open freckled face. He rubbed his hands together. "Ah, would you like a glass of water or something?"

"No," said Amberson. He sat down on the floor, and he rested his back against the toilet bowl.

"It won't be long," said Ralph Foster. "I'll stay here with you."

Amberson said nothing. He stared at Anne's face, and now the spittle ran in a sort of stream. He took out his handkerchief and dabbed at the spittle.

Ralph Foster leaned against the doorway.

Amberson was cold. He shuddered. He leaned over his wife and said: "Anne? If you can hear me, can you nod or clench a fist? Please, if you can do something like that, do it . . ."

Anne did not move.

Amberson watched her face and her hands and her eyes.

Anne did not move.

Ralph Foster spoke up. "Hasn't she been feeling well lately?"

"No," said Amberson.

"I . . . Benbow's is very good . . ."

Amberson did not look at Ralph Foster. He stared at his wife, and he kept watching for some movement of her face or hands. "Is Benbow's an undertaking parlor?"

"Yes sir. And it's Garrettsburg's best. It's called the Benbow-Ripley Funeral Home *officially,* but the town knows it as just plain Benbow's. My mother and dad were buried out of Benbow's, and I am here to tell you it is a fine place."

"That's very good," said Amberson, shaking.

"Ah . . . would you like me to call down for some coffee?"

"No."

Ralph Foster nodded. "It won't be long now," he said.

"Yes," said Amberson.

Sinclair came into the bathroom and sniffed at Anne's face.

Amberson watched Sinclair but made no move to keep him away from Anne.

"Well," said Ralph Foster, "a little kittycat, huh? What's her name?"

"She is a he," said Amberson, "and his name is Sinclair."

"Sinclair. That's a nice name for a cat."

"Yes," said Amberson.

Sinclair hopped on Anne's belly and stretched out. He licked his chest and forepaws. Amberson made no effort to remove him. He watched Anne's hands and her eyes, but nothing moved.

"I . . . ah, do you think that perhaps he, ah, shouldn't . . ." said Ralph Foster, and then he hesitated.

"How's that?" said Amberson, looking up.

"Oh . . . ah, well, nothing . . . I suppose you know best . . ."

"If you're talking about the cat, he loves her, and I believe he has a right to be where he is. She is like a cushion for him, and she always has been. And, as a matter of fact, she has been a cushion for all our cats. *Where is that ambulance?*"

Ralph Foster spread his hands. "Any . . . ah, any minute now," he said..

"*Did it break down? Has there been some sort of accident?*"

Ralph Foster's head jerked from side to side. "It'll be along any—"

"*Then where is it?*"

Ralph Foster opened his mouth to say something, but then there was a pounding on the outside door. Sinclair hopped off Anne's belly and scurried into the closet. Ralph Foster went to the door and opened it. Two men came inside, and one of them was carrying a folded stretcher. Amberson got to his feet.

"Somebody sick here?" said the man who was carrying the stretcher.

Ralph Foster nodded. He showed the men into the bathroom. Amberson stood back.

"Jesus," said the man who was carrying the stretcher.

"What happened? Did she faint?" the other wanted to know.

"We don't *know* what happened," said Ralph Foster.

The men opened the stretcher and set it next to Anne. They lifted her by the shoulders and the legs and placed her on the stretcher. Amberson went to her and tucked the blanket around her. He looked at the man who had been carrying the stretcher. "You be careful with her," he said.

"Yes sir," said the man. He was fat, and there were veins in his eyes.

"Don't worry about a thing," said the other man, who was quite short and wore a sort of smock.

"She won't fall out, will she?"

"No sir," said the fat man. "You just watch." Grunting, he and the short man lifted the stretcher. "You got her?" he asked the short man.

"I got her," said the short man.

The ambulance men carried Anne out of the room. Amberson followed them. The ambulance was parked next to the Pontiac. A red light flashed on the ambulance's roof, and the rear door was open. The men slid the stretcher into the ambulance, and Amberson crawled in behind it. Ralph Foster stood outside. "Good luck," he said to Amberson.

"Thank you," said Amberson, and then the short man slammed the door.

The men ran around to the front of the ambulance and scrambled inside. Amberson blinked at Ralph Foster. The fat man drove. The ambulance went hurtling in reverse, skidded to a stop, then went forward in a turn that just missed the parked Pontiac. "We'll be there before you know it!" the fat man hollered back to Amberson.

"When Charley drives this thing, he *drives* it!" hollered the short man.

The fat man turned on the siren, and the ambulance went careening out of the motel parking lot. Ralph Foster stood with his hands on his hips, and he was leaning back on his heels, and then he was gone. Amberson looked down at his wife, and his ears hurt from the noise of the siren.

"Let's pick them up and lay them down!" hollered the short man.

"You *betcha!*" shouted the fat man.

The ambulance weaved and skidded through traffic, and Amberson hung onto the stretcher with both his hands. The sunlight hurt his eyes, and so he pulled shut the side curtains. He said to himself: My ears hurt, and my eyes hurt, and my chest hurts. I am too old for all this. Will I survive it? Does it even *matter* whether I survive it? He reached for Anne's hand. It was warm. She had said last night she was cold. Well, she was not cold now. Amberson gently squeezed Anne's hand. He bent over her and kissed her eyes. He used his handkerchief to wipe away more of the spittle. There was an opening between the curtains, and he glanced outside and saw a bread truck and a Greyhound bus, and he saw two men in bib overalls, and the two men were leaning against a fencepost, and then he saw a mailbox that said SUGGS, and he saw treetops and mountains and a slash of the hard morning sky. He listened to the siren, and surely its loudness had penetrated Anne's sleep, or faint, or whatever her condition was. He shook his head, then again leaned over his wife, but this time his mouth was at her ear. "Anne?" he whispered. "Anne? Can you hear me? Can you move something so I know you hear me?" He pulled back and watched her closely, but she did not move. He gave a sort of groan. He rubbed his mouth. He placed a hand on her chest, but he could not tell whether she was breathing. He covered his mouth with a cupped hand. He breathed into the hand, warming it.

The short man grinned back at him. "There she is now!" the man hollered. He pointed with a forefinger. "Off there to the right! You see her?"

Amberson looked off to the right and saw a low brick building, painted white.

"It's a good place!" hollered the short man. "They took out my appendix last year, and they done a good job, and the food's good too!"

"You *betcha!*" hollered the fat man.

Amberson nodded and tried to smile.

The fat man cut the siren, and the ambulance made a sharp right at the hospital entrance. It rocketed up a long driveway that was lined with some sort of evergreen trees, and it came to a jouncing stop in front of a door that said EMERGENCY SERVICE. The fat man and the short man hopped out, ran to the rear of the ambulance, opened the door and pulled out the stretcher. Amberson came down after them. The stretcher had small rubber wheels on collapsible legs. The men opened the legs, then pushed the stretcher toward the door that said EMERGENCY SERVICE. Amberson hurried ahead of them and opened the door. He stood back, and they wheeled the stretcher inside. A doctor and a nurse came running. "This the woman from the motel?" the doctor wanted to know.

"Yes sir," said the fat man.

The doctor nodded. He pointed toward a set of large double doors. "Take her in there and put her on the table," he said to the fat man.

"Yes *sir,*" said the fat man. He and the short man pushed the stretcher toward the doors. The nurse held one of them open, and they pushed the stretcher inside. Anne's head moved loosely from side to side, but Amberson knew the movement indicated nothing. It did not come from *her.* It came because she was being moved so quickly, because she was lolling and flopping.

The doctor was tall and gray, perhaps sixty. He came to Amberson and said: "You the husband?"

"Yes. When I got up this morning, she—"

"Does she have a history of heart trouble?"

"No, but she does have cancer, and she's been very tired lately."

"What sort of cancer? Uterine?"

"Breast," said Amberson.

"Is she terminal? Do you know whether she is terminal or not?"

"Yes," said Amberson. "She is terminal."

The doctor nodded. He turned away from Amberson and hurried through the double doors.

Now Amberson was standing alone. He looked around. He hugged himself. He went to a wooden bench and sat down. He hunched forward, and he was trembling, and he told himself: Now, now, don't *do* this. Not *now.* There is too much to come, and you cannot afford to disintegrate. Not *yet.* Not quite *now.*

The ambulance men came back out through the double doors, and the short man carried the stretcher, which was folded. They walked to the bench and smiled down at Amberson, and the fat man said: "It's going to be all right, Mister. You got Doc Jasper in there with her, and he's the best doctor in the county . . ."

"Did you see her move? Did she move? Did she show any signs?"

The fat man shrugged. "I . . . I don't know. I mean, we just bring them here. We ain't no doctors or nothing like that . . ."

The short man rubbed his free hand against the smock. "We seen them a whole lot worse than her, but they come through okay . . ."

"Yessir," said the fat man. "Dave's telling the truth . . ."

Amberson became aware that he still was hugging himself. He unfolded his arms and leaned back. "Well," he said, "I do thank you for your help." He removed his spectacles and pinched the bridge of his nose. Then, after carefully replacing the spectacles, he said: "I wonder . . . how long will the doctor be with her?"

"No way of knowing," said the fat man.

"No sir," said the short man.

"Will he come out here and tell me as soon as he knows something?"

"Yes indeedy," said the fat man. "Doc Jasper is a good old boy."

The short man looked at his companion. "You got the papers, Charley?"

The fat man nodded. He pulled some papers from a hip pocket. "This here is your ticket," he said to Amberson. He opened the papers, took a pencil from a shirt pocket, then marked the papers. He handed them to Amberson and said: "Just sign where I've put the X's, and put down your address, too . . ."

Amberson looked up at the fat man, this Charley or whatever his name was.

"We got to have it for our records," said Charley, "so we know where to send the bill . . ."

Amberson nodded. He took the pencil from Charley and signed his name and address. Then he handed the papers and the pencil back.

Charley squinted at the papers. "Hey," he said, *"Ohio,* huh? I got *people* in Ohio. You live anywhere near Van Wert?"

"No. Van Wert is some distance from Paradise Falls."

"Oh," said Charley. "Well, I got a slew of cousins living in Van Wert —railroad people, most of them."

"May I ask you something?"

"Sure."

"How much is the bill? Could I pay it in cash?"

"Sure you can," said Charley. "It's thirty dollars, and if you give it to me now, I'll just mark these here tickets *paid.*"

"Fine," said Amberson. He reached for his wallet and extracted three tens. "Here you are."

Charley took the money. He scrawled the word PAID on both of the papers and handed one to Amberson. "Here you go," he said. "That's for your records."

"Thank you," said Amberson. He folded the paper and tucked it in an inside pocket of his jacket.

The short man, Dave or whatever, grinned at Amberson and said: "You must be a man who doesn't like to have bills hanging over his head."

"That is correct," said Amberson. "I have always believed in keeping my affairs balanced and neat."

"Yessir," said Dave, "that's what I've always been after, too—neat affairs. Yessir. Neat affairs." He nudged Charley. "Right?"

"Jesus Christ," said Charley, making a face. Then, to Amberson: "Don't you mind old Dave. He takes it in his hand too much, and he's got a soft brain."

"It takes one to know one," said Dave.

Charley sighed. "Come on," he said to Dave. "Let's leave this here man in peace."

"Just a minute," said Amberson.

"Yessir," said Dave, "there something else?"

"You are good men—do you know that?"

"Huh?" said Dave.

"How's that?" said Charley.

Amberson leaned forward. "I appreciate what you've done. I appreciate your taking the time to talk to me. You see, I've been married to that woman for more than fifty years, and it's not an easy thing just to, ah, sit here like this. You see, I . . ." A hesitation. Amberson's eyes were hot. He removed his spectacles, and again he pinched the bridge of his nose. He closed his eyes. "I . . . hope you understand what I mean . . ."

"Yeah," said Charley. "We sure do."

Then Amberson felt a hand on his shoulder. He opened his eyes. The hand was Dave's. And Dave said: "It's going to be okay. You and her will get in your car, tomorrow or the next day or whenever, and you'll drive out of here, and a year from now she'll say to you: 'Remember that little old place Garrettsburg where I had me my fainting spell? Wasn't that funny though?' Yessir, in a year's time you'll *laugh* about it."

"I . . . I hope you're right."

"You just wait and see," said Dave.

"All right," said Amberson.

Dave looked at Charley. "We got an airplane to catch or something? We can stay with this man a little longer, can't we?"

"Sure," said Charley.

Dave set the stretcher on the floor. Then he seated himself next to Amberson. "Ah . . . where you headed?" he asked Amberson.

"Richmond," said Amberson. "We have a nephew there."

"It's a pretty drive down that way this time of the year," said Charley.

"You going to stop at the Chancellorsville battlefield?" Dave wanted to know.

"We hadn't planned on it."

"It's something to see. Antietam, too, far as *that* goes, and Antietam ain't even that far from here. I always have enjoyed history. In school it was the only thing I was ever any good at. I liked to trace maps of the battlefields, you know what I mean?"

"Yes," said Amberson.

"If you got the time, you ought to stop at Chancellorsville. Antietam, too."

"Perhaps we will."

"The people who are all the time knocking this country, they don't know nothing about its history, and the things that's happened. They got no sense of how it all got put together, and that's a damn—"

The double doors were pushed open, and the gray doctor came out.

Amberson stood up.

So did Dave.

Charley looked at Amberson.

The doctor came straight to Amberson. "I'm very sorry," he said. His voice was too loud. He lowered it. "Ah, you see, she's gone . . ."

"What?" said Amberson.

"It was just general debility. You knew it was coming, didn't you?"

"What?" said Amberson.

The doctor touched Amberson's arm. "She must have died in the ambulance."

"She was *warm* in the ambulance."

"Yes. Well, then it was in the ambulance. Yes. She . . . ah, her heart simply stopped beating. The cancer had spread from the breast, hadn't it?"

"Yes," said Amberson.

"You told me yourself it was terminal."

"Yes," said Amberson.

"Are you all right? Would you like to sit down?"

"No," said Amberson.

"Jesus Christ, I'm sorry," said Charley.

"Me too," said Dave.

"Thank you," said Amberson.

It is all disintegrating now, and my search for logic has been a silly and schoolmasterish waste of time. (Much like my witless insistence that the past is so precious it cannot be permitted to expire. Enough of the past as the present; I am finished, and my world is finished, and I cannot avoid these facts by fiddling with grammar and adjusting tenses.) There is no rational way of measuring any of this, and there never has been. Patterns develop, but then they split apart. Logic keeps falling on its face like a rubbery clown.

For example:

Logically, Fred Suiter would have returned to Paradise Falls to pound out some sort of revenge against my bullying brothers. But he never returned to Paradise Falls, and we never knew what happened to him. Did the Almighty then intervene, striking down Ernest with celestial fire after causing Alvin Jr.'s daughter to be born with those dreadful hands? I doubt this. After all, had their crime warranted such severe punishments? No. I cannot believe such a thing.

Logically, I should have become involved with Regina Ingersoll back in 1927 when she made her outrageous inquiry. Some sort of sweetly romantic melodrama should have developed from it. Perhaps even a confrontation with Anne. But no such melodrama, sweetly romantic or otherwise, ever came to pass. Regina Ingersoll left town, and that was the end of her, and she became a foolish and laughable memory, amusing even to Anne.

Logically, I should have seen the cruelty Anne and I displayed when we named our cat Sinclair right after the death of our son Lewis. I should have deplored the name. But I did not. And neither did Anne. We had lost a Lewis but we had gained a Sinclair, and we never really gave serious thought to the implications of it. And, logically speaking, what we did was inexcusable. Were we afraid of Lewis? Was that why we would not admit him? How could we have been so callous?

Logically, I should hate my mother's memory because of her bigotry. But I cannot. I think of her with love. I remember her lap and her laughter, and I tend to ignore the encouragement she gave my brothers when they bullied Fred Suiter and the other Catholic children. I edit away the ugliness, and what remains is a nice lady who was a good cook, kept a neat house and loved her children. She was indeed all those things, but logic tells me she was a great deal

475

more, and it tells me I am entitled to dislike her, yet this I cannot do, and so the devil take logic.

Logically, there was no reason whatever for this final auto tour that Anne and I have taken. Frank Groh told me this, but I would not listen. She should have been permitted to die in her own bed. She should have been permitted to gaze upon the photographs, to pluck at old linens, to smile out her window at the autumn leaves spreading across her garden, to receive Florence and the girls, to chat quietly with me of our fifty years (*more* than fifty years). But I deliberately deprived her of all that. I deliberately dragged her along on my search for the definition of the apparatus. At the time, I thought it was reasonable that we measure our slice of the world, that we place ourselves within its context and try to come to some sort of logical conclusion. But this was all a lot of nonsense. Now, looking back on it, I can see that what I really was trying to do was spare her. Yes, spare her. Spare her the pain of leaving this life while all her beloved artifacts, her photographs and her linens and her old dresses and the rest of her things and memories, were within arm's length. By removing her from that environment, I thought I would remove that particular pain. If she died a stranger among strangers, would that not be easier? But this was an illogical conclusion, and now I know it, but now is too late. It is just as illogical and childish as the attempt to define the apparatus. Still, I am not altogether ashamed of my decision. It was illogical, yes, but it did give some evidence of compassion and of love. And what is more illogical than the human heart?

Logically, a great deal of the above is windbaggery of the purest ray serene. I set up a straw encounter with a straw adversary, and then I defeat him and go about congratulating myself. Apparatus, my foot! This "search," or whatever it has been, has been a rhetorical device shielding a central fact of my existence here in its last days. Namely and to wit: I wanted Anne to *myself,* without *photographs* and *souvenirs* and *nostalgia* to distract her from me. I did not want her plucking at her beloved *artifacts.* I wanted her to myself. Perhaps I am a selfish old man, but I wanted somehow to be free of competition with the Always Boy. This is a basic and final truth of my life, and I had better admit it. It is, I think, a sane and reasonable truth. I am not a lunatic. I have never been a lunatic. I have always been interested in behaving well. (I wanted her to myself. That is not difficult to understand, is it? I loved her, and I love her. I did, and I do. I know what I know.)

Logically, many people behave as though they are lunatics. Being what he was, why should Ernest have grieved so desperately over a dead bird? And why was Charlotte Krapf so afraid of death that she was willing to lie down with it? Was her life that rich? Has it been that rich since then? Where was the richness that day in those mountains near Latrobe, Pennsylvania, when that bus skidded off the road and five of her children were killed? Or take our son Henry. Why did he love the world so desperately when that world barely tolerated him? He loved his brother so much he played the coward to make Lewis a hero. Is it logical to give that much? Is it logical to love so strenuously? That day at Paradise Lake was extraordinary, and why did he give so much while receiving so little? Why was he chosen? Why did he die so early? Where was the logic in *that?* Dear God, there was a boy who mourned *streetcars* . . .

Logically, I should have been able to suppress the way I have felt about the encounter with Bernadette. It only happened once, and in a sense I was performing an act of kindness (and she tried to make me understand that). But I have never accepted it simply as that. By doing what I did that day thirtythree years ago, I violated an oath; I smeared dirt across my concept of myself, and there are those who would even call what I did incest. I have received forgiveness from Anne, but forgiveness is not enough. I must continue to punish myself, and this is illogical, and I know it is illogical, and perhaps I should count myself in the company of the lunatics.

We end up loving when logic says we should hate. We end up remembering when logic says we should forget. The clearer an answer, the more we question. Dull knives are sharp, and the world abounds with barking cats, cowardly heroes, and madness is the emperor of the universe. (All my life, I have sought to run faster than this planet revolved. Perhaps I have always sensed the madness and have sought to free myself from it. Is oblivion the only true logic? Or is it simply the ultimate surrender to all the madness? Anne is dead now, and she knows. Or, by not knowing, she also knows. What then of *me?* What do *I* know? Isn't it about time I freed myself of all these riddles and impossible quests? Is there not one final option that I have every right to exercise?)

I keep asking myself why I am here, and I keep insisting on a logical answer. The former is absurd enough, but the latter is an affront. I need to be freed from the convulsions of my mind and my *concepts* and all the other things that Anne, God rest her, knew stood in the way of the *essence* of what I am, and where I am, and whatever it is that will become of me.

Amberson cleared his throat. He turned from Charley and Dave and blinked at the gray doctor, whose face was blurred. Then Amberson realized he still was holding his spectacles. He carefully replaced them on the bridge of his nose, swallowed something heavy and lumpish, cleared his throat again and said to the doctor: "Ah, may I see her?"

"Certainly," said the doctor.

"We'll wait here," said Dave.

"Yeah," said Charley.

Amberson looked at them.

"Whenever you're ready, we'll give you a lift back to the motel," said Dave.

"We got nothing to do back at Benbow's that can't wait," said Charley.

"Thank you," said Amberson, nodding.

"Right in here," said the doctor, pointing toward the double doors.

Amberson followed the doctor through the double doors. The nurse stood next to a table where Anne lay. The motel blanket was pulled up to Anne's neck. Amberson and the doctor approached the table.

"It probably was some sort of infection," said the doctor. "Her condition made her quite susceptible to infections, as I'm sure you must know."

"Yes," said Amberson.

"And so it simply was a matter of her heart ceasing to function," said the doctor.

"Yes," said Amberson. "I surely do understand. I surely do." He stared down at Anne's face. It was gray now, as gray as the doctor. He had not remembered it as being so gray. Her tongue no longer protruded, and he could see no leak of spittle. He reached out and touched her forehead, and it still felt warm to him. The windows were unshaded, and perhaps the warmth came from the sun. He rubbed his dentures with his tongue. He looked at the doctor and said: "You tell me she is gone. Where has she gone?"

"Where?"

"Yes."

The doctor said nothing. He looked away from Amberson.

"Do *you* know?" Amberson asked the nurse.

The girl stepped back. "No sir," she said.

Amberson nodded. "Well," he said, "we'll all know soon enough, won't we?"

The doctor and the nurse said nothing.

Amberson looked down. He studied the flesh on his wife's face. Again he touched her forehead. Then he leaned over her and kissed her on the mouth, and her lips were warm. He straightened, looked at the doctor and said: "All right. Fine."

The doctor and the nurse ushered Amberson back out through the double doors. Charley and Dave were seated on the bench. They looked up.

"You'd better get the forms," the doctor told the nurse.

"Yes sir," said the nurse. She went out through another door.

Amberson walked to the bench and seated himself between Charley and Dave. They slid apart to make room for him. "Excuse me," he said, "but I just want to sit down for a little bit."

"Sure enough," said Dave.

The doctor went to the bench and stood over Amberson. "There are some . . . ah, formalities," he said.

"Of course," said Amberson.

"Miss Rossiter has gone to get the papers."

"Did you say Rossiter?"

"Yes."

"That's an interesting coincidence. Rossiter was my mother's maiden name."

"Oh," said the doctor. "Well, ah, do you have any relatives in this part of the country? I understand you're from Ohio."

"I have no relatives around here that I know of."

"I see. Well, perhaps Miss Rossiter's origins are in Ohio. I really don't know."

"It sure would be a coincidence," said Dave, rubbing his hands against his smock. He frowned at his fingernails. "Yeah," he said, "it sure would. I had a thing like that happen to me at a ballgame once. It was in Baltimore, and I sat down next to this here fellow, and we got to talking . . . you know how it goes. Turned out he was from Hagerstown, and him and me knew a lot of the same people, and I said to him: 'I got an Uncle Phil living in Hagerstown.' And he said to me: 'Phil what?' And I said: 'Phil Oliver.' And he said: 'This uncle of yours, he married to a woman named Trapp . . . Agnes Trapp?' And I said: 'Yes, that's a fact.' And then the fellow laughed and said to me: 'My mother is a first cousin to Agnes Trapp.' So, huh, what do you think of that?"

"It's quite remarkable," said the doctor.

"It was Fiftythree or Fiftyfour," said Dave, "and old Rocky Colavito hit four home runs that night for Cleveland . . ."

"Yeah," said Charley, "I remember that . . ."

"I never seen that man again," said Dave.

"Who?" said Charley.

"The man whose mama was first cousin to Agnes Trapp."

"You was like ships passing in the night," said Charley.

"Yeah," said Dave.

The nurse returned. She was carrying a clipboard. She held a pen. A number of papers were attached to the clipboard.

"This won't take long," said the doctor.

"All right," said Amberson.

The nurse's hair was black. It was pulled up in a bun under her cap. She was about twenty or twentyone, and her eyes were enormous. She was slightly built, and her teeth and mouth were too small. A badge was pinned to her bosom, and it said ROSSITER. Amberson had not noticed the badge before.

Amberson smiled at the girl. "Is it Miss or Mrs. Rossiter?"

"Miss."

"My mother's maiden name was Rossiter. Do you have any relatives in Ohio?"

"No sir."

"Oh," said Amberson. "I see." He still was smiling. His cheeks and gums hurt.

The nurse glanced at the doctor.

"Go ahead," said the doctor.

The nurse nodded. She tapped the pen against the papers, then looked at Amberson and said: "Name?"

"Howard William Amberson."

"No sir. I meant the name of the lady."

"Anne Georgia Amberson."

"Her maiden name?"

"Howell. And, incidentally, the Anne is spelled with an E at the end."

"Thank you. Her date of birth?"

"April 11, 1899."

"That would make her . . . ah . . ."

"Seventytwo," said Amberson.

"Yes sir. Thank you. Now, her home address, please?"

"120 West Cumberland Street, Paradise Falls, Ohio."

"Zip?"

"How's that?"

"The zip code for that address?"

"Oh. It's . . . ah, four . . . four something . . . I'm sorry, I just can't remember . . ."

"Miss Rossiter, never mind about it," said the doctor.

"Yes sir," said Miss Rossiter. Then, to Amberson: "Home telephone number?"

"Ah, 347–0108."

"Area code?"

"It's . . . ah, let's see . . . it's 614, I believe . . ."

"Now then sir, your name again?"

"Howard William Amberson."

"You are the husband, is that correct?"

"Yes."

"Was your wife covered by Medicare?"

"Yes."

"Did she have a personal physician?"

"Yes."

"His name, please?"

"Frank B. Groh."

"His office address?"

"Market Street in Paradise Falls. Something-something Market Street. I don't know the exact address."

Miss Rossiter nodded. "Thank you," she said. She finished writing, then handed the clipboard and the pen to Amberson. "Please sign at the bottom where I've marked an X."

"All right," said Amberson. He signed his name next to the X, then handed the clipboard and the pen back to Miss Rossiter.

Miss Rossiter handed the clipboard to the doctor. "Did I miss anything?" she asked him.

The doctor studied the clipboard. "No," he said. "Everything seems fine." He handed the clipboard back to Miss Rossiter.

She gnawed on her tiny lips with her tiny teeth. "I'm very sorry," she said to Amberson.

"Thank you," said Amberson.

Miss Rossiter turned and walked away. She hugged the clipboard. She went through the double doors into the room where Anne's body lay.

"She is a good nurse," said the doctor.

"Yes," said Amberson.

The doctor placed a hand on Amberson's arm. "Dave and Charley will take you back to the motel," he said. "You need to lie down and rest a little."

"Yes," said Amberson.

"Would you like something to help you sleep?"

"No thank you," said Amberson.

"Somebody will telephone you later today—about the, well, about the arrangements."

"All right," said Amberson.

"Would Benbow's be all right?"

"Yes," said Amberson.

"Benbow's is the best we have," said the doctor.

"So I've heard," said Amberson.

"They'll take care of the shipment. You'll be wanting the funeral and burial back in Ohio, won't you?"

"Yes," said Amberson.

"Is there anything else you would like to know?"

"Yes," said Amberson. "Pardon me, but where is the men's room?"

"Oh," said the doctor. "Wellnow, it's right out there." He pointed toward a brown door opposite the double doors. "Down that hall, second door on the right."

"Thank you," said Amberson. He stood up.

"You okay?" Dave asked him.

"I'm fine," said Amberson. He walked along a sunny corridor to the second door on the right and went inside. His feet felt peculiar, very light, as though they were encased in pillows, or perhaps bladders of air. He felt taller, knobbed, more fragile, like a pile of thin tottering sticks. He walked to a urinal, unzipped his fly, urinated, and it hurt. He stared straight ahead. KING KONG DIED FOR YOUR SINS was written on the wall. Amberson frowned. He finished urinating, but he continued to stand at the urinal. He fumbled in his pockets and came up with one of his Japanese pens. He uncapped it, then began to write on the wall. The pen moved carefully, and it wrote: IS UNDERSTANDING POSSIBLE? NO! I CRY. NOT HERE! Nodding, Amberson capped the pen, replaced it in his pocket, zipped up his fly, walked to a basin and scrubbed his hands with a bar of Lava soap. He returned to the reception area, and now Dave and Charley were standing. The doctor was gone. "We're ready if you are," said Charley.

"All right," said Amberson.

They walked outside to the ambulance. Dave slid the stretcher in the back, and then he and Amberson climbed into the front seat next to Charley, who again did the driving. Amberson sat in the middle, and he was able to smell the odors of Charley and Dave. They were warm and humid odors. Amberson sat erectly, his hands folded in his lap. He squinted into the sunlight. Charley started the engine, and the ambulance glided off down the drive and out onto the highway. Charley drove easily, and his breath came in placid grunts. "Be back to the motel before you know it," he said to Amberson.

"Yes," said Amberson.

"I could drive this here road in my sleep," said Charley.

"I expect so," said Amberson.

"When you get back to the motel, you get you a nice rest."

"Yes," said Amberson.

Then all three of them were silent for a time. The ambulance passed an automobile that had a Kansas license plate. It passed two boys on bicycles. It passed the SUGGS mailbox. Dave extracted a toothpick from a pocket of his smock. He dug at the openings between his upper teeth. Charley grunted, and his mouth hung open. Amberson saw cattle and a barn, and the ambulance passed an automobile that carried a bumper sticker reading SOCK IT TO ME. The concrete highway was in blocks, and the ambulance's tires went flup, flup, in a steady rhythm, over the openings between the blocks. Flup, flup, flup, flup, flup. Amberson tapped his tongue against the roof of his mouth in time with the flups. Dave dug and sucked. He removed the toothpick and stared at it, and it was pink. He returned it to his mouth and resumed the digging. Amberson saw a house that had lightningrods on its roof. He saw a brown cat sitting in a pile of leaves. He knew what he would do. He said to himself: I have an option, and I shall exercise it.

It was Charley who finally spoke. "Hey, Dave?" he said.

"Yeah?" said Dave, digging.

"You was talking about Rocky Colavito back there, and you said he hit them four home runs in one game back in Fiftythree or Fiftyfour."

"So?"

"So *I* say it was later than that. *I* say it was more like Fiftyfive or Fiftysix."

"You want to make a little bet on that?"

"Yeah," said Charley. "I don't mind if I do. I say he hit them four home runs *after* Fiftyfour."

"A buck?"

"You betcha."

"It'll be in Pete Tanner's baseball book. We'll go see him tonight after we get off."

"You betcha."

"He likes to think he's a sports expert," Dave told Amberson.

"I see," said Amberson.

"And I take a buck from him two, three times a week, just like clockwork," said Charley.

"Well," said Amberson.

"He's fibbing," said Dave.

"Oh?" said Amberson.

Dave grinned around his toothpick. "Well, maybe *once* a week—but not *two, three times* . . ."

Charley snorted. The ambulance passed a truck that was loaded down with logs. "Dave's got a memory like a steel sieve," he told Amberson, "and he adds to my beer money every week. Hell, when he goes off on vacation, I miss the little bugger, and no mistake. I miss him and his dumb bets."

"Don't start bragging just yet," said Dave. "We'll stop at Pete Tanner's place soon as we get off, and we'll just take a look at his little old book."

"You just better have your dollar ready," said Charley.

"Don't worry about *my* dollar," said Dave.

Charley grinned, then glanced sharply at Amberson. The grin went away.

"Oh," said Dave. "Yeah."

"You all right?" Charley asked Amberson.

"Yes," said Amberson.

"We'll be coming up on the motel real soon," said Charley.

"That's fine," said Amberson.

The highway widened, and now the ambulance was approaching the shopping area and the motel and the high school. It passed a bread truck, and Dave said: "Was that old Billy Green driving that Star Bakery truck?"

"I believe so," said Charley.

"I didn't know he was on the wagon again."

"Well, he must be. Old Man West wouldn't of hired him back otherwise."

"Yeah," said Dave, "I guess so."

"If I was married to what *he's* married to, I'd be a boozer twentysix hours a day, and that's the absolute truth."

"Yeah," said Dave.

"She looks like Phyllis Diller, only she ain't funny."

"Like a crutch she's funny," said Dave.

"You betcha," said Charley.

The ambulance slowed for the turn into the motel parking lot. Amberson leaned forward and looked across the highway at the high school. He looked at the football field off to the right. He folded his arms across his chest. The ambulance went bouncing up an incline, then coasted to a stop in front of Room Number One. Dave opened his door and got out. He held out a hand and assisted Amberson down from the seat. "You got your key to the room okay?" he asked Amberson.

Amberson reached into a coat pocket and pulled out a key. "Yes, thank you," he said.

Charley leaned across the seat and said: "You take it easy now."

"All right," said Amberson.

484

"And we're real sorry about your wife," said Dave.

"Thank you," said Amberson. His bones were cold.

"Mrs. Ripley'll probably come over to see you," said Dave.

"I beg your pardon?" said Amberson.

"About a dress for your wife. And the arrangements. Probably either me or Charley'll take her back to Ohio. Anyhow, Mrs. Ripley'll have to get the name of the funeral home in Ohio and all that sort of stuff."

"Oh," said Amberson. "I see." He walked toward the door of Room Number One. He was beginning to shiver. He should have worn a topcoat.

"You just lay down and try to relax," said Dave.

"Yes," said Amberson. "Thank you." He unlocked the door, then turned and smiled at Dave. "I really appreciate your help," he said.

"Never mind that," said Dave. "You just get your rest." Then, turning abruptly, he climbed back inside the ambulance, slamming the door behind him. The ambulance drove away.

Amberson watched the ambulance bounce out onto the road and turn toward Garrettsburg's center of town. He started to go inside the room, then hesitated and went back outside. He walked to the Pontiac, unlocked the trunk and pulled out the journal from its place behind the spare tire. He returned to Room Number One and closed the door firmly behind him. He took off his coat and shoes, wriggled his toes and seated himself at the desk. He began to write. He wrote of logic and lunatics and essence. He wrote of benevolence. He was interrupted once by a telephone call. It was Ralph Foster, who had heard about Mrs. Amberson's death and wanted to offer his condolences. Would Mister Amberson like some coffee and food sent to the room? Amberson told Ralph Foster no, that would not be necessary, thank you just the same. Then Ralph Foster asked whether Mister Amberson would be staying another night. Amberson thought for a moment, then told Ralph Foster yes, he would be needing the room for another night. Sinclair came out of the closet and sniffed at the telephone. Amberson moaned and hung up. He hugged Sinclair to his chest, and Sinclair's claws went in and out. Amberson had forgotten all about poor old Sinclair. Great God, what would happen to Sinclair? Florence and her husband had two German shepherds, and they would not be able to take him. Amberson pressed his face against the cat's neck. He jammed shut his eyes. Sinclair was purring. Amberson groaned, opened his eyes, brought his face away from Sinclair. "We're . . . we're going to have to do something about you, old fellow," he said aloud. Then he placed Sinclair on the floor, and the old cat curled up at his feet and took a bath. Amberson returned to his writing, and he worked until nearly one o'clock in the afternoon. He wrote carefully, and he sucked on his pen, and he thought of his children and his brothers and his sister and his wife. And he thought of Regina Ingersoll and Charlotte Krapf Haskins and dear Bernadette. The touch of his wife's mouth when she was a young woman. Henry's atrocious efforts to play the trumpet. Florence, the happy bride. Caroline and her dolls. Fred Suiter and his loquacious fish. The snort and chortle of the '29 Chevrolet. Anne's cascading jigsaw puzzle. Alice, with her smile and her breasts forever at the ready. Classrooms and track shoes and cinders and jubilation. Suspension of disbelief. Emerald White and Dr. Button. A Famous Buick and its Famous Shades and an innocently villainous horse. The sting of Anne's precious rhubarb against his tongue and throat. He summoned regiments of dead persons. His mind stumbled across a landscape of dead days. He squeezed his head, and he said to himself: I have arrangements to make. I must be orderly. I must function with neatness and precision.

It was just one o'clock when the telephone again rang. It was a Mrs. Greta Ripley, and she was calling from the lobby. "I hope I didn't wake you up," she said. Her voice was small.

"No," said Amberson, "you did not."

"Do you feel well enough to talk with me? I am here to pick up a dress for your wife. And there are certain other arrangements that have to be made. May I come to your room?"

"Of course," said Amberson.

"I'll be right there," said Greta Ripley. She hung up.

Amberson put on his shoes and coat. He looked around the room. It was neat enough. The maid had straightened it while he had been at the hospital. He went into the bathroom and bathed his mouth in Listerine. He swished the Listerine, and it stung. He spat it out, rinsed his mouth with water, then removed his spectacles and washed his face. He did all these things quickly, and he was just drying his face when there was a knock at the door.

He put on his spectacles, went to the door and opened it. The woman was quite tall. She was about forty, and she wore a plain blue dress with a short skirt. Her face was heartshaped. It was framed in blond hair, and it was rather pretty. "Mister Amberson?" she said.

"Yes," said Amberson. "Please come in."

Mrs. Ripley entered the room and seated herself in the chair at the desk. She crossed her legs. They were admirable legs.

Amberson sat down on the edge of the bed.

Sinclair came out from under the desk and scooted into the closet.

"Oh," said Mrs. Ripley, "a kittycat . . ."

"Yes," said Amberson.

Mrs. Ripley reddened a little. "That was a stupid thing to say. What did I *think* it was? A tarantula?"

Amberson said nothing.

Mrs. Ripley coughed. "I . . . well, I called from the lobby because I . . . well, I just don't like to come barging in . . ."

"Yes," said Amberson. "Thank you."

"I am . . . very sorry . . . about your wife . . ."

"Thank you," said Amberson.

Mrs. Ripley opened her purse and took out a notebook and a pencil. "We . . . ah, we might as well get down to it. I don't want to take up too much of your time."

"That's perfectly all right," said Amberson.

"Is there a dress that would be suitable for her?"

"I believe so," said Amberson. He nodded toward the closet. "Her suitcase is in there. You may pick whatever dress you think is suitable."

"Oh," said Mrs. Ripley. "All right. *Now.* The hospital has given your wife's full name as Anne Georgia Amberson, maiden name Howell. Is that correct?"

"Yes," said Amberson.

"Date of birth April 11, 1899?"

"Yes," said Amberson.

"Home address 120 West Cumberland Street, Paradise Falls, Ohio?"

"Yes," said Amberson.

"Is there a particular funeral home in Paradise Falls that you prefer?"

"Yes," said Amberson. "Zimmerman's."

"All right," said Mrs. Ripley, writing down the name. She blinked at Amberson, then said: "I assume you would want us to ship the remains back there."

"Yes," said Amberson. "That would be simpler than having them send a hearse here, wouldn't it?"

"Absolutely," said Mrs. Ripley, "and it would be less expensive."

"Fine," said Amberson.

"Now," said Mrs. Ripley, "ah, is there any particular price range you have in mind?"

"Price range for what?" Amberson wanted to know.

"The casket."

"I don't know," said Amberson. "I haven't thought of the price range."

"May I make some suggestions?"

"Of course," said Amberson.

"The price of the entire service is the price of the casket. Were you aware of that, Mister Amberson?"

"No," said Amberson, "I was not. Or, if I was, I have forgotten."

"Well, we could offer you a—"

Amberson held up a hand. "Please," he said. "I'm sorry, but I'm just not able to discuss this right now. Do you think you could do me a favor?"

"What's that?" Mrs. Ripley asked him.

"I have a daughter. Her name is Florence Portman, and she lives in Dayton. Could you telephone her tonight and consult her about all this?"

Mrs. Ripley nodded. "Yes," she said, "I'd be happy to do that. I can certainly understand why you're not able to—"

"She doesn't know yet that her mother is dead. You will have to be the one to tell her. And I don't want you to call until tonight. And I want you to ask her not to telephone me."

"I'm sorry," said Mrs. Ripley. "I don't quite—"

"I simply do not want to talk to her right now. I do not want to be the one to have to tell her. She and her husband will come here, I'm sure, and they can take care of the arrangements, and the coffin or the casket or whatever you call it."

Mrs. Ripley began to weep.

Amberson frowned at her.

Her mouth fell apart. She wept silently, and she hunched forward.

"What is it?" Amberson asked her.

She looked up. She snuffled. She pressed her hands against her knees, and her purse and the notebook and the pencil dropped to the floor. "I've . . . oh dear, you see, I've never been any good at this . . ."

"Now, now," said Amberson.

"My maiden name is Benbow," said Mrs. Ripley, "and I'm the last of the Benbows, and our little world sees me as . . . as carrying on some sort of a tradition . . . but I *hate* it . . ."

"I am very sorry to hear that," said Amberson.

Mrs. Ripley stood up. She lurched across the room and seated herself on the edge of the bed next to Amberson. She reached for him and embraced him. Her tears dampened his face, and she had a light fragrance. She embraced him tightly, and she was choking, but she managed to say: "I . . . it's supposed to be a business, and there's nothing *wrong* with it, I guess . . . but can't you see how it might chew me up? I mean, I am *no good* at this sort of thing . . . and I *never have been* . . . I . . . why can't *somebody else* do it?"

"Now, now," said Amberson. He patted Mrs. Ripley's neck and head and shoulders. "There, there. It's not such a terrible thing."

She looked at him. "What?"

Amberson smiled. "Endings are only sad when nothing precedes them," he said. "My wife lived a good life, and she made a contribution. I mourn her, yes, but it is not as though there is some tragedy involved. She is finished, but I still love her, and that counts for something. I have not wept yet, do you know that? But I shall. And when I do, I shall hold nothing back. She wore out, but she was not defeated. She was human, and she erred, as the saying goes, but her goodness overshadowed her mistakes. And so the least I can do is acknowledge the goodness. She was a complete human being, which means that her finish is no outrage. I loved her, and I love her, and I shall embrace her goodness when I remember her. Can you make any sense out of that?"

"I . . . think . . . so . . ."

"The world is *nothing* next to *that*," said Amberson, "and no horror or grief can defeat it."

Mrs. Ripley nodded numbly. She sniffled. Her ears were pink, and her mascara had run. She blinked at Amberson and said: "You really mean those things, don't you?"

"Yes," said Amberson.

"I am the one who is comforted, and you are the comforter."

"That makes no difference," said Amberson.

Mrs. Ripley pulled away from Amberson. She stood up, returned to the desk, sat down, retrieved her purse, pulled out a Kleenex and blew her nose. Then she dabbed at her eyes. "Why don't you want to talk to your daughter?"

Amberson exhaled. "I need to be alone," he said. "I need to get it all straight in my mind. I love my daughter very much. But for now I need to be alone. So would you telephone her for me? And try to explain to her how I feel?"

"Yes," said Mrs. Ripley.

"Thank you," said Amberson.

"Oh dear," said Mrs. Ripley, and she began to weep again. But this time she quickly brought the weeping under control. Again she dabbed at her eyes, and then she said: "You are . . . really . . . something . . ."

"Not hardly," said Amberson. He stood up. "I'll write down the name and telephone number for you." He went to the desk and scribbled Florence's name and number on a piece of motel stationery. He handed it to Mrs. Ripley. "And please don't telephone until this evening."

"Ah, may I ask why?"

"She . . . well, she is always out most of the day anyway . . ."

"Oh," said Mrs. Ripley. She stood up. She still was blinking. "Now, about the dress . . ."

"Perhaps it would be better if my daughter chose it when she arrived. I am sure she will be here by morning."

Mrs. Ripley nodded. "Yes," she said, "that makes sense."

"You are a very pretty lady."

"What?"

"You are a very pretty lady."

Mrs. Ripley stared at Amberson.

"Take my word for it," he said.

"And *you*," said Mrs. Ripley, "are a handsome gentleman."

"Thank you," said Amberson.

Mrs. Ripley stood up. She went to Amberson and took him by a hand. "You are the handsomest gentleman I know," she said. She embraced him. "Your wife must have been really something, too."

"Yes," said Amberson. Mrs. Ripley's hair tickled his nose. "That she was."

"A beauty, I bet."

"Yes," said Amberson.

Mrs. Ripley pulled back from Amberson. "I'll remember you for a long time."

"I'm glad," said Amberson.

"And I'm getting out of here before I bawl again."

"All right," said Amberson.

Mrs. Ripley leaned forward and kissed Amberson on a cheek. Then she brushed past him, opened the door and went out without looking back. The door slammed behind her.

Amberson crossed to the bed and lay down on top of the spread. He covered his ears with his arms and listened to the sounds of his heart. They were frail and exhausted sounds, and there was little rhythm to them. He gently touched his cheek where his friend Mrs. Ripley had kissed it. He placed his fingers against his mouth and kissed them. There was a thump on the bed, and he opened his eyes. Sinclair sat at the foot of the bed. Weh, said Sinclair. Amberson smiled at Sinclair. "Yes," he said, "I do believe I have an idea." Then Amberson again closed his eyes, and told himself: It was a brick house, and it had vines, and I shall have no trouble remembering it. He smiled. He surely did hope she would not brandish a pistol this time. The chenille bedspread was lumpy against his face. He said to himself: The option is mine, and there is no shame involved in exercising it. He lay there for perhaps an hour, not sleeping but not mourning either. Finally, gasping a little, he opened his eyes and sat up. Sinclair was asleep at his feet. Amberson carefully got out of bed and went to the suitcases. He searched them and came up with three more cans of the 9-Lives. He stuffed them in the pockets of his jacket, and then he retrieved Sinclair's dish from the closet. He took it into the bathroom and washed it. He glanced down at the floor and made a small trapped sound. He rinsed the dish and hurried to the bed. He held the dish in one hand and picked up Sinclair with the other. He let himself out of the room, went across the parking area and began walking along the road back toward the center of Garrettsburg. He walked on the left side of the road. One always walked facing traffic if one had one's wits about him. He hugged Sinclair, and Sinclair gazed at him sleepily. Sinclair tensed whenever a car passed, but Amberson held him tightly. Amberson walked loosely, and he tried to time his breathing with his steps. He had decided not to drive, and he was glad he had decided not to drive. He walked past a place that had a sign saying PIZZA, and he walked past a place that had a sign saying ECONOMY CAR WASH, and he walked past a place that had a sign saying KENTUCKY FRIED CHICKEN. He told himself: I should be hungry, but I am not. He stroked Sinclair behind the ears, and the old cat hugged one of Amberson's arms with his forepaws. "It's going to be all right," said Amberson, speaking loudly because of the rush of traffic. "You'll find kindness and loving hands." Then Amberson came to the place where the sidewalk began. His legs were more wobbly, and Sinclair was heavier, but Amberson moved as briskly as he could. He walked a block, then two blocks, then three, and leaves skidded at his feet, and then he came to the brick house that had the vines. He climbed the porch steps and rang the doorbell, and it was Sherry Muller who came to answer it. She wore shorts and a halter, and her hair was pulled back in a bun. She smiled when she saw Amberson. "Well, for heaven's *sake,*" she said, pushing open the screen door. "Please come in—if you don't mind my looking like Miss Dumb Cleaning Woman of 1934."

"No," said Amberson, "please. Can we just talk here?" He felt his control beginning to slip away. He cleared his throat.

"Is there something wrong?" said Sherry Muller.

"No," said Amberson. "Not really—but I was wondering if perhaps you would like a cat. He is a nice cat, as I believe you know."

Sherry Muller reached out and scratched Sinclair under the chin. "You . . . ah, you want me to have him? Well, for crying out loud *why?*"

"He is a nice cat."

"Yes. I know that. So why do you want to give him to me?"

"We have owned a great many cats, and he is one of the nicest."

Sherry Muller placed her hands on her hips. "Please tell me what this is all about."

Amberson moistened his lips. He did not want to weep. It would accomplish nothing, and perhaps it would even frighten her. "Could you take him just on faith?"

"Faith?"

"Yes. Could you take him without having to know why? He's not diseased or anything like that. He is simply a loving and gentle cat, and I want to see to it that he has a good home."

"But *why*? You'll have to tell me why." Sherry Muller brushed at her hair with the back of a hand. Her face was somber.

"Would you take him if I told you?"

"Yes. I believe I would."

Amberson nodded. He swallowed thickly. "All right. My wife died today, and he reminds me of her."

"What?"

Amberson said nothing.

"Oh my *God* . . ." said Sherry Muller.

"She has had cancer for some time, and she died this morning."

"But I just *talked* with her *yesterday.*"

"Yes. So did I."

Sherry Muller's voice was pinched. "You want *me* to take the cat, is that right?"

"Yes."

Sherry Muller blinked, and her eyes were brimming. She nodded. "All right," she said. "Yes. Fine. I'll take him. He's a good old fellow, isn't he?"

"Yes," said Amberson, hugging Sinclair.

Sinclair looked at Amberson. One of his whiskers caught in Amberson's coat. It pulled at his lips, giving him a sort of sneer.

Sherry Muller stepped out on the porch.

Amberson handed Sinclair to her.

Sinclair embraced Sherry Muller's arm.

Amberson fumbled in his pockets and came up with Sinclair's dish and the three cans of 9-Lives. "This is the brand," said Amberson, "most enjoyed by Morris of TV fame." He placed the cans in the dish and held out the dish to Sherry Muller.

She took it with her free hand.

"He is finicky like Morris," said Amberson, "but he's not as finicky as *some* cats I've known . . ."

Sherry Muller nodded. There were bumps on her arms.

"You're cold," said Amberson. "You don't have to stand here."

"But . . . don't you want to come in?"

"No thank you. I . . . there are still arrangements to be made."

"You're just going to *walk off,* and that's *it?*" said Sherry Muller, her voice thick. She stroked Sinclair's spine, and he rubbed his head against the crook of her arm.

Blinking, Amberson turned away. "He has all his . . . shots . . ."

"I'm . . . I'm so very sorry," said Sherry Muller from behind him.

Amberson nodded. He went down the porch steps. He barely was able to see. He did not look back. He had no idea whether Sherry Muller was watching him or what. He hoped she went inside before she caught cold. He shambled. He kicked leaves. He wanted to look back, but there was no way he could look back. He listened carefully, but Sherry Muller did not call out to him. He *was* walking off, and that *was* it, and she understood that was it. Amberson snuffled. His eyes ran, and the lenses of his spectacles were smeared. His arms felt light. There was nothing to hug, so he hugged himself. He shambled along as quickly as he could. He returned to the motel, and this time he did not bother to walk facing the traffic. He walked past the place with the sign saying KENTUCKY FRIED CHICKEN. He walked past the place with the sign saying ECONOMY CAR WASH. He walked past the place with the sign saying PIZZA. He swung his arms, and they felt so very, very light. The traffic rumbled past him, and it stank of gasoline and exhaust fumes, and now his knees hurt. He crossed the motel parking area and unlocked the door to Room Number One. He went inside and closed the door. He felt faint. He shuddered. He lay down. And then he wept. Amberson wept. He wept. His chest hurt. His head hurt. His dentures hurt. He wept for her sweet butchered body. He wept for her voice that forever was gone. He wept, and his sobs were cavernous, and so he pressed a pillow over his face. He wept for the deformed daughters and the martyred sons and the thunderbolted brothers. He wept for the forever dead days and he wept for vanished streetcars. He threshed against the chenille bedspread, and Regina Ingersoll smiled at him and said: It's a shame I never found out. And Bernadette said: I was helped, and I thank you. And Anne said: I love you. And Amberson's fists rubbed against his eyes, and he knew yes, yes, yes, it was proper that he mourn, that he make the acknowledgments, that he admit the benevolence and with it the termination. The option would indeed be exercised. Finally, blinking, he eased himself off the bed. He wiped his eyes, blew his nose, went to the desk, seated himself and wrote the final installment of his journal.

This has all been inconsistent and at times downright incoherent, *he concluded,* and I have often betrayed my promise that I would not

493

yield to exaggerations and melodrama. And I sought logic when there was none. And my attempts to define the apparatus were ridiculous. I am not large enough for such a task. No one is. And—beyond all that—I have concluded that it is trivial, and never mind its size. Then what remains? Could it be called a texture? Could it be called an essence? If, in preparing for my last moment, I have achieved a benevolence, then perhaps this journal has succeeded. And I believe the benevolence does exist. I believe it all has been worthwhile. I grieve, and I weep, and yet at the same time I experience no feeling of waste. I have done my best, and surely my life has had texture. I leave with guilts, yes, and a feeling of anxiety (call it fear, call it by its true and naked name), but at the same time I am not resentful, and I refuse to run flapping in thunderstorms.

I have known love. I have known good people. These last five days, Anne and I have encountered many kindnesses from strangers. We embraced, and we addressed ourselves each to the other's heart, and surely our love has counted for something. Surely that particular apparatus has been valuable.

But what remains to me now? Querulousness? Pain? Pain within pain? An enfeebled loneliness? Well, I will not hear of those things. I disaffiliate myself from them. I insist upon freeing myself from them, and I know just the method I shall employ.

I am going—but not in the sense of a man packing his bags and his household goods and moving to Syracuse, New York. I am going in the sense of dying, and it is that simple. I have done what I could, and there is no more I can do, and so why should I stay? I love the world, and I love the kindly strangers who befriended us, and I have wept for my wife and our cat and all the sweet memories that have sustained me for so many years. And so then all right. What remains? My life is done, so why should I not free myself?

And the method is to me so lovely. I shall finally defeat this planet. I shall finally succeed in flying. I shall realize my largest ambition. Oh, I love you all, you dead ones and you who still are alive. And it all has been worth the effort, believe me. Which means that there has been texture. Which means that there has been essence. Mourn me if you like (and I hope you do), but know that I am free. I have nothing further to say, and so I bid you farewell.

Amberson closed the journal. He stood up, rubbed his hands together. He walked to the front window and looked outside. It was past twilight, later than he had thought. He went to the desk and emptied the contents of his pockets. Out came his wallet, the books of Travelers' Cheques, his keys and his Japanese pens. He piled them on top of the journal. The telephone rang. He did not answer it. He frowned for a moment, then seated himself again at the desk. He took one of the pens and a sheet of motel stationery, and he wrote:

Dearest Florence:

This was right and proper, believe me. And also believe me when I tell you I have always loved you. I do not believe there is anything further that need be said. Read the ledger. Perhaps it will clarify some things about your old Daddy. Or perhaps it will not. But read it anyway. I love you.

The telephone rang fifteen times, then stopped. Amberson placed the sheet of stationery on top of the journal. Then he took another sheet and wrote:

My name is Howard W. Amberson, and I am a guest at the Cumberland Mountain Inn.

He folded this second sheet and tucked it in a pocket of his trousers. He walked to the door. He turned and checked the room for one last time. No, he could not think of anything he had forgotten. He went out of the room, and the wind caught the door, slamming it shut behind him. He walked to the road and crossed it. He walked across the damp grass in front of the football field. He let himself in at the gate. He walked past the bleachers, and he walked to the cinder track. His gums and teeth hurt. Grimacing, he removed his dentures and threw them away. He dropped to one knee, and his joints cracked, and the cinders scraped his trousers. He breathed deeply once, twice, three times. He looked up, and the sky was clear. He smiled. He rubbed his tongue across his raw gums. He pushed off, and he straightened, and he began to run. His coat flapped, and his arms churned. He shook a fist at the sky. To shake one's fist is to damage one's stride, but this did not concern him. He timed his breath with his stride, and his legs felt loose, and his knees felt loose, and his *feet* felt loose. He said to himself: My goodness, I am footloose. My frangicars are slarfing on all six. He laughed aloud. Now he had forgotten the sky and his fist. Again he grimaced. He circled the track once—a quarter of a mile. His breath whistled, and then his heart exploded, and he fell loosely, scraping his face against the cinders, and his grimace softened, resolving itself into a smile, buttery and benevolent, toothless and terrific and utterly free.